About the author

Also known as the artist ILYA, Ed Hillyer was editor of *The Mammoth Book of Best New Manga* (3 Volumes, 2006–2008), and his books include the award-winning graphic novel series *The End of the Century Club*, noir anthology *It's Dark in London* and, most recently, a daring adaptation of *King Lear* for Manga Shakespeare.

Ed Hillyer is a Hawthornden Fellow and was writer-in-residence in September 2004.

THE CLAY DREAMING

Ed Hillyer

Myriad Editions

First published in 2010 by
Myriad Editions
59 Lansdowne Place
Brighton BN3 1FL

www.MyriadEditions.com

1 3 5 7 9 10 8 6 4 2

Incorporating *The Life of a Greenwich Pensioner*
by Joseph Druce, 1779–1819.
As owner of the manuscript, The Mitchell Library,
State Library of New South Wales, has very kindly
granted permission for its usage.

A CIP catalogue record for this book is available from
the British Library.

ISBN: 978-0-9562515-0-3

Printed on FSC-accredited paper by
CPI Antony Rowe, Chippenham, UK

For my family

'This is not the era of sport,
but of martyrdom and persecution.'

~ Thomas Carlyle

I

Sport

PROLOGUE

King Cole is in motion, and that is all he cares to know as he dashes headlong through the streets of London. Blindly he runs, into a spin of lights.

Hills are lifted up, high towers, high mountains and fenced walls – such shapes as he has ever Dreamed. Behind the lights the buildings pile black on every side, threatening collapse.

One Big Ant-hill Creek, this is.

An Australian Aborigine, Cole is not daunted out Bush. His heart is open, his liver glad. He yells for joy.

Light to dark and dark to light, he races through the arches of the Adelphi along the Strand. The streets, filled with a riotous, milling throng, roar and whirl about at every turn. The window displays of bright-lit theatres and their print-shops draw the crowd – figurines no more real than the coloured shapes they stare at, looking-glass images of themselves.

He hears again the wheezing violins, strains of a waltz, sees the white men all in black, their ladies dressed as flowers, smelling not of flowers. They poke and prod and stare until he leaves them all behind, leaping from that cliff above Pall Mall.

A yellow whoosh of flame turns his head – fire-juggler. Cole collides with a column of smoke. A barrel-organ clatters and rolls. Impressions strike with physical force. His skull throbs and his scalp tingles. No matter – after the suffocating attentions of the Athenaeum Club, to be ignored is bliss.

Every few steps, scenes shift beneath his feet. They take on forms new and more clinging. Cole runs on the spot: it is the great globe that spins. He has to run to keep up.

Cityscape darkening, the frantic passage eventually slackens in its pace. Churning thoroughfares give way to ever-narrower lanes. Away from West End glory, night skies return, clear, with very little cloud.

The air, however, closes, rank with rotting vegetation. Hissing and growling sounds – King Cole finds himself in a downtrodden neighbourhood, much emptied of humanity. The front door of nearly every low, black house gapes onto the highway. Deep within dance kitchen fires, ringed with nightmare silhouettes. Queer animal shapes throw themselves across cracking walls and filthy floors.

He pauses a moment to catch his breath.

Were it not for the gas lamps marking the street corners, jutting from blackened brick, they would be no different from clumps of brushwood. By their flickering light Cole can make out other shapes crawling the street. Taking a step back, he disappears into a recess.

Their clothing much resembles the fine dress he is lately used to, but grown shabby, ill-fitting and old. Battered top hats fold in on themselves. Huge, filthy overcoats part to show second, no less ragged coats beneath. Baggy trousers, rope-tied at the waist, dissolve around gap-toothed remnants snarling at their feet. These stinking, outsize garments swamp the bodies of the pale and stunted creatures that bear them. Despite their obvious burden, they are spectral and insubstantial beings.

Under his breath Cole murmurs an incantation, a charm to ward off evil. He peels himself off the dank wall, lest he stick there, permanently, like a fly to a sticky-bud.

Borne on an east wind, saltpetre, sharp and corrosive, stings Cole's nostrils. The foetor of burnt flesh and charred bone catches the back of the throat. Beneath his feet, a black slime of damp pyrean ash coats the stone paving. Mixed with the ineffable charcoal scent is an alien tang Cole cannot identify – potassium nitrate.

In spite of it all, he senses the proximity of water.

A scattering of trees brackets a black-spired church, some almost as tall as the terrifying spike at its centre. With a trained eye Cole selects the most suitable. He reaches for one of its lower branches and hauls himself aloft. Setting the soles of his bare feet against the trunk, he grasps it firmly between both hands and, glad of the bark beneath his fingers, executes a nimble ascent. In a matter of seconds he nears the treetop.

Balanced between the high branches, King Cole swings back and forth, surveying the surrounding country – his eternal domain.

Immediately to the southeast he can make out a derelict marketplace, then scraggy patches of open ground. To the south lurk vast waterholes, deeper and darker than any salt lake. From these sprout entire forests of dead wood – ships with sails mournfully struck, tightly bound to skeletal masts. As he watches they in turn show indistinct, run aground amongst the misty ghosts of houses, houses of ghosts.

And beyond them all – to his horror – he sees, coiled and slick, the Great Serpent.

CHAPTER I
Thursday the 21st of May, 1868

THE HUNTING PARTY

'With Earth's first Clay They did the Last Man knead,
And there of the Last Harvest sow'd the Seed;
And the first Morning of Creation wrote
What the Last Dawn of Reckoning shall read.'

~ Rubáiyát of Omar Khayyám

In the beginning is the Song, and the Song is of earth, and the earth is Song.

And the earth is without form, and void: and the blank face of the void is white.

And the singers of the Song pick their way across that void, until another song should reach their ears. Faint, hard to place, it grows steadily louder. Brazen, discordant, the music is new to them – the theme all too evocative: a savage song fit to fire the heart, or to curdle the blood.

Song, and dance – barely discernible smudges separate out from the solidifying plenum. Dots here and there in the nowhere, the vibrations begin to take on physical form.

The brute chorus, more urgent now, is calling all of Creation forth.

Gnowee, the Emu's egg, is born from the land. The darkness divides from the light. Etched across this new horizon are the shadow-sequences of Dreaming. Silhouettes, they loom, assuming substance: becoming…

…a tree…

…a startled bird…

…a serried rank of scarlet jackets.

The North Downs of Kent, a lush, undulating landscape, lay couched in morning mists. No rain fell, but the clods of saturated earth exhaled moist breath. The sun was little more than a bright disc, suspended, its heat remote.

It took Time to burn a hole through the air.

Crisp, white chill gave way gradually to dew. Dawn opaque as pearl turned a translucent opal – a child's marble, red shift tense within.

Hue, and cry – a pack of foxhounds romped across rough pasture. Giving tongue, they announced their quarry cornered; a huntsman's horn quavered in reply – sounds neither of triumph, nor of mourning, but imbued with the hollowness of each.

In a copse at the base of a steep slope, the Master of Hounds caught up with his charges. Ringed tight about a dense covert, their white bodies thrashed like maggots in a wound. They yelped and snapped and scratched and howled.

'Ware Riot!' the Master called.

Crashing through barriers of undergrowth, the leading body lurched to a halt. Hunting pinks pulsing in pallid twilight, the West Kent gathered, eager for the kill. They could taste metal on the air.

The horses reared and circled, huge heads tossing, their eyes rolling; flared nostrils snorted gouts of steam. Something lurked in the clump of trees ahead, causing the animals to panic. Stabbing hooves churned the damp ground into a thick paste. Stumbling in the mulch, the frenzied hounds risked being trampled underfoot.

'Forrard!' cried the Master. 'Hoick to'm!'

But his hounds, whining, kept their distance. Smartly he dismounted, strode forward, and brought up his whip to part the curtains of vegetation. Dismayed, he hollered a caution. Taut reins restrained horse and rider from their sudden urge to flee.

Gasps and oaths escaped the ruffled company. Gentleman farmer, lord and lady alike stared, slack-jawed. There was the dead fox, lolling, back broken, held tight in the grip of a black fist. The hand belonged to a man – very obviously a man. A living soul, he rose up, as if of earth itself: formed of the dust of the ground, in their image, after their likeness – and yet shockingly other.

Stark naked in that glade stood a Stone Age relic – an Australian Aborigine.

'Not just one, but three of the buggers, black as sin!'

CHAPTER II
Thursday the 21st of May, 1868

BACK AND FORTH

'We must bear in mind that we form a complete social
body…a society, in which, by the nature of the case,
we must not only learn, but act and live.'

~ *Rugby Magazine*

'What the bloody fucking hell do you think you're playing at? Someone could
have been hurt…or worse!'

Athletic and powerful in his movements, Charles Lawrence paced the front
of a small provincial schoolroom. His honest face was thin and weather-beaten;
even so, he appeared younger than his 40-odd years.

From outside, the sharp smack of willow gave rise to cheers. Lawrence
raised his voice to match.

'That's right!' he shouted. 'Hang your woolly heads, you black sheep!
Hang 'em in shame, as well you might! All excepting you of course, eh, Your
Majesty?'

Scattered amongst the facing school desks sat the objects of his scorn: Dick-
a-Dick, Mosquito and King Cole were the three Australian Aborigines who
had startled the local fox hunt early that same morning. Each was dressed in
matching flannels, shirt, and waistcoat. Dick-a-Dick sported a jacket that barely
stretched across his muscles, and a vest considerably fancy. They otherwise
wore casual clothing of a sort that might as well have been sacking – baggy
and cooling, and perfectly anonymous. If not for their midnight-dark skin they
might have passed for ordinary workmen.

The infantile and exaggerated postures of the pair seated nearest to
Lawrence further distinguished them. Crouched at odd angles in a vain attempt
to hide behind child-sized desks, they raised folded arms and peered – yes,
sheepishly – through the chinks of their parted fingers.

The classroom was bright, built entirely of bleached pine, and redolent with
stale schoolboy sweat. Large windows down one side overlooked a playing field.
Closest to these perched King Cole, distracted by the cricket game beyond.

Sensing the approach of his interrogator, Cole snapped to attention and dropped his tousled head. Rapid heartbeats measured the silence.

Lawrence glowered. His clear blue eyes radiated both fire and ice. He took a swift step away.

'You can't get painted up and go parading your filthy particulars to all and sundry!' he said. A dramatic spin of his heel brought him once more face-to-face with the humbled assembly. 'And whose bright idea was it? Skeeter? Dick-Dick? Was it you, hm, Your Majesty?'

Lawrence waved his hands, imploring.

'Not that I expect you to tell me. Thick as thieves, you lot, thick as thieves. Wasn't *my* idea to bring you here.'

Lawrence's moods were quick, the darkest flush of fury already drained from his rosy complexion. Slackening, his strong tan hands began to fidget. He fingered the book on the teacher's desk beside him – *Tom Brown's Schooldays*, a recent edition.

Cricket was Charles Lawrence's driving passion: he was all but married to the game. Playing for Surrey since he was a schoolboy had led him on to Scotland, Ireland, Australia; and eventually back to his native England, shepherd to a most unusual flock. As coach and team captain Lawrence had in his charge a total of thirteen Australian Aborigines – the first ever professional cricket team to visit and tour from overseas.

They had travelled a long way together, and at close quarters.

Lawrence pictured himself, among the Aborigines, back on board the wool clipper *Parramatta*, the frigate-built ship on which they had endured endless passage from Australia.

He had brought with him a goodly supply of copybooks, and endeavoured to teach the Aborigines to read and write. Their fluency in English varied widely, along with their appreciable intelligence. Lessons had started out every morning, but could not last long, for the men soon tired, preferring to amuse themselves in drawing trees, birds, all kinds of animals and anything else they thought of. Fearing the limit to his own abilities, in the event Lawrence had exhausted their attention far sooner.

The Blacks liked to play draughts and cards, and also with the youngsters on board. They would charm pieces of wood from the carpenter and whittle away at them with admirable skill, making needles and lots of other little things for the ladies. They became great favourites with the womenfolk, who delighted in their spirited company, and whose children always wanted to be with them...

Church bells rang the half-hour. Focused again in the moment, Lawrence stood opposite an expectant trio. The Aboriginals were blessed with beguiling looks. Their dark eyes large and full, with a soft quality, there was, generally speaking, a degree of docility prepossessing, and expressive of great sympathy.

Faced with such generous and trusting pupils, he found it impossible to stay angry.

'Do you want to get me into hot water…into trouble?' stammered Lawrence. 'Well, then, eh? We might as well pack up our kit right away, climb back aboard ship and spend another three months in the bloody belly of the *Parra*bloody*matta*!'

A flash of white teeth from Dick-a-Dick and his bluster fell deflated.

The classroom became quiet. In natural communion, all four men began to watch the game going on outside.

The Aboriginal Australian Eleven had set sail from Sydney on the 8th of February, bound for the Old Land. They had finally arrived, docking at Gravesend, on Old May Day – May the 13th, 1868 – 81 years to the day from when that First Fleet, under Arthur Phillip, had originally departed to establish the new colony.

Leaving behind an antipodean summer's end, they had made landfall at the start of British summertime. The two seasons were of course hardly comparable. The omnipresent clouds and wearisome vapours of Merrie Olde England were most unlike the bright blue skies of Australia. The Blacks complained of double vision due to the weak light, seeing two balls thrown for every one. Fortunately, by local standards the recent weather had been unseasonably dry, some days freakishly warm – Friday last and especially the Tuesday just gone, with the thermometer hitting 83 Fahrenheit. Still, they'd had only just over a week in which to recover their land legs, and for the Aborigines to acclimatise.

The game in progress beyond the schoolhouse window was a practice session, a part of their brief round of training: after months of inactivity on board ship they had all gained an inch or two around the middle. The high plateau of the North Downs overlooked the pitch from one direction; the tall, tiled spire of St Mary's church the other. Four oasthouses, so characteristic of the Kentish countryside, directly bordered onto the sports field. Conical roofs bent forward, they too seemed to incline their heads the better to follow the action.

Laurence blinked, his concentration shot.

'Neddy will insist on leading with the wrong leg,' he muttered to himself. Making for the door, he turned to point a commanding finger. 'Wait here,' he said. 'We're not done. I'll return presently.'

'"*Bladdy facken hell!*"'

Laughter breaks out.

'Sounds proper 'Stralian there, inna?'

'Too bloody roit.'

Mosquito, the smallest of the three Aborigines, leaps from his desk and makes for the open door.

'Lawrence…' says Cole, 'Lawrence said we wait f'r 'im.'

Mosquito throws back a dirty look and keeps on going.

Dick-a-Dick, who has seniority, addresses Mosquito in their own language. '*Grongarrong*, him right,' he says. 'We should wait.'

Mosquito halts within the doorway. His homelands are at Naracoorte, also known as Mosquito Plains. A skilled carpenter and an ace with the stockwhip, he is, like Dick-a-Dick, a firm advocate of temperance – which is as well, since he is the devil with a drink inside him.

Sulkily, he returns.

'White men,' says Mosquito, 'have no manners.'

This spite is directed at King Cole: the simpleton has spoken out of line. Mosquito then presents his back. Facing Dick-a-Dick, he adopts a dialect only they share. 'Did you have to invite him?' he says. 'He brings bad luck.'

'*Na? Puru watjala?*' asks Cole. He understands well enough that nothing good is said of him. His lip curls. '*Mardidjali.*'

'*Miriwa,*' spits back Mosquito. 'Drop dead.'

Still favouring Dick-a-Dick, Mosquito resumes English for Cole's edification. '*He* is the one whose tongue is difficult.'

Feeling the hurt, King Cole rises instantly from his seat. Now all of them are standing.

'*Wembawemba,*' jibes Mosquito. 'Everybody know. Ancestors him no good.'

Cole squares with his accuser. Dick-a-Dick intercedes. Put in the position of children, it is hardly surprising they should act the same, but no less shameful for all that. Dick glares reproachfully at Mosquito.

Mosquito cannot believe it. 'You side with him,' he whines, 'against a brother? He is not *Jardwa!*'

Dick-a-Dick grimaces. *Jardwadjali, Mardidjali, Wutjubaluk*; the battles they fought over the Murray Lands are over 20 years past, as long dead as their peoples.

'So few blackfellas…' he sighs.

Dick calls to mind his birthplace, *Bring Albit*, the sandy spring close to Mount Elgin, and his family crest – *Kiotacha*, the native cat.

A lengthy silence ensues before Dick-a-Dick speaks again.

'Back in the World,' he says, 'we were Lizard…Crow, Eaglehawk. We were Pelican…Fire…and Emu.'

He measures his speech, taking long pauses. One does not speak lightly, nor too quickly, when dealing with weighty subjects. Words are anyway no way to talk. It takes time to summon the right ones.

'Remember where we come from,' he says. 'That is important…'

Taking his fellows each by the arm, Dick-a-Dick directs their attention beyond the window glass. He tells them, 'We are very far from home.'

Another pause.

'In this place,' continues Dick, 'it does not matter if we are *Gabadj*, or *Guragidj*, Blackheaded Snake, or...' his eye takes in Cole '...Southern Cross.' Dick-a-Dick lays a placating palm on each man's shoulder. 'White Cockatoo?' he says. 'Black Cockatoo? Here, whole mob just Cockatoo.'

Sad to speak his mind as if it belonged to somewhere else, Dick-a-Dick allows his words to sink slowly in. They watch Lawrence engaged in parley with their team-mates on the field.

'You want beat the whitefellas at their own game?' says Dick. 'Don't. Be proud who is your brother.' His right hand moves to cup the back of Mosquito's neck. He studies the face of each man in turn. 'Look after me an' him,' says Dick. 'That about all we got left.'

Mosquito sets his jaw. He drops his head. 'No good you talk English me.'

'Soon,' says Dick, 'all World become one England.'

King Cole's mouth hangs open. Belonging to no particular place, condemned to remain a boy, he has so much that he wants to express, yet nothing he dares speak of.

Lawrence returned, breaking the spell.

Dick-a-Dick, leading by example, made his way back to the desks and sat down. Mosquito remained standing, facing down Cole.

'*Tji-tji*,' he said. 'Child. I know my *miyur*... I remember my place.'

'Skeeter, Cole...please,' said Lawrence, 'be seated.'

His few minutes away had given him a chance to reflect on their situation. Lawrence was, if anything, even more contrite than the three Aborigines had contrived to appear. Ninety days confined to a ship – and often cramped and chilly quarters below deck – were akin to a prison sentence even for a civilised gentleman, let alone nomadic tribesmen.

Good morale inspired any team to play better; among players as instinctual as these, it was invaluable. The Blacks, reasoned Lawrence, had only sought to satisfy their characteristic urge to explore new surroundings. They did so in order to cheer themselves. The impromptu hunting party might have been a blessing – in different circumstances.

'I know you fellows to be responsible men...' Lawrence began, but faltered. Their actions, although justifiable, could not be condoned. They were in England now.

'Sorry, Lawrence,' the Aborigines chimed in singsong chorus. No need for talk. They understood. Charles Lawrence felt moved.

'I was of a mind not to let you attend Saturday's party,' he said, 'but I suspect letting you go will prove the greater punishment.'

The lesson concluded with a wry smile.

The Aborigines beamed broadly in return.

'Gave those ruddy toffs a scare did you, boys?' Lawrence's bushy moustaches failed to conceal so wide a grin. 'Wish I'd been there,' he said, 'to see the look on their faces.'

A muffled 'Howzie!' carried through the window-glass. Four heads turned as one.

The players did not have to be told. 'Go on, then,' shouted Lawrence after them, 'get back to practice with the others!'

CHAPTER III
Saturday the 23rd of May, 1868

PERFECT GENTLEMEN

'The Aboriginal black cricketers are veritable
representatives of a race unknown to us until the days of
Captain Cook, and a race which is fast disappearing from
the earth. If anything will save them it will perhaps be the
cricket ball. Other measures have been tried and failed.
The cricket ball has made men of them at last.'

~ *Bell's Life*

Town Malling, a quiet nook just to the west of Maidstone, made for the
Aboriginal Eleven's first base of operations. Tour manager Bill Hayman
exploited family ties, employing Kent County Cricket Club secretary William
South Norton – his brother-in-law.

Charles Lawrence paced the upstairs lounge of the Bear Inn. Hayman and
South Norton, both seated, looked on. Dressed to the absolute nines – white
dress shirts, crisp dark suits, black shoes polished to a bright blaze – they sported
Sunday-best on a wet Saturday afternoon.

The windows had been thrown wide open. Despite driving rain, the High-
street market bustled; the drone of trade and industry, carried from below, set
the small room thrumming. The day was extraordinarily close. Neckties loose
and top buttons unfastened, in concession to the heat as much as the hour,
all three gentlemen sweated profusely. Lawrence especially suffered. Humidity
aside, he had whipped himself up into a keen state of anxiety.

When their ship hove to, the national press had been obsessed with the
General Election, and then, as it docked, with Disraeli's ascension to the top of
his 'greasy pole'. Very little publicity had greeted the team's arrival. To ensure
the tour turn a profit they needed to attract the Great British Public. Journalists
from the influential London papers had been invited to watch the Aborigines at
practice, as yet without concrete result.

Their debut at the Oval was only two days away.

'"Attempt to Assassinate the Duke of Edinburgh".' South Norton read aloud from *The Illustrated London News*, the latest edition just arrived by train from London. '"The Australian mail",' he continued, '"brings copious details of atrocious attempt on the life of his Royal Highness on March 12."'

'Not guilty,' Hayman pleaded. Privileged by birth, the freckle-faced fellow was some years younger than Lawrence. He raised his hands in mock surrender. 'Our alibi, I think you'll find, is water-tight.'

'Pshaw!' said William South Norton. A sleek and handsome creature, dark hair slicked with oil, he somehow achieved casual dash even whilst soaked in perspiration and chewing on a piece of dried meat.

'"The wound of the Duke",' South Norton read on, '"has happily not proved severe, but it was extremely perilous. The bullet struck against one of the ribs on the right side, within a short distance of the spine, and passed around the body." Oh, I say! A close-run thing,' he commented. 'Fenian business, to be sure.'

Lawrence yanked at his over-starched collar. 'Yes, yes! That's all very well,' he said, 'but it is *old* news.'

Word of the attempt on the life of the Duke of Edinburgh – Queen Victoria's second son, Alfred Ernest Albert – had reached passengers aboard the *Parramatta* as soon as it dropped anchor off the coast of England. The Aborigines were deeply upset. The Duke had come to see them play at Sydney, just prior to their departure. The Blacks, honoured with an introduction, had testified to their loyalty with a true British cheer for the royal representative.

William South Norton snapped the paper in the air. 'It's news to me, old boy,' he said. 'Fresh detail!'

Bill Hayman's slender hand stroked his mutton-chop whiskers. 'You don't...' he said '...you don't think that it might have a deleterious effect on *our* fortunes, do you, Charley?'

'A what?' Lawrence looked especially annoyed.

Hayman retrieved a pocket handkerchief to mop at his dampened brow. 'We don't want folk thinking every Australian a murderer!' he said.

'It does not seem so great a stretch,' reasoned South Norton, 'since you are all convicts.'

A snarl of exasperation exploded from Lawrence's lips. Hayman snatched the newspaper from his startled *confrère*, skimming the section headlines. '"Nothing in the Papers",' he read. 'Hm, indeed!'

Abruptly let go, the pages separated as they swept to the floor.

Outside the open windows the rain fell without cease, the English climate reasserting itself with a vengeance. A polite knock at the hatch from below, and on the threshold stood the tavern's proprietor. He held out his prize – the *Sporting Life*, a copy they had so far failed to find.

Lawrence pounced like a starving man on a glazed ham.

'Much obliged, Mr Longhurst!' said Bill Hayman, to excuse him.

The landlord creaked away.

Lawrence tore through the paper, finding a passage marked for their attention. '"Arrival of the Black Cricketers",' he announced. 'Here we go: "…no arrival has been anticipated with so much curiosity and interest as that of the Black Cricketers from Australia." How-*ZAT*-uh! "They are thirteen in number, and are captained by Charles Lawrence"…' he trumpeted his own little fanfare '…"late of the All-England Eleven, who has been for some time at the Antipodes."'

Lawrence fell silent, his frown returning.

'Read on,' said Hayman.

'I am,' said Lawrence.

'Read on *aloud*, Charley!'

Charles Lawrence resumed his patrol of the threadbare carpet. '"Monday in the Derby week (May 25) is to witness their *début* in London,"' he read, '"arrangements having been made for them to play their first match against Eleven Gentlemen of the Surrey Club, at the Oval, on May 25 and 26; and on the Thursday after the Derby they will go through a series of athletic exercises on the Surrey ground."'

The pitch of his voice rose, excitedly.

'"The following gentlemen of the Surrey Club have been selected to play against the Blacks in their first match" … '

Hayman leapt up, to lean over Lawrence's shoulder. They went through the list of names, quizzing or else joshing where they had knowledge of an individual's form. William South Norton merely picked at his teeth. Presently, seeming mollified, Hayman dropped back into his seat.

Lawrence paced the bounds and read on. South Norton watched his progress somewhat glassily, excavating his fingernails.

Lawrence suddenly turned, batting the open spread with the back of his hand.

'"With respect to their prowess as cricketers,"' he read, '"that will be conclusively determined by their first public match. We hear, however, that Cuzens and Mullagh show considerable talent and precision in bowling, but, to use a homely phrase – the proof of the pudding will be in the eating." *Hah!*' He threw the paper down, where it joined others piled at their feet.

'Johnny Mullagh *is* our trump card,' said Hayman. 'And there's you, of course.'

Lawrence ignored the compliment. Crossing to the empty fireplace, he took up a dog-eared pocketbook from where it lay on the mantle, beneath a massive mirror.

The compact and well-worn room they occupied formed an antechamber of sorts to the quarters allocated to the remainder of the team. Communal lodgings seemed to suit the Aborigines best. Rather than split them into twos and threes to lodge with various households, Lawrence and Hayman had elected to keep everybody together under the one roof – even if it meant that of the local inn.

The players were either getting themselves ready, or dozing within. Should any of the Blacks quit their quarters, to venture downstairs or outside, they would first be required to pass through this room – and that accorded with Lawrence's preference. The arrangement afforded greater security, and laid to rest at least some of his crowding fears.

'Thomas Hughes writes about cricket,' he said. 'Here, what do you make of this?' Lawrence located one of his many scribbles in the margins. 'A schoolmaster says, "The discipline and reliance on one another which it teaches is so valuable, I think, it ought to be such an unselfish game. It merges the individual in the eleven; he doesn't play that he may win, but that his side may."'

Lawrence brandished the book, his cherished copy of *Tom Brown's Schooldays*. 'Should I try reading some of it out to the boys?'

Hayman laughed. 'The Gospel According to Tommy Hughes, is it?' he said. 'You square-toes. Old Blow-hard! Now you're being ridiculous! Our "boys" they may be, but still, they are grown men.'

South Norton picked at a piece of lint marring the pristine black of his jacket. 'I think *Tom Brown* quite correct in its sentiments,' he said.

Hayman was undeterred. 'You know as well as I do, Charles,' he said, 'that when it comes to unselfish behaviour, there's precious little we can teach them.'

Lawrence bowed his head and mumbled something unintelligible. He looked up, searching the face of his colleague.

'Do you think they will?' he said. 'Behave?'

South Norton sprang from his chair as if flea-bitten. 'When you came to my house that first morning,' he said, 'I had no notice of what time I was to expect you… So, when you all walked in, straight after breakfast as I recall, you, or rather your wild gentlemen, caused a good deal of excitement.' He moved to gather up his topcoat and hat. 'We served a little light refreshment,' he said, 'and my two young daughters were brought into the front parlour to inspect the Blackies. You two were, I think, occupied elsewhere…'

'I was in London,' said Lawrence, 'sweet-talking Burrup and the S.C.C.'

Filling the far doorway, William South Norton chuckled awkwardly. 'The little ones were not at all frightened, you know.' He spoke to Charles Lawrence directly, with all the kindness he could muster. 'Nor had they reason to be… And now I'm afraid I must leave you,' he said. 'So much still needs sorting for this evening! Bring your lads over for seven o'clock, prompt. *Adieu!*'

The clatter of South Norton's exit lapsed into brooding silence.

Hayman huffed, 'You don't have to make a song and dance over every little thing, Charley.'

'No,' said Lawrence, 'that's your pigeon.'

Bill Hayman whined, perplexed. 'They know how to dance the way the ladies like,' he said, 'waltz, polka, you name it. They know their way around a pack of cards…and they're bloody good at billiards.' He recalled with a twinge how Johnny Cuzens had fleeced him at the tables in Gravesend. 'Back home,' Hayman said, 'they acted perfect gentlemen.'

He coughed.

'Most of the time.'

Charles Lawrence glared at the younger man. His eyes threatened frostbite. Hayman had dared allude to their previous tours in Australia – before he, Lawrence, had taken up with them. 'Back home,' he said, 'they could go and visit relatives, those that still have them. Indulge in a spot of ceremonial dancing, or otherwise fill what leisure time they have hunting.'

'*Ih…*'

'They cannot do that here.'

'Charles, I'd rather not…not now…'

'It is imperative we keep them occupied,' said Lawrence, 'as much as we possibly can. We don't let them out of our sight, if we can help it.'

Hayman looked away, his lips pressed firmly together.

Lawrence closed with him as a swordsman would, fighting a duel. 'Make no mistake,' he said, 'I mean to go back to Australia. I want us to return with honours, not wreathed in shame, nor condemned as murderers.'

His resolve was iron-clad.

'I will not have any more deaths on my team.'

CHAPTER IV
Saturday the 23rd of May, 1868

BIRDS OF NO FEATHER

'Night and day the irons clang,
and, like poor galley slaves,
We toil, and toil, and when we die
Must fill dishonoured graves.'

~ 'Jim Jones at Botany Bay', traditional

'The hair is not wiry, like that of a Negro. It hangs in dark locks...something almost refined. A marble bust in the museum. Except black, of course.'

'And is it soft?'

'Heavens!' exclaimed Mrs South Norton. 'Am I to know that...? I would not touch them.' She returned her cup to its saucer with an emphatic clink. 'Should you?'

A number of heads shook all at once.

Mrs Hilary South Norton led the ladies of Town Malling in discussion and afternoon tea. Matronly and magnificent, she fairly basked in the glory of her primacy. The group gathered in close around a mahogany-framed sofa flanked by matching tubs. Each of them held a fan, spread, which they flapped in an attempt to cool their faces; the heat of the day so unusual and oppressive that all they achieved was to cut the air into slices.

Opposite Mrs South Norton bobbed Lily Perfect, by far the youngest present. 'The Black Cricketers,' she trilled, 'you've seen them already?'

Given the general air of excitement, the redundancy of Lily's query was excused. Hilary South Norton seemed only too happy to repeat her proud boast. 'Yes, I've seen them.' Her formidable chest was thrust further out, although it seemed scarcely possible. 'I have *met* them,' she corrected. 'And so shall you.'

She patted her elaborate coiffure. As the close friend of their hostess, Mrs Luck, she was the only woman not required to keep her hat on.

On her left, Lily's portly, cherubic aunt clapped soundlessly. Minute biscuit crumbs fell from her lips. 'So shall we all!' she crowed.

Sounds of a late arrival created a minor disturbance in the adjacent hallway. The hopeful cluster turned their heads in fluid unison: fed so many titbits already, they craved new sensation.

One of the servants appeared, and ushered into the drawing-room a slight, soberly dressed woman. 'A Miss Sarah Larkin, ma'am.'

The whisking fans ceased in their movements.

The exalted high priestesses crouched, awaiting their sacrifice. Seeing so much attention fixed on her, Sarah's insides contracted. She hovered in the doorway sideways on. As one the group cast their beady eye, a critical stare that ranged about her person with unkind freedom. Her face was deemed plain and undecorated, her forehead a touch too broad. The way the hair burst forth from her temples, only to double back under restraint, untidy. Dull hair it was, too – dark, no attempt made to disguise sweeps of premature grey. Long, tense fingers, entirely absent of the requisite languor or even a decent manicure, clutched at a stack of papers she seemed reluctant to surrender: she held them like a comfort, or shield.

The butler relieved her of these.

Her body, exposed, was lean but not so very elegant. She wanted for poise. The dress advertised total indifference towards the fashions of the day. She wore a mantle, for pity's sake! *And* she was too tall.

It was all they could do not to audibly tut.

Although a greeting worked about Sarah's lips, no sensible sound came out. She conceded neither bob nor curtsey, and thought for a moment that she might simply turn and leave.

'Come, my dear. Sit.' Too late – Mrs Hilary South Norton had delivered the dread command. 'Ladies,' she said, 'this is Sarah Ann Larkin, a relation to the Twyttens of Royston Hall…not that you would know it…'

Mute resentment broke into a flurry of welcoming smiles. The clutch parted to indicate a perch in their midst, if not room exactly. Even as she settled, Sarah sensed pitying glances exchanged behind her back. She began to shrink, until catching herself in the act.

The company of women was outside of her adult experience. She might as well have been nesting among flamingoes.

'ANNIE, YOU REMEMBER OLD LAMBERT LARKIN?' Hilary South Norton shouted across the room at alarming volume. 'THE VICAR OF RYARSH?' A palsied old crone, collapsed in a far wing chair, gave no indication of having heard. She gave no indication of being awake or even alive. Hilary South Norton persevered. 'THIS IS HIS ONLY DAUGHTER, SARAH! SARAH ANN HILDA!'

'Huldah', not 'Hilda'; and there was something unsavoury about having one's middle names bellowed across a room. Sarah blushed, to the neck.

Mrs South Norton turned to her with a look of grave import. 'How is your father?' she said.

'Too ill to travel,' replied Sarah, matter-of-fact.

'So I see. Poor dear. I do hope he is well looked after in London.' Hilary South Norton performed an abrupt aside. 'They still have the Cholera, you know.'

The remark was rewarded with a chorus of gasps, and one 'How awful!'. For all Sarah knew, there might yet be cholera in London, but it suggested their house itself plague-ridden! The battleaxe took her by the hand, to continue raining blows about her poor, undefended head. 'You must keep us apprised.'

Her commiserating tone made Sarah nauseous.

Mrs South Norton heaved a loud stage sigh. 'Such sad news from the Manor,' she said. 'The Captain was a fine man. Tea?'

Just two days prior Captain John Savage, latterly Justice of the Peace for the county of Kent, and Lord of the Manor, had dropped down dead.

At least he'd the good sense to do it on Ascension Day, thought Sarah. Wisely, she bit her tongue. For much of his early priesthood her father had served the locality. On his behalf, and in the family name, she was there to pay respects to a man she had never met.

'No,' said Sarah, recalling the offer of tea. 'Thank you.'

'Yes, indeed,' continued Hilary South Norton, 'events of recent days have caused us great concern. And how are *you* coping, my dear?'

Not being able to scream or hit out, the preacher's daughter couldn't rightly say. She did not care for the way Mrs South Norton conflated the subjects of her *conversazione*, nor the implication arising. Social convention dictated that she respond graciously. Her audience grew impatient. Sarah considered a moment: aside from a subtle fury, she felt nothing. She had anyway missed her cue.

A knot momentarily disfigured Hilary South Norton's porcelain brow, and then it became clear: Sarah's silence had returned the offence twofold. Swift as the drop of a veil, dismissal shadowed her stone façade, and the fearsome basilisk turned away. The other ladies twittered nervously, at no point uttering anything worth the breath.

Escape from their clutches took Sarah the worst of an hour, but escape she did, to walk through the heat haze of the flower garden, alone. The air outside smelled no less sour. All the same, she relished a moment's peace and solitude. Those two things lately seemed very much to go together. Sarah never felt so lonesome as when in company.

Her great fear, on the train journey there, had been that whatever she might say would seem too trivial, and yet nothing could match what she had lately endured. To be made so suddenly self-conscious was an awful thing.

The birds stayed silent, and the bees too. The humid heat could not suppress vibrant hues of leaf and petal. Doubly blessed, their responsibilities stretched to little more than looking pretty and inspiring calm.

Looking down, Sarah considered her miserable outfit – sufficient for a funeral perhaps, but never the impending party. She suddenly despised her appearance – that very thing she had come, over the years, to think nothing of.

Sarah's girlhood had effectively ended the night her mother died, half a lifetime ago.

'*You are the woman of the house now.*'

She had awoken the next morning to those very words. The words with which her father chose to inform were his only consolation. Overnight, a woman, even while her body and mind struggled to catch up. What that meant, in purely practical terms of course, was that Sarah became the housekeeper, with a helping hand from Mrs Beeton's invaluable little book. In very short order it had fallen to her to assume control of the household's tidy function.

Always and forevermore, her mother, Frances, would be the angel of the house. And a hollowed place it was in which to keep on living. There, the good daughter learnt her life's lesson – to settle for being less.

The first years following their sudden loss were close to unbearable. As the only real survivor of that night, Sarah gained the strength sufficient to stay weak, obliged to take on her new role, as 'an helpmeet'. It was not good that the man should be alone. She must be willing to crouch, to place the slipper on her father's foot – it was the least she could do.

And if her own girlish feet were thereby bound, in the Chinese fashion, then she herself had allowed it: for the greater good; for the sake of peace; to please.

Gently she cradled the heads of flowering blooms – camellias and lilies, wilting – listening all the while to the distant gurgle of the cascade, that delightful water feature across the front road.

She should not resent the other ladies so much. In adulthood as in childhood, society required that genteel womenfolk fill their idle hours with harmless amusement – a 'pass-time', so-called: music, or drawing – anything so long as it was of no real consequence. She could not begrudge her poor father his demands of her exclusive attention.

Sarah let the crisped bulb fall in a shower of petals.

She was briefly courted when young – younger: a single suitor had made serious approaches, seeking her father's permission. Lambert had turned him aside, citing lack of prospects. In paraphrase of the tract he shortly after tasked her to transcribe, an imprudent marriage might have taken its ill effect 'On Posterity'. It was prosperity rather that occupied his mind, so she felt – and said as much when the time came, deliberately misreading the text back to him. He hadn't commented.

As for the disappointed young man, he had undertaken mission work in the colonies, soon to die from an extreme tropical malady. Or so she told herself. Either way, she had never heard from him again.

This wound was old, however; the 'pangs of dispriz'd love' soon dimmed. Her infatuation had been but brief, and, Sarah decided, she had not loved. What, anyway, was love? As the Queen's own chaplain had only just recently decreed, from the chapel at Windsor Castle: 'The spirit of romance is dead.' It was official.

When it came to responsible womanhood, none less than Victoria Regina served as every feminine ideal: devoted wife and indulgent mother, a widow so dedicated in mourning that she had not been seen in public in years.

Sarah could hear voices from within the house, calling her name – the first guests must be arriving. Turning too quickly, she snagged her dress on the thorns of a rose bush. Urgently she pulled herself free, required to readjust folds of material in order to disguise the torn threads.

Making for the opened French windows fostered her greatest fear. Failing fortunes such as theirs presented a great many dangers. Daily she read proof of how the weak were shown no mercy. Domesticated hens sometimes turned on a sickly member of their brood to peck them literally to bits.

Sarah might be better off staying hidden from the world, were her coat any more ragged or in patches.

CHAPTER V
Saturday the 23rd of May, 1868

FORMAL INTRODUCTIONS

'Truly, we cannot help feeling that cricket has a humanising
and civilising influence, for Mr Lawrence's black team observe
all the courtesies and amenities of the cricketing field, and
privately both act and speak like gentlemen.'

~ *Bathurst Times*

William South Norton peeped around the door to the drawing-room. His
mother held court. Lily Perfect and her aunt were there, doubly worth avoiding;
the widow Ireson; the Millgate – begging their pardon, Viner – sisters; and one
other blackbird he could not put a name to, somebody from out of town up for
the grand funeral.

Ducking away before he might be seen, Norton collided with another man
at his back.

'Begging your pardon, sir,' the fellow said. 'Elias Luther.' He puffed out his
cheeks and fanned his headgear. 'Terrible heat, sir, don't you find? I do hope we
ain't in for another like '58.'

'What were you doing there?' demanded William South Norton.

'Examining these splendid portraits what are hung along the wall,' said
Luther. ''Quite 'squisite they are, sir. Very delicate. I fancy that I've never seen
the blush upon a lady's cheek caught quite so well, in my humble opinion. Why,
it's almost 'z-if they were alive.'

'You are a connoisseur of painting, Mr Luther,' said William South Norton.
'These pictures are the work of John Downman R.A., one-time resident here at
Went House. Our own Cade House served as his studio.'

'I am not familiar with the name as perhaps I should be,' said Elias Luther,
patting the back of his neck with his kerchief, 'but I shall be sure to make a note
of it, for future reference, yes indeed.'

Turning the brim of his bowler around in his hands, he checked up and
down the hallway, before leaning close in to whisper. 'Still, not quite the Manor,
Mr Norton, is it?' he said.

The original venue for that evening's reception, of necessity, had required eleventh-hour substitution.

'New money hasn't the same ring as old,' said South Norton, 'but neither can a beggar a chooser be.'

Realising he addressed the proprietor of a successful carriage service, William South Norton covered his embarrassment with a short cough.

Each man smiled, and turned to the contemplation of fine art.

An hour later, and the main reception room at Went House was filled with the milk if not the cream of Malling society. For higher echelons to attend, quite so soon following the death of Captain Savage, R.N., was inappropriate. Invitation had of late been extended to the wealthiest local tradesmen, or else to those long established in business.

Mourning dress universally observed, the gentlemen wore black armbands; the ladies, dresses uncharacteristically sombre. Town Malling and its environs being something of a military enclave, many of the men-folk wore Naval or Army uniform, polished medals proudly on display. Even so, the lowering of the beam promoted a more relaxed and convivial atmosphere than might otherwise have prevailed.

The music of a light chamber orchestra masked the stiff swish of crinoline and the tinkle of glassware. Adjoining rooms opened up to accommodate the swelling crowd, until it occupied much of the ground floor. The younger set mulled over gravitation towards the games room, when the sharp rapping of a cane announced the guests of honour.

The Aborigines filed in, to a polite ripple of applause.

They walked with grace and composure, and, in the habit of athletes, precise awareness of the space their bodies each occupied. The men stood up straight and thrust back their shoulders to give the best formal account of themselves, as they had been drilled. A casual line-up formed at the far end of the room.

The crowding citizens admired their absolute darkness. The skin of the Aborigines was not exactly black, more very dense brown: not at all reflective of the light, it had the dry, mellow quality of soot. Their hair was uniformly black and curled, just as Hilary South Norton had described. In stature, they differed as much as the same number of Englishmen might be expected to vary, ranging in height from about five feet four to five feet nine inches, or perhaps a little taller. Each of their faces appeared quite distinct, especially with regard to their sprawling, bridgeless noses; high foreheads, fringed, with whiskers and moustache rigorously groomed in the military style. A proud regiment, then, but not fierce – beneath beetling brows their large eyes appeared calm and kind. Smiles flashed, cheeky and shy. They were less 'wild gentlemen' than gentle men that had once lived in the wild.

Bill Hayman cleared his throat.

'Ladies and gentlemen,' he said, 'it gives me great pleasure to present to you – our team.' He bowed and stood to one side, to introduce the players in turn. 'Red Cap...

'Tiger...

'Peter...

'Mosquito...'

The next in line loomed noticeably broader than his fellows – a large, burly man. 'Bullocky.' The audience barely smothered their amusement.

Hayman indicated the big man's muscular, grinning neighbour. 'Dick-a-Dick.' Temptation too great unleashed loud titters and murmurings.

'King Cole...

'Cuzens.' Johnny Cuzens looked to be smallest of the company.

'Jim Crow...

'Twopenny...

'Dumas...

'Mullagh...' Identification of the tallest member set the men-folk rumbling. Conjecture from the *Sporting Life* engendered great expectations. Lawrence allowed himself a proud smile.

'...and at the end,' concluded Hayman, 'Sundown.'

The names that were given are the names that have taken.

Hands clasped behind his back, beard thrust forward, King Cole's manner is staid and dignified. 'Charles Rose' to the whites while working at their sheep station, his status has since been elevated – without having any genuine meaning at all.

He concentrates on the far wall, above the curious, crowding heads, and wishes himself anywhere, away from it all.

On cue, each Aborigine nodded, or bid the crowd a genial '*G'di!*' – the contraction of '*Gia Gindi*', a formal greeting in one of their own languages.

Hilary South Norton was tickled pink. 'They have been trained to say "Good day"!' she enthused. Her hand, clasped to her ample bosom, rose to her fond, blushing cheek as her favourite son stepped forward.

'The lovely county of Kent,' said William South Norton, 'is England's celebrated garden, also called "the Gateway to England"! And may I say, I am delighted to see so many of the good people of Town Malling present tonight...'

Noises of approval arose from all sides.

'Let me ask you all to join me in opening wide that fairest of gateways, that we might welcome to our shores these talented sportsmen, all the way from their – um – their native Australia!'

William South Norton led a brief round of applause.

'An additional toast is in order,' he continued. 'To Her Majesty, on the occasion of her birthday, which is tomorrow. Raise your glasses if you please. To our most gracious Sovereign Lady, QUEEN VICTORIA… Grant her in health and wealth long to live. The Queen!'

'The Queen!' echoed all.

'We wish our esteemed guests, the Aboriginal Australian Eleven, the very best of British during their stay,' said South Norton, 'not least this coming Monday at the Oval. And, for ourselves, a jolly evening's entertainments, overshadowed as they are by such grave and untimely misfortune among the – ah – among the Savages.'

Charles Lawrence's face turned ashen.

A general collapse ensued. Excited Malling residents rushed forward to shake hands, attempting to engage one or other of the team in conversation. The hubbub of small talk filled the air; the foreign guests slowly filtered throughout the room. Groaning platters of food and drink, carried from group to group, were offered up for their delectation.

The Aborigines had not yet learnt to ignore the serving staff. Every time their glasses were topped or plates refreshed, they showed their teeth in sincere appreciation.

Cuzens, caught up in the sensation of new tastes and smells, sampled freely from every tray.

'Steady on, Johnny!' Lawrence banged about like a sheepdog at trials.

William South Norton gathered up his brother-in-law and beckoned Lawrence over to join them. He wished to single out – and, where expedient, introduce – local notables.

'Elias Luther, by whose graces you will be escorted to Snodland Monday morning,' he said in passing, 'and… Ah! But you really must meet this gentleman. William, Charles, may I present…William Charles Viner. Oh, how perfectly absurd! And his wife, Adelaide.'

'Adelaide,' said Bill Hayman, taking a step forward, 'Lovely name. A favourite where I come from.' The colonist bowed his head charmingly.

A silver-haired man standing alongside made himself known. 'Excuse me, sirs. John Scotchford Viner. Delighted to meet you. My wife, Rebecca.'

A much younger woman with a passing resemblance to Adelaide took her place at his side.

'J.S. is cousin to William Viner,' South Norton explained, 'while Rebecca is Adelaide's sister.'

'We like to keep it in the family,' said the elder Viner. 'My card.'

A blazing rectangle was thrust into Lawrence's open palm. He paled as he read it.

J. & W. VINER
The High-street, Town Malling

'NOT DEAD, BUT GONE BEFORE'

Funerals furnished and a great variety
of coffin furniture

As soon as their backs were turned, Lawrence cast it into the fireplace.

The circulating food trays gradually ebbed away. Customarily shy, the Aborigines proved slow to join in general conversation, often failing to respond even to direct questions; but they were not ignorant as some of the townsfolk supposed.

Masculine talk favoured the subject of sport. As the evening progressed, the women withdrew into the adjoining drawing-room, there to await the menfolk who might join them as they wished. The ladies soon grew impatient, wilting like great dark flowers across the sofa-chairs. Groups including Black Cricketers were inveigled to follow on.

The Aborigines, growing more relaxed, peered in exaggerated wonder at the voluminous skirts worn by the English ladies: layer on layer cascading down, glaciated waterfalls that splashed, crystalline, onto the carpet.

'Dat not heavy?' said Twopenny, tugging at the hem of one such striking female garment.

Some professed doubts that these glamorous creatures possessed lower halves, or feet. They knew better of course, but relished the play. The native Australians employed a keenly developed sense of the ridiculous. They pretended to think cups and saucers shellfish, put them to their ears to listen for the sea, or had them 'walk' daintily across the teapoys. They pointed at wine bottles and enquired what kind of fish lived in *these* shells, where they might be found, and wondered aloud how there were none similar on their own beaches.

Charmed, the ladies proposed a round of simple parlour games.

'Hand-shadows!' someone cried.

One after another the wall lights were extinguished, until only a portable table lamp remained. In the semi-darkness the Aborigines, led by Dick-a-Dick, rolled the whites of their eyes. They hooted like owls, and spread wide their palms. Everyone laughed.

Adelaide Viner explained the concept of a 'shadowgraph', a pictorial silhouette made by various positions of the hands and cast upon the wall. Anonymous in the dark, 'spooky' voices called for her to show examples.

'Ooo-oo, we are creatures living in shadow!' they said. 'Set us free!'

'Yes,' cried another, 'bring the shadows to life!'

The likeness of a dark horse appeared, gaily tossing of its head and waggling the ears. A crab scuttled to and fro.

'Do the snail! The snail!'

A large black snail slithered ponderously on its way, until a pair of rabbits came bouncing. Lily Perfect, over-excited, suffered hiccups.

'Old Mother Hubble…that is, Hubbard!' shouted a local wag.

'Old King Cole!' suggested another.

At the appearance of a long nose and pointy crown, the Aborigines screeched and hollered so much that there was a rush to the darkened doorway and the lamps were ordered re-lit. They continued to cut extraordinary capers, some entirely helpless with mirth. Eventually they pushed forward the one among them called King Cole, and for those in confusion the penny dropped. The English sang the nursery rhyme in a rising chorale, while its namesake stood isolated and embarrassed in the centre of the room.

'Old King Cole was a merry old soul
And a merry old soul he was he!
He called for his pipe
And he called for his bowl
And he called for his fiddlers three!'

One fellow mimed the throw of a cricket ball at the appropriate moment, but no one else got the joke.

Young Lily Perfect approached the bashful Aborigine, and curtsied. With painful sincerity she asked, 'Are you really – *hic* – a king?'

He answered honestly. 'You say that I am a king.'

Cole shrank immediately back, retreating behind a nearby pillar. In short order he became at one with it, so successfully that he was soon forgotten by almost everyone.

Sarah Larkin, feeling awkward for him – almost as much as for herself – remained standing off to one side. She fingered the ormolu: genuine gilded bronze, not alloy, like that back at home.

'Dear brother, what is it?' enquired Bullocky.

'I don't know,' said Red Cap.

For the benefit of an eager audience, the pair of them discussed the merits of a large painted portrait of the lady of the house, Mrs Luck.

'Is it a ship?'

She did indeed resemble a ship in full sail.

'No, mate,' said Red Cap. 'I think it a kangaroo!'

Dick-a-Dick meanwhile mischievously lamented. He blamed England's weak sun for the loss of his colour. 'I spoil my complexion,' he said. 'When I go back my mother won't know me!'

Amongst Aboriginal farm-hands the Queen's birthday was known as a time of plenty, when bread, beef, and blankets would be distributed; anticipation of rewards had put them in higher than normal spirits.

An outburst in the hallway created a sudden stir in the main room beyond. Word spread like bushfire: against all expectations, members of the landed gentry were making a late entrance.

Rushing in from the opposite direction, William South Norton hissed at one of the servants. 'Nevills?' he demanded. 'Or Birlings?'

Into the lobby, larger than life, strode Sir Ralph Nevill, the West Kent Hunt's Master of Foxhounds. Two steps behind followed his sister, the spinster Lady Caroline Nevill. Their host, Edward Luck, quailed in his boots. Hilary South Norton was beside herself.

As confirmation reached his ear of the West Kent's arrival in force, Lawrence's heart shrank. Here they came, charging. Desperately he searched for an avenue of escape.

In the drawing-room the Aboriginal gentlemen were being entertained with music. Three blackfellows casually reclined on sofas while the ladies played and sang for them. Elsewhere hands dealt cards for whist. Addressed in broken English, Tiger was being explained gaming rules he knew very well. He let it carry on until he lost all patience. 'What for you no talk to me good Inglis?' he growled. 'I speak as good Inglis as him belonging you!' Tiger pointed out Peter, smoking the peace pipe beside the fireplace. 'Big fool that one fellow,' he said. 'Him not know Inglis one dam!'

Bill Hayman executed a hand signal, letting Tiger know that he should moderate his language: ladies were present. Turning back to an attentive Adelaide Viner, he continued to explain how Lawrence – actually, he and Lawrence – were teaching the Aborigines to read and write.

Tiger overheard, and snorted derisively. 'What's usy Lawrence?' he jibed. 'Him too much along of us. Him speak nothing now but blackfella talk!'

Charles Lawrence stood apart from the main gathering, nervous and distracted. Local gossip raged on, as he guessed it would about any strangers in their midst.

'They sailed away beyond the South China Seas, and came back with a grown daughter...'

'Who? *Hic...*'

'The Twyttens.'

Lawrence followed the speakers' sightline, alighting on a very pale young woman with streaks of grey in her bountiful hair. Although attracting his eye, she remained unaware of it. Watching, listening to events, she herself did not speak, and yet all the while she radiated a fierce intelligence. The crystal sharpness of her gaze was really something quite exceptional.

Lawrence caught King Cole also looking on, from the opposite side of the room. He stayed for some reason half-hidden, and then, meeting Lawrence's eye, ducked away.

They were the only persons silent within the general ferment. Lawrence wondered what should condemn this young woman to be so much of an outsider, or Cole – he too, for that matter.

Despite herself, Sarah Larkin had excited interest. The Aborigines could tell she was different. Not from her plain dress – they accepted people as they were, without judgement. They perceived the cold shoulder she endured from the other English.

Rebecca Viner was petitioned to introduce the 'him quiet one lady'.

'She lives in London, our capital city, where she works in the library at the British Museum,' said Mrs Viner. 'That's right, isn't it, Sarah?'

Sarah whispered an assent.

The information only led to further confusion, and more questions. How best to explain, to men who had no written language, the concept of a library? A museum? Following a brief discussion they arrived at a formula to explain away Sarah's role – imaginatively, and rather poetically – as 'a guardian of the words of dead men'.

'The living and the dead,' said Sarah. She felt secretly pleased with her new identity: it made her life sound interesting.

The curious Aborigines were impressed. Traditionally speaking, male elders were their guardians of law and lore. Sarah was comparatively young, and a female. They looked on her with renewed respect. King Cole felt his observation of her special character had been confirmed.

Mosquito openly expressed his satisfaction. 'Sarah. Pretty name,' he said. 'I'll 'member 'im.' He was literate, with a clear hand. To prove the point he wrote out her name a great many times over.

Lawrence oversaw, and approved, the neat intersection of cultures. He would have to learn not to feed his fears, to trust in the temperance and good humour of his *Akwerkepentye*, his 'far-travelling children'.

In the parlour, sickly Johnny Cuzens slumped in an armchair, long-faced companion standing guard by his side.

Peripatetic, Lawrence strolled over to join them. The team captain placed a comforting hand on Cuzens' shoulder.

'Not just one, but three of the buggers, black as sin!'

The voice of Sir Ralph Nevill boomed, carrying from the next room. He related, not for the first time, the occasion of his first meet with the Australian natives, out on the hunting field.

'…had 'em cornered in a covert! So I said to George, have your *punkawallah* bring his mount to the front for a gin-jabber with these savages. Couldn't get a word o' sense out of 'em. Surrendered the fox, though. Smack dab into the hands of Reverend Perfect, the original black beast. Came home from a good run, brush in one pocket, prayer-book in t'other!'

Rumbustious Sir Ralph concluded his tale. 'Too bad about the Captain, what? Same day. Sorry business.'

A brief period of contemplation, and then Charley Dumas spoke up. '*Eni na watjala?*' he asked. 'You know dat pella, Lawrence?'

'Mm?' said Lawrence. 'No, Charley. No, I'm glad to say I don't.'

Lawrence dreaded their sort – the kind who liked to exercise dominion over the earth. The hunt was meant for meat, not merely for sport. The Aborigines had taught him that.

'I am told the entire continent of Australia is little more than a desert.'

A stranger's voice in his ear, Lawrence turned. He recognised William Viner. 'What could they possibly do there?' the fellow enquired. He addressed him directly – as if the Blacks were deaf and dumb, or else entirely absent.

'Live off the land,' said Lawrence, 'take pleasure in the hunt…as do the wealthy of our own nation.'

He paused.

'Or they would, if only allowed to. Excuse me.'

Charles Lawrence realised: perhaps it was not the conduct of his players that he should be worried about.

CHAPTER VI
Monday the 25th of May, 1868

INTO LONDON

'Now Nineveh was an exceeding great city of three
days' journey.

And Jonah began to enter into the city a day's journey,
and he cried, and said, Yet forty days, and Nineveh shall
be overthrown.'

~ Jonah 3:3–4

The Aboriginal Australian Eleven made their way into England's capital by
train. Whilst in London, the team would be quartered in the Queen's Head
Inn, on Southwark's Borough High-street – just a short carriage ride from
Kennington Fields and the Oval. Their all-important first match was scant
hours and a few miles away.

Lawrence clung to the overhead racks, meaning to address the gathered
Aborigines. He jiggered and swayed in the centre of the rolling carriage, and
searched his heart to find the right words.

Their protracted journey together had begun nearly ten months earlier.

He, Lawrence, had spent a memorable first night, steeped in the rich
collective smell of them – thirteen Aboriginals, a cook, and the coachman, as
well as himself and young Bill Hayman – the entire troupe crammed into a
waggon-and-four wherever space among the tents, 'tucker' and other supplies
could be found. In this delightful proximity they left Lake Wallace, and spent
the next eight days trekking some 150 miles southeast.

It rained all the way from their base at Edenhope to the coast at Warrnambool
– a perpetual, torrential downpour. The accommodating Blacks fashioned
Lawrence excellent wigwams, and kept the fire up to his toes. Even so, the
rigours of Bush travel knocked him up something awful. On his third night
without sleep he discovered the reason: when not using it in place of a pillow, he
was spending the majority of his time perched atop a wrapped parcel – which

turned out to be the rotting torso of a kangaroo. His expressions of horror amused the natives no end. In one fell swoop he gained their confidence and won their affection, the neophyte team captain their confirmed New Chum.

On wet spring evenings, the Blacks engaged in shooting 'roo and opossum. Ever sporting, Lawrence had joined them – the sure-fire way to ensure fresh meat. Thunder and lightning writ large across desert skies, they traded jokes and stories around a big campfire; plenty of logs for seats, any amount of mutton chops cooking on the gridiron, and tea piping hot out of a little billy stove. All told, he had enjoyed himself immensely.

In the simple surround of that earthly paradise, Lawrence had introduced them to the life and teachings of Christ, and met with their curious interest. The Sunday following their arrival he took them all to the Church of England, Warrnambool, where they were very attentive, and when the collection plate was presented, each gave a little help. Evening prayers on board ship had continued in their Christian education…

'You remember, boys,' Lawrence said, 'the excellent Captain Williams.'

'Oh, *yes*, Lawrence!' the Aborigines unanimously agreed.

The captain of the *Parramatta* had proven very popular with them. During their lengthy voyage both he and Lawrence had taken it upon themselves to instruct their charges in the Scriptures. It helped overcome their fears of the endless sea. Captain Williams' leading of the prayers inspired confidence in their safety aboard his vessel: if the captain was so good, then they should never sink (*Matthew* 8:23–27). When the time came for good Captain Williams to take his leave, a few days prior to their landing at Gravesend, the Aborigines had become greatly distressed.

'You remember, then, his warning to you,' said Lawrence, 'when he came to your bunks to say goodbye?'

For the duration of their sea voyage, rather than be assigned the relative luxury of their own private cabins, all had crammed into intermediate berths situated between first and second class.

'He said, "Now, boys, I have to thank you for your good behaviour during this passage, and to give you a little advice. In England you will meet with as many thieves and vagabonds as hairs on your head, and they will tell you that you are very clever, and then ask you to have some drink and then rob you. So don't have anything to do with them, but do just what Mr Lawrence wishes you to do!"… You remember he said that, don't you?'

Emotions ran high concerning the early departure of Captain Williams, and there had been a good deal of crying. Fresh tears fell in the train carriage, so, clearly, the Aborigines well recalled. Lawrence, not for the first time, doubted the wisdom of what he had started.

Praying for the understanding heart of Solomon, he elaborated on his theme. 'He was afraid,' he said; 'he was afraid you might be led astray in England.'

Dick-a-Dick spoke up.

'You can trust us, Lawrence,' he said. 'We be careful.'

Dick-a-Dick, a natural performer who often played the clown for any sort of audience, was, at the same time, sober and wise, a highly respected member of his clan − and often an inspiration to them all. Amiably, he turned to his team-mates. 'Captain Williams and Mister Lawrence, they know Jesus Chrise,' he said. 'Jesus Chrise and the little pickaninny they tell us about that we saw in the picture.'

'*Uah! Ne!*' The others approved, nodding vigorously.

Lawrence joined in. Upturned faces all around wore expressions of calm and rapt attention. Bless you, Dick.

'They kill him,' said Dick-a-Dick.

The train lurched violently, and Lawrence almost fell.

Damn you, Dick. Lawrence shot the blithe trickster a filthy look. Was he being sincere, or sly? His mind raced.

'Jesus is in heaven now,' galloped Lawrence, unsure how to recover. 'And we pray to him to keep you all safe in England.'

Their train slowed to a crawl, beginning the final approach into London Bridge station. The stop-start motion took on the lulling tempo of a rocking cradle. The barest sliver of a low moon, still visible near to the horizon, loomed large.

A sulphurous taint as if from the ashes of a great fire billowed into the carriage. The Aborigines crowded at the windows for their first glimpse of the vast, smoking metropolis. Narrow streets swung by below the viaduct − mud, and stone, and soot. Following the wet, black Sunday just gone, all colour had been drained from the view: everywhere appeared lifeless. No longer green fields, for miles in every direction stretched only grey rooftops. It seemed as if they sailed once more an immense and unending ocean. One would have to be mad to leap into it.

Sound asleep, only King Cole remained in his seat. He grumbled somnolently, farted and shifted slightly, a frown on his screwed-up face. Those nearest to him turned and laughed.

'*Bripumyarrimin*,' they cooed.

'Him dreaming.'

CHAPTER VII
Monday the 25th of May, 1868

AT THE OVAL

'But for their colour, which is decided enough, the
spectators might have believed that they were watching
the play of some long established club eleven. The
best argument that could be adduced in favour of the
aboriginal race, it shows of what the native race is
capable under proper tuition and care.'

~ *The Australasian*

With three lusty cheers to announce themselves, and a warlike whoop in
salute of their opponents, the Aborigines swept onto the cricket field at the
Oval. Startled birds took flight. Like the rumble and crash of a great wave,
the massive crowd roared back from the stands. In the stadium ground's short
history, its enclosures had never been packed so full. The whole of London, or
so it seemed, had turned out to see them play.

Carriages without number ringed the pavilion. Grand four-in-hands pressed
in against dogcarts; springy and elegant phaetons nestled close to lumbering
stagecoaches; barouches, gigs, chaises, trucks and hansom cabs.

More women than usual could be counted among the spectators, from
common serving-wenches to fine ladies. The cautious watched from the
seclusion of their carriages. The bold sat side-saddle on their horses, perfectly
poised, programme in one hand and reins in the other. A great many more
mingled freely on the stands.

The newspapers were having a field day. 'A New Epoch in the History
of Cricket!' screamed one headline. 'Decidedly the Event of the Century'
pronounced another. Scattered throughout the crowd, vendors cried out their
own, often scurrilous variations.

A festive atmosphere prevailed, more sensational than strictly sporting.

The instant the Black Cricketers had appeared, synchronous motion created
a blinding broadside – the flash of sunlight reflected in a thousand spyglasses.
Everyone was determined to take a closer look, the majority interested more

in the physical confirmation of the Aborigines than they were their cricketing acquirements.

Their skin colour seemed to vary in shade, but they were most assuredly as advertised: 'Very Black: virtual photographic negatives of White Cricketers'. Lithe and athletic, slight of limb yet standing straight and upright, they appeared tolerably broad in the shoulders, if rather weak in the chest. Hair and beards were worn long, whiskers luxuriant. Particular remark was made of their broadly expanded nostrils. Some patrons found them handsome, others ugly.

As for their dress, the Aborigines wore white flannel trousers held up with blue elastic belts. Their Garibaldi shirts were of a fine military red, adorned with a diagonal flannel sash, and a necktie pinned under a stiff white linen collar. Beneath this finery they sported undershirts of French merino wool. A peaked cap, bearing the silver emblem of a boomerang crossed with a cricket bat, completed the ensemble.

Charles Lawrence had initiated the idea of a uniform, supplying the 'corps' with suitable raiment for their long campaign; he saw it as a means of fostering tradition – the team taking pride in itself – but also, of fashioning them into playing-field heroes. His chief inspiration was the system as first introduced, at Rugby school. Individual colour schemes further distinguished each player, caps ostensibly matching their flannel sashes. Pre-printed cards, offered for sale, tabulated names alongside corresponding tints. In this way spectators might tell one Black from another, even at distance; and a very good arrangement it was agreed to be.

The Aborigines of course had their own ideas, and swapped their caps around continually.

In the Reading-room at the British Museum, within the main Salon, Sarah Larkin sat upright in her usual seat. She looked high overhead, to where the light streamed in through the enormous dome. It was perhaps 150 feet in diameter; the lantern itself must have been at least 40 feet across. Her imagination fluttered at the enclosing glass.

Returned from Town Malling, Sarah did not at all like the perspective her recent trip had lent. Domestic life centred around little else than dirty pots and clean linen. The remainder of her days she spent here in the library. She might have been content to live chiefly inside her own head, except for the fact that her firing thoughts could go nowhere, led to nothing, and availed her naught.

Sarah closed up the text she was uselessly holding: this past quarter-hour she had not looked at it once. A trickle of dust leaked from out of the spine, piling a tiny heap on the desktop. With a sweep of her sleeve she reduced it to a moth-like smear. In the end, she had to admit: aside from her familiar routine, she had no idea what else to do. She was of practical use only – a tool, a mindless machine with no dimension of its own.

She closed her eyes and listened to echoes around the vast chamber: the thumbed rasp and ceaseless swish of turned pages; books, books as they banged, singly on tabletops or thudding in great piles. Each layer of sound, the padding feet, the leathery squeak of shoes, once noted, she filtered out – seeking further still. Snuffles, snorts, a stuttering cough, quiet conversation; these too were catalogued and put aside. Finally, she could make out muted echoes of the distant streets, solid evidence of a world beyond.

Real life happened somewhere else, far, far away.

Freshened by rain and solidified by the action of sun and wind, by noon the Oval turf looked to be in tip-top condition. Julius Caesar, a Gentleman of Surrey, served as umpire. Players from both teams shook hands and briefly huddled about His Imperial Highness. The Eleven Gentlemen of Surrey won the toss, and they elected to bat first.

Mighty Mullagh began the bowling, wearing a sash of dark blue.

An occasional mild shout from the English players inspired an echo among the stands – 'Well hit!' or 'Run it out' and, when the Aborigine Peter fumbled the ball, 'Butterfingers!' But the greatest excitement came when Mullagh pitched up a ripper, bowling out the first of his opponents. The unrestrained jubilation of the Aborigines reverberated right across the ground. They tore up and down, running barefoot between the wickets 'like deer', tumbling and rolling in the bare grass, and all the while screaming and shouting their native backchat. Play continued brisk. The audience agreed themselves highly entertained.

Between two and three in the afternoon the time came for a short luncheon break. As he made for the pavilion, the last Surrey Gentleman let opinion be known that the wicket had been insufficiently rolled.

'It's got all the qualities of a blasted billiard table,' he grumbled. 'Not just the colour, but the pockets! Bah! Let's drown our sorrows, eh, Jupp?'

Dumas, Twopenny and his brother Mosquito gathered around poorly Cuzens. The team were denied the services of its 'great gun': he suffered a bout of enteritis and was too weak to play. The rest mingled with the spectators, who crowded in eagerly. They were passed cakes, sweets, and baskets of homemade biscuits. Hipflasks offered freely, the men were encouraged to take a nip. Fearing precisely this, Lawrence strove to gather up his flock and guide them into the lunch tent, where the choice of beverage was limited to a very dilute sherry, or tea.

Following the interval King Cole, suitably regal in magenta cap and sash, and then Bullocky, wearing maroon, resumed the bowling. Neither enjoyed much success. After his energetic socialising at lunch, Bullocky in particular appeared somewhat the worse for wear, only redeeming himself later with a superlative catch. Charles Lawrence took over the bowling and made short work of the remaining wickets. The Aborigines bowled in the new over-arm style. By shifting gear to deliver a few slow and under-arm pitches, their captain gained pleasing results, at least until Surrey readjusted.

Next up, it was the Aborigines' turn to bat.

Their first innings were unspectacular. Only Mullagh achieved an appreciable score. King Cole managed half as many before being bowled out by Mr I. D. Walker of Surrey, caught out earlier by Cole for a single run.

And so ended the first day's play.

'We did all right,' said Bill Hayman.

Lawrence looked disappointed.

'The Blacks returned the ball quickly,' he said, 'but not with their usual precision. We might have fared better if it weren't for that idiot colonial at the interval, with his loud "coo-ee!" and our boys running over to him.'

Hayman laughed. 'That was Gerald,' he said. 'I know him from Adelaide. The town, that is. What he's doing over here, I don't know. Got talking to them in their own lingo, he did, and pretty soon they were jabbering round his wagonette like a barrel of monkeys! The corks flew out of bottles like magic, and the contents disappeared double quick!'

'I had to put a stop to it,' said Lawrence. 'It's no laughing matter! Thank the Lord I could use Cuzens as leverage, and got them over to the main tent, where we could keep a weather eye on 'em. And somehow Bullocky still got drunk!'

Bill Hayman blushed, but offered no answer.

CHAPTER VIII
Tuesday the 26th of May, 1868

BLACK GOLD

'Properly managed and instructed, the native race might
have been turned to much better account than has been
the case…instead of gradually dying off from the face
of the earth.'

~ *The Australasian*

'*AUSTRALIA:* The shipments of gold to England
during the month amount to 183,500 oz.'

~ *The Illustrated London News*

The next day dawned cold but clear. Recent rain had penetrated the hard
ground, freshened the herbage, and laid the dust. At last perfect weather
conditions prevailed – a warm sun and a cooling breeze.

Outside the main gate of Newgate Prison, with the crowd yelling 'Hats off!',
Michael Barrett was publicly hanged for his part in the 'Fenian Outrage': an
attempt to blow up the Clerkenwell House of Correction.

Numbers returning to the Oval cricket ground were only slightly diminished.
A strong muster came early, anxious to observe the Blacks at practice, their
murmurous presence audible from within the clubhouse.

'"The Aboriginal natives have entered with ardour into cricket,"' read Bill
Hayman. '"With ardour"!' he declared. 'Oh, I like that!'

'"They are the first Australian natives who have visited this country on such
a novel expedition, but it must not be inferred that they are savages",' related
Charles Lawrence. '"On the contrary, the managers of the speculation"…' He
put down the cup from which he was drinking. 'Oh, how I've come to hate that
word!' he growled.

'Savages?' said Hayman.

'Speculation!' said Lawrence.

Hayman shrugged. 'What else would you call it?'

Lawrence pursed his lips a moment. '"The managers of the speculation",' he read on, "make no pretence to anything other – "'

Hayman chuckled.

'No,' cried Lawrence, 'listen, Bill: " – other than purity of race and origin." What the Devil?'

His grimace gained a few extra creases.

'What sort of words are they putting in our mouths?' he said.

The team's captain and manager drank strong coffee as they examined the match reports from the first day's play. Early success could guarantee their tour, if translated into further bookings. The plan was to set up two- or three-day fixtures, almost back-to-back, for the next four months.

Out on the field the Aborigines were warming up, with a competition to see who could pitch the ball the farthest. For the moment all were in view, and out of harm's way.

Inside the clubhouse, William South Norton was keen to engender enthusiasm for the next day's Derby Sweepstakes. '"Here we are working ourselves up into a factitious interest in Lady Elizabeth, Rosicrucian, Blue Gown, and Speculum, and completing our parties for the Wednesday of Wednesdays."'

Lawrence made a point of preferring his colleague's choice of quotes. Bill Hayman read aloud from a copy of the *Daily Telegraph*. '"Nothing of interest comes from Australia, except gold nuggets and black cricketers",' he reported. 'Charming! I shall try not to take it personally!'

'Let me see that.' Lawrence grabbed for the paper.

'"The prophets",' countered South Norton, "tell us that their calculations are in a most complicated state, and they certainly approach the subject with the most catlike *circumbendibus*."' He turned in his chair. 'Ho, *ho!*'

'What new thing can be said about the Derby?' deadpanned Lawrence.

'None, I should say,' agreed Hayman.

South Norton sulked. No one could be more loyal to the gentlemanly art than he, but there were limits. He stood. This was the Derby, dash it all, the most famous of all horse-races! 'Then I'll leave you to your speculation,' he declared. And stalked out of the clubhouse and into the pale sunshine.

The others exchanged a glance over their respective broadsheets.

'Hm,' began Hayman. '"It is highly interesting and curious to see, mixed in a friendly game on the most historically Saxon part of our island, representatives of two races so far removed from each other as the modern Englishman and the Aboriginal Australian. Although several of them are native bushmen and all are as black as night, these indian fellows are – to all intents and purposes – clothed and in their right minds."'

'I should cocoa!' said Lawrence. 'In proper costume.'

'How about this, then,' Hayman volunteered. '"The Oval has distinguished itself by a day's financial operations rivalling that of a large theatre on Boxing-night. Seldom has any cricket ground been encircled by such a variety of vehicles as were counted yesterday in the less aristocratic enclosure…" ooh-la-bloody-la " …near the Stockwell Road."'

'Hmph. That'll be the waggon train,' grunted Lawrence, 'seeing off an attack.'

'Eh?' Hayman looked lost for a moment. 'No, Charley!' he said. 'They mean "indian" as in ink!'

Roses bloomed in Lawrence's cheeks. 'Oh good grief!' he said, 'Damn their eyes!'

'Share it.'

'"It will be a lamentable thing",' read Lawrence, '"if the game of cricket is to be degraded to the level of these sensational exhibitions that are so regrettably in fashion."' He faked collapse. '*Ungh!*'

They wrote of fashion, sanity, and spending – but what of sport? Where, Lawrence wondered, was able commentary about their cricketing skills? Admittedly they had not played their best, but even so.

'And did you see this one?' he asked, swapping between *Telegraph* and *Sporting Times*. '"A circus sideshow of racial curiosity…little better than a vaudeville turn."' His eyebrows rose. 'Then it mentions a match once played at Greenwich, the one-legged versus the one-armed! I hardly think comparison to a freak-show does us many favours!'

'I dare say it might,' said Hayman.

'Don't you dare!' warned Lawrence.

Bill Hayman supped his coffee and held his peace.

'The most ridiculous part?' continued Lawrence. 'This is the one article that goes on to acknowledge good play from our boys.'

'What paper is it?' said Hayman.

Lawrence held it aloft.

'The Pink 'un! Well, there you go. Serious interest in cricket is a new wrinkle for them. They'd much rather we played on horseback.' Hayman paused to consider the notion. 'Now that *would* be a sensation!' he said.

'Our aim isn't a sideshow!' railed Lawrence. 'It's about cricket, well played. Why, if a journalist dared show his ticket right now, I'd soon punch it for him!'

'Whoa, Charley!' said Hayman. He laid a hand to his partner's shoulder. 'You may take the boy out of Hoxton,' he said, 'but you can't – '

A bell rang somewhere within the enclosure.

'Ding, ding! Round two… We're on!'

~

At close of play on Monday the Aborigines had been four wickets down for 34 runs. Mullagh and Twopenny, the two 'not outs', presented themselves at the stumps just after noon.

Messrs Frere and Walker resumed the bowling for Surrey. Twopenny and then Lawrence were swiftly caught, before King Cole, in partnership with Mullagh, brought the score up to 65. For the best part of an hour Mullagh mounted a skilful defence, until defeated off a slow. The remaining wickets fell quickly. Their score being in a minority of 139, the Blacks were obliged to follow on.

Walker completed his revenge, catching Cole out for a duck. With the diligent assistance of Peter, Mullagh, strident, doggedly defended for another two hours. He met unflinching with a couple of nasty smacks from the ball.

At the end of the second day's play Mullagh's 73 runs accounted for half his team's second innings total, but it was not enough. The Aborigines lost by an innings and seven runs.

Due to his sterling performance on both days, Mighty Mullagh was declared 'man of the match'. Hoisting him aloft in a chair, the players carried him off the pitch to the cheers of an appreciative crowd.

Later, he was awarded a cash prize. He shared it out, equally, among the other members of his team.

CHAPTER IX

The 'Wednesday of Wednesdays', the 27th of May, 1868

THE CRICKET BALL

'The order of civilisation in the Christian sense seems
to be first to make savages men and then to make them
Christians... To convert the savage into a sheep shearer
was something, but it is more to make him into a smart
cricketer...the savage rises to quite a higher social level.'

~ *Ballarat Star*

Derby Day, a rare national holiday, interrupted the team's Oval engagement
during this action-packed 'week of sports'.

The weather supplied all that the heart of any racegoer could wish. The
Prince of Wales – Queen Victoria's beloved Bertie, her eldest son Albert
Edward – had travelled overnight from Scotland to reach the Epsom Downs
in time. Re-christened for the day 'Derby Sweeps', the Black Cricketers also
attended, Mullagh with his batting honours thick upon him. To their credit,
none of the Australian party took a potshot at the M.C.C.'s royal patron.

The Aborigines pooled Mullagh's prize money and bet on Forest King for
the Derby Stakes: the jockey wore a jacket, of red stars on a yellow ground, that
rather took their fancy. The eventual winner by half a length was the favourite,
Blue Gown. In second place came King Alfred, and third, Speculum. The
players lost their bet, and William South Norton his shirt.

The Sweeps, quitting the Downs early, were soon returned to their London
base. They had been invited to a high society ball, and needed to make ready.

Come the evening the West End streets were a-glitter, Vanity Fair turned out in
all of its *beau monde* flash and finery. With the Season at its height, everybody –
everybody who mattered – was in London to see and be seen.

The course of 'all England's day' saw citizens of every stripe commingling
on the Downs, a few hours' classless communion that kept everyone entertained.
Then, in the day's dying minutes, a purple velvet drape drew the length of
Pall Mall. Handsome cabriolets parked three or four deep soon clogged the

avenue entirely. Fine ladies and gentlemen swept into the hallowed portals of the awaiting Clubs – the Reform, the Travellers', the Athenaeum. Rolls of red carpet laid across the paving slabs showed the way. Ragged onlookers loitered, respectfully enraptured: the poor, gathered by the wayside. Each thin scarlet strip re-established the great divide, a gulf more impassable than any known to nature.

Down a dark alleyway a side door stood open, billowing smoke from the busy kitchens. Pots clanged within, frenzied master chefs screaming orders in broken English. Servants in black tie scrambled up concealed stairways, bearing enormous silver salvers. At the ornate carved doors each one would pause a moment, regain his composure, and then execute a sweeping entrance into the grand hall; the hubbub and hot air broiling out to greet them.

> 'Derry down, then fill up your glass, he's the best that drinks most!
> Here's the Athenaeum Club! – who refuses the toast?
> Let us join in the praise of the bat and the wicket,
> And sing in full chorus the patrons of cricket!'

'CAPITAL! CAPITAL!'

A thousand spoons made rollicking music on a thousand wine-glasses.

'The Reverend Cotton will, I trust, forgive adaptation of his verse,' exclaimed the speaker.

The illustrious Athenaeum Club boasted one of the best houses, and certainly the best club library, in the country. For the Aboriginal Australian Eleven to be invited to attend, even for one night, was indeed an honour and a privilege – a mark of respect for their efforts on the sporting field.

Or so Charles Lawrence preferred to think. From being the talk of Town Malling, overnight his little cricket team had become the toast of the largest city in the western world.

The Athenians and their guests sat at long banqueting tables arrayed along either side of the grand hall. Broad vertical stripes ran the ornate wallpaper's full height, beneath a vaulting curvilinear ceiling. Great glittering chandeliers, ringed with enough gas lamps to rival small suns, shone their brilliance down on an assemblage no less dazzling. Dukes and earls, lords and ladies, the witty, wealthy and highborn, sat alongside academics, scientists, fine artists, and well-connected authors – permanent residents all of the winner's enclosure.

Pausing between sumptuous food courses, the ladies fanned themselves and admired their neighbours. Their *décolleté* dresses were spectacular, decorated and colourful. Cut daringly low, they exposed white female flesh to a degree almost alarming.

'That generous kindness of the remote settlers has disclosed to the outer world a mine of undeniable talent in the Aborigine.'

Applause surged as the speaker bowed, first in the direction of Charles Lawrence and Bill Hayman, then turning slightly in order to salute the team.

'These coloured wielders of the willow,' he intoned. 'A sable troop, hunting the leather...'

'Oh, good grief,' Hayman groaned.

'They are by renown adroit hunters,' the speaker continued, 'skilled trackers, and now, evidently, we can also say born sportsmen. For all reports indicate they ride well, and, for savages, play cricket fairly.'

'Damned with faint praise if ever I heard it,' grumbled Lawrence. He leant in close to his confederate. 'Who is this pompous idiot?'

'A Mr Andrew Long,' Hayman whispered back. 'Or Lang. I'm not sure.' Each could smell the wine on the other's breath.

The next speaker rose to address the crowd, thick white hair whorled like whipped cream, a sallow dog's face above his canary-yellow shirt.

> 'Your swarthy brows and raven locks
> Must gratify your tonsors.'

His voice a nasal whine, grated on the ear.

> 'But, by the name of Dick-a-Dick,
> Who are your doughty sponsors?'

Hearing Dick-a-Dick mentioned by name, the Aborigines screeched their ridicule.

'A poet!' said Hayman.

'Of sorts,' said Lawrence.

The curious canary-hound continued.

> 'Arrayed in skin of Kangaroo,
> and deck'd with lanky feather,
> How well you fling the fragile spear
> Along the Surrey heather.'

Neighbouring Surrey must have scanned better than Kent, or so Lawrence supposed.

> 'And though you cannot hope to beat
> The Britishers at cricket,
> You have a batter bold and brave
> In Mullagh at the wicket!'

Barracking and booing all but drowned out the final lines.

The bard ended with a gestural flourish, thereby chancing to duck a chicken bone aimed expertly at his head. The Aborigines, having assimilated the poor fool's mannerisms as well as his delivery, performed wickedly accurate imitations.

The evening's entertainments had begun.

Between courses, couples took to the centre of the banqueting hall, especially cleared for the purpose, to delicately swish about. Corks popped, shoe leather creaked, and the string orchestra twanged their twine: the sounds of a cricket ball in full swing. A few of the Aborigines essayed their dance-floor skills to the obvious delight of all. Quadrilles, polkas, schottisches and waltzes – any style with which they were unfamiliar, and there were not many, they very quickly picked up.

Beyond taking mustard with their roast mutton, and the occasional use of knife instead of fork, the Blacks were noted to dine in full observance of the usual proprieties.

'This, however, is not to be wondered at,' reasoned one observer. 'As we have seen, they are admirable mimics, and readily adopt any pattern set before them.'

'I had the pleasure of playing a game of cribbage with three of the party,' assured a gentleman from Kent. 'They have mastered the intricacies of the game, generally so puzzling to foreigners.'

The Aborigines' additional reputation as prodigious eaters arose merely as the result of their showing off, a favourite trick rebounding of late on 'crook' Johnny Cuzens.

In bodily and mental calibre they were agreed top-drawer, 'as temperate as anchorites', 'as jolly as sandboys', and – in consideration of those dancers who confirmed their expertise – 'as supple as deer': Lawrence found himself congratulated so often that he began to weary of compliments.

'Bowling is like poetry. A bowler must be created with natural advantages if he is ever to shine. When found, indeed, he is like a *tenore robusto*…a price-less treasure.'

Through the miscellaneous din, Lawrence could make out the stentorian tones of an English gent who clearly fancied himself an expert. Only blandishments being served at his own table, Lawrence sought him out by eye.

'…although, by unremitting diligence, more for the pleasure of overcoming difficulties than anything else – one or two Englishmen may have taught the Australian native to present a more than creditable appearance, their existence is a mere phenomenon which has no significance.'

A bearded sage, perhaps 50 years of age – the man's head seemed huge, like that of a horse. Lawrence fancied that he gestured in his own direction, his broad brows sternly knotted. What had he just been saying?

'To my eyes the deportment of the dignified Aboriginal is that of a sapient monkey, imitating the gait and manners of a do-nothing white dandy. Both in attendance this night…'

'Some monkeys I have seen,' said one of his coterie, 'might feel injured by a comparison. They are the ugliest race of beings conceivable. Ugly to the point of disgust.'

'Excuse me…' said Lawrence. Addressing an elderly gentleman to his left, he indicated the other table. 'Do you know the fellow there?' he asked.

'Let me see,' the old man said. 'With Lucett? Why, I do believe it's Trollope, over from the Garrick. And I thought he was in America!'

Taking another gulp of red wine, Lawrence studied his target intently.

'He writes for the *Saint Pauls Magazine*,' continued his advisor, 'now the editor, I believe. And a deal to say on the subject of English sport.'

'I'm sure,' said Lawrence. The din of the party growing, he narrowed his eyes and hunched forward.

'Even Cricket has become such a business,' the writer-editor was saying, 'doubt arises in the minds of amateur players whether they can continue the sport, loaded as it is with the extravagance of the professionals. A countless body of cricketers, with nearly every name absurd, daily floods the columns of our newspaper…'

There could be no doubt where his comments were directed. Lawrence's face turned as crimson as a pillar-box.

'And this,' the nag's head pronounced, 'brings me to the monster cricket nuisance of the day. It is bad enough to see a parcel of ninnies airing a flaming ribbon and a sonorous name in the newspapers, and duly paying for the insertion. But it is far otherwise with the so-called Elevens that go caravanning about the country, playing against two bowlers and 20 duffers for the benefit of some enterprising publican. It's just not cricket!'

A swell in the music muted his torturer. Lawrence unsteadily refilled his glass and gulped its contents down.

His colleague, Bill Hayman, fielded enquiries at their own table.

'How has it come to pass,' wondered the pretty wife of an Athenian, 'that Aboriginal natives are playing the game of cricket?'

'Every big sheep station employs upwards of two, three dozen hands,' said Hayman, 'and every one of them plays cricket. Before he sold up, my uncle ran Lake Wallace South. Some of the Abos that lived on the swamps near Edenhope, they came to work on the yards. If a game were going in the evening, they'd come see what the ruckus was about. That's how they got into the sport. And they were good at it!'

He gulped, nervously. '*Are* good at it. As you'll see.'

'They became absorbed in the game,' said the lady's husband.

'Er – yes,' said Hayman.

'And how did you select these particular players, Mr…Hayman, is it?'

Hayman shrugged. 'Old Peter over there was a shearer at Lake Wallace,' he explained. 'Others came from around Lake Colac, and the Wando. Bullocky, from Balmoral, further down the Hamilton road…like that, I should say.'

'From Balmoral?' said a listener. 'Well, I'm blowed!'

Lawrence butted in. 'There is no such thing as an Australian Aborigine.'

That certainly got their attention. Surprised more than anyone, Lawrence found himself addressing the entire table.

'You might as well say, "He's a European", when a man could be Scottish, or Russian, or a Spaniard!'

'And what are you?'

'I'm serious,' insisted Lawrence. And he was. 'Aborigines are not one single people. I mean there used to be lit'rally hundreds of 'em, all over Australia… hundreds of tribes, leading the lives of nomads an' hunters.'

Bill Hayman looked at him quizzically.

'Hundreds,' Lawrence repeated. 'And each had their own language…' He went quiet.

'Please,' someone said, 'do go on.'

'By all means,' encouraged another.

'Our boys?' said the wine, talking. 'A couple were *Wurdiboluc*, from the desert, and the rest from the swamplands…or is it the other way around? I can never remember. Anyway, *Jadwaj…Jadwadjali, Madimadi*…'

Aboriginal speech was a stream's fluid murmur: softly spoken vowel sounds tumbling one over another. Interpreting the talk of even close neighbours, that lyrical flow would run into rocks. Foreign consonants dammed it altogether. Lawrence trying to formulate the same words sounded like a cat with a hairball.

'What extraordinary tosh!' one man complained. The remainder of the table, however, regarded Lawrence in wonder.

'You speak Aboriginal, Mr Lawrence?'

'No!' he said. 'Don't you see? That's what I'm trying to tell you. They come from all over, speaking different tongues. Charley is from Queensland. Skeeter, Cuzens and Tiger, South Australia…' He counted down using his fingers. 'Neddy an' Twopenny's from New South Wales…'

'Neddy's called Jim Crow here,' said Hayman.

'Oh, yes.' Lawrence blinked. 'And the rest,' he said, 'the rest is from Victoria. Cuzens was the first one to coach 'em. He was the one taught 'em cricket.' He was no longer sure of his point.

A sharp-faced scientist spoke up. 'You use the past tense when referring to their tribal derivation. Why is that?'

Lawrence declined to answer. Hayman filled the awkward silence.

'When we originally recruited the team,' he said, 'from Pine Hills, Brippick, Miga Lake and so forth, our choice was…limited. Many of the stockmen were the last of their clans, their mobs up-country numbering only a few old men and their *gins* – '

A high-pitched laugh interrupted. 'I'm sorry. Did you say "gins"?'

'Their womenfolk,' Hayman explained. 'The young women are *lubras*, the older women *gins*.'

'So they are, as I've heard, dying out?' said the scientist.

Lawrence and Hayman exchanged a look across the table.

'If there's a right time to make this tour,' blurted Lawrence, 'it's now or never.' His face burned. 'This team has played together,' he said, 'in some shape or form, for over two years now. When I came on board, after their previous tours, numbers were down.' He threw a dark look at Hayman. 'It fell to me to put a new side together…from the best of those remaining, and some other Blacks.'

'"Remaining"?' a voice queried.

'The ones that were still alive,' said Lawrence.

His seeming callousness drew gasps.

'You make it sound a massacre, Charles,' pleaded Hayman. Rallied to his own defence, he addressed the table as a whole. 'We lost only four.'

'A drop,' said Lawrence, lightly, 'in the ocean.'

The orchestra finished a popular number; the dancing couples separated and clapped to show their appreciation. Applause at such a juncture sounded sardonic in the extreme.

Before Cuzens even, the players had been coached by Old Tom Wills – a fine cricketer, but a dangerous drunkard. His influence had proven fatal: four of the Aborigines died from alcohol poisoning. Others, including Dick-a-Dick, took severely ill, almost dying. Wills had left the team in disgrace.

As his successor, Charles Lawrence utterly condemned the former laxity. History could not be allowed to repeat itself.

Nor should it be repeated in present company. In seeking a way out of their predicament, Bill Hayman succeeded only in digging them deeper.

'A glass of grog is a potent reasoner with a blackfellow,' he breezed. 'An Aboriginal will drink anything any time, and he calls everything "rum"… everything that he don't call "him"!'

The promising scent of scandal attracted a growing audience. Lawrence looked into the flushed pink faces gathered around. He stood abruptly, grasped Hayman firmly by the arm, and whisked him away.

'Well, I never!'

'Quite extraordinary!'

The eyes of all at table followed their retreat into the milling throng.

'Perhaps the orchestra struck up a favourite…'

As the partners passed Trollope, his sharp tongue cut Lawrence to the quick. ''Twas an evil hour for cricket,' it rasped, 'when shrewd men saw where money was to be got.' The literary giant seemed to turn and leer, baring vast yellow incisors. 'The English,' he sneered, 'are accused of reducing all things to pounds, shillings and pence. I trust the Abhor-riginals will reap some benefit from the revenue they have helped to earn.'

He knew he was right.

Charles Lawrence was almost shocked to find the world still turned on its axis. The ball swirled about them, orchestral music a speeding carousel. Resolving not to drink any more, he advised they both should stick to sober-water. Hayman sulkily announced his retirement to the dunny. Lawrence undertook a circuit of the room – to clear his head as much as to reassure the flock of his abiding presence. The soul of constancy he was, clambered onto the wagon, steady as a judge, temperate as an…as an ammonite.

He wanted to belch.

The grand occasion was not nearly so intimate as that enjoyed at Went House, by dint of its sheer scale. Scattered throughout the great hall of the Athenaeum Club, the Aborigines, finding themselves isolated, became subdued. Unfailingly polite when approached, they by and large sought to avoid direct conversation, grunting their responses with a surly sort of civility. Swamped by extravagance beyond their experience, they were simply overcome.

Stout Twopenny, encircled, took questions from the curious crowd.

'Are there no Aboriginal women?' a body asked.

'Course!' spluttered Twopenny. 'Course it true! Dem all back 'ome.'

'Are *you* married, Mr Tuppenny?'

Twopenny looked down at the shiny floor and shook his head.

'Then you are a stray tup?'

This rudeness was howled down.

'When I see me first whitepella,' offered Twopenny, 'many whitepella…I think you only men. Dem 'ave no *gins*. Makes no sense, men come all dat way alone, without wimmen to gather *mirka* and to *puck*.'

The gathering is bemused. '"Puck"?'

'Puck!' repeated Twopenny, his hair a woolly triangle.

Bill Hayman intervened. 'Use your loaf, Twopenny,' he said. 'These good people don't want to know about things like that.'

'Oh,' they cried, 'but we do!'

'No,' said Hayman. 'You don't.' He led Twopenny aside, still conferring. 'When speaking in a foreign tongue,' said Hayman, 'betimes we must needs employ greater restraint than that accorded to us.'

Twopenny screwed up his face. 'Boss,' he said, 'you talkin' shit.'

Lawrence watched as a grey-haired old spy, without so much as a by-your-leave, openly conducted a microscopic study of Red Cap's face and form. Bloody 'ethnologists' – they had already had to deter one from taking measurements at Malling.

At the opposite end of the hall, towards the enormous fireplace, fizz was found in the new descriptive nouns the Aborigines had coined concerning various European animals. Rabbits, for instance, were 'stand up ears' or 'white bottom'; pigs, 'turn ground'; and cockerels, 'call for day'. For others, they arrived at simpler solutions: cattle were 'boo-oo'; sheep, 'ba-ba'; and horses, 'gump-gump' or 'neighit'.

The nation's greatest minds, arm-in-arm with her most glamorous aristo-crats, took up the Christy Minstrels' standard 'Merry Green Fields', with its distinctive verse-chorus.

> 'With a boo-oo here, and a boo-oo there,
> Here a boo, there a boo...'

A fat man bursting out of his dinner-suit waved to Lawrence.

'The place is become a barnyard!' he called. 'Tell your man there!' He pointed at Red Cap.

'Tell him yourself,' retorted Lawrence. 'He's quite capable of under-standing.'

The ethnologist, if that was what he was, still loitered. The fat man, however, raced on past. Red Cap wisely melted away into the crowd.

The grey-haired spy broke his silence. 'D-d-dashed impertinence!' he stammered.

'Red Cap is his own man,' said Lawrence.

'I refer, sir, to *yours*,' the spy said. 'I expect and therefore excuse *his*.'

'Lord Hogg', meantime, 'oink-oink'ed here, there, and everywhere for all he was worth – doubtless a very large amount. Lawrence realised he might have judged too hastily. This new attack, alas, was a different matter.

The spy closed with Lawrence – a wounded old lion, dangerous malevo-lence lurking in his rheumy eye. 'A wild, untameable restlessness is innate with s-s-savages,' he said.

'They are not savages,' insisted Lawrence.

'Savages they are, and savages they shall always re-...always remain.'

They stood toe to toe. Neither had the advantage of height, but Lawrence began to quail before the older man's belligerent aspect.

'A puh-person's race can explain and justify almost anything,' the man spat. 'D-D-Doctor James Hunt, Puh-president of the...of the...'

Moustaches flecked with a stutterer's spittle, he settled for holding out a printed card.

Lawrence already despised such items. He studied the curious pyramidal emblem inscribed there – a triangle inverted within one larger, to produce four smaller triangles of equal proportion. In heraldic style, each of these contained a symbol. At the apex was an eyeball. In the three spaces below, reading from left to right: a human skull; a fat carrot – the depiction of an early tool, or flint, perhaps; and last and least, a brain, presumably also human. An inscription encompassed the entire design, one word on each of the emblem's three sides.

SOCIETAS / ANTHROPOLOGIE / LONDINENSIS

Nonplussed, Lawrence flipped the card over.

Dr James Hunt, Ph.D., F.S.A., F.R.S.L.
PRESIDENT,
Anthropological Society of London.

Lawrence looked back up, poised to introduce himself in return. During the interim, however, the contentious old cuss had gathered himself for a speech.

'I am quite aware who you are,' snapped Dr Hunt, cutting him dead. 'And let me tell you, I have collected numerous instances where children of a low race have been sep-puh-puhrated at an early age from their puh-…from their puh-…from their parents…and reared as pa-part of a settler's family. Yet, after years of civilised ways, they have abandoned their home, flung away their dress, and gone to seek their countrymen in the Bush, among whom they have subsequently been found living in contented bar-bar-bar…' Another pause enforced for breath, he appeared to quite lose patience with himself. '…bar-bar-barbarism!'

'I hardly – ' began Lawrence.

'And without a vestige of their gentle *nurture*! There…what do you say to that?'

Lawrence very much wished to contradict the old lion: separating children from their parents hardly seemed a civilised act. But, when it came to it, his heart simply gave out. 'If you will excuse me, "doctor",' said Lawrence, handing back the card, 'I feel sick.'

An unhappy Lawrence quit the room.

'They talk the moon down from the sky,' says Cole.

'*Garra Gnowee*,' Sundown sadly agrees.

King Cole and Sundown stand side-by-side some way apart from the press of the crowd. They hold on to an unlit cheroot, in contemplation of the gigantic chandelier suspended high above their heads. Kinsmen, they express their frustrations in the language common to them.

Too many faces – Cole can endure no more. He only delays a moment, to share his lament, and then leaves.

He makes his way up to an open balcony, just below the level of the roof. Alone at last, King Cole stands at the top of the Athenaeum building, perfectly still, like a strange phantom or statue. Light bleeding through the great hall's upper windows, at his back, reduces him to a slender silhouette; it gilds the outline of his locks, stirred by the stiff breeze, to lend a fierce coronal. For a silent hour – neither speaking, nor stirring – he takes in the vast panorama of the London night.

The flare of countless gas lamps overwhelms him.

At first he believes that he stares into an immense crystal cobweb, parent to those suspended in the false sky, below. Every surface shimmers aglow with light either direct or reflected: the city itself, burnished and blazing, blinds him with its glare.

Glowing like hot coals, his black eyes mirror the scene. Ringed with fire, he is afire.

And yet London, for all its burning, gives off no discernible heat – all of its energies spent on illumination alone; any warmth it might produce swiftly disappears into the night sky, to be swallowed up by the freezing vacuum of space.

In time, the semblance of a chandelier is forgotten: the dancing sparks and flickering tongues of flame become the bewitching firebugs of his Dreaming. He watches them as they dart in pairs, up and down the streets below. Edging forward until his toes grip the very brink of the balustrade, King Cole is newly aware of a shadow realm revealed at his feet. Beneath the coruscating nimbus of light lurks a black mass that spreads below and beyond like a dark stain.

He hears screams and shouts in the night, a countless multitude of different voices raised. Indifferent towards his eavesdropping, the ruminant city talks tunelessly to itself. Deeper still, and duller, an incessant grumble rises up from out of the depths.

Sleepless in his bunk, in the hollow bowels of the *Parramatta*, he would often listen to a sound very much like this – the restless swell of the oceans.

The longer he listens, the louder it seems to roar, as deafening as the crashing thunder. It is a cataract, onrushing, that hurls itself endlessly over the edge of some mad precipice.

His body quivers with vibration. His foot slips, and, with that sudden start, he knows. The noise that he feels more than he hears is matched by the frenzied drumbeat of his own heart. It is the pump and rush of his life's blood, answering the call – an odd familiarity; reminiscence, displaced; second nature. Before awareness even that he moves, King Cole is in motion. Seeking surrender, craving oblivion, he throws himself down.

The balcony stands empty.

King Cole is gone – only jacket and shoes, left behind in a small pile, to show that he was ever there.

CHAPTER X
Wednesday the 27th of May, 1868

TJUKURPA

'Once more within the Potter's house alone
I stood, surrounded by the Shapes of Clay.

And once again there gather'd a scarce heard
Whisper among them; as it were, the stirr'd
Ashes of some all but extinguisht Tongue,
Which mine ear kindled into living Word.'

~ Rubáiyát of Omar Khayyám

A waxing crescent moon leads the bright star Rex through the night.

As the hour advances, the ghost folk – or whatever else they might once have been – fade away. Either it is the absence of the crowds, or else the deserted streets grow wider than before, into a wilderness of hard, unyielding stone. King Cole alone seems to occupy the vast wasteland. Jogging quietly along, he welcomes solitude. He has at last space in which to move, and breathe.

What is it he is looking for? Does it have a name?

He is not hungry, trailing good game. He is not thirsty, in search of water. Spurred ever onward, instead he thinks himself the hunter in search of fresh knowledge.

What is it the Ancestor Spirits are trying to tell him?

Tombs carved from out of the rock, a numbing procession of side-streets passes him by. One after another, after another, the monotonous regularity numbs Cole's physical senses, but concentrates instead his inner eye – a glow-worm circulation that beckons him ever onward.

Overriding every due caution, Cole hastens down his lonely road.

His own hand held up in front of his face is without colour, turned translucent. Through it an image floats, suspended, in mid-air. Sometimes darker, sometimes lighter than its surroundings, only captured at certain angles, picked out in moon gleam, it radiates a fine web – a cracked windowpane, star-glazed.

Cole slows.

The air curdles, sluggish with a sweet and sickly stench. To the north, a long stretch of high wall blank-faces broken-tooth terraces, rotten with decay. Fixed on irons half as tall again as any man, infrequent oil lamps shed little in the way of light.

King Cole comes to a complete stop.

He stands before a hazy portal, threshold to an inner courtyard into which he feels compelled to go. The rot-stinking cavity stands clear before him, yet he cannot breach it. The syrupy air is itself a wall.

Feeling his way like one blind, four doors along he comes to the mouth of a narrow entrance; set close between two back-to-backs, a dark and stinking ooze seeps down its centre. Neither moonlight nor lamplight dare enter in, but Cole does.

He slinks down this back street, chilled innards aching, barely suppressing the urge to retch. Water streams from his eyes. The stink of shit spears his lungs, even as it slops over his toes. Were it not for evidence to the contrary, he cannot imagine such a place inhabited.

Oppressed on all sides, a bend in the blind alley lends no respite. The pressure crushing his insides only grows stronger. He has to crouch, loosening the belt that holds up his trousers, and evacuate his bowels.

No longer able to stand upright, Cole flattens against the filthy brickwork. It closes in. Eyes swimming, he can barely see a foot in front.

'*Aaaauuuughh!*'

His head pinned underarm, an invisible fist smashes repeatedly into his face. He's been in bad fights before, back in the woolsheds of South Australia. Never was any good in a fight. Snot clogs and tears fall. He wants to surrender.

In-gna! Demons!

'*Whsssht!*'

Mind no longer his own, he feels he must break free. Stumbling on, Cole emerges onto a wide street lined with shops. By day it would appear a major highway.

Breath returns in shallow gasps. He recovers slightly, vision clearing, yet his pulse gallops ever faster. Lifeblood pumping through arteries, the dead silence bangs at his ears.

He fears his head may burst.

One block, two blocks on – here, at the heart of his Dreaming, an unassuming street, down which he is impelled to go.

One…more…step.

Blessed relief washes over him. It is as if he has pierced an unseen veil. His head clears, and the leaden silence, once so fraught, is simple, peaceful, and absolute.

His body drifts, weightless. Air becomes wall, becomes windows. Windows become wall, becomes air. Black space alternating with blue sky, days cross paths with night and back again.

Cole glides through a realm that flows around him. This land should be a stranger. It is not. Sure now of himself, of his situation, he retraces a route that is more than familiar, certain of the direction he must take.

Hand caresses wall. Flesh strokes stone. Stone grazes skin. This is the image of Truth he has always known, but never until now realised.

He senses the faint stirrings of a sleeping presence; breath steadily drawn and exhaled, in darkness, by darkness.

Drawn closer to the hole in shattered window glass, he cranes forward to peer inside. Glass shards encircle his bare scalp. Stare keenly as he can, King Cole cannot conceive of what lurks hidden in the blackness, although something most certainly does. The frisson of another life, deep among the shadows, calls to him.

His body is cradled in the early morning. Mother's palm, warm and rough – he feels the touch of her firm, guiding hand on his forehead, then eyes, his nose, mouth, and on down to his feet. *Wuduu*, the warming of hands, is what he misses most of all.

Dandled in her lap, he looks up into sad and loving eyes. They blink him to sleep, so patiently.

Cole's face breaks into a broad, toothsome smile, then falls, lost to sorrow. It has been a lifetime since he was held.

Hot grief rolls down his cheeks. A sudden jolt – pain, deep down in his belly – drops him to his knees. He clutches at the bare walls, wretched and mewling.

This is conduct unbecoming a *bourka*, a full-grown warrior of the *Wudjubalug* – the man he most desperately wishes to be. Taking firm grasp of his resolve, Cole rips away at the knot of shame. He pulls himself up and forces himself back. Recovering the main street he sprints a hundred paces clear, determined to put as much distance as possible between himself and this dear, dreadful spot.

Never again will he return, to the Well of Shadows, to the stone cell there and not there – the pulsating heart in the darkness.

And the stranger in the London night is marked, fair game. Blood and feather, let him be led to the hive.

CHAPTER XI
Thursday the 28th of May, 1868

A REVELATION

'One man fastens an eye on him, and the graves of the memory render up their dead; the secrets that make him wretched either to keep or to betray, must be yielded.'

~ Ralph Waldo Emerson, 'Character'

First light struggles to penetrate the fug of an attic room, wherein most of the Black Cricketers lie sleeping. Drunken snores reverberate from more than one cot. A sneaking shadow parts the retreating darkness, makes its way towards the empty bunk. As it crosses the Aborigine the whites call Sundown, his eyes shoot open. He wakes with a start and cries out.

The face he meets is a horror mask – upper half white, the lower half black like his own. Dead white skin clotted and misshapen, two black orbs, livid-rimmed in scarlet, blaze within. The horror face bids him hush, before creasing into a familiar smile.

'Brother?' says Sundown.

King Cole rocks soundlessly in joyful assent. He grips Sundown by the shoulders and shakes him in a fit of breathless exuberance. More than happy to see his dear friend again, it almost seems he had not expected to.

'*Hnh,*' smiles Sundown, his broad face creasing, 'you lucky Lawrence him too drunk to count.'

Fully awake, he makes a rapid assessment of Cole's outfit – what remains of it. Mud gums the formal black trousers up to his calves. The dress shirt, crisp and white at the start of the previous evening, is blackened and ragged. Collar and cuffs have completely disappeared. Of his evening jacket and shoes there is no sign.

Sundown whistles appreciatively. He is impressed.

The white sediment spreads thick across the upper part of Cole's face.

'*Worum mwa?*' Sundown asks. 'Where you go? Some place good, eh?'

Keeping their voices down, they chat in their own native tongue.

'Out Bush,' says Cole. 'Been walking…sending the path out of myself. Went to pay respects to the Old Land. Sing a bit, dance a bit, say hello.'

Cole casts Sundown a sideways glance. A new element of caution out-distances filial ease. 'The Old Land' – New Chum Lawrence has used the phrase many times, meaning his England home.

Sundown does not know what to make of it in this context. Perhaps his ears are still asleep.

His sleep-swollen face betrays nothing.

'An' you still got your kidney fat?' he says, only half-joking.

Back in the World, if a stranger should pass through the territory of another mob without first seeking permission, he risked attack. Most likely he would be killed, and *yelo*, his kidney fat, removed – sweetmeats to be hung in a *wadderlikkie*, a small string bag worn at the throat, conferring strength and courage to the wearer.

So the old custom went. The World is changing fast.

As if a cloud passes overhead, Sundown's lazy smile upends to a frown. He flops back on the bed, and with a liverish sigh stares up at where that open sky should be. He should not have thought of home, not even for an instant.

His voice, when it returns, is slurred and sullen.

'This country,' he says, 'doesn't suit me. I'm a stranger here. I like to be in my own country, where I was born. I am now miserable.'

King Cole smirks, indulging his kinsman. He has heard this sulk from gloomy Sundown on many occasions during their touring together – the first time, expressed with no less conviction, when the team lodged but two days' walk from their base at Edenhope. And look at them now!

They left everything behind, two winters gone – two-fellow cold time ago. Sundown's unhappiness strikes him full measure.

'*Teiwa*,' Sundown moans. Glassy with loss, his deep brown eyes fill with yearning. Silent tears fall.

'*Ballrinjarrimin*,' says Cole, softly. He strokes his clan brother's abundant curls. For a timeless time, they sit together in perfect sympathy.

Nestled on the low eaves overhead, a drowsy wood pigeon pronounces the occasional throaty '*oom*'. Tiny white feathers, from its downy underbelly, drift, gently, to the flagstone floor.

Done with their sad meditation, Sundown turns to Cole, expression grave. 'Brother,' he says, 'this unsung land…him a dead place.'

'*Eora?*' says Cole, brightly. 'I know! All night I walked along this big place. He's no end to him! One big stone garden…'

Cole rubs his aching shinbones. He pictures himself, wandering the hollow quiet – street after street, grey rows all the same.

'Mounds, everywhere. Burial mounds!' he says. 'In the dark time, they shut themselves inside…shut themselves in and set fire to everything! Can you believe it? But today, there it is all back again…and they built even more in the night!'

Sundown looks entirely sceptical, but Cole is sure of himself. He leans in, words barely a whisper. 'I been walking in the footsteps of the Ancestors!'

'*Atpida*,' Sundown says flatly. He won't accept it. 'You are mistaken. Not here.'

'Even here,' nods Cole. 'Here especially!'

Sundown almost gets up, before huffing and settling down again.

One land cannot be changed for another. And it should remain untouched, just how it was at the time of Creation. The scarified country around Malling town, much altered by the hand of man, was bad enough. London City is far worse – an unimaginable hell.

'*Worum mwa?*' Sundown repeats his question, almost abruptly. Eyes narrowed, he searches the face of his friend.

Cole takes a cautious look around. Everyone else in the room is laid flat out.

'*Tjukurpa*,' Cole says.

The word hisses out from between his teeth. They shake their heads vigorously, and place their hands before their mouths.

Tjukurpa, 'Truth' – the Dreaming. Sundown is scandalised. King Cole struggles to excuse his words.

'You know, brother dear, my Truth has always been…different. I cannot explain it,' he says. 'But this is my Truth.' No longer able to contain himself, he exults. '*Deen, Deen! Eora*,' he cries, his voice a thin reed. 'My Truth…it is here! This place, this "London", One Big Ant-hill Creek.'

'*Na!*' says Sundown, startled. 'What?'

'This dark time, I saw my Truth. I walked it, as I always walk it. But now it is around me in the bodyworld too!'

Cole's second skin cracks, part flaking away, resulting in a shower of white powder. He grips the edge of the hard wooden pallet that serves as Sundown's bed.

'I see it and I *know* it!'

After a lifetime of confusion and concealment, he has at last the freedom to be himself, to know himself.

'I think,' says Cole, exhilarated, 'I got my call…to go to the Big Place…swap songs around the campfires of my Ancestors!'

The *Nurrunbung-uttias*! Sundown looks skywards.

'Songs, old and new, to be sung here,' Cole enthuses. 'Much to be explored… understood.'

The city he sees in his Dreaming is both the same and different.

King Cole smiles.

'What else is there,' he declares, 'but to know one's Dreaming.'

The room is very quiet.

'But...here?' Sundown asks, aghast. 'This dead place! Why here?' Eyes wide, he searches each corner of the room, seeing beyond the bounds of the bare stone cell in which they squat – reviewing, in that same instant, the unceasing horrors without.

When, finally, he speaks again, Sundown's voice fills with portent.

'This is not the World!' he warns. 'We are outside of the World... These men...they are no brothers of ours!'

Cole remains silent.

At Sundown's touch, Cole's dried clay mask crumbles all away to dust. Delicate wisps, sent up like smoke, circulate in a ray of sunshine high above their heads.

'*Bunjil-nullung*,' Sundown calls him. 'Mister Mud.'

In his soft, rich voice, Sundown begins to recite a favourite story.

'There is a boy...a very stupid young fellow. On his Walkabout, the boy comes to a lagoon. Wide body of water there...and the day, he's mighty hot. This boy, he goes to wet his body in the lagoon. And the great brown snake that lives there eats him up, the stupid boy.'

The Great Serpent uncoils in Cole's memory.

'*Bimeby*...' starts Sundown.

His clan-brother laughs, unsettled.

'By and by,' Sundown repeats, 'that great brown snake, he shits out the stupid boy. But the boy not blackfellow any more...

'Him a *GRINKAI*!'

One of their companions grumbles in his sleep. Both hold their breaths, until his loud snoring resumes.

'When I wake,' Sundown says, face to half-face with his errant team-mate, 'I think *you* a *grinkai*, come to kill me.'

Among themselves, the Men often jokily refer to whites as *grinkai*. Their pallid, pulpy complexions resemble nothing else quite so much, in their experience, as a flayed corpse – the dead body peeled and pink, once the outermost layer of skin has been removed.

They are blackfellows who think themselves sophisticated, poking fun at the beliefs of simple Bushmen, fathers and grandfathers dead and gone. Yet the web of many lifetimes still ensnares them. Doubts, deeply rooted, persist. As they sailed away from the World they knew, all certainty drowned in their wake; their ship's course inverted. At the end of their long journey, who can say they have not travelled to the Spirit World across the oceans?

Is this the fabled land of the dead?

Are these white men dead men?

Are these dead men kin? Or are they even men at all?

'Are you a *grinkai*?' asks Sundown, pointedly.

King Cole hesitates. He suddenly collapses, his body disappearing below the level of the cot. Sundown gasps and scrambles up to look over the edge. His brother's body lies inert on the cold stone flags.

He is only playing possum. In a trice Cole pops back to life. 'Lay down black man, jump up white man,' he mocks. 'Plenty sixpence!'

He jangles some loose coins in his pocket, and they both fall about, laughing recklessly. As skilfully as Dick-a-Dick parries a fast-ball, King Cole's jest has turned the tricky issue aside.

'Good on yer, mate.'

Sundown takes up his clan brother's hand and presses it between his own. Cole has spoken unwisely, of an impossible advent. It goes without saying: what has passed between them stays in this room.

All around, the other team members begin to stir and rouse.

As far back as Cole cares to remember, *Ballrinjarrimin*, whom the whites call Sundown, is the closest to a companion he has known – his only true friend and confidant. Looking deep into his eyes, he shows him a brave face.

'*Min-yelity yarluke an-ambe, Aly-elarr'yerk-in yangaiakar!*' smiles Cole. 'What a fine road is this for me, winding between the hills!'

'*Baal gammon*, blackfellow,' says Sundown. '*Budgere* you.'

King Cole takes great solace in this blessing.

The World is anyway lost to him – willingly, he gives it up.

'I think,' he says, 'to go…into whatever Dreaming lies ahead.'

CHAPTER XII
Thursday, the 28th of May, 1868

SLINGS AND ARROWS

'I am as free as Nature first made man,
Ere the base laws of servitude began,
When wild in woods the noble savage ran.'

~ John Dryden, *The Conquest of Granada*

Following Derby Day, the team was returned to the Oval for a day of Australian Sports. Handbills promised 'a thrilling exhibition of Aboriginal athleticism'. On normal match days, native displays directly followed close of play, and always drew a larger gate than any ordinary game of cricket.

The English crowds still attended in force, gratifying the tour's organisers. Events began modestly enough, with some running, jumping and hurdling – feats billed 'pedestrianism'. The athletes appeared in outfits anything but.

Matching trunks complemented their individually coloured caps. Beneath these they wore long tights, fleshings dyed an approximation of their skin colour, underwear the English press delighted in dubbing, 'Oh-no-we-never-mention-'ems'. The garments were intended to represent, as near as decency allowed, 'the light and airy apparel of the native Australian' – in other words, no clothes at all.

The 'One Hundred Yards' Flat Race' opened the show. Then came the various jumps and hurdles. The winner of each contest received a cash prize and a warm round of applause. Thereafter followed 'Vaulting with Poles', 'Throwing the Cricket Ball', the 'One Hundred Yards' Backwards Race', and the 'Water Bucket Race'.

Fidgeting in their seats, idly chatting amongst themselves, the crowd grew restless. A nice enough excuse for a day out, it was generally agreed, but nothing special.

The best, however, was yet to come.

At the far end of the ground emerged a curious little figure, wrapped in a blanket. With measured step, he processed towards the middle of an otherwise emptied playing field. Attention gradually fixed on his slow and steady progress.

An expectant hush fell over the heaving stands. Only once the tiny performer had reached the centremost point did he let the blanket fall. A loud, collective gasp preceded an 'ooh' of appreciation.

Painfully thin and black as pitch, Charley Dumas stood no more than five feet four inches in height; the extraordinary costume in which he was clad, however, added immeasurably to his stature. Long, straggly hair covered his limbs, head and face, a doublet of animal skins worn over his hose – not kangaroo skin, but opossum. A broad plaited band of cabbage leaf encircled his brow, a head-dress surmounted by a crest of plumes from the impossibly colourful lyre-bird. The feathers of an ordinary wood pigeon filled these out, the unfortunate creature, captured that same morning, making for a fine bush-tucker breakfast.

The resplendent savage stood, poised, a length of carved wood curving forth from one raised hand, before, returned to his blanket, squatting down on the ground. Propelled without visible effort, the implement moments before seen in his hand now hurtled through the air, high above the heads of the crowd, whirling so rapidly that it appeared a semi-transparent disc. Having completed a circuit of the entire stadium, it returned, with uncanny precision, almost to the same exact spot.

The boomerang, or *callum-callum*, looked to be about the size of a man's arm, but quite thin – a strong, curved lath cut from a very solid wood, convex on its upper surface, and flat on its underside. Retrieved and thrown rapidly forward, it cut through the air with a loud whirring sound, advertising to one and all its deadly potential.

One end striking the ground, the wondrous device shot up, like a startled bird taking flight. Presenting its flat blade to the eye and then its sharp edge, the weapon turned invisible in the brightness of the sky. Appearing again as its plane of rotation changed, it began to glide rapidly about, first in one direction, then another, as though guided of its own volition. Sailing like a swallow, circling like a pigeon, spinning and twirling at a great height, it continued to gyrate in a most extraordinary manner. On its third throw the boomerang suddenly ceased in mid-flight – hung high and immobile as the lark – then swooped downwards to bury itself among the margins of the crowd.

The applause was thunderous.

'Cracking!' the crowd cheered. 'Bloody marvellous!'

A bright spark commented, 'That's the nearest to a gun that shoots round corners I should ever hope to see!'

Thus began the main event, 'Throwing the Boomerangs and Spears, and Kangaroo Rats, by the Blacks'.

Likewise adorned in possum and lyre, fur wrapped around their loins and a sort of fur cap on their heads, various others of the Aboriginal team joined

Dumas on the field. They walked with a proud and elastic swagger, notably in contrast to their former modest gait. In the laying aside of their ordinary clothes they underwent a positive transformation, as if they had thrown off disguises that rendered them commonplace.

In their skilful deployment of arms, the native Australians enthralled the baying crowd. Dextrously, they manipulated the *weet-weet*, or 'kangaroo-rat'. Made of whalebone tipped with wood, from a distance the device resembled a huge tadpole. Gripping it by the end, the Aborigines would swing it backwards and forwards so violently that it bent quite double. Taking a short backward run and then wheeling around, at the last they gave a quick underhand jerk and let fly. The low-flying slingshot cut the air with the sharp and menacing hiss of a bullet. Properly thrown it struck the ground more than once, a movement approaching the long leaps of its namesake; English observers were put more in mind of a skimming stone at 'ducks and drakes'. A skilled throw could send the 'kangaroo-rat' completely across the Kennington Oval: Dick-a-Dick repeatedly scattered spectators on the far side, striking the fence beyond.

Half a dozen warriors proceeded to stage a mock battle – three living targets, at a distance of nearly 300 feet, completely hemmed in by the accuracy of spears thrown by the other men. *Dará* or *teipa*, six or seven feet in length, each hardwood shaft was tipped with reed so as to fly point-foremost. The butt was fitted into a wooden pin then expertly whip-lashed, launching the spear into its terrifying trajectory. With leverage more than doubling the power of sinew, the wielder was able to propel his spear with unprecedented force and accuracy.

Bloodthirsty and warlike demeanour rendered the drama even more acute. Before throwing, each warrior hoisted his spear aloft so as to make it quiver, the loud clashing vibrations seeming to excite his fury. Menacing the foe with trembling spear, the aggressor would leap and yell, raving like a madman.

Each spear, thrown, gracefully writhed through the air, a thin black snake undulating – beautiful, and just as deadly. Unless their living targets dodged aside, they were certain to have been impaled.

Ethnographers present kept frenzied notes, enjoying the display for its own sake. Sports pundits expressed an equal satisfaction. Echoes of cricket within these arts of war went some way towards explaining the Aboriginal team's fine out-fielding and throwing-in, the accuracy and rapidity with which all able Australians threw the ball being much admired. Sure at the bat and deft at blocking, their wonderful quickness of eye and precision of muscular movement greatly enhanced their game.

Their team captain, too, entered into the spirit with 'Lawrence's Feat with the Bat and Ball', an impressive balancing act *à la* Tommy Dodd on the London stage – Lawrence appearing to catch a ball, thrown by Bullocky, on the narrow edge of his bat.

Dick-a-Dick, natural showman that he was, had delighted many with his antics, winning the backwards race by a few good lengths. His return to the field met with loud cheers. The programme described the next feature attraction, 'Dick Dick Dodging the Cricket Ball'.

Carrying in his left hand what appeared to be a short, thick stick, he stood out in the centre of the ground. The audience adjusted their binoculars: seen in close-up, he held a small shield, no more than four inches wide and decorated with carved designs. A curved wooden club, his *leowell*, extended from Dick's right hand – a formidable-looking weapon that should raise a nasty bump on anyone's cranium.

'Throw 'em ball!' he cried, beckoning. 'Throw 'em ball!' Screaming out his challenge, Dick-a-Dick cheekily invited all comers. Three burly fellows leapt forward, to be supplied with a heap of hard cricket balls. For the benefit of their audience, Lawrence loudly instructed they throw these at the 'human wicket' from a distance of less than fifteen yards, at will, all at once if they liked, and as hard as they possibly could.

The volunteers dutifully began to pelt Dick-a-Dick, using nothing less than lethal force. A flurry of activity broke out among the crowds, odds laid and bets taken as to how long he might survive.

Taking no notice of any ball passing more than an inch or two away, Dick baffled every straight ball with a keen intuition. As if blessed with sixth sense, he foretold the precise direction of each attack. Blows accurately aimed at his head and body, he parried with the shield; those on target for his legs he struck at using the club. Sometimes, throwing his club and shield to the ground, he would drop down on one knee, or simply dodge the balls with an elegant sidestep. Those sure not to hit he treated with contemptuous indifference, merely lifting an arm or moving his head a little to allow that the ball might pass, though it ruffled his hair in doing so. Whether standing still or dancing, his attitudes remained at all times picturesque. Jumping, ducking, falling now and then, parrying with the *leowell*, Dick-a-Dick defied all three throwers until they were completely exhausted.

Not a single ball had found its mark.

He had worked himself forward almost under the very noses of his opponents. Pulling grotesque faces, he grinned and yelled for victory. Excitement grew very great; his impudent assurance incensed and amused the crowd in equal measure.

Amidst the din of cheering, a rough element, their blood up, began to pour out onto the pitch. The entire ground erupted in chaos, and Dick-a-Dick fled.

Sarah Larkin sat high on the stands. Furies screeched all around her. Strangely cool, she lost herself in thought.

She had not told her father of her plans to attend, although, ostensibly, she acted on his behalf. An ardent cricket-lover, Lambert would have welcomed eyewitness reports of a day's play, especially as an unexpected treat. She really should have paid more attention, and come on an actual match day. If only the idea had occurred to her earlier.

Sarah wasn't sure what to make of the exhibition just witnessed, even less what her father might think. And, were she completely honest, her presence was owing to no account but her own. Why she felt the need to see the Aborigines again, and quite so soon, she was sure she had no idea. A mild curiosity, that was all.

Thus absorbed in the general mêlée, she was overtaken by a somewhat stranger sensation.

Out on the playing field stood one of the Aboriginal players, immobile as a statue, though wild figures on every side ran to and fro. Hard to tell at such distance, but Sarah thought him the one they had called King Cole. And he looked straight at her. Not around her or through her but right into her. She stared into brilliant black orbs. From beneath a brow broad and severe, pupils black as jet returned her looks. It wasn't possible: he couldn't have singled her out in this vast crowd, let alone recognised her. No, she was mistaken.

She blinked and shivered. He stood too far away after all. Hard to see how she might have made out the finer details of his face – and so pin-sharp – let alone meet his eyes.

And then he was gone. There were just blind bodies, rushing back and forth across the grass, and everywhere tumult.

She would remain in her seat until calm once more prevailed, and then make her way quickly home.

CHAPTER XIII
Whit Sunday, the 31st of May, 1868

CUTTING REMARKS

'Still thou upraisest with zeal
The humble good from the ground,
Sternly repressest the bad!
Still, like a trumpet, dost rouse
Those who with half-open eyes
Tread the border-land dim
'Twixt vice and virtue…'

~ Matthew Arnold, 'Rugby Chapel'

'Your mind is not on your game!'

Charles Lawrence berated King Cole for the poor quality of his most recent performance. A brisk day's play at Maidstone on the 30th had ended, unsatisfactorily, in a draw. 'We should have won that match.'

'Sorry, Orrince,' mumbled Cole.

'And as for you…cap it all!' Lawrence turned on Bullocky. He thrust forward a half-empty whisky bottle. 'Say black's your eye,' said Lawrence.

'Him not belonga me.'

'You've not seen this bottle before?'

Bullocky regarded the evidence sadly: it was still half full. Carefully he weighed his answer.

'Dat bottle,' he said, 'belonga some other pella.'

The merry-go-round whirl of the metropolis behind them, the entire company had returned to the Bear Inn, Town Malling, spare in its comforts. Friday's violent thunderstorms had abated, turned to drizzle.

'It's this sort of day I hate the most,' sighed Bill Hayman.

'Pentecost?' said William South Norton.

The pair stood looking out of the casement window. They occupied the antechamber to the first-floor lodgings reserved to the Aboriginals – a room they had begun to refer to, strictly between themselves, as 'L's guardhouse'.

'The sort of day,' said Hayman, labouring his point, 'when the hour of nine in the morning cannot be distinguished from five in the evening. The gloom neither lifts, nor the damp ground dries. It's like living in a cloud!'

The far door exploded inwards. Almost taken off its hinges, it ricocheted off the wall, shuddering furiously. In stormed Lawrence, knotted up with rage. South Norton raised a weary eyebrow.

'The maid found *this* in Bullocky's bed!' shouted Lawrence.

They stared at the whisky bottle clenched in his fist.

'Perhaps it was there to smooth his pillow,' Hayman suggested.

Lawrence slammed the bottle down next to the fireplace, so hard it was a wonder nothing broke.

'Let's hope he remembered to toast Her Royal Highness,' said William South Norton.

'The Melbourne Parliament has passed a law against sedition,' Hayman explained. 'It is now an offence even to boast of refusing to drink the Queen's health!'

'No separation for the colonies...'

'And they have executed the Duke of Edinburgh's assassin.'

'Would-be assassin.'

'It was a mistake,' said Lawrence, 'to attend church this morning.'

'You insisted,' said Hayman. 'Said it was important. "Whit Sunday, when the Holy Spirit descends upon its disciples."'

The priest had taken his sermon from the *Acts of the Apostles*, chapter two. 'A prophecy of fire and brimstone, signs and wonders?' said Lawrence. 'It's stirred up the Blacks something awful.'

'Put, quite literally, the fear of God into them,' said Hayman. He had never much approved attempts to Christianise or Anglicise the Australian natives, even in order that they might be saved.

The unhappy pair communicated their differences by addressing themselves to William South Norton – whose back was turned.

'Even I found it terrifying,' Lawrence admitted. 'A blood moon...the Spirit poured out on all flesh.'

'Perhaps,' suggested Hayman, 'you might disallow Bullocky from this evening's outing.' One Mr Allerton, 'an amateur of distinction', was to present the tragedy of the Danish prince at Town Malling's Assembly Rooms.

'No,' said Lawrence. 'I'd much rather have him in hand...'

His voice trailed away. William South Norton had magicked a tumbler from somewhere, and casually poured himself a generous measure of whisky. Swirling the golden liquid around in his palm, he took his turn holding forth.

'My wife and I have enjoyed nursing Little Johnny Cuzens,' he said. 'He has, I think, the makings of a first-class player. And that fellow Mullagh, *he's* quite the Pilch of your Eleven…up to county form! You work very hard for them, Lawrence, you do. It's most commendable.'

He raised a toast, no irony intended.

Lawrence's face threatened thunder.

'To Her Imperial Majesty!' said South Norton. 'Long may she reign.'

He drained his glass. As the contraband warmed his cockles, he warmed to his original theme.

'Minnie tended Cuzens with her special recipe chicken soup. She says his ears went up like a sow in beans. But the others?' he said. 'Odd, superior sort of savages… It's hard to get friendly with 'em. You've a good wicket-keeper in Dick Dick. Big old Bullocky does solid stick-in-the-mud business, all right. As for the rest? Boomerangers and Shake-a-spear-ians. The fielding's good, but, Mullagh excepted, there's not a third-rate batsmen among them!'

His emptied glass, upturned, hit the occasional table with a thwack.

'And that, as it turns out, is the pudding in the bowl…'

South Norton meant well, but it had come out all wrong.

Lawrence's face darkened: three in the afternoon, and already the grease-merchant was full of new wine.

'You simply have to get to know them better, William,' said Hayman quietly. 'And that takes time.'

Charles Lawrence said nothing. Face turned away, he had begun to brood. The sentiments expressed by William South Norton unwittingly echoed many of the match reports published in his adopted homeland, clipped from the newspaper articles Lawrence followed so avidly – in *The Australasian*, the *Hamilton Spectator*, the *Melbourne Age and Argus*, and the *Illawarra Mercury*. Following a game played in the sweltering heat of Boxing-day, the *Bathurst Times* had seen fit to comment on the Edenhope Cricket Club's new uniforms: how greatly their intelligent appearance stood in contrast to their debased brethren, skulking in the Bush.

Lawrence recalled how, some months earlier – during their first game following his engagement, in the mid-August of 1867 – the fielders had been unable to keep their feet on the ice.

That was how it was in Australia: everything topsy-turvy.

'We must have a stowaway on board,' said Lawrence. 'Is there some Maori tribesman we don't know about?'

'Oh, you're not still harping on about *that*, are you?' said Hayman.

Saturday's edition of *The Field* had reported, 'A variation in the black hues of their skin, these men represent the colonies of Victoria, Queensland, South Australia, and New Zealand.'

'Obviously, they meant New South Wales! I'll get on to them to print a correction,' said Hayman. 'That way, we get another mention.'

'Art is of no country, indeed,' huffed Lawrence. 'Why pay attention, when everyone's a Johnny Foreigner!'

'The niggers begin at Calais,' said William South Norton.

Lawrence rounded on him.

'For your part,' he snapped, 'you might at least keep Malling's underworld at bay.'

'You're not in Pall Mall now, old boy,' said South Norton, sleek as a cormorant. 'It's always pronounced "Mauling" by natives of my age.'

'*Aul* the same, dear chap,' said Hayman, 'see if you can't keep that felt-monger Seagar away from the lads.'

Further overtures from the roguish local pelt merchant must needs be discouraged.

'Last week's fox hunt was very regrettable,' said Hayman. 'We'll have no repeat of it.'

'They have need of our protection,' said Lawrence. 'They're like children.'

'And, like petted children,' said Hayman, 'not quite so docile and obliging as on first arrival. They have been rather spoiled by their good reception in this country.'

'You could both try harder,' said Lawrence.

Their heads turned, all amazed and in doubt.

'To do what?' said South Norton.

'Keeping Bullocky out of the Bull, for one thing. Or the Prior's Arms...' Lawrence sighed. 'The King's Arms, the Swan, the Cricketers...so many opportunities for drink in this puddle of a town,' he said, 'I've lost count!'

'It can't be helped,' said South Norton, 'if we are famously hospitable.'

'Oh, yes,' said Lawrence. 'To the point of finding someone else's bottle of whisky under one's pillow!'

'The honeymoon is over well and truly,' said South Norton. He moved to recharge his glass. 'You are annoyed with me because I played for Maidstone, against your precious Blackies,' he said. 'I'm not on the opposing team now, you know!'

'I wouldn't be so sure,' said Lawrence.

South Norton threw back the tumbler of whisky, and then set it down. 'I'll gladly serve my country,' he said, 'and see you on the field!'

And with that, William South Norton swept out of the room.

Bill Hayman laid his head to one side.

'Don't piss him off, Charles, there's a good fellow,' he said. 'He may yet come in useful in the days ahead.'

The sounds of song and laughter bled through the partition wall from the next room. No fans of the English rain, all the Aborigines sheltered safely indoors, engaged in some worshipful rite of their own.

'You should congratulate yourself,' said Bill Hayman at last. 'All that hard practice has paid off. The Blacks do very well, everything being taken into consideration.'

'Don't they, though?' said Lawrence. 'Remembering to pass the port widdershins, and good for parlour tricks!'

Hayman's breath escaped. 'Confound it, Charles! *You* confound me!' Every attempt to pay the team captain a compliment was turned on its head, and its pockets emptied.

'You know, my own belief was that their manners should be improved,' said Lawrence, 'at first.' He thought of their time back in Australia, when all seemed right, and good – and everything the other way up. 'Increasingly, I find myself more attached to the Blacks' natural character.'

'Sorry, Lawrence?' said Hayman. 'Blow me down!'

A fan of the theatre, Bill Hayman occasionally indulged a sideline as amateur entertainer, his forte being pastiche, or comical ditties in character. Drawing on these skills, he started to strut in front of the fireplace. In mellifluous but mocking tones, to the tune of 'The Battle-Hymn of the Republic', so popular of late, he improvised a marching song.

> '*Tom Brown*'s body lies a-mouldering in the grave!
> *Tom Brown*'s body lies a-mouldering in the grave!
> *Tom Brown*'s body lies a-mouldering in the grave!
> His soul goes marching onnnn!'

Hayman teased Lawrence over his favourite text, and in the parlance of civil war, to boot. They no longer spoke the same language.

Bill Hayman clasped at the small of his back – injury, added to insult. The damp was proving no good for his bones. Smarting, he departed, following South Norton down the stairs.

Lawrence drew closer to the only company remaining.

The edges of the old mirror above the fireplace hung ragged, where the silver flaked. He seized South Norton's empty glass. So as not to take up the bottle, Lawrence reached into his pocket and clutched hold of his cherished copy of *Tom Brown*, like a charm.

Heaven only knew, idle hands got up to no good when left to their own devices. They took to pilfering, poaching and in-fighting, where they might be better controlled by organised games.

His far-travelling children were not blank, like slates. But, otherworldly in their innocence, while neither good nor evil, they seemed of capacity for either – their characters malleable, like clay. Thus impressionable, they might be led anywhere – along the straight and narrow path of righteousness, or else astray. Ultimately, however, it all amounted to the same end. Even with good intentions, they could only be taken advantage of.

Lawrence swirled and spat disgust into the ashes of the fireplace. Rising, he again caught sight of himself in the flyblown, corroded mirror. His face, warped, bloated, stretched across the uneven surface of the glass. Shirked in places, shifting with his slightest movement, it shrank even from itself.

'"To be, or not to be: that is the question…"'

Onstage, before a full house, Hamlet made his immortal Third Act entrance. A thrill of excitement rippled throughout the theatre audience: young or old, nearly everyone knew these famous lines, even if they did not entirely understand them.

Lined almost the complete length of the second-to-front row, the Aborigines sat agog. It had been over a year since their last trip to watch the 'drama', Bill Hayman having taken them to a double-bill of *Rip Van Winkle* and *Nan, the Good for Nothing*, at Ballarat's Theatre Royal.

Hayman glanced down the line and wondered, as he had then, what the show might possibly mean to them. Some of the team members had since departed, and new ones joined. Some at least might never have seen the like.

Dick-a-Dick had used his share of the team's prize monies to hire an extravagant costume for the evening, looking more Genghis Khan than Aboriginal cricketer – nothing he need learn about dramatics. As for the remainder, was it more or less to them than mere play-acting?

Hayman felt wary of Lawrence, seated stolidly by his side. Nanny Lawrence, Good for Nothing, stared fixedly ahead; still in his almighty sulk. Bill Hayman returned his wandered attention to events onstage.

'"To die,"' rhapsodised Mr Allerton, '"to sleep. To sleep: perchance to dream. Ay, there's the rub."'

Neither of the team's guardians noticed, at the very end of their row, an emptied seat.

'"For in that sleep of death what dreams may come…"'

CHAPTER XIV
Whit Sunday, the 31st of May, 1868

BUGARAGARA

'The world is mind precipitated.'

~ Ralph Waldo Emerson, 'Nature'

Mityan, Brother Moon, emerges from the Shadow Lands. Between the bars of a blue gate, Dreaming streets give way to Dreaming fields, dim borderlands lit by His pale face.

After jogging concrete miles beyond a train journey's many more, King Cole has arrived at the edge of the city, at least as he knows it. From here on, the stone desert should peter out, like the ash at the end of one of Bullocky's cigarettes. Instead the hard roadway beneath his feet scrolls on, splitting as it spreads ever further out. From each dividing branch more buildings sprout forth. Every blade of grass is flattened, every tree felled. All earthen tracks are paved over. Smoke fills the air, bringing the horizon ever closer.

Any hope of open country denied, Cole stands at a crossroads, confounded by a barren wilderness that never ends. Into this latest aberration he will not stray. Keeping within known margins, he makes his way along what the *walypela* markings call 'New Road'; even before lessons with Lawrence, he could read a little.

Weak gas lamps, posted either side at regular intervals, taper away into the darkness.

All is silent, but it broods.

A new sensation disturbs, something unfamiliar, the shadow of a shadow unseen. All the same he feels it there, enough to acknowledge a lurking presence – the fear that creeps beyond a campfire's bright circle.

Cole shudders. He catches a faint whiff of it; the burgeoning guilt a dog must feel, dragged before evidence of its crime. The same as for any yellow dingo, he cannot comprehend the misdeed, beyond that implication of wrong relayed by his remote accuser.

This slippery notion either escapes him, or else he shakes it off.

He recalls his parting from Sundown, and, last thing, the secret he shared. 'Ancestor Spirits have led me here, and I must find my Way.'

Words a melody on the tongue rattle an urgent tattoo inside his skull.

Step for step, moving soundlessly, Cole heads south.

Passing through a succession of inner courtyards, evil-smelling and indiscriminate in character, King Cole gains ground by degrees. Sibilant beings loiter close to each obscure entrance or exit, bodies pressed close to the sticky walls. He keeps to the middle of the pathway as it finds him.

Looking down at his formerly smart evening-wear, foot-stinkers and jacket again discarded, he sees the shirt is smeared with grease and soot. His trousers are sodden. Cole recalls that earlier night's incantation, and supposes it to have worked. He is now as they were, those pale and stunted spectres. The splash and reek of the streets have rendered him unremarkable. At one with his surroundings he is beneath notice, and therefore safe.

One must first seek permission to pass through any hostile country. He should very much like to keep his kidney fat!

Having skirted the Well of Shadows, Cole means to pick up his previous trail. Before him squats a mean red-brick building, longer than it is broad, and bordered by a thicket of trees. A low, square tower tops the church, as it seems to be, decorated with globe-like ornaments that resemble huge chess pawns.

He looks on in wonder as the roof falls in. Through the collapsing body rises a monumental spearhead. The black tower springs up straight and true, an enormous nail, only stopping once its sharpened point has sliced through a bank of low cloud. Succeeded, the ornate old structure at its base crumbles away, until not a sign of it remains.

A single strike of the church bell dies in the air. Not even the promise of dawn colours the night sky.

Stairs dripping with filth lead the way down to the river, running shallow towards low tide. At their base, he crouches low over the exposed bank, close to the water's edge. He dips nimble fingers into the nightmare sludge, repeatedly daubing the upper parts of his face, neck and breast, until caked with a fearsome ritual garb.

King Cole stands tall in the presence of the Great Serpent, *Mindeye*.

Mindeye eats up clay and spits it out again. Masked in the stinking slime that trails in His wake, His lowly follower seeks to honour and placate the great Spirit Ancestor. Cast from the mud, in His image, they are one. His scent is the same.

Cole holds the vast body of water in awe. He stares a while across the turbid expanse – the sheer breadth of the river, in the dead of night, accentuated by its emptiness.

On the opposite shore, the darker side, a lightless mass cleaves to the river-banks. Likewise moulded of tidal muck, it rises from the slick silt – bricks and mortar black with the dust of coal-ships, and soot from the smoke of squat hutments there compacted – an impenetrable wall.

Marshland this was, and always would be.

Cole traces the progress, swift progress, of a broken bough bobbing in and out of sight among treacherous currents. The wide mud-tide flows thick and fast. Under what is again a moonless sky the river is a deadly torrent of ink. Surface taut with menace reflects nothing. It is like staring into empty space, a bottomless pit – an immense and unquenchable hunger.

Darkness calls to darkness.

East is the direction in which Cole is drawn, and so eastward he goes.

Massive warehouse walls blinker his vision, affording only glimpses of the Serpent's course. The path is wrong. He feels certain he should walk with the river on his left side, not the right.

King Cole retraces his steps, until standing once more at the head of Pelican Stairs. He turns west. Looking back, a wavering form shimmers briefly, and disappears from view – a place he knows well drowned beneath two great waterholes. Taking this as a promising sign, Cole advances. His temples throb with foreboding. Just ahead rears an apoplectic grey tower, penitential and severe.

He paces nearer the wall's great curve. Dull, metallic vibration – power bound by the bleak stone circle – causes him to tremble. Cole reaches out a cautious hand, establishing contact. The presence is physical, solid and undeniable. Cracked plaster, peeling paint, meaningless slogans scrawled across the surface; the tower bears outward signs of neglect. The place, so it seems, is abandoned and ignored. He spies a doorway, partly concealed. The gate that bars the way is flimsy. Beneath layers of clogging dust and trailing broken cobweb, hangs a notice.

Property of East London Railway Company
KEEP OUT

With fluid ease Cole squeezes through a broken slat, low to the ground. By the wan light he can make out, immediately to his right, a modest wooden cabin. The window-glass throws back a smeared reflection. He searches his pockets for a stray coin. This he places on the ledge of the phantom tollbooth, amongst delicate spider-spun filaments. Passing inside, he stands and waits for his eyes to adjust.

His keen night vision gradually discerns differences in density. Within the total blackout of the tower's interior, he senses volume and scale. High overhead, an immense domed ceiling shuts out the sky. Only a couple of paces in front, a balustrade curves away to either side. Open space yawns below.

Cole peers over the edge into abysmal gloom. A gaping maw at least 50 feet wide eagerly waits to swallow him up. No telling how deep down into the bowels of the earth the great shaft might sink; there is no certainty it even has a bottom.

An urge to flee furiously battles the intense compulsion spurring him on. Lure eventually overcomes dread. Cole turns to one side, grips the raw-bone rail and, guts tightened, braces to launch himself into the void.

He runs, full tilt, hollering at the top of his voice. Hysterical echoes accompany him all the way down, inexorably down.

Twinned stairwells sweep back and forth, traversing the sunken circumference. The stone pathway splits, only to reconvene, and then once more part company – the cadence of a falling leaf.

King Cole, swept to the bottom, slows.

His bare feet slap onto a paved platform, a subterranean road. Colliding with a fixed length of iron track, he stumbles. His flailing hand meets with clammy plaster. The walls run cold, rivulets chill as the sweat that streaks Cole's forehead. He is down, under the ground, farther than he ever believed he could sensibly go.

Reaching for his *waddy* club, tucked into his belt, he withdraws it.

Ahead of him in the gloom, a light flares above two massive, horseshoe-shaped arches, each more than twice his height and wide enough for a single carriage. Burning overhead at some nebulous mid-point, the gaseous star too soon winks out. Twin corridors stretch out before him, into everlasting midnight – a hope-devouring darkness.

The dismal black lanes bring to mind the holes of shipworms, bored into the soft wood of the *Parramatta*. He faces perhaps the Great Serpent's lair, or, worse, His interminable gullet. He perceives ribs, diminishing with distance. They lead to *Mindeye*'s foul black belly.

Is that the stench of His guts he can smell? From far off in the distance comes a faint churning sound, the racked workings of waterlogged lungs. The foetid vapour suggests the impossible: the breath of a corpse.

Beyond fear, King Cole passes the point of no return. Choosing a side at random, he starts into the left-hand tunnel.

Positioned at fixed intervals, flame-jets of gaslight spark into fitful life. From some way ahead, snatches of a queer, mechanical music waver amidst ghostly echoes: weak, female voices; scuffles and scrapings that come from the frequent little alcoves conjoining the paired passageways. As he approaches, Cole perceives – deep within the darkness – termite forms. From the shadows of their dirt caves they whisper and beckon, pitifully eager, sadly imploring.

The dead city seethes with such horrors. It has no space that is not filled. Even here, thousands teem, groping blindly. Some seem to tend humble stalls for penny wares. Others have nothing to sell except themselves. Withered scraps and faded charms – shopkeepers, whores, but nowhere any customers.

Fast travelling between worlds, Cole often witnessed phantoms in some sense or another existing. None he can recall is as pathetic and forgotten as these white-haired, pale-limbed creatures. Dully aglow in the intense gloom, they wear glass marbles for eyes. Be they relics of the past or figments torn from some dread future, he neither knows nor cares. Sensing they are not as solid, as constant as he in the Dreaming, he chooses to ignore them.

Doggedly, he drives himself forward.

At a junction where the tunnels widen, a miniature steam-driven organ plays without any audience. Garlanded with artificial flowers, all choked up with dust, it grinds out indeterminate tunes, ceaselessly and carelessly. Cracked and dirty orange-coloured tiling surrounds a complex array of mirrors, lamps, and lenses. Billing itself the 'Cosmorama', the elaborate object idles, extinguished.

King Cole finds it increasingly hard to draw breath.

The passageways are suddenly choked: with ancient silt; bygone sands; or fathoms' river-flow. He struggles on through suffocating murk, his arms and legs flailing desperately.

Globes of liquid light swell and burst before him. Cole runs. Every insubstantial spectacle intended to delay and doom, he ignores, stopping for nothing. A treadmill pace gains the far stairs; he ascends swiftly, bursting through barred doors.

Flopped like a landed fish, convulsing, vomiting a little, King Cole lies sprawled on the dry paving. He rests a while.

Above and behind snores a sleeping giant. Hand pressed to his chest, Cole turns to look. The sounds growl out of a bump on the skyline – all that shows of the great nest below.

His heaving lungs eventually calm, rising and falling in tune.

Regaining his feet, he surveys new surroundings; another distinct region, cognisable from other days' and nights' Dreaming – yet, again, subtly different. As he turns east, the river is now on his left. The great black beast stretches out, skin scabbed by countless dark barges.

Cole searches for some trace of the road bridge he has just crossed. There is no sign. The city, divided in two, is all alike one piece of dry land. A warrior of the *Wudjubalug*, he has walked beneath the waves without getting wet! Resolute, he resumes his passage eastward.

Ahead lies a cold, black swamp.

Cole picks up the pace. He runs along a strip of dry land, sees a strange stone house on legs. Turn-turn fetch-the-water, a windmill rises to his right.

He runs on into a maze of smaller streets, dense overgrowth almost impenetrable. Sharp left, hard right, the lie of the land is a complex set of rhythms. Ahead, two lanes converge. Another course joins his own. The only way forward lies straight ahead. At every junction his choices are predetermined. He is being driven, like a sheep to its pen.

A narrow causeway crosses over a whiplash twist of creek, where the air reeks worse than swamp gas. Cole is returned beside the Great Serpent.

A scattering of vessels drifts unmanned on the low-lying waters. Their criss-cross cables drip, slathered over with tar, draped with weed.

From behind high cloud, a lambent screen, reappears *Mityan* – a good hunting moon. Bone-stark, every detail of the Dreamscape gains in definition. Moonlight ripples the currents, white to black and black to white – the scales of the Great Serpent, writhing.

Impetus turns Cole inland.

The streets converge on an open marketplace, above which rises a complex of tall, rectangular buildings. Glowing white in the night, it is a moon palace.

He approaches closer, along a riverfront terrace. The tranquil galleries, lined with stiff columns, recede into middle distance. They seem to float on a slight ground mist, as if becalmed on cloud.

A restless crowd emerges from among the sturdy pillars. Steadily they stream, pouring forth from all points of the compass. Croaking voices harsh and grating, they call like crows, occasional laughter dissolving into fits of racking cough. Dressed in uniforms of ragged blue, some wear hats cocked with three corners, others, knitted caps. In all shapes and sizes they come – men, and the remains of men. Limbless, peg-legged, one-eyed or one-armed, some bend so low they resemble lobsters or crabs. They drag themselves through low oceanic mist, strangely undisturbed by their laboured progress.

Gradually, they disperse, to sit in clumps by the river steps, as useless and cluttering as fallen leaves, or else to roll about their palace grounds.

Returning along the terrace, past the heady, commingling scents of brew-house, bakery, and stable block, Cole comes to a fence bordering on to formal gardens. The woods are thick, the trees very big. They shake to warn him away. Something else, pressing close, insists he go in.

This part of the garden is neglected and overgrown. It is, he sees, a burial ground. Cole's head throbs. He trips, and falls.

Is someone there? He feels afraid, a small child again.

Regaining his feet, Cole drags himself across the rough turf. The grass gives way with a brittle crunch, wasp bodies crushed underfoot. A sudden chill scoops out his lungs. Limbs shivering, he can feel the marrow inside his bones; taste blood, on his tongue. It is the very edge of night and the end is near.

Cole lurches to a dead halt.

Breath comes in puffs of white cloud that blow back into his face. Dried clay caking his features and upper torso, the Thames mud begins to crack and disintegrate. Crumbling, it falls away in a shower.

He stands at the base of an old grave, unkempt and entangled with weeds. The uneven earth at his feet has been turned long ago. There is no headstone, just a short wooden stake driven into the ground. King Cole falls to his knees, clutching at the soil.

Raising his left forearm, he takes up a small blade, concealed in his back pocket, and slits open the largest vein.

His hot blood spatters, smoking, on the turned ground.

King Cole falls back into the long grass, relishing the embrace of earth, the sensation of sinking back in. His night's journey is ended. Taken together with his first London Dreaming, it has been a life's journey, womb to tomb – from birth to death and beyond; a vital link between opposite shores of existence found and forged, without his having the least idea why.

He opens his eyes. He has left the old grave behind, making the steep climb up a nearby hill. In appreciation of the elm at whose root he relaxes, its unique outline, he follows the coil and twist of branches. The tree stands alone on the hill. Venerable link between earth and sky world, its limbs thrust upwards, reaching outward to gather in the stars.

Bark fingers weave in and around constellations only semi-familiar. The campfires of his Ancestors, the *Nurrunbung-uttias*, dot the galaxy. Their smoke threads its milky way. Differing entirely from the night skies of his homeland, the cosmic alignments diverge only slightly from the stranger-skies of his Dreaming.

A dark red orb rises but brings no dawn.

Cole wonders if what he has heard is true: that the starlight itself is but a trace of long ago and far away. Looking past the branches overhead, beyond even the light of the planets themselves, he contemplates – with sad longing – the blackness in between the stars.

The sun was strong, back in the World. When he left, summer was at its height.

He mourns the loss of his former team-mates, his clan brother most especially. And then, sinking deeper, he remembers his people, and tries desperately hard not to think of their fate.

Leaving all mortal thoughts behind him, he falls into a deep and dreamless sleep.

And still, the darkness looks on.

CHAPTER XV
Whit Monday, the 1st of June, 1868

AN AWAKENING

'And, lo, hath the Fiend Infernal most craftily and unduly
gotten the honest Name and Fame of one extraordinary
Studious Gentleman of this land within his Claws…that
this gentleman shall, with this English or British State, either
(during his life) be counted a good Subject, or a Commendable
(nay, scarce a Tolerable) Christian.'

~ Dr John Dee, *The Perfect Arte of Navigation*

The sky to the east turns pale. One by one, the pinpoint lights of distant stars wink out. All the dark solidity of night drains away, troubled memories no more than a haze of sadness.

Before anyone else is abroad, King Cole walks the riverside streets. His limbs ache with the lingering bite of cold. He can count his bones individually, a sensation not entirely unpleasant, for it reassures he is alive, and in brief respite the air seems almost fresh.

He examines the wound, fresh on his arm, the large vein pierced as part of his sacred ritual. The earth gives life, and takes a body back when it dies. He is bound, now, to the earth, the earth atop the grave where he shed his life's blood; but why this grave over any other?

Dawn announces itself cautiously, sending out a single radiant beam to pierce the dense forest of masts along the waterfront. Awash in monotones, a single ship, broken away from its brethren, sails the leaden tide.

Barefoot, Cole treads light, yet his keen ears mark the noise he does not make. His footfalls, so it seems, go not unaccompanied. Step for step a displaced echo knocks some way behind him. One ear cocked, he minds the steady beat. It rebounds back and forth between surrounding warehouse walls. He pauses to look around and about – but when he stops, so, too, does the echo. No sign, no scent of his counterpart; he stands alone.

King Cole proceeds swiftly, where to, he isn't sure. He has been following a marked trail; of that much he is certain. He needs help now to interpret the signs.

Past the mid-point of a narrow alleyway, something darts from the shadows at its far end. Cole freezes. No time to turn, to run. It advances too rapidly towards him – a strange, hollow figure. Tall, hunched over almost double, it barrels down the passageway, scraping one wall then the other as it lopes from side to side. A bundle of sticks hoisted over one shoulder, from its scabby claws radiates a burst of filaments, the seedling of a great dark thistle. Only as they close does Cole see it is a man, face blacker than his own. From under the brim of a soot-caked hat, his yellow eyes stare, bloodshot.

The chimney sweep, as he trundles by, salutes with a filial nod.

The retreating figure dwindles, ultimately swallowed back into the brickwork. King Cole checks himself over before continuing, relieved to have survived the encounter.

Solitary cartwheels creak in the distance, and then nothing. The silence that follows is huge and terrifying absence, a vacuum about to be filled.

Faint tremors begin beneath Cole's feet. The vibrations travel throughout his body, like breeze through a grove of eucalyptus. He sets his jaw, but cannot stop his flesh from quivering. As he hurries towards the alley's extreme the disturbance only mounts. Metal grinds stone; clashing sounds, like a rapid shower, not of rain but shattered glass fragments.

Cole stumbles into a main thoroughfare. London is alive, the first wave of workers already busy. Massive carthorses strain slab-like muscles, pulling at wagons piled high with fruit and vegetables, sacking, fish; the wheel-rims crunch against cobbles and kerb, while their iron-shod hooves pound, shooting sparks.

Just off the beaten track, a crowd gathers at a coffee-stall. Another warms itself around the oven of a baked-potato man. Still more workers scuttle from out of the side streets, pulling on their outer garments. Bent low with purpose, they add their weight to the turbulent mass.

Cole thinks of the other great cities he knows. Built and inhabited by numberless thousands, they have their own workers, and soldiers, and queen – whole societies, blind, exhausting their lives in darkness, hidden from the eye of *Gnowee*, the Sun. White ants, they scrape out holes to build up their towers, bite after bite, extracting clay particles from the sand. This they mould into upright slabs, hardening one with the rock. Chamber on chamber, piled one above another, they are forever building, building, building, adding to the mound. They never tire of it, and they never stop.

And he thought he had left the nest behind. He is still deep within it.

Performing a neat circuit of the Reading-room, Time looped back around on itself. Wall to opposite wall, like Narcissus in the Styx, the Wisdom of the Ages troubled to stare at nothing bar its own reflection.

Sarah Larkin sat beneath the ceiling dome in her customary chair. Bored stiff, she had meant to calculate the total range of her freedoms, but could not find a number low enough to start.

The British Museum's library had accumulated texts throughout more than a century of rapid expansion – this latest Reading-room, vast and circular, its seventh successive incarnation. By exceedingly skilful arrangement, it was supposed to enclose shelf-space for a million and a half of books; more than sufficient, one would have thought, to fix her so firmly to one spot.

The curve of the dome sprang from a massive cornice, almost entirely gilded, a golden ring that topped three encircling tiers of bookcases. By her reckoning, these 'presses' must contain upwards of 80,000 volumes. Those at ground level, within reach of the public, numbered perhaps 20,000 alone.

Four further bookstacks surrounded the main chamber, a labyrinth running across several floors; perforated iron walkways allowed natural light to filter through from glass roof to basement. Only staff members might retrieve items from the rows above, via these upper galleries. Access doors from external passageways had been artfully concealed, with a variegated stripe pattern simulating the spines of books. Strips of the same design covered over the iron piers supporting the dome. The given impression was of an unbroken circumference of books; intended as an inspiration, no doubt.

Taken all together, the present library obliterated what had once been an open quadrangle within the museum complex. As a small child, Sarah had sat upon the grass there, fashioning herself chains from daisies.

A clerk entering through an upper doorway appeared to step out of the bookcase, a literary phantom. A great clutch of keys hung suspended from his waist.

Looking around at other inmates, scattered amongst neighbouring tables, Sarah recognised many faces – strangers, every one. Oh, she knew their features well enough, but that was all. Their characters remained unknowable. Hearts closed, minds occupied, they met on nodding terms at most.

In the dim light their skin looked old and grey, as hers must do. In this place, only the book-bindings kept their colour.

King Cole finds himself penned, closer than he can stand, between filthy brick walls. He scales the nearest to scurry along the top of it.

''Ere!' says an objecting voice, rapidly outdistanced.

Lofty black viaducts span in either direction. Terraces stretching beneath squirm with indifferent life. Even to the topmost windows, flung open wide, the mealy bodies bulge and spill: listless smokers; small children, protestant at being shut indoors; washerwomen hanging out their sopping rags. Women and children by the dozen are squeezed into every back yard. They kiss at gurgling babies, corralling more in makeshift pens as they themselves toil, scrub, stir and grind. The menfolk stand in the corners, filling or emptying the great slop-barrels there, or squat on the doorsteps, whittling. Others crouch in outhouses joined to the back of each chimneystack, tending smaller chimney-fires between their lips.

Every funnel great and small belches thick smoke.

A goods train screams across the land-bridge overhead. Shocked by the deafening noise, Cole almost falls from his perch. A suffocating shroud, dense and poisonous, descends. The air completely fills with choking fumes.

Straddled, dwarfed, chaos and clamour at every turn, King Cole flees. He runs and jumps from wall to backyard wall. Up ahead, women with gammon limbs queue at a standpipe, blocking his way. Cole spies a square of empty dirt. He drops down, weightless.

It takes but a moment to catch his breath. He has outdistanced the evil black cloud.

Incomprehensible sights and sounds now fill his days as well as his nights. Is this Dreaming? Is he fast travelling, or slow?

King Cole stares, wide-eyed, at the ground: no earth beneath his bruised feet, only more concrete. A stubborn weed pushes up through a crack it has forced in the man-made stone. Is this all it is, his greater Truth? He cannot tell. A parade of imagery, of no consequence, without sympathy, is mere sensation. He is lost: a wandering eye, choked lungs, goose-bumped skin and running feet – nothing more.

In Malling, Sarah had been described as working here at the library. Only men were allowed on staff, truly employed. Mind having no sex, her sex was of no mind.

She had been coming to the Reading-room since the age of sixteen, solely at the behest of her father. Her basic function amounted to little more than that of Lambert's copyist and personal secretary. In service of the Frankenstein's monsters that made up his sermons, she laboured over what was, in effect, a work of endless transcription. She trawled through Scripture for stitchings-together of deathless prose, the purloined wisdom and hand-me-down inspiration that had long ceased to be their daily bread and weekend butter.

Sarah had never enjoyed working for her father, most especially not since Lambert had taken somewhat definitively to his bed; in all likelihood, he would never again have the strength to deliver another of his anyway unpopular harangues – not in public. Thus, an exercise she had always felt essentially dishonest had become futile as well. And if it was God's will that he not recover, then she toiled in vain. Still, she kept coming to the library out of – what? Force of habit, sense of duty; or was it in pretence that his health might improve?

Her everyday visits were enough just to get her out of the house, and its stifling atmosphere of ill health.

She loved her father. She would do anything for his quiet life.

Lambert had always suppressed the works of certain authors, encouraged a chosen few. Working daily in the round, there was of course little in the world of books that could escape her – a bargain binding both ways. Emancipation, in terms black and white; Thomas Huxley had discussed womanly beauty, 'so far as it is independent of grace and expression'. Sarah knew which she would rather – and that was independence.

The university college in Bloomsbury, she heard, held evening classes opened to women. Maybe, one day, she might allow herself to investigate. What she wished for, most of all, was to be put to proper work – devotions that might amount to something.

No dream was worth having, unless it were impossible.

King Cole pulls together his scattered fibres.

Derby Day, exhibition cricket matches, are nothing more than idle fancies to him now. There can be no going back, only forward.

The shoving and the arguments are almost too much. Treading boots, hooves, cow-shit, and sour, angry faces; he dare not stop, even to think, for fear of drowning. To every side the bodies crush in. It is hard to keep one's feet. Vehicles, people, animals, impossibly dense, beyond number – moaning bullocks, sheep, and massive pigs – great flocks and herds are being driven down the street. The drovers-boys call and shove, and the dogs snap at their heels. The trusting creatures, though they may mill and complain, let themselves be steered to their doom. Knackers' carts return in the opposite direction, loaded with carved flesh all lifeless and bloody.

So much dust is kicked up that vision is down to a matter of feet, in front and behind – no telling which is which. Cole keeps an eye to the animals' backs, and, when in doubt, follows them.

The air clears a little. Cole stumbles to the wall. Looking over, he sees rapid waters far below. He is crossing the river once more.

Somewhere in the crowding city lives the Guardian. She is the Guardian of the Words of Dead Men. He saw number-writing on that stick, driven into the ground above the grave.

He will seek her out, and ask for her help.

Determined to upset her routine, Sarah decided to break early for lunch, perhaps to get some air.

'Have you finished with the book?' the Returns clerk enquired.

Sarah considered a moment. 'I have,' she said. 'Thank you, Mr Evans.'

Passing through the Museum doors, Sarah topped the broad stone flight of steps. Following a grey morning the sky had not brightened, nor the air warmed any. No point pausing over a scene she knew too well.

Hurrying, head down, she only marked oncoming feet in order that she might avoid collision; to the well-mannered tip of any gentleman's hat, she remained oblivious.

'The Museum', 'Mus-e-um' – asking of directions by intermittently mooing at passers-by, King Cole is directed to the place he most wants to be. A double stockade of spear-points blocks his path. Such is the urgency of his case, he overcomes even this fierce deterrent. Once inside the gates, he waits for her on the stone steps, uncertain she will come – but then she does come!

As Sarah Larkin reached the base of the broad descent, one flickering shadow detached from the rest, to sweep along in her tracks. As she paused, so paused her mimic. Even with her sharpest wits about her, she would never have noticed the hanger-on – not unless he wished it.

Reaching the Museum's main gates, she turned sharp right, making her way along the outside railings. Looking across Great Russell-street, Sarah regarded the frontage of No.38 – Mills and Wellman, the furnishing ironmongers. The same premises served as a Post Office Receiving House, Money Order Office and Savings Bank – a threshold she only crossed, these days, in order to withdraw funds, never to deposit. Life, the newspapers complained, had become cheap: not last she looked. To run a six-roomed house required a minimum £200 *per annum*. With no longer any income to speak of, she could only watch as their savings evaporated.

It was the first of the month. Sarah tabulated their needs, balanced them against her obligations, and resolved that it was not due time – not quite yet. The inevitable might be put off for a few days more.

Running the final few steps, Sarah reached the front door of No.89 and presented her key to the lock. She paused a moment in the lobby. Dr Epps did not appear to be in. The door to his waiting room was shut, as was the way to his surgery.

She needed to replenish the coal supply, at least in her father's room, and would rather not be seen tripping back and forth from the back yard. First, however, she would need to change clothes; these few items she wore were the only ones fit for public appearance. Gathering her skirts, she sped up the narrow staircase.

Sarah looked in on her father, only to find him sleeping. Her nose wrinkling, she opened a window. On his overcrowded bedside table, she left behind a sheaf of her most recently transcribed notes, placing a fir cone from one of his collections as an ineffectual paperweight.

King Cole follows the Guardian, unsure of his approach. She disappears into another set of buildings close to the first, slender by comparison, but almost as tall. Part, he is disturbed to note, goes down under the ground.

She is somewhere inside. He must gather up his courage and make his way to her.

A stone bridge leads to the doorway through which she went. The ditch that separates building from street is only a few feet wide, but deep and dark enough to threaten disaster. He steps gingerly – one foot, then the other – making sure it takes his weight; that he won't be tipped to his doom.

He examines the door, and imagines it open, and the Guardian standing there before him.

Returned to the landing, still unchanged from her street clothes, Sarah experienced a curious magnetism. She had found herself drawn back down the stairs. From the first floor landing, she considered the door to the street. Was it properly shut? She was sure – so why this bizarre compulsion?

Open the door.

The loop-holes of retreat held their pleasures in reserve, 'to see the stir of the great Babel, and not feel the crowd'. Or was that in itself denial? All morning, for just such cowardice, she had taken herself to task.

Sarah opened the door.

CHAPTER XVI
Whit Monday, the 1st of June, 1868

HIS MAJESTY

'AND the LORD God said, Behold, the man is become as one of us…'

~ *Genesis* 3:22

She knew neither how, nor why, but Sarah Larkin was in no doubt that the dark stranger standing in the shadow of the porch had come for her.

The figure moved into the light – not light so much as the leavening of London's greater gloom.

A wild man, he showed even blacker than before. Dark waistcoat and trouser caked with indescribable filth, his shirt, worn without a tie, gaping open at the neck: it might once have been white. Shock-haired and red-eyed, his appearance might have excited greater alarm had she not recognised him instantly.

His name was King Cole, and he was one of the Aboriginal Cricketers.

The threshold, raised a foot or so above street-level, was enclosed by an iron railing, the broad stone slab levelled like a drawbridge beneath their feet. Sarah stood within the doorway; he hovered on the step.

On her doorstep, an Australian Aborigine! A visitor had come to see her, come all the way from the bottom of the world; and looking, for the life of him, as if he had run all the way.

His expression was one of total bewilderment. Shaded by long, dark lashes, his pupils were great black marbles flung in her face – haunted eyes, pleading with her.

How had he come to be there? Was he lost?

'*Ngayulu…*'

King Cole spoke. Head inclined, his manic stare searched the ground at his feet.

'*…ngayulu nyanga teiwa pitjangu.*'

Sarah's own lips had formed no question, yet his appeared to make answer. She marvelled at the beauty of his language, words 'more soft than rain'.

He looked away down the street. From somewhere deep and rich inside heaved the most affecting sigh.

'*Teiwa*,' he said, '...*teiwa*.'

A carriage sped past, wheels rattling. The length and breadth of Great Russell-street rang with vendors' cries. King Cole's gentle phrases all but drowned in the surrounding din. He seemed so sad.

Their eyes locked for a split second, with the force of a thump to the chest.

His face brightened.

'*Jangan-djina-njug!*'

Dodging a sudden missile, quite invisible to the eye, Cole staged a brief pantomime – the exaggerated placement of one foot before the other.

'*Jangan-djina-njug*,' he shouted. '*Jungunjinanuke!*'

'I can't...I can't understand you!' said Sarah.

Less than two feet away from her danced a near total stranger – not perfect, and none so strange. She had no guarantee the man was even in his right mind. With a reach of his arm he might...

No, she would not give in to fear. The black orb of his eye was that of a dove, not a hawk.

Passers-by concentrated largely on their own affairs; his loud actions, however, his dishevelment, had begun to attract notice.

'Comealong comealong comealong comealong comealong...'

Hypnotic rhythm rolling, thick and throaty, King Cole burbled pleasantly by her side. '...comealong comealong makim makim Serpent.'

Thirpent? Lulled by his banal narrative, Sarah barely noticed as the flash flood of native language eased into a guttural approximation of her own: an Aboriginal sort of English.

'Goalong goalong goalong goalong PINIS!'

His sudden spit brought forth a flush of hot blood to her face and cheeks. He was staring again. People were staring. Some had stopped in their tracks just to stare. Sarah grasped King Cole by his sleeve and pulled him inside the quiet house, closing the door to the street behind them.

Having bidden the fellow enter, she could not very well refuse him welcome. Nothing to be done about the mud all over, but it was mostly dried. As directed by her good conscience, Sarah mounted the stair. She signalled, shyly, that he might follow.

She moved carefully, her tread deliberately light. The Aborigine followed on without making a sound.

They gained the upper floors and the relative privacy of Sarah's own family apartments, where she led him into the front parlour. A four-square chamber of medium size, their 'morning' room, so-called, was an embarrassment, but no more so than any other. Neither fixtures nor fittings had been improved in the fourteen years since her mother's death. Even in the old days, they had only received guests on rare occasion.

'Welcome,' said Sarah.

Politely but promptly she excused herself. A dubious reflex action demanded that she wash her hands. She then lit the stove and put a pan of water on to boil.

Sarah rushed further upstairs to check on her father. Although it was gone eleven, almost twelve noon, he remained sound asleep – a small mercy.

Repairing downstairs, once again to the kitchen, she rapidly gathered all the makings of a tea tray – the Staffordshire Porcelain – teapot, sugar-pot, milk jug, two cups, and a delicate slop bowl. She fretted all the while. Lambert overslept, meaning that he must have suffered another restless night. And what would he have to say, if he only knew that she entertained a man; especially such a man as King Cole. Better to think of herself as entertaining royalty!

Sarah returned to find Cole engaged in particular close study of a picture frame. The antique map was of London. Surely aware of her presence, he nevertheless paid her no heed. Instead, with his fingertip, he traced the course of the River Thames, marked as a long, looping ribbon of blue. Seeing a matching trail inscribed in the thick layer of dust on the picture-glass, Sarah felt deeply shamed.

She went to arrange the tea service on a tabletop caddy, only to find it missing. Hesitant to put the tray directly down, Sarah scanned the room before approaching her guest.

'Tea?'

Her strangulated voice sounded ridiculous, the hoarse squeak of a house mouse. She cleared her throat as delicately as she could. 'Tea?' she repeated.

The dark face turned, the lost, wild cast from before replaced by a beatific calm. Cringing no longer, King Cole stood erect, if in relatively relaxed fashion. Were it not for the raggedness of his clothing, the darkest copper of his complexion, he might suit formal surroundings as well as any gentleman. Lest she be completely beguiled, he wore no shoes. She might have noticed sooner were the colour of his feet not so intrinsic.

'Will you take a cup of tea?' said Sarah.

He moved to take the obviously heavy tray from her arms, froze, and then bowed slightly. When it came to social graces they appeared equally rusty; in more relaxed circumstances she might have granted it amusing.

'Please,' she said. 'Have a seat.'

He hesitated. She nodded towards the balloon-back velour, its cabriole legs carved from mahogany. This he spurned in favour of a much-worn easy chair. Deep-buttoned chenille stuffed with horsehair, the spongy upholstery swallowed his narrow flanks. Struggling to rearrange himself, he perched on its edge.

'How do you like it?' persisted Sarah. 'Your tea?'

She set down the tray, picked up the pot, and with a faint tremor poured from it. King Cole had again failed to respond, but when she proffered the tiny silver-plate jug he nodded eagerly. She poured the milk, understanding from his bashful smile to add a more generous measure. The most curious expression on his face, he watched as the white swirl circled in the dark liquid, finally taking up his teaspoon and blending it in.

He sipped his tea, thoughtfully.

Sarah occupied herself with the makings of her own cup. The brittle clink of crockery seemed to fill every corner of the room, until they eventually sat in mounting silence. That blasted grandfather clock in the hallway – she could have died between its every tick, and tock.

Cole scarcely looked at her, and spoke not a word. She wondered what he could possibly want – for her to begin with the introductions, perhaps.

'Sarah,' she said.

However much she felt she should, she did not extend a hand.

He did not react.

Sarah smiled, feeling slightly foolish. More of a context might be required. 'Sarah,' she said again. 'My name...is Sarah.' Wincing, she gave herself a light tap on the shoulder.

The reticent Aborigine nodded curtly, but would not meet her eye. After a little delay, he mumbled a single word.

'Thara.'

'S-Sarah.'

'Thara,' he said.

With the gentlest lisp on the sibilant 's', he repeated her name, she was sure of it. She must allow it.

'And – uh...you?' Sarah made what she hoped was a reciprocal hand gesture. 'Your name?'

He was examining the carpet, testing it with his bare black foot. His feet and hands too were surprisingly slender.

'Your name is...Cole?' she asked. 'King Cole?'

She knew full well what he was called, but suspected it a given name. Still, he nodded.

How was she meant to address him? 'King'? 'Mr Cole'?

'I hear the team will play at Lord's,' Sarah said, meaning nothing by it. She knew very little of cricket, other than that her father very much liked it.

A further pause before Cole grunted agreement. '*Uah.*'

'How is the tour going?' she asked.

His hand waved: it goes.

'You are in London playing another engagement?'

According to the latest report she had read, the team had returned to their base in Kent. Why had he come?

'Is everything all right?' she asked.

No answer was forthcoming. Evidently, his life was his own.

Enough of this! She spoke bluntly. 'How may I be of assistance?'

The whites of his eyes flared slightly, black pupils arcing in her direction.

Sarah had not meant to sound so unfriendly. At least his looks, she noted, were no longer quite so bloodshot. He remained relatively calm – content, so long as left in peace. She lapsed into a similar quietude, simply waiting for him to speak. 'King Cole' could explain himself, and in his own good time.

Once again, Sarah became aware of the noise of the city: filtering through glass, through bricks and mortar, bluntly it forced its way into her home. Even held at such a remove the sweep of traffic was a constant. Closing her eyes, she chose instead to picture it as waves, breaking on a distant shore.

She made one or two moves of the tea things, tacitly making sure to meet her guest's every want and comfort. She availed herself of these opportunities to study him at close quarters – aware, and not unpleasantly so, of his subtle reciprocal investigations.

Cole had a flattish sort of nose, and a wide mouth. Both lip and nostril were thick and fleshy. She did not find it an especially attractive face; it was too alien for that. Hair lustrous and crow-black made it difficult to guess at his age, his unruly mop a mess of curls. He looked years younger than previously, while upset: he was perhaps around the same age as she was – not yet 30. All the same, life had left its mark. The deep knots in his brow aged him prematurely.

Here was a man who harboured a secret, whose dreams were troubled.

He suddenly spoke.

'You,' he said, 'help me.'

'Help you, how?'

Cole stood, pointed to the far corner, and led her to the map hanging there. Talking nineteen to the dozen, with his finger he retraced the line of the river two, three times over in quick succession. He stabbed at the map so forcefully that it jerked and rapped against the wall. Sarah reached and in one smooth motion lifted the frame off the nail. She brought it to the nearby table, into the light.

He made a plaintive animal sort of noise.

Short of any available rag to wipe it clean, Sarah dragged her sleeve across the glass. As the fold of dark material cleared the frame, King Cole yelped. He began to clap loudly, shouting out more of his nonsense.

'Please! Please be calm,' entreated Sarah, and then, more sternly, 'Be quiet!' She looked up, mindful of her father: as if she might see through the ceiling! She looked down again.

Outside, the sun had finally emerged from hiding. The room was momentarily illumined: loosened threads of dust swirling around the interior caught the light, surrounding them with a bright halo.

He was pointing at a smaller image, revealed in the far corner of the chart. The illustration was of the Royal Observatory at Greenwich: not the Great Equatorial Building – the sallow old map pre-dated its construction – but the quasi-Jacobean frontage of Wren's Flamsteed House, topped with its characteristic time-ball.

'The Royal Observatory?' she said.

He didn't understand her.

'The Royal Observatory,' Sarah repeated. She pointed to the picture. 'You want to go there?'

'YES!'

Cole straightened up, apparently expectant of their immediate departure. It was plain if not so simple: he wished them to go to Greenwich – the pair of them.

Sarah Larkin was not sure quite what else to say.

'Yes.'

CHAPTER XVII
Whit Monday, the 1st of June, 1868

GUARDIAN OF THE DEAD

'The entrance of a friend adds grace, boldness, and
eloquence to him; and there are persons, he cannot choose
but remember, who gave a transcendent expansion to his
thought, and kindled another life in his bosom.'

~ Ralph Waldo Emerson, 'Character'

The Guardian stands in the open doorway. It is her: a caterpillar, wrapped in so much cloth. King Cole crosses over, out of the shadow and into the light. He can't help staring. It is the worst rudeness.

The situation demands a proper introduction. Cole clears his throat.

'I am…' he says.

He is careful to keep his eyes turned towards the ground. To show respect, to not presume, he feigns a casual uninterest.

'I am a man,' he says, 'who comes from a land far away.'

He looks away, down the street, sees that place so much further distant.

'Long way…long way.'

Kantillytja warara – beside the mountain range. He has travelled further than the sunlight is from the star. His liver aches, sick at the thought.

It does no good, to retreat inside of himself. She is about to speak. The questions form on her lips. He must stay in the moment.

'Walking feet,' he says.

The words are amusing. They remind him of Dick-a-Dick; sounding a little like his true name. 'Walking feet,' he says. *'Jungunjinanuke!'*

The Guardian cannot understand him. His talk is all wrong for her ears. Stupid, he must select a new notch along the talking stick. While tongue and brain engage, he re-enacts Dick-a-Dick's challenge at the Oval, how impossible he was to hit with a cricket ball. Caused a big smash-up all round, by Christ. She will know it. She was there.

He should impress on her the great lengths he has gone to, simply to find her.

In the same casual talk as the croppies use, Cole tells her of his latest journey, through night into day, start to finish.

In conclusion his tale seems shocking to her, surprising him in turn. He openly admires her blush, a whitefellow phenomenon that always fascinates.

And then, before he knows it, he is inside her house.

Curtains part-way drawn lace the dark parlour in shadow. The room has a high ceiling, and two tall windows overlooking the street, but is so busy with objects that it feels small and dim. Piano, writing desk, dining table, bench and chairs, stools – so much dead wood. While he understands the purpose of at least some of the scattered objects, many others remain a dull sort of mystery. There is a musty smell, as if something crawled into one of the corners and died there.

The Guardian leaves him alone for a time.

King Cole makes closer study of his new surroundings. He trails fingertips along the rim of the shelf above the fireplace, eyeing, but careful not to touch, the crowding ornaments. More line the piano top. They cover every available surface – china figures, jugs, little baskets, and books; books, books, books. This place is much like other whitefellow houses he has seen, filled, too filled, with trappings; all of it dust, gathering dust.

The walls are a pale yellow, marked with a delicate scrawl, a repeating pattern whose meaning he cannot decipher. His attention turns instead to the many mirrors, large and small, hanging there. Most of them turn out to have paintings under their glass.

One in particular catches Cole's eye. Part-hidden by the open door, it hangs in the corner furthest from the light.

The Guardian returns.

Walypela art is hard to decipher. Is that the Great Serpent? He thinks so.

'Please,' she says. 'Have a seat.'

Too many choices present themselves. He follows the direction of her nod, selects something sturdy; squat low on bended knee, its clawed feet should hold firm. A bad choice – it tries to eat him! He plucks his behind from its eager mouth, and sits further forward. His thirst very great, he is ready and indeed most willing to accept the ceremonial tea.

Contented, Cole prefers not to rush into speech; the favour he must ask concerns matters most delicate. Even to speak to her is very trying. She is the Guardian. And she is also a woman. How should he address her, in a way that will not offend? He cannot call her mother. He cannot call her sister.

Her nose is long and straight. Her large eyes, filled with shy looks, are clear and honest. The skin, though, is very pale, milky, even whiter than he is used to seeing; unlike most of her kind, she keeps it clean. Not even any blood is visible there, unless she is angered or shocked, when she turns positively pink.

Already she has many grey hairs. It is because of her great wisdom.

She speaks. She says to call her 'Sarah'.

The word is difficult, as her tongue is difficult.

She is pointing at him. That will never do. To save them both the embarrassment he looks down at the floor.

Undergrowth flowers there. It has been pressed flat by the passage of many feet; or possibly the same feet, many times. Bright green leaves on dark green ground look something like the hedgerows seen around Malling town. Hot red flowers sprout from stems yellow and thorny, thorns he can see but not feel, though he palpates them with his foot. Blunted, they do not pierce his flesh.

'Your name is Cole?' she asks. 'King Cole?'

He nods, not wishing to contradict. This she appears to find acceptable. That is good. Better than to pursue the subject.

King Cole is not a name that suits. Among the elders on the team, he is yet accorded no respect. He has the advantage of years, but no distinction.

A unique, inexplicable Dreaming has been his lifelong burden; until this last week of days, its essential topography was always not just different, but totally irrecognisable – not remotely resembling the land of his birth, nor any single feature of his mundane life. And then, suddenly, it exists, bodied forth, and he within it. In his excitement, the desire to share this revelation overrode all due caution. And who could blame him?

The Red Ochre Men, that's who.

He cannot afford to make that mistake again.

The Guardian's thick brows arch, insistent, asking of their questions. Her pretty lips, berry-red, naturally red, spoil on a mouth pulled small and tight.

He sees more than hears how his reluctance to speak makes her angry.

Her eyes are winter; the pupils icy grey, almost colourless, and ever so slightly glazed. As transparent as they seem, they are silica crystals in a desert. When their looks clash, the collision is so direct he experiences pain – so much so, he can't even be sure whose it is.

Thara.

She seems curious about him, in her way. None of this helps to solve his predicament.

Her body is of little interest. Inside her cocoon of dark cloth, the precise outline stays uncertain, except to say that she is long, and thin. It is the fire in her spirit he most admires, her obvious intelligence. What he needs is her advice.

Still, the Guardian is a woman. This involves compromise. The value of silence must be duly considered. Not all knowledge is permitted; in religious matters, in particular, women are stupid.

He may tell her nothing of his recent experience, reveal none of his past. The Way of the Law strictly forbids it, an offence punishable by death – that of the hapless female.

Eventually, he accepts there is no other choice. He must take the risk.

'You help me,' he says.

'How?' she asks.

The cave painting! Cole leads Thara to the map behind the door. He tries to explain. She surprises him by taking down the frame, and carrying it over into the light.

The long blue animal described there is surely *Mindeye*, the Great Serpent. He examines the surface of the drawing, looking for some way to recognise the Well of Shadows, or Moon Palace, anything that might indicate his trail. The mark-making is too obscure.

He lets out a weary growl of frustration.

And then he sees the red ball, knows the image for what it is meant to be: the false sun he first saw, early that same morning. Yes, it is that thing, he is certain. It has significance!

'*Eora! Eora! Deen!*'

Thara's eyes look skyward, filled with fear. Is her god angered?

Quieter now, he points at a corner of the painting. He searches her expression, patiently, earnestly, longing for a spark of recognition.

'Yes,' she says.

She says yes.

The matter is settled. Thara will return with him, to the place she calls 'Grennidge'. What else can they do? He is desperate. In the city whose shape he has known all his life, still, he is a stranger.

She is the only one qualified. He knows no one else.

Her colour overcomes his grave doubts. This alone lends distance, and hopefully pardons the offence – as far as he is willing to commit. It is only by persuading himself that her womanhood is irrelevant, that Cole has finally been able to speak.

Her sex is of no account.

As long as he remembers that, the danger of their damnation is not so great.

'Yes,' Sarah said.

But then she asked, 'Why me?'

King Cole looked very serious.

'Guardian,' he said, simply.

Ah.

Rebecca Viner had described her as 'a guardian of the wisdom of dead men'. Or was it 'words'? A pretty fanciful attempt to explain her away; Sarah had dismissed the overblown suggestion, even as she thrilled to it.

Hearing the title again, and in such admiring tones, she found herself quite taken with it – such a glorified elevation of her self.

She took a moment to savour this newfound sensation, this very female vanity.

CHAPTER XVIII
Whit Monday, the 1st of June, 1868

THE REJOICING CITY

'Wherever he turned his wandering eyes
Great wealth he did behold –
And peace and plenty hand in hand,
By the magic power of gold.'

~ Charles 'The Inimitable' Thatcher, 'Look Out Below'

When Sarah Larkin reappeared in the doorway to her father's bedchamber she found him bright and busy. He sat at his desk, in nightshirt and dressing gown, surrounded by books and papers. She felt immediately concerned. Had he been disturbed? Was he aware they had a visitor – that *she* had a visitor?

'How are you, father?' she asked.

He expelled only a short grunt by way of acknowledgement.

Men were impossible to talk to. Sarah entered the room and hesitated, before advancing to the foot of his bed to declare her intentions.

'I am going out for a few hours,' she said.

Only then did Lambert Larkin look at his daughter. Seeing that she was already dressed for departure – not realising that she had already been out that morning, and without opportunity to change – he took it as sure sign of her determination. His eye returned to the matter in hand.

'What was all that infernal noise, a few minutes ago?' he said.

Lambert meant only to express disapproval: he had woken from an unbearably poignant dream, one that pained him still.

Sarah saw that his breakfast tray lay untouched. Her father wasn't in the habit of taking lunch; but neither was he likely to go hungry, at least not through any neglect of hers.

'Oh, you heard that?' she said. 'A picture frame. Downstairs. It fell off the wall.'

'By itself?'

'Mary. Mary was dusting it.'

Sarah looked away, down at the skirting boards. She was hopeless at lying. Some days before, upon her return from Kent, she had been obliged to dismiss Mary, the last remaining one of their servants. At seven shillings and tenpence a week, the simple truth was that they could no longer afford her. She had not yet dared to tell her father.

'Is there anything else you might need?' she asked.

'"Else"?' repeated Lambert. 'If there is, I shall get Mary to bring it to me.'

Sarah swallowed. 'Oh, but Mary has gone,' she said. 'For the day. She had to go to Islington, for…'

Panicked, she could not think of a good reason to go to Islington.

'Do not say "oh", child. It gives you a fish's mouth,' chided Lambert.

Sarah already wrestled second thoughts. If Dr Epps was absent and the surgery closed, with neither herself nor Mary on hand her invalid father would be alone in the house, for who could say how long? Greenwich was not a short trip. 'You will be all right, won't you?' she said.

'I am busy,' said Lambert, simply. 'You will not be needed this afternoon. You may go.'

She had only sought to be excused. He neither acknowledged her latest delivery of transcripts, nor thanked her for them.

Sarah swept out of his throne-room, entirely glad not to have mentioned the mysterious gentleman waiting downstairs.

Brighter skies had brought the crowds out in force. Taking to the streets, Sarah Larkin and her shadow were obliged to push their way through heavy pedestrian and horse-drawn traffic. Each absorbed in private thought, they hardly spoke at all.

What on earth should make him want to visit the Royal Observatory? wondered Sarah. Perhaps the reason would become apparent once they were there.

The worn pair of her father's old shoes on his sleek feet suited the Aborigine rather well; the parson's black coat, less so. It was not long enough in the sleeve, and fell noticeably slack around his shoulders. King Cole's slender frame and narrow chest failed to fill the jacket out as her father once had; or did, rather.

She did not like falling into that trap – admitting Lambert's active life might be over.

As they walked, Sarah took pains to observe the reactions of her associate to his surroundings. Were she to drop back a step, she found that he would stop and wait patiently for her to catch up. If she walked on ahead, they remained in tandem: she could not see him at all without turning around. It all became rather obvious, and anyway impolite. They proceeded side by side.

Via surreptitious glances, she approved Cole's splendid skin tone. Beneath the black surface glowed depths of burnished bronze – as if, like some Regency holdover, he was fashioned from ebonised wood. Sarah caught sight of their reflection in a shop's window-glass; how her own grey flesh suffered by comparison. Hardly the tall, dark stranger of fairground fortune, he stood slightly shorter than the average height appropriate to his sex; she, somewhat taller than hers.

He wore a grimace.

'How do they fit, the shoes?' Sarah asked. 'I hope you do not find them too uncomfortable.'

Cole merely smiled.

With a waft of her hand she gestured that they should cross the road.

How shabby Bloomsbury looked: the busy street congested with smoke and dirt, every exterior was of the same filthy grey. What must he make of it? She noticed how infrequent carvings in the surrounds to doors and windows would arrest his attention, the soot-caked structures otherwise showing very little ornamentation.

They stood within the shadow of the Parish Church of St George. Its dark tower had terrified her ever since she was a little girl. Sarah disliked it still – a reproduction of the tomb of Mausolus at Halicarnassus, one of Seven Wonders of the Ancient World: by what right did a pagan monument squat there?

Blackened by coal-smoke, the entire building was benighted, a match to the naked brick fronts of the surrounding tenements.

'Bin big bushfire here,' said Cole.

He was right. The church itself looked burnt, more Satanic than Christian. Her entire neighbourhood was on the slide, a decline all too familiar. The horrors of *Gin Lane* crept nearer every day. What sort of a household was without at least one servant in its employ?

Sarah shuddered and turned. She beckoned to Cole and with a sudden leap they were in the road, in the path of oncoming traffic. Luckily, a recent ruling obliged London General Omnibuses to pull in to the side to pick up their passengers.

Sarah hoisted herself up, ducking through the still moving doorway. King Cole followed on. He had to bend almost double to enter. Bodies were packed close within the interior – a damp little lodge, air wet with breath. The smell of oranges did not entirely disguise sour odours. The gentlemen within sat bolt upright, their top hats scraping the low ceiling; ladies tilted heads in a more decorous incline.

Sarah and Cole hazarded a path through a dozen or so feet, avoiding the poke of umbrellas, folded like broken-winged birds. Gaining their seats at last, they ended up near to the front. None of the passengers would meet anyone else's eye; gathered too close for comfort, their bodies jerking helplessly in time.

Sarah worried briefly that Cole might be taken for her Pompey, or a Caesar: in truth, the fashion for black manservants had long passed. She felt slightly surprised, but nonetheless relieved, that no especial notice was taken of them. Not for the first time, she followed his eye-line. Painted daubs above their heads celebrated the white man's hunting – advertisements for scent and trouser, Stearine Sperm Candles and Ivory Soap ('It Floats').

The conductor appeared next to them.

'Where to?' he asked.

He shouted too loud. Sarah was measured in reply. 'Where do you go?'

'Ludgate!'

Sarah had had in mind the St Paul's Pier for their first port of call, so that was perfect. Purse in hand, she paid the minimum fare, sixpence each. She thought to check for at least two more coins with which to pay the ferryman, and enough again to get home.

It took them over half an hour to make even partial headway down High Holborn. When they turned into Chancery-lane, the road stood completely snarled. King Cole evinced mild bemusement, but Sarah's cheeks were burning.

'It's the Holborn Valley works, m'am.' The conductor, stooped at their side, peered ahead. 'They have just now finished a circus at the far end,' he said, 'at least as wide as that at Regent Street.'

The conductor surveyed the immobile chaos without emotion, resigned to his lot.

'Is there no way through?' said Sarah.

'We go down Chancery Lane, that's our normal route,' the conductor stated, still shouting. 'But with all o' that goin' on, so it is for every'un else!'

Red-faced, Sarah declared that they should quit the omnibus. King Cole, mute, complied.

They walked the boundaries of Lincoln's Inn, and then cut across the Inns and Chambers of St Dunstan's. A maze of walkways and passages, this part of the city, with its gabled shops and galleried courtyards, was still almost medieval in character.

'Dear me,' exclaimed Sarah, 'now I think we are completely lost.'

A tug on the sleeve, and she found herself following the Aborigine through the antiquated district. He strode forthright and imperious, an impish hand resting on the lapel of her father's black coat.

The narrow alleyways out of the law courts soon gave way to a much wider thoroughfare, lined with a curious admixture of the old and new. They emerged a little west of the wedding-cake steeple of St Bride's, 'the Phoenix of Fleet-street': Fleet-street named for the Fleet river, whose former valley it bisected, a sluggish ditch entirely submerged. A seething quagmire of mud and horse-dung, the road had even less chance of living up to its name. Omnibuses, four-wheeled broughams, hackney and hansom cabs, as well as merchant carts of every size and description – a thousand vehicles were held in furious stasis whilst their drivers bickered and swore, whips ineffectually cracking the miasmic air. All attempted to squeeze through the stone archway of Temple Bar, boundary marker between the Cities of London and Westminster.

To the north and west of that giant frog-mouth lay the signs of a vast demolition.

A massive Imperial programme of improvements, being conducted throughout the nation's capital, required the equally radical destruction of its past – London's oldest surviving parts. The city simultaneously ruined and restored, all remnants of earlier lives were being transubstantiated, into limestone, into brick and terracotta. The latest and greatest public buildings towered high overhead, ornate with frescoes, statuary, and stone carvings. From all sides figurines gesticulated and faces leered, as if extruded from the rock itself.

Seeming overwhelmed, King Cole – formerly so confident – baulked and trembled in the balance; no longer sure which way to turn, after all.

'You do not know this part of town?' asked Sarah.

His wide eyes turned her way, a reply so long in coming she thought he had not heard the question.

'No,' he said.

Sarah Larkin recovered the lead, and they stumbled on towards St Paul's Cathedral. A new bridge at Ludgate Hill cut straight across the cathedral's western approach, obscuring even this mammoth landmark from view – just one of many rail networks scratching fresh scars across the face of London. Dust and fumes clogged the atmosphere, the smog of a million chimney fires in addition to the filth disgorged from hell-mouth excavations north and south. As the result, the uppermost swell of the dome could not be seen, even from as close as Ludgate Circus.

Only when an immense shadow fell across them did King Cole look up towards where the sun struggled to pierce the murk. Sheer, perpendicular shock – hundreds of feet above their heads, filling the slender strip of sky, frowned a massive giant.

Sarah heard the loose scuff of borrowed shoes – her father's shoes – abruptly cease. Cole's fingers brushed lightly against her sleeve.

Turning, she followed the flex of his outstretched arm, pointing beyond them in solemn wonder.

She had to raise a hand to shield her eyes against the light.

She thought of snow, snow on coal. Portions of the cathedral walls had been blackened by soot, others washed clean by rain – a permanent etching in sunshine and shadow. This chequered appearance was common to Portland Stone, out of which so many of London's grandest buildings were crafted.

'Piebald,' said Sarah.

'*Uah*,' King Cole agreed, 'like Him g'nort!'

She looked to him, uncertain.

'Neighit!' he declared. He imitated the sound, and then raised and stamped his foot.

'Oh, horse!' Sarah laughed.

His teeth shone brilliant white in his black face.

Moving south of the cathedral, they soon found themselves fenced in by hoardings and deafened by the roar of heavy machinery. Workers wielding picks and shovels tunnelled deep underground, laying railway lines, water and gas pipes. Vast subterranean tracts had been exposed, timber sleepers shoring up their excavations. Unremitting roadworks forced the unhappy pair to forsake and re-mount the pavement countless times; a potent mix of ordure squelched underfoot, their route necessarily roundabout.

'Half of London is being torn down,' lamented Sarah, 'the other half, torn up!'

Coming finally to the end of the twisted narrows of Paul's-wharf, the trekkers met with a heartening sight – a glittering expanse of bright water. The river at high tide, although fouled and stinking, seemed to them the very breath of life.

'Old Father Thames!' said Sarah, cheering.

'*Uah*,' nodded King Cole. 'Serpent.'

They stood alone on the St Paul's Pier, and for a time Sarah worried that she might be mistaken. Then from among the crowding wherries and river-barges appeared a dingy little steamboat, the *Nymph*.

A rush of suits, materialised from nowhere, filed past them from the dock, clerks and bookkeepers, frock coats and stovepipe hats a uniform black.

Sarah paid the ferryman, and she and Cole took seats near to the prow. The *Nymph* swiftly gained the centre of the channel. As the engines changed gear, the funnel coughed up a small black cloud. Suspended overhead, it stayed with them, and proceeded to shower them liberally with smuts.

They passed beneath the granite mass of Rennie's London Bridge. From the Tower onwards, London best resembled a seaport. Wharves and warehouses in a continuous line concealed the enormous dockyards beyond. The shipping lanes either side were thoroughly overcrowded; with coasters, dredgers, galleys and lightermen; freighters, tramps, clippers and brigs. River traffic had tripled inside of a century.

Lulling vapours curled from off the surface of the Thames. Beneath a roiling oilskin, scorning all light, the polluted river ran deep and dark. Making repeated attempts to break through, a sickly orange sun performed feats of alchemy, suffusing impure airborne particles with gilt.

Into this daze the *Nymph* went gliding, everyone on board in a shallow trance.

CHAPTER XIX
Whit Monday, the 1st of June, 1868

JOURNEY'S END

'London begins at Greenwich Hospital.'

~ Anon

In his dark time Dreaming King Cole has walked beneath the waves. Never would he have thought to dare ride the Serpent's back.

Hand holding fast to the iron railing, Cole gazes long time long into the dark shadows beneath their boat. Fireflies float through the belly of the beast, far below. Greens, blues, vibrant pinks and purples; the bizarre costumes they wear are coral-bright – quite unlike the pale phantoms of his recent adventure under these waters.

A gentle nudge from the Guardian, and King Cole rights himself. All the blood gone to his head makes it spin a moment. Spots throb before his eyes.

Thara's mellow voice is there to soothe and guide him.

'Did you hear me?' Sarah said. 'We have arrived.'

The *Nymph* slowly drifted with the tide. Preparatory to docking, their boat was turning in the great river bend of Greenwich Reach, a sweeping curve that swallowed the tongue of land known as the Isle of Dogs, behind. The manoeuvre gave them ample time in which to consider their prospects.

Elevated on a riverside terrace close to a thousand feet in length, framed by parkland, stood the most beautiful palace. Instead of presenting a broad front to the river, it was split into two horns, or wings, of equal size – mirrored images, only slightly asymmetrical: nearly 300 feet apart, they divided either side of a broad green lawn. At their nether reaches, a little way inland, two further piles arranged themselves in elegant alignment with the first, buildings if anything even more stirring in their design. Stacked pediments led the eye irresistibly upwards, to twin clock-towers topped with golden weather-vanes, the drum of each cupola reminiscent of the dome of St Paul's, doubled and expressed in miniature. Unlike the sullied cathedral, however, here the Portland Stone shell remained brilliant and white.

A court fit for a king – Sarah Larkin looked across to observe her Aboriginal companion. He blinked against the bright blaze, uncertain. Greenwich was once a principal Crown residence, the first and last port of call for visiting ambassadors. She could well imagine him an emissary of sorts, a foreign dignitary, if not an actual king. It seemed only appropriate that they pay a visit here.

The entire complex flanked a breach boldly cut through its centre. Perpendicular to the river a spacious avenue ran inland, adorned either side with Doric colonnades. As it hove into view Sarah pointed up the hill beyond, assuming this was where her fellow traveller intended for them to go.

'The Royal Observatory,' she said.

King Cole grinned broadly.

Vessel docked at the Steamboat Pier, they gladly disembarked. Alongside lay waiting-rooms: mindful of her eventual return, Sarah consulted the schedule on a painted board there.

WATER CONVEYANCE
Departures every half-hour
8am–5pm winter, 8am–9pm summer

It could not be later than two, two-thirty at the most.

To the south, in sunshine, stretched the green hills of Greenwich Park. With every mile's distance from the smoky city, visibility had improved: the air hereabouts was relatively clear.

Sarah looked towards the eminence of Blackheath. A branch of the Larkin family resided there, enjoying considerable wealth. Her father disapproved the means by which they had amassed their fortune, Sarah even more so. They were slavers. She resolved, there and then, that she would never go to them for support, no matter how lean their finances.

King Cole in turn studied the palace before them, the long fence separating it from the main thoroughfare, and a trim lawn beyond. Trees in full leaf nestled against the outer margins.

'That building,' said Sarah, 'is a hospital. A hospital for sailors.'

Faint hope of appreciating anything for what it was, simply by looking at it: in the minds of the majority Greenwich was associated with nothing more ambitious than a fish dinner.

Standing to one side, her arm extended, she invited that Cole take responsibility for their next move. The Aborigine strode inland, face grim with foreboding. He followed the line of the ornamental railings that enclosed the Hospital complex, his narrow palm trailing, testing their substance. Sarah straightened her skirts and followed on.

Heading up King William-street, he led them to a large, cast-iron double gate. A monumental ball of stone, easily six feet in diameter, surmounted each sturdy gate pier. The globe to their left displayed 24 meridians – tropics, circles, equinoxial, and ecliptic – indicative of a celestial sphere. To their right a terrestrial sphere, similarly copper-inlaid, bore a different cross-weave – the parallels of latitude.

'*Bugaragara.*'

King Cole mumbled something Sarah did not catch. Gripping the iron bars, he looked from the gateway towards a building south of where they stood; then, eastward of their present position, towards the far end of the same block; back again; and, finally, up at the gates.

He seemed perplexed, as if the barrier was unexpected, or perhaps not where he expected it to be.

'You…you want to go in?' Sarah asked.

His eyes in reply were more than eloquent.

She approached one of the smaller wicket gates intended for pedestrian traffic. A gatekeeper dressed in a plain sort of guard's uniform appeared.

'Can we go in, is it possible? Into the Hospital?' she enquired. Vaguely, she indicated the grounds.

Just then the main gates swung wide, to permit exit of a shabby horse and cart. From the window of the lodge-house opposite, a second guardsman waved it through.

'Only persons of decent appearance and the carriages of gentlemen permitted to pass,' announced the gatekeeper. 'No dogs, and no beggars, vagrants, piddlers or other idle disorderly persons…of either sex… OY, PUT THAT AHHT!'

Sarah jumped at his sudden shout. A man passing through the opposite gate obligingly extinguished his cigarette. The gatekeeper tugged the peak of his cap.

'Just a bit o' fun, ma'am, don't mind me,' he said. 'Visiting?'

'Errrm, yes.'

As the guard stood to one side to let her through, he caught sight of Cole, lingering at the far side of the gate pier.

'Away from there, Uncle Tom!' he said.

'He's with me,' said Sarah.

'Ma'am?'

She had spoken too softly. Sarah cleared her throat. 'He's with me.'

The guard eyed her curiously before conceding. 'Begging your pardon.'

Sarah and Cole strolled a few yards into the Hospital grounds, and then, as if by prior arrangement, both picked up their pace. Sarah was convinced they would be called back at any second. King Cole subtly assumed the lead. They continued past a quadrangular building of stuccoed brick, further enclosed by its own set of railings and identified as the Infirmary. Cole eyed it with suspicion.

Turning right at its northeastern corner, he led the way up the far side until they were out of sight of the West Gate.

Up ahead, a couple, well-dressed, wandered arm-in-arm. A small man dressed in a business suit took his lunch, seated on the lawn. Other than that, the neat grounds were deserted. Amid such wide open spaces, the monumental scale of neoclassical architecture combined to eerie effect: they walked into a scene whose perfection evoked, for Sarah at least, an unsettling preview of the afterlife.

Where they walked, they went alone. Sarah's feet began to drag. She had no idea where she was being taken, and by a man she knew next to nothing about. All at once it occurred to her: no one knew she had come to Greenwich; were she disappeared, nothing would ever be heard of her again.

Passing behind the Infirmary, they approached a second lodge. This one looked broken-down, fallen into obvious disuse. A caution formulating on her lips, Sarah cast a quick glance behind them. Turning back, her heart froze. They had walked into the middle of a graveyard, overgrown and in ruins.

'God's acre,' she heard her own voice whisper, 'forsaken.'

The burial ground was quite large, closer to two and a half acres. The vast majority of monumental stones lay broken. King Cole scampered ahead, scanning the earth for a sign of some kind.

Sarah struggled for breath. Graveyards made her nervous.

'Forsake me not,' she prayed.

Cole crouched low and pointed ahead towards a certain spot. His other hand urged her forward: she should go to it. Tall trees creaked and groaned overhead, the breeze prowling their leaves picking up speed. She looked back, uncertain. He shooed her more to the left – there. The trees sighed and the wind died. She faced an old grave, one among many. Little better than a hole in the dirt, it lacked a headstone.

Sarah swayed a moment, examining the plot. King Cole drew up silently alongside. She leant precariously across to part the grass at one end, revealing a short wooden stake driven deep into the earth. There was no name on it, just a number, barely legible. With her fingertip she traced the faint impressions.

'One... Four... Two... Nine.'

The ground was intact except at the eastern corner, where an animal of some kind had recently been scratching at the soil. Strange that, after the lapse of what must have been many years, so little grass yet grew atop the grave.

Sarah closed her eyes a moment. Opened again, she caught sight of something –

'AAAAAAARGHHH!'

Sarah slid in the burial mud. She stumbled, almost losing her footing as she tried to turn, scrabbling for purchase, for balance, her every instinct screaming.

Arms wide, his hands spread, Cole cut off her only route of escape. Eyes big as saucers, he pursed his lips. His palms bobbed up and down, a calming gesture.

Sarah stood, awkward, all fingers and thumbs, clutching first at one elbow then touching a hand to her face, unsure where to look. She flinched a little.

Atop the old grave lay crumbled shards of clay, a fine dusting of off-white powder, and something else – something dried and dark, seeped in deep and crimson.

'It all right,' said King Cole. 'It all right. Him my blood.'

His voice was gentle.

'My blood,' he said. He touched the earth, brought up his fingers to show her, stained scarlet.

'Same colour you.'

CHAPTER XX
Whit Monday, the 1st of June, 1868

A NAME

'The grave, great teacher, to a level brings
Heroes and beggars, galley slaves and kings.'

~ Horace Walpole, 'Epitaph for Theodore of Corsica'

Who was buried in plot 1429? Sarah Larkin wanted to know.

'Chockie-man.'

'I'm sorry,' she said. 'What?'

'Deadman,' said the Aborigine. His body jerked as if connected to a galvanic battery. He expressed a hissing sound.

'Yes, but who is…who was he?' Sarah repeated. 'What was his name?'

King Cole looked a little abashed. 'I don't know,' he said.

'You don't know?'

'I forget.'

'You've forgotten. So you did know it?'

His looks no longer askance, Cole appeared to resent the questioning. His voice, however, sounded convinced. 'He had none.'

His habitual evasions had exhausted Sarah's patience. 'We'll see about that,' she said.

The desolate graveyard stretched between Romney-road and King-street. A broken down sign near to the entrance identified it as the 'Royal Hospital Burial Ground'. The site belonged, as Sarah had rather suspected it might, to the adjacent white stone complex.

King Cole flatly refused to approach the Infirmary building. They were obliged to return to the gatekeepers' lodge.

'That's Goddard's Garden, that is,' said the guard, sitting at the open window. 'No bodies been put in the ground there in years. They all go up the Pleasaunce nowadays, a ways east of here.'

'You should have a word with Matron, ma'am.' The first keeper they had spoken to, at the gate, appeared in the adjacent doorway. 'Mrs Georgiana Riddle,' he said. 'You can find her through there, in the starboard wards.'

He advanced sufficiently to point out a single-storey building Sarah had not noticed before, partially obscured by a stretch of brick wall, and abutting the Infirmary's west end. The guard indicated a small doorway set within the wall.

The other man leapt to his feet. 'Fred, no...' he said, and moved to block the path suggested. 'You don't want to go that way, ma'am. Through there's the Helpless Ward.'

He looked at his colleague, filled with reproach – but not without the shade of a grin, also. 'There are sights beyond that wall,' he said, returned to Sarah, 'sights a lady such as yourself don't wish to see. Some of the Helpless, they're allowed out of doors into a little garden there. For the benefit of the air, like.' His voice fell to a whisper. 'The most miserable and shocking objects on God's earth.'

Despite herself Sarah shivered a little. She looked at King Cole. His eyes stayed fixed on the ground at his feet.

'Where else might I direct our enquiries?' she said.

The portlier of the two gatekeepers, the one who had already attempted some fun at their expense, took Sarah by the arm, a touch impertinent. He began to escort the pair of them a little way further down the main drive.

'Mister Dilkes!' he said. 'Mister Dilkes, he'll know what to do with you. Oh, yes. One of our longest-serving members, he is.' The uncouth fellow rolled the words around his tongue. 'Long on the staff is old Mister Dilkes. Eh, Eddie, lad?'

Comments directed back to his colleague, the gatekeeper tipped him a wink.

'Started out clerk in the Out-pensions, so he did, and well before my time! There's precious little Mister Dilkes don't know about this place...and don't he relish every opportunity he gets to spread it around!'

He stopped and pointed clear of the Infirmary, over towards the southeast. Not much more than a garden gnome at this distance, a figure sat on the grass lawn next to one of two small dolphin fountains – the same little fellow in the business suit Sarah had noticed earlier.

The gatekeeper made his way back to their lodge, chuckling as he went. 'Dear old Dilkesey. He'll like you.' He shouted ahead. 'Won't he, Eddie?'

Crosswise paths divided the fountain lawn. Nothing else for it, Sarah set a course over to the little man, King Cole trailing behind. Gales of laughter broke from the lodge at their backs.

The clerk had been monitoring their back-and-forth progress for some time, and with a keen interest. Seeing the odd couple directed his way, he hastily thrust the last of his sandwich crusts into his mouth and stood, ready to attend them.

Drawing near, Sarah could see he was small indeed, barely five foot tall. Balding, rotund, very pink and with doughy flesh – late middle-age had put him on the slide back towards infancy. She marked the eagerness of his poise. The man balanced almost on the balls of his feet. He stooped a moment to brush the crumbs and creases from his suit, adjusted his *pince-nez*, and ran a hand through thinning strands of hair.

'Got a couple of strangers, *have* we?' he said.

His tone, bright and jocular, was thoroughly welcoming.

'*Anyone* not Navy is a "stranger" around here!'

'Mr Dilkes?' said Sarah.

'Loveless.' He nodded. 'Dilkes Loveless. Clerk attached to the Admiralty, faithful servant of this Hospital, and at *your* service. How might I be of assistance, madam?'

No ice to break, Sarah felt degrees of both heat and moisture in his handshake. Promptly she introduced herself and 'Mr Cole', explaining their situation – insofar as she understood it herself.

'Plot number 1429, you say? Hmm,' said the clerk. 'A Greenwich Pensioner, almost certainly. He would have been a Royal Navy man. And what is your *connection* to the deceased, may I ask?'

'None at all.' Sarah answered perhaps a little too frankly. 'On…on my part,' she added, and wavered a moment before indicating King Cole. 'That is to say, we hope to discover it. The plot was otherwise unmarked, but… as to the identity…' Her voice rose an octave, without directly framing the question.

'You will need to consult the Burial Register,' said the clerk. 'Held, under *normal* circumstances, by the Hospital Secretary. And, really, you should apply to the Governor for permission. In *writing*. Only, he is absent at present.'

Oblivious towards her attendant, Dilkes Loveless eyed Sarah through the thick lenses of his glasses.

'It is not something we generally allow, you see,' he continued. 'Not without following *correct* procedures…'

More than used to these ingratiating tactics from staff at the British Museum, Sarah patiently waited out the clerk.

'In the Governor's absence,' said Dilkes, '*I*, however, am empowered to decide issues of access. I think therefore I might be able to look it up *for* you.'

'Good,' she said.

There was a slight hesitation on his part. Sarah stood firm.

With a grandiose gesture Dilkes Loveless directed that she follow him across the grass towards the main buildings. He body-swerved the gurgling fountain, a spring to his step.

'You were lucky to *catch* me today,' said the clerk. 'The Lords Commissioners of the Admiralty have abolished the separate "Military" and "Civil"

Departments. Nowadays, we *all* muck in together! I myself am designated for duty at Somerset House. It's not often I'm to be found here any more…'

Rustling and bustling, the breathless clerk threw back a look inviting of sympathy.

'In short, we no longer *have* a Secretary. But I can take you to his former office, and there we shall see what there *is* to see!'

Sarah Larkin had trouble keeping up; heaven only knew what King Cole made of it all. They were about to enter into one of the grand colonnades, starting at the rear of the nearest main block.

'Here is the Court of King William,' said the clerk. 'King William the third, for whom *this* block is named, and *there*, his queen, Mary.' Dilkes indicated the next building along. 'It is, I must emphasise, a *Royal* Naval Hospital, the land granted by Warrant in *1694*!'

He pronounced the date *most* emphatically, as if the lapse of years alone made it impressive.

They passed beneath the eaves of the nearest colonnade.

'A hospital in the sense of an *alms*house. The Pensioners who are the objects of this noble institution must be seamen or mariners disabled by age, or those *maimed* in the King's…or *Queen's* service…those veterans of the main who on our widest Empire bleed.'

This last said leeringly, Dilkes rolled his eyes for melodramatic effect.

Sarah saw once more the door, the door in the wall that enclosed the secret garden of the Helpless Ward.

She checked again for Cole's reactions, hoping for the slightest clue as to what they might be doing there. He placidly examined stone-carvings directly above their heads, floral designs set into the portico ceiling: oak; daisy; sunflower or buttercup? Thistle…

Sarah yelped. A massive carriage lamp seemed to swing too low overhead as she passed beneath. It was bigger in the body than she was. As they turned the corner, great oak doors on their immediate left towered more than twice her height.

'A royal palace,' Dilkes was saying, 'provided *solely* for the solace and repose of those Pensioners…'

More than a palace, Sarah thought, they intruded on a colossal temple, fit for the gods of ancient myth and constructed on their scale.

'As a gesture of munificence, it is unsurpassed!' cried the impassioned clerk. 'The very *conscience* of civilisation!'

Looking at the place, at its very generous extent, Sarah decided that it must be a guilty conscience.

Just across the way, to the east, loomed Queen Mary Court, a matching double of the building they skirted. In viewing the colonnade opposite, Sarah could better appraise the details of their own: Doric columns standing 20 feet tall were paired in a long row – gigantic open cloisters, equally, breathtakingly beautiful. She looked across into a mirror in which they themselves did not appear.

King Cole, at her side, began to act most peculiarly. Twitching and jumpy, his dark eyes darting about, he appeared seized with convulsions. Faced with the Aborigine's eel-like contortions, Sarah felt almost relieved to have the Hospital clerk for company.

'What on earth…?' stuttered Dilkes. 'Does he suffer fits?'

It seemed prudent to confront the issue.

'What's the matter?' she said to Cole. 'Are you all right?'

'One dark ago,' said the Aborigine, 'manypella this place. Many many. Sickpella, sailorpella, around, around, around, around.'

King Cole turned the four points of the compass and threw out his hands at each one.

Dilkes Loveless stared at these curious antics, the even curiouser language. This was by far the strangest stranger he had ever been obliged to escort.

'Arm gone pella, leg gone pella, all drinkin' pellas,' said King Cole.

Pausing first to roll up one trouser leg, he enacted a crazed mime-show of amputation and deformity. One sketch, highly convincing, featured a drunken sailor; a balancing act in search of equilibrium, elastic limbs all at sea.

Startled, Sarah's breath caught, before exploding in a burst of laughter. Its immediate loud echo silenced her just as swiftly.

Dilkes Loveless clutched at his jacket buttons. His mind boggled.

King Cole fixed the pair of them with his large black eyes, genuinely spooked, his whisper barely audible. 'Everypella gone.'

He leant in close to confide, darkly. 'Manypella,' he said, 'manypella him pinis in dem 'ouse.'

A great many men had died there.

With admirable aplomb, Dilkes Loveless confirmed his story. 'He's quite right,' said the clerk. 'At one time, you would have felt these ambits intolerably crowded. The Hospital in former days housed many more patients than it does now. A great *deal* more. I say, how do you know that?'

Receiving no answer, Dilkes carried on regardless.

'The old Pensioners would idle out their days, sitting about the place, smoking and chatting amongst themselves…'

Unexpectedly, Cole took up the thread of yarn the clerk was about to spin. 'Manypella old and sad,' he said. 'Very tired. Him like a lizard on a rock, lying on him back and him belly…'

He moved towards one of the alcove seats, spread his limbs slightly, and directed himself towards the sun, as if to soak up some of its heat and energy.

His body again folded in on itself. He motioned further along the deserted colonnade.

'An' him, slither up an' down all same. Him got head in a sling, and him got head in him hands.'

He pointed in specific directions, as if the figures described were arranged in a sort of tableau in front of them.

'All sad,' he said. 'All tired. Is one big cage for them, this pretty place.'

Sarah stared at him in both alarm and wonder. The empathy in his soft voice she found moving; the slight sibilance that made 'thad' of 'sad', endearing.

Cole overtook the lead, just as he had when she became lost amongst the side streets of the Fleet: until this moment, it had not occurred to her how odd that should be.

Who was the stranger here, who the guide?

Cole continued to bob back and forth, interacting with the various persons that, for him perhaps, still populated these stone corridors. His descriptions were so vivid, his disturbed imagination so infectious, she could almost see for herself the figments he narrated.

Sarah looked again to the colonnade opposite, at an empty spot exactly the same as where they were standing. She knew then, for certain, that the Aborigine perceived the world in ways she could not understand. If only she could see the world through his eyes.

'They…uh…yes,' said Dilkes Loveless, clearing his throat. 'They would gather here in scores and loll upon these benches, the old sailors, smoking the while, and entertaining the strangers, *visitors* such as yourselves, with their *fanciful* stories…'

Dilkes eyed the other man warily.

'The only occasion they bestirred themselves for would be mealtimes,' he continued, soon recovering his stride. '*Or* when going over the details of some long-ago engagement led to disagreement, and they fought their old sea-battles over again…'

What more the Aborigine could see, Sarah was not to know. Thanks to the untimely intervention of the clerk, King Cole had withdrawn back into himself.

The little busybody set off across the grass lawn between the twin courtyards of William and Mary. As they approached the adjacent Queen Mary building, open ground afforded a splendid view of the domed clock-tower. Sculpted faces roared from each of its corners – Neptune the sea-god presumably, wearing shells for ears.

Sarah felt provoked to ask an obvious question.

'The Pensioners, sir, the gentlemen you speak of, whom Mr Cole tells us he saw this last night,' she said, 'where are they all now?'

'Last night?' said Dilkes. 'I'm not sure I follow.' He took his glasses in his hand, and nervously rubbed at the lenses with a pocket-kerchief.

Sarah wasn't sure she followed either, but that was what he had said – in the night, or perhaps the day before. He had been there before?

'Where are they all now?' she persisted. 'The Pensioners.'

'They are all below,' said Dilkes.

'…Dead?' said Sarah.

'Heavens, no…at their lunch.'

A thunderous roll and a clatter loud as cannon-shot rent the air.

The sky was full of cloud, but not dark; and anyway the noise seemed to come from somewhere beneath their feet. Dilkes Loveless started laughing, and then so did King Cole. Rather than delay their mission any further, Sarah resolved to overlook her frayed nerves, in fact all further phenomena: she preferred they press on.

Arriving at the East Gate, they passed out of the Hospital complex and across Park-row, a perimeter road. The Hospital's Civil Offices lay directly opposite, housed in a relatively modest two-storey outbuilding.

They made their way through the lobby and up the stairs, entering into a plain and undecorated suite. As he passed an open doorway, Dilkes Loveless acknowledged an inquisitive glance from one of his industrious colleagues.

'Horatio,' he said. 'Still on lunch! I'm escorting these strangers to the Secretary's office.'

Arriving at the relevant door, he turned a key in the lock and bade them enter. Once all were settled within the cramped confines, he began to rummage around, sorting through mounds of paperwork and the bound volumes carelessly heaped on every side.

'The former Secretary would have taken care of all deeds and documents relating to the Hospital, kept all the necessary books, and…ah, here we go!'

Dilkes carried a few dusty articles over to the main desk, and started to leaf through them, opening and discarding them at great speed. Sarah watched King Cole, who waited patiently – but also, she felt, dispassionately.

Dilkes heaved an impressive tome over to one end of the table and laid aside the others.

'These are the relevant Burial Registers for the Hospital,' he said. 'If there was no monumental inscription, and indeed no stone, then we are dealing with a Naval rating, an ordinary seaman. The marker on the plot you are enquiring about…' The clerk seemed to have arrived at a relevant page. 'Fourteen twenty-nine, did you say?'

Sarah sat forward. 'Yes?'

Dilkes Loveless stabbed the open page with his finger, and began to read aloud. '"Burials in the Parish of Greenwich in the County of Kent, No.1429.

Greenwich Hospital, 12th February 1819."' His eyes flickered over the top of his glasses, examining Sarah's face a moment before he resumed his reading. "'George Bruce,"' he said, "'age 41, ceremony performed by William Jones."'

'George Bruce.' Sarah repeated the name. She looked towards King Cole in the hopes of some sort of response. He blinked perhaps, but that was all. He looked at Sarah – equally hesitant, equally hopeful.

The clerk sat with his chin in his hand. The name seemed to mean something to him, at least.

'Bruce,' he said. 'Yesss, George Bruce. I've heard talk of him, once or twice. Not in many years, mind.'

For a silent moment or three, the clerk researched his excellent memory. Seated facing, Sarah Larkin and King Cole teetered on the edges of their seats, postures comically identical.

'If I am thinking of the right man,' said Dilkes, slowly, 'and I *am*, then his face was most *horribly* disfigured.'

Sarah was taken aback. How terrible! 'Was he…was he very badly wounded?' she asked.

'George Bruce…there's more, there's something else,' said Dilkes. 'I'm sure it will come to me, given time.'

Leaning forward, he deigned to show to them the open page of the Burial Register, even as he snapped it shut. Dilkes Loveless spoke with total confidence.

'No further details here,' he said. 'Nor, I doubt, to be found anywhere. A great many sailors, you will appreciate, have lived and died here at the Hospital over the years…*hundreds* of years. Unless there were *exceptional* circumstances, the records will not enter into any greater detail than what you are already privy to.'

Dilkes paused a moment while his audience slumped.

'If I were to look at the *Admissions*,' he went on, slyly, 'I dare say I might find out the name of the last *ship* on which he served, and so forth. There is nothing to indicate he was anything out of the ordinary, for an ordinary seaman… although I *have* heard the name before…

'It does not mean anything at all?' He addressed the question directly to Sarah.

King Cole's wide eyes met hers, open, trusting. It was up to her, then.

'Yes,' she said, 'would you look to the Admissions, Mr Dilkes? I think it might help us to know a little more.'

'*Hmph.* Very well.'

Dilkes Loveless only pretended to be irked. He smartly located another, larger tome on a high shelf, brought it down with mock ceremony, and began to leaf through it carefully.

'This is the rough entry book of In-pensioners, from 1846 all the way back to 1756,' he said. 'Of course I don't *know* the year in which he came to the Hospital; we are tackling this somewhat *aft about*. But if I make a start from the date of his burial in 1819…'

Beginning somewhere around the final third, scanning each page as he flipped them over, he studiously worked back towards the middle of the great book.

'This *may*…' he hummed '…take some time…'

Sarah idled awkwardly, monitoring proceedings. She felt indebted, surely the clerk's every intent. Since the moment he had entered his office, he had adopted a manner more official. She had preferred him, if that was the word, when officious.

King Cole still wore his trouser-legs hitched at half-mast, the muscles of his lower leg appearing almost wasted. Discreetly, Sarah motioned that he should re-adjust his clothing.

Dilkes Loveless' clearing his throat caused her to stare guiltily down at her shoes. With a slight intake of breath she saw how terribly muddy they were: she must have tracked mud throughout the office suite.

It came from when she had stumbled about on the grave.

If she understood Cole correctly, the fresh blood she saw there was his own – red, like hers. Why should he have thought that detail reassuring?

'Ah!' announced Dilkes. 'Here we are! "April 18, 1817. George Bruce,"' he read. '"Age: 40. If married: no. Girls: 1. Born: Shadwell. Last residence: Glocester Court." I can't make out the next word.' He smiled. 'It should, by rights, be the name of the admitting doctor…'

Dilkes continued with the reading.

'"Number of years in King's service: 17. Trade: sea. Last ship: *Congo*, sloop. If ruptured: no."'

Sarah had produced a small scrap of paper from an inner pocket, and with the worn-down stub of a pencil hurriedly took notes. These extra details might later prove valuable clues. Assuming, of course, that any of this should lead anywhere.

'Here there is an additional note…' he concluded. '"Lost 2 fingers right hand."'

Sarah looked up to see the clerk studying her.

'Thank you,' she said. 'Thank you very much, Mr Dilkes. You've been very helpful.'

Pish posh, some slight concession seemed in order.

'Dilkes *Loveless*, Mrs Larkin,' he said. '*Lieutenant* Dilkes Loveless.'

Sarah bridled at the firmness of his correction. The air temperature in the office palpably dropped a degree or two.

'*Miss* Larkin, lieutenant,' she answered.

Dilkes Loveless, immediately regretful of his tartness, thrilled at the cold spark of her temper. He took delight in confirmation – and from the lady's own not unlovely lips – that she, too, went unmarried.

'Please,' he said, '*Miss* Larkin. Call me *Charles*.'

She was no great beauty, to be sure, but her peal of unguarded laughter had brought the old colonnades – and him – to late life.

'Would you like to take the grand tour?' he said. 'Really, one cannot visit the Hospital without seeing all of the glorious sights it has to offer.'

Sarah considered their position for a moment. The Observatory was all but forgotten, if indeed it had ever been a part of the Aborigine's original design. For some unfathomable reason, events now appeared to revolve around the occupant of an anonymous grave.

The baldness of Bruce's identity was disappointing, appearing to mean little as it did to King Cole. From his abiding silence, all she could assume was that they should carry on.

'We have barely scratched the surface, thus far,' chimed in Lieutenant Charles Dilkes Loveless.

Indeed.

'And it would help to walk off my lunch,' he added, patting his belly.

Instead of answers, only more questions presented themselves. With the clerk's help, perhaps…

'Of course,' said Sarah. 'We would be happy to.'

Who knew where it might lead?

CHAPTER XXI
Whit Monday, the 1st of June, 1868

OMPHALOS

'...this Petty Navy Royal is the Master Key wherewith to
open all locks that keep out or hinder this incomparable
British Empire from enjoying, by many means, such a
yearly Revenue of Treasure...'

~ Dr John Dee, *The Perfect Arte of Navigation*

The Admiralty clerk escorted his guests across a wide, green lawn – the Royal
Naval Hospital's Grand Court, where their promised tour would begin. They
came to rest near to the middle, close to the banks of the Thames.

Sarah Larkin glanced over at King Cole. He watched intently a small
gathering, sitting on the river steps some way behind them, smoking – a few of
the uniformed Pensioners, the first they had seen; even at this distance, Sarah
could hear their pebbledash-dry coughing. Looking around, she spotted more.
The sailor-gentlemen emerged from a recessed doorway built into the base of
the King William building.

'Ah,' said Lieutenant Dilkes Loveless. 'You see our good masters *are* at
home. They've had their lunch and are now coming up for some air. What's
today, *Monday*? Boiled beef and broth! A meal well garnished with vegetables
and potatoes, the same to be enjoyed on Wednesdays. We shall proceed to the
chapel.'

Their guide sped towards the broad stone steps to the upper lawn, making
for the Queen Mary building – and away from the Pensioners as they finally
materialised. He led them through the west door into an octagonal vestibule. As
soon as Sarah and King Cole entered, a uniformed guard sprang up.

'Tickets,' he rasped.

Dilkes Loveless waved him aside. They advanced into the middle of a lofty
antechamber, putting them – as Sarah calculated it – directly beneath the clock-
tower of the eastern dome. Four tall Coade Stone maidens occupied niches in
the stonework, one to each angled corner. Plaques beneath bore inscriptions,
carved in bold type.

FAITH IS THE SUBSTANCE
OF THINGS HOPED FOR
THE EVIDENCE OF THINGS
NOT SEEN

Faith, on their immediate right, held aloft her book and cup. Hope, opposite, leant decorously on a ship's anchor.

WHICH HOPE WE HAVE
AN ANCHOR FOR THE SOUL
BOTH SURE AND STEADFAST

Meekness, the other side of a descending stairwell, clutched a bunch of lilies and exchanged loving looks with a lamb. The plaque beneath this statue had been obscured.

Sarah threw the clerk a quizzical frown.

He quoted, sight unseen. '"Blessed Are the Meek, for They Shall Inherit the Earth".' Dilkes smirked. 'The text was ordered covered up,' he said.

'Whatever for?' asked Sarah.

'Her Majesty's Navy does not *approve* the sentiment,' said Dilkes.

He was not joking. Extraordinary!

Sarah looked across to the fourth figurine, Charity, who suckled and cradled various infants. Troubling not to meet the glare of the thwarted sentry, sat below, she missed out on the final verse.

Something else had caught her eye: a painted plaque, occupying a recess in between Faith and Hope, listing the names of 'CHAPLAINS'. Among these, Sarah noted 'Samuel Cole D. D. (1816–1838)'. A man by the name of Cole, in service at the same time George Bruce had been an inmate! Turning to King Cole, she remarked on the coincidence.

He seemed unfazed.

Out of politeness, she thought to explain to the clerk.

'My friend goes by the name of Cole,' said Sarah. 'I thought there might be a connection…'

Dilkes Loveless, giving her black-skinned companion a briefly appraisal, visibly doubted it. 'Coal, you say?'

Sarah finger-tapped the wood of the plaque.

'King Cole is currently visiting England as part of a cricket team,' she said. 'The Aboriginal Australian Eleven. Maybe you've read about them. They are all over the newspapers.'

'Cricket, hm?' Dilkes feigned interest. 'Is this your *first* time in England, Mr Cole?'

A very good question, and one Sarah wished she had thought to ask herself.

King Cole nodded, somewhat curtly.

Sarah's finger, trailing down the board, came to rest on the name of the incumbent just as Dilkes Loveless happened to pronounce it aloud.

'Our current chaplain is the Reverend William G. Tucker, M.A.'

'Tucker!' blurted out Cole. His body suddenly bucked and contorted, in the grip of violent amusement. 'Tucker…! Tucker! Tucker!'

The Aborigine cackled, patting his distended belly as it poked through a gap in his shirt. Sarah blushed, embarrassed. Dilkes Loveless scooted them up the short flight of steps, through folding doors of mahogany.

'Sir.' He shushed. 'You are in a House of *God*!'

Once inside the nave, Cole immediately quieted.

The chapel itself contained plenty of interest, rope-chain and anchor designs within the flooring, waveforms abounding. Sarah's ears pricked up when the Hospital clerk invoked St Paul: already more than once that day he had made his saintly presence felt. Coade Stone medallions within the body of the pulpit represented scenes from his life, and in the massive dark altarpiece painting that enclosed the apse, *The Preservation of St Paul*, Sarah recognised events recorded in the *Acts of the Apostles*.

They turned and left by a different door, situated next to the list of chaplains – 'Tucker!' King Cole barely suppressed a giggle – and climbed down a flight of steps into the basement. Queer sounds rumbled down the sub-corridor: a succession of dull thuds, as if somebody was upsetting furniture. Sarah shivered. Even on a relatively fine afternoon the air was very chill underground, and she felt a strong draught.

A large refectory room, deserted and dusty, extended to the east. Turning to the south, they entered a subterranean piazza.

'This,' said Dilkes, 'is the former Chalk Walk.'

The crypt-like archway was both long and narrow.

'A Smoking Gallery,' he said, 'so-called for the vast quantities of "chalkies", those long clay pipes the sailor-Pensioners favour, being dropped and crushed underfoot. On wet and wintry days the old tars would stow themselves away in the stone lockers you see lining the walls, where fires were always kept burning… the *only* place they were allowed to smoke indoors, due to the obvious fire risk. As you may have gathered, sailors are very great smokers, forever *spitting*.'

From his expression, Sarah understood the clerk was not a smoker.

'Common rooms are discouraged, for this very reason. We have a *library*…' Dilkes Loveless turned to her, his face twisted into a smile '…but old sailors, although great smokers, are *not* great readers. And so the Governor proposed the provision of a Bowling Alley.'

Two young men wearing stained white aprons, having the appearance of cook's assistants, trundled their bowling balls lazily down a wooden track – the source, Sarah divined, of that previous and alarming roll of thunder.

Presumably, that put them somewhere below the eastern colonnade.

Turning at right angles, the clerk ushered them along another corridor even narrower than the first; an undercroft, he explained, connecting the William and Mary Courts. They walked at this very moment beneath the upper lawn.

Whether or not he understood their situation, King Cole gave no sign.

They approached a second dining hall beneath the King William block.

'Here,' said Dilkes, 'you may see one of the more *domestic* parts of the institution, not so generally known to the public…'

Unlike the other refectory room, it showed signs of recent occupation. Serving staff still cleared the long barrack-tables. The air retained a certain pungency.

Dilkes Loveless backed out of the doorway, seeming surprised. A dribble of inmates limped past them, silent with famished concentration. Be it knife, fork, or spoon, each man carried a clinking utensil, and also – by hook or by crook, where they lacked for a hand – some sort of makeshift container; tin can, jug or basin slopped a-swill with a steaming stew.

Sarah remarked on the lateness of the hour.

'Some prefer to take their meals *apart*,' said Dilkes. 'They may fetch rations, returning with them to their cabins, but only once the main sitting is done.' The clerk shrugged. '*These* days,' he offered, 'we tend to let them sleep late.'

That same mournful lassitude seemed, Sarah thought, to pervade the Hospital's entire fabric.

As the last awkward straggler staggered by, he revealed a diamond-shaped design on the back of his blue coat. Divided into quarters, each contained initials, lettered and numerical. Sarah's curiosity was piqued.

'These correspond to an individual's *quadrangle*,' confided Dilkes, 'his ward, cabin number, *et cetera*, so that we may readily identify where each man belongs. Accidents, you understand, are of frequent occurrence given their, um… *constitution*.'

He leant in close to dispense another exclusive dollop.

'A man dies, on the average, daily.'

'An' yellowcoat?' asked King Cole.

'Offenders against Hospital rules were called "canaries",' said Dilkes. 'They wore a yellow coat and performed menial tasks…but…' the clerk stared at the Aborigine, mystified '…*that* punishment was abolished many decades ago…!

'Their uniform…has altered of late,' he said, 'the original design felt to be outmoded. Knee-breeches have been exchanged for full-length trousers, and round hats allowed for daily wear, instead of the old tri-corner.'

Long after the Pensioners had disappeared from view, King Cole continued to stare into the depths of the corridor. His concern, Sarah observed, was for the Hospital's inmates – the people not the place, exactly the opposite case to when they walked the streets of Bloomsbury.

She herself wished to know more about how the old sailors lived; the evidence of things seen preferred to that hoped for.

'Mr Dilkes,' she said, 'would it be possible for us to see more of the domestic arrangements? One of the wards, perhaps?'

'We shall visit the wards, *yes*,' he snapped, 'all in good time. First, you must witness the Painted Hall. It is the *jewel* in our crown!'

They mounted another stairwell, ascending into a second vestibule, below the dome of the King William building. A prominent notice declared an admission charge. Sarah reflexively reached for her purse, neither desiring money of King Cole, nor stopping to consider whether he carried any.

Dilkes Loveless shooed her coins away. 'You are my *guests!*' he said.

Climbing more steps, they entered the Great Hall. Over 100 feet in length and at least 50 high, *trompe l'œil* painted arches suggested a ceiling twice its actual height.

'Whitepella!' exclaimed Cole, and expressed a click of wonder.

Everything else they had seen was as nothing compared to the astonishing painted ceiling, which was all the clerk had promised and more. A lavish Baroque masterpiece, thunderously it trumpeted the manifold virtues of Imperial monarchy. Neck straining, Sarah could hardly tear her eyes from the lofty pageant, an orgy of allegory. Peace handed King William an olive branch; he passed the red cap of Liberty on to Europe. Old Father Time flexed his muscles and held naked Truth up to the light, while impervious Minerva thrust a spear, and Hercules swung his mighty club in a ferocious arc.

'Time exposes Truth,' proclaimed Dilkes Loveless. 'And Wisdom and Strength destroy the Vices.'

Vices represented, in this instance, by Louis XIV of France, being trampled under the royal foot.

Much like the other tourists scattered about the Great Hall, the small group slowly drifted across the open floor-space. Upwards of 200 framed paintings lined the walls, arranged in tiers three deep between towering Corinthian pilasters, themselves almost hidden by long crimson hangings: the Naval Gallery. The walls also were painted. The nearest arch presented a life-size man-of-war, gunports open and threatening a blast; the other held captive a treasure ship piled high with booty, the spoils of military conquest. Amid potent symbols of England's Naval power – cannon, coils of rope, spars, drums, and muskets – eight gigantic slaves broke their backs in support of the massive oval frame depicted overhead.

A riot of fleshy figures tumbled in and out of the heavens above, the tableau abundant with plump, pink nudes. Out of nerves, fatigue, or both, King Cole finally succumbed to a prolonged fit of giggles.

Irked, Dilkes Loveless smacked his lips. He rushed them onwards, passing through an arch – genuine, proscenium, by Hawksmoor – into the Upper Hall.

'Your quest,' he said, 'might once have brought you *here* more directly. What *used* to be the Hospital's Record-room now contains pictures and relics appertaining to Lord Nelson.'

Mural paintings bracketed the archway through which they had just walked; Dilkes proudly narrated their details.

'Plenty pours riches into the lap of Commerce,' he said, 'whilst Britannia, trident at the ready, ensures Public Security. It is the might of the Royal Navy, above all else, that protects Mother Nation's merchants, and sustains in turn the Divine Right of Britain's Royal Family.'

Sarah began to feel a little dizzy from the surfeit of imagery; she would have relished a cup of tea and a chance to sit down.

King Cole approached the far wall.

'"*Iam Nova Progenies Coelo*",' Dilkes read aloud the Latin inscription there. '"Now a New Race from Heaven."' The vast wall-painting portrayed the Hanoverian royal family, King George I surrounded by his children and grandchildren. The image of St Paul's Cathedral loomed large behind; what Sarah assumed had caught Cole's eye.

'The West Wall,' said Dilkes, 'celebrates the Protestant Succession. No, please *don't* touch!'

Cole obeyed. He pointed at the figure of a small boy: Frederick, Prince of Wales, dressed in a bright red coat, stood with one hand on the King's knee. In the other, he held out a royal orb. King Cole grinned. 'Howzat!' he cried.

The orb did resemble a cricket ball. What was more, the boy in the painting had Cole's eyes, those same dark pupils, eerily ablaze.

'Yes, it's ironic,' said Dilkes. 'Cricket was supposedly the death of him.'

According to popular tradition, Frederick, in line to the throne, was slain by the pitch of a cricket ball. Sarah recalled the cruel Jacobite verse commemorating the event:

> 'Here lies Fred,
> Who was alive and is dead.'

She turned aside.

The ceiling of the Upper Hall was no less impressive than that in the Grand Hall. From the four points of the compass, the Four Corners of the Known World, feminised, paid homage. To the west, Europe was accompanied by a white horse; Asia, in the north, adorned with a particoloured turban, presented a camel; Africa, east, a lion at her side, modelled a nonsensical elephant hat; and finally, to the south, rose the Americas – personified by Pocahontas, the Indian princess who had so tragically fallen for a stranger to her shores.

If London, the nation's capital, was the seat of Empire, then standing in the middle of this room effectively situated them at its dead centre.

'Where is Australia?' asked Sarah.

'When this painting was done?' replied Dilkes. 'My dear, *Australia* was yet to be discovered.'

Sarah Larkin looked from the Naval clerk to her Aboriginal companion, but said nothing.

CHAPTER XXII
Whit Monday, the 1st of June, 1868

PALE SHADOWS

'For you, ye Naval warriors, you whose arms
The trident sceptre of your Country's power
Fearless sustain, and with its terrors shake
The shores of distant nations – yes, for you
Your grateful Country frames the fondest cares.'

~ Thomas Noble, *Blackheath*

No sign of his energies flagging, Dilkes Loveless turned to face Miss Sarah Larkin.

'You were hoping to see life on one of the *wards*, were you not?' he said. 'King Charles is closest. Let us go *there*.'

The Hospital clerk opened a small door and stood aside to let them pass. In the lobby area, a fine stairwell of dark wood curled its way up and around the interior. As they began their ascent, Dilkes Loveless regained the lead.

'Just as it would have been for your man George Bruce,' he said, 'the daily routine for Pensioners remains *much* the same. *Excepting*, of course, their various comforts.'

He pointed to wall fixtures, overhead – the gas-lamps.

'When I joined staff here nearly 30 years ago,' he said, '*many* areas, these staircases for instance, were only lit with oil…whale for the officers' corridors, and fish for the ordinary seamen. *Only* the Painted Hall and Chapel had gas. Eventually, we hope to extend it to the wards as well.'

On entering the room at the top of the stairs, Sarah's first impressions were of scale: the doorway itself must have been at least eight feet across, wide enough for them to walk all three abreast.

'Accommodation,' Dilkes was saying, 'is a mixture of smaller rooms, space for between four and eight curtained beds, and large wards such as *this* one, either side of the spine wall.'

In support of the lofty ceiling, a double row of pillars neatly divided the spacious interior. At the centre a large fireplace dominated, with wood-panel surround. A room of such size, thought Sarah, must be very hard to heat in the wintertime.

'The old sailors have never found these quarters much to their taste,' confessed Dilkes. 'Too *big* for their liking. Lest we forget, these men have spent years of their lives at sea. They become inured to life on board ship, where conditions are *cramped*, to say the least. In concession, a system of smaller enclosures has been introduced, reducing the available space to something more *palatable*.'

The clerk indicated little wood cabins dotted about the room, suggestive of a haphazard street of tiny shop-fronts: wainscoted and curtained, their glass windows were filled with prints and knick-knacks, as if on sale. The group approached one of these cabins, the curtain of which was drawn aside. About a dozen feet in height and the same in depth, but only nine feet across, there were four bed-spaces crammed inside – very homely. Canopied with curtains, the individual iron-framed beds each included a sea-chest to the side, covered over with a cluster of sentimental keepsakes.

Sarah had one, just the same, at the foot of her own bed; it had belonged to her mother. She ran her fingers over the gnarled wood, and gently warmed the brass.

'Lockers for their worldly possessions,' said Dilkes, 'and souvenirs of their sea-voyages.' Other chalets they passed contained anywhere between one and eight berths. Hammocks sometimes slung across in preference to beds reinforced the illusion of life below decks. It struck Sarah as immeasurably sad, that conditions at sea had left the old sailors so institutionalised; equally, that they lived out their days evidently wishing themselves elsewhere.

'But, where is Mr Cole?' she said suddenly.

Even as the words left her mouth, he reappeared at her side. His ability to blend into any background could be at times disconcerting.

He looked, and with obvious interest, towards the far end of the ward: only here were any of the beds actually occupied. Sarah noted the subtle presence of a few womenfolk, not so much in attendance as they were idly hanging about.

'Are these…are these nurses?' she asked.

'Oh, heavens, *no*,' said Dilkes. '*Widows*, mostly.'

They drew close to a bed somewhat marooned out in the open. A body lay on it, insensible.

'Having dropped anchor, and snug-moored,' said Dilkes, 'our patriot and hero finally earns a modicum of peace here in a Greenwich harbour.'

Sarah almost begged for the clerk to stop, but he continued.

'As you see, the old sea-dog lacks for vigour.'

They looked again at the body inert in the bed. The man had no legs.

The clerk cut for himself a slice of Hazlitt. '"Stung with wounds, stunned with bruises, bleeding and mangled, an English sailor never finds himself so much alive as when he is flung half dead into..."' Dilkes Loveless froze, mid-quote '"...the cockpit."'

The Greenwich Pensioner lay awake, staring at them. His beady eyes, bloodshot, glittered with suspicion.

'WHO ARE YA?' he shouted. Although minus a pair of legs, he retained a healthy set of lungs.

'*Salty* old sea-dog...' said Dilkes. He moved to the head of the bed and laid a hand on the old sailor's shoulder. 'Many of our residents exhibit a *supernumerary* vitality...'

'BUGGER ORF!' yelled the sailor. 'Who are ya?' The inmate's body jerked in the bed as he tried to get a better look at who stood beside him. 'Lieutenant Loveless!' he said. 'Beggin' y'r pardon, sir, only I was sleepin' and not expectin' ta meet with anyone. I didden know quite wheres I was f'r a moment!'

'That's quite all right, Siddon,' said Dilkes. 'Settle down.'

Sarah gave a gentle smile. King Cole peeped out from behind her skirts.

'Siddon,' said Dilkes.

'Sir?'

'This is *Miss* Sarah Larkin. Oh, and a *Mister* Cole.' The clerk bowed on his ward's behalf. He said, 'May I present Percival Siddon, R.N.'

The inmate's beady eye rolled over them, exploring Sarah's charms only briefly before settling on Cole's black face. He squinted in a most unfriendly fashion.

'Siddon celebrated his 75th birthday less than a week ago,' boasted the clerk. 'Didn't you? And that is nothing unusual. At the turn of the century, records state we had near to a hundred inmates, disabled, mind, at well over 80 years of age. One particular fellow was still going strong at 102!'

'I remembers him,' grunted the sailor. 'Awkward old – '

'Then,' Dilkes said, 'there was John Rome, the signalman of Nelson's *Victory*. "England expects", and all that! The *very* man to hoist the flags before the Battle of Trafalgar. He passed on only *eight* years ago.'

'*Arrrh*,' roared Siddon. 'The Battle of Trafalgar! I was there! We showed those F – '

'Now, Percy,' said Dilkes, 'you know that isn't true.'

'Those flaming Frenchies had – '

'Percival.'

'*Ahhh*...' Siddon rolled his head, defiant to the last. 'Well, Rome isn't 'ere to tell it any more, iz'e?' he said. 'So I might as well! If it warn't for our spinning a yarn now and then, why, sir, we should spit and sputter at each other like a parcel of cats in the gutter!'

Disconsolate, the old seaman started to cast around. 'Who's got my bottle?' he shouted.

Sarah worried over which end of him had need.

'Anybody seen my bottle? Who's nicked my drink?' roared Siddon. 'Blarm me, I needs a drink! Me stumps is plaguin' somethin' rotten!'

'The Governor recognises,' galloped in Dilkes, 'that for many veterans, life can be a little dull – '

'Yurrr, the Guv'nor,' Siddon interjected. 'Tha's very big of 'im. More of a man than me…he's still got hisself a leg to stand on!'

'Unavoidably,' Dilkes persevered, 'shut out from *wholesome* interests – '

'I saw 'im,' said Siddon. 'In the middle of the night it was, only a day or two gone.' He flicked his head towards one of the east windows.

The clerk's face dropped.

'They'd sat me in a chair and forgot me,' Siddon shouted. 'Sat there all night I was, staring out that damned window like an owl! Saw him out on the Court. Raisin' a toast to King George, he was, then fell over backwards!'

Dilkes Loveless rushed at them. Before they knew it, Sarah and Cole were through the next set of doors.

The old sailor could still be heard, blaspheming away behind them. 'Arsy-varsy, ha HA!' he cried. 'Such a laugh came 'pon me, I 'ad like to beshit meself!'

'Admiral Sir James Alexander Gordon, the Governor,' gabbled the clerk. 'Roses in his cheeks, lovely fellow, very kind. Heart of gold, but wooden-legged… Not a *well* man, sadly.'

Dilkes Loveless smiled and frowned and looked about, assessing their next move.

'You will find it *quieter* out here,' he said.

'The man's bottle?' said Sarah. She searched the face of the clerk. His eyes met hers, and in that fleeting instant she witnessed a spark of panic.

'The Pensioners,' he said, firmly, 'are given a daily allowance, *much* as they were in the service. They have ways and means of getting their hands on more, of course, and are often found…' His voice trailed away. 'The Trafalgar Tavern,' he said, recovering, 'the Red Lion, the Man in the Moon, the Victory…all a hop, skip and a jump away. When it comes to pubs and taverns, we enjoy a *surfeit.*'

Sarah recalled the Chalk Walk: perhaps the men needed places where they might smoke in company, and keep warm at the same time. What with the grog, and the London fogs, it was no wonder that their chest ailments were aggravated.

'Things in general, however,' said the clerk, 'are not as *bad* as they used to be.'

He led the way down a back staircase, smaller than the first.

'And how *did* they used to be?' said Sarah, a slight note of challenge in her voice.

The angle of the dim stairwell was tight, the party almost turned back on themselves.

'Drunkenness, quarrelling…fighting…' Perhaps for the first time, Dilkes hesitated to speak. They had rather left behind his regular patter. 'It was, in truth, an absolute pandemonium,' he said. 'A personal filthiness prevailed that would stand your hair on end.'

They emerged into a stone-flagged foyer of sorts, open at one side to the grassy sward of the Grand Court.

'The Surgeon-General himself made complaint,' said Dilkes. 'Unless he be a patient in the Infirmary, it was difficult to find a Pensioner who washed his feet or body from the time of his admission till his death.'

'They were not made to wash?' said Sarah.

'There was no *means* of washing back then, other than in the chamber pots they had just emptied,' said Dilkes. 'There are washbasins in the wards *now*. Conditions, I assure you, are very much improved!'

The clerk pointed out a set of stone troughs at one side of the lobby. Underneath each, Sarah noted a second trough intended to capture and recycle the spilt water.

'The water-closets originally stood outside, a good hundred feet or so away from any building. In consideration of sanitation, you see. That did prove a trial for many of our less *capable* veterans…'

To say the least – Sarah tried, but not too hard, to imagine their struggles in the depths of winter. She shivered.

Dilkes entertained only fond memories of his own designated toilet, out on the west lawns. It was in the same approximate spot where he chose to take his lunch.

They passed through another set of double doors, into a ward that was completely empty.

'Lieutenant Loveless…' said Sarah.

She heard the echo of her own voice, and looked around the stark white room. 'You – um – you refer to the inmates as those "remaining". May I ask… where have all the others gone to?'

'Dear lady,' he replied, 'to the only better place there is.'

'I'm sorry?' she said.

Dilkes Loveless threw open the next set of doors with a flourish. 'My office,' he said. 'Or my sometime office, I suppose I should say now.'

The room was spacious, under-furnished, and utterly charmless.

'Please, sit,' urged Dilkes. 'May I offer you some light refreshment?'

Already his hand clasped a small bell. Sarah consented. The bell was rung, and in short order a smart young purser appeared through a smaller side door to receive his orders. They were soon settled and, indeed, glad of the rest.

Dilkes Loveless leant forward across his desk.

'The Hospital opened 100 years already, it was following Trafalgar that numbers reached their peak,' he said. 'We hit full capacity by 1814, housing nearly 3,000 sailor-Pensioners!'

He felt gratified to see her thickish eyebrows raised.

'The end of the Napoleonic war brought with it *peace*,' said Dilkes. 'Our source of income was sharply reduced, just when the payment of pensions was at its greatest. Out-pensions especially cut into our capital at an alarming rate…two million pounds *wiped out* inside of four years!'

This, then, would have been around the time that George Bruce was admitted; and shortly thereafter died.

The clerk took up his teacup and slurped.

Sarah's cheek twitched, while King Cole idly twirled a quill feather between his fingers.

'Our resources stretched,' resumed Dilkes, 'affairs struggled on in this un-Bristol-fashion for the next 30 or so years, before the men began to die off. You'll forgive my bluntness. These last two decades have seen a sharp *falling off* in numbers.'

Dilkes Loveless gathered up a sheaf of papers and tapped them briskly on the desktop, before moving them over to the opposite side.

'Disarmament, you see, cuts down Royal Navy ships,' he said, 'while the Merchant Service ever expands. All part and parcel of increased settlement of the colonies, the very *fruits* of our exertions. The real problem is we haven't had a Naval conflict worth its salt in over 50 years!'

'You speak as if that were a bad thing!' said Sarah.

'Oh, but it *is*!' Dilkes Loveless took another urgent sip of tea. His cup rattled in its saucer. 'Valour, duty, honour, loyalty,' he said, 'our national symbol, Jolly Jack Tar, is but a pale shadow of his former self!'

Sarah thought of Lambert in his bed.

Entirely uninterested, King Cole monopolised the sugar-bowl.

'Of necessity,' said Dilkes, 'we are obliged to maintain Hospital security, and management, of course. Where once there were *20* officers in charge, today there is only the Governor, a captain, a commander, and three lieutenants, including myself. Seven wards closed, two out of the four blocks no longer in use… The expense! You can't imagine! Annual running costs have doubled in the last eight years, to 114 pounds *per capita!*'

Sarah gasped. An entire family might be supported on half as much. She and her father survived on little more: only because there were just the two of them could they class themselves better off.

Dilkes, carried away with the matter of accounts, looked a little abashed. He finger-traced the lip of his teacup.

'It is the payment of out-pensions,' he said at last, 'Government's previous great mistake, which may finally do for us. Recently reinstated, they have proven too popular, two-thirds of residents taking up the Duke of Somerset's offer. Out-pensioners, you see, can draw their money whilst living with their families. It is tantamount to an *inducement* to leave…in search of those consolations, dear lady, which only social and domestic affection will bestow.'

An odd sort of transparency appeared in his wide blue eyes: he was looking at Sarah through bottle-top lenses with what might, in another, have passed for a soulful expression. She looked away.

For a breathless moment or two, Dilkes Loveless fell silent. His empty gaze shuttled around each wall of his office in turn.

Abruptly, he stood.

Sarah turned around to find that King Cole, too, was standing. She turned back. The clerk, his hand outstretched, was showing them to a small side door.

'Shall we?' he said.

They made their exit via a small antechamber, and then across a dark corridor. Outside once more, they paused, standing within what appeared to be the inner courtyard of the King Charles block. King Cole's attention had begun, rather obviously, to drift. Sarah wondered how to bring their tour to a close without offending the clerk unduly.

'Just 371 inmates survive,' he was saying, 'including those in the Infirmary. That's what we have left, *rattling* around, in an institution built for 3,000.'

Dilkes Loveless moved on, the gravel grinding beneath his heel.

They passed beneath an archway at the riverine end. The clerk came to a halt beside a length of railings that, bordering the Hospital grounds, overlooked a narrow strip of pathway beside the Thames.

The tide was coming in.

He talked incessantly, like a tap that could not be turned off.

'We would be closed *already*,' he said, 'were it not for the "Guv'nor", bless his old boot. Closed by the suffrage of those for whom the Hospital was originally founded!'

Curiosity got the better of her; Sarah advanced a few steps to peer through one of the lower windows of the riverside apartments. The superiority of fixtures and fittings to anything seen in the wards was immediately obvious. The ceiling was vaulted, the handsome door-cases carved from stone.

'What' she asked, 'is through there?'

'Why, the Governor's apartments,' said Dilkes. 'Even if their posts have been abolished, the majority of officers and their families have of course chosen to remain in residence.' Dilkes Loveless seemed to indicate the entire southeast pavilion.

'Of course,' echoed Sarah.

She was wrong in her earlier assessment: no guilt of any sort found its expression here.

'The conscience of civilisation' was not troubled in the slightest.

King Cole, head dreamily inclined to one side, listens to faint strains of a weirdling music. He feels it in his liver as he knows it in his bones: this sad place contains too many dead. Reason enough for the site to be abandoned. It is contaminated, destined to lie empty forever.

Sarah felt a slight panic rising in her breast. King Cole, who always lingered a little too far behind for comfort, was missing.

She hurried back, passing through the courtyard to the centre of King Charles, just catching sight of his muddied trouser-leg as it disappeared through a doorway.

Sarah followed on, back to the stone-flagged foyer where the water troughs were gurgling. No sign of Cole.

A door stood ajar opposite that to the deserted ward. It had not been open before. She ran to the threshold.

The Hospital clerk, puffing along behind, struggled to keep up. When he came to the inner doorway he found Sarah just inside. The Aborigine gentleman hesitated a few steps further on, at an apparent loss.

Brows pleading, King Cole communicated his vexation to Sarah.

'Where are we?' she asked of Dilkes.

'The Peacock Room,' he said.

A sculpted bust topped an ornamental fireplace, below which knelt the melodramatic figure of an angel, weeping abject tears.

'There we are,' Dilkes suddenly announced. 'I knew it would come to me. George Bruce!'

Looking again at the bust, Sarah performed a neat double-take.

'No, no,' gasped Dilkes. '*That* is Charles Dibdin. Died 1816...so the pair, to my knowledge, will never have met. Not in *this* life.'

'I don't follow you,' she said.

'Dibden was the author of a great many sea-shanties, and the like,' said Dilkes. 'One of which was "The Greenwich Pensioner".'

Sarah nodded, still unsure of his logic.

'George Bruce,' he said again. 'I *knew* the name was familiar to me from somewhere! He wrote a *book*, you see, detailing his own extraordinary story.'

'A book?' she asked.

'Yes,' said Dilkes. 'He called it *The Life of a Greenwich Pensioner*!'

Sarah scrabbled for her stub of pencil.

'Well, I *say* extraordinary, never having *read* the thing,' added Dilkes, 'but he crossed the oceans more than once. Every sailor has his stories, and his poor face must have got like that somehow!'

Excited, Sarah looked from the clerk to King Cole and back again.

'*Guruwari*,' hissed Cole. '*Guruwari!*'

The meaning behind his expression was a mystery, yet he too seemed provoked by the mention of a book. And something must have sent him racing in there at such a clip.

'Do you know where I might find a copy of this book?' she said.

'Let's see,' hemmed Dilkes, squinting. 'No longer *here*, I'm sure of that. No, I must confess, I'm not sure *where* it might be. Most likely among the paper ephemera we've cleared out along the way. Your best bet would be the library at the British Museum.'

CHAPTER XXIII
Whit Monday, the 1st of June, 1868

ONE TREE HILL

'Fixed on the enormous galaxy,
Deeper and older seemed his eye:
And matched his sufferance sublime
The taciturnity of time.'

~ Ralph Waldo Emerson, 'Character'

Fresh and lovely-sounding, Sarah Larkin's laughter echoed throughout the flagstone lobby, and – louder, longer – inside Dilkes's loveless head.

The clerk returned his guests to the grass lawns of the Grand Court, the Royal Naval Hospital's open quadrangle, and the spot where their official tour had begun. Sighing loudly, he turned to observe the incoming river traffic. A flotilla of trade vessels crowded their way upstream.

'Greenwich Hospital,' Dilkes Loveless said, 'is much *endeared* to an Englishman's heart.'

He twinkled meaningfully at Sarah. His transparent looks lingered; she turned aside.

Raised on a plinth beside them was a statue of King George II, face worn away by the action of the elements. King Cole regarded it suspiciously.

Met with awkward silence, the clerk returned to looking out across the waters, his attention drawn by the sailor-Pensioners still huddled or hobbled at the riverside.

'Little accustomed to kindness of any sort,' said Dilkes, '*wanting* everything that tends to enliven or endear a home. It is perhaps the monastic character of the place that has proven distasteful to so many.'

Self-pity had crept into the clerk's droning voice, and Sarah felt he eyed her ring finger, gloved though it was, with rather too much significance.

'Well,' she said, 'thank you, lieutenant.'

They had what they needed. King Cole drifted, patently keen to leave.

'Charles,' said Dilkes.

'Charles,' she said. 'Thank you. You've been *most* helpful.' Sarah was backing away even as she spoke. 'We both appreciate,' she said, 'very much, the time you have taken to show us arou – '

'I extend myself to you,' spluttered Dilkes. He saw the alarm in her eye. 'My continued *service*, I offer you, in whatever way it, might be…' he wanted to say desirable '…most *useful*.'

'Time is getting on,' said Sarah. 'We mustn't keep you from your work.'

'I can take a look through papers at the Admiralty, if you'd like?' said Dilkes. 'Let me take your address. In case I should find anything more concerning Bruce. That is, if you should wish me to look…'

Sarah raised one eyebrow – it was a sound idea, at least in part.

'Maybe…' She thought aloud. 'Well, maybe,' she said, 'in that case, I can take *yours*…'

Their relief almost palpable, Sarah and Cole entered into the grounds of Greenwich Park.

Sounds of birdsong and laughter carried on the breeze, across glorious acres of wide-open space. They could see a trio of boys with feathers in their caps, running in delirious, diminishing circles, until one caught another and they all tumbled headlong to the grass. A maidservant navigated a three-wheeled baby cart along the main path. As with any popular amenity, the place had become a little frayed at the edges, but these signs of wear and tear, if anything, only added to its charm. Long boulevards stretched forward, planted with exotic trees of extraordinary girth. Sarah and King Cole soon found themselves idling at a central point, a sort of shaded crossways. In the midst of this semicircular grove, fine lawns and thicketed woods surrounded them, the park a curious patchwork of the cultivated and wild. A few tame deer, allowed to wander freely, grazed nearby. Their scent was strong. King Cole eyed them hungrily.

A party of children rolling down from the brow of the nearest hill landed almost at their feet, breathless with laughter. As they turned to climb back up, the curious couple followed their lead.

The Royal Observatory crowned the hilltop, a guiding principle for weary travellers far from home. Commanders of all vessels sailing from the Thames set their chronometers by the red leather ball atop Flamsteed House: the great globe measured, from the Greenwich Meridian, degrees of east-west longitude providing the basis for all British maps and charts. According to the public clock outside the gates the hour was nearly five. Whatever else King Cole might have in mind, Sarah knew she would soon have to make her way back to the house.

They turned to admire the view.

The broad sweep of the Thames valley stretched out before them. London was just part of a wider panorama, a great dark smear alleviated by the occasional protuberance: the Tower; the Monument; the tallest city steeples. Beyond rose the hills of Hertfordshire, Buckinghamshire, Bedfordshire and Surrey. Smoke piled from out of a hundred thousand chimneys, but at sufficient remove so as not to obscure everything. Rather than brood beneath the metropolitan canopy, for once it was possible to look across to it – even to discern the smell of clean air.

They seemed almost on a level with the clouds.

Screaming children charged to the edge and launched themselves into thin air, pitching themselves down the sharp incline. Sarah very much wished to be a child again, and free of her encumbering skirts. She might then find the courage to join them in their violent, tumbling game.

Instead, Cole led her away from the crowds to climb a nearby promontory, one he appeared to favour. A solitary elm stood proud at the apex. Side-by-side on the grass, they sat beneath its shade.

The banks of neighbouring hillocks extended rich and green. The crest of One Tree Hill, in contrast, was but sparsely covered. Yellowed grass faded between patches of bare earth, the blue haze of fir trees skirting its lower margins.

King Cole grunted.

'Leg rain coming,' he observed.

It was true. Piled high along the far horizon, great dark thunderheads gathered. Distant showers fell in fitful curtains.

A little way along, the owner of a telescope had set up shop. Every now and then, his peddler's cry could be heard. 'A look through my spyglass, penny a go!'

A way below, their picnic forgotten, a gentleman entertained a lady on the slopes. His hat was off. Every now and then the man with the telescope succumbed to temptation and gave the pick-knickers a closer look. Otherwise, Sarah and Cole were completely alone.

In a single afternoon, they had covered more ground than many Londoners did in a lifetime. They relaxed and rested.

The Aborigine sat with one leg thrust out in front, the other folded back under and supporting his body. He began to scratch away at the soil between his feet.

Looking up at Sarah, King Cole spoke excitedly.

'In the dust,' he said, 'I write.'

He started to draw with the displaced earth. Sarah could not hope to understand; even so, she was fascinated. The longer they had remained at the Hospital, the more its palatial confines had seemed to sap all of their vital energy – Cole's especially. Apparently revived, he drew with both hands, using the index and middle finger one after the other to create a double dotted line. He drew a number of these lines, each one different, and erased by a sweep of the palm. In the last of these line drawings, she perceived a familiar shape.

Unless she was mistaken, he outlined the loop of the River Thames, just as it was laid out before them.

King Cole grunted again. He inscribed an almost perfect circle, and then with an air of finality struck a line through it, to effect something like a capital Q.

Sarah deliberately held her tongue. Attempting to adopt his gestural 'body language', she allowed her facial expression to deliver the full force of her enquiry.

His dark eyes flickered. Seeming nervous, he would not meet her quizzical glare.

She noticed some sort of marks on the bark of the elm tree behind him. Fresh and injurious, the carving had been made only recently. It was a figurine, human, arms extended and legs spread, as if dancing. Eyes, nose, even the joints of the knees were boldly marked, but there was no mouth. Immediately that he saw she had spotted this thing, King Cole shifted his position to block her view of it.

His hands raised and held flat maintained a perfect stillness. He began to move backwards and forwards very gently, seeming as if to indicate all of the land that stretched out before them, as far as the horizon, perhaps even further. Fingers spreading, his hands fell. A small word combined with this dismissive gesture to convey something negative, something *not*. He touched the grass at his feet – not. He indicated the trees – not. The deer where they grazed and dozed, and all of the people wandering the park – they too were denied. The entire earth lay empty, without any of these things.

Narrating the while in his singsong native language, Cole either spoke in hushed tones, or alternately gabbled in staccato bursts.

His gestures almost preternaturally slow, one thin arm nosed sinuously, gracefully forward – no mistaking the movements of a snake. Cole's musculature tightened. Instinctively, Sarah understood the concept of great size imbuing this 'snake'. When it set to shuddering, she trembled. One eye opened and sly, the snake began to gather and rear itself up. Slowly, slowly, it turned its head, taking in the view.

Formerly so quiet, King Cole babbled like a brook. Sarah, beguiled, yet found herself distracted. Storm clouds, building higher in the sky, approached fast; sun breaking out from between them transformed the dirty brown river into a glittering wreath.

King Cole's snake-arm began to weave its way forward, across the land. Back and forth it slithered, his other hand close in behind it, making short sweeping motions away from the elbow. Sarah thought at first it shed skin. Continuing, the signals seemed more likely to emphasise progress. At a certain point, the snake met and matched the exact course of the Thames.

She had a boat to catch. The steamer service ran late, but her father would be expecting his supper sooner. The library closed at six: if she were absent much longer, he might begin to wonder where else she had got to.

With a snap the big snake retreated, back, back, returning to the place from which it had emerged. The great head turned, pointed towards the ground, and began to…spit? No, speak. Cole called out, the opening and closing of his hand synchronous with his shouts.

'*Mia! … Mia! … Mia! Gala!*'

The late afternoon light laced everything with silver. Sarah wanted to stay, but knew that she could not. Already the view-peddler had packed up and gone, and so had the lovers.

'I must go!' she said.

King Cole bucked and jerked, popping a loose fist – another, and then another.

Sarah stood.

Cole's body hunched forward, his tongue protruding slightly, blowing out his cheeks. The expression on his swollen face was comical, ridiculous.

Although no one else was near to see, Sarah blushed. She took a step backwards, retreating unsteadily.

'You'll…you'll be all right, making your own way?' she said.

King Cole answered with a loud croak. Entire body bloated with mime, he hopped, a big fat frog. Lightning fast, his whole form shifted. Once more the snake slid over his belly, brushing up against it.

Sarah forgot herself a moment.

Again the frog, Cole's mouth sprang wide, his swollen shape contracting. He began to heave and void himself out of his mouth. And to laugh! Vomiting. And laughing. Sarah, perturbed, took another step away.

Ten fingers sprouted, questing upward, arms flinging towards the treetops as his hands fluttered away. Faster now, physical forms shifted and changed, his lips moving but the torrent of words barely audible.

'…*arkooloolalaranakaratharagarshayarrawa…*'

He jumped, hiccupped, and flew, swam and galloped and slid, populating the landscape with a thousand different animal likenesses.

The great snake reappeared and spoke in an angry voice. '*Wia ma pitja,*' it shouted. '*Nungkarpa lara pupinpa!*'

Such fantastical nonsense, after all the help she had so selflessly extended, unnerved and annoyed Sarah. Absorbed in the telling of his mystic tale, Cole acted as if she were no longer there. Why tarry?

Their joint quest, whilst inconclusive, had not been entirely fruitless.

'I hope that some of what we learned today has been of use to you,' she said. 'Shall I see you again? To…tomorrow, perhaps?'

The Aborigine fixed her with a fierce black eye, as if he could turn her to stone.

'Read in book,' he said, 'like whitepella.'

'Yes,' she agreed.

Sarah tripped haphazardly down the hill. The tumbling children had all gone. Making towards the park exit, she allowed herself one look back. Filtered through the trees, the sun threw long dark shadows far across the grass, claw-like talons that seemed to reach for the huddled figure of the Aborigine. He sat immobile atop One Tree Hill, dwelling on his deep, unknowable thoughts.

King Cole abruptly removes the shoes he has been given, stiff and sopping as pig snouts, and throws them carelessly aside. With a swipe of his bare foot he erases the dirt drawing. The tale of the Rainbow Serpent is done. He stretches out, flexing his toes, no longer fervid, but pensive. He cannot recall the last occasion on which his spirit knew peace.

Spirit Ancestors walk the land, as they have since the dawn of Creation. They sing the World into being. This is Truth. Nothing exists that does not also exist in Truth – where it is, in fact, more real. In order to honour his debt to the Guardian, for all the help she has rendered, he has tried to gift Thara a little of this ancient knowledge. This he has done in the manner of a story best fit for children, as much as the limitations of her sex allows.

An invisible weave, he knows, coheres the World: a network of pathways formed throughout the Dreaming, the footprints of the Spirit Ancestors. Such is the fund of learning he has been taught. The path an Ancestor takes when forming the land becomes a Songline, or Dreaming trail. These Songlines both define the World and maintain its integrity, handed down the generations of man to be replenished through their Dreaming for all eternity.

This is *Bugaragara*, 'the Way of the Law'.

If a person such as himself hopes to walk any Songline, he must first learn the corresponding song. In singing the song, he becomes one with both Ancestor and path, and contributes to the continuing cycle of Creation. That then is the purpose behind his going Walkabout. For, without song, the land would cease to exist; just as surely as the Men die, when denied the birth lands they belong to.

Only now that he is outside of the World has he finally located his Dreaming. *Bripumyarrimin* ponders this.

Afternoon light fades slowly into evening. A striking sunset flushes the river in shades from bronze to crimson. An entire fleet of merchant ships sails in on the blood-tide.

Smaller barks darting in between, the galleons come gliding, stately and assured as swans. Their wide, white wings are fat and full; the vessels drift, deep-freighted. As each sea-worn prow cleaves the waters, the waves catch the sunlight, sparking. In the path ploughed behind every ship's keel settles a trembling shadow.

King Cole's weary head dips forward. He recovers.

Rust-coloured clouds brew up a storm. The numberless buildings are set afire by the low sun. A single shaft strikes the lip of One Tree Hill, *Panatapia*. The searching orange ray moves on, dappling the deer that graze peacefully in the meadow, before illuminating the gleaming white buildings of the Hospital. They shimmer and disappear, replaced with an ancient palace brick-red in colour.

Lulled, laid back, between pillows of cloud, King Cole looks into pools of deepening blue. A few birds circle there, way up high.

He listens to their evensong. A chorus of church bells answers. He hears the barking of a dog, somewhere off in the distance, and then, faint music At the base of the statue of King George, two Naval cadets take their stand. Sounding the tattoo on drum and fife, they signal the close of another day.

King Cole rests his tired eyes. Glowing lids gradually fade to dimness, a pale grey that soon darkens. Occasional coloured lights bloom and sparkle in the murk, crashing like the spray of waves ashore. His liver, the seat of feeling, opens out like a flower, his consciousness suffused with a delightful fluorescence – the Dreaming.

When at long last his eyes reopen, the moon smiles down, and all is silent. The threatened storm has passed over. Only thin wisps of cloud remain, skimming swiftly by.

'*Ballrinjarrimin?* Y'alright?'

No response. Dick-a-Dick stands at the foot of Sundown's bunk, Cuzens close behind. The whole day through, Sundown hasn't stirred. Dick-a-Dick kicks the wooden leg of the bed.

Jogged, Sundown rolls over. It is clear enough he hasn't been sleeping. The others look him over.

Dick-a-Dick grunts.

'*Bripumyarrimin,*' he says. 'Ain't here, eh.'

Dick jerks his chin towards the empty bunk next door. Dark circles under his eyes, Sundown only looks sheepish, and hangs his head.

It is nearly a full minute before he answers.

'Him...gone.'

'Where?'

A shorter pause lingers in the air.

'Walkabout,' Sundown murmurs.

Cuzens snorts.

'*Deen?*' asks Dick-a-Dick, equally incredulous.

There follows another steady silence, before Sundown shakes his head. 'Him London.'

Dick-a-Dick whistles, and shifts his weight to settle on the opposite hip. He runs fingers through his thick hair, almost seeming to drag his brow up with them. Gloomy Sundown starts, very quietly, to cry.

One of the others approaches, to see what is the matter. Dick-a-Dick shrugs. He relates the news in their *Jardwa* tongue. No one asks when Sundown thinks his clan brother will return. His silent tears speak for him.

Where King Cole has gone, he isn't coming back.

II

Martyrdom

CHAPTER XXIV
Tuesday the 2nd of June, 1868

A NEW WORLD

'Our birth is but a sleep and a forgetting:
The Soul that rises with us, our life's Star,
Hath had elsewhere its setting,
And cometh from afar'

~ William Wordsworth,
'Ode: Intimations of Immortality'

At first, there was only the void.

Then, hard to place, faint sound, growing steadily louder – the clatter and churn of carriage wheels beyond number, a newsboy's hoarse cries.

Sarah Larkin awoke with a start. Her sleep had been deep, and apparently dreamless. All the same she felt dizzy, somewhat light-headed, as though woken from dream after all. Still for a few minutes longer, she listened to the world outside, and wondered at what she might have missed.

She recalled with relish her adventures the day before. A whole day spent in crossing the city, in spite of which she had returned home feeling energised. Sarah thought amiably of King Cole, her erstwhile companion. His skin; gestures more eloquent than words; and the great black pupils of his eyes – she had met with an Australian Aborigine!

Upward and onward! It was early but she rose anyway, keen to get on. Her neck felt stiff, and, suffering a little gastric discomfort, she summoned a delicate belch. Better.

Sarah noticed splashes on her shoes where they lay beneath the dresser. They were encrusted with shapes of clay – mud from the burial mound. Taking them to the sink, she began to wash them, gently. It would not do to scrub: this pair would have to last. She doused them with cold water, rubbing at the stains with her fingers.

The wet brown leather glistened.

Seeing her face in the mirror, she gasped then laughed. Nose and cheeks smudged with great smears of soot, she looked as chequered as St Paul's. Her unwitting fingers must have done that dirty work on feeling the black snow settle.

There, good as new.

She propped the shoes up to dry, and went to heat water for a bath.

'"In the beginning was the Word, and the Word was with God, and the Word was God."'

As Sarah gathered together a breakfast tray, she heard the rich bell tones ring out from overhead. Mounting the stair, she gave thanks that her father's speaking voice should sound so fiery, so strong. Invoking awe of heaven as surely as threat of hellfire, it still had the capacity to scare her a little – delightfully so.

'"The same was in the beginning with God. All things were made by him, and without him was not any thing made that was made."'

As she entered his room, knowing how it would please him, Sarah supplied the rejoinder.

'"In him was life, and the life was the light of men,"' she said. 'You look well this morning, and sound better!'

Lambert Larkin sat up in bed, as craggy and grey as a mountain. His open mouth widened into a rare smile.

'Amen,' he said. 'And all the better for seeing you, my dear.'

Sarah placed the tray and the morning's papers at her father's bedside, needing first to move a few of the large books piled there: various volumes of Thomas Carlyle's monumental *Works*, and Lambert's beloved Kingsley. Down with the lamb and up with the lark; plainly, he had been busy for some hours already.

Eyes askance, Lambert watched her as she worked. He pulled another quote.

'"All the seeds of yesteryear",' he said, '"are today, flowers."'

'Or weeds,' Sarah said. She curtsied.

The shadow of doubt crossed the old man's face. Almost immediately he noticed the change in her. His smile died a little.

She noted the candle, burnt completely out, and feared he had not slept the night at all.

'Here,' said Sarah. 'I brought you some lighter reading.' She presented fresh copies of the *Daily Telegraph* and *The Times*, the journals he best favoured.

'You will be going to the library today?' he asked – flatly, as if it were a matter of course.

'I shall,' she said.

But not for his sake, not today – rather, on King Cole's behalf, perhaps even her own.

'Stay a little,' he said, 'and read with me, daughter.'

It was not framed as a request. She hesitated.

'If you would be so kind,' Lambert added.

His voice warbled a little. Faltering, he concluded with a pathetic little cough.
'A little while, then,' she conceded.

They sat in silence. In perusal of the morning papers, he ate the breakfast she had prepared for him. Lambert reached over to turn a page. Below the sleeve, rolled up so as not to trail across his plate, the snow-white cap of his elbow appeared cracked and flaking, the inside of his forearm almost translucent, blue tracks and exposed sinew working within. In between the ferrying of mouthfuls he laid down his fork, and rasped together the tips of his thumb and index finger. Lightly pressed, the powder-dry digits circled first one way, then the other – a habitual, ruminant action. The persistent scrape could infuriate if she let it.

Unable to finish, he broke his leftovers into pieces.

'Scatter these crumbs on the sill for me,' he directed.

Watchful not to dislodge the windowbox, Sarah did as she was told. She noticed that some of the plant stems carried dead leaves, and crisply removed them.

'"To cultivate a garden",' he said from the bed, '"is to walk with God."'

Sarah smiled to herself: that was the voice of her father, all right. As a church minister he liked to keep abreast of every topical debate, but his choicest philosophy embodied all of the theory sufficient to a sundial.

Lambert looked suddenly morose.

'I miss having a garden,' he said.

In Greenwich Royal Park, at the tip of a slope not far from the Eastern Gate, towers an ancient oak. No other tree in London is so huge.

In the final stages of its decline, age has hollowed out the great giant. From the upper reaches of that wooden crater where he has spent the night, King Cole emerges. Face creased with sleep, he looks down from his perch into the unexpected interior. His expression distorts with a mounting horror. The morning skies are cloudy yet luminous. By their spectral light he is witness to acts of desecration.

Instead of standing tall, the grandfather tree staggers. Out of his side a doorway has been carved. Rough innards worn smooth, the earth below is tiled over, and there is a table, placed at the centre of the dying tree.

Appalled, King Cole descends and quits the scene.

'I'm so bored with the Abyssinian Expedition!'

Lambert Larkin snatched across the pages of his newspaper. He held it rudely, like a screen, entirely obscuring Sarah's view of him.

How typical – demanding of her company only to ignore her.

'Who, to entice me, with more ease
To cross the room and reach his knees
Held plums in sight, his child to please?
MY FATHER.'

Recalling verses from William Cole's *The Parent's Poetical Present*, Sarah recognised little in them concerning her own upbringing. The threat of punishment had always been much more Lambert's style. 'Do not rush, child. It is sufficient to proceed at a walking pace.' That, an admonition occasioned by the breaking of an ornament, had been about his only direct address of her in childhood.

Always there had been a hardness of shell between them, quite impossible to penetrate, she never certain it was not her fault. Neither their temperaments nor intellects matched. Beyond the texts she was obliged to transcribe for him, they did not even read the same books.

Her mother's death had been so abrupt, so unexpected. One evening she was alive, the next morning, dead. Ever since that evil hour, Lambert's very gradual decline made his own passing an eventuality that no longer seemed quite real. Over time, they had established separate routines whereby he, at least, could affect self-sufficiency. Sarah counted her blessings, even on the one hand: without the Museum library so close by, she would have been entombed in that house.

Their single shared enthusiasm was for *The Illustrated London News*. Saturday mornings would normally be spent *à deux*, poring over the latest issue and supplying a running commentary. Only after noon – weekend opening hours at the Museum – could she resume her duties following a morning 'off'. A thin patch of common ground, to be sure, but sometimes it could be made to last out the week.

With this in mind, perhaps, or as some perverse show of favour, Lambert had retrieved the last weekend's edition from the bottom of the pile. He no doubt saw entirely different virtues within its pages, but without the evidence of the newspaper's many engravings Sarah might have doubted the larger world existed at all. She could read there about the galas and gatherings, the theatre shows, gallery openings and lectures, and stare long and hard at picture representations of faraway lands…places and events she would never see for herself.

Sarah studied the ornamental logo on the front page as it was presented to her, almost as if truly seeing it for the very first time. A part of the design depicted the annual Oxford and Cambridge boat race along the River Thames. The shining dome of St Paul's Cathedral, transcendent, speared the heading with splendour. A block of waterfront buildings marked out the foreground: warehouses in deep contrasting shadow, likely under a cloud.

Lambert stabbed a finger at the open page, startling Sarah from her reverie. She took it up.

'You want this?' she asked. '*Nocturne for Piano, "A Dream of Enchantment"*?' He had pointed to a list of adverts under the heading 'New Music'.

'Nooo,' he scowled.

Sarah stared at the page. 'Which?'

Impatiently, he snatched the paper back.

'Just tell me,' she pleaded.

'The book they are advertising, by a Dr Doran,' he said, scribbling out a note. 'I want you to fetch me a copy.' Waving it a second or two in the air to dry, he thrust the inked scrap into her hand. 'Vain fantasy,' he muttered.

Sarah looked down at an unsteady scrawl that few could hope to decipher. The book she wanted to search out was another entirely, yet this presented the perfect excuse for her to leave.

'Abyssinians,' Lambert rattled on. '*Pchah*! Sinners from the abyss! Sin the very fulcrum to their name!' He wrestled the oversized pages about. 'First the Indians,' he said, 'then the Negroes and Jamaicans…abysmal beasts, all of them. They deserve what's coming!'

His eyes, having clouded over a little, just as suddenly cleared. 'Oh,' he said, 'Sarah.' He looked at her, seated by his bedside, as if unsure of time or space. 'My dearest lily! Forgive me…I'm tired. I think I shall take a nap.'

Despite his outburst, Sarah was more annoyed at herself. She had lost yet another chance to assert herself, by leaving of her own accord.

She was always free to go; it remained within his power alone to release her.

Quitting the house, Sarah half-expected to find King Cole waiting on her doorstep. She was disappointed to find that he wasn't.

The sky was low, the cloud dense, the air thick. Just a day like any other. She turned and walked the short distance down the street to the British Museum. Passing into the entrance hall, she headed directly towards the Reading-room, fumbling in her purse to find the small pink card that was her means of entry.

NOT TRANSFERABLE.

THIS TICKET ADMITS

Sarah Larkin

_____

TO THE **READING ROOM** OF THE

BRITISH MUSEUM,

FOR THE TERM OF SIX MONTHS

From the *26th* day of *March* 18 *68*

Appended on the reverse were a few rules and regulations she knew by heart.

The Ordinary Reading-ticket, once a cumbersome and inconvenient full-sheet affair, had been much reduced in size. Sarah was presented her first on turning 21, as if it were the keys to the kingdom. Little did she realise, then, how the lock would be turned behind her.

Looking at her card, noting her name down in the register, the attendant allowed her to pass. Sarah left her coat in the ladies' cloak-room and her brolly in the umbrella-room, making use of the water-closet before proceeding into the main Salon.

The distinctive odour of the Reading-room greeted her at once – leather and cork-carpet. The floor covering, chosen for its sound-absorbing properties, was kamptulicon, that peculiar compound of rubber, cork and gutta-percha, a greyish rubber-like substance obtained from the sap of various Malayan trees. The elastic composition made it exceedingly pleasant to walk on.

Thirty-five tables – nineteen long, and sixteen short – converged towards the centre of the Reading-room, all covered with splendid black-japanned leather. Two on the near inside, designated A and T, were exclusively reserved for the use of lady-readers: hassocks, cushions for kneeling as found in church pews, being provided to accommodate the voluminous skirts *à la mode*. Sarah exercised the feminine privilege of taking a seat wherever she pleased. She selected a suitable vacancy, one located an agreeable distance from her nearest neighbour, made a mental note of it, and went to consult the New General Catalogue of printed books. This was stored amongst the semi-circular desks that made up the centrepiece to the room, a diminishing ring of three concentric circles.

The smallest, innermost stand, its floor raised, enclosed a space apportioned to the superintendent of the room, and his immediate staff. The attachment of a glass-enclosed avenue, up and down which the attendant clerks ran their errands, widened as it extended from this mid-point. Seen from above, the arrangement might suggest a giant keyhole, the readers' tables radiating outwards like a spider's web.

A pair of novice members, newly constituted, stood adhered to the spot. They seemed at a loss, bewildered by the complexity of the arrangement, the great arcs and galleries of books that lined the expansive and airy dome.

Sarah, shy and concentrated, was inclined to keep her head down. She walked around the outermost of the central bars, renewing acquaintance with its banks of red and blue catalogues, their several titles arranged under general headings – *Academies* – *Bible* – *England* – *Shakspere* (sic).

Handwritten slips, pasted-down, filled the pages of these bound volumes. Sarah soon found various entries under 'Bruce' or 'Greenwich Pensioner' that promised much. She followed a cross-reference leading to a garland, chasing it down in that forest of dark-green binding housing the *Music* catalogue. Satisfied, she at last proceeded to the very centre of the room, where she filled out a pre-printed form for each item, before depositing them with one of the clerks at their raised desk.

'A-5?'

'E-3.'

The clerk looked up. 'Fancied a change today, did you?' he said.

'Yes,' said Sarah. 'Thank you, Mr Baynes.'

The junior assistant retreated up the avenue behind the glass screens and disappeared through one of the two small doors at the north end of the Reading-room. These led to the old libraries of the Museum, quite closed to the public, where most of the request materials were stored.

With time to kill, Sarah turned her attention to the open presses that lined the Reading-room walls. Divided into sixteen distinct classes – *Law, Philosophy, Fine Arts*, and so on – these could be accessed by readers *ad libitum*, without the trouble of writing out requests. She concentrated her efforts on *Biography*, and then *Geography, Voyages, & Travels*, but without significant result. Having made reference to ordinary or standard works, she rambled freely for a bit. Often, one simply fell across the very thing, even when unsure what it might exactly be. No such luck this time.

There was little else she could do except wait.

The horizon always hangs too close. One after another, bloated shapes crawl over it – enormous monsters made of metal or wood, crushing stone giants bearing relentlessly down on him. Soot-caked, they are indistinguishable one from the next.

King Cole's frustration mounts. The city, vast and timeless, is unremitting, beyond reason. It has no end and no beginning. Unless he forever remains atop One Tree Hill, he fears he will never again see more than a few hundred paces ahead.

Without the Guardian tripping along beside in her formidable female armour, he is no longer obliged to moderate his pace. Cole strides out.

About 45 minutes following her submission, the first of the requested materials was delivered to Sarah's desk.

'Thank you, Mr Tate,' she said. Sarah made a point of remembering everyone's names, and using them; the favour was not often returned.

She turned the small octavo booklet over in her hand. A disappointingly familiar object, it was a compilation of religious tracts. The paper quality was poor – coarse, chipped with flecks of wood pulp, and frail to the touch. The original publications, taken individually, would have been short pamphlets: cheaply printed, mass-distributed, designed to be given out on the street – an antidote to the proliferation of penny-bloods. Copies might be left atop inn tables to instruct travellers strayed from the path, or to catch dissolute drinkers in an impressionable frame, and remind them of the error of their ways. For 'wide *is* the gate, and broad the way, which leadeth unto destruction', and 'strait *is* the gate, and narrow *is* the way, which leadeth unto life' (*Matthew* 7: 12–15).

This looked to be a set of twelve chapbooks written by Robert Hawker, the famous pulpit orator, and grandfather to Robert Stephen Hawker, the poet-vicar of Morwenstow popularly known as 'the Sailor's Friend'. The publication date given was 1806. In intervening years, the method and means of wayside proselytising had changed very little.

As she flicked back and forth through its pages, a portion of the book's brittle back broke away. Sarah felt frustrated. This was not the book she sought, merely a general commentary of some sort, unconnected to George Bruce. Still, she located the frontispiece to the second entry, and began to read.

> *No.XX. The GREENWICH PENSIONER:*
> *Being An Earnest and an Affectionate Address,*
> *Proposed to the Serious Consideration of many of*
> *That Brave Body of Seamen Which Belong to the*
> *ROYAL HOSPITAL at GREENWICH.*

The title page featured a simple engraving, such as one might find in a children's storybook, of a sailor-Pensioner, resplendent in tricorne hat and greatcoat. A singular fellow – one-armed, one-legged, one-eyed – he tottered unsteadily, walking stick clutched in his remaining hand. Sketchily indicated behind, evoking Greenwich Hospital, were the twin domes Sarah had admired the day before.

The document might have some bearing after all. She read on.

Prefatory remarks sang the praises of both the Royal Navy and its 'noble Institution', sentiments that conjured the charmless face of the clerk, Dilkes Loveless. Reading through, she could almost hear them expressed in that whining voice of his.

Then, before her eyes, the address transformed into something else, an accusation of drunkenness against the 'Greenwich Pensioner' of the title: 'the prosecution of a path so evil' that the author ventured to present an extract from *The Sailor Pilgrim*, a small work, lately fallen in his way, on the subject of intemperance. But of course, Robert Hawker was not about to address the worthy Pensioners other than to berate them for their sins. She had seen and heard more than enough sermons on the evils of the demon drink in her time, and from far less estimable sources. Sarah lent the remainder but a cursory glance.

She thought it a shame King Cole could not see for himself the engraving of the wobble-legged Pensioner – his instability, as she now understood it, attributable to more than the sum of his missing parts. Whilst rambling the colonnades, the Aborigine had described just such a person, mimicked him even, right down to the antiquated mode of dress; a level of detail he couldn't possibly have witnessed first-hand.

As to the character of their mystery man George Bruce, she entertained no ideas. He might well have been the kind of drunken sailor who could fall intemperate, and in Robert Hawker's way. This particular 'Greenwich Pensioner', however, probably held little significance for her Aboriginal friend.

In case her father should ever wish her to compile another sermon on the subject of intemperance, one of his very favourite hobbyhorses, it would, however, be wise for her to summarise the text. Sarah slid one of the supplied blotters under a crisp new sheet of paper and took up her steel pen. Scribbling notes with skilful speed, she had made significant inroads on *The Sailor Pilgrim* itself by the time another of her request items arrived.

It was a small, pocket-sized volume, another collation of popular printed circulars dated *circa* 1800, the pages very grey and semi-transparent – *A Garland of New Songs*. Beneath the list of contents, and registered very poorly, was another jolly little engraving, this time of a galleon tossed on the high seas.

The very last entry accredited a song called 'The Greenwich Pensioner'.

> ''Twas in the good ship Rover,
> I sailed the world around,
> And for three years and over,
> I ne'er touched British Ground;
> At length in England landed,
> I left the roaring main,
> Found all relations stranded,
> And went to sea again.'

These must be the lyrics as written by Charles Dibdin. Recalling how King Cole had been drawn to that strange and empty room within the Hospital, containing his bust, Sarah felt moved to transcribe them.

> 'That time bound straight to Portugal,
> Right fore and aft we bore,
> But when we made Cape Ortugal,
> A gale blew off the shore;
> She lay, so did it shock her,
> A log upon the main,
> Till, sav'd from Davy's locker,
> We put to sea again.

'Next in a frigate failing,
Upon a squally night,
Thunder and lightning hailing,
The horrors of the fight,
My precious limb was lopp'd off,
I, when they eased my pain,
Thank'd God I was not popp'd off,
But went to sea again.

'Yet still I am enabled
To bring up in life's rear,
Although I'm quite disabled,
And lie in Greenwich tier;
The King, God bless his royalty,
Who sav'd me from the main,
I'll praise with love and loyalty;
But ne'er to sea again.'

Sarah could only guess at how faithfully this bittersweet song represented the sort of men who put to sea to serve their country, adventurers who saw so many wonders, yet suffered so much.

Another attendant interrupted her labours.

'Th-thank you, Mr…'

Too late – whoever it was had already stolen away.

She held in her palm an unremarkable bound volume, blandly designated *Tracts*. Sarah nevertheless became faintly light-headed. Promptly she forgot every other item pending on her desk.

'*BRUCE, George, of Ratcliff-highway, London. Memoirs of Mr. George Bruce, of Ratcliff-highway, London, naturalized New Zealander, &c.*'

The catalogue entry had included the right name, but other details had made it seem an unlikely match for the text she hoped for. The publication date of 1810 fell too early by a decade: George Bruce had been admitted to the Hospital in 1817, and died there in 1819. The total document was only sixteen pages long; too little for a *Life*, surely. And the mention of New Zealand had thrown her.

'*Born: Shadwell*', Bruce's Hospital records had stated. Ratcliff-highway was in Shadwell.

Could it be?

She leafed through the yellowed pages urgently.

MEMOIRS

OF

Mr. GEORGE BRUCE

OF

Ratcliff-highway, London,

NATURALIZED NEW ZEALANDER,

AND

HUSBAND TO THE LATE PRINCESS AETOCKOE,

Youngest Daughter of

TIPPAHEE,

KING OF NEW ZEALAND.

LONDON :

Printed by T. PLUMMER, Seething Lane, Tower-street

Sarah began to read.

I was born in Ratcliff-highway, in 1779…

Keen though she was, her responsibility towards King Cole took precedence: she would rather not face him again empty-handed. She returned to the beginning, transcribing the *Memoirs* even as she read through them. So much time had already gone by: Sarah soon realised she would not be able to complete it all before the close of day. The library stayed open until 6pm, but her personal deadline loomed closer. She could not very well leave her father unattended, not two entire days in a row. At the very least his suspicions might be aroused, that Mary, the servant girl, was no longer with them.

'REQUESTS FOR MATERIAL TO BE DELIVERED TODAY,' announced a booming voice, 'MUST BE MADE IN THE NEXT FIFTEEN MINUTES.'

The appointed hour came and went. Sarah's furrowed brow broke out in a light dew of perspiration. She had got as far page eight – exactly halfway. Flicking ahead very quickly, she noted some ominous-looking verse in bold type. No time, no time.

With a last stab of the pen she completed her closing sentence, and at the risk of smudging the latest page of notes began immediately to pack away her papers. She carried the various books to the central dais.

'Do you wish for any of these books to be reserved,' enquired the clerk, 'or are you returning them?'

'Yes,' said Sarah. 'Oh, except for that one!'

Sarah pointed to the *Tracts*. The book containing the *Memoirs* she very much intended to recover the next morning.

The clerk held the book aside from the others, as she had done. 'This one?' he said.

She saw that he held up the right book.

'Mmm, yes,' she said.

So scattered were her thoughts that Sarah entirely forgot to thank the attendant. They parted in a flurry of nods and smiles, semi-automatic on her part.

What a day for false starts! Still, she had transcribed a fair amount from the varying materials, and believed herself to have gathered something useful. A pearl of wisdom for her very own sundial: 'It is the search that teaches, not the finding.'

Even if this curious memoir was not George Bruce's purported *Life*, it seemed more than likely that she had found their man.

Home again, and with no sign of Cole, Sarah checked in on Lambert. His interest only extended to an enquiry about dinner. Dinner was duly prepared and served.

As evening fell she lit the lamps, and changed clothes. The paved backyard housed an outside toilet for the use of Dr Epps' patients, a rainwater barrel, and a coal-bunker. Loading the scuttle, Sarah struggled up the stairs with it, and into their various rooms. After filling the fireplace in the front room she heaved the cast-iron grate back into place, readjusted the hearthrug, and gave the white marble surround and the floor-level fender a quick polish. She did the same in Lambert's room, and thankfully he offered no direction.

She wiped down the tilework in the halls, stairways and kitchen, but decided to leave the cleaning of the rooms until before breakfast. Too much activity at once would only draw attention to the fact that she discharged all domestic duties herself.

The first of the servants to go had been her governess, then the cook, and finally their housemaid. Without even a daily girl to help out, Sarah was more than ever the lady of the house. Despite her own straits, she felt more conscious of having crossed a line in failing to provide employment.

She proceeded to shut the house up for the night, pulling across the thick outer and lace inner curtains, sealing out the world and cosying the interior as best she could.

Nine o'clock came and went, and still no sign of Cole, though she listened out ever so carefully for his knocking at the front door. They had parted the previous day in such disarray that she had not even thought to enquire where he was staying, or how she might contact him again, should he not reappear. Perhaps she had spent the whole day on a wild-goose chase after all – a Greenwich Goose! She noticed the framed map of London, still laid out on the table in the front room, and resolved to put it back up – just as soon forgetting to do so. Bruce's story and the question of what it might mean preoccupied her thoughts.

She read a little of nothing to her father until he drifted off into sleep, and then, extinguishing the lights room by room, repaired to her own chambers to read a little more herself. Sarah felt saddened that King Cole had not come, and wondered where he might be. She recalled him on their step, in his distressed state. Knowing London's reputation, she even worried a little after his safety.

They hadn't made any explicit arrangement. Not out loud…

Preparing to retire, Sarah attended to a few night-time ablutions. Looking into the mirror and combing out her hair, she suddenly noticed her shoes again: not the old buckle shoes she had settled on for the library, but the pair cleaned that morning and left out to dry. They stared at her most accusingly. She turned to take a closer look. In rough spurts, speckles and chalky white arabesques, the clay chalk splash-marks had returned – or rather, bothersome phantoms, they persisted. Taking the shoes to the water-bowl, she once again began to scrub, much more forcefully than before. Feeling not unlike Lady Macbeth, Sarah worked hard to remove all trace of the stain that, lest she forget, she had picked up sliding around on an anonymous grave.

She was still very wide awake and, truly, not quite herself – as if in a dream state.

A sudden tap at her window made her spin around, spraying water in a wide arc. Her heart fairly leapt into her mouth. On the other side of the glass, pantherish on the slim sill, crouched King Cole.

What on earth?

She slid the catch aside to let him in, as readily as one would admit a dove into the cote, and he knelt, panting, beside her. He was inside the house before it even registered – they were four storeys up from the street!

His clothing, presumably that same outfit as worn the day before, was even more ragged and filthy, his feet again bare. Where her father's shoes had got to, heaven only knew.

'H-how…?' she spluttered.

Questions still forming on her lips, Sarah saw that he was bleeding. His left trouser leg was ripped open, his exposed knee as well as his hands raw with cuts – from scaling the building?

She led him to the water-bowl, ready to soak and treat his wounds, only to realise the clouded water was filled with dirt. They met in her bedchamber, and she clad only in her nightdress: the peril of her situation for the moment escaped her. Pressing one cautious finger to her lips, she briskly passed him the bowl, took up the candle-lamp, and led her obedient intruder around the narrow twist of the top stairs, along the lower landing past her father's door, and down another flight to the kitchen.

King Cole is already familiar with the layout of the house, all the rooms looking to him much the same. An Aboriginal habit, or tactic, is to gather intelligence – whether concerning a place, person, or animal – through prolonged observation, remaining oneself hidden. Prior to his appearance tapping at the window, he has spied on the Guardian for some hours from the rooftops opposite. Selecting various different vantage points, he has observed her movements about the crowded house with a keen interest, she tripping up and down the stairs between perches like a bird in a cage.

Cole follows Thara now, as they walk together down the stairs. He wonders, silently, at the tumbling cascade of her loosened hair. How subtly the abundant silver threads reflect the delicate light of night.

They stood pressed close together beside the kitchen sink.

His strong brown hands, once cleaned, showed little more than a criss-cross of minor scratches, but the wound across his knee required that Sarah staunch and dress it. The gash was nasty, and yet he bled only a little – thin blood, more like red water. She expected his skin must be thick, to be so swarthy, yet his prominent veins beat with the strongest pulse. He was all visible life and energy. Although slight in the body, Cole was put together admirably well. He carried no lumber, as the delightful phrase went.

To work by the lamp's dim light, Sarah was obliged to stoop her head. Dabbing with the cloth at his bare black flesh, she was careful to avoid any direct sort of contact, or to press a second longer than was strictly necessary – taking equal care not to appear overly reticent about it. She could not look him in the face till it was done.

All this they achieved in near total silence. His eyes glittered all the thanks she needed. But no, in fact, she required more.

'Most of their names are polysyllabic,' Saturday's edition of *The Field* had reported, 'and not very euphonious. In order, therefore, to meet the exigencies of the times, each man has adopted a sobriquet under which he will doubtlessly be recognised in this country.'

Sarah rather doubted the Australian natives themselves had anything to do with their summary Anglicisation, or the choice of simple, slang names. She was finding it almost impossible to address King Cole directly – by that title, at least: to refer to him in nursery rhyme surely trivialised his person, and mocked his truer identity.

He stood back and flexed, showing appreciation for her handiwork.

She folded over the bloodied cloth in her hand, and regarded him directly.

'If you would be so kind,' Sarah said, 'tell me your real name. I am sure that I should try and pronounce it carefully, if not so very correctly.'

She only wished to spare him, as well as herself, further embarrassment.

'*Bripumyarrimin,*' he said, without hesitation.

Oh, dear.

Floundering somewhat, she tried a different tack. 'Do you mind very much being called King Cole?' she asked.

'*Bripumyarrimin!*'

He all but shouted it out. Valiantly, Sarah tried to get her English tongue around the Aboriginal word. The undertaking was tortuous.

His black eyes twinkled a moment or two before he let her off the hook she had so earnestly swallowed.

'Best you call it Brippoki,' he said.

'Brip…Brip-okay.'

'Brippoki.'

Another attempt and she got it. 'Brippoki,' she said.

Brippoki – formerly King Cole – exulted. '*Brrrrrrrrrrrrrrrrrrr!*'

The labio-palatal sound, produced by the rapid vibration of his tongue, surprised her. Sarah's delighted squeal filled the modest kitchenette – more joy than it had contained in over a decade. She clapped a hand across her open mouth and instantly went quiet. Her eyes bulged, a brief snort escaping between her fingers.

Brippoki beamed.

His teeth were very regular, perfect in fact, even if the rest of his features were not so terribly attractive. His dark face shone from within: and it was inner beauty that impressed her the most.

Sarah instructed him to wait in the parlour, where it was more appropriate to receive guests. She lit a paraffin table lamp, and a couple of the gas-lights along the inner wall, in preference to the five glass shades of the central gasolier.

When Sarah returned she had dressed again. She brought with her an old pair of her father's trousers, indicating that he should change out of his own; stopping short, however, of offering to repair the damage with needle and thread. Stepping out to allow him privacy, she returned shortly after with a knock at the door and full tray of tea. In case he should be hungry, she had brought him the leftovers of their evening meal. Brippoki was required to hold the trousers up at the waist. Sarah went to fetch a belt.

Once sure that he was comfortable, and giving only the briefest outline of her day by way of an introduction, Sarah sat by the light barely illuminating her half of the room, and produced her notebook. She knew very well what he had come for: a reading of her transcript regarding George Bruce, the Greenwich Pensioner. She prevaricated slightly, more out of politeness than anything.

'I cannot,' she said, 'declare with absolute certainty these are the words of the same man, the fellow as described to us yesterday at Greenwich…'

Brippoki nodded and gave his congratulations, instilling her with his every confidence. 'You pindim, eh, dat pella,' he said.

'I'm rather hoping *you* might be able to confirm that, one way or the other, once you have heard what I'm about to read out. What I can say is that it is a most remarkable story, although many details may, unfortunately, be rendered unremarkable by my narration.'

Brippoki looked faintly exasperated.

'I should begin?' she said. 'Very well…'

CHAPTER XXV
Tuesday the 2nd of June, 1868

DISTANT VOICES, STILL LIVES

'How death-cold is literary genius before this fire of life!'

~ Ralph Waldo Emerson, 'Character'

Sarah began to read.

> I was born in Ratcliff-highway, in 1779, of creditable parents, who bestowed on me a liberal education. My father was at this period clerk to Mr Wood, distiller, Limehouse. In 1789, I entered on board the *Royal Admiral*, East-Indiaman, Captain Bond, as boatswain's boy. Sailed from England for New South Wales, and arrived at Port Jackson in 1790, where, with the consent of Captain Bond, I quitted the ship, and remained at New South Wales.
>
> At Port Jackson, I entered into the naval colonial service, and was employed for several years under Lieutenants Robbins, Flinders and others, in exploring the coasts, surveying harbours, head lands, rocks, &c. I was lastly turned over to the *Lady Nelson*, Captain Simmonds, a vessel fitted up for the express purpose of conveying Tippahee, king of New Zealand, from a visit which he made to the government at Port Jackson, to his own country.

'*Rangatira.*'

'What was that?' Sarah asked. Brippoki had suddenly spoken. 'Ranga…?'

'*Rangatira,*' he said again, and nodded approvingly.

'*Ranga-tee-ra,*' repeated Sarah. 'What does that mean?'

He made a waving motion with his hand, and then splayed fingers behind his head, as if to show a crown. '*Rangatira,*' he said again.

'You mean the king?' she asked. 'You mean Tippahee?'

What else was a crown, but a hat with a hole in?

Presuming it a word in Cole's, Brippoki's, own language, Sarah continued with her reading.

> The king embarked, and the *Lady Nelson* sailed on her destination. During the passage, Tippahee was taken dangerously ill, when I was appointed to attend him. I acquitted myself so highly to the king's satisfaction, that I was honoured

with his special favour, and on our arrival, the king requested that I should be allowed to remain with him at New Zealand, to which Captain Simmonds consented, and I was received into the family of Tippahee, where every effort was used to instruct me in the language, customs, &c. of the inhabitants.

Being very circumspect in my conduct from an early habit, I was fully determined to persevere in acquiring the knowledge prescribed by my patrons. I accordingly communicated to Tippahee my wish to travel to the country, with a view to become completely acquainted with its local situation, languages, and the customs of the Inhabitants. Tippahee, with the greatest cordiality, acquiesced to my proposal, and added that his son Pouver should accompany me; we accordingly proceeded on our journey, which we continued for seven months.

I found the country healthy and pleasant, full of romantic scenery, agreeably diversified by hills, dales, and covered with wood; the people were hospitable, frank and open, though rude and ignorant, yet worshipping neither images nor idols, nor aught that is the work of human hands, acknowledging one Omnipotent Supreme Being.

Sarah paused, ostensibly to make a note in the margin. She looked the Aborigine over. He calmly returned her gaze. She read on.

On my return from making the tour of the country, Tippahee proposed to place me at the head of his army, and invest me with every authority of which he was himself possessed; this proposal was sanctioned in one voice by nineteen of the principal chiefs. It was however necessary that, prior to my taking the command, I should undergo the ceremony of being tatoow'd, without which I could not be regarded as a warrior: the case was urgent, and admitted of no alternative. I therefore submitted resolutely to the painful ceremony, my countenance presenting a masterly specimen of this art.

The Hospital clerk had said of Bruce, 'His face was horribly disfigured.'

Being now tatoow'd in due form, I was recognised as a warrior of the first rank, naturalised as a New Zealander, received into the bosom of the king's family, and honoured with the hand of the Princess Aetockoe, the youngest daughter of Tippahee, a maiden of fifteen years of age, whose native beauty had probably been great, but which had been much improved by the fashionable embellishments of art, that all the softer charms of nature, all the sweetness of original expression, are lost in the bolder impressions of tatoowing.

I now became the chief member of the king's family, and was vested with the government of the island. Six or eight months after my marriage, the English ships *Inspector*, *Ferret*, a South Sea whaler, and several other English vessels, touched at New Zealand for supplies, all of whom found the beneficial influence of having a countryman and friend at the head of affairs in that island; they were liberally supplied with fish, vegetables, &c. &c.

I and my amiable consort were now contented and happy, in the full enjoyment of domestic comfort, with no wants that were ungratified; blessed with health and perfect independence, I looked forward with satisfaction to the progress of civilisation which I expected to introduce among the people, with whom, by a singular destiny, I seemed doom'd to remain during life. While enjoying these hopes, the ship *General Wellesley*, Captain Dalrymple, touched at a point of New Zealand where I and my consort then chanced to be. This was some distance from the king's residence. Captain Dalrymple applied to me, with a view to assist him in procuring a cargo of spars and benjamin, and requested specimens of the principal articles of produce of the island, all which was cheerfully done.

Captain Dalrymple then proposed, that I should accompany him to North Cape, about 25 or 30 leagues, where it was reported that gold dust could be procured, Captain D. conceiving that I might prove useful to him in the search for gold dust.

With great reluctance, and after many entreaties, I consented to accompany Captain D. under the most solemn and repeated assurances of Captain D. that he would, at every hazard, re-land us at the Bay of Islands, the place at which we embarked. Being at length all on board, the *Wellesley* sailed for the North Cape, where we soon arrived and landed. Finding that we entirely had been misinformed as to the gold dust, the *Wellesley* made sail, in order to return to New Zealand, but the wind becoming foul, and continuing so for 48 hours, we were driven from the island.

On the third day the wind became more favourable, but Captain D. did not attempt to regain the island, but stood on for India. I now gently remonstrated, and reminded him of his promises; to which Captain D. replied 'that he had something else to think of, than to detain the ship, by returning with a valuable cargo to the island; besides, he had another and a better island in view for me'.

On reaching the Feegee, or Sandal Wood Islands, Captain D. asked me if I chose to go on shore, and remain there, which I declined, on account of the barbarous and sanguinary disposition of their inhabitants. Captain D. desired that I would choose for myself, and then took from me several little presents, which he himself and his officers had given to me at New Zealand; these were now given to the natives of the islands in the boats then alongside.

Leaving the Feegee Islands, we sailed for Malacca, where we arrived in December, 1808. At Malacca Captain D. and I went on shore; I was anxious to see the Governor, or commanding officer, to state my grievances; but it was late in the evening when we landed, and I could not see him till the following morning, by which time Captain D. had weighed from Malacca Roads, leaving me on shore, and carrying off my consort on board the *Wellesley*, to Penang.

I then acquainted the commanding officer at Malacca with the case, expressing my wish to regain my consort, and return with her to New Zealand. After waiting for three or four weeks, accounts were received of Captain D.'s arrival at Penang, upon which I obtained the commanding officer's permission, and left Malacca in the Scourge gun brig, for Penang, where, upon my arrival, I found that my consort had been bartered away to Captain Ross.

Kidnap, and worse! As far as she could tell from his sphinx-like composure, Brippoki was willing and able to follow the drama, even through such a tangle of names, dates and events. She cleared her throat.

On waiting on the Governor of Penang, I was asked what satisfaction I required for the ill treatment I had experienced. I answered that all I wanted was to have my consort restored, and, if possible, get a passage to New Zealand. Through the interference of the Governor, my consort was restored to me. With her I returned to Malacca, in hopes of the promised passage to New South Wales; but as there was no appearance of the expected ships to that port, I was now offered a passage for myself and my consort to England, in one of the homeward-bound Indiamen from China. By getting to England, I hoped from thence to find a passage to New South Wales, but I could not be accommodated with a passage to Europe, without the payment of 400 dollars. Not having that sum, nor the means of raising it, I came on with the *Sir Edward Pellew* to Bengal, where I and my consort, the affectionate companion of my distress, were most hospitably received, and where our hardships and long sufferings were forgot in the kindness we experienced.

Sarah turned the page.

'*Literary Panorama* for May, 1810.'

'The following passage is shown within quotation marks,' she explained, 'taken, I imagine, from the above-named document.'

'Aetockoe, the Princess of New Zealand, was presented on Monday, June 19 last, at the Government House, to the Right Honourable the Governor General. She was introduced by Governor Hayes, and was most courteously received. The Princess appeared slightly embarrassed at the first moment of introduction, but she soon recovered her usual ease and affability of manner. She has made such rapid progress in English, that she clearly comprehends whatever she hears in that language, and gives a distinct and intelligible answer in the same tongue. The dress of the Princess had a striking and shewy effect: it was formed of ribbons, and other materials, so as to resemble, as nearly as possible, the dresses of fine flaxen matts, and ornamental feathers of the ladies, of the highest quality in New Zealand. After a short audience, the Princess took leave of Lord Minto, highly gratified with her reception. Aetockoe is an interesting girl, of about 18 years of age, sensible, and far superior to what could have been expected in an unlettered native of New Zealand.

'The lady is of an interesting appearance, remarkably fair, – but her features rather of the Malay cast. Bruce is not much above 30: – he is completely tattooed, according to the custom of the Southern Islanders.'

The impartial tone did not accord with the remainder, suggesting a newspaper report, or similar. Portions only of the *Memoirs* rang heartfelt and true.

'I suspect,' declared Sarah, 'the hand of more than one author.'

Precedent aplenty existed among street literature such as this, often compiled from many sources. In truth, she wasn't sure what to make of it; for that, Sarah relied on Brippoki. She laid the papers down flat.

'And that, I'm afraid,' she said, 'is as far I was able to get today. *The Memoirs of Mr. George Bruce*…sounds like our man, wouldn't you say?'

He would not.

Feeling short-changed, Sarah shuffled her various papers. George Bruce – from Shadwell, one of London's poorest hamlets, a 'naturalized' prince of New Zealand – presented indeed a most singular destiny.

New Zealand, however, was not Australia.

'Why do you want to know about this man?' asked Sarah. Understanding well enough that Brippoki disliked direct questions, she saw no way around them. 'What is he to you?'

Apparently unable to look her in the eye, Brippoki just shrugged.

Sarah slapped her notebook shut. Whatever Bruce meant to the Aborigine remained unclear, yet the text or else her line of enquiry had taken effect – an effect too profound for him to entirely conceal. Seeing his hackles bristle, she demanded to know the reason.

Brippoki rolled his eyes by way of special pleading, or else as a warning: their whites flashed through the gloom in a lighthouse rotation.

'Red Ochre Men!' he gasped. He clamped a hand over his mouth. This was not simply a matter of mimicking her actions in the kitchen, but something far more serious.

Brippoki got up to leave.

Sarah understood the man to be terrified out of his wits. Mystified, somewhat taken aback, she felt all resentment instantly drain from her. It was gone midnight. Where could he go, at this time of night? She still had no idea of his lodgings. With Mary gone they had a spare room, but…

Instead of the door, he made for the window. He waited alongside, anxiously willing for her to open it. She moved to comply.

'London is so large,' she protested, ineffectually. 'To think of you out there, alone…'

Brippoki had hopped onto the sill, and crouched within the frame of the open window. He turned, the expression on his face unreadable.

'Not alone,' he said.

He leapt, disappearing into the dark. Sarah could not bring herself to look after him. She stood for a time, blinking, thinking to pinch herself, and then reached out to close the sash window.

She sealed the window-frame firmly shut. She would have to discourage such dramatic entrances and exits.

The notebook still in her hand, Sarah recovered her seat. She turned over the leaves of later pages. Bruce's adventure was leagues distant from that 'polite' literature suitable for a lady, fit for the drawing room, to be read aloud – and thankfully so.

The Princess Aetockoe.

Sarah yawned. She recovered a crumpled scrap of paper and smoothed it out – her note scribbled in the civic offices of the Royal Naval Hospital, Greenwich.

> *George Bruce.*
> *Age: 40.*
> *If married: no.*

A consort, yes – by English standards he was unmarried. And there was mention of a child, a daughter?

> *Girls: 1.*
> *Born: Shadwell.*
> *Last residence: Gloucester Court.*
> *Lost 2 fingers right hand.*

The relation of Bruce's *Memoirs* had badly shaken her visitor. She wished to make doubly certain of the man's identity. They had, at present, only half the story. Enough – she was overtired, bed calling.

Tattooed on the face. What must that look like?

The large framed map of London still lay on the occasional table. She took it up, carried it across the room, and restrung it to the nail on the far wall. Since taking the sleeve of her *blouson* to it, she barely recognised the old heirloom. The sickly and yellowish tinge erased, delicate lithographic hues refracted what little light reached them with a subtle brilliance she rather admired. Catching sight of her reflection in the glass, she noticed the heightened colour in her own cheeks.

'Read in book like whitefellow' – that had been his only instruction. She had little hope of understanding Brippoki, and yet she felt compelled to help. Unsure of his reasons, let alone hers, it was enough to know that he relied on her.

Sarah took the map down again. Keeping it hidden behind the opened door seemed too great a shame. She would seek out a new situation, somewhere more in the light.

CHAPTER XXVI
Wednesday the 3rd of June, 1868

LOST, AND FOUND

'Strange friend, past, present, and to be;
Loved deeplier, darklier understood;
Behold, I dream a dream of good,
And mingle all the world with thee.'

~ Alfred Lord Tennyson, *In Memoriam*

Sarah could not sleep.

Sailor. And princess.

Fingertips rasping on dry fibres. Queer fabric. Indefinite shapes.

Something nagged from the shadows of sense memory, something long lost; an emotional recall more than any specific event or action, close enough to touch, yet remaining just out of reach. The suggestion alone was enough to make her heart ache.

The sailor and the princess, rough paper held in her hand. Bright colours.

George Bruce's story provoked her on a level deeper than any she consciously understood. She had never before been acquainted with the text, she felt sure – and yet, somehow, she knew better. She had the feeling that she already knew the tale. How, then, and where?

Sarah churned in her bed, frustrated. Taking up her pillows, she turned them over, one, then the other, hoping for a cool side that might yet soothe her to sleep.

Eyes open, she stared into the blackness of night; eyes closed, into inner dark. Maybe if she went over it, one more time.

Brippoki. Brippoki had led her to a grave. According to records, the grave belonged to a sailor-Pensioner, one George Bruce. Brippoki appeared as mystified as she was, yet urged her to uncover his life story; the story of his *Life*.

The sailor. George Bruce.

According to the Naval clerk Dilkes Loveless, prior to his death George Bruce had presented the Hospital secretary with the book of his life story, a book entitled *The Life of a Greenwich Pensioner*. So far, she had been unable to trace a copy. There was, however, his *Memoirs*, and Sarah felt sure…

But wait a moment. All along, she had assumed that she was looking for an item in print. What if…? Of course! If the book had never been published, it would only exist as a manuscript. There might only be one copy.

Her heart sank even as it leapt: unearthing a single artefact presented that much greater a challenge. If it survived, there was of course no guarantee it would have found its way into the library collection of the British Museum. It could lurk almost anywhere. Even so, even so, a manuscript! Fool! The likelihood was much too great to have been so simply overlooked – Bruce's book, an unpublished manuscript!

Opening hour at the Museum could not come soon enough.

The princess.

Sarah imagined Aetockoe herself, floating directly overhead. Wearing a feathered headdress, she exactly resembled the Indian chieftainess from the Naval Hospital's painted ceiling.

Disappointed at such a limit to her imagination, Sarah Larkin finally slipped into unconsciousness.

Dawn, barely perceptible, threatens to break.

Brippoki hasn't slept in three days. Drawn as before towards the dread Well of Shadows, he resists the urge. Those parts of the city most familiar to his Dreaming are too filled with sadness. Instead, he lets the wind dictate direction.

He wanders beside London Docks. Next to the River Thames, the Great Serpent Himself, here alone he finds space for contemplation.

The huge, unnatural lakes stretch as far as the eye can see. From in amongst these trapped waters sprouts a forbidding forest, limitless, and petrified. A low wind whistles through the leafless black spars.

Stern brick formations rise to either side. Even so, the taller mastheads and yardarms overtop their roofs. This puzzle of angular rhythms mesmerises, yet makes Brippoki sad. The bolt uprightness of clay and wood betrays the hand of man, as do the squared sides of each deep lagoon. The curve and flow of natural forms is nowhere to be seen, nowhere a single natural growth, not plant, or living flower.

Played out in great long lines, the bowsprits stitch each ship to shore. Brippoki prefers them swamp and woods, as once they were.

In the empty early morning, amidst so much timber, the pungency of turpentine is almost overpowering. His keen nose is able to detect an underscore of subtler aromas: the welcome fragrance of coffee and spice, plus headier fumes of rum, tobacco, and rank, untanned hide.

Beneath Tobacco Warehouse, and the stacks of the South Quay, lurks a labyrinthine complex of stone cellars. From their unventilated depths, the fermentation of wine mingles with a fungal smell, the dry rot that coats their ceilings black.

Brippoki lingers over the threshold, at the lip. In the same instant that he is repulsed, he finds himself further attracted – just as it is with the city as a whole.

From east to west the wind switches direction, turning brisk. Brippoki puts his face into it. Progressing eastwards, he covers good ground, in that desolation before dawn. Only the occasional guard dog rouses itself as he pads past, to deliver a desultory bark. Rats and cats interrupt their pitched battles, startled by his silent approach. Everywhere is bare of human life.

He seems quite alone.

The Museum library's manuscript collection was extensive, rare, and in nearly every subject could be declared exceptional. Confident of her claim on the *Memoirs*, Sarah spent the first part of the morning delving into the relevant catalogues. She stood, almost at the centre of the Reading-room, within the innermost circle of the three concentric stands, where ranged the Cotton, Harley, Sloane, and Lansdowne collections. Moderately familiar with their contents – most especially the writings on Scripture – she had, by the same token, never needed to search for anything so specific.

There were in excess of 25,000 manuscripts catalogued, to date. Without knowing the year in which a work might have been presented, Sarah would be obliged to go through them all. Assuming such presentation where Bruce's manuscript was concerned, the posited event might conceivably have taken place at any time since its completion in 1819.

It rather looked as if she would be required to renew her contact with Lieutenant Dilkes Loveless.

Sarah continued to trawl through the various subject-headings that seemed the most appropriate – Navy; Travels; Voyages, &c. (Journals of Voyages and Travels) – but had to concede this was searching for the proverbial needle in a haystack exceeding large.

Never before had she wanted to lay her hands on a book so urgently.

Turning about, Sarah faced key members of library staff. They sat arranged at stations along both sides of the central dais. Business proceeded quietly beneath the watchful eye of George Bullen, superintendent of the room. Keeper of the Department of Manuscripts was Edward Augustus Bond, the Egerton Librarian; in spite of all her years in dealing with him, or perhaps because of them, Sarah was not overly fond of the man. She coughed politely, before directing her enquiry towards the nearest of his senior assistants, Harry Ward.

Ward ceased to make notes, and squinted at her. He met her even gaze crookedly, with every air of a man not relishing the interruption. With his pen, he pointed towards the folio volumes she had just that minute abandoned.

'On these two stands the catalogues must be referred to,' he said, the advice perfunctory, delivered by rote, 'and the tickets, of which there is a plentiful supply, made out for the works required.'

'Yes…yes, I know,' Sarah patiently explained. 'I've tried the main catalogues, and those for the Additional *and* Hand – '

She cut herself short. 'Without success,' she said. 'I was wondering if you might…'

Ward's one good eye swivelled in its socket. He threw a withering look at one of his juniors, eavesdropping further along the platform, and then back to her. His mouth was set. Sarah could appreciate his annoyance: every day she overheard other readers make the most outrageous and ignorant of demands. She changed tack, trying not to sound so vague.

Look confident. State the facts.

'The title of the book – the manuscript,' she did not say 'perhaps', 'is *The Life of a Greenwich Pensioner*, and the author was Bruce, George Bruce. It would have arrived in the form of a bequest from the Royal Naval Hospital, at Greenwich…but I don't know the year.'

The senior assistant had returned to his writing. She stared at his bald crown.

He spoke once more, with weary but firm finality. 'Readers must conduct their own searches,' he said, 'for which the catalogues are provided. Staff are unable to undertake a search on behalf of a reader.'

He deigned to look up, briefly, thereby declaring a conclusion.

'If we were to do that,' he said, 'nothing would ever get done.'

Eyes dull with disappointment, Sarah moved away.

Turning a corner in relative quiet, Brippoki faces, head on, a ship bearing down in full sail. Conjured as if from air, countless small craft busily crowd the riverfront. They weave back and forth, criss-crossing each other's passage, a thousand collisions every minute only narrowly avoided.

Running along the riverside, Brippoki seeks the glimmer of dark waters, through tangles of chain, rope and crane, else covered over with spars and gangplanks. A heavy barrel swings at head-height, almost dashing out his brains. Only nimble reflexes save him. He stops to watch as it is winched aloft. High overhead, numerous bridges run warehouse to warehouse, spanning the narrow lane in which he stands. The air is filled with barrels, bales, and boxes, creaking and swaying all about – the larder of a giant jungle-spider. Hungry black mouths piercing walls either side are served gobbets by wheezing windlasses.

London, it appears, is being fed.

'You cannot,' said the junior assistant. 'It is in use.'

'In use?' said Sarah. 'But it was reserved to me!'

The library staff seemed suddenly determined to frustrate her every effort. She brandished articles relating to the 'Greenwich Pensioner' from the previous day's investigations. 'I didn't want these again,' she whined. 'Not these ones. *That* was the book I wanted.'

'Madam, please...'

'Is there a problem?'

A senior assistant took an interest. Sarah laid down the wrong books and hung her head while Dorset Eccles, the junior, explained. She had sounded more petulant than she had intended.

'The book is in use, miss,' the man confirmed.

'Yes, I thank you, Mr Graves,' Sarah snapped. 'The book was in use to me. I had asked that it be reserved, but these were reserved in its stead.'

She touched the small pile on the desk before them. Uncertain whether she had dealt the day before with Dorset or his brother Gregory, she couldn't accuse them of any wrongdoing, and it was anyway not in her nature.

'There has been,' Sarah stated, 'a misunderstanding.'

'I see,' said the senior assistant.

It did not help that in any dispute one's face was level with a man's midriff: Sarah felt like a small child scolded, or a criminal brought before the judge. The volume of *Tracts* containing the *Memoirs* was doubtless wending its way back into the bowels of safekeeping. She would have to re-apply for it again, later.

The two men regarded her steadfastly, and without pity, until she backed away.

Sarah had no other choice but to return to her notes from the previous day, locating, without too much trouble, a bound copy of the periodical cited in Bruce's narrative, the *Literary Panorama* for May 1810. 'A review of books, register of events, magazine of varieties, etc.', the octavo bound volume presented a comfy handful in neat brown binding.

'Turning with easy eye thou may'sdt behold... All nations.'

In every number of the *Literary Panorama*, the frontispiece was the same. Sarah thought she recognised the epigraph as a quote from Milton – *Paradise Regained*, or perhaps *Paradise Lost*.

The article therein reproduced the very same text as in the *Memoirs*. Ironically, it stopped short at around the same point reached by her transcript. Half as much again, again denied her; Sarah's groan of frustration caused a couple of nearby readers to look up.

Written in the third person, the *Panorama* entry had been accredited partial source for the *Memoirs*, and so must have appeared first. Who else could have written it, if not Bruce?

A short preface to the article was suggestive from any number of angles. 'Of the following narrative we have seen two accounts, differing in some trivial particulars. We have chosen the present, as being the most perspicuous and copious, with less of crimination than the other. We have added a few incidents, from equal authority.'

Taking up her transcript, Sarah made a closer comparison of the two texts. An additional fact immediately leapt off the page – the name of George Bruce's father! 'George Bruce, son of John Bruce, foreman and clerk to Mr Wood, distiller at Limehouse, was born in the parish of Ratcliff in 1779.'

Sarah double-checked her transcript: the detail was absent from the *Memoirs*. '*John Bruce*'. She made a separate note of the father's name and underscored it.

Interposed after a constellation of asterisks, the same article ended with a further editorial aside. 'We have not seen Capt. Dalrymple's statement of events; and therefore deem it justice to suggest the propriety of not determining on his conduct, which appears to have been both unwarrantable and cruel, till that officer has been heard in his justification.'

'Miss Larkin?'

Benjamin J. Jeffery, another of the junior assistants, hovered beside her desk. She had noticed him before, his hair a vertical shock, and he boggle-eyed, or so she thought, at ungracious Mr Ward, who had no right to treat her as if she were a foolish novice.

Young Mr Jeffery held out a book.

'I think…' he began. 'I couldn't help hearing before. I think this may be the manuscript you were looking for? *The Life*…' uncertain, he checked the item '*The Life of a Greenwich Pensioner*?'

Sarah's free hand flew to her throat. She laid down her pen and turned in her seat, nearly knocking over the ink bottle.

He held a plain sort of a notebook, as one would find in any stationer's, the right-hand corners at both top and bottom quite battered and worn away. She read the grubby label on the front.

The Life of a
Greenwich Pensioner
1778 to _____
Presented to John Dyer Esq.
Secretary to Greenw'h Hospital

From the worn cover she looked up into the freckled face of the young clerk. He smiled awkwardly.

She reached out for the notebook and, trembling, took possession of it. The birth date was right – well, close enough. The details were right. She turned it around and around in her hands, hardly daring to open it up.

'How…?' she said. 'I mean, wherever did you find it?'

Circumspect, the junior assistant glanced around, so pale and awkward, he couldn't even stare at his own oversized feet with composure. 'It was – um – it was among the manuscripts that had been filed incorrectly?' he said. 'There are a number without their correct details, and this was among the pile.'

Benjamin J. Jeffery finally managed to look up.

'It's not a big pile,' he said in earnest.

Three times a year, the library was closed for a week in order that it might be thoroughly cleaned. Such opportunities were taken to check and update the book stock: always a number of items had been misplaced, or gone astray.

'Some of the entries lose their numbers and have to be checked individually?' said the junior assistant. His voice often rose at the end of his sentences, as if doubting even of itself. 'That is,' he said, 'if it isn't immediately clear where they should go. We are each of us given a few to check through, when we have a spare moment. When I overheard you repeat the – uh – title to Mr Ward, it sounded familiar. It was in my…in my pile, but I hadn't got around to looking at it just yet.'

Benjamin J. Jeffery flapped his long hands in her general direction.

'You can…you can read it for me.' His sheepish grin indicated a joke. With a fearful twist his head suddenly jerked around, and back again. 'Don't tell Mr Ward! Or Old Bullen,' he urged. 'Please, miss. I shouldn't really be giving out the book, not until it's been located within the catalogue.'

Sarah was only half listening. He veered away. She turned the slim notebook over in her hand, feeling a little queasy. Had she ever found the correct entry, somewhere in the catalogues, the book itself, misplaced, might still have eluded her grasp.

She turned over the first page and began to read.

Sailors slung over the sides of ships apply fresh coats of paint. Others work high in the rigging. The outlines of human figurines are reduced to a smudge, to a blur, lost in shadow or motion. The cranes swing, and on every side more labourers trudge to and fro, backs bent and heavy-laden. In raucous crews, smocked and hatted, the dock-workers of the great Port of London labour hard to unload enormous merchant vessels. The quayside swarms – men with red faces, yellow, brown, and black faces; even men with blue faces.

Brippoki cannot get used to the deafening levels of noise. Emptied barrels, rolled across cobbles, emit a deep bass rumble. The hammers clank as coopers fashion brand new casks. Greased lengths of chain, let out link by link, clink clink in steady repetition. Their loads cast loose, they whizz free, rattling in a manner most alarming. Long ropes, freed, drop down into the waiting water with a satisfying plash.

A ship's captain cups both hands to his mouth, voice suitably amplified to relay his orders.

'Whippers,' he cries, 'tackle them barges! Ballast, to the colliers they've emptied! Attend to that cranky one first. Fill the hold good and fast. It's pitching like a proper lushington!'

On his command each team scurries forward, toting great sacks of gravel.

Brippoki looks away to an upper level, where sweating workers slug on clay bottles of beer. They gather close and shifty around the pedlar. Nearby, another man dips his long brass beak into a cask of spirits, a hummingbird at a flower.

More ships arrive, groaning, full bellies submerged, flags of many colours flying from their masts. Quayside crowds clamber down to the decks on long ladders, to begin the unloading. Bales of goods emerge, unreadable scripts and symbols classifying their contents: camphor and cocoa, hardwood and jacaranda; jute, molasses and tin; spices from Java; ice from Norway; tobacco, timber, rice, and rum.

A long open shed spans the waterside, waiting to receive these discharged cargoes. Here, under cover, coopers, weighers and measurers beetle forward to meet them, and attend to their several departments. In weighing stations positioned beside each loading bay, the large beam scales tilt back and forth. From the riggers to the dockers a polyglot chorus is spoken and sung, but in these check cabins, no one speaks except in numbers.

Cranes hoist the valued goods up and out of sight. Dwarfed by the huge blocks of intricate machinery, their operators have to work hard and fast, just to keep up. The machines set the pace, not the men.

Idly, Brippoki looks across the surface of the waters, stained a dark rainbow: black with coal dust; blue with indigo dye; purple with wine; white with flour; and brown with tobacco. Contents disgorged, the ships rise up, their decks now high above the quay.

Brippoki sees a pair of mounted constables advancing in his direction. They carry guns. Men like these he associates with the cruelties of the Native Police. Casting around in alarm, he turns aside, abruptly disappearing into the depths of the nearest warehouse.

The floor is sticky underfoot, the cavernous interior thick with a hanging mesh of knotted rope and strangling chain. Crossbeams and wooden planks recede into forbidding depths of shadow. The chaotic black space echoes with cries: a hurly-burly jumble of orders, cautions, and yankee-nigger songs, blending into one monotonous drone. He can just about make out the bodies of men, tugging and straining at their bonds.

A square of daylight extends inward from the open entrance. At its furthest edge, a crooked line-up stands before an array of heaving trays. Ancient old men prop themselves up against the edges of the long work-tables; their elderly faces haggard, empty as skulls.

'Where the hell is he?'

In a righteous fury, Charles Lawrence flung aside an empty chair.

'Catching Captain Boycott at slip like that,' said Bill Hayman. 'Is that what gave their game away?'

No sooner had Lawrence cast off one set of chains than he would set to work forging new ones: Hayman sought to distract his colleague from brooding.

'I mean,' he said, 'Cole is a fine player. But he was never that sharp!'

Their latest engagement had returned the touring cricketers to Gravesend, their first port of call, playing against Kent.

In spite of their sudden straits, Lawrence smiled wryly. 'You know what it was?' he said. 'I could hear Tuppenny grinding his teeth at the bat.' His face fell. 'That's when I thought to look under the cap.'

'Ha! I just thought he'd put a bit of weight on!' said Hayman, a touch too eagerly.

Lawrence regarded him sourly, face red with shame enough to share. He looked down and away.

'It's not like it's a new problem, Charley, this absenteeism, or whatever you want to call it,' continued Hayman. 'Their clearing off without a word of warning, it's the plague o' the sheep stations and the welfare both. One day you'll see them happily working the herds, and the next, *poof*, vanished, without a trace. It can be anything up to a year later and they'll return, nary a word of explanation, and acting as if nothing has happened.'

Or never to return at all; Hayman dreaded to think it, let alone make mention.

'One has to remember,' he persevered, 'they're not like us. Not, by nature, given to sitting around.'

'This does, I think, present a new problem,' said Lawrence, darkly.

'What I mean is, they're nomads, wanderers,' said Hayman. 'That's their lifestyle. Stick them in one place too long and their spirits flag. They'll soon get restless, if not sick, in their longing for a change of scene.'

Introducing games of cricket to the Wallace yards had been of great benefit, going some way towards countering the Aborigines' temperamental depression, and the problems arising. They were no longer so tempted to stray off into the Bush, for one.

Hayman shrugged. 'You know,' he said, 'that's why touring seemed such a good idea. But they don't like to work. Not all of the time.'

He seemed to surprise himself with that rare moment of insight, and looked the guiltier for it.

Lawrence knew full well about their nocturnal habits, the Aboriginal foraging for Bush tucker. He had done his best to suppress these urges while they were on English soil, but, in the night, he guessed they went ahead anyway.

And now one of their number had run off.

Teaching, controlling, reproving, governing…had he been too harsh?

Only when Sarah lifted her head to look at the clock did she realise the hours that had passed, so absorbed was she in George Bruce's book. If she didn't soon begin her transcription, she would have nothing to show Brippoki on his next visit.

There could be no doubt – *The Life of a Greenwich Pensioner* was the work of the same man. Given what she had already understood from his pamphleteered *Memoirs*, Bruce had been the first white man to live amongst the natives of New Zealand, as one of them. He had even gone so far as to marry their princess, and possibly to father her a child. Whatever became of them all, Sarah soon expected to learn for herself.

She turned again to the opening text of the first page.

> *The most. Wonderful. Adventrs of A man Ho was born in sant Pols Shadwell London. the frist of my remembrence. was That my father hilt a satuation under. mrster woodhum a disteeler at Limhous. I. was one of thirteen Children Wich God was pleased to Bless my Father and mother with. all so I was The greatest favouright of that family by an icstronory ad vent at my birth.*

As used as she was to both antiquarian language and handwritten scrawl, the wording of the manuscript was hard to make out at first.

Resisting her eagerness to skim ahead and discover all, Sarah directed her energies towards initiating a transcript. As per her normal working practice, she started out with an assessment, a brief note describing the book itself.

A labelled notebook, the pages had been numbered by hand, 119 in total. The flyleaves were watermarked 1847, indicating an approximate date when the pages had been assembled between covers: somebody had cared enough to look after it. That in itself perhaps furnished a clue as to when the Museum might first have acquired the original manuscript.

The work was principally of one hand, but with at least three differing scripts alternating. It seemed fair to presume George Bruce illiterate, dictating his story for others to record. A service performed most likely by his fellow inmates; they were, unfortunately, not so very literate themselves. The text, however, looked to be complete, in good condition, and – excepting occasional idiosyncrasies in spelling or grammar – relatively easy to decipher.

Steeling herself, Sarah began her transliteration.

> The most wonderful adventures of a man who was born in Saint Paul's, Shadwell, London.

She made a separate note – '*St Paul's, Shadwell*'. His birthplace had already been given as 'the parish of Ratcliff in 1779' – a parish centred on the Highway, that notorious stretch of slumland struck through the riverside hamlets of Stepney and Limehouse. St Paul's was presumably the parish church there, St Paul himself a persistent echo worth investigating.

> The first of my remembrance was that my father held a situation under Mister Wood, him a distiller at Limehouse.

'*Wood? Woodham?*' Sarah made another note in the margins. Thus, details rendered in both *Literary Panorama* and *Memoirs* were confirmed.

> I was one of thirteen children which God was pleased to bless my father and mother with. Also, I was the greatest favourite of that family by an...

'*...icstronory ad vent. Icstronory ad vent.*' Sarah repeated the confounding phrase over and over under her breath, before making additional notes. All that seemed necessary to solve each riddle was to read the text out loud, if discreetly. It made sense, if the words had been dictated in the first instance.

> An extraordinary advent at my birth. That was, I slept for twelve months on my face, taking no refuge but the suck from my mother's breast and returning to my sleep. This wonderful event caused my mother many (a) time to sigh and say I was born to a most horrid and dreadful life, or a good fortune.

Every new line started with a capital letter; other random capitals were scattered throughout the text. Following careful consideration, Sarah elected to record the exact wording, peculiarities and faults intact, although eliminating the unnecessary capitals. It made for harder going and slowed her down, but better preserved the narrative's antiquated charm. The unlearned, almost phonetic nature of the original transcript was quaint; more than that, intrinsic.

> At the age of eleven years, my father failed in business, and Death entered our family when burying ten out of thirteen children.

Sarah halted again.

> *This Propety Drove the famely in the utmost distrees.*

'*Propety,*' she hummed, '*propety.*' Property? Poverty! Like Brippoki perhaps, Bruce could not pronounce his Fs and Vs.

I then to mrster ballmney His Rope Groond To turn the weeill for A woman Who wos Spining of twin. hear wos Clasekly hadcakted With all sorts of infemeny in short I Soon be came A quanted with the most Noterast gaan of thieefs and murdres that ever existeed on he face of the Earth.

It was going to be a long day.

The Isle of Dogs is a truly terrifying place, where impossibly tall chimneys vomit clouds of thick, black smoke. Circulating among the swirling crowds of workers are bluecoat constables: burly men with thick necks, dressed in dark uniforms. They brandish staves, and snarling dogs restrained on short leashes. Gatekeepers and watchmen patrol the high walls, or check the rolling carts, in and out. Each of the dock-gates and various entrances is heavily guarded.

None of it presents too much of a problem for Brippoki. When he doesn't wish to be seen, he is quite invisible.

The air rings with the constant din of a smithy. The clangour of the hammer shapes iron across anvil, and mandril, and quare. Wind and water turn to steam. Wooden vessels become ironclads.

Turned in a gradual circle, Brippoki makes his way back towards the docks at the top of the island. Outside the main gates an enormous crowd gathers, blown in, as surely as the ships, on the westerly wind. Inquisitive, he joins on at the fringes. With every passing second more bodies arrive, amassing behind. Desperately, they press themselves forward against the chain barriers. Before he knows it, the swollen crush pens Brippoki in.

Skin of one beast, within its enclosure the crowd snarls and strains. When the calling foremen appear, a primal thrill ripples through the throng. Then they take to nearby platforms at the front of the crush: there is a rush and a push, a sudden great step forward. The scuffling begins, and the scrambling, the stretching forth of countless hands. For a moment Brippoki's feet no longer touch the ground. Instinctively, he lets his body go limp. Should he be knocked to the ground, he knows, it would be the end of him.

Strict and ceremonial, the foremen begin to select their work gangs, calling out from a register of names. Men in the crowd volunteer their own names. Others, if they know them, call out the family names of the foremen, and some their Christian names. Faces twist into masks of anxiety. For many this is a struggle fought twice daily, with each and every turn of the tide.

Everyone begins shouting at once and the noise is fearsome. Unable to move, Brippoki's head soaks with perspiration. He gives off a low, animal stink.

'Harry! *HARRY*!' a man beside him calls. 'For the love of God...'

Hapless thousands stand ready. Jobs await only a fraction. As each selection is made, every man's chance of a payday dwindles. The competition becomes more severe. Frantic, the castaways begin to leap up and down, waving their arms and kicking out with their legs, pushing and tugging frantically to get nearer the front. There is savage jostling for position. Fights break out all around. Some men jump onto the backs of others, the stronger ones literally grinding those weaker under foot. The crowd as a whole begins to pitch and roll, circulating furiously. A whirlpool forms. Brippoki too has to thrash in constant motion, just to keep his head above the undertow. Carried away, quite literally, he also feels compelled to cry out his name.

'Bripumyarrimin!' he shouts, gasping for air. *'Bripumyarrimin!'*

Raised aloft opposite the last of the foremen, and turned bodily in the air, he is confronted by a maddening sight. Men fight tooth and nail, but they are drowning, all of them, death etched on a thousand screaming faces.

'BRIPUMYARRIMIN!'

He is overwhelmed.

Before she knew it the time had come for Sarah to return the book.

The admonition, printed on the reverse side of every Reader's Book-ticket, was quite clear.

READERS ARE PARTICULARLY REQUESTED:

Before leaving the Room, to return each book, or set of books,

to an attendant, and to obtain the corresponding ticket,

the **READER BEING RESPONSIBLE FOR THE BOOKS**

SO LONG AS THE TICKET REMAINS UNCANCELLED.

Seeing Sarah approach, book in hand, Benjamin J. Jeffery's face gently glowed.

'I would like to keep the book out for a few more days, if I may,' she said, polite but firm. 'Do you think that would be possible?'

The young man fingered one of the Reader's Manuscript-tickets. Since no green ticket had been filled in the first place, there was none to cancel. Nor could one be filled *ad hoc* without either Press Mark or individual catalogue entry number, both of which the vital manuscript lacked.

The junior assistant visibly wrestled with the problem.

'I would very much like it,' Sarah quietly insisted.

Loath to be parted from it, she gripped the book tightly. She did not wish the manuscript misplaced, not even temporarily.

A light sheen of sweat beading his forehead, Benjamin J. Jeffery drew closer. He phrased his words carefully. 'You may want to leave it out. For today,' he said. 'Among the catalogues, perhaps.'

Sarah turned and considered. The catalogue shelves seemed awfully close to the attendants – under their very noses.

'I could place it in an unfrequented part of the open shelves,' she suggested.

His eyes glazed over, and she saw his Adam's apple bob up and down. 'Whatever,' he gulped, 'you think best.'

Hidden in plain sight, the risk of discovery appeared minimal. Were the misplaced manuscript found, nothing connected her to it. The worst that could happen – and most certainly, it would be terrible – would be for it to disappear, returned to an anonymous pile.

Done, and done.

She passed him by.

'Thank you, Mr Jeffery,' she said, most sincerely.

Sarah strode out of the Reading-room, an unusual spring in her step. She rather relished their collusion – her own small act of rebellion.

CHAPTER XXVII
Wednesday the 3rd of June, 1868

STORYTELLING

'Shades of the prison-house begin to close
Upon the growing Boy...'

~ William Wordsworth,
'Ode: Intimations of Immortality'

'How are you feeling, father? How was your day?'

Lambert Larkin let out a long, grey moan.

'Oh, dear,' said Sarah. Her lips formed a *moue*. Laying a chill palm to his forehead, she winced. His bedchamber long since filled with that peculiar sickbed smell, her father had lately developed quite appalling bad breath.

Neither warm nor cold beneath its blanket of low cloud, the day was moderate: opening the window a while presented no great risk.

'I have been to the library,' she said.

Thank you for asking.

'No great news, I know.'

There, fresh air. Well, air anyway.

He flapped a hand towards the remains of a bread roll from his largely uneaten breakfast, and she knew what to do. Ever since boyhood her father had always loved to watch the birds, and was a careful observer of their habits.

Family tradition held that he acquired his lifelong interest in birds and animals from Sir John Downman, the illustrious portrait artist and Royal Academician. Between 1804 and 1806 or so, the painter had briefly made his home at Went House, Town Malling, leaving behind a number of his pictures still on the walls there. Lambert would have been seven to nine years old, his deep and abiding love of nature encouraged, in childhood's formative years, by the quiet and solemn old artist, who would have then been approaching 60 years of age.

Ordained as a curate a decade later, Lambert had planted his vicarage gardens with red cedars, limes, Turkey oaks, and Tulip trees: by all accounts, they yet flourished. On the 20th of July, 1831, he married Frances Twytten,

Sarah's mother, dear departed. Sarah herself was born another ten years on, almost to the day.

She stood, staring down into her empty hands. Broken bread lay scattered all across the windowsill.

Lambert, who was anyway not in the best of moods, squirmed in the bed, obviously irked by her lingering. 'Where is your mind, child?' he said.

Sarah battled an overwhelming temptation to confide in her father concerning Brippoki. And yet, from experience, she knew it could rebound in a fashion most unpleasant. Following her trip to the Oval the week before, she hadn't known what to say – whether to admit to her mistake in missing the cricket, or not mention the day at all. In the end she had told him almost everything. Having witnessed the astonishing flights of the boomerang, how could she not? He had deemed her colourful tales regarding the Aboriginal Sports far too frivolous…so, to reveal her subsequent association with one of the cricketers themselves…? The thought of them meeting provoked and terrified her in equal measure.

It was not that she ached to tell her father, specifically; more, she craved to share her news with at least someone. And who else was there?

When Brippoki showed up at their front door he looked wan and dejected, something even the proverbial cat would discard, slumped on the step. His red-rimmed eyes were once again bloodshot. He smelt strong and strange.

A woman of lesser character might not have invited him inside so readily.

Sarah offered him a hot drink, for which he appeared grateful, and a portion of their evening meal. She had been considerate enough to make extra. This he refused, but she kept the covered plate to hand in case he should change his mind.

News regarding Bruce's book inspired Brippoki's almost immediate recovery. His spirits revived, he appeared very keen to hear the dead man's tale.

Sarah's reading of the text was slow going but, out loud and in company, much more effective than when she had tackled it alone. Having Brippoki for an audience brought the story to life. The relation of the infant's year-long sleep, in particular, held him enthralled. Then, when he heard of the loss of ten out of the family's thirteen children, he became so wretched with sadness that heavy tears rolled through the dust on his cheeks.

I then to Mister…

'Ballmeany?' said Sarah. 'Bellamy, possibly…'

Mister Bellamy's rope ground, to turn the wheel for a woman who was spinning twine.

She read to Brippoki those very same words Bruce himself must have spoken, half a century before.

> Here I was classically educated with all sorts of infamy.

'Really, *ahem*, I'm guessing,' she said. 'If you could see a sample of the handwriting I have to unravel!'

Reflexively, Sarah held out her old notebook. Brippoki flinched.

'Well,' she said, 'it's the spelling presents the greater obstacle…'

Her voice trailed away. Sarah looked her guest over brightly, in a trice, before bending her head to resume with the reading. She'd had an excellent idea, but it could wait.

> In short, I soon became acquainted with the most notorious gang of thieves and murderers that ever existed on the face of the Earth!

Sarah felt gratified to hear Brippoki gasp. And this was but one, early indication of George Bruce's colourful way with words. He turned quite a phrase for an illiterate sailor.

She continued.

> Here the serpent took a hold of my heart…

Brippoki sprung forward, nearly falling off the edge of his seat.

'Yes,' she confirmed. 'He means Satan… You know who Satan is, don't you?'

'*Uah*,' said Brippoki. 'Debbil-man!'

'Yes, the devil.'

'The black man!' Brippoki shouted, excitedly.

The… Why should he say that?

> Here the serpent took hold of my heart, charring me up in every wickedness.

'He means, I think, that he was…blackened by fire. By hellfire, as it were.' She thought the coincidence odd.

> So I went on for two years. My poor broken-hearted father and mother by this time became acquainted with my horrid life and strove their utmost power to stop me, but it was in vain.

'Horrid life!' Brippoki intoned. '"Horrid and dreadful life"!'

'Why, yes, his fate,' remembered Sarah. 'I hadn't noticed.' According to Bruce's own mother, his long sleep in infancy ramified either his fate or his fortune: Brippoki had requested, nay, insisted, that she repeat this part over and again. She read on.

> Many a time I cursed my dearest mother to her face. One day, when she was chastising me for my wickedness, she pronounced on me a few words as follows:

– You wicked wretch, for your disobedience to God you will wander in the wilderness like a pilgrim seeking for refuge, and will find none!

A fulsome curse for a mother's lips; Sarah had already made note of it. The effect on Brippoki, however, she could not have predicted. Clasping his head in both hands, he cowered and wailed in abject distress. His upset was so severe, it took several minutes and a second cup of tea to soothe and quiet him again.

It was, perhaps, Sarah's own fault. Her delivery inherited a little too much fire and brimstone from the Reverend Lambert Larkin.

Calm restored, and with half a mind to the ever-present risk of disturbing her father, she suggested they take a short break. George Bruce's fortunes did not improve in the pages ahead, and his fate only worsened. Brippoki, however, preferred for them to continue.

> Shortly after, I should have murdered my poor father with a brass candlestick, which I threw at him, but he, putting his hand, prevented it. I was put into the workhouse, wherefrom hence I was bound apprentice to Joseph Frogety at Barking. I went several voyages to Holland with my master dealing in fish. My master treated me with every kindness. But alas, this happiness was but for a short time, for one day at Limehouse where my master lived, my mistress made me put my clothes with my fellow apprentices.
>
> When taking them on board, I found them covered with vermin. This curse surely was sent by God on me for my wicked deeds. I ran from my master. My young master brought me back the following night…

Distracted, Sarah paused. The literal transcript was '*Foulling Night*', the unwitting poetry of which she had rather liked.

> …and I was put down in the cabin in the charge of an old man. He told me that my master would flog me for running away. That same night, when the old man was asleep, I went to the companion…

'…the window at the top,' explained Sarah. Brippoki was nodding, almost mechanically.

> Then, putting my head to the top part, I forced it open and set off for London, where I resided for a few weeks.

'London,' Brippoki repeated.

The incident with the '*vammont*' – the varmint, or vermin – sounded closer to genuine misfortune than offence. Bruce's only real crime had been the fear of consequences. Added to an already lengthy list of misdemeanours, however, his running away must have reflected badly: in the minds of his accusers it would have only confirmed his guilt. Warranted or not, the threat of flogging had driven him to flee a second time.

Setting off for London, from Limehouse – Bruce made the city sound so far off! In those days, Sarah supposed, it was. She returned to the text.

One day, my mother met me on Tower Hill, and compelled me to go with her to the North Country Pinks, Limehouse, where I was left with Master Wheatley, who was in partnership with my master. I was treated with the most tenderest usage that ever a child was dealt with. My employ was to go out with beer. One night I went to a widow's house to carry beer, when I saw on her table lay a silver watch. I had in my company one of Master Wheatley's sons with me, so that I could not accomplish my wicked thought I had in my head at that time. But soon after we both arrived at his father's house I left him, and made my way for the poor widow's house with that wicked intent that I had the first moment I see the watch laying on her table. At my return to the widow's house, she was at that minute going out. She locked the door and shoved to the window-shutter. As soon as she was gone some distance from the house, I pulled the window-shutter open, and jumping in the window I ran to table, where I caught up the watch and put it in my bosom. Then jumping out of the window with my booty, I ran to Master Wheatley's house. The watch was going and I was frightened that some person would hear it tick.

I immediately went out of the house and hid the watch in among some logs where it remained till the next morning. I was very restless during the night for fear that the widow should come to my master and enquire for the watch. The next morning when I went downstairs, to my great surprise I see through the window some men moving the logs where the watch was hid. I then took in my hand two stones and began to play with them till I throw one of them on the spot where the watch lay. I took up my booty and went to London where I met with one of my old companions.

'This, presumably, must be one of that "notorious gang" of yore,' Sarah commented.

'Not mine,' said Brippoki quickly, vigorously shaking his curls.

'No,' Sarah said, 'I meant…' She smiled, letting the breath out. She read on.

He conducted me to his father, to whom I gave the watch. He received it and told me I was a good boy, asking me at the same time to come and live with him. I told him Yes.

I remained with this man for a few weeks. My employment: with his son, day and night, in thieving all we could catch. His father and mother received all the stolen property.

One morning, passing a cookshop, I went in and found on the counter a very large plum pudding, which took my attention. But the suspicious barking of a little dog, who was in charge of the shop, prevented me for some time. Finding no assistance to the little dog, I jumped on the counter, then, dragging a very large dish of chitlings to the edge of the counter, threw some of them to the little dog. This stopped his noise, and was his death, for as soon as he

189

came to the edge of the counter to fill his belly, that moment I turned the dish upon the poor little dog, which completely smothered him. Finding everything quiet, I got down off the counter and carrying with me the plum pudding on my head, I went into St George's Fields, where in a little time I had so many companions that I did not know what to do. The pudding was soon devoured, and I returned to the poor old sinner who encouraged me to thieving with his own son.

My ruin was but for a short time, for soon after, my eldest brother met me in the street, picking pockets on the Sabbath night. I then stopped with my brother for some time. I was soon overtaken by justice. Many times I was caught thieving, but I was so small that the Ladies and Gentlemen all pitied me, and let me go. But at last I was caught in the fact, and cast for death at the age of twelve years. It was for breaking a window and taking out two pieces of handkerchief.

I remained in Newgate for some time, and from thence to the hulks at Woolwich, where I remained till the year ninety-one.

Captured in these simple lines was the delicious moral mix of turpitude and innocence that must be the experience of every young thief. The lost *Memoirs* quite forgot, they had been catapulted back into the earliest days of Bruce's misadventures.

Sarah looked over at Brippoki: expression rapt, utterly transported. Did he know any Dickens? Here was young Oliver Twist, encouraged by a corrupt Fagin into thievery. Along trotted Bill Sykes's unfortunate dog, Bullseye. Or perhaps Bruce was rather an Artless Dodger. The essential difference being, this tale was first-hand – banal, untutored, and utterly authentic.

Just so long as poverty and deprivation maintained their distance, not simply in years, Sarah took a perverse sort of pleasure in peeping at such a world, 'for the imagination of man's heart *is* evil from his youth'.

Sarah settled back into her seat, and closed the notebook.

'Hopefully,' she said, 'Bruce's manuscript found, we may make better progress tomorrow.'

Brippoki's face looked plaintive, his brow creased. 'He is in...Wool Itch?' he asked.

'In one of the prison ships at Woolwich, yes,' she said, slightly hoarse. 'They are still there, as far as I know.'

'He is imprison?'

Brippoki's black pupils rapidly darted around the room. In his dismay he seemed to look at everything and nothing. She found it impossible to read his thoughts.

'Is...' she said '...is this...?' She searched for some way not to ask it as a direct question. 'It has been in some way helpful to you?'

He did not answer. His habitual silence was unnerving.

In place of the manuscript itself, Sarah brandished her notebook. 'We've found the book!' she said. 'Bruce's book. Aren't you pleased?'

'Oh, *yes*, miss!' he said.

Brippoki's utmost sincerity disarmed her.

'His early life…' she said. 'He records everything in such detail, I wasn't sure you would want to hear it all.'

'I want to know all things,' said Brippoki.

In the wake of so firm a declaration, Sarah proposed her earlier excellent idea. 'Come with me to the Museum,' she said. 'As a member of the ordinary public you may attend, on certain days in the week. We'd have to obtain for you a viewing pass, of course, but then…you could see…for yourself?'

Brippoki looked aghast, and violently shook his head. Fidgeting, he stood and paced about the room.

Sarah was nonplussed.

The clock in the hall began to chime. The hour was more greatly advanced than she might have guessed; it would not do for Brippoki to remain so very late into the evening. Sarah leapt to her feet. As she struggled to summon the correct phrases, her hands motioned him outside.

'Until tomorrow, then.' She blurted the words. 'We'll have to continue tomorrow.'

She made for the door, only to turn and see Brippoki heading for the window. It gaped only slightly, in order to air the room, but, grasping the rim forcefully, he rammed it open wide. The drapes guttered in the sudden breeze.

'Oh!' she gasped.

Gathered in the interstice, Brippoki turned and nodded a goodbye.

He was gone.

Standing within the frame of the open window, the strands of her hair trailing, Sarah took some moments to gather her wits. She heard the strangulated yowl of an alley-cat, a short distance away.

The woodsy smell of her gentleman caller imbued the air. She dared breathe not a word to her father concerning Brippoki's nightly visitations. Let him remain her very own secret: to savour, even when stinking; to reveal – or not – as and when she saw fit.

Lamps extinguished, heading upstairs, Sarah put her ear to the crack of Lambert's bedroom door. His loud snores for once reassured: he remained fast asleep.

Her face broke into a wide and self-satisfied smile.

The dove of deliverance had brought her an olive leaf, pluckt off.

At long last, she held on to something exclusive; that precious something never before experienced – a life of her own.

CHAPTER XXVIII
Thursday the 4th of June, 1868

'HORED AND DREDFULL'

'At Newgate I was tried and cast,
My Guilt was plain and clear,
Sentence of death on me was pass'd
But Mercy my life did spare
For fourteen years to New South Wales
I was straightway to go,
Thus Justice did at last prevail
And brought me very low.'

~ 'At Newgate I was Tried and Cast', traditional

The players confined to lodgings, their custodians in the main lounge, the Aboriginal Australian Eleven made ready to quit the Bat and Ball Inn, Gravesend.

'Our third match, and already two men down,' railed their captain, Charles Lawrence. 'If it ain't one thing, it's another. We haven't played at full strength since we got here!'

William South Norton raised one eyebrow: not having forgiven Lawrence his slights the previous Sunday, he implied a sore loser.

'Two?' he queried. 'Who else is it has gone missing?'

Lawrence turned away, lest he be tempted to smack South Norton's smarmy face for a six.

'Not missing,' Bill Hayman clarified, pouring oil on the waters. 'But may as well be, for all the use he is.'

South Norton gawped, clueless.

'Sundown, lad,' said Hayman. 'Laid low by some mystery illness. It's all we can do to turn him in his bunk.'

South Norton began to chortle.

'What's so funny,' growled Lawrence.

'Sundown,' he said, 'tied to his bunk. Very thoughtful, considering how much you've to pay for the things.'

Thomas Elt, proprietor of the Bat and Ball, proposed to charge £40 for their accommodation, a small fortune well above the average. Further, he had applied to the local Board of Guardians to supply beds and bedding – the hotel's existing linen too good for the black cricketers.

Lawrence balled a fist and stepped forward. Bill Hayman intervened. He motioned for his brother-in-law to back off. William South Norton was, for the moment, wise enough to hold his peace.

Charles Lawrence seethed. He had altogether too much on his mind of late, not least this most recent unpleasantness. King Cole was still missing. He struggled to recall the last occasion on which he had seen him. Despite interrogation, neither Sundown nor any of the others would admit to anything. His corps had closed ranks: if they knew where Cole had gone to, they weren't saying. At times like this Lawrence resented their otherworldliness, the secrecy inherent in their faith, their complicated code of brotherhood.

'They said the blasted idiot's gone "Walkabout"!' he ranted. 'For no damn good reason.'

Bill Hayman paused in the packing of his bags. 'They said that?' he asked.

'For no good reason that *I* know of,' said Lawrence. 'You know what it's like, blood from a stone…'

So they might take off for days, weeks, months on end, and who knew why? In order to join up with their kinfolk, somewhere out in the Bush. For the sake of some unholy communion, or whatever else constituted the rhyme and reason of their ritual life.

'Don't he realise he has prior obligations?'

'If he could spell it,' said South Norton, 'he might realise it.'

Lawrence ignored the remark. 'From now on,' he said, 'they'll have to return to their sleeping quarters each night, and we'll have to make double sure of it.'

'Or there'll be Elt to pay!'

Lawrence went for William South Norton, stabbing finger-first. 'Mention that blackguard again,' he shouted, 'and…I'm warning you!'

Bill Hayman, steadfast between them, spoke *sotto voce* to his kin. 'And I warned you,' he said.

Turning, he took hold of Lawrence by the shoulders and spun him halfway about. 'More to the point, old chum,' he said, 'what are we going to do about it?'

All Lawrence's air went out of him. When he spoke again, his voice seemed pathetic and small. 'What *can* we do?' he said. 'Inform the press?'

'And tell them what, exactly?' Hayman, sounding very take-charge, had obviously been thinking things through. 'Cole's only been missing a day or two, at most. And he may come wandering back at any moment. Then how would it look? No, publicity-wise it would be a disaster, and that's something we don't need. I'd go to almost any lengths to avoid it, in fact.'

Hayman raised his right shoulder and, stretching one arm out behind, tried to iron out a kink in his back. 'Best,' he advised, 'to say nothing, just yet.'

William South Norton nodded curtly.

Lawrence pursed his lips, reflecting.

'Outside of ourselves,' said Hayman, 'who would even notice if Cole doesn't appear on the pitch?'

'Instead of "not out",' South Norton quipped, 'we may say "never in"!'

Hayman offered up the most practical solution, since it seemed entirely down to him. 'We'll keep their caps swapped around,' he said. 'Nothing the Abs themselves haven't done before now…'

Lawrence walked to the window, attempting to cool off.

'What on earth does he think he's playing at?' he said, mostly to himself.

Charles Lawrence looked out over Gravesend, not even seeing it.

The booming notes sound, deep and low. They resonate throughout Brippoki's body. Trembling, he has to clutch at the walls for support. In the aftermath, the air yet vibrates.

Craning his neck, he marvels at the Piebald Giant.

Buried to His chest, He is yet massive above. Aside from the gunmetal blue of His bald head, the skin is either very black, or very white. The markings fall in uneven patches, half a bone here, the swell of muscle there. Wreathed in smoke, stacked like a thunderhead, He is the stone-silent master of all He surveys.

Brippoki feels daunted, but in the same moment reassured by the sight of an old friend.

Even here, Truth is. Spirit Ancestors walk the land, as they have since the dawn of Creation.

That a land where Ancestor Spirits walk could be created any less than perfect is unthinkable. And yet, from everywhere around there comes the noise of busy digging, digging, digging. Brippoki looks back in the direction he has come. Droves of labourers teem over great mounds of displaced earth. Others, high overhead, clamber across a wickerwork of scaffold. He emerges only gradually from his daydream. The scene is one of very great destruction.

Brippoki's face twists and falls.

He moves closer to the precincts beneath the cathedral. To every side throngs an army of darkness, entire suited regiments on the march. At each road junction the dense clusters amass and disperse, a mirror to the flight of crows, crying overhead.

Crushed in the midst of such impersonal mass, Brippoki lets events flow over him.

Without the Spirit Ancestors' enduring presence, he would be lost in this false London.

~

Sarah Larkin checked in on her father, made the breakfast, cleaned up a little from the night before, and then set out for the Museum. A short queue of patients coughed outside the front door, waiting on the late arrival of Dr Epps.

The dense cloud cover of the last few days persisted, sky almost settled on the rooftops. Sarah's blouse stuck to her flesh from the unusual humidity. She let none of it dampen her mood. She breezed into the Reading-room, eager to set off on her travels.

Bruce's manuscript remained where she had carefully chosen to leave it, in between *A Dissertation on the Properties of Pus* and *Essai sur le Dyssenterie Putride*, a spot surely little frequented. Sarah caught sight of Benjamin J. Jeffery, watching. Jaw set, she blinked a subtle acknowledgement. He shied away.

Sarah soon found her place within the text, the point at which their juvenile hero was to be deported to Australia; the sentence of death commuted to transportation for life, for the stealing of two silk handkerchiefs.

The tale of the '*plumpuding*' and the '*poor little doge*' had been at once both horrible and amusing. Sarah felt rather fond of the young George Bruce, so shameless, yet so filled with shame that he should admit to picking pockets on the Sabbath!

The *Life* seemed as honest, in its way, as a confessional.

> *...then I went put on Bord the royal hadmarl east indamen. to Go to portjacksen. my imployment. during The yage wos to see all the boys cleen to Muster every moring be for the captin. the Ship arived at hir Respictef port. wih the Loos of sevan Soles out of four houndred And thifty. wich captin Bond had on bord. Captin Bond was one of the most Nobelist harts that ever Existed on Earth. For he be haved bouth A father and frind To all on bord. during A passage of four Mounths and four days. I left the ship. And wos sent to towngabbe. my imployment Was carring water to the men. that was fellin The trees to clar that part of the countrey For agerculter. in A few mounths after I Was Seest with the feever. I then wos cuk Hospital. in A short time I recovred my Helth.*

Events moved apace. Sarah primed her pen.

Port Jackson was a main port of Australia; 'Towngabbe', she guessed, the name of another settlement of that colony. As for the ship on board which he travelled, following a few whispered experiments she settled on the *Royal Admiral*, East-Indiaman – as identified in the *Memoirs*. Regardless of the dates' conflicting by as much as two years, it seemed safe to assume the vessel was the same. The captain's name, Bond, sealed it.

According to the *Memoirs*, Bruce had served as 'bo'sun's boy', with no mention of his trial or imprisonment. Calling muster on board ship or carrying water on land – he might have been employed in either situation, even as a convict.

Sarah turned to the continuation of her transcript.

I then employed myself in ranging the wilderness collecting of all sorts of insects for the doctor of the hospital. This lasted a very short time. For, one day, as I was taking a bird nest out of a large tree, I fell down on the ground, where I lay for a considerable time, the blood running from my mouth, nose, ears, eyes, and every part of my body where it could find vent.

Oh!

I was reported to the doctor by a little boy that was with me. The first of my…

…*relicttion*…

Recollection?

wos That I found my self. ling on my bck in The hospital. and the docter standing by my Bad side. asking me if I know him. I Answerd in the infirmtith.

Horrific circumstances notwithstanding, Sarah smiled at the happy accidents of language; his 'bad side' for bedside; 'infirmity' – well, almost – for affirmative.

He asked me what I did with the young birds. I told him that I let them all go. He said I was a good boy, and bid me go to sleep, for as I had slept so long that it was a pity to wake me. I asked the doctor how long I had been asleep. He told me fourteen days.

In one year I recovered my health. I then was sent to Richard Fichgeril (*Fitzgerald?*) who was Superintendent of that settlement. He took me for his body servant. After a few months I was sent to the Governor General of that Colony, whose name was Frances Groos (*Grose? Or Gross?*). He asked me my name, and where I was born. I told him. He said that he well know'd my friends (?), and if I was a good boy that he would make me a free man in a short time. Which he did.

'A good boy', 'good boy' – the phrase kept recurring. The Fagin-type character from the Limehouse passages had also used it, but in a sense quite distinct – in praise of his efforts in stealing the widow's watch.

as soon as the Govner Had pardained me. I then went onbrd his Majesty scooner. hir name the cumbellin she wos imployed Carring packits to nofick iland commander Lieutenant Bishworth.

On that separate sheet of paper where she had written 'Royal Admiral, East-Indiaman, Captain Bond?' Sarah added '*the* Cumbellin – *a schooner, commander Lieutenant Bishworth*', and then '*Norfolk Island?*' The library was not exactly short of reference books, and at this stage any detail could have relevance.

And was a 'brig' – in the *Memoirs* – some sort of a prison ship, as it sounded? She would have to ask someone more familiar with nautical terms.

The Greenwich Hospital clerk, Lieutenant Loveless, had offered to enquire after George Bruce at Somerset House, something she had largely dismissed. She could do worse than to write him a quick letter. She might then forward a brief questionnaire.

Sarah returned to the manuscript.

> *I was in this imploy for five years. then Lieutenant robins cuk command of hir. and went On a yage of discovery. I went with him. the First strange land we mad. two small islands To the wast of portjacksin. the name of thaese islans. are the new year islands. be cases. thay wods discovred on A new year is day. those islands are A bounded with seals. see Elfint bagers porkpine and in the morning and Evening thay both are covred with birds. after We had invested those two islands. we went to invest A harber named port fillips. The enterince of this harbor is very narrow for no ship can go in A ganst the tide. this harbor from the enterince to the head of it His Fifteen houndred miles.*

~

Sarah was trying to concentrate. There had been a spattering of rain earlier in the day, while she was still working at the Museum. She recalled the intermittent thrash of it, drumming on the glass lantern of the dome, and how the wind, having risen, had hurried her home. That one brief shower had been the only rain all week. The winds howling outside might hopefully blow the clouds away.

> It is a most beautiful harbour, and abounds with a vast quantity of black swans in all times of the year. As soon as Lieutenant Robins had explored this port, he then returned to Port Jackson. I have forgot one remark. On the voyage that was ingoing on shore the boat was upset with eight men. I was one of the number. Two of them was drownded.

'Ahem…"were drowned".'

Sarah found the rattling of the window-frame distracting. Apart from anything else, she worried the noise might disturb her father.

'Would you mind awfully shutting the window?' she said. 'Just for a while.'

Brippoki took a moment to comprehend that she no longer read from the manuscript. He jolted forward from his seat, happy to comply. As he approached the casement the curtain billowed up to meet him.

The window had been left partially open all day in order to air the front parlour: it had seemed hardly surprising when Brippoki entered in that same way, unannounced, and at his customary late hour. Sarah began to appreciate there were certain benefits to this arrangement.

'Thank you,' she said. 'Now, where were we?'

> At our arrival at Port Jackson we found Captain Flinders, who had lost His Majesty's Ship *Porpoise*. He immediately took the schooner and turned all the

crew on shore. Taking with him as many of the men that he could stow in her, Captain Flinders sailed for England, leaving behind him half his ship's company. I was left on shore with the crew. I then took on me the duty of a police officer.

Sarah tilted one eyebrow in exaggerated fashion.

I did not hold this office long, for one day I made a seizure of spirits. No sooner had I got it in my possession but drinked it, for which crime I was sent to hard labour for six months.

Before I had been one month at this labour, a quarrel rose between the Englishmen and Irishmen. I was one of the Englishmen that was in the fight. The battle lasted four hours. One of the Englishmen was past recovery. Several of the Irish was in the same state. The battle ended at night. The next morning when enquiry was made who was the first aggressor, the Irishmen with their false oaths soon turned the Englishmen. I was one of the number that was found guilty. I was sentenced to 200 lashes.

When the time appointed for my punishment was come, I made my escape into the wilderness. It was in the evening when I made my escape from the hand of my tyrant.

Bruce had run from a flogging, just as he had when a small boy, in London.

The first night I slept without fear.

Sarah noticed another recurrence, but only because Brippoki had reacted so strongly to it before. Following his fall from the treetops, and his bleeding from every orifice, Bruce had slept a fortnight through. His prodigious, death-like sleep echoed a similar occasion, the 'extraordinary advent' at his birth.

Ever since the earlier reading, Brippoki had been distracted, jumpy. Sarah knew better than to expect any explanation. His spirits were palpably intense, but she could not, it seemed, know his reasons – if reason even prevailed. At every pause, she searched the mysterious depths of his dark eyes, and wondered how she might unlock their secrets.

Compared to the state in which she had found him the previous evening, he had at least flattened down his hair, and straightened his ragged clothing. He had also cleaned the supper dish.

The next morning at the appearing of the blessed light from Heaven, I was awakened with the melodious voices of the beautiful birds whom God had made. Here, for the first time, I looked in the lap of Nature, and there I found God in His power and His Wisdom, His Knowledge and his Mercy. I rose and began my pilgrimage.

I went on my travels through the woods. In the evening I promiscuously met a man who was a settler. He asked me where I was going. I told him:

– To look for work.

He employed me and that night introduced me to two men that he was supporting in the day time; and in return, at night, those two men went to the different settlements thieving, and brought him the stolen property. He also told me that it would be better for me to join them than anything he could recommend me to. I consented and went with them.

Every night, we used to go to the different stock-yards belonging to the Government, stealing sheep, goats, pigs and geese, ducks, fowls – or anything we could catch. In a few days after, we were joined with three more poor miserable sinners like myself. Now being six in number, we went on in a most dreadful way of thieving.

'Most horrid and dreadful,' Brippoki confirmed, his expression grave.

Indeed – what progress for a pilgrim, from policeman to a rustler of livestock.

'*Premiskisly*', the original text had said. 'I promiscuously met a man.' How old would Bruce be? She guessed not far off twenty years of age. The man he met in the woods had turned out another Fagin, and he had fallen into bad company.

In about two months after, one of my late companions proposed to go to one of his friends to procure some tobacco and salt for all the gain. It was agreed on, and that night we all accompanied him to the border of the settlement, where he told us that his acquaintance lived. We gave him half a sheep to present to his friends. He took his departure from us with that vow to bring us what we then stood in need of. But alas, he betrayed us all. For by this time there was a most desperate hue and cry throughout the whole country, and great rewards for all our lives. And when his friends told him this, he went to the police and put them in a way how to take our lives.

Her energies flagging, Sarah struggled to interpret her own scrawl.

The plot being laid, he returned to us. We then went to our place of abode in the wood and there remained till the next night, which was the time that this Judas appointed for our lives to be taken. The tent which we all sleep in, it was in a thick part of the wood, so that no person could get to it without great difficulty, and before it was a large fire from which the heat came so strong that we could not bear any clothing. We were all naked. It was to be so. I could not sleep, for that Great and Merciful God, in whom I put all my trust and hope, He never left me in all my distresses. O my dear brothers, that I could display to you all in net that lively faith I have in that God who made and Created me, then you would not be surprised when you came to hear how many times I have escaped from the hand of my enemies, who sought my life and thirsted after my blood. Nay, I was in Hell, but the blessed Lord Jesus Christ brought me out of it.

Sarah glanced up, to gauge what effect, if any, the impromptu preaching might have on Brippoki. Hunched in concentration, he listened – intent as always – but made no sign.

About the midnight hour I thought I heard the sound of a human foot. I with the greatest of care began to awaken the untimely mortals who lay by my side asleep. But the poor weak-hearted creature, who well knew his appointed time to which he had betrayed all our lives, he momently jumped up to his feet and began to shout as loud as he could, and immediately jumped over the fire. This was his agreement with the police officers on the night he first betrayed us, but he was deceived, for half went over the fire and half run through the thick part of the woods. Those three that went over the fire was immediately taken, and in a few days two of them was executed.

As soon as I got through the thick woods it began to rain, and the night turned so dark that I was glad to sit down by a large tree, where I remained till the morning. I had with me two of the untimely creatures. It was in the wintertime, so that my joints was set with the cold that in the morning, when to rise, I could not, till I was helped by both of the men that was with me. We were all naked.

Sarah shifted uneasily in her seat. The imagery of men, naked, lost in the woods, evoked something primeval. If the Australian Bush was the Garden of Eden, then these lost souls had been cast into the outer darkness, into a wilderness of night.

But as soon as I recovered myself, I then went on my travels through the woods, for a settlement named Prospect, which we made in a day and a night's journey. Our legs and feet was tore in a most dreadful manner by the brambles and briars. There lived a man at this place in whom I thought I could trust my life with the greatest of confidence, but alas when I entered in his house his very countenance displayed the Judas heart that he had in his bosom. Now the Devil had locked his jaw as he does all his servants when he finds their labour in vain. That morning saw the grand archangel with his flaming sword in his hand guarding my poor sinful soul. However, the body of destruction that he had for a partner, she told me that anything I wanted of her husband he would it immediately. I then asked him to go to George Pell that lived in Towngabby.

'*Toongabbe*,' said Brippoki suddenly.

'Toon…' she repeated. 'How do you say it?'

'*Toongabbe*. Place near water.'

The suggestion that Bruce travelled through country Brippoki was familiar with excited Sarah beyond measure. She read on even faster.

I told him to tell Pell that I and two more men was naked and I wanted clothing for all three. Luker then took his departure from us, and we returned into the wood, carrying with us a large cake made of flour, and a good piece of pork, which his wife had gave us. As we was lamenting the horrid state, almost perished with the cold it being in the depth of winter, we being all naked and as ravenous as wolves with the hunger, one of my unfortunate companions asked me if I know any more of the settlers. I told him I did, for during the time I had been with Dr Caley collecting insects, that I had been from one end to the other of all the settlements that Government had.

Farr said:

– Alas my dear boy, your travelling was different then to what it is now. When you was with Dr Caley you was free to travel, but now all our lives is in danger.

'This is one of his companions,' Sarah explained, 'a man called Farr, whose speech is here reported. And here Bruce makes answer...' She assumed a different voice.

– Well, faith, what you say is right. But let me ask you, don't you think that I was in as much danger when I have been all hours of the night collecting curiosities? For you know, Farr, that there is plenty of snakes in the wood, and wild beast that would devour a man. But, Farr, you think of the danger that our lives is in by the laws of man, but you don't think on that Great and Merciful God that brought us three out of the gulf of Hell. I mean, Farr, the night before last night: how that providential God brought us out of the hands of our enemies. Farr? Don't despair, God is good.

Brippoki was nodding.

Farr said:

– You astonish me, Bruce, with your discourse, and I am sure that God has gave you a great gift. But it is no time for preaching now.

Sarah allowed herself a wry smile. 'Bruce replies again.'

– Well, Farr, both of you are very cold. Come, let us go and I will take you to a house where you both will get a good warm at the fire. For my part, thank God, I am quite hot.

Brippoki sat suitably agog. This was as well: sorting out dialogue scenes from a single breathless paragraph had taken up much of Sarah's day.

The handwriting at this point had taken on a noticeably different character. It looked to be the work of the same hand, in bigger, bolder print. Maybe nothing more than a fresh writing implement – but if George Bruce, strangely warmed, was beginning to rave, as it appeared, then the note-taker would have been required to write faster, just to keep up.

I then went to the house of Joshua Peck, where we was received in a most efficacious manner. Mr Peck immediately brought us some old rags to cover our nakedness. Mrs Peck having a large family of children she burst into tears, and taking me by the hand and kissed me, she also told me that Joseph Luker was going to inform the soldiers and police officers that we were on that spot, and she expected them every moment.

– Mrs Peck, you surprise me, for I sent him to George Pell to bring me clothing for us three.

Mrs Peck said:

– Yes, my dear child, I know. For he came to this house to light his pipe about an hour ago. And he told me and my husband that his wife had gave you three bread and meat enough for one day. But he exclaimed that it should be the last that you should eat, for he would have you all shot that day before twelve o'clock, and he swore a most desperate bloody oath.

I said:

– Well probably that oath may be his end. Come, Farr and Meredith, let us go. You hear what is said. Goodbye, Mrs Peck. God bless you for what you have done for us men this morning.

Sarah modulated her voice a little higher, to signify the change of speaker back to Mrs Peck.

– Goodbye, dear children. But you had better go up on that high hill and stop for a little while, to satisfy yourselves with the truth in respect of what I have told you of Luker. I then…

No, Bruce had resumed his narrative.

Sudden weariness threatened to overtake Sarah. She had been working hard for far too long. It was time to speed things to a close.

I then took my leave of this bright and efficacious soul Mrs Peck, and complying with her last sentiments I went on the said high hill above mentioned, and in a short time I was perfectly convinced of what I had heard of Luker. For I see him with about 30 more poor untimely creatures like himself, filing through the woods on search of my life, and the other two poor wretches that was with me. Now they danced round the house of my dear loving sister Peck, just like the serpent round the garden of Job, when God gave him permission to tempt Job.

Here my weary bowels yearned, when I saw the deception of mankind one to the other.

Sarah closed her notebook. There was more, but her voice had begun to give out.

'I'd like you to meet me, just across the street, tomorrow morning at a nine o'clock,' she said, smartly. 'Will you do that?'

Brippoki nodded, mutely.

Sarah stood, and indicated the window.

'Very good then,' she said. 'Until tomorrow.'

CHAPTER XXIX
Friday the 5th of June, 1868

THE BUSH OF GHOSTS

'For in and out, above, about, below,
'Tis nothing but a Magic Shadow-show,
Play'd in a Box whose Candle is the Sun,
Round which we Phantom Figures come and go.'

~ *Rubáiyát of Omar Khayyám*

Crestfallen, Brippoki returns to his nest on the roof. The previous night, his audience with the Guardian and Deadman ended, he had never left the house, but crawled up over the eaves and out of sight; collapsing, at long last, into a deep and dreamless sleep.

Brippoki tucks himself again into that same recess, out of the chill winds.

Having slept there for much of the day, he can do no more than rest awhile. Some hours before dawn, he drifts into the Dreaming.

The paper yabber makes him liver-sick with memory, of stringy bark, gum and peppermint trees, towering above dogwood, tea-tree, and honeysuckle. Brippoki yearns for an open landscape, the rhythm of a different drum. His belly misses more than ever the sugar-bags, *nardoo* and witchety grubs, all proper *oonjoo*. He tongues for them.

The night is crisp and clear. It has been two and two and one more dark since he last saw the face of *Mityan*, hunter moon. Thin and hungry then, Brippoki worried that He had since wasted all away. The hunter has only been Walkabout, trailing the game He has eaten all up. *Mityan* is back, and blazes, full-up *bingee*.

The bright sky tastes sharp of another moonlit night, when the elders had stolen him away. The boy inside should have died the next day, and been reborn a man – an entirely different being, worthy of both new appearance and new name – a proud warrior of the *Wudjubalug*.

His people.

Where are they now – his father? His mother? Where, his brothers and sisters? More than a world away – their souls belong to another place.

Seeing as it is a full moon, and in an effort to cheer himself, Brippoki starts to sing the hunting song of *Wile*, the opossum.

> '*Kawemukka minnurappindo, Durtikarro minnurappindo,*
> *Tarralye minnurappindo, Wimmari minnurappindi!*
> *Kirki minnurappindo…*'

> 'If pris'ner in a foreign land,
> no friend, no money at command…'

Brippoki hesitates, before continuing.

> '…*Wattetarpirri minnurappindo…*'

> 'That man thou trusted hast alone,
> All knowledge of thee should disown…'

There it is again, distorted by echo. A man's voice, much harsher than his own, and yet faint from being carried on the wind unknowable distance.

> '…*Worrikarro…*'

> 'If this should vex thee to the core,
> I prithee Messmate stay ashore,
> There like a lubber whine and blubber
> Still for thy ease and safety busy.'

> '…*minnurappin…do…*'

> 'Nor dare to come where honest Tom,
> and Ned and Nick, and Ben and Phil,
> and Jack and Dick and Bob and Bill
> All weathers sing and drink the swizzy!'

As the rough and roaring voice launches into a chorus, the whistling wind snatches it away, just as suddenly as it had arrived – a raucous sailor song, the likes of which Brippoki heard aplenty while on board the *Parramatta*. The good Captain Williams preferred to teach them only church hymns.

Brippoki advances a step or two, meaning to follow, only to halt and think better of it.

A full moon, and yet – he is not the hunter.

Listening out for some feather-light tread not his own, he sets off in an opposite direction.

~

Dear…

Dear Charles,

Setting pen to paper, Sarah Larkin wrote to remind the Royal Naval clerk of his 'kind and generous' offer. She declared the manuscript found, outlined a little of the extra detail discovered, and requested copies of what, if any, documentation concerning George Bruce might be held at the Admiralty.

Conscience kept returning her to the top line, entirely too familiar for her tastes. She hardly knew the man, and in all honesty preferred it that way: it would be wrong for her to encourage him.

A formal address would be best.

~~*Dear Charles,*~~   *Sir,*

Sarah scrapped the letter and started again.

Half an hour later, her endeavours completed, she crossed Great Russell-street to the posting-box outside No.38. She had forgotten her gloves. Feet balancing on the edge of the kerb, poised to return, she found herself looking up at No.89 as if a stranger to it.

A relic of the Regency era, their house was typical of its kind: five storeys tall, including the cellar floor, and narrow, perhaps only 25 or 30 feet wide at the most. A terraced property, simply constructed, it had but two main rooms to each storey. Two and sometimes three windows at the front overlooked the street. Those at the back faced the unattended yard behind.

Wavering, unsteady, Sarah examined each floor in turn. John Epps, physician, occupied the ground and below-ground floors and, as landlord, owned the entirety. On the first floor, at the front, was their parlour, or lounge, the kitchen and a small bathroom out of sight at the back. Directly above was her father's bedroom; his study at the front now largely neglected. The top front room of the house was her bedroom, with the maids' former sleeping quarters behind. The sweep of the stairwell, towards the rear of the house, significantly reduced the breadth of each back room.

Though she searched it for any sort of associate feeling, her heart was empty. Bodies filled the crossing, buffeting her as they bustled past. Still she stood, eventually staring into the open sky. A beautiful clear day, the clouds were gone: her wish granted.

Another break in the traffic – without further ado she hurried on.

As she approached the Museum, the figure of Brippoki appeared as if by magic. The moment he separated from the crowd, Sarah noticed a wild glint in his eye.

'I'm sorry if last night ended somewhat abruptly,' she said. 'Only I felt so very tired all of a sudden.'

He said nothing. She walked on, almost immediately turning.

'Thank you,' she added, 'for agreeing to join me this morning.'

Without comment Sarah handed him another pair of her father's shoes, stockings too. Brippoki accepted them obediently. As he bent to slip the shoes on, she saw his left trouser leg, half torn entirely away. The bottoms were shredded beyond repair, impossible even to tie with bowyangs. She couldn't give away Lambert's entire wardrobe!

They stood alongside the tall black railings, shortly before the main gates to the British Museum.

'I thought we might take a look at the manuscript together,' announced Sarah. 'The original.' She took care not to pronounce it a suggestion: her mind was made up.

Through the gates, they approached the main building. She flourished a sheaf of notes. 'For ease of reference,' she said, 'I have prepared an abstract of Bruce's story. As a ranger in the wilderness, for instance, he collected insects for a Dr Caley.'

As they closed with the Museum steps, the broad shadow of the looming building fell across Brippoki. He appeared to jolt.

'This,' said Sarah quickly, 'was most likely Dr George Caley, botanist and explorer, a *protégé* of Sir Joseph Banks…' She regretted the foreign term. 'His student, I should say.'

The Aborigine's wild eyes widened further. She was losing him.

'Toongabbe, as you say, was the base for his activities at this time.' She spiked the familiar word like bait to a hook.

Before they could mount the steps leading up to the main entrance, Brippoki dug in his heels. Determined to achieve her goal, Sarah skipped ahead, talking faster. 'The Governor General of the colony was a Major Francis…Grose…' Keen to egg him on, she made a slight return.

'Thara,' he said. 'No go there.'

'It's all right,' she cooed. 'It's a Friday. The general public are admitted.'

She held out her hand to him. Brippoki retreated a step backwards, violently shaking his head.

Honestly! He was just like herself at three years old, being forced to attend church.

'Brippoki!' she said. 'I'll still take notes! I just want you to see for your-self…'

His head shaking all the faster, he looked ready to bolt. Sarah smiled, kindly. 'Not being able to read is nothing to be ashamed of,' she said.

She thought she was being very clever, but misread him completely. His hands waved, imploring, in the air. She suddenly grasped one in her own. As shocking to him as it was to her, their flesh touched. They sprang apart.

'Not enter dat place,' he insisted. Without raising his voice at all, Brippoki spoke with ultimate conviction. 'Place for dead men,' he spat.

'A "place for"…? A few days ago you led me into a graveyard!' she protested. 'How could this be any worse?'

This hollow mountain does not exist in his Dreaming. And as for what lies inside…

Guruwari.

Brippoki thrusts his chin forward, underscoring his decision with one final shake of the head.

Turning a deaf ear to the Guardian's cries, he jogs swiftly away.

With a slight tug of resentment, Sarah pulled the manuscript from the *ad libitum* shelves, where it nestled between two taller, slimmer volumes, *A Lecture on the Extreme Folly and Danger of Servants Going on Errands before they are Sent*, and *The Adventures of a Pincushion*.

Ungrateful heathen, more stubborn-headed than a mule – if he had only agreed to accompany her, Brippoki might then have seen for himself what lay ahead, and given her some vital direction. It would have made her present task so much easier.

Rather than resume the transcript, she went over her abstract, and continued researching the related gazetteer.

Bruce and his *Life* dated back to the very earliest days of settlement. Major Francis Grose, Commandant of the New South Wales Corps, had arrived in the colony in 1792: acting governor on first Governor Phillip's departure, he soon retired, due to ill-health, in 1794.

Matthew Flinders, English navigator and explorer, was the first to circumnavigate Van Diemen's Land, and the man said by some to have given Australia its name. The *Memoirs* asserted that Bruce had sailed with Flinders; the *Life* gave the impression he had not. Which was false?

With regard to lesser individuals, common settlers – a few previous acquaintances of Bruce in some capacity or other (fellow convicts on board the *Royal Admiral* perhaps?) – they would have already been forgotten by history. Starting on a fresh page, Sarah anyway initiated an entry list.

> *George PELL*
> *Joshua PECK ('joshsire peck') or PEEK, variously*
> *Joseph LUKER*

Sarah tapped her teeth with her pencil.

She had imagined the Aborigine's skin would be hot to the touch, and damp. It was entirely opposite: smooth, certainly, not unlike the dark wood it best resembled, but also cold, and dry. She knew what it was: Lambert had once described to her the sensation of handling a snake. Brippoki felt reptilian.

Quitting the Museum grounds directly, Brippoki makes his way south. He feels he must attend to Thara's advice, in all things. She is the Guardian. In interpreting the words of the dead, he relies on her completely – yet there can be no exchange.

He can see that it hurts and annoys her. But only a fool would further risk the wrath of the Red Ochre Men. Their sole function is to punish Lawbreakers. Women exist outside of religion. All ceremonies are *meilmeil – tabu*. And if the woman is also whitefellow?

He cannot be certain that two wrongs make a right.

No longer following the compulsive paths of his nights' Dreaming, he prefers to stick close to those regions best resembling them, as the Guardian's own house does. Elsewhere, everything looks wrong.

Past the burnt black church an endless stream of vehicles confronts him. Hazarding his life more than once, he eventually crosses over. A few streets further south and west and their rolling thunder no longer breaks on his ear with such pain.

All burial-places are liable to be haunted by evil spirits, and therefore to be avoided. The brick holes rich with wine, the ancient oak, the walking beneath the water; the city is riddled with such portals. The graveyard, too, was filled with trees, rich with links between Lowerworld, earth, and sky. Allowing himself to be led there before was a mistake, quite possibly compounded by leading a woman there in turn.

And now, in trying to lead him inside the mountain, the Guardian further diverts him from a wise course.

Any person, when guiding a stranger through their country, is often required to misdirect them. They must be led away from sites of spiritual significance. Were their situations reversed, he would do the same.

Here, in this place, the cold stone smothers all life. Somewhere beneath the stone sleeps the earth. Earth, giver of life, of a man's food, the repository of his spirit and thought, whose gentle embrace awaits him on the day he will die.

In an entire city of the dead, it is hard to know where to begin, and when to end. But even within these mystery parameters, there are limits.

To trespass on their sacred sites is something he cannot afford.

'Chestnuts all 'ot, a penny a score!'
　'Buy, buy, buy, buy, BU-U-UY!'
　'Fish, fried fish! Ha'penny. Fish, fried fish!'
　'D'you want me, Jack?'

Brippoki stares at the young boy. From the gruffness of his voice, his mock gravity – dressed exactly like his elders – he thinks him a grown man, stunted by deformity.

Eliciting no response, the boy turns aside.

'Oy, cocksparrer,' a street-seller calls him over. 'You odd-jobbin'? Over 'ere, then.'

'Want a boy, Bill?' says the youngster.

'Just said, didn' I? An' me name's Jack,' croaks the barrow-merchant. 'Come an' cry the goods for me. Me voice is all but broke. There's bunse in it for ya!'

The youngster's face shines. For a split-second, he is a boy again. Tugging proudly at the trailing corners of his neckerchief, he proceeds to hawk the weary coster's wares.

'*Fish, fried fish!*' he shouts. '*Tuppence f'r three!*'

The barrows clog pavement and road alike with oranges, onions, herrings and watercress, cheap second-hand furniture, old iron, and rabbit skins. Brippoki is obliged to step over the heaving baskets as they spill out into his path.

'*Soles, oh!… Live haddick… Ee-ee-eels alive, oh! Mackareel! Mack-mack-mackereel!*'

'*Oranges, two a penny!*'

Spoiled fish and fruits form a greasy mash underfoot. Brippoki's senses reel. He jams a thumb into each ear, and cross-weaves the fingers of both hands across his face to press his nostrils shut. The din and confusion melts into a low background hum, accompanied by the sounds of his own steady breathing.

Through this fleshy mask, he watches as the people float past. Mouths open and close, issuing their dumb, indifferent cries; baby birds and gasping fish.

Passing behind the stallholders, he looks into the avid faces of the crowd. They find their meals in the streets, and eat them on their thumbs.

Brippoki makes his way down Dudley-street, a mart for old clothes, second-hand boots and shoes. He sidles up to one of the displays, slips off the footstinkers that Thara has most recently gifted him, and leaves them there.

A bird-fancier parades by, tame songbirds perched along each outstretched sleeve. An eager line of waifs and strays follows on. Intrigued, Brippoki joins them.

They arrive at a point where seven streets meet.

Brippoki turns on the spot, dumbfounded. Seven paths to choose from, and each looks much the same as another.

Which way now?

He squats with his back to the pillar raised at the centre of the Seven Dials. He dares not move forward. Brippoki looks around, and around, and around.

In all directions the markets proliferate, street vendors offering up for sale every possible trinket – cutlery, old clothes, rat poison, toys and spectacles, pet goldfish. Bird- and dog-men, singers, peddlers of prints, the makers of doormats, the blind hawking matches or needles; each pursues his trade with a single-minded fixity, verging on obsession.

'*Buy, buy, buy, buy,* BU-U-UY!'

Insistent and repeated, their individual calls are those of birds in a forest.

Back, then, to the manuscript. Having worked a little way further than the material thus far conveyed, Sarah was at a slight loss how best to proceed.

The transcription itself had become easier. Someone else had worked alongside Bruce and his 'secretary', correcting spellings, inserting missing letters. And, once an amended spelling had been introduced – 'police', 'was', 'thieving' – it was invariably kept to: they learnt from the correction. She appreciated the will towards self-improvement.

Conversely, the narrative began to unravel. Bruce's flight from justice through the woods continued, but dissolved into a stupefying sort of delirium. His calls on God were many, and repeated.

For Bruce, waking in the wilderness had seemed something akin to a religious experience, God found in 'the lap of Nature'; exactly where her father best liked to commune with him. Emerson, a favourite of hers, wrote of an occult relation between man and the vegetable, one that allowed him to never feel alone in the universe. In the woods, where he was returned to reason and faith, Man was always a child – in the woods, and of the woods.

In her own early childhood, Sarah had much enjoyed their family excursions to Epping Forest. She could not help but see the Australian Bush, through which Bruce made his 'pilgrimage', in much the same terms: leafy and oaken. Brippoki, she supposed, envisaged things somewhat differently, and entirely more accurately.

She fancied they all of them trod a single path through that same wilderness. Bruce went first, plotting the route they must follow. On his trail, she would forge ahead, and then, for the sake of her importunate guest, backtrack and show him the way.

It was only at rare times that they might happen to walk side-by-side.

On one of several street corners opposite Brippoki, under the inn sign of the Crown, loiters a gang of three brawny lads. A mean fourteen or so years of age, they stand dressed in black frockcoats and caps. Thieves seldom work alone. Brippoki understands instinctively they are up to no good, and should be avoided.

A coster's boy strolls past, banging on a drum, an innovation to draw attention whilst saving of his voice.

Brippoki turns.

Queen-street. A man sits making flowers. His hands move faster than the eye can follow, reaching up, on occasion, to pluck dried grasses from the bundles strung overhead: crimson, yellow, blue, and brown. Birds sit stuffed and mounted, sealed in glass boxes stacked behind. Eyes unblinking, their frozen postures suggest not life, but sudden death.

The loitering trio steps off the kerb. Without uttering a word, they move, as one, into the middle of the street, tailing their latest victim.

Brippoki turns again.

Little Earl-street. While her husband waves his fat arms about and parlays his pitch, a farmer's wife crouches beneath the trestle table. She applies a fresh lick of paint to make rosy turkeys' legs. A wolfish dog cleaves to her side.

From Little White-Lion-street, an appleman in his stuff-coat swings out wide, side-pockets loaded. Doing brisk business, he turns to his young helper. 'Hurry it up with them gawfs!' he hisses. The boy redoubles his efforts, frantically rubbing at the red-skinned fruit to make it look brighter and feel softer. He drops them into a waiting basket, which the apple-man snatches up, burying the bad in amongst the good.

'*Hot eels, O! Eels O! Alive, alive O!*'

Brippoki looks down Great White-Lion-street, into the writhing depths of the tub. He estimates four dead eels to every live one. No odds – they are snatched up with a flourish and cooked before hungry customers may tell the difference.

Little St Andrew's-street. A haggard fellow trundles a knife-grinder, offering to sharpen up blades. Great St Andrew's-street. Brippoki looks after where the thieves' gang set off to, and shudders.

He turns one final time.

Humming gently to the tune of 'King John's Song', Brippoki stares into Great Earl-street, the seventh of seven roads. Just close to the urinal, he sees the strangest apparition of all.

Layered sleeves all dangling in ribbons, the vendor's long coat frays into cobweb at collar, cuffs, and elbows, unravelling at its lower margins. He holds forth sheaves of caramel and honey colour, and mutters more than shouts in the way of his fellows, as if, unlike them, he would rather pass unnoticed.

A rat pack of dirt-black boys scampers around the stinking urinal, leaping and snatching thick handfuls of air. Tilting at the tall spidery-man, they fling their arms out. Catching flies, they toss them at his fly-papered hat. If their aim is true, and one of the insects should stick, the *warrigal* caper and send up a mighty shout. Often as not they miss. Dead or alive, the flies lodge in the man's thick hair and beard – the long and greasy threads of the miserable man-spider stuck fast with little black bodies, some struggling, mostly still.

Wheresoever Brippoki looks, all is false and foolish. There is nothing but the frenzy of buying, of selling, of eating and drinking, of noisily fighting, and dying.

~

The tendons of Sarah's right hand ached, her fingers black with ink. She had transcribed as much of the manuscript as she could manage for one day.

It had been hard going, compared to what had gone before. Her temples fairly throbbed from wading through a welter of prayer. The text's urgent tempo had accelerated to a fever pitch almost unbearable, but at its height had come astonishing revelations. The secret was perhaps unwittingly revealed, its significance unclear. She could hardly wait to share the news with Brippoki.

Giddily, and only a little guiltily, she moved around the book presses, looking for another location, suitably remote, in which to conceal the manuscript.

Ah, perfect.

Evening draws in. London's West End lights up.

Brippoki has gathered courage sufficient to quit Seven Dials, and drifts further south, then east. Brought to a pause consistently now, he very gradually traverses the length of Long Acre.

Rouged cheek by sunken jowl rise the national theatres: the Alhambra Music Hall on Leicester-square; the Pavilion, the Royal Italian Opera, the Queen's Theatre, and the Theatre Royal, Drury-lane. The beggars themselves grow more artful, singers and pavement artists, but also circus strongmen, acrobats, jugglers and conjurors. There isn't a crossing-sweeper or shoeblack, it seems, who cannot turn his hand for an extra coin.

An old blackfellow mutely holds aloft a sheet of newsprint: the paper, so oft-handled, is stained quite tan, almost falling to pieces. He wears a dark-coloured shooting coat of tweed. As with so many London faces, his eyes sink into hollows above cheekbones sharp as blades. When Brippoki approaches he shies away, to display in a new direction. The tragic old gentleman will not engage with anyone. He acts through old habit or instinct, a diehard having long ago lost the reason behind his actions.

Back in the World, Brippoki would think nothing of him. Among the Men, those who can no longer fend for themselves are considered a burden. He searches through his inner pockets. He still carries a little of the *walypela* coin. Grasping the old fellow's free hand, he turns it over, and presses his last shilling into the creased palm.

Brippoki's progress slows even further. At times he comes to a complete stop, letting the flow of commerce pass him by, or else to observe a peculiar character, an incident attracting his attention. Other times he stops for no reason, and does not care to look at anything in particular, but enters into a solitary trance. The noisome environment then fades from his sensation, and he, also, merges with it, to pass quite unnoticed – an individual spark, lost within a greater fire.

CHAPTER XXX
Friday the 5th of June, 1868

UNTIMELY CREATURES

'Who hears, who understands me, becomes mine –
a possession for all time.'

~ Ralph Waldo Emerson, 'Friendship'

'Blackpella bin big-pella worry-pella.'

Brippoki hung his head in apparent shame. He shook his locks in earnest.

He said, 'All sorry-pella, by cripes!'

Sarah reached out and patted the arm of his chair. Something must have happened that day to inspire such humility: that, or else he knew just how to get around her.

'I'm the one who should be sorry, *Bripumyarrimin*,' she said. 'I didn't realise the Museum would disturb you. Where did you go?'

Brippoki looked up and grinned, winningly.

'You say my name, miss,' he said. 'You say my name just right!'

He began to hum a distracted tune.

Sarah noticed more white in his eyes than usual, an effect perhaps of the dim light. In spite of their conversation – he was suddenly talkative – Brippoki only seemed to grow more faint and distant.

'I walk him road, longa town,' he paused to say. 'I walk and walk. Now it has tired me.'

He spoke, as always, with feeling. Brippoki shook his head some more, his staring eyes never lifting from the floor.

They sat in silence for a while. Sarah hesitated to begin with her reading, in case he might open up to her a little. She also felt nervous of tackling some of the headier passages to come.

'It a strange thing,' said Brippoki, perking up. 'Saw a man-spider.'

Sarah showed interest.

He raised an arm high above his head, his eyes following, even to the point of pulling him up out of his seat. 'Tall man, him hat,' he said. 'Tall hat, like chimeney-spout. Smokin' too!'

Sarah smiled a dark and doubtful smile. He began to waft his other hand around and behind the arm that was raised, as if spinning a cocoon of some diaphanous material.

'Sticky smoke,' he insisted. With a finger, he stabbed into it here and there, up and down. 'Black dots,' he said. 'Liket sticky bun!' Forearm held out at a right angle, he mimicked exactly the croak of a street-vendor. 'Three sheets! Three sheets!' he said. 'Catch'm live!'

Brippoki flopped back down into his chair.

'Bloody mad mob, dem pellas,' he said. 'Head spin so much, me think him broken. No more belonga me.'

Sarah laughed. 'I know how you feel,' she said. 'I felt much the same, the day after our trip to Greenwich.'

'"Grennidge",' Brippoki repeated. He looked thoughtful.

'Some tea,' she said, 'might revive you.'

Sarah excused herself.

In the Guardian's absence, Brippoki further examines her trappings.

The greater part of the chamber is in darkness – as on previous nights, Thara has only troubled to light a single lamp – but Brippoki's night-vision is keen.

Somewhat mystified, he considers a tiered stand or 'whatnot', the walnut legs spiral-turned. Each of its three shelves is topped with a delicate ornament. The same ritual figurines as run along the mantel also cram a side cabinet; he sidles up to the nearside wall, peering behind it.

Crouched and quiet, a spider patiently waits in his white thread-kingdom.

Sarah returned, bearing a full tray, to make ready for their nightly tea ceremony. Her notebooks were, she noted, untouched. Had it been she alone in the room, and their positions reversed, she would surely have sneaked a look. Brippoki appeared not to have gone near them.

'You like it with milk, that's right,' Sarah stated, 'and plenty of sugar.'

She pushed the silver bowl forward.

'*Bunjil*,' he said. 'Your pappa…him bery worry-pella.'

Her father, he said, afraid? Sarah didn't know why Brippoki was right: only that he was.

'What makes you say that?' she asked. She steadied the sieve, and tilted the teapot, pouring a cup for herself.

Brippoki looked around the room at great length, and regarded her a little insolently. He said, simply, 'You would not understand.'

Sarah returned the pot to the tray with a testy bump. Reaching for a spoon, she suddenly dropped it. The teaspoon clattered across the tray.

Brippoki knew about her father?!

Sarah flinched, checked herself, and then mopped up the spillage. She acted as if nothing had happened. She merely said, 'Let's see how our "wicked wretch" is doing, shall we?'

Abruptly she took up her notebook, and held it open in her lap. She scanned down the page, all afluster.

'Last we left off, Bruce and his luckless companions, Farr and Meredith, were betrayed by a man named Luker. They narrowly escaped capture, and were being pursued by a large group of about 30 men...'

'Untimely creatures,' Brippoki recalled.

'Just so,' said Sarah. 'The pitiable "untimely creatures" that were hunted are now the hunters.'

She cleared her throat and started to read.

> But oh, my dear readers, only think on the words of our Blessed Saviour Lord Jesus Christ: 'O ye men of faith, call on me in the time of your trouble and I will deliver you out of your woe.'
>
> Quite sensible of that horrid state of life that my sins had plunged me into, from the very bottom of my soul did I cry unto the Blessed Lord for my deliverance. My prayer was as follows:
>
> – O most Merciful God who made and created me. You know that I know nothing of Thy sacred words, nor for what end I was made. Therefore, Gracious God, I hope you will pardon me this morning for calling on You for mercy. What I now speak comes from the bottom of my soul, with the most liveliest faith and hope that ever a poor muck-worm like me possessed.
>
> – Behold them wicked men in the valleys beneath this mountain, how eager they seek my life. And they have brought with them dogs to devour my flesh.
>
> – O Lord, give not my soul to the Serpent nor suffer him to steal it by night. I call on Thou to raise from the earth a poisonous smell to the nostrils of those dogs which at this moment are tracing my footsteps to devour me. Suffer them not to follow me this day. Neither suffer those wicked men to behold me with their eyes, for if they do, Thou knowest they will separate my poor soul from the body. Then she must sink, for my sins are so heavy that my poor soul would not be able to bear them up.
>
> – O spare me, that I may repent me of my wickedness and save my soul. Amen.

'Amen,' said Brippoki.

> The reader will soon know that God surely heard my prayer that morning, my life was so closely pursued. I watched them till they went into the house of Luker, as I suppose to refresh themselves, after a tiger's hunt after my life. I then rose on a most careful manner, and went from the high hill into the woods.
>
> You will understand that my father and mother used to quarrel about religion. My father was a man who followed the Church of England, and my

mother used to go to what the people call Methodist meeting. This used to cause a dispute, for my mother would never give in to my father, but that both church and meeting was one by the will of God to Jesus Christ.

In the weekdays he would come home drunk and call her an Old Methodist Dog. Then she, on a Sunday, would what we call 'roast' him.

You shall hear what funny discourse they used to have about me, on a Sunday morning, when my father used to take me to church. For they both loved me to excess. And you may depend upon it, that my father and mother loved God better then ever they did their children, though they loved them dear enough.

Sarah turned the page a little too briskly.

Before my mother would let me go she would roast the old man a bit, in this manner:

– Ah, you are very Godly today. You forget how you come home every night in the week drunk, and call me an Old Methodist Dog. So now, Mister Godly Man, today I shall call you an Old Church Lion. So, Old Church Lion, don't think that you are going to take my favourite child with you to that playhouse of yours, which you know by the behaviour of the people is not much better. Have I not been there myself, and seen the actions of the people? There is one nodding, and another winking, and all of them looking round about them, and laughing and admiring the different dresses. And there is another thing. Don't you know that God will have nothing to do with you, Old Lion, without you are introduced to him by his Son Jesus Christ?

But my opinion is that God is well pleased with all people that go to church and meeting, for it is a good sign that they are jealous one of another who loves God best. I assure you that my father was devotedly fond of me as well as my mother. God bless them both, and I hope I shall meet their souls in Heaven, together with all my brothers and sisters, friends and relations, for I don't expect to see them any more on Earth.

Sarah took up her pen to make an adjustment, and in so doing missed how severely moved Brippoki was by the expression of these most recent sentiments.

I have run a long way out of our discourse about my father and mother, but this is a way that I learnt, by my poor old mother dragging me every night in the week from one meeting to another to hear the Gospel of Jesus Christ preached.

I never was taught anything by man on Earth, only what my poor old Methodist mother would tell me in her wrath. That is, God would punish me for my wickedness to my father, and her, my mother. For by rebelling against my father and mother I also rebelled against God. But, if I would pray in the midnight when I woke out of my sleep, and in the morning and at night when I went to bed, God would forgive me for all my sins and wickedness. And not only that, but by constant prayer night and day, that in all times of my trouble my blessed Redeemer would take me out of the hands of wicked men every time they sought my life. And I am sure those words are true.

For when we were in Luker's house, we had no thought of going to Mrs Peck's house. Farr said how dangerous it was going, so many people venturing our lives. But still I would go. This was that Great and Merciful Jehovah, for my poor mother's sake, who so constantly prayed to His Blessed Son Jesus Christ.

And well I know it, for when I was at home with her in London, she used to tire me with running to meetings every night in the week.

Parental roles reversed, this was Sarah's own experience in childhood. She smiled.

But to tell you truth, at that time I was too young to know much of God.

And this, too – her smile quite disappeared.

But I tell you, every time I went with her to meeting the old woman gave me a ha'penny. So you see, I used to go after her for the sake of the ha'penny. And praise be for it! For through the drunkenness of my father, she could not pay for schooling, so I could neither read nor write. But she used to tell me that if I minded what them good men said, it would be better than all the reading and writing on Earth. So it's true, for many a man that can read and write, when you come to discourse with him, you will find he knows nothing of Christ Jesus.

'Amen!' said Sarah.

She looked a little startled with herself. 'I'm so sorry,' she said, before continuing.

It was almost night, and we were nigh the road that leads to the River Oxbury, and those poor wretches so closely pursued our lives, that if they were on the road they would hear us. Then we all three should have lost our lives.

– O Farr, said I, I was born to live and not to die, so night and day I to God for mercy cry.

At those words we entered the road, where we travelled all that night in silence. About the hour of ten o'clock the next morning we arrived at the Oxbury amongst the settlers. When Farr discovered two men with whom he was well acquainted, we all three went into their barn loft for a short time, when Mark Dammers came to us and told us that we could not stay there, for that he expected the police officers and soldiers, who was seeking our lives night and day. This man was one of Farr's friends. Robert Hobbes was the other. While Dammers was talking to us, Hobbes came and called Farr and Meredith.

They went into the dwelling house of Hobbes and held council how they should leave me.

In a few minutes after, Dammers came and called me in a violent hurry. Farr and Meredith were with him. He told us we had not a moment to stop, for that the enemy was on the adjacent farm. But he only said this to frighten me. He told us to follow him, and he show us a place where we should be safe from our enemies. We all left the house and went into the woods. Farr had with him a large cake and a piece of meat, which Hobbes his friend had given him. He gave me the bread and meat to carry, because he knew he was going to leave me.

Sarah thought she heard Brippoki utter a curious little noise, but, purposeful, she pressed on.

As soon as we had left sight of the house, Farr and Meredith stopped behind, as I thought to ease themselves. Dammers went with me to the side of a large lagoon, where we sat down. But after a time Dammers went back, to see, he said, what was become of them.

I now was left by myself.

Here grief swayed me down to excess. Nay, as I thought, my very soul was melting. But the floods of tears that flowed from my eyes soon gave ease to my grief, and I, after a solemn praying, rose.

Necessarily, Sarah took a breath.

My prayer was as follows:

– Merciful God, look down from Heaven, and have mercy and compassion on me, a poor wretched sinner, and conduct me what either I shall go or what I shall do. For behold, I have now fulfilled my mother's saying to me in her wrath – that I should wander night and day like a pilgrim in the wilderness, seeking refuge and should find none.

Sarah marked Brippoki's own sharp intake of breath.

'Yes,' she confirmed, 'his mother's curse has become his truth.'

– But O, grant me the later prayer of my mother in her calm, for well I remember both that prayer in the wrath, and that prayer in her calm. Behold her later prayer, most merciful God:

– O most merciful Redeemer of all the world, I pray and beseech thee that all of my family who are shut up in darkness by sin may by the light of Thy blessed spirit find their relief. I also am informed by the planet of my dear son Joseph that he is to live and suffer for all the sins of this family.

There.

Sarah glanced up. Brippoki had been rocking back and forth, as if in contemplation of the prayers; he did not especially react to the different name.

She persevered.

– Come Blessed Jesus, come and take this child of mine into Thy charge, and convert him for Thy Heavenly use, O Lord, that his soul may become in Thy sight like a spark that flieth from a fire and kindleth the whole house.

– I further implore You, tell me what is this that I see in the countenance of my dear child. Is it persecution or Glory? O Holy Jesus, permit me to say the latter.

– Goodbye, my dear Joseph.

Sarah stopped to deliver what she hoped was a significant look.

– I shall not come to you any more, but may God send His messenger to you to abide with you forever, and help you through all your troubles of this life that is before you. For you have got a most wonderful high mountain to climb. And if ever you are cast away in the wilderness, do my dear Joseph call on the Blessed Lord Jesus Christ, and put all your faith and hope in Him. And now you see, my dear, I can't stop any longer with you, so goodbye. But may the Grace of Christ, and the blessing of God Almighty, and the fellowship of the Holy Ghost be with you for ever and ever, amen.

'Amen,' Brippoki said again.

'Amen, indeed!' Sarah snapped. 'Don't you hear what has happened?'

She stared into his patient face, before casting her head down a moment to cool off.

'Forgive me,' she murmured. Without her intending it, Sarah's voice had been raised with all of the fervent preaching, and with it her temper. She looked up, and carefully measured her words.

'Listen,' she said, 'to his name. George, George Bruce. In her prayers his mother is calling him *Joseph!*'

Stumbling across the discrepancy in the library that afternoon, she had at first been unsure who spoke: who, and about what to whom. But then came the second and third repetition of the same name.

'Joseph, Joseph, Joseph,' she said. 'Three times, in his mother's prayer.'

It had never occurred to her that he might have changed his name, but of course, in light of his criminal record, it made every sense that he should.

'You don't think it odd?' she said.

Brippoki appeared to think about it, yet still said nothing.

Sarah tried and failed to mask her disappointment: this was not the reaction she had hoped for.

'I find it odd,' she declared. She shuffled her papers. Did she want for his attention? She had made a deliberate effort to cut the most repetitive '*pritching*', without losing entirely its delirious aspect. Had it been too heavy going, even so?

'You believe in God,' she said.

Brippoki considered. Patiently she waited him out.

'The Truth,' he said at last, 'is the Way. It is life.'

As good a way of putting it as any she had heard – but not enough.

'You speak of truth, when I asked you about God,' she said. 'The Christian God.'

Brippoki took up the challenge. 'Me believe...' he said. 'Me believe in the land of your God. Here, God hold the most power.'

The gift, certainly, was not refused, but was not necessarily accepted.

'And you pray...' she said.

'Lawrence often say this to us. "Boys," him say, "we must pray to God to forgive us." We must pray to God to forgive us all them wicked things and mischief that we done.'

'Lawrence?'

'Our captain.'

She recalled him. 'Oh, yes.'

'All day...' continued Brippoki, 'all day I try to think about good things. We must not do those things that are wicked. They are wicked. We must pray to the Almighty Father, try to please 'im.'

Sarah approved.

'Almighty God, if it please him,' Brippoki said, 'then he will be good to me.' Raising his hand a moment, he corrected his previous remark. 'Whatever him do to me, it must be good.'

Sarah found no fault in him at all.

'I shall continue,' she said. 'Bruce returns to his story...'

> I have not repeated this prayer with ambitious thoughts, but by bearing those prayers in my heart to this day, I am in hope to obtain Thy powerful pardon from death and Hell. If I lay down in these woods I shall be dispersed from this stage of life by snakes or adders. And if I go forward, man-tigers will devour my flesh and drink my blood. O sweet Jesus Christ, have mercy on my never dying soul. O come my blessed Saviour, and lead me through these woods, for without your assistance this day, I perish.

Brippoki stirred in his seat, excited by mention of man-tigers.
Sarah settled back.

> Saying those words, I looked up to Heaven, and saw one of the most beautifullest sights that ever mortal eyes beheld. It was an enormous body of geese. The number of them was six or seven thousand. It is a most wonderful thing, for such a sight was never before that day seen in all the great South Seas, nor has it been seen since.
>
> I stood confounded, with my eyes fixed on the object. The flock descended so low that I perfectly beheld them in their elegance. They were perfectly

white as snow. They entered the east side of the lagoon where I stood. The circumference of this body of water was about three miles, out of which these beautiful creatures covered one. Without moving a feather on wing they went their circuit three times round the lagoon, distant from the water about 90 feet. Yea, my dear brothers and sisters, this sight appeared to me as if Jehovah had made a string fast to each of those beautiful creatures and was playing with them out of the window of Heaven. The powerful sun was in his full lustre of the day, and pressed with all its might on the down of those beautiful creatures. The reflection of them dazzled my sight. I could no longer look up.

But with my face towards the ground, swift as lightning my wondering thoughts run round. My heart with grief was arkless bound, and my wretched soul with fear was almost drowned.

Brippoki whimpered quietly to himself.

But while I confounded stood, a whispering voice to me did say:

– O wicked sinner do not despair, lift up thy head and behold the road thou art to take this day, for the Great Redeemer has heard thy cry, and sent thee word thou shall not die.

With those thoughts of inexpressible joy, I again looked towards the amenable birds, when with astonishment I see them all of a cluster, and as straight as a line they followed one another so that before the last took his station I positively lost sight of the first.

I set out through the woods in the same direction as nigh as I possibly could steer. For I said in my heart that God had surely sent them on purpose, to show me what road I should go. So it was true, for by going after them I saved my life.

Sarah closed her notebook.

'"Mine eyes have seen the glory!"' she exclaimed, a trifle ironic. 'Who would have thought.'

She drained her cup, and then looked at Brippoki.

'Revelation,' she said, 'upon revelation.'

He did not respond. Sarah elected to be more explicit.

'George Bruce is, in all probability, an alias,' she said. 'Not his real name.'

Who, then, was he really? Joseph…? Joseph who?

Sarah found it hard to credit: that Brippoki could appear so blithe and accepting of this latest turn of events.

He should be dying to know.

Brippoki, who was *Bripumyarrimin*, who was King Cole.

CHAPTER XXXI
Saturday the 6th of June, 1868

GETTING AND SPENDING

'A living body is of necessity an organised one – and what is organisation, but the connection of parts to a whole, so that each part is at once end and means.'

~ Samuel Taylor Coleridge, *Literary Remains*

'…spirit and body together, one single flower in bloom.'

~ Johann Herder

Sarah parted the curtains. Another warm and bright start to the day; sunlight filled the room. The sudden contrast was too much. She tugged on the drapes, closing the breach a little.

'I heard you,' croaked Lambert, 'in the night. Saying your prayers?'

Sarah took a moment to find her answer.

'Father,' she said, 'you know I always say my prayers.'

Rather than depart immediately for the Reading-room, she had decided to spend her morning at home, with Lambert. She had neglected him overmuch the last few days, and companionship must form a certain portion of his care.

Turning to where he lay in the bed, Sarah squinted. A streak of sunlight fell across the pages of a book, open on his bedside table; dazzled, she frowned, and closed it up.

She made him a present of *The Illustrated London News*, 'hot off the press'.

'Is it Saturday?' he said. 'I had thought it would never come!'

Lambert struggled to sit higher on the bank of pillows. These Sarah rearranged and freshened until he arrived at a more comfortable posture.

He did not take up the newspaper.

He said, 'Would you read to me, my darling? The print has become too small for these ancient eyes of mine.'

'It is the same size as it ever was,' she said. 'You wear out your eyes by reading through the middle of the night!'

'My mind must be occupied somehow,' sulked Lambert. 'My sleep is often disturbed. I am too restless.' Sudden antagonism made him raise his voice, distorting it unduly. 'I lie in this damned bed all day long!' he gargled. 'Is it any wonder that I cannot sleep at night?'

'Hush,' said Sarah. 'Let us not argue. I will read to you. There was never any doubt that I would.'

She hoped her voice, more well used this last week than it had ever been, would hold out.

'The National Sports if you please,' said Lambert. 'The noblest of all pursuits.'

He meant the cricket.

'If *you* please,' said Sarah. '…I have it.'

'Well, then!'

She chose a report on the Australian Eleven.

'"Mullagh",' she read, '"seems to be the 'all round' strength of the Aboriginal cricket team, as Cuzens, the bowler, did not take a wicket in the first innings with the gentlemen of Kent. None of them seem to like the Surrey slows; but, with the exception of a little lack of dash, Mullagh is a rare batsman. 'They catch,' so an able critic observes, 'a ball at long field by a snatch as it passes them, throw in and long stop well, and keep wicket by making one man into very near short slip and wicket-keeper as well.'"

'Hm,' she joked, 'how's that?'

Despite the many hours Lambert had spent impressing on her the finer points of the gentlemanly game, it was all Greek. All the same, Sarah felt gratified to learn something of the progress of Brippoki's team. She pondered the logistics of his recent appearances, and their frequent matches; surely even a man of his talents couldn't be in two places at once.

Lambert sucked at his teeth. 'This weekend's match is at Deer Park, versus Richmond, is it not?' he said. 'I dare say their quality will be decided.'

The morning light, combined with his enthusing, smoothed the creases from his habitually stormy features. He looked almost a boy again; that same boy clasping bat and ball alongside his sisters Emily and Fanny in their formal portrait, sketched so long ago – sepia over charcoal, with red chalk on their faces.

Sarah suddenly wished to divulge her secret.

Her great fear, however, was for Lambert to decree that she should never see Brippoki again. Awareness of his expressed views regarding Abyssinians and such overtook her inchoate impetuousness; the same black contempt would surely be extendable to an Aboriginal native, or anyone who chose to associate with them.

'…Grace…'

A stirring from Lambert saved her nausea from curdling.

'You said "grace"?' she asked. Was he still thinking of the cricket?

'Those,' he said, 'blessed with a natural gift must use it well.'

'By that you mean…?'

Lambert turned his head to stare at her, owl-like.

'By that I mean the Black Cricketers, yes,' he said. 'Of course.'

He gave the concept some further thought.

'But not exclusively,' he said. 'As grace is Nature's gift, so is a natural gift a Grace…God-given.'

The milky veil previously cloaking his gaze had been abruptly yanked aside. He regarded her, unblinking, with alarming clarity.

'I speak of physical Grace,' he said. 'There is but one true Temple in the World, and that is the Body of Man.'

Lambert gathered his energies, raising himself higher in the bed.

'The Soul – *ungh* – placed in the Body,' he said, 'is like a black diamond…the edges need sharpening in order to shine. It is the duty of every good Christian to make best use of the faculties, both mental and physical, that God has given him. Put them…to good purpose, and improve on them, if he can. *Spiritus Sanctus, corpus Christi*, mind and body in perfect harmony. Good health…to the greater glory of God.'

'Amen,' said Sarah.

She didn't entirely agree, but found agreement generally easiest.

'Men glorify God with their body, as in their spirit,' he continued, 'for matter and spirit are one…natural reflections of each other. This is as clear to me…as to one who gazes into a rock-pool, and sees the heavens, opened.'

His wonderful voice had begun to break apart. Lambert inclined his head a little, and looked away.

'Or is it,' he said, sounding bitter, 'that your soul makes the body, as the snail its shell?'

Before she could protest he started shouting. The preacher's voice, raised, filled the modest chamber to the very corners.

'"What?"' he said. '"Know ye not that your body is the temple of the Holy Ghost *which is* in you, which ye have of God, and ye are not your own? For ye are bought with a price…therefore glorify God in your body, and in your spirit, which are God's."'

Sarah watched as his rock-face shimmered and dissolved into a mess of creases. His distresses were unbearable to her, most especially when she could not divine the cause. She wanted to fly to him, but could not will her trembling body to move.

'All,' he said, 'all is held accountable to God! And yet look at me…! Little strength in my legs…my trembling hands, my vision so cloudy at times, I can't even read any more…and my lungs! My lungs rattle. Do you hear them? What *good* am I?' Lambert wailed. 'Of what use? A bishop-bird! Well housed, better fed, and higher-priced, that utters no note to speak of to redeem his keep. Jamrach himself could not sell me now!'

Even in the midst of his abject misery he could force her to smile –

'"But they're the fashion, sir," says he, knowing full well how every fashion shall pass away!'

– and kill that same joy in an instant.

With an offhand gesture Lambert cast aside these mortal thoughts.

'Forgive me,' he said. 'My mind is weak and slow.'

She took up his hand: it was hot. 'Every word disproves it,' she said.

His hand grasped hers back firmly, and gave it a shake.

Sarah watched, fascinated, his great cable veins at work. He had a strangler's hands. She admired them a little, even as she feared them, and then felt sorry either way. Their skin was puckered, blotched and discoloured, and in places the flesh gathered in tight folds. All of the force they had once contained was gradually shrinking away.

Lambert's first love was for cricket. Often throughout his life it had provided a refuge, in some sense, from reality. After a protracted illness – his health, in old age, shattered beyond recovery – there was no longer any escaping the inevitability of death: not even here.

'Sarah,' he said, 'my darling…all things must pass…'

He spoke of her mother, of course. She knew that.

'Hush,' she said, 'do not speak of it.' She would dearly love to hear him talk about her, but not at such a cost to himself.

Lambert rewarded his daughter's bravery with a bravery of his own. He insisted. 'All things,' he said, 'must pass.'

'If…if it is God's will,' she tremored.

Lambert's other hand closed around theirs both. 'It is God's *plan*,' he said.

No charcoal and no chalk; the innocent radiance earlier transforming her father's face had been wiped out.

She searched through the newspaper for something else to read out – almost anything would be suitable – but on hearing the rustling pages Lambert raised an imploring hand. He was too morose even to speak. Sarah glanced up, and saw that his eyes were closed. She understood.

'It's all right,' she quavered. 'I have business at the library.'

Sarah waited for a counter-command that never came. Putting down the newspaper, she made ready to leave.

'Are you sure there is nothing I can get you?' she said.

He nodded, faintly.

She could not leave him. She must leave him.

'Mary…'

His eyes flicked immediately open: Lambert was many things, but he was no fool. 'You have this month's rent money for the good Dr Epps?' he asked. 'It is due Monday.'

'We do.'

'Well, then…'

His eyelids closed again. He no more wanted the subject of their financial straits raised than she did. Sarah allowed herself a gasp of relief – but only once his bedroom door was shut, and she stood alone at the top of the landing.

Charles Lawrence strode into the Richmond clubhouse in full gear.

'We're almost ready for the off!' he called – only to face William South Norton, alone. 'Is he here?' said Lawrence bluntly.

South Norton pointed to the opposite doorway. 'The king,' he said, 'is in the counting house.'

The look engendered on the team captain's face was priceless. William South Norton realised his mistake.

'Oh!' he said. 'You thought I meant old Cole-face, didn't you? I'm afraid not.' South Norton made the sound of gathering spit, and mimed the anointing of his thumb. This he applied to his trouser front, at the groin. 'Him, we made a freeman of.'

Overgrown public schoolboy! Lawrence pushed past him. He made his way to where Bill Hayman sat at a desk in the outer office. 'We are ready,' he announced.

'Hi yo, Charley,' said Hayman, not looking up. 'Coping?'

'We'll be glad of the rest, tomorrow.'

Hayman hummed. 'Just going over the ledger for Graham,' he said, marking up a column.

Lawrence cleared his throat, ready to speak. 'I'm not happy about – '

'You realise,' Hayman interrupted, turning the foolscap file around, 'we're well on our way to making our first thousand?'

'What?' said Lawrence.

'Receipts are already there,' Bill Hayman said, 'just about. But look at our surplus!'

Lawrence looked. The Oval had brought them over 600 pounds, outlay accounting for around half of it. Maidstone had made just 35, again halved by their not inconsiderable expenses. Still, 300 pounds for a week's work was not to be sniffed at.

'And this week,' said Hayman, 'the odds have improved! Less than half off nearly 200 from Gravesend, even with the bedding fiasco. And we look to do as well here!' He patted the lid of their moneybox with a broad smile. 'Whisper it… over 500 pounds!' gloated Hayman. 'The future of our tour seems assured.'

He laid a friendly hand on Lawrence's shoulder.

'Perhaps ours,' he said, 'is the only little corner of Empire wisely governed just now.'

On her way to the library, Sarah stopped at the Post Office opposite to enquire after the receipt of any mail; but there was none.

She recovered the manuscript from the previous evening's place of concealment, tucked inside *Our Friends in Hell, or Fellowship Among the Lost*. A member of the library staff sprang to intercept her.

'Oh!' said Sarah. 'You made me jump!'

She felt hugely relieved to see that it was her co-conspirator in the affair, the junior assistant, Benjamin J. Jeffery.

'Miss,' he stammered, 'Miss Larkin, I take it you have seen the notice of closure.'

She had not. With a sweep of his arm, he indicated the nearest example; she could clearly see that copies had been liberally posted around and about the shelf units. He summarised the essential details, chancing once or twice to let his eyes alight on the offending article, clutched in her hands.

Within earshot of the superintendent, they were obliged to communicate in a sort of code.

Sarah's heart fluttered in a slight panic. She had been vaguely aware that May's scheduled closure had not occurred. Postponed by Museum authorities, it was rescheduled for the week beginning the 22nd of June, a fortnight hence.

Playing Lionheart to his Blondel, she spoke softly.

'I understand,' she said. She laid one slender palm across the top of Bruce's manuscript. Her voice shrank further, to barely above a whisper. 'I hope to be done with it sooner. I just need a few more days.'

This, evidently, was not the answer he had hoped for. Mr Jeffery's eyes conveyed all that he wished to say, eloquently enough. His life was in her hands.

He spoke through gritted teeth.

'Just so long,' he said, 'as you know.'

A lady-like cough from somewhere behind her, and he walked on abruptly, without another word. Sarah lingered a moment before turning.

A lady stood by the far exit doors, as helplessly as a cow at a gate. Instead of her raising her hand to the door, manners decreed that a gentleman must perform the operation, even had he a hundred-yard walk to do so.

Sarah took up her station for the day.

Brippoki clings to the undersides of eaves. He shelters in the darkest doorways, and deepest pools of shadow. Pale and ghostly shapes, endlessly parading, shimmer through the streets in sunshine.

In the cold light of day, parts of the city are so different as to be unrecognisable. He better understands the city by starlight, or moonlight. At the height of noon, features familiar from his Dreaming, double-exposed, rapidly fade – leaving only discrepancies: strange, monumental eruptions, insistent crowds.

Blinking, Brippoki stumbles, less sure in his movements for being unsure of his whereabouts. His Truth is mixed with falsehood, to the point where they are hard to tell apart.

Over the course of the recent week Sarah had been working ahead on her transcript, only in increments, but far enough to sow seeds of doubt.

The convenience of some of the names made them read almost like those in a novel. There was Luker, for instance, as in 'filthy lucre' – but also, perhaps, Lucifer.

Fiction was never so strange as the truth, supposedly, but it crossed her mind that the entire story might be just a fabrication, a fabulous invention. From the heaven-sent flock of birds to crossing paths with a shepherd boy, Bruce presented pious imagery neat as a pin. Running in remote and silent woods, through the dark night, in the wintertime, he was Blake's Bard, 'That walk'd among the ancient trees'. Martyred, naked, on thorns – '*Our legs and feet was tore*' – Sarah wondered at the power of his visions in the wilderness, the immaculate imagery they conjured: exceeding Popish raptures, all of the self-torturing punishments so beloved of Catholicism. Bruce was obviously a capable-enough storyteller, even something of a dramatist, to judge from recent notes. Yet, if his own identity were suddenly open to question, the *Life*, perhaps even the man himself, could be an elaborate fake; like Ossian, like Chatterton's works of Thomas Rowley.

For her own satisfaction Sarah felt she needed verification of some sort, one piece of hard evidence that could establish as fact the narrative lately overtaking their lives.

An alarm sounded. It was almost six o'clock. The entire readership within the library grumbled and prepared to end their studies for another day.

Sarah took up the blotter. Prior to closing up the notebook, she gently massaged her most recent lines. The text of the manuscript had become complicated, the most recent section having morphed into something of a playlet, fraught with unpunctuated dialogue that needed to be picked apart and carefully attributed.

Sarah went gliding amongst the shelves, seeking another hidey-hold for her precious cargo. She found what she adjudged a suitable haven, nestled up against another, eminently obscure title, *Public Performances of the Dead* by George Jacob Holyoake.

~

Saturday is payday for the workers of London. As evening advances, the streets throng ever deeper with itinerant market stalls and the eager shoppers who attend them. The barrows offer up ''ot taters' and sheep's trotters, fresh bread, milk and other sundries; every delight, in fact, on which it is possible to spend a week's wages. Spirits are high. Many of the men are paid from tables arranged at the public houses, and wives will be lucky if they do not drink their earnings away.

As natural light wanes, the gas taps and candles are lit. The streets flare up, self-generating gas-lamps giving off a fierce and intense white light. Vendors make sure to situate their stalls underneath them, the better to set off their wares. Strung out either side of long streets busy with amusement, the markets take on a fairground air.

Brippoki stands snake-charmed by tendrils of smoke that rise and curl in the cooling air. They come from the red flame of an old-fashioned grease lamp, set smack in the middle of a pickled whelk stand. He looks across a spread of silver herring, glittering by candlelight. The saliva is so thick in his mouth that he has to turn away.

Weaving, in a daze, he has once again wandered the whole day through.

Coloured lights bounce and strobe, pink, and red, and yellow. Brippoki closes his eyes and jerks his head, side to side, until their after-images judder to a halt. Spectres promenade twilight's unearthly beauty. They grin, their trails glowing green and blue, fading to purple as they pass. He thinks of the Great Serpent's gullet, and the forlorn creatures there. These are different, more like the coral-dressed mer-people that walked the river's depths, only closer now, and brighter still. They are fireflies, and dancing lightning bugs. Their laughter and squeals of drunken delight echo, as if from afar.

This weak yellow sun is incapable of baking his brain; Brippoki reckons himself to have slipped sidelong, into the Dreaming – when he is only faint from hunger.

Brippoki arrived a little earlier than usual, just as Sarah was finishing her supper. She had begun to leave a window open on the first floor, their tacit agreement being that this was all round the best way for him to perform his subtle entrances and exits – such an arrangement as one might have for a tame bird, or half-domesticated cat.

He saw that she was still eating. Brippoki casually reached out of the window to retrieve something from an adjoining sill – something unspeakable.

'I join you,' he grinned.

It was a piece of meat, charred and blackened, and, from the gamy smell, more than a few days old. Declining to sit on a chair, he squatted on the floor and began gnawing at the gross object, lips smacking in contentment.

'Dat *putjikata* proper good tucker, my word!'

Very much his word; Sarah hadn't the faintest idea what it meant.

'Where…' she hated to ask '…did you get that?'

Brippoki wiped the back of his hand across his greased lip and pointed up, towards the roof. His eyebrows danced a jig.

The meat was definitely off. She remembered, two or three nights before, as he was leaving, the sound of a strangulated yowl…

Putjikata.

Sarah pushed aside the plateful of leftovers, unable to finish her meal. She promptly cleared away the supper table, ready for them to reconvene with the text of George, *né* Joseph, Bruce – if Bruce he was.

He wandered the wilderness like a pilgrim. As the attributes of civilisation were stripped away, so he seemed to gain in spiritual awareness. The 'wicked, wicked wretch' was preparing to make his peace with God.

Brippoki chewed on a piece of stick tobacco, having stirred it first amongst the fine white ash in the fireplace. He refused his usual chair, preferring instead to stay on the floor. That made it seem all the more like story time in the nursery – only what a curious fable, and curiouser child.

Sarah stared at the pages ahead. She barely knew how to begin.

CHAPTER XXXII
Saturday the 6th of June, 1868

DOUBLE LIVES

'Then ev'n my buried Ashes such a snare
Of Vintage shall fling up into the Air,
As not a True-believer passing by
But shall be overtaken unaware.'

~ *Rubáiyát of Omar Khayyám*

Sarah took a deep breath.

In a short time after, I met a boy who was minding sheep. The child was much terrified, but I soon consoled him. He then gave me every information that I wanted, and directed me a nigh way for crossing the river that led through the village, which was my intent.

I went on in a most cheerful manner, and in a few hours came to the riverside, where I met a man who asked me my business. I told him I was going to banish myself from all society of mankind, and trust to the mercy of God in the wilderness.

He then insisted I should go into his house which stood close by. I consented, and as I walked by the side of him, I perceived that his heart was full of grief, pitying me, for the tears from his eyes rolled down his cheeks rapidly. This moved me. I replied:

– Friend, you are but a stranger to me. Therefore think not of my troubles. You see I don't fret for myself.

A good reason why, my heart was so full of grief, it would hold no more, and my soul was so light with faith in God that I dared every insect on the Earth to touch a hair of my head.

I entered his house. No brother could ever have treated me better, and he insisted that he would so do everything that lay in his power to save my life. I remained with him three weeks, during which time I related to him all my pedigree. And he, in return, every Saturday would bring me news what report was flying through the country about me.

The first Saturday when he came home from the green hills, he told me that there was a proclamation, for all persons that had absconded from the law to surrender themselves up, or in three days they would be outlawed. And he also told me that he had met with Hobbes, who informed him that Farr had written a private letter to a Colonel Fairfax concerning it, and by the answer of the said letter he was sure that if I would go to Colonel Fairfax with him I should not die. And, if I consented, that night I was to go with him to Hobbes' house. I immediately despatched him with the answer, to tell Farr that if he chose to trust his life to a rotten staff, I would not.

The next Saturday he again went to the green hills to draw his ration from His Majesty's stores, and at his return he gave me a full account of the death of all my companions. For they had given themselves up to the law and were hanged.

The third Saturday, he told me that there was a most desperate outcry about me. But he had good news to tell me. That was, he met a man that day who knowed me in England, and that he also would do all that lay in his power to save my life. I asked him the man's name. He told me Thomas Dargane.

I then thanked him for all his faithful kindness to me, for that night I should leave him and go to Dargane, for I well recollected him. And that night I with my friend went to the house of Dargane. Here I took leave of Charles Bell, who was my friend. I then remained with Dargane for some considerable time, during which time there was diverse of robberies, all of which I was accused. Nay at last there was a murder committed on the road that was also linked to me, although it was 40 miles from the River Oxbury that the murder was committed.

However this report, being rose on me, was the separation of Dargane and me, for as soon as he heard it he came to me in a violent hurry, and burst into such a fit of laughter at the lies that was told about me that I could not get one word out of him for some time.

But as soon as he recovered himself from laughing, he uttered these words:

– Bruce, I give you all that I possess, farm and wife, children and all my money, if you tell me how you do it.

– Do what, Dargane?

– How you fly, Bruce.

– Me? Fly? Dargane, I wish I could. But tell me, what do you mean, Dargane?

– Why, I can't help laughing, Bruce, when I hear what horrid lies they tell of you. There was a man murdered yesterday on Dick River Bridge, and there is one of the most dreadfullest liars in my house you ever heard tell of. He's just come from the green hills and positively swears that he saw you yesterday on the bridge, alongside of the murdered man. And that he would have caught you, if his foot had not caught a stump and he fell down! But he vows, by all the virtue of an old cabbage stalk that he has with him which he calls a gun, that he will have you Dead or Alive before this day week. So, come in and talk to him, for I am sure that he don't know your person at all. For he is not been in the country three months, so how can he know you? But mind, Bruce. Before him, call me 'Faithful', and I will call you 'Swift'. Because if we call one another by name he will discover you, and then you will be obliged to put him in the river.

We both entered the house.

– Come, my dear, is dinner ready? For I am sure poor Swift must be hungered, for he has been hard at work. Ain't you hungry, Swift?

– Yerse, Master Faithful, I am.

– Well, come, my man, sit down and fill your belly. Thank God for it, here is plenty. Come. I don't know your name, Master, but come and have a bite with us.

Here we all sat down to meat, and after we had all eaten our fill, I thus addressed my accuser:

– I presume you know Bruce, that you are in pursuit of him?

– Know him? Ah, that I do. And if ever I see him again, I be bound he don't get away.

– Ho, then you have seen him?

– I see him yesterday murder a man on Dick River Bridge, but he didn't know that I knowed him. But I did, though.

– Well, my friend, but if you see Bruce murder a man, you are as bad as him if you didn't strive to stop him.

– I did, sir, but he run away from me.

I turned to Dargane.

– Well, Master Faithful, what do you think of it?

– Why, Mister Swift, I think what a dreadful thing it is, if this poor man is mistaken in the person of Bruce.

– Yes, Master Faithful, that is what I was thinking of myself. But this man says that he is sure he knows Bruce. And Bruce don't know him. Those words, Master Faithful, puts me in mind of a few words that I heard a doctor of the blessed elect say once, when I went with my old mother to hear a sermon preached. The old man took his text about St John the Evangelist, and these was the words: 'Behold, my dear brethren, St John was in the world, and the world knew him not, but he knew the world.' Do you understand those words, my man?

I was speaking to the stranger once more. He replied:

– No, sir, I don't. It is like a riddle to me.

– Well, my man, I will tell you. Understand that St John the Holy Evangelist is as God, and God is as the Holy Evangelist St John. For whatever one said, the other agreed to, together with the Holy Ghost when they made your seed and mine. And then made they a garden to sow that seed in, which is this world, that you and all people are in. If you mind and look out sharp, you will become a freemason by my discourse to you.

– St John was one that was with God when he lay the foundation of this world. Therefore the Holy Evangelist knowed the Heavenly works as well as the Earthly ones. But the world, and the people that were in the world at that time, knew nothing about how Heaven or Earth was made. So, how could they know anything of St John the Holy Evangelist that was at the making of all?

So it is with you, my man. How can you know anything of Bruce, when you told Master Faithful that you have not been in this country four months? And to my knowledge Bruce has been in the country above eight years, for I came in the ship with him.

– And there is another thing. I am sure Bruce has been in the woods this five months. So how can you say that you know a man you never saw? And when you do see him, you don't know him! Why, I might be him for all you know.

– No, I am sure you aren't him, sir.

– Why, what makes you think I ain't him?

– Because you would run away, sir, for fear I should shoot you.

– Ho, Master Faithful! Do you hear this?

– What is it, Mister Swift?

– This poor man says that if I was Bruce, I should run away for fear of this old candlestick that he has with him… Putting all jokes aside, I tell you what you had best do, my man. That is to go home, and pray to God to give you Grace, that you may know better than running about seeking a man's blood for the sake of emancipation. That is what you are to have, my man, ain't it? If you take Bruce dead or alive.

– Yes, sir. And I aim to have a farm, as that is a settlement in this life, for a short time.

– But look here, my man. What a shocking thing it will be for you, if by seeking the life of Bruce for the sake of your emancipation you lose your free pardon from Christ for your immortal soul, and drop into Hell, where you will have a settlement forever.

Sarah turned the page.

At those words, all in the house, instead of laughing as they had done, they all burst into a flood of tears. Because Dargane and his wife well knew my spirit, and expected every moment to see the poor midget wallowing in his blood. But Dargane see the fire of my soul darting through my eyes, and exclaimed with a loud voice:

– O Bruce!

That was a little too loud.

Sarah leant in closer, to render the shout instead as a sort of stage whisper. Brippoki sat further forward, on tenterhooks himself.

– O Bruce, consider my dear children, and don't take his life in my house!

Brippoki jerked backwards, as if losing his balance.

'Are you all right?' Sarah asked. She continued.

At those words the poor miserable wretch turned quite pale, and got up and left the house. Whatever betide him, I don't know, for neither Dargane nor me ever heard of him after. But for the safety of Dargane and his family, I that night went down the river to Samuel Woodhum, a freeholder to whom Dargane had recommended me.

I stopped with him till the cries became furious through all that country about me. All through I was hard at work for my living. But when I heard those horrid lies that daily rest on me, I said in my heart: 'Behold, old merciful Redeemer. It is not men that tell lies on me, but devils. Therefore I will again return to thy desert places, where thou hast ordained for a wicked wretch like me to wander.' I told Woodhum my intent. He pressed me to stop a few days, and then he accompanied me back to my first friend by that riverside, who received me with great joy. It was at night, but, it being too dangerous to stop in his house, he then took me to an old house half full of straw. It had no doors, nor window-shutters. Within the immense body of straw there were hundreds of snakes, adders, vipers, rats and mice. I was inexpressibly tired. Now, the responding eases fell from the loud cries of my soul, filled all the chambers of my heart, and hushed all my worries to sleep. I fell down amongst the straw, where I remained till the next night, when I went down to the riverside with that intent to cross it, and go up among the mountains of that country.

'Go…up among mountains dat country?' Brippoki queried.

Sarah nodded, 'Go up among the mountains.'

Having entered fully into the drama, Sarah enjoyed the taking on of different character parts. She had varied the tones of her voice to suit the supposed manner of each. Just as her father had lived much of his life by nature outward-bound, her mother had best enjoyed the diversions of theatre, and it was perhaps these instincts that ran thickest in her blood – another innate talent lain dormant.

With his wide grin, or frown, or expressions of shock as appropriate, and the occasional steady nod, throughout her performance Brippoki had egged her on.

'Thomas Dargane,' said Sarah. 'Does that name mean anything to you? No? What about Hobbes?'

Brippoki merely extracted the stick he had been sucking at and tucked it away behind his ear.

Of course not – wasn't it Hobbes, in the *Leviathan*, who wrote that man was a naturally selfish unit? Sarah consulted another of the lists she had made on various slips of paper.

'Mark Dammers,' she said, 'Charles Bell, Samuel Woodhum?'

What was in a name? Brippoki shook his head to each one. He sported a daft expression, as if they played at a game.

'How about the River Oxbury, or the River Dick?' she pressed. 'I was wondering if either of those places were familiar to you.'

No. She supposed the Aborigines would have their own names for such places.

'No matter,' she said. 'Carrying on… Something happened in the middle of this sequence that I don't fully understand, an interruption of sorts to the ongoing narrative. It reads as follows…'

Just as I was about to relate to the world this part of my life, where Dargane laughed so hearty at the lies that was told behind my back in New South Wales, then three of Beelzebub's gang jumped up in the house of Greenwich, where I was in the year 1817, June the 16th, about this work. It was eleven o'clock in the day when the three devils came about me, and all of them being in authority over the rest of devils, they demanded I should go with them to their master, to answer for a quarrel that I had with the she-devil that was one of the three. As I went with them to their master, every now and then I would look them in the countenance, and they all three looked like an old tame baboon that I saw once playing with a child. When the child gave him a smack of the head he would twinkle his eyes and screw up his mouth as if he was sucking plums. So were the faces of those vipers. They twinkled their eyes and screwed their mouths, being crammed with infernal lies by the Serpent, which they vomited before their master.

'And there,' said Sarah, 'the digression as suddenly ends. It reminds us, I suppose, that he is in the Hospital while dictating all of this. We then return to the main story, and the account of Bruce's dialogue with Dargane.'

According to her calculations, performed earlier that day, the reported events took place just after the turn of the century, around the year 1803.

'Oddly enough, Dargane shares a joke with Bruce over precisely this: his ability to be in two different places at the same time.'

Brippoki looked guarded. His face, drawn, seemed a shade paler than before. He had definitely lost a touch of his former pristine colour.

Whilst enjoying his grisly supper, and whenever she looked to him as they read, he had seemed much at ease in her company. It was only when she caught sight of him out of the corner of her eye – when he was not concentrating, not overly conscious that she observed him – that Sarah sensed collapse in his posture.

He looked so very far away, lost among his private thoughts.

However hard she worked, she really was no wiser than when they had first met.

'If you don't mind,' Sarah said, 'I think that's where we'll leave the reading for tonight. It has been rather a long day…as I'm sure it has been for you, too.'

He should have been at the cricket match, in Richmond.

'Tomorrow,' she continued, 'I shan't be able to read to you. The Reading-room is not open on Sundays. And anyway, I should spend the day with…with my father.'

Sphinx of black quartz, judge my vow.

'He is not well,' she said.

Brippoki stood, and bowed. Sarah stood also.

'Are you…I can get you something,' she suggested. 'Perhaps a drink. You can stay a while longer, if you like.'

He shook his head and made for the open window. The night was mild and the curtains hung slack.

'We can reconvene on Monday, in the evening,' she told him. 'There is some way I can contact you, in the meantime?'

'I will come,' he said.

'I can't fetch you anything? You're sure?'

Sarah had intended passing him a few coins: the man was reduced to eating cats! But he was already gone. He had got all that he wanted, which was for her to continue with Bruce's story. She returned to the table and gathered up the various texts.

Dargane had very obviously feared that Bruce might strike, or even possibly kill his accuser. It seemed all the more remarkable that Bruce, while protesting of his innocence, should freely admit the same; a lively bit of drama, relived in the moment, and, Sarah felt, played successfully to much the same end.

> *In a short time after I met A boy who was Minding sheep. the child was much terfied. But I soon consold him.*

As in the library, when first reading these innocuous-seeming phrases, she was struck by a vivid mental image – that of the escaped convict beating the boy; not praying, but cursing God the while. Why continue to doubt the truth behind what she read?

Sarah began to suspect herself of base prurience.

> *…my Heart was full of grief it whold hold no mor. And my soul was so light with faith in God. that I Deared every insick on the earth to touch A Heaire of my head.*

Bruce sounded beatific, resigned to his fate or his fortune. She wondered how he must have looked – probably wild, his flesh torn, and horribly burnt by the Australian sun.

Sarah closed the window, and climbed the stair. She would clean up the supper plates in the morning, making sure to dispose of those bare bones Brippoki had left behind.

Feeling a little queasy, she stopped on the middle landing, next to the door to Lambert's room. She couldn't hear anything.

She opened the door a crack. It was too dark to see within.

'Father?'

She barely breathed the word. Opening the door wider, she peered towards the bed. It was so very dark.

'Father?'

Her throat caught. Sarah saw the shape of him, sat up in the bed. She caught the glint of his eye, and heard a faint sound.

'…Lambert?'

A chill finger ran the length of her spine.

Lambert Larkin was sound asleep. The rattling in the darkness was his lungs as they laboured.

CHAPTER XXXIII
Sunday the 7th of June, 1868

'UMBRA SUMUS'

'The feelings are blunted, [...] the future a blank;
in the dirt they are, and in the dirt they must remain.'

~ George Godwin, *London Shadows*

All is without form. Then comes red brick and hard paving, the sting of grit on flesh, in eye. The street swirls into focus for a few rapid heartbeats, before layers of burning gauze again strip it away.

Brippoki jogs through billowing swells of vapour: the white mist at the base of a storm-fed cataract, turned acrid and choking. It leaks from every open window, through hot grilles underfoot. He glimpses the bodies of men, below the level of the ground, stripped naked against fearsome heat. They stir at great vats of boiling red liquid, a stew of raw sugar, blood, and charcoal. The smell is astonishing, and soaks into everything. Brippoki beats at his sleeves and chest as he progresses from one cloud to the next.

All turns white, then again red. The earth shakes, and the air fills with hammering and screams from a sky plunged into sudden darkness. He feels his clogged lungs about to burst.

Sweet sticky steam – the same taint he suffers to linger since that first night, deep in the Well of Shadows – threatens to swallow him whole. He is not Dreaming. Here is death, physical death.

Turning aside from the main street, Brippoki runs through a small square. He takes this brief opportunity to breathe, only to be faced with more of the same. Unwilling to backtrack, he has no other choice but to plunge headlong, deeper into the miasma.

For all of the reasons the manuscript brought back to mind, Sarah Larkin no longer went to church, not even – most especially not – on a Sunday.

Throughout her childhood she had been forced to attend twice daily on the Sabbath, in addition to at least two visits during the week. Her own father was ever the main speaker, and Lambert would speak at the pulpit in the same way he did at home – stern, didactic, above all disapproving, inspiring more of fear than devotion. His business often seemed less about heaven and happiness than the threat of banishment from the same. Petitioners and practitioners of other religions, notably the multiplying sects within the Anglican faith, were his particular targets.

Above all reproach when it came to his own moral conduct, he had never to her knowledge touched a drop of alcohol. And he never, ever went out at night. Between the hours of eight and nine o'clock in the evening the curtains would be drawn and the holy candle lit for family worship; she was taught early to kneel separately, in private prayer. A Bible reading, then a half-hour's discussion concerning the text, and she would be put to bed.

On rare occasions, at least while Sarah's mother was still alive – Lambert being somewhat highly regarded within his own professional circle – they would receive other ministers as their dinner guests. Conversation after the meal invariably turned to examination of doctrine and a re-establishment of principles. At needlework and such in the same room, Sarah and Frances were allowed to attend, but only on the understanding that they were strictly forbidden to speak, unless spoken to.

And as for the 'blessed elect' themselves, her father was a rare bird among them. Although ministers of God who lived by His Word, many obeyed nary a syllable of it. They held no qualification, to pass judgement on the behaviour of others. Prideful thought though it might be, Sarah recognised in herself, by true nature – in her spirit or soul – what they were only by profession.

Her upbringing, then, had made her perfectly faithful, a cynic and a sceptic resistant to any and all indoctrination. She knew her own mind, and in her own mind she trusted. The dutiful daughter, compliant and obedient, was no sheep to follow blindly in her father's footsteps, without question.

Thus far, at least, Sarah hoped that Lambert could be proud of her.

Brippoki gulps air, careful not to take in too deep a draught of an atmosphere still noxious and repellent. He filters each small mouthful, before swallowing it down. Unsure how far, or for how long, he has sprinted and shouted, he has at last outrun the awful corruption. It clings fast to his hair, and to what remains of his garments.

Come to rest a little way west of the London Hospital, he sits at the foot of a curious-looking hillock. Whitechapel Mount is a dust-heap, a truly enormous accumulation of every sort of household refuse. Hogs snuffle and root at the base. Children delight on its artificial slopes. They run up and slide down, joyously rolling in the muck below. Elsewhere about the sides, solemn and solitary, clamber the adults. Each carries a sack, collecting from the discarded materials that form the mound: horse-dung, cinders, and scraps of cloth. Scavengers, they never raise their eyes from the ground.

Brippoki runs at the heap and in short order gains the summit. From the top he can see, further north, the mesh of railway lines, and enormous factory chimneys smoking. Turning, he faces the imposing hospital building and its grounds. Everywhere else, as far as the eye can see, street after street after street, are the endless piles of brick, carelessly and randomly deposited.

The sky hangs low. Buffeted by the strong winds, Brippoki begins his descent. Near to the mid-point his way is barred. The dirt itself stirs and rears in front of him. A grubbing toiler, rags greased with marrowfat, caked in dust and birdlime, totes its bag of slime. Brippoki recoils. A claw-like hand extends to lift a long, dirt-yellow shaft. Bone-pointer! In a blind panic he swerves. Losing his footing, he tumbles head over heels the rest of the way down.

Landing in a thrash of limbs at the bottom, Brippoki leaps to his feet and immediately runs. Hitting a busy street, one of the widest he has seen, he flings himself across both lines of roaring traffic.

He runs a good thousand yards before daring to even think of slowing down, and never once looks back.

Little distinguishes a Sunday morning in London. Fewer omnibuses operate and there are no 'cabs', so the roads are quieter, yet by no means quiet. The pavements remain as crowded as ever. Bodies spill over into the street at less risk of being run over, that is all.

The markets from the previous night continue, and Brippoki loses himself, gladly, in the crowd.

'Awright, guvnor?' A Whitechapel man tips his hat and gives a wiggle of his moustaches. Whether he is polite or poking fun, Brippoki has no way of knowing. Unaccustomed to the least acknowledgement of his presence, he merely smiles and walks on. Compared to the intricate web of taboo that governs the British Islanders and their drawing room rituals – which Hayman and Lawrence have thoroughly schooled them in – there appears to be no etiquette for the street.

Along Brick-lane, the crush of bodies becomes intense. For minutes on end no one is able to move in any direction, neither forward, nor back. A whiskery man on his right-hand side, thin and shabby, reeks of alcohol, others of mildew, old sweat, and indigestive breath. Brippoki tries ducking forward, to no avail.

As they draw level with Thrawl-street the bottleneck begins to ease. From the back, a gang of young boys squeezes through the crowd, the smallest of them seeming to wriggle out from beneath Brippoki's arm. His upturned face whines for spare change.

'*Gerahtavit!*' shouts a stern voice.

Another grinds out a warning. ''Ang onter yer purses, ladeez and gents!'

The beggar boy, whip-smart, sinks from view. He pops up again a few yards further forward, rags fluttering. Minutes later, at the kerb, Brippoki sees him again. He stands proud among his peers, childish chest puffed out. An older youth taps his shoulder and again he sidles into the crowd. Brippoki follows the sightline of those remaining. They observe the opposite side of the street, where an old *gin* runs a fruit stall, a red-spotted handkerchief tied around her scrawny neck. A hand shoots out from the crowd, grabbing at her apples. The gang shout, betraying their agent. The stallholder turns, and, with a speed surprising for her age, lashes out with both her stick and her tongue. The small boy repays her foulest curse twofold and, unashamed, pitches a rosy pippin directly at her temple. The old woman falls, more from shock than from the force of the blow.

The crowd churns, and, though many hands grasp for the thief, none is able to catch him before he slides away. Sympathetic supporters gather up the victim of the assault. Grey hair in disarray, her dark eyes curdle to mud.

'I'm an old woman!' she shouts, indignant. She wipes at the dirt on her cheeks as if to dry an imagined tear, and wails pitiably

'Where's old Bandy Shanks?' someone demands to know.

'Niver around when yer needs 'im,' comes the reply.

Brippoki has to admire the gang's cunning ploy. In all the excitement, no one misses the red-spotted handkerchief.

A teenaged coster, seeking to escort his gal in some semblance of fine style, delivers a sudden sharp dig to his ribs. A moment later the lad happens to shove the wrong person. With a butcher's shop smack of flesh on flesh, he is sent rolling into the gutter. He rises up swinging. Evil on their minds and in their hearts, the ugly mob gathers around. Broken-veined and wild-eyed, they howl for blood. Brippoki knows the signs of drunkenness all too well.

A stocky middle-aged man in a dark blue uniform intervenes. Finger stabbing, he cautions the complainants. Brippoki especially marks his pointed headgear. The majority he meets on the streets resemble to some extent those spirits that populate his Dreaming, but not this one.

Seeing there is to be no bloodshed, an old man next to him turns away. 'Jest in time to prewent it,' he scowls, 'the warmint.'

Grumbling and sour, the crowds move on. Brippoki no longer struggles, but goes with the flow. An accumulating lethargy has crept into his bones. Something deep inside him gives up.

The wailing ting-ting of a thin bell wheedles and cajoles from a small gospel hall, hidden down a nearby side street. In the opposite direction, and then from a few blocks north, the summons is reinforced. The hour of eleven has arrived, and with it the chorus of church bells begins in earnest. Brippoki winces with each successive crack and clang.

'Move along,' orders the policeman. 'Move along now.'

Two dark-blue-suited colleagues wearing bright white gloves join him, to shoo the market away. The shopping crowds are swiftly dispersed. The traders wheel away their barrows, and retire to count their blessings. Within minutes the streets are emptied. Only Brippoki remains, rotting fruit at his feet, a scrap of waste paper, caught in the breeze, jerking before him like a fish on a line.

A new group slopes out of a side doorway. Young men, they wear their caps so far forward on their heads that their eyes are no longer visible. Eager yet wary, they creep about on the dead lurk, sizing up which of the surrounding shops or houses might be emptied during church services.

Brippoki wanders onto a patch of open ground, stretches himself out on the threadbare grass, and leaves them to it.

Eyes closed, he tries his best to envisage George Bruce. An English seaman, his weather-beaten face is the same colour as the brick. His actual features are a haze, impossible to resolve, soon dissipating, lost to the city.

Brippoki sits up. A bank of cloud has stolen away the sun, and in the chilly gloom he realises he is no longer alone.

The disused graveyard is bounded by the long side wall of a public house, and also the back end of a ramshackle terrace. A gravel path stretches down the centre. In amongst threadbare trees scattered either side drift maudlin figures. Anonymous bundles of rag, they eventually come to rest against the marginal walls, faces turned, obscured in shadow. In fear of the bone-pointer smuggled among them, Brippoki stays rooted to the spot.

From the west, out from beneath the terrible spire of Christ Church, a general hubbub arises. The congregation, outpouring, begins to filter onto the gravel path. As they draw near, the scrap piles animate. They drag themselves closer to where the worshippers file past, pious and hopefully charitable.

Looking at the folk coming out from the church, it is obvious that few are any the better off, yet many drop a penny where they can. One beggar, a blind man, has trained his dog to grip the begging bowl. The novelty secures extra success.

Gathered not far from where Brippoki stands, the same four thieves seen previously sing a saintly psalm; feet and heads now bared, a couple hold their jackets apart to assure that they possess no underclothing. The passing crowd loudly dismisses them; in comparatively rude health, they are branded 'shallow coves'. Black looks aplenty are thrown in their direction, but no coin.

Once the last among the stragglers have quit the scene, the barefoot young men stride over to Brippoki, shoving him to the ground by way of an introduction.

'Dog on it!' says the bravest. 'Yew ain't no anvilhead nor Abr'am-man, any more'n we are!'

'There's nowt for you here, Tom,' snarls another. 'Beat it!'

One of the group slyly coming up behind, Brippoki is struck a sharp blow on the back of the neck. They close in around his prone form, teeth bared, balling their fists.

'Yer in the 'Ditch nah, mate, entcha,' one snaps. 'In it up t'yer neck!'

'This is *our* patch!' The last one to speak delivers a swift kick to Brippoki's belly, for emphasis. '*Right* queered our pitch today, you did!' he says. 'Filthy cunt!'

Before Brippoki can catch his breath or reach for the *waddy* tucked in his belt, they bear down as one to redouble their assault, punching and stamping him into submission. His feeble moans and outstretched hand only spur them to greater ferocity. With every impact, bright starbursts of light fill his vision, until there is only blackness.

When he comes to, the first thing Brippoki registers is surprise that he still lives. He dares not open his eyes, but waits for the pulsating cycle of colours to slow. His conscious mind explores his various aches and pains. Checking bodily extremities, he assesses the damage. His breathing is fine, if a little ragged. He has probably suffered bad bruising, but nothing seems broken – at the most, perhaps, a cracked rib. Lucky.

Brippoki's eyelids flicker open. A ladybird walks the length of a stem of grass. That same green grass covers over half a world, turned on its side. He can hear the scratch of ants, busy below. With an effort he sits up.

Bone scrapes along bone.

The shadows have lengthened considerably, and the day is almost done. He can feel the tautness of congealed blood around his nostrils, dried along his top lip. From a nearby bush, he carefully selects a couple of broad leaves. He wipes his face clean, cracking and applying the moisture from another plant as a salve.

Backlit by the setting sun, the black tower of Christ Church darkens the rectory garden. Brippoki quails beneath the sharp shadow thrown down. He crosses into quiet Church-street, a dark vale, also largely consumed, and makes for the far corner. At the tip, he has to stop and hold his aching sides.

Best to take things slow at first.

He looks up. A flare of orange light illuminates the front of another church building. The dramatic sideways slant of a dying sun's rays illuminates each pit or protruding part of the brick and plasterwork. Brippoki feels glad to have survived, to be alive. He senses himself suspended, between the states of life and death, on the verge of some grand discovery.

Brow creased, he studies the stone relief of a sundial within the chapel's elongated pediment, set high overhead. The hours are clearly marked with roman numerals. He knows enough to understand the *walypela* look to these letterforms as a means to quantify time. A pair of sticks, somewhat like a water-diviner, protrudes from the upper centre. The shadow it casts points off the dial, directing his attention towards more characters that cap the design: four digits, like those on the grave marker, only different.

Carved beneath is a brief inscription, '*Umbra sumus*': mysterious words that he cannot understand.

CHAPTER XXXIV
Monday the 8th of June, 1868

THE ROAD TO DAMASCUS

'So it's roll up your blankets, and let's make a push,
I'll take you up the country and show you the bush,
I'll be bound you won't get such a chance another day,
So come and take possession of the old bullock dray.'

~ 'The Old Bullock Dray', traditional

Turning to greet his tenant, John Epps raised his hat, a faint medicinal whiff for his cologne.

'Miss Larkin!' he said.

'Dr Epps,' said Sarah. 'I was about to leave this for you.'

She presented him with a plain brown envelope.

Amid the morning bustle of Great Russell-street, they met outside the front door to No.89. The landlord was diminutive, a well-groomed man of middle age. They stood almost eye-to-eye, he on the front step and she the pavement. In taking up the envelope he glanced across her right shoulder. She had approached from the direction of Mills and Wellman, Ironmongers, Post Office and Savings Bank.

Rent money in hand, he squinted up at the low sky. 'It seems almost unfair,' he said, 'given the preternatural warmth of recent weeks, that today should start out so uncommonly cold.' He gave a genial little shiver, before addressing her more directly. 'Uncommonly cold... I trust you are wrapped up warm against the elements?'

Sarah smiled weakly. He saw lines of anxiety on her face, and that she clutched a second, much larger envelope. 'If you'll excuse me...' she said.

'Certainly.' He stood aside and she rushed in through the open door. 'And, thank you!' he called after.

Sarah Larkin's slender, retreating figure had already disappeared around the stairwell. Dr Epps retrieved his key, still dangling from the lock. He turned to face the queue of patients for morning surgery.

'All right,' he said. 'Who's first?'

~

Without pausing to remove her bonnet or outside garments, Sarah tore at the seal of the large envelope. The correspondence came direct from the Admiralty, from the office of the clerk Dilkes Loveless.

'Dear Miss Larkin,' it read. 'Thank you kindly for your recent letter. I count myself delighted to have this further opportunity to assist you in your endeavours. To whit, please find enclosed a Navy-Office list of those ships on which George Bruce is recorded as having served.'

Sifting through the appended papers, she found a table of sorts, copied out in the clerk's elegant hand. This she gave a cursory examination before returning to his cover letter.

'Further references to this same individual,' he went on, 'are found among articles of gubernatorial correspondence held at the Admiralty. He writes to the Secretary of State for the Colonial Department, presenting his Memorial.

'Records returned by Lachlan Macquarie, governor of the colony at New South Wales at that time, detail his response concerning George Bruce, "who went by the name of Dreuse in this Country".'

George Bruce had once gone by an entirely different name. Only now was she in possession of both halves – 'Joseph', according to a slip in the relation of his own *Life*, and 'Dreuse'. Joseph Dreuse.

Sarah penned an immediate and hasty reply. Making sure to thank the clerk profusely for going out of his way to assist her, she then requested – if he would be so kind – the full text of the correspondence. Bruce's 'Memorial' must, she felt, bear relation to Bruce's *Memoirs*.

Sarah valued complete information in a way that only a clerk might appreciate, and said as much. And then, since it nominated vessels additional to the Admiralty List, she traded in her own tally of those ships on which Bruce said he had served, as recorded from the manuscript thus far.

She referred herself to the additional comments Dilkes's transcript had included: written against the first ship listed, the *Lady Nelson*: 'No books'; and later: 'Vol. Sydney, deserter from *Lady Nelson*'.

'Deserter'…this one word went so entirely against what she understood from Bruce's earlier *Memoirs* that she very much wished to know more. She would have to see what accounting was yet to be given in the more honest-seeming *Life*.

Finally, thinking that it could do no harm, but might indeed be arousing of the clerk's curiosity, she made declaration of her suspicions: that 'George Bruce' was a false identity, latterly adopted by man whose real name was almost certainly Joseph Dreuse, or else something very similar.

Sarah quit the house again. She posted the new letter, and then, making her way down Duke-street, continued south. No time to retrieve the manuscript from where she had last left it – she would not be reading it today. The author's very identity being in question, she meant to trace Bruce back to his literal source, his birthplace. Her intent was to proceed directly to St Paul's, the parish church of Shadwell.

Catching an omnibus from New Oxford-street, Sarah sensibly sought travel advice from the conductor. She remained on board accordingly, until the start of Whitechapel.

Alighting there, she cut down Leman-street on foot. Once before, while her mother was still alive, they had ventured here as far as the Garrick Theatre.

Hard alongside, at times overhead, the steam trains rattled past constantly; London and Blackwall Railway passenger locomotives serving Fenchurch-street station; goods transports to and from Wapping's wool and wine warehouses.

The air grew thick with fumes. Sugar refineries, prevalent hereabouts, generated an atmosphere most unnerving. Gratings, set in the pavement, revealed lurid aspects of a hell, sufficient almost to make Sarah turn tail and run. Handkerchief pressed across her nose and mouth, she maintained her course.

The Ratcliff-highway – a coagulate of older, lesser roads – ran across the top of Wapping Island, from Little Tower-hill in the west almost to the Regent's Canal in the east. Running parallel with the river and hard by the docks, it was of a piece with London's port and its commerce – so utterly notorious, following a series of murders early in the century, that it had since been renamed. St George-street only existed on maps, however; everyone still referred to it as of old.

Sarah's ideas concerning 'the Highway' persisted from her childhood picture-books, as a broad avenue of elms: the area had not been built as a slum, as could be said of Shoreditch, or Bermondsey in the south, but a slum had been made of it. The houses collapsed together in a cheery yet filthy disorder, each drunkenly supporting its neighbour. The populace, clinging to their porches, eyed her suspiciously as she passed.

As she approached the corner of one tumbledown street, a group of sturdy women-folk all but filled the pavement. Dark shawls gathered up over their heads, they resembled mourners, and stood with their faces pressed to the dark surface of a window-glass. The white lettering above their heads read 'CREAM GIN'. One turned aside to sit on the kerb dejected. She cradled a tiny infant.

Chancing the gutter, Sarah passed by.

The streets being unpaved and with no guttering to speak of, heavy raindrops fell splashing in filth and puddle alike. Sarah regarded a strand of grimy rabbit-skins. Her boot heels skidded in the nightmare sludge. Even in decline, Bloomsbury was a paradise by comparison. She had often overheard other Londoners speak of going 'up West' and 'down East', without ever really understanding why, not having seen the imbalance for herself.

Thinking on her mission, Sarah redoubled her courage. She marked the multiplicity of churches by their visible signs. A spire here, a bell-tower there, they sprang up in swift succession – Mission, Episcopal, Swedish Protestant – the notoriety of the former Ratcliff-highway was such that it required the services of every single denomination. Any one of these eruptions might be the St Paul's Church: she really should have referred to a Kelly's Directory before venturing forth, only she had not expected the road to be so very long...

Adjacent to the bustle of a cab stand was a turning into Ratcliff-street. Sarah stood at the gate to a graveyard. The grind of wheels at her back reduced to a dull murmur, a spooky hush settled over the place. Mighty St George in the East reared to her left. Pale sunlight, playing on the stained glass of its rear window, threw patterns across the acreage of cold stone. Abutting to the northeast, through the shade of a grove of trees, she glimpsed a second church, a Wesleyan or Methodist chapel. Other potential candidates clustered close by. Tucked away down side streets, they were perhaps more immediately accessible, but only by cutting across this burial ground.

Sarah shivered, turned, and made her way back to the main road.

The next turning, about a hundred yards on, was nothing more than a dark alleyway, enclosed on all sides by high brick wall. She could see that it opened out after a short interval by the way that it grew lighter ahead. Not entirely insensible of the dangers, but inclined to recklessness, Sarah gathered her skirts from where they trailed in the muck and ducked in.

A gutter ran down the centre, where a lean young pig stood sniffing at a mouldering stump of turnip. Someone from an upper window gathered spit. Thuggish-looking women, mottled arms as thick as hams, crouched beneath the windowsills, knees up to their flabby chins. Naked babies wallowed at their feet, pink, puny and underfed, like worms.

In this jungle of the senses the stink of humanity was almost metallic.

Sarah hesitated at a junction within the network of small passageways. By the stark blackletter of signs screwed to the walls she at least knew their names: Palmers-folly lay behind, Perseverance-place ahead.

First bypassing a Rehoboth chapel, Sarah briefly contemplated sanctuary inside tiny Ebenezer Church.

She crossed into Angel-gardens, a squalid slum terrace of back-to-backs accessed by a blind alley. This led to and from an inner courtyard, enclosed on all sides by high brick wall: the Chancery. A suffocating pocket universe that had surely never known light, or air, its brickwork was black, as if shadows of night clung there. The walls pressed in so close that the sun, when it shone, might only blanch their very tops.

Sarah was instantly struck by the absolute silence: to not hear the sound of anything in London was exceptional. At first she assumed her ears had popped, as with altitude gained, instead of her having sunken to these great depths. Among such ghostly haunts, she could not be certain she was not herself the ghost. The stench was truly overpowering. Enervated, becoming faint, she felt she might fade entirely away.

This must be Shadwell – Dreuse's London, barely altered since the day he was born.

The enclosed courts slid invisibly one inside another like a succession of trick Chinese boxes. Figures filled the doorways, faces leering; it was enough to see their lips working to know that they traded in slander and gossip. The risk was great in pressing on; greater still in staying put. Sarah's pulse, already racing, set to a mad gallop. Gathering all her strength, she advanced into an even darker passageway, no bigger than her coal-cellar, to emerge within a bare yard, long, and thin, and ruined.

Altogether down and out, the poorest of the poor, the residents swarmed like lice in crumbling wood. The staggered outlines of an agglomeration of hovels, close-packed, begged for a conflagration to wipe them out. No gardens here, and no angels; these were the precincts of the damned: bodies that suffered, spirits that fell, souls that were lost. Sarah could scarcely believe whole families made their homes in this way – not living, mere existence.

She looked out at scenes as if steering a tiny craft that merely sailed through them. Danger, perhaps even tragedy, hovered in the wings. One or two of the stunted creatures were stirring. Listless blanks before, the masks of their faces began to twist and take on new shapes. Broken-veined and empurpled, they exhibited blunt interest, even the stirrings of anger. From out of the generalised grumbles sprang an occasional loud oath.

Sarah wanted to bring out her purse, slip the few coins into an open hand, if only for the sake of a child – but feared such an action might bring the rest down on her head like a pack of hungry wolves. She was no ghost, but flesh and blood: if she did not pull herself together, she risked being torn apart.

She turned and fled.

A dark figure pulled away from the shadows in her wake, moving almost as swiftly in pursuit.

Popped like a thorn squeezed from a wound, Sarah rejoined the main Highway. Crossing the busy road to the south side, she passed by entrances to the docks. Over the tops of shorter buildings the tall spars of a great many ships were visible at anchor, and she could almost smell the salt sea on the air.

Van horses toiled the length of New Gravel-lane. A roughneck crew of sailors swaggered past, doing the rope-walk. Dark-skinned, they wore red shirts with broad sashes tied around their waists. They seemed hopelessly exotic, like foreign pirates, the air boiling in their wake redolent of rum.

Sarah examined the shops, marine-store dealers. They were bright with brass fittings: quadrants and sextants, chronometers, all sorts of other navigational paraphernalia. A mariner's compasses nestled among ocean-going charts. A sudden gleam in the window-glass caused her to spin about. The light reflected off the polished buttons on the jacket of a custom-house officer. Standing tall by her side, he nodded politely. Sarah hurried on.

Crude hand-written notices read, 'LODGINGS FOR SAILORS – OWN BUNKS', 'LETTERS WRITTEN AND SENT', or, 'MONEY AND BILLS EXCHANGED'. Sitting at the threshold to a ship's chandler, one fellow in particular caught her eye. Hands dyed a deep orange colour from the handling of rope and tar-bucket, he wore a bright satin waistcoat, and pulled at the most enormous pair of boots. His face glowed red, but not, thought Sarah, through strain: his tanned muscles worked comfortably. Twisted around his head, worn as a sort of turban, was a cotton kerchief. Dark hair, extruding beneath, was artfully curled into ringlets, and flattened with grease. He was, every inch, a model sailor: Bruce, as first pictured in her imagination.

'Not everyone is what they seem, down the Highway.'

The voice of a stranger at her shoulder made Sarah jump. A dark figure peeled away from the shadow of the lobby and advanced to stand beside her. His face was full – if not as florid as the other man's – and his gingery beard was flecked with white.

''Tis a fiddler's green, miss, beyond compare,' he said. 'Oh, some may look the part, dressed in their Guernseys 'n' blue jackets, but in a mess of y'ars they'll've sailed no further than the alehouse on the corner. Turnpike sailors they are, and that's all. Lurchers, idlers, beggars and thieves, the Sons of Abraham!'

The man barked out loud, as if for the benefit of all. Sarah looked around, embarrassed, and saw that 'Bruce' had gone, leaving behind only an empty stool.

'They sell a little fish fried in oil, or else keeps a lodgin'-house, but they're no more sailors than you or oi, moi dear. They only mime the maritime.'

At that the man bunched his fists and performed a little jig, the hornpipe, stopped short as suddenly as begun. He leant in closer, as if to confide – she saw the freckles of his cheeks – but then his voice rang out loud as before, causing her to flinch.

'One such beggar I knew with only the one arm,' he said. 'Every day he stood at the gates down in West Garden, the London Dock gates as you'll understand me, and took up enough to live like a lord! The great idle selfish brute.'

He would not stop talking. Backed into a corner, Sarah felt a trifle alarmed.

'Had a parrot, so he did, to sit on his one arm, and even then it had to do his begging for him! Language, warse than his own. Ev'ry sart a blasphemy an' obscenity, the Twelve Unprintable Monosyllables!'

His pale, bushy eyebrows worked up and down like two birds in a mating dance. Seeing that he had her full attention, he settled his face almost at once into a more serious expression, the tone of his voice modulated to match.

'Sargint Padraig Tubridy, ma'am,' he said. 'A water-rat operating out of Leman-street Police Station. An' it'll not be me you must be wary of.'

His fingers tapped the rim of his helmet. He turned to indicate their surroundings.

'This here's Tiger Bay, and here be tygers all right. No sart a place for the likes of you.'

He saw that she took offence.

'Oh, no, milady,' he said. 'The fault lies with the place, not with your good self.' Tubridy sniffed and wrinkled his nose, in what seemed a friendly fashion. 'I dare say you'll have noted the pertic'lar…atmosphere. T'ings go on here in Sailortown, such t'ings I scarcely durst mention. A reservoir of dirt, drunks and drabs, Mr Dickens has called it, and that should tell you sufficient. A respectable lady…a lady, that is, such as yourself…should not be out walking on her own.'

Sarah misunderstood. 'No,' she said. 'I should.' She decided to ask for directions. 'I have business here,' she said. 'I am in search of a particular house of worship, only, I didn't expect to see so very many – '

'Yus, ma'am,' he cut her off, 'one at ev'ry corner…'

She was smiling, nodding in agreement.

'The Bridge of Sighs,' he said, 'Ward's Hoop and Grapes, the Albion, the Prince Regent, the Effingham Saloon…' He pointed just behind them, and then just ahead of them. 'There's the Duke O'Yark's.' He smiled. 'And there, the White Hart.'

Sarah glared at him.

'You may think the Highway bad,' said Tubridy, 'but the neighbourhood's warse. Angel-gardins, Chancery-lane, Albert-square…' The police sergeant gently let her know he had been following her progress for some time. 'The genuwine sorry face of London's East End,' he said. 'Streets filled wit' houses of the vilest description, an' frequented by those who call demselves the Farty Teevs, alley-barbers who'll slit yer throat soon as look at you.'

'The Forty Thieves' – Sarah wondered if they bore relation to the child Bruce's gang.

'Lucky for you that you run into me,' declared Tubridy, 'before someone undesirable has done the same for *you*.'

She did not care for his familiar tone. Sarah thought to walk on.

'You may count on being the innocent bystander,' he was saying, 'but they are as much at risk should a fight break out and the sea-knives flash. These forin sailors are a danger, a-stabbing with their Bowie. A gin-mad Malay goes running amok, a-waving of his glittery creese, bot a tiny Greek stiletto is all it takes, for eyes that were of a colour, ta turn one red, while de udder one stays blue.

'Anyone,' he said, 'wishing to visit the Highway, or any other part of the environmint, is, for their ain safety, recommendit to gain permission from the authorities at Scotland Yard. Then they shall have an officer or inspector provided for their escort. Even a Metropolitain perliceman would be unwise t' walk these by-ways alone. An' here's me, a sargint without ma carp'rill. I shall have to ask that you accompany me, miss, ta prevent me from comin' ta harm…'

He touched his helmet again, in deference, and flashed a wicked smile.

'Or ma'am.'

Sarah smiled but shook her head, and began to pick up the pace in order to put some distance between them. 'I do thank you for your concern, sergeant,' she said in parting, 'but I think I shall be all right.'

'As you like,' he said. Following on at a discreet distance of about twenty paces, he called out after her. 'Oi'll feel safer, all th' same, if I might keep you in sight. We are but travellers on the same road, after all.'

Pointedly, Sarah crossed onto the north side of the street.

Barely a block further on, with each swing of its doors, the Albion public house belched forth more of its clientele, swelling a sizeable crowd. Forced back out into the road, Sarah slowed. At the centre of the disturbance she spied a woman, spectacularly fat, and dressed in pantomime costume. The buttercup-yellow finery, filthy and torn, suggested Dick Turpin, Jack Sheppard, or some equally likely hero-villain. The vision sat astride a wooden hobbyhorse, and performed a halting gallop in tiny steps.

Sarah walked on past. A general hiss issued from among the spectators.

'Cool 'im,' she heard someone say, in their peculiar backwards slang. 'Cool the esclop.'

Turning around, she was not the only one surprised to see the policeman walk by the crowd as if nothing were happening. He continued to dog her steps, at a distance no longer discreet. Her cheeks burned.

In this fashion the two of them continued on down the Highway.

Around King David-lane the street became yet more riotous. Whereas before she had been glad of Tubridy's silence, Sarah soon found herself grateful of his company. First the Admiralty clerk, then young Jeffery, and now, further, this policeman – all positively falling over themselves to assist her. She had never known herself the object of so much male attention. It was a flattering sort of novelty, to be sure, a situation so absurd she didn't know what to make of it.

Thus beguiled, yet innocent of vanity, Sarah discovered herself precisely where she wished to be.

Across the street lay the rectory and Vestry Hall; up ahead, rising over the tops of the surrounding trees, the piercing black spire of St Paul's Shadwell.

Sarah turned to address her acolyte.

'Much obliged, sergeant,' she said. 'I have arrived at my destination.'

'Ma'am.'

Tubridy looked up at the tall spire; the monster Union Jack, flying atop.

'I'll wait for you,' he said, 'out here.'

'Really,' she assured him, 'there's no need.'

'Along here?' he said. 'Believe me, there is need.'

The church itself was a very plain structure, a box of brick in the classical eighteenth-century style: large slates on its roof, tower and plaster-rendered steeple at the west front, but otherwise unadorned.

Sarah opened the gates and walked through, past a wooden board that read 'St Paul's Shadwell, The Church of the Sea Captains'. The screams of small children rent the air: the adjoining Vestry Hall doubled as both school and orphanage. Sarah checked that she had closed the gate properly behind her. In the midst of a clutch of the smallest foundlings stood a friendly-looking figure, dressed all in black. She could not get closer than a few feet, so they were obliged to shout their introductions over the nursery din.

Augustin Mellish, the vestry clerk, indicated another fellow a little farther on. He crouched beneath a rosebush – in the very middle of the graveyard. Steeling herself, Sarah picked her way in between the crowding stones. The rector wore a sun-hat. Pruning his roses, he remained unaware of her approach, even when she stood right beside him. The sharp beak of his shears worked nimbly. She cleared her throat.

'Reverend... Reverend Kingsford?'

Perspiring slightly, he stood and removed his hat, revealing a shock of grey hair. He was a tall, thin man, with kind eyes.

'Brenchley Kingsford,' he said, 'ye-e-es?'

The last vowel, elongated, sounded out a note of enquiry.

'My name,' she said, 'is Sarah Larkin, daughter of the Reverend Lambert Blackwold Larkin.'

'Oh, yes?' he said. 'And how may I be of assistance?'

Sarah said, 'I should very much like to consult the church's Baptismal Register, if I may. I have travelled some way in the hope that I might.'

Less than four miles distant from New Oxford-street, she had travelled to the ends of the earth.

'Certainly, certainly, that we can do.' The rector nodded; most readily, as if fully expectant of her request. He started to remove his gloves, finger by finger. 'It has been quiet for most of this last week,' he said, 'but you are the second today!'

'I...I'm sorry?'

Brenchley Kingsford paused to look at her a moment. 'My dear,' he said, 'you are not the only one. He has quite the fan-club, don't you know.'

Sensing her confusion, doubt crept into his voice. 'You *are* here for Captain Cook?' he asked.

'Captain…?' Relief swept across her face. She was almost laughing. 'I'm not interested in Captain Cook!'

The rector bridled, a touch peevish. 'My dear, we would never have heard of the Pacific Islanders, let alone attempted to convert them,' he said, 'were it not for men like Cook!'

'No,' she said. 'I meant…I didn't realise. It's another man I'm looking for, a different name.'

'Forgive me, Miss Larkin,' the rector said, 'for jumping to conclusions. The names of over 175 sea captains and their wives appear in our registers. They surround you.' He waved his gloves at some of the plots that they passed. 'Not only sea captains and their families,' he said, 'but shipwrights, rope-makers, pursers and chandlers. Gone aloft, I hope, most of them, gone aloft!'

Navigating carefully between the islands of moss, Sarah noted stones sculpted with designs of compass and sextant, and tiny sailing ships. Beyond the far wall, the bare masts of vessels moored in Shadwell New Basin towered like skeletons over their tombs.

Unable to compete with the noise of the children, the two of them fell silent until the church steps were climbed and the door to the lobby closed. Sarah had been studying the fabric of the building.

'I can't help observing, reverend,' she said, 'the church does not look so very old…'

Brenchley Kingsford smiled. 'Indeed not,' he said. 'The building is not the original.'

The rector having laid aside his hat and gloves, they entered into the main body of the church.

'Thomas Neale, a speculator in the docks with interests in East India, oversaw the construction in 1656.' He pointed upwards. 'By the early years of this century,' he said, 'the church had become very dilapidated. One Sunday, a part of the ceiling fell in. The church was finally demolished in 1819, and rebuilt the following year. The vestry books were lost, so it is fortunate the registers were not. Shall we?'

'Mmm,' Sarah agreed. 'But first, could I possibly trouble you for a glass of water…and avail myself of your water closet?' She smiled, bashfully. 'I should like,' she said, 'to wash away the dirt of the street.'

The reverend looked past her, in the direction of the Highway. 'That, my dear,' he said, 'requires a flood.'

He apprehended the look on her face, and stood aside. 'Through here. Through here.'

Sarah took the opportunity to check a small notebook, in which she had scribbled, in pencil, the most pertinent 'facts' – a compilation from Bruce's *Life*, his *Memoirs*, and the *Literary Panorama*:

> *Born Ratcliff-highway, St Paul's Shadwell, 1779*
>
> *George Bruce, son of John Bruce, foreman and clerk to Mr Wood,*
> *distiller at Limehouse*

Not least, she looked to the note taken from that morning's correspondence.

> *G.B. = Joseph Dreuse?*

His exact date of birth conflicted according to accounts. Strict accuracy in such matters could hardly be expected, however, of people from impoverished backgrounds who could neither read nor write. Official figures within the Admissions and Burial Registers of the Greenwich Royal Naval Hospital recorded 1777, and, logically – from his stated age – after February 12th of that year. What any investigator should ask, Sarah believed, was whether a person should ever be required to give false information. In his *Life*, 'Bruce' or Dreuse had been sentenced to death at the apparent age of twelve, 'so small that the ladies and gentlemen all pitied me'. Appearing a year or two younger than he actually was, and perhaps pleading the same, had saved his life. For all of these reasons, Sarah elected to initiate her search from February 1777 onwards.

The Baptismal Register was immediately located, being the same volume as that for Captain Cook's eldest son, already well thumbed. Brenchley Kingsford happily chattered away while Sarah pored over its pages. Within less than five minutes she had confirmed all that she wished to know, and more.

> *July 6, 1777 – Joseph and Josiah twin sons of John Druce Distiller*
> *and Mary Lightfoot in ye Malin Walk Born May 14.*

The alternative spelling to 'Dreuse' threw her only slightly; Governor Macquarie had had no reason ever to have seen the name of Druce written down. Sarah copied out the relevant details.

Twins!

'And she called his name Joseph; and said, the LORD shall add to me another son.' Mary Druce had named her son Joseph, meaning 'may God add' – for the sake of his twin brother? Or was it perhaps after the husband of the Virgin Mary, the man who played no part in Christ's conception.

'They are relations of yours?' the rector enquired.

'Yes.' Sarah blushed. It seemed easier to tell a lie than to try to explain the truth.

They quit the vestry, retracing their steps along the south aisle. Sarah, all aglow, congratulated herself on her persistence, her thoroughness; hang the sin of pride! Two, committed in as many minutes!

The main body of the church was lit by two tiers of square, domestic-looking windows, surrounded with Bath Stone. Sarah gazed at the triplet window high on the east wall, and across to the organ gallery above the west end, the entrance beneath the steeple. She tried hard to imagine how the original church, Druce's church, must have looked. Her eyes fell on the fat wooden pulpit. Even under several coats of varnish, and with much damage to the carving, it was the best piece of furniture there, stolid and dignified, and not without a certain presence.

'You are admiring our pulpit,' observed Kingsford. 'John Wesley preached here on a number of occasions, during the late decades of his life.'

'And was it a part of the old church?' Sarah asked.

'I believe so.'

Sarah was reminded of the tragi-comic arguments between Druce's parents, his mother the 'Methodist Dog', and his father the 'Old Church Lion'. Mary Druce might well have brought the boy child along to meetings here. Wesley had died in 1791, the same year Druce was sentenced to sail aboard the *Royal Admiral*, East-Indiaman, a deportee. That must have come as a double blow to his poor mother.

She looked to the ceiling. His local parish church, in which Joseph Druce had been baptised, had been demolished in the same year that he died.

'The roof fell in, you say?'

'Yes!' said the rector. 'Gave the congregation quite a turn, I should imagine. As the area fell into decline, so I suppose did its church.' He shook his head. 'The banns had to be called and marriages performed at St George's, until the rebuilding,' he said. 'A dreadful state of affairs. The Bishop of London granted us a special licence, and for four years services were held in the parish workhouse. Still, better a living dog than a dead lion, as they say.'

They had returned to the lobby area. Brenchley Kingsford came to a halt, his hand resting on his chin.

'Your father,' he said. 'Tell me, my dear, is he a ritualist?'

Sarah hesitated to answer.

'He...does not hold with it, no.'

The Reverend Kingsford drew close, to whisper in conspiratorial fashion. 'At St George's,' he said, 'Father Lowder and his cabal...' he checked over his shoulder a moment, and then hers '...they process, they genuflect, they make the sign of the cross.' He implored heaven. 'They swing thuribles!'

The rector drew back, assuming his full height. His eyes were no longer kind. 'The wearing of vestments alone is abhorrent enough, without the lighting of candles upon the altar, and...incense!'

He might as well have pronounced it 'incest'.

Within the Establishment Church, much attention was currently focused on forms of expression, considerable antipathy fermenting between the low Church, of which St Paul's Shadwell was a prime example, and the high. The rectory of St George's in the East, among the foremost proponents of the celebration of the sacraments and the preaching of the gospel, had, in recent years, been the *locus* for a series of scandalous riots: protestors releasing packs of dogs and even pigs among the pews.

In the face of such misery as she had witnessed that day, Sarah thought, obsession with the minutiae of doctrine was worse than meaningless. Schisms within the Church all but destroyed its effectiveness. How much more might be achieved if, rather than divide and sub-divide their efforts in the face of sin, or rather in the face of mortal need, they were to present a unified front, give coherent direction towards a supreme form of worship, all-embracing, all-encompassing.

Or perhaps her notions of universal succour were naïve. Her business concluded, all Sarah knew for sure was that she wanted to leave.

She stood framed within the light of the doorway, while the rector retrieved his outdoor gear. Something said earlier coincided with something else she had read: Joseph Druce had been sent to the workhouse while very young.

'You mentioned the parish workhouse, reverend,' said Sarah. 'Where was that?'

Brenchley Kingsford fixed his hat just so and snipped his shears. 'Angel-court,' he said, 'in the Chancery, off what is now Albert-street.'

Sarah's eyelid twitched.

All had gone quiet behind her, and she turned. Classes must have reconvened: the yard was empty.

'And Malin-walk?' she asked. 'Do you know it?'

Brenchley Kingsford took up a position by her side, standing at the top of the porch steps. 'Yes, I have heard of it,' he hummed. 'Let me see. It was to be found along Mercer's-row, now Mercer-street. It no longer exists.'

A mercer was a dealer in cloth, most especially silks: a remnant, perhaps, from the days when Shadwell was but a hamlet, and relatively well-to-do.

'Mercer-street,' mused Sarah. 'Is it close?'

'Oh, yes,' said the rector. 'Just across the road.'

'Sergeant!'

Hearing Sarah's voice so strong, so filled with vindication, Tubridy started.

'Ma'am?' he said. 'Your mission was, I take it, a success?'

'Very much successful,' she declared. 'Yes, and not quite done. I would be most grateful if you could direct me towards Mercer-street.'

'Certainly, ma'am,' he said. 'We have passed it already.'

With a slight lean of his upper body, he indicated for her to follow on. She should still have her police escort, it seemed. Sarah's attitude softened slightly.

'Thank you,' she said, 'for waiting for me, sergeant. I would have expected you had better things to do than to be my guide.'

She spoke modestly, pleasantly. He returned a broad and cheery smile.

'Other t'ings, ma'am, maybe,' the policeman admitted, 'but none better.'

In close alliance, they re-crossed Shadwell's High-street, walking west, back towards the city. They had gone about five chains, less than 400 feet, when they met with a familiar sight. The same turbulent crowd as before had swelled, entirely blocking the road.

Tubridy uttered an impatient oath. 'Excuse me, ma'am,' he said.

Advancing with intent, he forced his way through the outer ring, the more idle part of the mob. Sarah tripped along behind. Faces turned to stare, malevolent glitter in their eyes. The noise level was excruciating. Sarah crept closer to the sergeant's dark uniform, to peer over the broad blue expanse of his shoulder.

She was astonished to see, in the hollow at the heart of the matter, that same impromptu sideshow as passed previously. Events had processed but a short distance, across a side street and one or two doors on from outside of the Albion: her performance still ongoing a full half-hour later, Gaiety Gertie reprised her role as the Ratcliff Highwayman. She supported herself, barely, against the closed shutters of a shop, James Jelly Perret the baker's. The wooden hobby-horse, dropped, lay forlorn at her feet. It appeared her necessary prop in more ways than one. Despite all manner of hazy endeavour, she was either too drunk, too fat, or some combination thereof, to pick it up – or even to locate it. Head nodding beneath the outsize hat's broken plumes, her fleshy features were flushed and drooping. Her arms dangled useless at her sides, as if weighted with lead cuffs. The miserable woman was hopelessly besotted – drearily, desperately, falling-down drunk.

A ridiculous object in quite so many ways, she had, not unsurprisingly, gathered up an enthusiastic audience. The cackling pack of hyenas circled, baring yellow teeth, to snarl and snap at her heels. She feebly struggled to keep them off with a little halfpenny cane, wielding it like a miniature riding whip, and all the while pathetically weeping, great cow tears rolling down her cheeks.

Her chief tormentors were mostly small boys. Jeering, they offered choice cuts of advice as to how she should recover her mount.

'Hit 'im on the 'ock!' they cried; and more explicitly, 'Shove 'im up beyind!'

Having grasped the tenor of the event, Sarah had no wish to tarry.

Tubridy assumed a more commanding aspect. '*See here naow,*' he bellowed. '*show's over!*'

He spoke to the mob in an entirely different tone from that which he employed with her: and in a colloquial sort of idiom that might as well have been Greek or Chinese for all Sarah understood by it.

'*Let hir alone!*' shouted the sergeant. '*Moo falong naow, moo falong. Leave hir be. Lift Leg and Stride Wide!*'

A rattle of wheels and a sudden screeching behind them all, and Sarah turned to glimpse a shock of feathers, spangles and rouge: Tattercoat's Ugly Sisters, piled in a hansom cab. Others drew up alongside, seemingly part of a small fleet, having spent the night at the same tuppenny *bal masqué* as poor Gertie and only just now surfaced. Spidery arms reached out from the nearest carriage window, eager to snatch her up into its recesses. There was hardly room.

The sergeant caught hold of Gertie so that they all stood together, arm in arm, a picaresque tableau. Her would-be rescuers kicked up a hail of abuse, not only verbal, but also flinging whatever came to hand. The injustice was plain, from both sides.

Somewhere in the uproar, a wag began to sing a Gentleman's Song, a version of 'The Amiable Family', otherwise known as 'The Irish Policeman'.

> 'The cats on the house tops are mewing, love,
> Inviting each other to cooing, love.
> And softly inclined, is each cat to get lin'd,
> By each amorous mewing conveying, love.'

Tubridy caught on immediately. The first verses were rude enough; the last, as well he knew them, Unprintable Monosyllables almost entirely. He stood tall and sang loud to drown out the scandal of it.

> 'Still though oi bask beneath their smile,
> Their charms qoite fail t' bind me
> And me heart falls back t' Erin's Isle
> T' the girl oi left behint me!'

Not a shred of pity in his face, Tubridy snatched up the moll's trailing hobby-horse and thrust it roughly between her legs. He then grabbed her dull, questing hand and made sure that it firmly gripped the handle.

'See here, my Dandy Lion, y' feel that?' he roared. 'There's yer damned 'obby 'oss! G'wan naow, get y'self back home to Hairy-fud Shire!'

Roundly he slapped her horse's arse, to send her on her way. Game Gertie fair leapt into the clutches of her bosomy confederates. At their signal the cab pulled away, Gertie half in and half out, bloomers and cloak flapping three sheets to the wind.

'Blowzybellas! Doxies! Beggin' y' pardin, ma'am.'

Tubridy removed his helmet to mop his brow. 'I needs a drink.'

The grumbling crowds dispersed, variously scheming or proclaiming their fresh intentions.

'Le's up Wilton's, or Paddy's Goose.'

'Enny penny wot's goin', wir th' performince ent enter-feared wiv by no oaf-vicious black-beetle!'

A spit. '*Bleedin' Peeler.*'

Tubridy replaced his headgear, tapping it for good measure. ''Tis a good fortune,' he said, 'that we both be wearin' our bonnets.'

'I don't follow you,' said Sarah.

'Well,' he remarked, 'you should!'

Pulling his jacket taut, Tubridy marched straight into the nearest pub.

Sarah, still in tow, for the first time in her life entered into a public house. The degree of heat, smoke and noise was truly intimidating. Peripherally aware of the gayest and rummest goings-on in every dim corner, Sarah kept her head down. She dared not look too closely, but cleaved to the blue of the sergeant's uniform.

'Tubridy! Most welcome, sor!'

The manner of the man who spoke was the pink of politeness. He laid a proprietorial arm across the array of barrels, and cast a bold eye over Sarah's huddled form. 'A touch of Angel's Food for you, is it?' he said.

'Have a care, Clewley,' growled Tubridy.

The barman would have none of being cautioned in his own domain. 'Ah! What then is your poison, sargint?' he said.

Turning to meet Sarah's eye, Tubridy's face brightened.

'Hivens, James, h'what are you thinking?' he said, his accent much altered. 'Hai'm on duty. Can't you see hai'm on duty?' He twirled his moustache, before reverting to a stern blast of Irish. 'Oi'll 'ave you up in front of the aldermaaan!'

Clewley chuckled, Tubridy winked, and Sarah felt much older than her 27 years.

The police sergeant looked along the bar, considering.

'I'm for a touch of Mad Dog, if you please, Jim,' he said. 'And a pint of whativer the lady wants.'

Sarah's eye lit on a bottle of bright blue liquid that all but glowed in the dim light. The landlord, following her line of sight, put his hand to it. Seeing his eyebrows raised, she shook her head. She spoke to the policeman's sleeve.

'I don't...I don't drink,' she said.

'Very wise,' said Tubridy. 'Leave out the gin, try our ginger beer. It's local-produced, froma Signor Agostino Rolando ata numero twinty-tree.' To the barman, 'She'll have a ginger beer.'

'*Gin blear,*' a strange voice mocked.

At first, Sarah was unsure who had spoken. Only an old soak propped up the bar, and he seemed beyond all speech.

'*Ark!*'

She looked up. An enormous acid-green parrot patrolled the timbers above their heads. It bobbed and turned its head, fixing her with a single, wicked eye. The bright curve of its beak was cruel, like the blade of the Reverend Kingsford's secateurs.

'Cutlass,' cried Tubridy, 'you old rapscallion!'

Hearing itself addressed, the creature arched its neck backward and produced a volley of sounds, exactly like the popping of a multitude of corks. *'Go on wit' yaself! What's the time? What's the time? Find yer frying pan!'* The bird studied the policeman for a moment, then began to bob up and down excitedly, executing a rapid series of glottal clicks. It sounded exactly like a large clock being wound. *'Now we're busy!'*

'"Frying pan"?' queried Sarah.

Tubridy pulled his beer-pot aside. His mustaches wet with froth, he looked a mad dog indeed.

'Those vaaast silver watches the tars do wear,' he said. 'Sure 'n' you've seen 'em? Jolly Jack cannot pass a church tower without checkin' yon vane and givin' his pan a wind! Them's the two things thought worth knowing by every mariner worth his salt…which way the wind blows, and the roit toime!'

Sarah squinted through the thick haze of smoke at sailor-folk collapsed around the pub. Every one of them seemed to be pulling on a short pipe, regardless of whether it was lit, or they were themselves awake.

The sergeant, however, was on the move.

They threaded their way through to a corner table. All of the street folk appeared to be on the best of terms with Sergeant Tubridy. More than one insisted he join them for a drink, but he politely declined. In deference to the sergeant, little notice was taken of Sarah.

Resettled, she returned to examination of the seafaring gentlemen that surrounded them. The nearest sprawled but three feet away, lids at half-mast, and both hands thrust deep into his pockets. She recalled a favourite saying her mother would often repeat, on those days when they scanned cloudy skies in hopes of brighter weather: 'just enough blue to patch a sailor's trousers'. Legs outstretched and pockets distended, this sailor presented canvas aplenty. His shirt was open at the neck, and she could almost count the black hairs swarming thick across his chest.

Another man leaned forward and spat on the floor, before replacing his pipe. He affected all the airs of a crude philosopher. Around his table, a loud discussion raged in several languages all at once; each man seemed to wear a different national dress, lending the everyday scene a carnival aspect.

'You hear the babel, don't you,' remarked Tubridy. 'Up and down the Highway they go a-strolling, the sailors of every cuntery under hiven. The Greyks, Norway-gens, the Eye-talians and Purtu-geese. Vikin' Danes and Uncle Toms, Spaniards and Chinees. Men who warship a thousand gods, and men who know of none. Sailors, yes, of all kinds…and wimmen but of one.'

He leant heavily across the table, his voice falling to a dark croak.

'The Marys,' he pronounced.

As in Mary Magdalene?

His eyes roamed the tavern. Hesitant at first, she followed suit. There was no shortage of women present. Of undeniably low character, they intermingled shamelessly with the men. The alcohol, presumably, inclined them to fatness.

'The social evil, as 'tis rightly known,' said Tubridy. 'Shall I tell you, miss, how to spot a whore?' His blood was up and the beer was downed: he spoke indiscreetly.

Sarah flushed and stared at the table-top, but said nothing. She was keen to know.

'White dresses, and white shoes, that's what they likes to wear,' said Tubridy. 'Not that they're apt to keep clean for very long.'

Sarah saw evidence of a grubby sort of muslin, cheap blue silk, but nothing recognisably white. It could be as he said.

'Their cheeks, they redden with a little rouge, to give 'em life.' The burly policeman daintily patted his face.

Sarah conjured a mental image of the termagants shrieking from their cab, the hoops of their large skirts – an imitation of high fashion – splayed. As the carriage flew away, she had noticed one whose chignon had fallen loose, hair trailing like a streamer. What was that he had said about her bonnet?

'And always, near always, they walk twirling a small ha'penny cane in thir mitts. 'Tis a sly form of "advertisemint".'

Tubridy thwacked his beer-pot down on the table, sending up a whale-spout of ale.

'Red rag to a bull, it is!' he said. 'Spy a lady in the street without her bonnet, and sure you are to see her pocket-hankerchiff worn across her back. Their heads they keep bare, and instead drape it thus around the shoulder. Silk, those as what c'n afford it. Cotton will do the rest.'

Silken handkerchiefs: for the theft of a few such items, the boy Joseph Druce had been imprisoned and sent halfway around the world.

'Unfortunates, so some folks do call 'em,' Tubridy was saying, 'to earn thir fortune in such a way. Hellcats, says I. Beggin' yer puddin', ma'am.' Clutching his beer close to his chest, he leant in a little. 'They serve men's baser passions. Men, mark you, of every colour betwixt black and white.' His free hand swung in a wide arc. 'A whole world a races an' religions gathers here, for express purposes of profligacy and sin. That, or else I can't tell their pastime. An' each man idle worships in his own way.'

He had begun to talk in a circle.

The desperate clutch of churches strung along the Highway was perhaps a necessary evil, to cater to men's various needs, their spiritual comfort, in as many familiar and traditional forms as possible. Necessary evil – Sarah shuddered at the compact.

Tubridy, however, had in mind another sort of ministry altogether. He swung back.

'Oh, when his vessel is landed in the docks, and Jolly Jack Tar is a-port, the Highway's his *peed-a-terre*, his "tempawrary residawnce".'

He screwed up his mouth and dangled his beer-pot daintily, as if it were a tea-cup.

'The goodly folk of Ratcliff, they do live on Jack, as fleas on a dog,' he said. 'Twice as numerous. He arrives pockets full, an' they're jest as soon emptied, long before he must leave. He gets hisself into awful debt, poor Jack!'

'*Poor Jack!*' A high-pitched echo filtered down from the rafters.

'Jack may even pick up with his Jill,' Tubridy drawled. 'Some doxy to whom he will give in trust all the money he has earned from his latest voyage. They live with the wimmen until th' money is gone, an' consider themselves married, *pro tem*. He thinks himself in his element, does Jack, but his thinking's all at sea…

> 'I've a spanking wife at Portsmouth gates, a pigmy at Goree,
> An orange tawney up the Straits, a black at St Lucie:
> Thus whatsomever course I bend, I leads a jovial life.
> In every clime I finds a friend… In every port a wiiiife!'

The sergeant exhibited a fine bass voice, soon joined by others. Applause followed, and laughter. Pausing only to draw another cork, from back above the bar Cutlass launched into more of his rowdy repertoire – swearing and laughing, then screaming and swearing some more. Sarah spotted his green crest weaving deliriously side to side.

Tubridy searched the bottom of his beer-pot in hopes of finding a dreg. Sarah had hardly touched her own drink, and, seeing Tubridy smacking his lips, rather feared he was about to order another. The ginger beer and the pipe-smoke were burning in her throat.

'Mercer-street, sergeant,' she insisted. 'I must find Mercer-street!'

'Mercer-street?' He looked a little surprised. 'You are there!'

If, for the sake of argument, they were said to have entered the Albion by its front door, then they left by that door at its side. It opened directly onto Mercer-street, formerly Mercer's-row, and Joseph Druce's birthplace. Unsure what she expected to find there, Sarah felt obliged to visit.

The road, wider than many she had seen that day, ran north to south, perpendicular to the Highway. To the east was a shipwright's yard, and another, belonging to a builder. Attractive to the eye, a little way north, stood a tall building with a grand frontage: the commanding façade resembled somewhat that of St Martin-in-the-Fields.

'What is there?' asked Sarah.

Tubridy's attention had wandered. 'What?' he said. 'Oh. British and Foreign Sailor's...something something.' He stroked his beard, throwing longing looks back into the Albion. 'It isn't good,' he said, 'f'r you t' stay out here alone.'

'But I'm not,' replied Sarah. 'Am I?'

She knew well enough by now the root of his concern. Respectable women didn't venture out unaccompanied, unless married, and, married or not, never after dark. She had seen him, unsure of her status, checking for rings.

She wore gloves.

Her eyebrow arched.

'I think I'll take a closer look,' she said.

Tubridy waggled his little finger. 'Oi must needs perform...a wee investigation of me own,' he said.

He disappeared inside the pub. Instantly his head popped back through the doorway.

'Oi'll keep me ears open,' he said.

Sarah headed for the tall building. A high tower raised above its centre looked to be a minaret or belvedere, with a balcony rail for a lookout. Atop a row of four columns, beneath the carving of the large, central pediment, she read a bold inscription, 'BRITISH & FOREIGN SAILORS' INSTITUTE', dated 1856.

One of the lower window-panes was broken – starglazed, perhaps, by a thief.

Long before he fell by the wayside, Joseph Druce was born on or near to this very spot. It seemed somehow appropriate, that a means of salvation might present itself precisely here. Had his health been improved, then his spirit might also have been: and, had he survived, he might yet have returned to end his days – happily – where they began.

The street fell curiously quiet. As sunlight stole across the front of the Institute, before her eyes the Portland Stone began to glow. She turned, shielding her gaze, to stare up at the sky.

Just enough blue to patch a sailor's trousers.

If she concentrated just a little, she could still hear her mother's voice. She blinked, temporarily blinded by tears – from staring at the sun, or too much pipe-smoke.

Sarah started back towards the Albion. Tubridy was waving her over from where he stood outside. She felt cheered to see him again.

'You have suffered another bite,' she observed.

Abashed, he wiped the foam from about his moustaches. 'No, ma'am, oi'm all right, oi'm all right.' Helmet tilted back on his head, he showed empty hands.

The barman from before stood by his side. He seemed to glare across the road in the direction from which she had come. ''Tis a noble institution,' he sneered, viciously insincere, 'most deserving of our cordial support.'

Tubridy furnished an introduction. 'James Clewley, ma'am,' he said. 'He is boss o' this grog-palace.'

The gust of raucous laughter that blew through the doors between them declined into shouts and curses.

'Don't get me wrong, lady,' the landlord grunted. 'Gawd bless the Sailors' Home…but I would not choose it for a nay-boor.'

'Surely, Mr Clewley,' said Sarah, 'you cannot begrudge what is a charitable society.'

'Charity? *Wisht!*'

Tubridy's eyes boggled. 'Don't let Jack hear you speak of it like that!' he said. 'He's aw'fy high-spirited…an independent so't.' He wafted his sausage fingers back and forth in the air.

'I can,' replied Clewley, 'and I do. Between the railways an' Do-Good Societies there'll soon be no livin' off the Highway. It's no good for business when a sailor buttons up his pockets, I tell yer, or makes a dart f'r the railway an' never says nuffink to uz.'

The view through the open door to the saloon bar belied the landlord's gloomy comments: the pub appeared more full than ever. To the accompaniment of screeching fiddles, bodies flung their selves about in reckless abandon, boots beating out a tattoo across the boards. Dancing, and singing: drunken sailors, and women who knew very well what they should do with them.

Affable strangers would keep offering the sergeant drinks, and once or twice a disreputable-looking female creature approached to demand that he join in the dance.

'Oi'm all right,' he repeated. So used to the assertion, Tubridy sometimes volunteered it apropos of nothing and no one. 'Oi'm all right.'

The sky was growing darker. More drunken sailors went racing down the street on hired donkeys. They spat out a harsh vocabulary that, once communicated, one would be hard-pressed to forget; Sarah thought it a mercy that she could not better comprehend their speech.

Tubridy suddenly lurched forward.

'Check y'r frying pan, missy,' he said. 'Time to go!'

Catching hold of her arm with a surprising tenderness, he directed her bodily up the street. 'Oi'll be seein' you to the station,' he said.

Sarah protested – she did not know the way by rail – yet he would brook no argument.

''Tis but a short step to th' north, 'n' time you went,' he stressed. 'High time! *Upps*, pardin! Evenin' will soon be fallin' an' events is rapidly declinin'!'

He kicked at a large stone. A crude painting, marked 'Douro', lifted from the pavement at their feet. A disaster-beggar scrabbled to gather in his canvas, as Tubridy bellowed after him. 'AHTAVIT!'

At the top end of Mercer they turned left into Cable-street, and then very soon after swung a right. Up ahead was a raised viaduct, signal box just in view within the gap between houses. The air smelled of oysters and slow-baking potatoes. Shops were shutting, ready to be turned into 'gaffs' for the night, makeshift dance-halls and theatres, admission one penny. Provocative posters were being arranged outside to draw the punters in: lurid portraits of their star performers, caught 'in the act', and flash-card announcements scrawled in colour combinations gaudy enough to induce a headache.

'Astounding!' they screamed. 'Startling!! Don't miss it!!!'

But miss it Sarah would. Tubridy was walking almost too fast for her to keep up. 'Monday,' he said. 'Th'll be as many as six performances at each gaff, and every one bringin' 200 gawkers. Y'll want to be home before ony o'that, and so will oi. They know my face well f'r partic'lar reason.'

The whites of Tubridy's eyes showed dreadful proof of his sincerity. Sarah knew those staring looks: Brippoki's face lately wore that same expression. He was scared.

'Clewley, an' his sort,' muttered Tubridy, 'oh, they appear awl friendly-loike, but they'll turn you in an instant if they sees their chance. That they will!'

Squeezing into Station-place, he all but ran her up the steps to the platform.

'An onnatural instink stews in their hearts,' he said. 'For vengeance! An' once they think themselves wronged, they niver forget. Niver!'

Only once they had reached the top step did he relax hold of her. He forced a little kindness again to show in his face.

'Thank you…' Sarah struggled to catch her breath. 'Thank you again, sergeant,' she said, 'for escorting me today.'

Tubridy bowed and tipped his helmet, ever the gentleman. 'Always a pleasure, miss, escortin' a lady to church…or ony other house o' worship!' His damp red whiskers curled into a devilish smile. 'And in a heathen city such as this?' he said. 'Why, oi was only doin' m' duty!'

As he trotted away down the steps, Tubridy again began to sing.

'Saint Patrick was a gentleman and came of decent people,
He built a church in Dublin town, and on it put a steeple…'

A shrill whistle drowned out the rest of his verse. A train was about to pull into the station. Sarah was torn, whether to run onto the platform before he was properly out of sight, or wait and watch his departure. An icy claw raked her insides: after all he had done for her, all their time together, she had never thought to let him know her name.

'…'Twas on the top of Dublin's hill Saint Patrick preach'd his sermon,
That drove the frogs into the bogs, and banished all the vermin!'

Already out of sight, she yet heard his fine, true voice and took it as a comfort, before a gush of steam and a clatter of doors swallowed her up, and it, too, was gone.

The train journey from Shadwell Station into Fenchurch-street took only minutes. Sarah sat and stared out of the window. The low black housing, sweeping by, merged with her blank reflection. A lock of her hair had fallen loose and she curled it in her long fingers. Seeing again the fear in Tubridy's eyes, she finally appreciated what appalling risks she had taken; yet, feeling the heat of blood in her cheeks, she also thrilled to it.

The crowding walls abruptly fell away, to disclose a broad cityscape.

Soon enough, Sarah discovered the omnibus route for her journey home. She sat on board, much as she had on the train, in a daze.

The bus was bypassing the vast cathedral. Affairs seemed to circle St Paul continually, as moths did a flame.

The son of a Jew, the man Saul had been both blasphemer and persecutor, long before being recast St Paul, 'Apostle of the Gentiles', and one of God's principal proponents. But then by equal token, Lucifer, Bringer of Light, had been an angel of the Lord, and ended up no less than Satan, the Devil Incarnate. The traffic, so it seemed, might flow in either direction.

Sarah leant forward in her seat, the better to admire the great dome.

She looked up into an emptiness of sky, and had to raise a hand to shield her eyes from the glare. Her thoughts ran swift as lightning, to Joseph Druce, the wicked wretch, and his revelation in the wilderness; his lawless heart, lost in grief; his fugitive soul, drowned with fear; and then a mile of geese, the sun reflected on their down, temporarily blinding him.

The rim of the dome, lit from beyond the encircling clouds, deflected the subtle rays of early evening sun: she saw the head and shoulders of a colossus reduced to mere outline, the imposing mass an empty shadow, little more than a dream.

The sight of St Paul's Cathedral should have revived a good Christian. Instead, from this extreme angle, the entire fabric appeared to shift on its foundations, almost as if it might topple at any instant.

Anything might yet be possible, anything at all.

Sarah recrossed her own threshold with a profound rush of relief.

At some point during the day, her father had suffered a seizure and soiled himself. With Mary no longer present, nor herself in attendance, there had been no one to come to his aid. Heaven only knew how long he had lain enfeebled, and in an appalling state.

Lambert Larkin was mortified, beside himself with shame. He ran a slight fever, moaning and mumbling unintelligible nonsense as Sarah cleaned him and changed the bedding. The mattress was damp but she could not move him, not by herself, and neither did she think it in his best interest. A few layers of extra bedding would have to serve as a barrier. Once he was made comfortable again, she ran downstairs, hoping to find Dr Epps still in his surgery. The house was empty, the doctor gone for the day, as well as his staff. She would have run direct to his home in Hanover-square, or arranged for a message to be sent, but not at risk of leaving her poor father alone again.

Sarah fetched some coal and set a fire in his room. She made him soup, and helped him to eat. Little was said, and at length his mind seemed calmed. He looked up at her with such pathetic gratitude that it drove a lance through her heart. Not long after, thank the Lord, he drifted into sleep; Sarah did not leave his side, even for some hours after that. She simply could not forgive herself.

One floor below, Brippoki sits in darkness. Window and curtains gape open. The glowbug lamps in the street light up the ceiling for a time, until they are extinguished. Following his latest bout with London life, Thara's front parlour seems ever more an oasis of calm and serenity. At long last, he is able to relax.

The old man clock in the hallway chimes the hours. It is past midnight before a familiar shadow darkens the doorway. Guardian. Drawn with cares, she wears that same exhausted look he is all too used to seeing on the infinite faces that the city presents.

Brippoki speaks softly, so as not to alarm her.

'Thara,' he says.

To see her makes his liver glad.

'*Nei*-Thara. *Ba-been!*'

'Bri...Brippoki?' whispered Sarah. 'Oh, there you are. Hold on a moment while I...'

Rather than light the gasolier in the centre of the room, or even the paraffin table-lamp, she returned with a solitary candle.

The Aborigine was no more than a silhouette. Sarah drew closer. She immediately noticed a further change in his appearance, mistaking it a moment for an effect of candlelight. His features had always seemed fleshy: but then she gasped, almost inhaling the flame. Brippoki's face looked to have been smacked with a shovel.

'What,' she said, 'what's *happened* to you?'

Her terrible guilt forgotten, she ran to get water and a clean towel.

Bruises did not show on his black skin, but she could tell where it was puffy and swollen. There were visible cuts to his cheek, and brow, and lips. She bathed them, making sure they were clean, but there seemed no point applying bandages; she would have had to wrap his entire head, like an Egyptian mummy.

'Are you hurt anywhere else?' she asked.

Stiff movements and grimaces showed that his sides ached, but Brippoki impatiently waved her away. 'Him nutten,' he declared.

Sarah stood back a pace, feeling useless. He sat in his rags, looking completely worn out. The contrast from when he had first fetched up on her doorstep was sad, and she had thought him weary and dishevelled even then. That very first time she had seen him – at Went House, Town Malling – he had attracted her attention by being quieter than his compatriots: shy and retiring, like herself, the lines of his face drawn deep.

They yawned deeper still. That air of unknowable tragedy always lurking behind his eyes seemed almost nakedly revealed.

For a period they sat, saying nothing. At length, Sarah picked up her notebook, more for distraction from their separate woes than anything else.

'A lot has happened, since last we saw each other,' she said.

She opened up the book.

'I myself,' she said, 'have not been idle. I found something out today that I think you may find intriguing… George Bruce.'

She suddenly had Brippoki's complete attention.

'The name never seemed to mean much to you. Nor any of the others I have mentioned. Only the man. How about…' she flourished a piece of paper '…Joseph Druce?'

Brippoki looked a little wary, but did not otherwise react.

'*Josiah* Druce?'

No.

Sarah grew a little impatient. Getting to the bottom of the mystery man's identity, she had thought that she might at last be getting somewhere.

'I received a letter this morning from the Admiralty in London,' she said, 'presenting me with certain evidence, evidence that corroborates a suspicion held for some time now.'

Brippoki looked confused.

'You bin dancing?' he said, his tone disbelieving.

'I…eh? No.' Sarah barely masked her annoyance. She strove to measure her words. 'I have been to look in the…in a very special book,' she said. 'A sacred book.'

Guruwari.

'*Uah*,' he nodded. 'You Guardian!'

She followed his train of thought. 'Not in the library,' said Sarah. 'I was in a church. I went to that place where the man calling himself George Bruce has

270

told us he was born. I went to the church there, where he was blessed and given his name. His true name.'

Brippoki raised his hands. They were cupped, as if he meant to clap them over the flickering flame of the candle. The deep shadows that filled the room behind him jerked crazily; as, she supposed, they did behind her.

'George Bruce,' she said, 'is a fiction, a phantom. He is an invention.'

She checked to see that he followed, that Brippoki understood.

'He isn't real,' she said. 'He never existed. At least, not by that name…'

She belaboured the point, wanting him sure of it.

'His real name was Joseph Druce.'

Brippoki's lips shaped themselves as if he were about to repeat it.

'George Bruce and Joseph Druce,' emphasised Sarah. 'Two different names. One and the same man.'

Brippoki clapped his hands over both ears.

'Yes,' she said, 'it's true. I have it written here. Exactly as it is written in the sacred book.'

Brippoki's eyes opened wider. They were huge bloodshot orbs. He looked truly disturbed. Sarah almost wished she could take the words back, but she had come too far to stop short.

'"July 6, 1777, Joseph and Josiah, twin sons of John Druce, Distiller, and Mary…"'

'*WA-DAY!*'

She got no further. Brippoki flinched and fell to an awful trembling, then suddenly arose, shrieking. His limbs struck out in every direction as he stumbled from one piece of upset furniture to the next. The candle was blown out.

Sarah stood, speechless, hearing a voice, but seeing no man.

'*WA-day,*' he cried out in the darkness. '*Wa-daaayyy!*'

With another crash and a bang he made the open window, and in an instant was gone.

'BRIPPOKI!'

Sarah heard a wail from upstairs. All of the great commotion had woken her father.

'Who?' he hooted. 'Who is here?' The pallor of his face, dark around the eyes and open mouth…his head shone like a skull in the blackness.

Sarah brought the candle forward. 'It's all right,' she said. 'I'm here.'

'Frances?'

'Sarah.'

'Who else?' demanded Lambert. 'Who else is here?'

Sarah could not tell if he shivered from cold, fever, or fear. He had kicked off the main part of the coverlet, and was clad only in a thin sheet. It wound around his sweat-damp limbs and clung to him like a cerement, the shape beneath defined by its shallows and protuberances. She retrieved the blankets from the floor, and tucked them in around him.

'No one,' she said. 'There is no one else here. Only me, Sarah.'

'I heard a noise,' he said. 'An awful cry.'

'Yes,' she said. 'I'm sorry. That was me. I knocked over a table in the parlour. I was clumsy and the lamps were out.'

She couldn't bear lying to him.

'There was a voice,' he insisted. 'It didn't sound like your voice…'

'Hush, don't think of it,' she said. 'Don't worry yourself. Try to get some sleep.'

'Such a terror in the sound…' he said.

'*Hushhht.*'

'…such terror…'

III

Persecution

CHAPTER XXXV

Wednesday the 10th of June, 1868

THE DARK SIDE OF THE MOON

'There was a Door to which I found no Key:
There was a Veil past which I could not see:
Some little Talk awhile of ME and THEE
There seemed – and then no more of THEE and ME.'

~ *Rubáiyát of Omar Khayyám*

'*I should not like a son of mine to be born and bred in Ratcliffe-highway. That there would be a charming independence in his character, a cosmopolitanism rich and racy in the extreme, a spurning of that dreary conventionalism which makes cowards of us all, and under the deadly weight of which the heart of this great old England seems becoming daily more sick and sad – all this I admit I should have every reason to expect, but, at the same time, I believe the disadvantages would preponderate vastly.*'

Sarah Larkin laid down the book she was re-reading. She drew her shawl a little tighter about her shoulders. Out of the open window the night sky seemed less obscured by cloud than of late; the moon looked more than usually far away.

From the hallway, the grandfather clock sounded quarter-to. The hour would soon be ten, and for the second night in a row there had been no sign of Brippoki.

Her father having taken badly in her absence, Sarah had not dared leave the house since. Had she not been away to Ratcliff she would anyway have been in the library, but still, she could not forgive herself.

Tuesday morning first thing, Dr Epps had graciously paid a house call. Having only to climb two flights of stairs, he had charged for it nonetheless. She would have paid any price if only to gain peace of mind, and speed her father's recovery.

The doctor had assured her Lambert would recover in good time. She should turn his body frequently in the bed, so as to avoid his getting sores. Nothing much else could be done, except to administer sleeping draughts and let him rest. And so Sarah sat and maintained her lonely vigil: by day at her father's bedside, and every night at the open window one flight below.

She pluck'd a hollow reed.

As for her task at the Reading-room, she remained a little ahead of the material so far relayed to Brippoki. Her intent had been to read on to the end of Druce's manuscript; also, to complete her transliteration. Except that she had lost her reason.

Sarah smiled a bitter smile – true enough.

A night-cry brought her to the window; animal or human, Sarah could not say. Down below, a single creaking carriage meandered by. Otherwise the street was empty.

Sarah collapsed back into her chair. The book in her lap was *The Night Side of London*, by J. Ewing Ritchie, author of *The London Pulpit*: Lambert had purchased for himself a first edition. Radical in parts – from previous readings the introduction in particular stuck in her mind – the text as a whole amounted to little more than a guide to entertainments found at the more risqué establishments in the celebrated London night (The Mogul Drury-lane, the Cyder Cellars). The slim volume had been slotted away on a high shelf, and Sarah forbidden to look at it.

If Eve had never eaten of the fruit, she and Adam would never have discovered their capacity to act with free will in the world. Aged only sixteen, Sarah had devoured the text – as bitter for the daughter as it had been to the father, although for entirely different reasons. Like so many authors of his sex, Ritchie's love and passion was for dry statistics. One chapter however, the fourth, happened to concentrate its fetish for lists on Ratcliff-highway. According to Ritchie, in the passages she presently lingered over, a stroll there was sure to shock more senses than one. Having experienced for herself something of the same provocation, Sarah knew this very well to be true. A certain sense of it, the smell most assuredly, would never again leave her thoughts.

Then, as now, men of every colour and creed walked the Ratcliff-highway. George Bruce, *né* Joseph Druce, had been citizen of a 'rich and racy' Cosmopolis, a region wherein even an Australian Aborigine might not be considered so very out of place.

J. Ewing Ritchie discussed another common sight along the Highway, women 'fond of praise, of dress, and pleasure'. He evoked prostitution, simply, as the lesser evil – the slavery and drudgery of the workhouse providing the unpalatable alternative.

Hinting, forcibly, at the sham made of marriage, the author's commentary rang with at least one harsh and home truth: so long as the ideal of good prospects defined 'good' as 'gold', great expectations often fell in the way of a successful suit.

Or perhaps she was being a cross old maid.

No city, stated Ritchie, could be more corrupt than London. He pointed the finger of blame squarely at figures in authority: stern parents, divines, and schoolmasters – in short, all forms of government. Lawmakers imprisoned the young alongside the old. '*You take the little Arab of the streets, and, for acts of levity and wantonness which all boys commit, you send him to prison, at an age when you confess he is not a responsible creature, and then idiotically wonder that he turns out a criminal, and that he wars with society till he is hanged.*'

Thus the poor lads received their education, and grew up Ishmaelites.

'Street Arabs', just as Sarah had heard Tubridy refer to them, were identified with the sons of Abraham: Isaac was one, and the other Ishmael. *And he will be a wild man: his hand will be against every man, and every man's hand against him.*

Inculcating credo, teaching children catechisms – vaguely telling them to be good – only led to trust in forms rather than truths. Vice, though practised, was scandalously denied. Religion shut its eyes wilfully, refusing to look on life as it was: the Word undermined when not reflected by the act.

'*Is this the way seriously to set about moral reform?*' Ritchie asked in conclusion. '*Routine and officialism in church and state have made the outside of the sepulchre white enough; do we not need a little cleansing within?*'

'*How long will men look for grapes from thorns?*'

Sarah laid the book down. She did not feel much like reading any more.

The practice of one's own preaching, heaven knew, was rare enough; she had witnessed evidence of that in her tenderest years. Not from Lambert – he was unimpeachable – but in the behaviour of their guests. Ecclesiasts, by word or action each would offend; and, having offended, would be ejected. Every year fewer and fewer visitors had been admitted, until there were not any at all.

A person's outward conduct best defined their spiritual character. In setting themselves up as middle-men for God, priests often as not stood in the way of the ordinary person, blocking out the light – because, in their own sinning, by mere profession, they were unqualified. Truth was made for the laity, and Falsehood for the clergy.

Checking in on Lambert, Sarah found him almost too still and quiet. Appalled at herself, she picked up a hand-mirror she had laid aside for that very purpose, and held it, hovering, close to his mouth. She took it up. The glass was smoked. As it cleared, she was left staring almost dumbly at her own reflection: how grey her hair looked, how thin her face.

She returned to the parlour; stood, looking into the empty chasm of the street. Often, staring out of that same window, she had believed she could see all of life and London passing her by. It was not nearly all.

The *nachseite* or 'night side' of existence was that which was invisible, or sublime; the visible might allude to it, but only if one but knew the signs. She knew them now: the cheap white muslin, the halfpenny candy cane.

Following the theatre-show and suppertime lull, the vast multitudes of carriages returned. Their wheels ground and set the walls to a slight tremor.

Sarah recognised the true sound of the city. Too consistent for ocean breakers, it was the roar of a cataract endlessly pouring down a gulf.

CHAPTER XXXVI
Thursday the 11th of June, 1868

THE DREAM THAT IS DYING

'As a meteor shoots athwart the night,
The boundless champaign burst upon our sight,
Till nearer seen the beauteous landscape grew,
Op'ning like Canaan on rapt Israel's view.'

~ W. C. Wentworth, 'Australasia'

By the following morning Lambert Larkin appeared to have staged a minor recovery – back to the shadow of his former self. He acquiesced to Sarah's shaving his whiskery chin, an operation he would normally perform himself. There was much less blood to staunch, her hand being considerably steadier than his own.

Neither one made mention of Monday's events.

Other than to buy in fresh provisions and a newspaper, his dutiful daughter seemed reluctant to leave him alone for too long, yet by morning's end Lambert all but insisted she go to the library.

Returned to the British Museum, Sarah made straight for the manuscript. Halfway across the Reading-room she thought better of it. Without breaking her stride she overshot its place of concealment, performing a neat circuit of the outer catalogue stand. From this central vantage point, she discreetly searched the room. Benjamin J. Jeffery, the junior clerk, was nowhere to be seen.

Sarah placed herself within direct sight of the manuscript. It remained precisely where she had left it. She did not take it up. Instead, she selected a seat where the accommodation was least crowded, and made for the section of open shelves designated *Geography, Voyages, & Travels*.

She had been foolish enough to imagine they all walked the same path – Druce as the author of the manuscript; she, its narrator; and Brippoki, their keen listener. Wherever it was they might have been going, their roads had since separated. The figure of Druce, advancing, had cast Brippoki into the shade. Yet Druce was long dead, whilst Brippoki was alive – alive and in the flesh and night by night presenting himself in her parlour; and just as suddenly gone – as mysterious to her as when he had first appeared.

The world that she knew was the world of books.

Sarah resolved to read whatever material she could find on the continent of Australia and its Aboriginal inhabitants. She would go up among the mountains of that country.

She primed her pens and jotted down quick notes as she read.

Surrounded on three sides by vast oceans, for thousands of years the continent of Australia had remained uncharted, its very existence held in doubt. The buccaneer William Dampier became the first Englishman to visit those far-flung shores, washed up on the north coast in 1688. It had taken the deliberate efforts of Captain Cook to circumnavigate and definitively chart the nether land.

A full century after Dampier, the First Fleet of eleven ships sailed from Portsmouth and Gravesend, establishing the first British settlement at Port Jackson, a few miles north of Cook's landfall at Botany Bay. Church services were compulsory for convicts and emancipists – almost half of the new populace. Not long after it was built, the new chapel mysteriously burnt down.

The Second Fleet, much more diseased and unfortunate than the First, arrived in June of 1790 – and Druce only two years after, a deportee. Even unto the present day the disagreeable practice continued. Luddites, food rioters, Chartists, and not least agitators for Irish independence, a total in excess of 160,000 souls had been transported there as convicts, almost a fifth of them women.

According to the Reverend G. Strickland, writing in *The Australian Pastor*, a European population of less than 80,000 in 1840 had increased fourfold by 1851. Since that time the discovery of gold had provoked considerable rush and fever, exponential numbers of Europeans travelling to Australia in hope of making their fortune.

What, then, of the original inhabitants? Histories of the colony were presented as the history of the country: Sarah found almost as little mention of the natives there as in the manuscript.

Dampier, the first Englishman to meet with the Aborigines, reacted with disgust. Virtually the only remarks passed regarding them in his *New Voyage Round the World* were disparagements. 'The Inhabitants of this Country are the miserablest People in the World,' he wrote. 'Setting aside their Humane Shape, they differ but little from Brutes.' He thought the unknown land the most barren place on God's earth.

In the April of 1770, Captain Cook had witnessed evidence of occupancy. In addition to hollowed logs, and bark huts, steps had been carved into the trees for climbing them. He himself cut an inscription into a gum tree, raised the flag, and claimed the territory for England, calling it 'New South Wales'. Cook reported the natives few in number. They were primitives who went 'quite Naked', living in caves and hollows in the rock, having no proper place of abode. Nomads, knowing nothing of cultivation, they wandered from place to place in small parties in search of food.

The men and women of the First Fleet expressed less charitable opinions. Not only primitive, the Aboriginals were 'ugly', and 'stupid', 'the most wretched of the human race', 'the most miserable of God's creatures', 'the most miserable of the human form under heaven' – and so on, and no more. James Dredge, a Wesleyan, testified to the awful predominance amongst them of 'sins of the most obscene and revolting description', without revealing what they could be; proof nevertheless that they were without God in the world, 'entirely lost to all oral and spiritual perception'.

No crops, no houses, no clothes…and no religion either? Could Brippoki's heritage really be as bereft as all that? This was not at all her impression. Sarah felt sure she knew better – that he knew better.

Could he really be so different from the rest of his people?

Still in search of her elusive quarry, Sarah consulted the journals of early explorers into the interior. The Reading-room maintained an impressive selection. Surely here she would find the Aboriginal natives worthy of more than passing mention.

Major Sir Thomas Mitchell, surveyor-general for the colony of New South Wales, wrote of his journey, undertaken in 1836, across rivers and mountains no white man had ever seen. Passing into what subsequently became the crown colony of Victoria, he described a country wide open and ready to be possessed. From Mount Hope to rocky Pyramid Hill, its apex a single block of granite, he reported the view over the surrounding plains exceedingly beautiful. 'Shining fresh and green in the light of a fine morning… A land so inviting, and still without inhabitants!'

Bounded by the ocean, it was traversed by mighty rivers – the Murray, Glenelg, and Wimmera – and watered by innumerable streams.

'I was,' he wrote, 'the first European to explore this Eden.'

He named these rich and fertile pastures 'Australia Felix', and pronounced their potential for grazing unsurpassed. When Mitchell returned to Sydney with this news, it started a land rush. The following year he was rewarded with a knighthood.

He related little of the Aborigines, other than to say that they were 'friendly'.

Sarah went to retrieve Druce's manuscript. This time she maintained a steady course. If it were noticed at any time, and handed in or reported without its shelf-mark, the work would be lost to her. She preferred to have it in view, relocated among those same shelves where she had already spent the better part of her day, alongside books more suitable to its category. Perhaps then, even if seen, it might not otherwise call attention to itself for being out of place.

Shelving Mitchell, cross-reference led her to Ludwig Leichhardt and his *Journal of an Overland Expedition in Australia*. She liked the name because he had the same initials as her father.

In 1844–45 Leichhardt had trekked some 3,000 miles, from Moreton Bay to Port Essington. His party of ten included: a lad of sixteen; 'a prisoner of the Crown', presumably emancipist; an American Negro; and, intriguingly, two Aboriginal native guides. Their trip started out in a manner light-hearted enough, a rousing rendition of 'God Save the Queen' delivered as they wound their way around the first bend. The further they ventured away from the 'squatter' (or colonist) settlements, however, the more the details came to resemble Druce's experience.

Life in the Australian Bush was assuredly one of hardship and privation: hunger, desperate thirst, afflicted bowels, the shortage of a ready water supply and brutal exposure to the elements. The vicissitudes of heat and cold, an extreme variation in ground temperature between night and day, enforced their own brand of punishment. Swarms of mosquitoes and flies clung to the sores on their fingers, to the lips and ears, and even to the corners of their eyes, while small black ants crept all over their bodies and bit severely, falling into soup and tea and covering their meat. Happily, this was but part of an overabundance of wildlife in general: kangaroos and wallabies, brush turkeys, partridge and bronze-winged pigeons in particular were very numerous. A great many scenes of natural beauty also compensated for their sufferings. Rich in game, the open country was well grassed, simple river channels flowing between chains of lakes and lagoons where the huge flocks of ducks and pelicans were said to resemble islands of white lilies. Woodland was relatively scarce, where plumed cockatoos would precede them, swooping from tree to tree and filling the air with shrill cries. They shot them for the makings of a fine soup.

One of the gentlemen scholars, a Mr Gilbert, returned from an exploratory ride having observed the sign of an anchor cut into a tree. This he supposed done by a shipwrecked sailor, or else a runaway convict from Moreton Bay, a former penal settlement.

Sarah held fast to her fancy that, in some sense or other, they all of them followed in Druce's footsteps. Left to her own devices, she had at first pictured him travelling through bucolic scenery much like Epping Forest. Only later had she modified her conception in the innocent terms of a toy-theatrical back-drop; an all-purpose jungle of lush, tropical undergrowth – what, as a small child, she had called 'jumble' – but without any sense of the heat and flies, the blinding glare of a too-bright sun, or the twisted trunks of trees and their sticky, shining leaves.

Leichhardt and his party adapted to Bush life with admirable swiftness. To allay hunger they swallowed the bones and feet of a pigeon as well its sweet flesh, or the blunt tail and knobbly scales of a sleeping lizard. Lacking in provisions, their clothes and harness also wore away. Without flour, without salt, miserably clothed, all were yet in good health, showing how congenial the climate was, in fact, to the human constitution. As their basic comforts declined, so their desires became more easily satisfied. Necessity taught them economy.

There was hope, then.

In other respects they clung to the semblance of their former existence. At night they would stretch themselves on the ground, almost as naked as the natives. Leichhardt and his two blackfellows preferred to sleep out under the stars; the others insisted on erecting their tents. Mr Phillips planted blossoming lilies before his tent, in order that he might enjoy them during his short stay.

How like Lambert, who, denied a garden, fashioned for himself a blooming windowbox.

Aside from the neigh of a tethered horse, and the distant tinkle of a cowbell, the stillness of the moonlit night would gradually fall across the camp. A lone cricket might chirp along the waterholes, while the melancholy wail of the curlew issued from the neighbouring scrub. As the bright constellations wheeled silently overhead, the dying fire smouldered under a large pot in which their breakfast meat was simmering.

And yet, night by night, the lonely travellers revisited the lands they had left behind: in their dreams, they returned home.

By day, over the crest of each new hill or around the bend of a dry riverbed, the vista, ever expanding, opened up before them. Between waterhole, creek and lagoon stretched great wastes of sandstone and scrub, much of it bleak and intractable. In places the geology sounded truly alien: high basaltic plains pebble-dashed with white quartz and an iron-coloured conglomerate, or stripes of blue clay. Lumps of coal lay readily about, like lettuces or cabbage, ripe for the picking. The landscape was one of great contrasts, some parts swamp, and others desert. Following a few hours of rain, one might wholly transform into the other. Regions that appeared barren only lay fallow, ready and waiting to spring suddenly to life.

Hollows lay across the dry plains, pockets of rich black soil – the sediment, she assumed, having built up over time. Filled with water by a sudden thunderstorm, the seeds of the grasses and herbs that lay dormant there would instantly germinate, covering over everything with their rapid and luxuriant growth, as if by enchantment. In spite of its strange character, noted Leichhardt, this country could be most beautiful, if only watered consistently.

Sarah relished the image.

In his *Journal*, Leichhardt described fully the many and varied species of fauna and flora his party encountered. At last she was able to conjure the far-off landscape as it really must have been, and she thought it more wonderful yet.

In Leichhardt's account, as with Druce's manuscript, the Aborigines were conspicuous only by their absence. One time only was a lone figure observed, running at prodigious speed across moonlit plains in the distance.

Remote columns of smoke might be sighted in the daytime, distant fires at night, but Leichhardt's party only ever came across native camps that had been deserted. Trees appeared recently stripped of their bark, hives with the honey cut out. The 'Blackfellows' who never showed themselves were meantime acknowledged as holding the intruders under frequent observation. Sarah imagined this might also have been the case with Druce; the fugitive shadowed, that shadow unseen.

In one region, large heaps of mussel-shells covered over the sloping riverbanks, indicating a sizeable population, and one spanning successive generations. The prevalence of kangaroo and emu bones over the scarcity of human remains suggested the practice among them of the burial of their dead.

Sarah felt somewhat reassured: Brippoki's people were not completely without ceremony.

She read on deep into the afternoon, until her enthusiasm began to flag. So little mention was made of the Aborigines. Even the description of Leichhardt's own native companions never went beyond the names 'Harry Brown' and 'Charley'. And then, just at the point when she was about to give up, finally they made their appearance.

Near to a river, the sound of a stone tomahawk was heard. Guided by the noise, Leichhardt and his party discovered three black women: two digging for roots, the third perched atop a gum tree. These emitted dreadful screams on seeing the strangers approach, and swung their sticks and beat the trees as if it were wild beasts they were attempting to frighten away. The two diggers immediately ran off, and nothing could induce the lady in the tree to descend.

The next time they approached a native party, Leichhardt sensibly quit his mount. Horses were not indigenous to that country any more than the cattle they drove with them; even the wild Bush creatures did not know how to interpret them at first sight. And yet, despite precaution and their own superior numbers, the tribesmen fled as before. Blackfellows, it seemed, could not bear the sudden sight of a white man.

The Aborigines appeared a gentle people. On one occasion when the white camp was surrounded, and might easily have been taken by force of arms, the trekkers kept them in good humour merely by replying to enquiries in respect of their true nature and intentions.

And yet, as it turned out, the spirit of exploration was far from Leichhardt's only motivator. Over the course of their travels he had gone about naming and claiming the natural landscape for his many sponsors and supporters. Commercial interests underwrote almost all of his botanical notes regarding the suitability of pastureland for cattle grazing, and ultimately settlement. He had been commissioned to assess the lie of the land with an eye to its future development.

Leichhardt, in summation, confidently declared: 'We shall not probably find a country better adapted for pastoral pursuits.'

Fully aware of those who would come following in his footsteps, he proceeded in total ignorance of those who already walked the open country before them.

The natives apparently considered that same loamy black soil most especially favoured for ploughing to be the work of an evil spirit, 'Devil-devil land'. The fertile country they perceived to be under enchantment was seen – perhaps correctly – as their curse.

Sarah felt queasy, a knot deep down in the pit of her stomach.

When the natives suddenly attacked, she was almost ready to admit their actions justified. Following the swift and bloody death of Mr Gilbert, however, she felt the immediate sting of remorse. The spear that terminated the poor man's existence entered the chest between the clavicle and the neck, but made so small a wound that, for some time, Leichhardt was unable to detect it.

The colonial authorities equated the shock of the party's sudden reappearance in Sydney 'to what might be felt at seeing one who had risen from the tomb'. Few had expected them to survive their year-long trek through the interior – as indeed not all did. Thus, their adventurous spirits were commended among the land's first conquerors, by whose 'peaceful triumphs' an empire had been added to the parent state.

Sarah closed up the book, and returned it to the shelf.

Four o'clock. Intent on preparing Lambert something extra special for his evening meal, she quit the library early.

Moving to close the window, Sarah froze. The sill was still filled with crumbs.

'No birds came today,' said Lambert. 'They sense…my mortality…come.'

Sarah took what was merely the delayed end of Lambert's sentence as an instruction. Moving obediently to his bedside, she laid a hand to his dear head. Very aware of the age in his face, she attempted to smooth out the creases. 'I am sorry,' she said, 'that you don't feel well.'

'The machine is made to wear well,' he said. 'That it does not, is my own fault.'

'No…oh, no.' She lightly stroked his white hair. White. It had been grey before. Even that vestige of colour had gone out of it, and she had not even noticed.

For a time they fell silent.

'There was another report,' announced Lambert. He reached across to retrieve the newspaper from where it had fallen. 'The Australian Eleven…have played another engagement.'

The relevant page was thrust into Sarah's hand as if an urgent bulletin – and, in a way, it was.

'Read it!' he said.

'"June eighth–ninth,"' she read. '"Australian Eleven versus Sussex."'

'Not to me, you trout!' chided Lambert. 'Read it for yourself.'

The fifth match of their tour already. The popularity of the team as both novelty and draw was undiminished: Hove played host to the largest number of persons ever seen on that ground at a cricket match. A galaxy of beauty and fashion, so the article read, had graced the subscribers' marquees. Their scarlet shirts distinguished by coloured sashes, the Aboriginal team's form was remarked muscular and full of vigour, although several were noted rather sluggish between wickets, which was felt surprising, given their energy in other respects.

'Johnny Mullagh played something fierce again. It says that, doesn't it,' encouraged Lambert. 'You can read it out to me if you'd like.'

Sarah obliged, smiling. '"Mullagh,"' she read, '"by the way in which he opened his shoulders at the commencement, showed that he meant mischief"… "at the tail end were Peter and Dumas, the latter being run out for one, and he certainly did give Peter pepper for it, and no mistake."'

Eyes popping, her jaw dropped.

'What is it?' asked Lambert.

'Nothing,' said Sarah, blushing. 'It… I swallowed a fly, or something. I'm all right now. No, thank you, I'm fine. I'll carry on.

'"Young…"' She hesitated, disbelieving even as she read the words. '"Young King Cole then went in, and scored three off the first ball. He and Twopenny were in for a considerable time, but the merry young soul was ultimately bowled."'

Sarah reached across the bedside table, pouring herself a glass of water from the jug she replenished twice a day.

'A fly, you say? Silly trout,' said Lambert – fondly this time.

The probability that Brippoki had resumed his touring was one Sarah hadn't even considered. In retrospect it made perfect sense: he couldn't possibly have strayed all this time in neglect of his other engagements. How foolish!

She cleared her throat.

'"Eight guineas and a fob watch",' she read, '"awarded to Johnny Mullagh on the ninth of June, 1868, with the inscription *Presented to J. Mullagh by the gentlemen of Sussex for his fine display at Brighton.*"'

'Yesterday, and today,' enthused Lambert, 'the Blackies have been playing at Ladywell, versus Lewisham. And on Saturday, the M.C.C. at *Lord's!*'

Sarah worked hard to show no reaction.

'"By cricket",' he declared, '"are the prince and the peasant united."'

Saturday, at Lord's – did she dare?

Later, all of her chores done and a light supper served, Sarah again sat with Lambert. He seemed lost in thought, or else skirted the verge of sleep. She pretended to read a book, meanwhile listening for sounds from the floor below. Lewisham was not so very far distant.

'…muscular…and full of vigour…'

'Father?' said Sarah. 'Did you speak?'

'I was young once,' he said. 'Only the once.'

'And I have seen the picture that proves it!' she said.

No response. Lambert had drifted away again – if ever really there.

God's plan: *Go forth of the ark, thou.*

'No birds came today'…

A dove, but black. God's plan.

It was late. Very tired, Sarah lay in bed, staring at the ceiling in place of stars.

'Australia Felix' was the Promised Land, her wild beauty unspoiled…and then exposed.

Sarah tried very hard to picture the country Brippoki had left behind. She had seen it described as a land of limitless horizon…

There was a vision worth dreaming of.

CHAPTER XXXVII
Friday the 12th of June, 1868

THE DARK TWIN

'Ye suppose that there are men walking all the earth
over with their feet opposite the feet of other men.'

~ *The Christian Topography of Cosmas,*
an Egyptian Monk, circa 547 AD

Bunjil Ting-ting, one, two times, two times, two, two more – very many, *Bool-tha-bat*.

Dead of night swallows one last echo, the final strike of the tolling bell.

Riverside, open sky, hunted moon. Plenty shadow, more plenty light. That good.

Sky dark. No dogs, no piccaninnies. That bad.

The wide dark stream glides far below, blacker even than sky. Moonlight shivers on the troubled water. Shipping idles, the trees on the water, a dark forest silent by night.

In the distance, the Piebald Giant watches over all.

Ice-cold fingers steal through hair at the root. Across the bridge ghostly horse-men ride in file. They shimmer, unstable: in the half-light, by the sliver of moon, the tall buildings and distant hills show through them. The fall of their ghastly hooves makes no sound.

At length the bell sounds again, a single toll.

That prickling sensation returns. Something prowls the outer dark. The subtle hunter stalks; forever present, always just out of sight.

Wide eyes sweep the gloom, aching for the new day's piercing diamond – fearing the glimpse of a greater darkness, finding form in darkest hour.

The vault of sky turns a deep, dark blue. Dawn comes.

Less than a mile downriver, on the south shore, the stale piss-stink of tanneries fouls the air. A moat of stinking sludge encircles a bleb of housing, so tightly it oozes a poison. The open channel, a wound knit by a dozen or more wood-scrap bridges, fills with every high tide.

The sun's first rays striking the sides of their dens, the native islanders emerge. As bugs scuttle to ground after the lifting of a rock, they gravitate riverwards. Cloaked in oily rag, wreathed in smoke, their movement between houses is hard to track. All along the shoreline, the blackish dots congregate – *gins* and *lubras* mostly, from near-infant to decrepit crone. They roll their trousers and bunch their skirts, as if eager for a swim. Clustered about the various stairways leading down, impatiently they wait for the churning waters to recede.

Tide running low, they scatter along the exposed mudflats below the wharves, in either direction. Submerged to their ankles, they begin to feel their way forward with their feet. On both sides of the river, scores of bodies, mired, knee-deep, wade into the shallows, even up to their thighs. As outlying vessels become becalmed or beached, they struggle forward and disappear among them.

One youngster lifts another up, between barges. Soon she is on board, a little girl. She skips about the deck, knocking lumps of coal over the side into the wet mud. The older boy races backwards and forwards to scoop them up before they sink without trace. The girl in her big bonnet kicks over the wrong side from her brother, and he hollers and stamps in exasperation.

Eora, this place, is a smudge, a swamp. Everywhere *ngamaitya*, toiling in the thick of Serpent's cast. Wanting for grubs? Mussels? *Nung?*

Everywhere, dead people, washed up on the dead shore. They come from dirt, and they return to dirt – clay people, made of muck.

Lambert Larkin could taste his own tongue. His nostrils flared as he licked the air.

'My mouth is hot and dry,' he said, 'as it is every morning.'

'And I have brought you tea,' said Sarah. 'As I do, every morning.'

She laid down his breakfast tray and parcelled out the contents. He glared at her disapprovingly, as only a parent could, before his features softened.

'You must learn to let me complain, my dear,' he said.

'Never.'

His appearance improved appreciably with his mood, as if having reaped the benefits of a good night's sleep. Sarah opened up the curtains and then the window, quick to brush away the crumbs remaining on the sill.

Lambert professed a hearty appetite. 'Today I shall eat all of the toast you can bring me,' he said. 'Crusts as well!'

It was indeed a beautiful morning.

Sarah proposed to sit in company a while. Lambert accepted. Once breakfast was cleared, rather than commune with the morning papers, he requested that she open the drawers of the far cabinet, and bring to him various specimens from his collection of natural phenomena: sea-shells, dried broad leaves, pine cones and so forth. Each of these items he handled gladly, turning them over and over between his large hands. He ruminated with a soft and chesty rumble, exhaling gently.

'"No longer dead, hostile Matter"…' He looked to Sarah, smiling. 'Nature,' he said, 'lends to our everyday a small portion of the eternal.

'This pine, I picked up on one of my many high mountain walks, the same as with the small rock samples. I can recall precisely when and where each one came into my possession. Each one may be read, as easily as a book…and what's more, learnt from.'

He handed her the pine cone. Sarah nodded, absently.

'Every fragment of splendour means something dear to me, for being part of that greater continuity…' Lambert held a shell aloft between the tips of his fingers. 'Omni-potent.' He pronounced the word carefully, as a separated compound, his eyes twinkling at his daughter. 'This shell you see,' he said, 'comes from the shoreline near to Clovelly, in Cornwall, where your dear mother and I spent our honeymoon. The briefest of happinesses…'

Lambert drew a fingertip down the shell's serrated spiral edge. Bringing it close to his gimlet eye, he lightly traced one of the crisp ridges which themselves formed threads of colour around its circumference. His fist closed lightly around the shell, and he kept ahold of it as he sorted among the other objects gathered in his lap.

'All carries life within it,' he said, 'and is itself the meaning of life. Indivisible and one, just as you are, my dear…another link in the great chain which binds us to God.'

Sarah blinked and stared at the sea-shell. She took the compliment, but he'd never before made mention of their honeymooning, nor Clovelly. Her parents had been married ten years before she was ever conceived.

The pine cone resting on her palm, she examined the repetition of its form, neat and regular – the seed fallen close to the tree.

'"We dream",' said Lambert, '"of journeys through the cosmos… Eternity…"' He lost his thread. 'Novalis,' he said simply.

Age betrayed him. With not much to occupy his latter days other than thought, his penultimate fear was the loss of mind.

Sarah began to gather up the clutch of objects. They made the bed untidy, and she was scared they might roll to the floor and be lost.

'You are Nature's priest,' she said.

'Leave well alone, you fussbudget,' he snapped. 'Stop scrabbling!'

Roughly he slapped her hands aside.

She should have known better than to interrupt one of his raptures. Her real mistake, however, was in invoking Wordsworth.

'There are no halves in Creation!' Lambert stormed.

Jaw jutting, Sarah snatched away the last of the stray items.

'With every age,' he persisted, 'man conceives for himself some new illusion regarding his relationship with Nature. This is especially true of poets.' He leant his head to one side. 'We may be part of God,' he snapped, 'but we are not *as* God.'

Shamed by his sudden burst of ill temper, the old preacher essayed humility.

'Forgive me,' he said. 'I promote ideas above their station. The work of *my* hand, I neither commend nor grieve. I do God's work…' Staring into his open palms, at the flexing of his fingers, he appeared to trouble in their reflex action. 'It is all I know…'

Lambert fell silent. When he spoke again, his words were barely audible.

'I didn't hear you,' said Sarah, flatly.

'Put them away…' he said.

Sarah retrieved the precious shell from where it had fallen. He seemed about to plunge into another of his monumental glooms, and she wished to catch him whilst still on the brink.

'Oh, father,' she said, 'don't be sad, not today. The day is too bright for you to be sad.'

Lambert inclined his face towards the open window and took in a deep draught. 'You are right,' he said. 'I miss my life in the open air, that is all. I mean my former life…'

He sighed.

'I pine.'

Father and daughter exchanged a brief smile.

Sarah envisaged manhandling him into a bath-chair, wheeling him down the several flights of steps, and fighting their way through crowded city streets in search of a park or a train into the countryside, or at least the leafier outer suburbs; all of it of course impossible, a madcap scheme.

She settled for clearing the mess the room was always getting itself into.

'A beautiful summer's day,' mused Lambert, seeming sufficiently distracted. 'Hot enough, do you think, to encourage the Aborigines?'

Caught out, Sarah stopped and stared.

'You should go and see them play,' said Lambert, 'a proper match this time. Then come home and tell me all about it.'

Sarah returned to her tasking. 'I couldn't,' she said, quietly. 'It was wrong of me to leave you alone so much, before…'

'You know I prefer it!' snapped Lambert.

'But…what if…?'

'I will be all right!'

Sarah flinched.

'I believe I am quite recovered,' he said. His face was stone.

'If you believe,' she said, 'then I must too.'

'I am…glad you think so,' he replied.

Sarah regretted sounding so peevish.

'Will you go today?' he asked.

Could she?

'Perhaps…'

She would not leave him for an entire day. And it would take at least some planning. 'Perhaps tomorrow,' she said.

To go to Lord's, and to see Brippoki again…was it really possible – and with her father's blessing? She would pray for it.

'Then let today be glad, also,' said Lambert. He reached out a bare arm, fingertips skimming a ray of sunshine where it streamed into his bedchamber. 'The air has warmth,' he said. 'Take yourself into it. I insist!'

Sarah laid down her burdens, took up his outstretched hand, and kissed it. That was all she had really wanted: to be set free.

'Enjoy it,' he said, 'for my sake.'

She left the room.

'Fetch me back, if you can, some small measure of eternity.'

Lambert Larkin let the mask fall. No longer secretive in his sorrows, he looked more deeply stricken than ever.

Before resorting to the Museum, Sarah took a turn around Russell-square in the noonday sunshine, happy, for once, to obey her father's behest, as much as to act on his behalf. Strolling across the park, she picked him out a spectacularly fine leaf and, taking great care, secreted it within the folds of her skirts.

Naked beggar children splashed in the fountains. Buttoned up in sailor suit and pinafore, others stood protestant in the grip of nursemaid and governess. They looked daggers at their penniless cousins.

Her father had spoken of former life in the profound sense – the Garden of Eden, before the Fall, when mankind was content in its ignorance.

The weekend could not come too soon. As long as Lambert's health held up, then, God willing, she might look forward to taking a trip.

Pale imitation at best, it seemed too great a shame to have replaced a rare blue sky with the vaulted dome of the Reading-room.

Moving Druce's manuscript around the various bookstacks had developed into something of a nervous habit. This time Sarah transferred it between categories; from *Geography, Voyages, & Travels* to *Biography*. The previous classification had seemed appropriate only because of her familiarity with its content. A glance along the shelves from any casual reader – or worse, staff member – and the title they would see was simply *The Life of a Greenwich Pensioner*.

Still in search of the Australian Aborigine, Sarah grazed the available stock in haphazard fashion. Rather than be bound by one man's experience, or limit herself to any single, lengthy account, she elected to flit back and forth between titles, indices and cross references. The *Travels* section alone held more than 30 books concerning the crown colonies of Australia.

Amongst other things, Lambert Larkin had ever been a tireless antiquarian; Sarah inherited at least this much. The fanaticism for veracity lay at the very heart of her morality. In quest of absolute accuracy she would exhaust every available source of information, and hunger for those that she suspected beyond her reach. Only frustration with herself, with what she perceived as her own shortcomings, might slow her down.

Sarah utilised all of her skills, her practised eye and sharp practice. A promising reference in one volume might send her darting in search of another. Speed-reading, she quickly came to rely on a handful of names whose testimonies she returned to again and again – Captain Grey, William Westgarth, David Collins, the Messrs Jardine, and John MacGillivray – not admitting their opinions definitive, but the tools that she had to work with. She saw a copy of the *Journals* of Edward John Eyre, but this she purposely disregarded. The controversial ex-governor of Jamaica, Eyre had flogged, tortured, burned and hanged the slave descendants of that Caribbean island; only recently had he been returned to England to be put on trial for murder.

She cast him out of mind and sought to concentrate.

The available evidence suggested that there were coastal, marshland and desert Aborigines, each group differing from the others in terms of their physical attributes, degree of friendliness, and dialect most completely of all. Every tribe, no matter how small in number, appeared to have a distinct language of its own. In matters of custom and belief, however, all were broadly similar – insofar as their beliefs could be ascertained, which was not so very far. Beards, for example, found universal favour amongst full-grown Aborigine males; beardless men in European parties they met had been obliged to drop their trousers in confirmation of their sex.

More advanced than Captain Cook had given them credit for, if not by much, they commonly sheltered in hovels not much bigger than an oven, made from pieces of stick, or bark and grass; and only in the wet seasons.

Direct confrontation and displays of overt curiosity were considered the very height of rudeness, a trait absolutely confirmed by Sarah's own experience. Almost any line of enquiry would be politely rebuffed, making it almost impossible to establish anything for certain. By the same token, a conversational gambit such as revealing talk about oneself appeared to be as unwelcome as it was uninvited. Aborigines disliked contradiction, so unfailingly polite that they would agree with any argument presented to them – a suggestion Sarah found most concerning. In consequence, ever since the days of first contact, blacks and whites had continually wrongfooted one another.

The immutability of the otherwise docile savages was widely remarked on. New South Wales governor Lachlan Macquarie – the same – found them to be frank and honest, but he observed with regret that they wasted their lives in wandering. J. A. Turnbull pronounced their habits nomadic in both practice and temperament, concluding the New Hollander physically incapable of civilisation. The Jardines complained at how their unsettled nature presented a very great obstacle: they themselves had nothing to offer. Nor were they much interested in foreign objects, beyond a brief novelty value. This inability to be drawn forth, quite unlike the other native peoples British explorers had thus far encountered, proved a constant source of frustration. Without trade there was little hope of developing a greater understanding, no give, and no take.

Positions eventually relaxed and the white men prevailed on the Aborigines, who took a renewed fancy to comfort goods, pouring into the new towns in quest of tea, flour, sugar, and alcohol.

Sarah felt pleased to read of a possible reconciliation, but greater shocks lay in store.

Chastity was a virtue unknown to them: for a loaf of bread, a blanket or shirt, their women gave up any claim to it, and many were the white men who held out the temptation. Yet according to Westgarth, writing in 1846, the prevalence of illicit intercourse between black females and colonists was a fruitful source of misery to the Aboriginal population, not only from the introduction and spread of disease, but due to the hostile feelings engendered among the males.

Common-law relations aside, intermarriage between the races remained out of the question. No similar repugnance prevailed towards the half-caste children that resulted; they appeared acceptable to either side. Reverend George Taplin reported the Aborigines actually preferring to have white children: since the colonists had greater sympathy for them, they were the least trouble. Complications only presented themselves in later life. At some point, part-blood sons brought up amongst the settlements met with an immovable obstacle: no European woman could be found who would consider a native. Generally despised, they were obliged to go into the Bush for companions. Whether or not they found a welcome there, Sarah was unable to resolve.

She felt curious. What then, if anything, did Aboriginal males make of white females? Surely it must have been known from the start that such an exchange could not be tolerated. Were they repulsed, as the ladies of Europe were? Did they despise?

Among the Aborigines every man was considered equal, and given the opportunity to have his say. They recognised neither rank nor title. In all of their many and various languages, there was not one word for 'chief', nor one for 'servant'. The only term of respect that might be found signified 'father', and was applied to any of their old men. The idea that one man could be considered higher than another proved difficult to get into a blackfellow's head, and yet local government desired equal representatives to deal with. This led to the institution of the 'King Billys': Boongaree, pictured, wore a little tin-plate badge of office. He looked severe but at the same time hesitant, insecure, and quite naked without a beard. The ennobling experiment was a failure. Given no real authority by the administration, the Billys became figures of straw, disrespected in both camps. Many took refuge in the bottle, and could be found sprawled in the gutter, still in their royal vestments.

The name 'King Cole', in retrospect, seemed ever less appropriate. Sarah felt glad to have abandoned it.

One custom in particular arrested her attention – their strict code of retributive justice. In the tradition of *Exodus*, the Aborigines took an eye for an eye. 'He exists,' wrote the Reverend Wood, 'in a state of perpetual feud, his quarrels not being worthy of the name of warfare; and his *beau idéal* of a warrior is a man who steals upon his enemy by craft, and kills his foe without danger to himself.'

In an observation made decades earlier, David Collins was perhaps more precise on this same point. 'They are revengeful, jealous, courageous, and cunning. I have never considered their stealing on each other in the night for the purposes of murder as a want of bravery, but have looked on it rather as the effect of the diabolical spirit of revenge, which thus sought to make surer of its object than it could have done if only opposed man to man in the field.'

Blood-debts sometimes festered for many years before a ripe opportunity presented itself. Sarah recalled to mind Sergeant Padraig Tubridy's uncharacteristic fear of dusk, legacy of the many grudges held against his badge of office.

Pitched battles were not unknown, but, in the case of a killing, an oddly formal punishment seemed the most common settlement of any dispute. The accused must take his chances, submitting himself as a willing target for the spears of the aggrieved. The relatives of the deceased, as if they too were somehow implicated in the affair, would then be compelled to undergo the same trial. Sarah had seen the exact stunt performed at the Oval cricket ground, and then again with cricket balls substituted for their spears.

Nor were their vengeance killings limited in scope. According to the Aboriginal philosophy of revenge, if the accused were beyond reach, any associate of theirs would do. In one given instance of a sentry shooting an escapee, relatives of the dead man made reprisal not on the white man who had fired the shot, but on a native he was on good terms with, killing him instead. An entry in naturalist John MacGillivray's *Narrative of the Voyage of H.M.S.* Rattlesnake suggested that the killing of Mr Gilbert was just such an incident – revenge on an innocent for outrages committed by others of his party, the two blacks belonging to the Leichhardt expedition having seized on a local tribeswoman.

When interracial conflict broke out, it was sheer, bloody and protracted, a vicious cycle of killings. Woodland imps became the 'sable terror'. If the European party were weak, the natives would rob and murder them; if not, then the whites would commit wholesale butchery on the natives: survival of the fittest, in all its gory colours.

Evening comes down like a wolf.

South of the Thames, a mile downstream from London Bridge, sundown brings a second twilight to Jacob's dark Island, carbon copy of the first. Hearts hollow and bones weary, the shades of day unpeel themselves from the brickwork where they have idled away the hours between low tides.

The young girl from the coal-barge kicks over the remains of a campfire she finds abandoned. Her brother tries on some clothes, discarded there in a pile, his brief nakedness a patchwork of ghost-white flesh and black dirt.

The tide, newly turned, will not wait; they wade into the foul waters, enough receded for them to resume their scavenging.

As the last lick of sun scorches the timbers of the surrounding wharves, the little girl strays near to the outlet of St John's Great Sluice, a great black hole in the flaming wharf wall. On the threshold of the storm drain she half-turns, frozen in fear. A monster black shape rises up before her, hair matted and greased.

Screaming all the way, the two siblings slip and slide across the mudflats, falling up Horselydown Steps in their haste to escape. The boy shoves the girl on ahead of him. From the end of the alleyway he checks behind, attention fixated on a sliver of red, all that remains of the day. All at once there comes a loud cry from Pickle Herring Stairs; in the other direction, over Island-way, all the dogs set to howling. An almighty bang from the Tower echoes and re-echoes along the waterfronts.

Framed alone on the near horizon, in the welter of a dying sun, stands the dark outline of a man.

Brippoki sees it too.

Sarah sorted through the vegetables in the larder. Rather than throw anything out, she pared off the black parts and made a large soup. She ladled out a fair portion and then set the rest aside to congeal. Whatever her father could not finish she would have for herself, but no more. The soup would have to last them until at least Monday.

Lambert hunched forward in his bed, kissing at the spoon. After twenty tortuous minutes he laid the bowl aside. Sarah, realising that she was glad to see it half full, swore on the instant to spend their remaining funds as and whenever necessary, to make the most of life until it was gone – until the money, she meant, was gone.

Lambert Larkin patted his lips with a napkin. 'I know you are suffering,' he said. 'We must keep faith. The Lord will provide…'

Sarah hated herself all over again for not better masking her emotions. 'There are many,' she said, 'much poorer than we.' She refused to suffer exclusively. Her pity encompassed the world.

'Quite so,' agreed Lambert, 'and poorer by far than we could ever become… yet they do not suffer as you do, dear heart. They are not so sensitive, or else would have long since bettered themselves.'

'Why do you say that?' asked Sarah. 'Because they do not know God?'

Lambert was surprised at the edge of contempt in her voice.

'Though we might consider them the poorest of the poor,' he reasoned, 'many are found to be content with their lot. They languish outside of the church…literally, sometimes, outside the church…strangers utterly to religious ordinance. As irreclaimable as the heathen savage, yet not half so clean.'

'Even without God he has a soul,' she insisted, 'he still has feelings!'

Sarah became guarded. She did not wish to sound quite so specific.

'Any poor man,' she continued, 'any poor man under his lot, suffering. His feeling is infinitely higher than in a man who knows comfort. Of any sort.'

She meant faith, of course. Lambert pondered. Did she dismiss it?

Sarah saw herself back along Ratcliff-highway, in Chancery-court.

'How?' she demanded. 'How can pious feelings be expected of anybody in the absence of dignity…their daily bread so dry, it needs a thorough soaking before it can be eaten!'

Stunned silence. She realised she had been shouting at him. At *him*!

Lambert looked at her then with something akin to paternal pride.

'You are…a wise child,' he said.

His expression suddenly altered to one of infinite sorrow. Sarah was horrified to see him well up with tears. Unsure if she had been complimented or insulted or something else entirely, she fled in confusion, guilty only of having spoken out of turn, and, in an excess of feeling, in tears of her own.

A little later that same evening, recovered from her pitch of sentiment, Sarah returned to her father's bedside. He appeared to be sleeping. She dimmed the light, and, stomach growling, retrieved the remains of the soup. Not even bothering to warm it through for herself, she drank it down.

She lit the candelabra in the parlour, and sat reading through her notes from the day. Study as much as fear had inspired her outburst: she read through the jottings again to excuse the truth in what she had said.

Seven decades past, David Collins had written of the Aborigines local to the first settlements, finding them living in a state of nature, that which must have been common to all men prior to their uniting in society and acknowledging but one authority. No country had yet been discovered without there being some trace of religion: Collins pronounced Australia the exception. The natives, he said, worshipped neither sun, nor moon, nor star. However necessary fire might be to their survival, they did not adore it; nor did they venerate any particular beast, bird, or fish. If any conception of an afterlife existed among them, it was not connected in any way with religion, for it had no influence whatsoever on their lives and actions; he never could discover any object, real or imagined, that might impel them to the commission of good actions, or deter them from perpetrating what we would deem crimes.

'They have no idea of Divine Being', 'no words for justice or for sin', 'no object of worship, no idols, nor temples, no sacrifices' – the commentary of all observers tended towards the same conclusion – 'nothing whatever in the shape of religion to distinguish them from the beasts of the field'.

According to *Nahum*, one of the smallest books in the Bible, there once was a place called No, 'situate among the rivers, that had the waters round about it, whose rampart was the sea, and her wall was from the sea'. Brippoki, it appeared, came from the veritable land of No.

Obscure in their beliefs, the Aborigines yet appeared terribly afraid of visions and apparitions. Considering the manner in which Brippoki had most recently departed, Sarah felt this was obvious in itself.

After every page or two she would look up, searching hopefully out of the sash window.

The star constellation known as the Southern Cross, unique to the night sky of the southern hemisphere, must have been of desperate comfort to the earliest settlers. Against such great odds, and flying in the face of indifference, they had made it their mission to spread the gospel; to include this lovely, dreadful, Godforsaken land of No within His Kingdom, His Power, and His Glory. They would make of it the New Canaan.

Thus was paved the way to hell, with good intent.

For the Aborigine to be redeemed he first had to be converted. And yet, before attempting to save souls so blissfully unaware that they were lost, the colony's spiritual enforcers should have looked to themselves, and put their own house in order. They had taken an unpopulated paradise and made of it a penal colony. By their behaviours, the convicts, escapees, and emancipists – men like Druce – put to shame their men of light and leading.

The record of evangelism to the natives only added to the list of their failures. There was little that was noble about it. Every attempt made to civilise them – as students, as servants – had failed. Sooner or later they would return to their nomadic lifestyle, or worse.

'We saw them die in our houses.'

The statement's awful simplicity chilled Sarah deeper than bone. The deaths of even their most promising protégés confounded well-meaning reformers. The European lifestyle itself seemed inimical to the Aborigines.

The Bishop of Adelaide, no less, had gone on record saying that he would rather they die as Christians than drag out a miserable existence as heathens: either way, he believed their race would disappear. Civilising influence threw up its hands, giving up the ghost – something Sarah was convinced she would not do. Was he not a man, and a brother?

If the Aborigines were so impervious to the teachings of Christ, she felt they must hold to a sacred ideal of their own, and, what was more, put greater stock in it. Brippoki was conversant with Christian theology, but this appeared merely politic, or polite. She suspected that he retained the unhealthy conviction of his own gods or demons – but what? Was there any way that she might know?

Sarah chewed on the end of her pencil for a while. She wanted to know at least something of Brippoki's own life back in Australia, that ancient, sun-baked country that was his home; and from his own lips. How could she be expected to help, if she could not understand him – if he would not allow it? Study of the Aborigine was no less puzzling for having met one. She might as well have pulled figments out of thin air and made him up herself.

Much later still, Sarah lay in bed, again unable to sleep.

On many an occasion Lambert had enthused about what was known in the Highlands of Scotland as 'leistering'. Leistering involved night-fishing, with a spear in one hand and a torch in the other. With the torch, one would illumine the shallows, and thereby dazzle the fish. The risk was of blinding oneself, from the glare on the rippling waters.

Reading contemporary wisdom regarding the Aborigine seemed to involve very much the same hazard: she gained knowledge, but very little insight. Without the flesh of direct experience, words on paper lacked for true substance.

Brippoki's behaviour was neither simple, nor pathological, but rooted in profound difference, an opposite extreme. Try as she might, Sarah could not grasp his inner workings, any more than she might take hold of him in person.

Zebra was to ass as Aborigine was to white – some distances too great for any sort of bridge.

And where, oh, where could he be?

Tomorrow. Perhaps she would see him tomorrow.

CHAPTER XXXVIII
Saturday the 13th of June, 1868

RETURN OF THE KING

'In the progress of civilisation the direction has ever been from the east towards the west. The Romans overran the Grecian as the Greek had overrun the Persian, and civilisation abandoned Eastern Asia to find a home in Western Europe. Cricket takes another course. Its path is from the northern to the southern hemisphere; from the verdant lawns of Lord's at St John's Wood to the banks of the Wimmera River and the sheep-runs of distant Australia.'

~ *Bell's Life* (London)

'Victory!'

'What do you mean?' asked Sarah. 'Who has won?'

'Two days ago,' said Lambert. 'The eleventh of June, at Ladywell.'

Lambert Larkin wiped toast crumbs from his buttery whiskers. He blinked, hard, and snapped the paper to readjust it, a copy of that morning's *Illustrated London News*.

'"The Australian Eleven celebrate victory",' he read, and then performed a curt aside. 'Lewisham never were very good.'

'Oh, father,' said Sarah, unable to hide her smile. 'Perhaps the Aboriginals are better men than you allow.'

Lambert regarded his daughter over the top of the paper a moment, and then there was only the back page for her to look at.

'Isn't that who you are going to see today?' he said. He sounded impish. '"The team – " *huk...hurm, churrm...* Oh, dear. *Hf...* Would you mind reading it for me?'

'"The team",' she read, '"has adapted itself to the individualism and science of the modern world. Watching the 'native' eleven thus enjoying themselves, one remarks the perfect good humour which prevails throughout the games: no ill-temper shown, or angry appeals to the umpire, as is generally the case in a match of *Whites*."'

'Of course not,' retorted Lambert. 'They were winning!'

'"We – "'

Noisily he blew his nose.

'When you've quite finished…' she said. '"We are reminded of one of our own former *Sketches in Australia*, as graciously supplied by Dr Doyle (October third, 1863), freely adapting the end of a successful hunt to the quitting of the cricket field in the afterglow of victory, the sportsmen, 'laden with the spoils of the chase, wend their way campwards across the rugged hills, forming a single file as they go, adding greatly to the picturesque effect of an Australian sunset'."'

'*Bravo*,' mocked Lambert. 'No, you keep it. I think I shall close my eyes for a few minutes. They are rather tired.

'You can stay.'

Sarah was keen to make ready, but there was an hour or two yet before she would have to leave. The second day's play at Lord's would begin around eleven; allowing for travel time, she should easily make it by at the latest three o'clock, when play resumed after lunch.

Too preoccupied during the previous week to have much enjoyed the news, she took the opportunity to catch up. One article in particular caught her eye.

'*ROYAL INSTITUTION LECTURES: Sir John Lubbock, Bart., F.R.S., gave the first of a course of six lectures* On Savages *on Thursday week, the 4th inst.*'

On Savages! She had missed this!

'*In his opening remarks he stated that, in the gradual progress of civilisation, we find several principal stages – 1, the omnivorous, in which man lives on fish, roots, fruit and insects; 2, the hunting stage, in which he feeds on the produce of the chase; 3, the pastoral, in which he consumes the milk and flesh of his flocks and herds; 4, the agricultural, in which he adds grain to his diet; and, 5, the stage when letters and coin come into use.*'

How could she have missed this?

'*Ignorance, said Sir John, is the characteristic of barbarism; the application of knowledge that of civilisation. In his apology for savages, he noticed their want of any means of cleanliness and comfort; their great resemblance in language and habits to the children of superior races of men; and, in regard to their moral character, he expressed his opinion that considering their whole mental condition, they ought not to be judged by our standard, if judged by us at all.*

'*The idea that savages are free is erroneous.*'

Lubbock then, according to the report, described a variety of excessively minute regulations fettering their daily social intercourse, such as a woman's being prohibited from looking at or speaking to her son-in-law, these many restrictions being based on their universal dread of witchcraft.

One of Lambert's eyes was open, like that of a lizard, watching her. Sarah pretended to ignore him.

'*As an initiatory rite to admit them into the tribe, young men are tortured. Their dances take on a religious and theatrical character. Commenting on cannibalism, Sir John adverted to various reasons assigned for the practice, it being adopted by some for the sake of food; by others from motives of revenge, annihilating the enemy so that he might not be met with in the world of spirits; or with the expectation of acquiring the wisdom, courage, and other qualities of the deceased. Sir John concluded with a discussion of the language of savages. He noticed the occasionally complicated grammar, a deficiency in abstract terms, and finally, the use of the fingers in counting, which he considered to be the true basis of the decimal system.*'

'What are you reading?' asked Lambert, finally. 'Obviously it appeals to your imagination.'

'A lecture, given at the Royal Institution,' Sarah informed him. 'Sir John Lubbock, *On Savages*.'

'*Humph*,' he said. 'Cannibalism and such, I don't doubt.'

'Yes, as a matter of fact.'

'I saw that,' he said. 'Read some to me.'

'"Second lecture, Saturday the sixth."' She paused. 'Should I…?'

'No, no,' he said, 'from wherever you were is fine.' His eyes closed again, as if in meditation.

'"In his second lecture,"' she read out loud, '"delivered on Saturday last, Sir John Lubbock contrasted the paucity of the language of savages with the great variety and excellence of their weapons and their skill in using them, since on them they depend for their food from day to day – their very means of existence itself."'

The comparison came across as a little fatuous, but perhaps one had to have been there.

'"Comments on the implements of savage life he illustrated by a numerous collection from all parts of the world. The singular curved Australian weapon, the boomerang, was shown. It has the special characteristic of returning to the point from which it is thrown, if so desired. Mr Eyre describes the weapon as 'particularly dangerous, as it is almost impossible, even when seen in the air, to tell which way it will go or where descend'. He once nearly had his arm broken by one whilst standing within a yard of the native who threw it and looking out purposefully for it."'

'Mr Eyre?' queried Lambert, sleepily.

'Governor Eyre,' said Sarah, 'I presume.' She recalled the book overlooked at the library.

'Oh, well,' mumbled Lambert, 'perhaps he had the fellow hanged for it.'

Sarah flicked back through the pages until she found the corresponding news item. The next lecture in the series was advertised for Thursday the 18th, at three p.m.

Lambert's breathing had become loud and steady.

'Father?'

He was asleep.

She searched around the bed to find the 'CALENDAR' feature from the previous week's edition. Her lax housekeeping could, at times, be of benefit.

She had narrowly missed the third lecture. The fourth would take place that same afternoon. If only she had seen the announcement earlier. Could she make that? No, of course not. Lord's it was.

Next Thursday, then – stealthily she tore out the timetable of future dates.

'Pay no mind t' what the newspapers say. Your lads acquit themselves very well, aye, an' shown conspicuous skill at the game.'

The accent was Bristolian, the speaker powerfully built for such a young man. His jaw was almost blue with the beginnings of a ferocious beard.

Charles Lawrence managed to look a little less pained. *The Times*, England's sniffiest newspaper, would insist on referring to his team as 'conquered natives', and the day was infernally hot.

Bill Hayman nudged him in the ribs. The burly giant was still vigorously shaking his hand.

'Theys'll change their tune soon enough,' the fellow persisted. 'Always do. Saw you at the Oval too. Athletic fellows! Like to challenge some of 'em to a long throw after the match, if you're game.'

Lawrence smiled weakly. He released himself from the upstart's grip. 'If *they* are game,' he said.

Hayman stepped forward. 'Certainly, certainly,' he said.

'Jolly good. Ta-ra, then.'

'Bye!'

The door closed behind him. They were alone again. Hayman wheeled about. 'You know who that was, don't you?' he said.

'He was only a boy,' deadpanned Lawrence.

'Grace!' said Hayman.

'Which one?' said Lawrence. 'There are three of them.'

Hayman frowned, tutted, and then shrugged.

Lawrence looked out of the window at the sun shining on the Lord's ground, the green of the pitch, and the heaving stands. 'I think we should set the trap on our bolter.' He spoke in monotone. They found it easier somehow, not mentioning Cole by name.

'Involve the police?' said Hayman. 'You're cracked!'

'It's been nearly a fortnight.'

Bill Hayman chewed his lip.

'God only knows what's become of him,' Lawrence said. 'Or what might. Their morale suffers. They need a boost… You've seen the match reports. Even

the newspapers have noticed! That bloody commentary in the *Brighton Gazette*…
seems like it was picked up and repeated by half the papers in the country!'

'Which is a good thing,' Hayman observed. 'Or would you rather have all that
free publicity discourse on how we're so inept that we lost one of our own?'

'Why should the press have to know?' said Lawrence. 'We'll just go to
the police.'

'Oh, yes, that'll stay a secret,' said Hayman. 'Don't you know how anything
works?'

Lawrence looked abashed.

'I worry about it all as much as you do, Charles, but must we risk everything?
You know how they do. He'll probably walk through that door at any moment,
as if nothing's amiss.'

They found themselves both looking at the door in expectation.

'Besides,' breezed Hayman, 'we're not doing so badly! Mullagh's taken
what, five for 82 off 45 overs. He's bowled the Earl of Coventry, and Fitzgerald
too. That's their top scorers gone! 185 plays 164, in our favour. We may beat
them yet. The M.C.C.! Our second victory in a row!'

'Don't get ahead of yourself,' said Lawrence.

'I'd say His Lordship's playing very well, considering. Eleven runs at
Ladywell.' Hayman's jest met with no response. 'Even better than Dick-Dick,
the "merry young soul", why not sub Johnny Mullagh instead?' he suggested.

'They would spot Mullagh,' said Lawrence. 'I can't believe they haven't
spotted Dick. Why are you laughing?'

'Sorry.'

Lawrence looked worse than ever.

'How's the leg?' asked Hayman.

'Badly strained,' admitted Lawrence. 'I'll need Cuzens as a runner.'

'Charley, we *won*. Have you forgotten that already, or the good word it
generated? No, let's everybody concentrate solely on the things that go wrong!'
Hayman momentarily lost his veneer of good humour. 'Look ahead, man,' he
chided, 'look ahead.'

'I do.'

They had won. The team was adapting itself, as the newspapers said. But
Lawrence could not help thinking – the mutual support of the group was what
maintained their integrity, and, explicitly, Cole was denied it.

'Sub Twopenny,' he said.

The umpires, Grundy and Farrands, would never know the difference.

The interval for lunch is little more than a half-hour long. The Aboriginal team's
guardians take up the time in arguing, or else they would surely be alarmed to
find the majority of their men disappeared.

Throughout the latter part of the morning they have been engaged in frantic finger-talk with some distant object behind the outfield blinds. Now, and as directed, they crowd into a tiny broken-down shed on the far side of the ground.

Inside an arena surrounded by six thousand or more pairs of eyes, eight grown men accomplish this unobserved.

'By Chrise, whitepellas habin' a proper bust-up ober it you,' says Neddy.

'Smash it up all fall down!' adds Tiger.

They exaggerate, of course, for effect. All look into the shadows, in wonder, a little in fear. They speak to make themselves brave.

'Orrince bant ta set the plukmans on ya,' intones Peter, and sets himself to nodding.

'Lawrence, him gonna to give you the bullit,' chips in Twopenny, advancing to point. 'Take up a holemaker an' tchoot you deadpella! *Ptchoo!*'

'If ain't already.' Tiger's words have the ominous ring of truth. Everyone takes a step back.

Dick-a-Dick spanks the empty air in front of their faces and frowns. Turning to the corner of the hut, he attempts to reassure. 'Yeah, so Lawrence said!'

'Wha'chall doin' in this 'ere *gunya?*' Cuzens, a latecomer, appears in the doorway. The shadow in the corner flinches. '*HOLO!*' Cuzens cries out, alarmed. Startled at first, his eyes swiftly adjust to the gloom of the interior. All delighted smiles, he strides forward. 'Mate!'

The others gather round to block his path.

'*Ma pitja! Ma pitja!*' wails the apparition.

For some reason he does not want any of them to come near. Gladly they respect his wishes. He keeps to the shadows, almost out of sight behind a broken upturned table, in amongst the muddle of a ground-roller, stacked wooden planks, and a thicket of handles to rusted tools.

He has made his way to Lord's, as ever, by his own brand of magic.

'What up, *Bripumyarrimin,*' says Cuzens. The others look to their irrepressible team-mate and shrug. 'Bet you banting some tucker, eh,' he adds.

Brippoki's shadow moans. Each man searches his pockets and throws various scraps in his direction. A grateful hand reaches out to gather them up. It appears shaky. He gurgles, thrusting the foodstuff at his unseen face.

Patient for the most part, they wait him out.

At length, their erstwhile colleague utters a plaintive mumble.

'*Na?*' demands Red Cap. He speaks a little *Wergaia* – the tongue of the *Wudjubalug,* and of other mobs that once roamed the eucalyptus scrublands of the *Malleegundidj. 'Puru watjala…putuna kulinu. Na?*'

'He said "many days, no sleep",' snaps Dick-a-Dick, showing annoyance. 'Keep to English.'

His protective instincts are to the fore, his main concern for the greater good.

'*Bael? Bael Nangry?*' says Red Cap. 'You sure?'

'Yes.'

'Look like it.'

'*Gulum-gulum,*' someone sniggers. 'Him gone wild.'

'You let us down, mate,' says Dick-a-Dick, firmly.

Dick reflects; Neddy comes from somewhere near to Sydney, Cuzens down south at Rose Banks. *Brimbunyah* – Red Cap – like him, come up from Bringalbert woolshed. Tiger and Peter are *Marditjali* from Lake Wallace South. Most belonged to sand, and some belonged to swamp. The survivors of many distinct clan groupings, as a team they are only loosely affiliated. But wherever they might be from, all of the totem crests respect his word. In questions of behaviour, and in dealing with the whites especially, the others most often take his lead.

'King Richard', the white men dubbed him. 'King Dick'.

The names that are given are the names that take. Even before the coming of the white man, this has always been true of their society.

Since those earliest days between black man and white, many have adopted European names, their identities doubling, or halved. A man might become lost or die, but his namesake could live on, a ghost of sorts of his former self.

In the exchange of names, of clothes, manners, language, any joke, often enough repeated, becomes fact. They are stuck with bastard English as a common lingo not because it is worth believing in, but because it is easier to pretend. Their arts of mimicry ensure their invisibility.

Dick looks around at his fellows and their paled faces. Johnny Cuzens, Tiger, Mullagh, Jim Crow. They are people with names of their own, but nobody alive left to speak them. They might exist, but do not live.

It is survival, of a sort.

King Dick. His name is *Jungunjinanuke*.

'We looked for the smoke of your fire, *mate*.' Dick puts an unkind stress on the last word. 'Couldn't make it out.'

'*Murry murry* pire this place, how we spot his?' asks Neddy, incredulous.

Twopenny clips his ear.

'*Ball...Ballrinjarrimin? Ba-been!*' Brippoki cries out for his best friend and only real kinsman. He cannot see him anywhere in this crowd.

'Him not 'ere.'

'Sundown? Him not feelin' too good,' explains Cuzens. 'He's back in Town... *Nung*, eh?'

He adds, as an afterthought, 'They look after 'im good.'

Slinking deeper into the shadows, Brippoki begins keening. He asks for *Ballrinjarrimin*, insistently, repeatedly, only to be told – quietly, sympathetically – that he is absent.

'We bloody tellin' you,' says Neddy finally, '…'e's not 'ere!'

As Brippoki moves about they can see glimmers of white. They smell the animal fat on him, and their curiosity is piqued.

All things being equal, a man's authority and influence increase in proportion to his years. This is not true with regard to Brippoki or Peter, who are both considered foolish – for entirely different reasons. Cole, with his child's penis and his peculiar ignorance in matters of the Truth, is *mainmait*, the perennial odd man out – whereas Peter is merely stupid.

As full-grown men, however, they are left to their own devices, Brippoki not excluded any more than is necessary.

'Bet you wanna know how we doin', eh,' says Cuzens, brightly.

He seeks to change the subject. The others, cottoning on, chime in. Despite their fears, they mostly feel sorry for Brippoki.

'Yeah! We doin' bloody alright!'

'Keep on winnin'! Shoulda seen 'em Win-dy. Bloody mad mob, dem pellas!'

'It Purs-die!'

'…Win-dy, me bleve.'

'Pursdie!'

'*Pssssh!*' With a curt gesture Dick-a-Dick bids them cease.

Mullagh steps forward. He unwinds a chain from around his neck that holds the fob watch, and places it on the ground amid the food crumbs. At length the piteous sobs quieten, and then a skinny hand reaches forth to take it up.

Within the darkness, Brippoki reads what he can of the inscription on the casing. '"Pine",' he repeats, '"pine gentlyman".' He replaces it, paying his respects. '*Budgere pella!*'

A flash of teeth from the shadows is returned, six or sevenfold.

Mullagh stoops to take up his prize, and leaves something else in its place. This he pushes forward, to signify that it is a gift for keeping. Not a gift, to his mind, but Brippoki's rightful share of recent winnings.

'Plenny tic-pent,' smirks Peter. 'Some it you!'

The spidery hand steals forth again and claims the large coin. Everybody approves. Mullagh is clapped on the back for his good sense.

Dick-a-Dick reaches for Twopenny's back pocket and retrieves a magenta cap – King Cole's colours. This he also offers. It is not taken up. As both player and personality, 'King Cole' has already made his final appearance.

Someone else thinks to put down his skins, or 'fleshings', the close-fitting black leggings worn for their athletic demonstrations; another his boomerang, one of a cache of over a dozen that Charley Dumas has brought into the country, many of them already sold. These are taken up.

Brippoki shuffles back behind the tabletop, out of sight.

'*Bripumyarrimin. Worum mwa?*' Dick-a-Dick gently enquires, his tongue tackling *Wergaia*. 'Where ya bin, mate?' In the spirit of giving, he hopes for a reply. None comes. 'Got hisself a *gin*.' Dick grins. Even this provokes no response.

Cuzens flips a coin of his own. 'C'n buy y'self a *gin* now, b'ra!'

A few of them laugh.

'*Ludko.*'

The disembodied voice shatters their levity. 'Shadow', it says, meaning soul: the part of a man that leaves the body at death and travels to the Spirit World, where he will never have to die again.

The room plunges into absolute silence. For a minute or two, the beehive mumble of the crowd outside is all that can be heard.

From where he is crouched, out of their sight, Brippoki's voice again croaks. 'I walk the streets,' he says. 'A shadow…walk in mine.' Carefully he picks his way among the words, until he almost sounds like his old self. 'Mine, others,' he continues. 'Shadow to shadow, it walk. It hunt me in the dark.'

Dick-a-Dick does not like the turn events are taking. 'Solid…?' he asks. 'Solid shadow?'

'*Uah,*' confirms Brippoki. 'Not all there yet.'

'*Atpida! Brrrraaah!*'

An outbreak of whispers and the urgent shaking of heads, much hissing – the players are possessed by all the shivers and shakes of extreme anxiety.

Dick-a-Dick speaks, matter of fact. 'It want something.'

'Dunno,' says Brippoki. '*Arlak… In-gna.*'

'*In-gna!?*' Tongues click teeth. They all repeat the words, terror-stricken to varying degrees.

'Crack my bones, pro'ly,' mutters Brippoki. 'Gnaw on them, tomorra.'

To a man they have shrunk back, and cluster around the door. Brippoki is lost to them, and they to him. He lives in another world now.

'There is,' whispers Brippoki, 'a man. Man, I think. Deadman. His shadow cross mine. I need to pind him…pind him pirst.'

First, or fast – his voice is so quiet they can't be sure.

'Deadman?'

Who was it? Watty? *Bilayarrimin.* Jellico? *Unamurrimin.* Everybody starts talking at once. The deceased may not be mentioned by name, and so must be described by other, more roundabout means. If they are to list all possible candidates, they may as well stay forever: the litany will itself bring their lives to an end.

Was it Sugar?

Brippoki puts them out of his misery. 'Him no body we know,' he says.

'You seen 'im?'

Heard him first, singing his song. Hunter moon. Stupid. Defied the Law. 'Yes. I see him.'

More clicks. A couple of the men, the ones who have hardly spoken at all, they turn to face the wall. All of them most desperately want to leave.

'Speaks through his eyes,' says Brippoki. 'Burning fire…darts, through his eyes.'

Dick-a-Dick wishes Bullocky were there to back him up, instead of off getting drunk. 'Y' got a *woorie?*' he asks, only faintly. Dick-a-Dick touches his anus. A nervous reflex – Brippoki cannot see him.

Brippoki shakes his head sadly. His continued silence is answer enough. Filled with shame, bitter in disappointment, he begins to dissolve into the dark.

No hope for him, then. Deadman.

One by one, without another word, his former companions file out and creep away.

In the darkness, Brippoki hugs himself and begins to rock on his heels. They are a mass of cuts, and bleed afresh. His cries are very quiet. Sundown is gone. '*Ba-beeeen. Ba-beeeen!*' He is totally and utterly alone.

Once deserted, all eventually falls quiet in the old shed. The dust settles. Brippoki crawls into the light a little, to rest his head on the dry splinters of the window-frame. The paint, peeling, scratches his cheek. He doesn't care. Light shreds of cloud race through the sky. Brippoki searches out a single patch of blue, a hole in the white lace of upper atmosphere. The clouds speed past one by one.

Blink.

Blink.

He stays like that for hours.

CHAPTER XXXIX
Saturday the 13th of June, 1868

LORD OF MISRULE

'Incapacity for civilisation is one thing, and
unwillingness to submit permanently to the
restraints of civilised society another.'

~ W. B. Tegetmeier, in *The Field*

Sarah Larkin moved as low on the public stands of the Lord's ground as she
dared. Ready and waiting for the Aboriginal Eleven's second innings, she was
almost on a level with the pitch, on a good eye-line with incoming batsmen.

After some delay they began to stream out of the enclosure, showing
themselves off prior to their batting in pairs. Sarah clutched the team colour
card she had purchased, leaving just enough for her bus journey home.

'KING COLE (CHARLES ROSE / BRIPUMYARRIMIN) – ' it read,
'Magenta.'

'Charles Rose'? He had yet another name?

There was no magenta cap in sight, but the man in McGregor plaid wore a
sash of magenta. It was not Brippoki. She scanned the other faces of the team, the
card, the faces again. Brippoki wasn't among them. He was nowhere to be seen.

Play might go on until seven in the evening. She could not wait that long.
Where was he? The match began, Sarah too miserable to take it in properly.
She feared losing sight of him altogether.

Even though she left early, the traffic was bad coming away from Lord's.
When Sarah finally got home, Lambert was asleep. It was as well – he would be
disgusted with the inadequacy of her match report.

The impostor had been run out for seven. He did not look so bad at the bat,
but quite corpulent by comparison, his hair a ridiculous triangle of frizz. The
crowd seemed none the wiser that Cole's crown had been usurped.

Sarah warmed up a bowl of soup, and sat in the kitchen with it. She
sprinkled a little water over a stale bread roll and freshened it in the heat of
the open flame. When she had done, she wiped the last of the crust around the
bowl, and then wondered what else to do.

Night had fallen and the wind was getting up. She checked again on Lambert, still fast asleep. He was sleeping more and more these days, which was probably a kindness. In the parlour, the candle in the window she had earlier lit was out. The curtains jerked like the starched dresses on a chorus-line of string-puppets. The opened window banged in its frame, so she shut it.

As Sarah turned there was movement, a scrabbling in the fireplace. She shrieked.

After five filled days, Brippoki had returned to her.

Monday night had been a pandemonium, in the aftermath of which his appearance was almost completely transformed. The dark stranger sat among the ashes, completely nude, smearing his body over with white powder and streaks of black soot. Wide and bloodshot, his feral eyes glinted like those of a fox.

Following her initial shock, Sarah remained strangely calm. The last thing she wanted was for him to disappear again, into the night. She walked to her usual chair and sat down, without comment, acting as if there were nothing untoward about the occasion. To be in the same room with a naked man, a naked black man…what could be more normal?

He wore feathers in his hair – all of his hair. She took great care not to look too directly, nor even to glance at him for more than split seconds at a time. Looking thinner than before, he wore a whitened face, like the first time they had met. What was that, clay?

Feathers, snake and feathers…no, don't look!

Brippoki stayed where he was, framed within the dark wood and stone mantel. Humming and muttering to himself, he rooted around in the grate, appearing to rub some found substance across his gleaming teeth. Eventually he emerged, very much in the flesh. Sarah gasped a little before covering her open mouth. By the flicker of candlelight she caught glimpses of a network of raised scar tissue: a swath of fleshy ribbons cut across the entire length of his torso, his long torso, marring the pristine bronzed skin. Dark within the darkness, he shone at points, reflecting light.

Brippoki crept a few feet into the room then curled his body in on itself. Close to her, almost opposite, he squatted on his haunches, impassive, staring straight ahead. It was more of an effort this time, but Sarah kept up her affect of casual disinterest.

Even in relaxation the curves of his musculature expressed movement, latent force, bicep hanging like a swollen fruit, ripe inside the supple flesh. He was compact, but powerfully built, the symmetry of proportion near perfect in such a relatively small man: admirable, were it not for the horrific scarification of his skin – mottled glaze on a misfired vase. In addition to the ash and soot he was greased with some sort of glutinous paste, like beef dripping, and pungent to say the least.

Freed of crumple and restraint he recovered his natural advantage, a vital and fully remarkable creature once more. Sarah thought she might never care to see him quite so muffled in cloth or trouser again. There could be no accompanying him in the street, however. Something had to be done about his…about his…

She hurried to the kitchen, rattling cups in saucers and decanting a bowl of soup. Improbable, she knew, but if Lambert were to come walking down the stairs… She laughed, giddily. Short of breath, she had to stop a moment; hold on to her midriff to stop it climbing up out of her corset. Calmer now, she swallowed hard.

Sarah spared no thought for herself, too naïve to be sensible of the risks.

Brippoki sat just as she had left him. She took the tea tray to the table, near to the re-lit candle, and placed a setting. Only once she had returned to her seat did he rise and glide over to investigate. He was graceful more than naked, a shower of stars, the elasticity of his gait a constant marvel. He strolled more than ever rich and royal – lord of the forest, most natural of monarchs, the Emperor in his New Clothes. Standing erect at the table, he took tea.

Feeling that she made good progress, Sarah went in search of further offerings. On her return she lingered outside the open doorway. She spied on him, through the crack, inspecting and then discarding the dried bread. He dangled a hand in the soup to retrieve a chunk of vegetable. Sniffing at it, he broke it apart. She breezed in.

'Here,' she said. 'I've brought you some things.'

Sarah drew as close as she dared. He turned to face her. She saw the trace of disgust leave his open expression – the very same as she had once wiped from hers. Beneath the level of the table his fingers opened and dropped a soggy chunk of carrot. Although masked, his features creased when he saw the gift she held out to him.

'Pretty-pella stink!' he cried. Brippoki grasped at the bar of French scented soap in unclouded joy. 'Gibbit!'

Brippoki no longer stank like a beggar, only foreign – stronger, if anything; nature unadorned adorned the most. Sarah hoped that he might at least wash some of the animal fat from his poor face.

They both sat at table – near to one another, as they had before. Circumstances were only a little different. She withdrew the few coins from her purse and slid them across the dark wood in his direction.

His fingers sorted through the loose change. 'One-pella shilling,' he said, 'an' three little pella belonga him.' Brippoki picked up one of the coins and grinned. 'Ticpents, Thara!'

'I know it's not much,' she said, embarrassed. She rose halfway out of her seat. 'Should I get you…something to carry them in?' she asked.

'Thit,' he said.

'I'm sorry?' she said.

'Thit.'

She sat.

'How have you been?' Sarah asked. 'That is, I am fine. I hope you are feeling fine too. Only it has been a few days. I'm sorry about…about before.'

After a dreadful long pause, Brippoki nodded. 'Pine gentlyman!' he grinned.

His accent seemed thicker than it had been.

'You look…well,' said Sarah.

She lost control of her sightline, not knowing where to look.

Delicate of feeling, Brippoki achieved some measure of self-awareness. He took up the nearest likely covering, a tea towel, and laid it across his lap. 'Torry, Thara,' he said.

She stood. 'Should I…' she stammered. 'That is, would you like me to…?'

'*Uah,*' he said. 'Read. Read in book.'

Gladly, Sarah fetched her notebooks. They were laid to one side, for some days awaiting their chance.

'I'll pick up where we left off,' she said. 'We left him…' mentioning no names '…still a fugitive in the outlying settlements of the colony, presumably New South Wales. No exact date is specified, but around the turn of the century. He has been sleeping in some sort of makeshift barn, an "old house full of straw", and is about to cross a river to go into the mountains. You remember so far?'

Brippoki crossed his legs. He took hold of the raised limb with both hands, and his body began gently to rock. Were it not so dark, Sarah might have recognised the sorry state of his feet – run ragged – and quailed.

She cleared her throat and read.

> I was met by a man, who whole with the will of God preserved my life. He asked me who I was, and from whence I came. I told him everything. He told me he would visit Dargane the next day, and if I was with him when the man was murdered, that he…

The name written was '*Geelbethoth*', like that of some minor demon. Sarah, struggling to readjust, consulted her own marginal notes.

> …that he, Gilbethorpe, with the assistance of that great and wonderful Redeemer Jesus Christ, would save my life. He conveyed me to a large hollow tree at the back of his farm where I remained for some time.

Brippoki, ceasing motion, looked a little circumspect. Sarah pressed swiftly on.

> Every night I used to work with him, burning the trees off of his land, till I cut my foot in a most dreadful manner. I was in a dreadful state, for by the leaders of my leg being cut I could not move out of the spot where my friend placed

me, where I was confined in one pasture, for fourteen days sitting in the woods. I wanted for nothing. My friend came to me every night with every thing my heart could wish for. But, at the end of fourteen days, the bandage fell off my foot and the wound was closed, but the use of all my right side was gone, so that I could do nothing without help. My friend, seeing this, exclaimed:

– My dear creature, I feel for you. What a horrid state you are in to die. And what a pity it is that you cannot read.

I said:

– Don't despair, my dear brother, I shan't die yet. So you would say if you had seen what I have seen in my sleep, during this fourteen days and nights that I have been lying here. You know, Gilbethorpe, that you have many time told me I should sleep all my senses away. But I have been sleeping to get sense and knowledge.

Brippoki made a sudden noise and shifted his weight, luckily distracted in doing so by having to adjust his makeshift breechclout.

In the midst of so much else that was unsettled, Sarah had to confess it a relief to fall back into their respective roles, as previously defined: the simple certainty of what was required, and the provision of it.

– So you will understand when I tell you what signs God has shown me, both asleep and awake: which I will tell you, my brother, if you will stop and hear it.

The next day he came to me, and brought with him his wife.

Gilbethorpe said:

– There, my dear, you see how this poor creature is afflicted. Look, love, what a desperate cut he received, helping me to put wheat in the ground by the moonlight. Kiss him, my dear, that we may have a good crop, for there is some quarts of his blood sown amongst our wheat.

I replied:

– My dear brother and sister. You both tell me your thoughts very easy by your looks and behaviour. You both think I shall die, and are come to take your last farewell. But I tell you again, Gilbethorpe, I shall not die yet. So now I will tell you the signs that God showed me, about eight years ago, when I lived with the Superintendent of Toongabbe.

– One night at twelve o'clock as I was watching his house, I saw my own person stand before me. And with astonishment, I closed my eyes' lids and opened them immediately, and behold, it was gone.

Breath exploded from between Brippoki's lips. He was all of a sudden restless and shaking, his hands trembling like moths.

Sarah almost despaired, not knowing whether to read on or to cease.

'You understand what has happened,' she said, in her normal tone of voice. 'He says that he saw his own self, stood before him. Bruce, that is Joseph Druce.'

Brippoki leapt up. He spat, almost dousing the candle, which fizzed. He spat and made a queer noise that sounded like an owl or wood pigeon – '*Pooh!*

Pooh!' – and, clutching onto the tea towel and his modesty, eloquently expressed his great disgust.

'I don't – '

'*Wssshhht!*' A finger leapt to his pursed lips. Brippoki crooked the same clay-stained digit, black and white like a variegated worm, and with it inscribed various drawings in the air. He turned away from the table.

The harm, so it seemed, arose from her naming Druce – as if, by pronouncing his name out loud, he might be conjured to appear. It occurred to Sarah that this reaction had only been so since they had learnt the man's true name.

Brippoki leaned in with a long neck. Eyes extraordinarily wide, his fixed stare was a challenge, a caution to her and whatever she might say next. He edged forward to recover his seat, not releasing her from his insolent gaze.

Sarah felt like a fish stalked by a heron. She suffered the heat of her discomfort.

'Please…' she said.

He backed away a little.

– Then the cold sweat ran down my face. This was my poor immortal soul that had leapt out of her chamber, to ask me what I meant by loading her so heavy with sins. No sooner had she left her chamber with the assaults of my sins than the Satan placed one of his imps in her seat, so at her return to her chamber she could find no place of rest, only the base walls to cling to, as a bat clingeth to a white sheet of a dark night. The powerful grasp she gave my veins at that moment drove all the cold water out from among my blood in torrents.

– O, my dear brother Gilbethorpe. God's guardian angel over poor weak souls like mine was passing by, and heard her pitiful cries about her chamber. That night I see myself, He rebuked the evil spirit and gave my poor soul her seat again. This was the first sign, Gilbethorpe.

– The second was here where I lay in these woods, at about the same hour of the night. I was laid on the broad of my back, perfectly awake, looking up to Heaven. And I see the Heavens part asunder in the centre, the distance of about six feet as I suppose, and the Light of Heaven shone on earth, just like the light from a blazing lamp through the crease of a door. I thought I heard a soft voice say, 'Despair not. God Himself orders this sign to be shown to you, that you shall live and not die, for you have long life and great sufferings to go through on this earth. And the miracles of thy life shall be recorded through all nations. Among the heathen also shall you be honoured. Yea in your old days the Lord will lift you up, and raise you above all your enemies, so them that hate you shall fear you. Therefore praise the Lord.'

– At those thoughts the Heavens closed. This, Gilbethorpe, was the second sign that God showed me.

– The third was in a dream. I fell down a dreadful steep hill, and came with great violence against an iron stanchion. It gave me such a shock that I said in my dream, 'Surely I am not in a dream now. For if I had been ever so fast asleep, I am sure that I should have waked with the tremendous blow that

I have received on my right side. And there is another thing that makes me know I ain't asleep. It is daylight, and there is a man, the other side of these rails, and I will go and ask him what place this is.' And as I went round to the old man I looked under the rail, and it looked like a furnace that was at its full heat. I asked the old man what furnace it was. He told me it was Hell. But there was no person in it yet.

– I waked. And this was the third sign God showed me.

– Another night in my dream, I went into a house that had windows in the top of it, one of which was open. And two Grand angels were in the house, and three Goddesses. I advanced to a glass case full of inexpressibly rich diamonds. While I stood gazing, the Goddesses came to me, and the centre one, pointing to a gold crown covered with diamonds, told me that that crown of diamonds was for me.

– And this was the fourth sign God showed me. So you see, my dear brother Gilbethorpe, that it is not to creatures sleeping in their beds full of thoughts of this worldly business that God manifests Himself to, but to poor miserable sinners like me in their pilgrimage.

– I can tell you of one remark I made, when I was in London with my mother.

– One day four of us children run about my mother crying for bread and butter. She took us into the front parlour, where the bread was. And to try our patience, she gave us a small slice apiece. But, as all young 'uns do, we pouted our lips, and all throw down our bread.

– The old woman in a most cordial manner took the bread up which we threw down, and expressed these words: 'If you ain't satisfied with a little, you shall have less.'

– And at that moment a beggar came to the window, to which she gave all the bread and butter before our eyes that was in the house, and locking the door at the same time told us we should not go out that day, and that she meant to have given us all the bread and butter if we had been content with what she give us first.

– So you see, Gilbethorpe, how it is with greedy persons rich or poor. They are not satisfied with what God please to give them, but they want the whole world to themselves…

My friend now took leave of me for that day.

Brippoki stood.

'No, no! That is what is written in the book! *He*,' said Sarah carefully, 'means Gilbethorpe.' She indicated his seat. 'You are welcome yet,' she said. 'There is only a little more to go.'

The next day, Gilbethorpe laid me, with my lame side upmost, on the body of an old tree that was exposed to the heat of the sun, best part of the day, and told me to mind the crows didn't run away with me till he should come at night to remove me. He constantly attended me night and morning, and at the end of six weeks I got the use of my side so as to walk. And in a short time after I again assisted my friend with his daily labour, till one day a man whose name is Joe Wright came to the place where I was at work. He knew I was a stranger. He advanced to me. I rose up with that intent to take his life, but he saw the axe in my hands with which I meant to kill him.

He then turned about and run home to his house and told his wife that he would go immediately and inform of Gilbethorpe for harbouring me. Gilbethorpe came to me and told me that I had not a moment to stop but be gone from there, and at the same time, appointed a place where he would meet me. I went immediately and set fire to the place where I slept by night, which was formed by the hands of nature. This caused great confusion in the whole settlement. For it was so, before I set light to my place of rest, there was not a breath of wind. But as soon as I had kindled my tent with fire, the wind rose and the fire ran, violently consuming everything that stood before it, so that when my enemy returned the whole place was in a flame.

Every night at twelve o'clock Gilbethorpe came with provisions to me in the woods, alongside a most beautiful stream of water. I remained in this situation for five months, till the new Governor arrived, whose name was Philip Gidley King. My friend Gilbethorpe went to him and told all my sufferings and that for five long months he knew me to be hard at work. The Governor immediately gave him my free pardon. I cannot express to the reader all my heart felt at that time. It was in the dead hour of the night when my friend came to me with my free pardon in his bosom.

'Good mate, Gilbeythrop!' enthused Brippoki.

'Yes,' agreed Sarah, 'a very good man.'

'Liket you!'

'Not quite…but thank you.'

A good note for them to end on, and a blessing; for that was all there was. She would have to return to the library and transcribe the next part of the manuscript before they could carry on.

'Over?' he enquired.

'Yes,' she said, 'for now. More tomorrow, if you'd like. No…'

The next day was Sunday. The Reading-room was closed on Sundays.

For once, even with the story done, Brippoki showed no immediate wish to leave. He seemed glad of her company. She would have been gladder of his, if he only wore a single stitch of clothing. One would do.

His fingers twinkled in the air, a magic trick like she had seen him perform once before. Hey presto, a large golden coin glittered between them. It threw off sparks of candlelight.

'Where did you get that?' she asked.

More to the point, from where on his naked person had he retrieved it? Better perhaps not to know.

Brippoki explained that it was his share of the team's winnings – which allowed he was still with them, after all. Maybe she had quit Lord's too early, and he had come straight from a post-match display of exhibitionism – so to speak.

'It you,' he said.

'I beg your pardon?'

'It you,' he said. 'You help me.'

He thrust it forward, almost under her nose.

'No!' she said. 'No, I couldn't possibly.'

'Me gibbit you,' he insisted.

Sarah studied the coin, but did not take it from him: it was a genuine golden guinea! A relic of Regency England, a 'spade-guinea', the side presented bore a shield shaped like the playing card suit of spades. This was most likely someone's idea of a tasteless, if extravagant, joke – gold, King of Metals, given in prize monies to a mock dignitary. Sarah wanted no part in it.

'No,' she said. 'Really. I won't accept it… You don't owe me anything.'

Brippoki held the coin out, silently pleading, until she stood and moved away.

'Keep it,' she said.

Sarah instantly felt that she understood the reason why it had been impossible to trade fairly with the Aborigines: just as the notion of reciprocity lay at the very heart of their morality, so did they base their economy on generosity, the giving of gifts. He only tried to pay her money because he thought of it as something she might value, when already he had gifted her something far more precious. All she might share in return was her reading from the manuscript, a very poor exchange.

Sarah forgot herself. All of Brippoki's expressive body language had wilted. He slumped with melancholia. Was it her refusal of the coin?

Brippoki went to the window. He wanted out.

Sarah moved to comply.

'When will I see you?' she asked. 'I can't retrieve the manuscript until Monday, and we've exhausted the notes I have. I'm awfully sorry.'

He could come again tomorrow, but what then should she do with him? It seemed an improper suggestion: and she had anyway promised her Sundays to Lambert.

Brippoki merely shrugged his shoulders. He would not look at her.

'Mun-dy,' he said.

'Monday, you're sure? I'll have some more to read you by then. But come tomorrow, if you'd like.'

According to their match schedule, printed in the morning papers, the Australian Eleven were due in Southsea Monday and Tuesday, and again in Stortford later in the week. The tour continued apace.

'You will be able to make it?' she asked. 'You have cricket all next week.'

'*Bael* mo' cricket,' he mumbled. 'Cricket…over.'

'But, the team?'

'En't my clan brothers,' he said. 'En't my kin.' With a petulant flourish he threw his loincloth high into the air. Without exactly meaning to, Sarah caught it on its way down…just a tea towel again.

'I'll pray for you,' she said.

'Pray,' he said, 'tomorrow.'

And with that, he was gone.

Sarah felt her forehead: it was hot, and a little wet.

She had made him unhappy.

Whatever Brippoki made of Druce's story, she could not say, but he certainly took the man's words to heart. The way he sat, coiled like a spring. The way he stood, and oh, the way he moved, so swift, scarcely seeming to move.

He went naked, as truth goes.

Sarah looked from the empty fireplace to the seat at the table he had only just vacated, disbelieving almost. An unearthly illusion of character; painted, fancifully wild – she had wanted to see him so very much these last few days. The mess and the soup bowl lent proof where proof was needed.

The strong wind gripped the entire window-frame and seemed to shake it with both hands. Temperatures outside must have dropped; it was certainly chilly indoors. Wasn't he cold, like that?

She folded her arms and rubbed them; well past time she snuffed out the light and went to bed.

Leaping from the high window, his nimble fingers grip the brickwork and he pulls himself up around the corner, out of sight.

Brippoki scales the drainpipe, as if it is a thick black creeper running up the side of a tree. He sits on the roof, in contemplation of the distant stars, bittersweet.

Mityan, hunted moon, is already half eaten up. What little high cloud remains scoots past, driven by the high winds. The streets themselves are howling. Sleeping, to get knowledge – he dares not go into the Dreaming, scared of what might find him there.

He listens for sounds that he feels more than hears above the rising gale; the interior clicks and shuffles of the house beneath, preparing for sleep. The last of its tiny lights is extinguished.

Brippoki loses some hours.

Three days without sleep. Three days of running without pause, without direction, running in circles around the Piebald Giant, eventually slowing, to enter into the wormhole of the Great Serpent – wandering into West Monster Abyss. The rock formations here astound, alien and terrifying in their regularity: high mountains and deep chasms, a valley of brick threaded through with a torrent.

Grey days, and featureless, spent tripping back and forth across the Serpent's back.

Brippoki, coming to, snaps to wary attention. He searches the blackness for signs.

Wicked impulses, gathered, have become shadow, the shadow becoming substance. From Dreaming, it spills over.

Time to slither.

Thinking it no longer safe to stay, he gathers up his *waddy*, his boomerang and skins from the cranny in the chimney, and goes in search of a new fireside.

He runs from roof to roof. It is easy. The houses are all connected. When they are not, distances one to the next are always small in one direction or another. He finds, driven into some walls, row on row of large spike nails: one set to hold on to, another for his feet to race across. Hopping one to the next he barely has to slacken his pace.

Passing into districts less solid to cling on to, he risks being blown off the more crooked rooftops. He slides down towards ground level, sprints along the tops of alleyway walls, the yards behind each tumbledown hollow linked in endless lines. Slathering dingo-dogs lunge at their chains as his heels fly by.

He avoids turning south, towards the Well of Shadows, or west into unknown parts. Instead he heads east, towards that territory best remembered.

He is but a dot etched on the horizon, a blur against the cloud-dimmed sky.

The Guardian has refused him. He has no mate, no one to turn to, nor place to belong.

'*Bael Thara,*' moans Brippoki. '*Bael ba-been.*'

Without warning, he faces an apparition, his opposite. In shock, Brippoki's vocal cords clench, the blood freezing in his veins.

A white face, blackened by soot, stares into a black face crusted with clay, ash, and chalk. Cold sweat and hot tears trail contrary streaks across their cheeks.

Met with a May Day lillywhite, the chimneysweep's eyes roll, perplexed. His hair is dusted with powder, caked in meal; but he wants for his glitter, his gold leaf-foil and ribbons.

White-black hands out, Brippoki backs up, and edges around the black-white man.

The sweep is alarmed to see his nakedness. He bangs together his brushes and tools, crying: 'Weep weep! Weep weep!'

Brippoki runs on.

And he does.

CHAPTER XL
Sunday the 14th of June, 1868

THE DEVIL'S FOOTPRINTS

'And Shaphan the scribe shewed the king, saying, Hilkiah
the priest hath delivered me a book. And Shaphan read it
before the king.

And it came to pass, when the king had heard the words
of the book of the law, that he rent his clothes…and wept
before me.'

~ *2 Kings* 22:10-11/19

A slight lifting of the curtain brought light flooding into Sarah's room. An
hour or more yet, and then she would get up, spent from a night of dreams
without sleeping.

In the gloom of darkness, in the still hour of the night, that deeper shade
had lingered. Ash and soot, a king couched among charcoal…a black snake
crowned with white feathers.

Sarah rolled over onto her back, properly awake and thoughts busy.

Belatedly she realised the Biblical Joseph that Druce was named for was
most likely not the husband of Mary, mother of God, but Joseph 'the dreamer'.
From the signs God had shown him in his fever, it was clear that he knew to
identify himself with his namesake.

Joseph had dwelt in the land of Canaan, the favourite of his father, Jacob,
and hated by his brothers for his self-aggrandising dreams. Sold into slavery,
Joseph had been entrusted with the superintendence of his master's house.
Falsely accused and cast into prison, implicit confidence was again placed in
him when the keeper committed the other prisoners to his charge.

The circumstances echoed Druce's own life story, if somewhat in reverse
– the boy criminal had been given the responsibility of mustering his fellow
prisoners while on board the *Royal Admiral*, subsequently serving an army officer,
and then the botanist Caley, as his masters in the new colony.

Under Pharaoh in Egypt, the faithful servant Joseph had eventually risen to
a position of great power owing to his skill at interpreting dreams. All Druce's

talk of dreams, his 'sleeping to get sense and knowledge', quite possibly exposed him as a charlatan of the first order. He would often solicit pity via expression of his piety, finding impressionable souls, like the Gilbethorpes, and dazzling them with vivid stories of sin and redemption. That was likely his means of survival, the method by which he had always survived. Perhaps he was not even conscious of doing it, fooling himself with that same brand of biblical signs and wonders he had been raised in; the same as had been burned into her.

So God performed His works through sinners, more than those meek and mild: she would have to take that on advisement. Sarah did not doubt it. Or did she doubt too far? For so many years locked up inside her own head, she envied the active and simple-minded.

She should strive to be more like Brippoki.

Joseph Druce, by his own account, was a character filled with intrigue. His travels had taken him to the opposite ends of the earth. So, too, had those of Brippoki, a fellow equally intriguing. More so, she felt, for being that much less transparent.

He remained, to her, a closed book.

What Sarah wanted most of all was for the Aborigine to sit back and tell her *his* life story. He got his learning by entirely other traditions – and could, no doubt, do wonders by the power of imagination. If only she could see the world through his eyes.

She suspected a whole host of secrets to which she was not privy.

Well before noon yet, and she sensed that the air temperature outside was the highest it had been since the start of the week. The incessant wind was a *scirocco*, hot and heavy as breath. Sarah rose, washed, and began to dress.

Tidying the parlour, she discovered a trail of minute stains marking the carpet, from window, to fireplace, to table. Scrubbing at them, the cloth and her hands showed up fresh scarlet. They were traces of blood.

Brippoki has made an open secret of his sacred shame. And been rejected. His manhood still appears that of a boy. Seeking out a means with which to smother his boyhood self, he raids the wash lines across the backyard walls of Whitechapel for a 'shammy leather'.

Travelling through this far country, conjuring up the landscape in His wake, an Ancestor Spirit has left behind a trail – a narrow causeway made from scattered words and musical notes. Even as they shape the earth, these Songlines form a map. Only by taking the right path could Brippoki have hoped to meet others who share in his Dreaming, from whom he might have expected hospitality. But he has lost his way. He has strayed from the path…

Brippoki touches the bruises on his face, only now healing. He still feels the ache in his sides. These clay people, many cannot be understood at all, with their growling and their bits and spits of words. From their stone and wood chambers piled high in a heap they arise, bird-shrieking, dog-howling, the flesh of their faces, stripped red and raw, burst like lizard guts on the fire.

He has entered into hostile territory, at risk of losing more than his life.

During their travels, Ancestor Spirits scatter *guruwari*, shards of Dreaming. Seeds of life, these forms persist, withstanding all ravages of time, death and decay. Anything so imbued with the power of Truth is a *tjurunga*, a most sacred object.

The *tjurunga* is as one with the Ancestor, the house of his Spirit, to be cherished and hidden away. If not, strangers may be tempted to come and steal away the very essence of life. Their campfire tales are filled with such stories of robbery and revenge.

To speak of one's Truth in the presence of any female is against the living Law, but showing a *tjurunga*? That is blasphemy. A blasphemer's life is forfeit. They must be killed, or at the very least savagely beaten. If they do not accept their punishment, and flee, as fugitives from divine justice they will be mercilessly hunted down. Either way, their souls are sure to be damned for all eternity.

But if it is a woman, a white woman showing a *tjurunga*? Brippoki's head hurts.

The impossibly hot day presented Sarah with a quandary. However much her father's bedroom needed an airing, the window could not be opened because the wind was too violent, whipping all of his papers around. She opened other windows in their part of the house. The fresh air forced through them might eventually circulate. She could attend to any damage later.

Sarah read aloud from the Sunday papers, coverage of the match at Lord's, relieved, if slighted, that Lambert should prefer the official version of events to any of her own observations.

'"Saturday's play",' she reported, '"was in marked contrast to the Friday, when the Blacks had been adjudged to have begun indifferently, only to improve until the point where their performance was agreed the superior."'

'So they were in the lead?' said Lambert. 'Well, well! A rum do.'

'"Misfortune, however, seemed to attend the steps of the second movement of the Blacks",' continued Sarah, '"at the very outset of their second innings. Dick-a-Dick was clean bowled, and Tiger was doomed to a speedy retirement. Lawrence made but one hit that counted. Cuzens came in and by vigorous but not always wise hitting got up the score to 28."'

'Twenty-eight? Ha-hah!' His enjoyment of their collapse brought much-needed colour to her father's cheek. 'Continue!' he ordered.

'"Mullagh – "'

'Johnny Mullagh!' cried Lambert. He clapped his great hands together in anticipation of grand doings.

'" – the greatest card,"' she read, '"was then played, but not with the spirit and style of the day previous. He seemed to hit anyhow. At the fall of the sixth wicket for 40 runs it required no prophet to foretell the issue of the match. Bullocky was absent without sufficient reason being assigned, and, to make short work of what may be called a travestie upon cricketing at Lord's, the Blacks were defeated by 55 runs."'

'Dear, dear. A travesty?' Lambert gloated. 'I knew they were getting ahead of themselves.'

'I thought cricket allowed the peasant to play the prince.'

That was impertinent: Lambert was shocked, but not so much as Sarah. She had betrayed her partisan feelings.

He looked a little stormy.

'The lamb may lie down with the lion, but that does not make them equal,' he said. 'You misunderstand me, my girl.'

Sarah felt her bonds tighten, but was equally convinced that no apology was necessary.

'"Marylebone",' she read on, '"were the eventual winners, but not without facing a sterling piece of bowling from Johnny Cuzens, who took six for 65 runs of a second innings total of 121."'

She refused to look at her father's face.

'"At the close of the first day's play",' Sarah read, '"Dick-a-Dick caused a sensation by inviting members to pay up to a shilling to try to hit him with a cricket ball from 10 paces. Cuzens is showing more batting form, but the Blacks are not doing much, and bid fair to be only a fleeting attraction."'

'Whatever happened, I wonder,' mused Lambert, 'to Johnny Bullocky?'

Sarah continued her reading, and not purely for Lambert's benefit. Among the related news articles there appeared a curious sort of commentary, journalist responding to journalist between their respective papers. Making mischief, she chose to share it.

'"To those",' she read out, '"who have any doubts as to the identity of the manhood in the white- and black-skinned races, it may be satisfactory to learn that the same *hopes* and *fears*, the same *zeal for the honour* of the Institution, the same *pride* in the cricketing *uniform* and *colours*, the same complacent *vanity* in looking 'the thing', animated on this occasion the *quondam denizens* of the wilderness – "'

'Is this to be one of those sentences without an end?' interrupted Lambert.

'It is,' admitted Sarah. 'The emphases are theirs. " – the cricket match at Lord's proving incontestably that the Anglican aristocracy of England and the 'noble savage' who ran wild in the Australian woods are linked together in *one brotherhood of blood* – moved by the same passions, desires, and affections – "'

'*Tcha!*' scoffed Lambert.

'" – differing only because in His wisdom God had ordained that His revealed truth should travel *westward* from the hills and valleys of Canaan, until at the appointed time the stream of Divine knowledge should turn eastward, and cover the whole earth 'as the waters cover the sea'."'

'What on earth…?' he spluttered.

She was perhaps being unnecessarily provocative; still, there it was, in black and white.

'Let me see that!' Lambert snatched the paper. He merely checked for himself – as if she could have made it up – and then threw the pages down.

'*Pshaw!*' he complained. 'A savage is not so simply turned citizen.'

Patiently, Sarah gathered what had scattered and slid to the floor.

'You can take a horse to the water,' said Lambert, 'but you cannot make him drink. We are finding, as a general rule, that the dumb beast has to be coerced.'

'You are cruel,' Sarah observed.

'In order that we may be kind,' smiled Lambert. 'It is often necessary.'

'An influence amounting to the same as authority might be arrived at through a system of kindness,' Sarah asserted. She looked her father over, coolly. 'A person might accept almost anything,' she said, 'from one to whom they were suitably attached.'

Lambert considered for a moment.

'We must take direction from *our Father*,' he stressed the words unkindly, 'the Almighty Disposer of Events. The pious Israelites could not build the walls of Jerusalem without holding the trowel in one hand…and a sword in the other.'

Brippoki knows he has strayed from the correct path. It is not enough to follow the way that is already there – that is the wrong way. It is necessary to sing, and to send the landscape and the road out of oneself. This is *Bugaragara*, the Way of the Law.

During his first nights' fast travelling in a city of the dead, he forgot the importance of this distinction. He fooled himself into thinking that he forged a path, when, all along, he has been following one – his course somehow directed.

He might as well have worn a ring through his nose.

He has not followed in the footsteps of any Ancestor; instead, a devil.

And now the devil is following after him.

CHAPTER XLI
Sunday the 14th of June, 1868

IDYLS OF THE KING

'Days and nights of fervid life, of communion with angels of darkness and of light have engraved their shadowy characters on that tear-stained book. He suspects the intelligence or the heart of his friend. Is there then no friend?'

~ Ralph Waldo Emerson, 'Nature'

Inland from the coal jetties, dockside, heads the Regent's Canal. Tracing the borderline between Stepney and Limehouse, it passes beneath the London and Blackwall Railway, then in swift succession bustling Commercial-road and quieter Salmon's-lane. Above Stonebridge Wharf is the Salmon's-lane Lock. A stone's throw beyond, opposite the towpath, stretches waste ground. Marshland overgrown with reed and tall swamp grasses, it is effectively cut off by the brick-span arches of a viaduct.

Tucked away well out of sight, behind this retired spot, a semi-circle of branches has been arranged: fallen from the surrounding, sickly trees, they are struck into the ground against the prevailing wind. Constructed from materials to hand, the rudimentary shelter blends entirely with the landscape, invisible to within a matter of feet.

Brippoki keeps his bare head to the leeward end. He does not sleep, but rarely moves, except, whenever the sun makes an appearance, to roll forward and bask, like a reptile warming his blood. Every now and then he wafts a switch of goose feathers tied with gut, to brush away the flies. All comes from that same bird whose fat and plumage have furnished the basis of his ritual 'hero' costume. The rest he has eaten raw.

After many days of running in a blind panic, the simple pleasures of staying still cannot be overestimated. In a city so filled, empty of life, finding any suitable place to rest has been almost impossible. The small mud creek in which he first settled turned out to be a tidal inlet, his encampment washed away. Without a source of fresh water, his every effort at digging a well was frustrated by the thick and cloying muck. His second choice, the Serpent's lair, was no better.

Milling children had disturbed him. Too many bodies, too close for comfort – even there they had come intruding.

No more streets. No more people. He's staying put.

Happy elbows, here is better, *balla-duik*. He's lying here quietly.

High ground would make for a better outlook, but low ground scrub, this secluded grove, is best for hiding out. In such a high wind, a natural hollow beside a water-course is the choicest option.

Not that this place, *eora*, is without its faults. The water flows unnaturally straight, as if bewitched. A hillside pocked with caves overlooks from the opposite shore. And there is the willow tree. Yet a small brook weaves through the banks of tall reed, there is sand as well as clay underfoot, and, to alleviate his crowding miseries, the bliss of being able to sit, at long last, skin to the bare earth.

'What would you say, if you were to meet with one of the Aboriginal cricketers?' asked Sarah.

'I should say nothing,' Lambert replied, 'unless they were willing to visit me in my bed.' He thought for a moment. 'I don't deny they have a pleasant, a sympathetic sort of a face. It is not, however, a look of great intelligence.'

Sarah moved to speak, but Lambert cut her off.

'Meeting one on the street,' he said, 'I would raise my hat. I might even challenge him at the wicket, yes. But invite one to supper? Dine at the same table? No, daughter, I think not. Wisdom allows that a man may recognise his opposite. In association, there is none.'

The lion lay down with the Lamb. Imperfect sympathy indeed!

'From all that I have read of our missionary efforts,' he went on, 'the Black races seem incapable of being brought out of darkness into light. And by darkness I mean the power of Satan. All is vain.'

'All is vain?' repeated Sarah, unsure of his meaning.

'In vain.' Lambert threw up his hands. 'The animal's thirst may be quenched, but, be sure, it remains a horse.'

The insistent rattle of the window, closed against the battering winds, caused their heads to turn in unison. Lambert barely paused in his speech.

'The savage is an infant,' he said. 'Incapable of self-control, innocent of the knowledge of good and evil – '

'Not – ' Sarah tried and failed to interrupt him.

' – destitute alike of foresight and experience. What might be learned from them?'

Nothing, if our mouths were perennially open and our ears shut.

'As a child,' he continued, 'he is helpless. And if not properly attended, his moral state does not elevate in and of itself. He rather becomes degenerate. In this respect, Messrs Hayman and Lawrence are heroes. The performance of their native cricketers, on and off the field, does them credit. Would that I could say the same for their countrymen, that "Colony of Disgracefuls", convicts, escapees, and emancipists…'

He evoked men like Druce. Sarah, who had begun to tidy the room, turned.

'…and now that detestable term, "squatters". By their behaviours, they put to shame their men of light and leading. How eagerly they abandon their mother country. Men of all classes, wilfully, demoralising themselves. Grubbing, for gold…

'Here is the descent of the species!'

Sitting up higher in the bed, Lambert Larkin paused to wipe away the phlegm gathered on his lips.

'God gave man dominion over all other creatures,' he said. 'Why, then, sink below the level of brute creation? Through folly, intemperance, the indulgence of his evil lusts… The seething mass of humanity, drawn together by the love of gold! Is *this* progress? Have we evolved?'

'Father – '

'Victory, the golden crown…goes to the man least mindful of clambering atop the heads of his fellows, in order that *he* might gain it for himself. Be sure, it is the only way and the only time that he will ascend.

'Have we learnt nothing from that dreadful spectre of Civil War?' Lambert asked. 'As if war,' he said, 'could ever be "civil"! Shall the strongest survive this struggle for existence? Or will it be the most foolhardy, the most greedy, the most ruthless, the most venal who alone succeed? There,' he snarled, 'in the land of the lazy Doasyoulike.'

Eighty degrees. Brippoki keeps to his *gunya*, *waddy* close at hand. He sits and soaks up the heat, replenishing his energies, remaining invisible. Waterholes are dangerous for the same reason they are delightful – all living things congregate there. The dead, he hopes, will stay away.

Through half-lidded eyes he relishes the liquid sparkle of sunlight, at the same time keeping watch; glad to the brink of fear.

Deadman, Dreaming, got speared in the foot, numb in the side. Laid him out on the old tree. Mind the crows don't pluck him.

Brippoki's head droops. He is so tired. But no sleep! Sense and knowledge – Deadman comes for him when he is sleeping. Shadows claim him. No catching him sleeping. He's still got his spirit. Keepin' it.

The surface of the waters glitters.

Despite his equitable feelings, Thara cannot be entirely trusted. She may not deliberately seek to mislead him, but…

Brippoki's jaw works in a chewing motion. He chews at length, then spits, chews, and spits. He makes a pause to examine the results. Each sample in his lap is of a different sort of bark, which he has begun breaking down into fibres with his teeth. Having selected the best, he places it into his *coolamon*, his dilly bag. Noting the type, he knows where to find more.

He has made the dilly bag from his skins, the leggings torn into strips, looped and tied at the waist. He uses the string-pull there to seal it.

Brippoki settles back on his haunches and looks deep into the sky. He fingers the golden guinea *Unaarrimin* has gifted him. In trade, the practice whitefellows so much enjoy, such glittering objects are highly respected. More coins in a man's pocket means better treatment from the *walypela*.

All of his adult life, back in the World, he has worked the sheep stations, in what is now called 'Western District'. He never saw so many of these valued tokens as he has since joining the team. They pick them up regular, following feats of hunting prowess and showing their skill with weapons, mimes played out at the end of each public game of cricket. Even when at play it is to earn, doing it over and again as necessary, for 'prize money'. Play without pure joy or laughter.

He turns the pretty coin over and over in the sunlight. Brippoki likes the way it shines, but is otherwise indifferent. What shall he buy with it?

'An inferior creature knows its place and abides by nature's laws. Man was created a superior being…and yet he continually abuses that divine potential, choosing to sink instead. He wars with himself…thieves, commits adultery… and other crimes too horrible to mention.'

Lambert became misty-eyed.

'Blood-letting,' he said, his voice breaking, 'more shameful and sinful, because committed by men who profess to know better!'

Some reflection beyond his words appeared to rip him to the core.

'Even an angel is not, of necessity, a civilised being,' he whimpered. 'Not even an angel.'

Sarah had seen these same distresses distort his features ever more frequently of late. They would come over him like a rash, knotting his brow, writhing his lips – plunging them both back into those unbearable, unwanted years, when they found themselves newly alone; on their own in that house.

The heat in the room was fierce.

'Civilisation,' he rallied. 'We are perhaps more at risk within these walls than ever we were without them.'

'These walls?' she asked.

'The city walls,' he said. 'Any civilisation…in which morals are forgotten, ceases to advance. Yes, yes, I see what they are saying. It will instead stagnate, fall into decline. Babylon, Medo-Persia, Ancient Greece, Egypt, Rome: history provides us with many examples…empires whose great cities are in dust.'

He made explicit reference to that queer editorial piece she had read to him that very morning. Sarah searched among the pages at the bedside in quest of it. She took up the paper, only to discover the report on Sir John Lubbock and the lectures she had missed. Casting her eye over the paragraphs again, what seemed obvious was that Lambert must have read and digested these too.

She was once more reminded: how much her father already knew of matters she had only yet begun to discover.

Civilisation implied the development of arts and science, but what were those worth offering without enlightened and moral conduct? They had taken an unpopulated paradise and made of it a penal colony. Before attempting to save the native Australians, souls blissfully unaware that they were lost, the colony's spiritual enforcers must of necessity look to themselves, and put their own house in order. Equitable treatment was necessary to society, if it was to be at all recommended.

Was it this gap alone between reality and the ideal that deranged her dear father's mind? Sarah wondered what could be said that might put him at ease.

"'The fear of the Lord *is* the beginning of wisdom,'" said Lambert, once more sounding confident, "'and to depart from evil, that *is* understanding.'"

Fear…really, the rule of fear? He had expressed this before: Jerusalem, built by the sword.

'A proverb of Solomon, the son of David, king of Israel,' he confirmed. 'And here's another… "Righteousness exalteth a nation; but sin *is* a reproach to any people." Christ came also as the Healer of Nations, and to take away the sin of the world. Stretched out upon the cross of Calvary, He offered himself a Holy Sacrifice for the sins of the whole world. He died, but the grave could not hold Him!'

The Word was irrefutable: Lambert often preachified when seeking to conclude an argument, even one largely conducted with himself.

Out of breath, he lapsed into silence, for which Sarah silently gave thanks.

She was no pretty meadow flower, nor any ugly sort of weed; she was the blackberry, clinging to a thorny bramble.

Sundown. Brippoki is alone.

He casts fearful looks across the choppy waters. All day long the scorching wind has blown hot and fierce. The twisted willow shakes, speaking through its leaves.

The broken building beyond, a towering tenement, is honeycombed with caves, a hive as big as a hillside filled from top to bottom with bloodsucking bats and other predatory creatures, waiting for the sun to fall before they will emerge. Brippoki senses their massive dozing presence as a sinister background buzz.

Dread plucks at his liver. Twilight is the worst time, the spirit especially vulnerable. As the last of daylight disappears, the shadows gather in close. Joining up. Under cover of night they will come to remove him.

Back in the World, his mob would wait out the day, only coming out once the heat had died down, the plaguing insects taken to their own *gunyas* among the spike grass. Then it was time for them to congregate around the campfires, to sing, and tell stories, and fuck – time for them, but never for him.

Night falls, the dark time. Night alone is not good; and he is so very alone.

Dark and stormy, the night has no moon. All is in shadow. Trees creak and groan to the blast, threatening to break. None is very near, but he can hear them, moaning. Wickedness and vengeance are abroad.

Spirits in darkness will murder him in his sleep. And so he will not sleep.

Brippoki thinks to get moving. He needs to move if he wants to stay awake. Best, though, not to travel at night, unless there is a good moon. If he can't see where he is going, he might fall down a ravine, become lost beyond recovery.

He misses having his campfire. A fire by day is a danger, a sure way to be spotted, the thin trail of smoke leading his enemies right to him. They will be watching for it. But fire at night can appease the Spirits of the dead. The fire is life, that quality they lack. Fire keeps them away from the campsites of the living.

Tea-tree is good for a fire-stick, and may be found in swampy regions – a light wood, brittle, with resin. It burns with the fiercest flame, smells sweet, and gives off almost no smoke.

A short jog to the west and there are many trees – but in a burial ground, best avoided. A dash northward from there, *mokepille*, not many trees, but the high winds have brought down *murry* boughs. Among them Brippoki finds wood suitable to his needs. He thinks to risk a small fire, and refresh his spirit make-up. Not only a disguise, it helps to ward off evil. A bath of grease and ash better contains the heat of day absorbed into his body.

Returning to his resting place, he builds a tiny, smokeless fire. Crouched over it, he listens intently to the cries of night, and makes ready to run.

CHAPTER XLII
Monday the 15th of June, 1868

STATIONS OF THE SOUTHERN CROSS

'And the king commanded...

'Go ye, inquire of the LORD for me, and for the
people, and for all Judah, concerning the words of this
book that is found: for great is the wrath of the LORD
that is kindled against us, because our fathers have not
hearkened unto the words of this book, to do according
unto all that which is written concerning us.'

~ 2 *Kings* 22:12–13

Brippoki holds aloft a smouldering fire-stick. He knocks off the charred end
with a sharp blow to the brick of the viaduct, performing a few circulations in
the air to bring it back to life. The remainder of his campfire extinguished with
a kick of earth, he takes up his *waddy* in the other hand, and sets off.

Patches of soft ground are rare, but, when met, he avoids them. If obliged
to cut across, he pulls his feet. Clear prints would proclaim his presence.

'*BRRRAAAH!*'

In-gna or *Arlak*, with loud breaths he discourages evil Spirits. Brippoki chants
words of power as he runs.

An *Arlak* may take on a man's shape. They catch stragglers in the night –
those fools who separate from their fellows. At any moment black arms might
fling out of the dark to seize and carry him off. The best protection against the
Arlak is fire.

The dark-time cries of the dead are a torture. Melancholy moans come
from deep underground. Hollows whistle high in the air. *Mityan* moon at last
shows His face, the largest of His hunting dogs faithful by His side. With every
passing hour, He shrinks thinner, His light dimming.

At the end of a long run, *Gnowee*, red sun, comes to chase Him away.

One time, the World was only dark – dark-time all the time. The Men, to
see, had to light bark torches if they wanted to walk about. In those days *Gnowee*
was just a woman like other women.

One day she leaves her little boy asleep in a hollow in the ground, while she goes out to dig roots. Yams are scarce. *Gnowee* wanders so far in her search that she reaches the end of the earth. Continuing in her wanderings, she crosses over and comes up the other side. It is dark there, and, not knowing where she is, *Gnowee* cannot find her little boy anywhere. She climbs up into the sky carrying a great bark torch. She still walks there, and sometimes under the earth, looking for him.

Or was it that *Courtenie*, the native Companion, had hidden Emu's egg? The old stories are all mixed up and confusing to him.

Only as dawn breaks does the hot wind finally die down. Virtually all trace of cloud has been blown from the skies. After the long restlessness of night, Brippoki is glad to return to his *balla-duik*.

Forty days, and forty nights – time is running out.

First post brought with it a second letter from the Admiralty clerk, Dilkes Loveless. At Sarah's request he had ferreted out more documents regarding Joseph Druce, patiently copying them down in his own looping longhand. She rather feared it a labour of love.

'Dear Miss Larkin,' he wrote, 'it is my distinct pleasure,' and so on and so forth. Sorting through the sheaf of appended papers, Sarah felt herself suitably indebted, if no more endeared. The lieutenant had been in correspondence with one of his opposite numbers: the name Druce was confirmed in ship's musters for the *Royal Admiral*, East India Company, listed as a convict among 'Persons transported as Criminals to New South Wales in the *Royal Admiral* in the month of May 1792'. His 'form' – presumably, crime – drew a blank, but the date and place of his conviction had been recorded as 'Middlesex, 14 Sep, 1791', and his sentence, '7 years'.

Further attached were extracts from the log of His Majesty's Australian Ship *Lady Nelson*, a Royal Naval vessel on which Druce had later served. The enclosure numbered many pages – the gallant clerk indulging Sarah with some irrelevant-seeming background, sentimental notes on the ship's various voyages and eventual fate – drawing her attention, however, to two entries in particular.

Sun 13 – heavy sea running in the offing – noon – strong gales – sent boat on shore for Greens for the Brigs Company – punished – Jos: Druce with four dozen lashes for theft, disobedience and embezzlement.

Tue 22 April – made sail at noon, strong breezes, heavy rain + swell from the Eastward – Run from the ship Joseph Druce.

The year was 1806.

The clerk mentioned a similar incident, taking place on board during a voyage from Sydney to Norfolk Island in 1804, one 'J. Druce' punished with 24 lashes for theft. He had apparently sold on the after-effects of a shipmate, drowned less than two weeks previous. Oh, Joseph.

The log excerpts supplied indelible proof of his wretched character. Joseph Druce, a.k.a. 'George Bruce', was confirmed a deserter – a deserter and a liar too.

A convicted felon, he had been pardoned and employed as a sailor in His Majesty's Navy, yet – as Sarah well knew – remained a thief, drunkard, rustler, fugitive from justice, and swindler, embezzlement merely the latest addition to an entire catalogue of his crimes.

Dilkes went on, 'I relay this material to you as a private matter, rendered in the strictest of confidences, and I beg your utmost discretion in this regard.' And all of this great favour, she was led to surmise, fell due to impressions made during 'the very pleasant afternoon' of their 'all-too brief' acquaintance. 'Any further assistance that I might furnish,' *etcetera*.

As ever, he tried that little bit too hard. If Dilkes expected some sort of reward for his efforts, then heaven help her.

Last and by no means least, he forwarded a full transcript of the letters that had tipped her off to Druce's alias, including the text of his pleading *Memorial* to the Colonial Department. Its opening sentence flourished a most extraordinary, entirely new assertion, and bare-faced lie:

> *The Memorial of George Bruce most humbly Sheweth, That your Memorialist is a native of Scotland.*

Outrageous. For the moment Sarah cast it all aside.

Hideous scars distort the willow's bark, across the water. The tree whispers foul curses, and droops its limbs.

Brippoki's flimsy *gunya* has collapsed in the night. He rebuilds it, introducing a few improvements to see him through another day. The earth within he beats with a large flat rock, to make it level. Any loose stones, protruding roots or grass stems, he removes. The wind having died down, he gathers up dry leaves, spreading them across the smoothed earth to make for a comfortable couch.

The air is chill. Brippoki relents: he will build a daytime fire. He clears another patch of earth, just in front of his new shelter, scooping out a shallow trough at its centre. He thinks of *Gnowee* and her lost baby, and then goes in search of more wood.

Taking out a metal barb that he keeps up his nose, he begins to bore a hole into the bigger of two fire-sticks. A quarter-hour of patient exertion, and his fourth attempt to ignite a tiny flame meets with success. He lays the fire seedling on the cleared ground and feeds it more dry grass and then, finally, bundled twigs.

A piercing cry overhead makes him leap for cover. As loud war-drums beat, he buries his face in the dirt and quivers with fright. The terrifying sounds soon recede. Peace prevails, but Brippoki stays rooted – much like the storybook ostrich, believing that it may not be seen even as its posterior waves in the air.

Almost immediately, the almighty commotion repeats. He fears that he must find a new camp. Lifting his head at last, Brippoki discovers his mistake. Train services have resumed across the viaduct above. In fact, he feels greatly reassured: such deafening noise may well daunt the real demons.

The frequent passing engines are soon enough of little consequence. If anything, the regularity and tremor of their progress becomes more soothing than alarming. Brippoki still freezes every time the whistles blow, a black statue, carved in an endless variety of poses.

Lulled, content, he returns in his mind to the sheep runs of Western District, Southern Australia. He works the flocks there, and dwells on Brippick Station – drives sheep, plays cricket, and dreams his mysterious Dreaming.

He has, the last eight years or more, been a shearer and a herdsman. Having given up his sad wanderings, he settles down, wearing the costume of the stringybarks, the croppy one whites, eating same food, smoking some pipe. His talk turns to whitefellow talk. New skin.

Restless, he once in a while takes off into the Bush, wanders a bit. There aren't any longer the great gatherings to head for. Every summer, the fires in the hills are fewer.

His Dreaming is as strange and remote as it has ever been. In the end, he no longer bothers with his Walkabouts. When the quiet times come and there is no work, he sits by his hut and gathers dust.

Sarah looked in on Lambert. He was awake, sitting up in bed and reading intently. He only spoke in answer to her, and then in monosyllables, not looking up at all. She had no time for sulk or silence, and so did all that she had to do and then left him to it. Swiftly but surely she dealt with all her various chores around the house, and then shopped to replenish their stores.

It was late morning by the time she reached the library and recovered the manuscript. She got straight down to transliterating another chunk of Druce's life story. The copy of his *Memorial*, just received by post, showed the date 1813. Her own efforts at his chronicles lagged by perhaps a decade.

It took Sarah only a short while to get back into the swing of deciphering the illiterate scrawl, her patient efforts soon rewarded with interest. She very much hoped Brippoki would pay her another visit, come the evening.

By lunchtime the Reading-room had filled considerably.

Sarah overheard an article of gossip: that Benjamin J. Jeffery, the junior assistant who had been so helpful to her, had been let go. The unofficial story ran: improper advances towards a female reader, advances being returned, and on the premises too. No official version existed. He simply wasn't there any longer. Sarah felt sorry for him, whatever the truth of it.

She checked the time. In another hour or two she should return to the house, make sure Lambert had eaten his breakfast, and perhaps even find his mood improved. She returned the manuscript to the shelves, patrolled those surrounding it, and let her fingers be her guide.

The noonday sun pulses overhead. Brippoki's mouth is dry. Motionless, he sits.

He cares little for his time on Brippick Station, nor relishes the work, but no other choice exists. If he wants to eat, he must work. The land *walypela* leaves to them offers no means of support. The old and the sick receive their handouts. Everybody else has to do whitefellow work. The borrowed clothes, wet in the rain, do not dry. The old sicken until buried in their new skins. The white life is no life for them.

The young men live, the old men die. Learning is forgotten. As lines of kinship turn to dust, *Warri* the wind blows them away. Few traces are left. The loss of life means that the Way is lost. And loss of the Way is the loss of life. Not many new children are now born. No childhood for them.

Brippoki is just one among the many lost and lonely. He works the station. Life lacks meaning. *Tchingal* squats overhead, a giant black patch among the constellations. *Waa* the crow turns Argus.

'God' introduces himself. He ain't much cop. Just another bloody shepherd.

Seated in the midst of the white man's Dreaming, Brippoki crosses himself – just in case.

The lost generation, they are the last generation. No people no more. No kin.

These unhappy thoughts are nothing good. Don't go there.

The cricket is a way out. He takes it. Up *Bring Albit*, down sandy spring, Billy Hayman and Tom Hamilton learn them how to play the game. Wills a good one. Lawrence too. When playing there at Pine Hills, balls go in all four lagoons. The team come from all over – Benyeo, Hynam, Struan, and Fulham – come to Bringalbert Woolshed so they can beat the whites. Speaking in many different tongues, their speech abrupt, hard to understand, from stations all over, they come – Lake Wallace South, Mullagh, Rose Banks, and Brippick. Some of them, liking their drink too much, are gone now. *Murrumgunarriman, Pripumuarraman, Hingingairah,* Jellico.

Travelling immense distances, passing through the territories of a great many rival mobs, they adopt the white man's naming to ease their passage.

And that is the only meaning of the name he has been given by the *guli* not his brothers, not his kin. The men and women of *balug* soil, the *Wudjubalug* clan of the *Wergaia*, the 'No' people, all are gone now, no more No. He is the last of his motherline, the last of his tongue.

Bripumyarrimin means 'The one from Brippick Station'.

He hasn't any other name than that, a name without No meaning. No true name. No true name for which he is qualified. He is the one from Brippick Station, a man without a name. And a man without a name isn't any real sort of man at all. Unfit for ceremony, unfit for company, only fit to be ignored, he is still considered a boy – *tji-tji*, a child – a child in a man's body.

Team all gone now. No more cricket. Nowhere left to run, to hide.

He is the last.

Boraingamin, all is ashes. Brippoki's fire has no heat in it, only sadness. Back and forth the trains scream past, back and forth.

To cheer himself Brippoki plans for a feast of *joogajooga*, fresh pigeon, served on a broadleaf platter with a side of lily root, and, as an appetiser, baked tadpoles on grass.

He clears a narrow path through the *mallee* scrub down to the creek. One hundred paces in from the water's edge, he constructs a bush break of foliage, behind which he crouches in readiness. As the sun goes down, birds swoop down for an evening drink. For ease they follow the line of his clearing. The whirr of wings warns of their approach. A branch suddenly appears, thrust into the flight path. A bird drops stunned at his feet. He takes it up and breaks its wings.

Brippoki catches three birds in this way.

Breaking larger sticks over his head, he builds up the fire. He uses his barb to pierce a small hole in each pigeon's belly, and hooks and withdraws the entrails, closing the aperture with a wooden skewer so that the juices are retained whilst roasting. Feathers singed off, the birds are broken apart and thrown on the fire to cook. Their entrails make for a tasty snack, an accompaniment to the tadpoles.

He knows a woman's work well enough, but in all his grown years Brippoki has never known their company.

Brippoki presented Sarah with the scorched carcass of a plump, fresh pigeon. She offered him a serving of the supper she had prepared. Both share and gift, put to one side, were then politely ignored.

Sarah found Brippoki's choice of evening-wear not so very indecent as it had been on the previous night. He wore only a few feathers in his hair, daubs of red and white on each cheek, and a necklace that seemed fashioned from hollow stems of reed. A lambskin chamois concealed his manhood; flesh, against flesh.

She served the tea. Taking her time, and with that same searching look often met in the mirror, Sarah studied the face of the stranger in the candle. She searched in vain for the least vestige of that mild serenity once observed there.

Despite his ash coating, Brippoki glowed slightly with the sheen of perspiration. For the first time ever in Sarah's experience he appeared to be short of breath, showing every sign of a man whose blood was overheated.

He grasped at the proffered teacup and drank it down with urgent gulps, somewhat obviously burning his throat, more thirsty than wise.

Steadily, Brippoki calmed. Pacing the room a while, he eventually settled – thankfully beside the unlit fireplace, rather than in it. She joined him.

The evening was warm, as the day had been. Neither Sarah, playing host, nor Brippoki, her guest, made the slightest attempt at small talk. Instead they sat together in comfortable silence, slowly perfected – worked at these last two weeks – their relative degrees of modesty shyly endured until arrival at this mutual, wordless accord; finally able to enjoy one another's company.

To spend a fireside evening reading quietly, else aloud for amusement, was such a very normal activity; the closest approach to domestic habit Sarah might hope for. At this, the very height of her flight of fancy, their present situation amounted almost to a vision of married bliss. It differed only in certain particulars.

'Thara,' said Brippoki, fetching a worm from between his toes. 'Tell story roun' the *boree* log.'

She said, 'You first.'

Although she had carried her notebooks when she came to sit in her chair alongside, they remained deliberately unopened. Sarah laid them aside.

Brippoki didn't immediately respond to her challenge. She, however, had sufficient strength of purpose to maintain her silence. By looking every now and then down at her books, she encouraged in him the very letter of reciprocity. He owed her that much.

'Tell me,' she said, following a lengthy pause, 'tell me something of your home, in Australia.'

Brippoki remained quiet for a little longer time, and then, rising, began ever so gently to caper and mime. He turned his back to her, and for a minute or so nothing seemed to be happening. She saw the musculature shift in his narrow back, as his blade bones slid from his shoulders. Then, as his hands rose into view, Sarah saw that his fingers were joined at the tips. His arms continued up above the level of his head, until nearly at full stretch. Excitedly, she perceived what was perhaps an attitude of prayer – and to a god of his, not hers.

Shuffling his toes by tiny increments, he gradually rotated, a groaning song issuing from deep inside his throat. Turned almost completely, he lunged forward with an explosive breath.

His neck cricked, ever so slightly. '*Kurura*. Comepella,' he said, smiling pleasantly. 'Bring, bring, up *Langanong-joruk, Longerenong.*'

Brippoki pointed, his eyes growing wider.

'One Big Ant-hill Creek,' he whispered.

'Ant?' queried Sarah. 'Ant-hills?'

'*Murry*,' he assured her. 'Big! White ants!'

Sarah frowned a moment, before feeling she understood. He meant termites. She had read vivid mentions of them, in Leichhardt's *Journal* among other places. His actions had described one of their extraordinary nests. She resisted her slight disappointment – no religion yet, unless Aborigines worshipped termites.

Brippoki looked her way only infrequently, and when he spoke it was in broken sentences, spread across great pauses – deliberate, and thoughtful.

'Big...' his arms rose and fell, describing a great arc '...cities.'

Brippoki's knuckles at tapped his temple, and he made a 'toc, toc' noise with his tongue.

'Hollow inside,' volunteered Sarah, and he nodded.

His mouth began working without making any sound. He appeared to spit into his hands, before smoothing them onto some imagined surface, creating castles in the air.

Brippoki repeated the cycle of actions, touching various of the objects around the room. Whenever he lacked the English words, Sarah nominated terms according to his suggestive shapes and gestures – a parlour game of charades.

Wood, they fed on wood, wood and...sand, to make their rock, stone, no... clay...clay, through the chewing of their jaws, clay that hardens into stone, strong enough to defy a...'*karko*'? Spade, it looked like.

The nests became vast networks of little passages and cells. The sounds Brippoki then made, in addition to the twinkling of his fingers, perfectly suggested countless thousands of busy bodies, working unseen inside their mound.

'White ant nest filled him ants *murry* different kind. Workers, building...no wings, no eyes.'

'No eyes?' gasped Sarah. 'They're blind?'

'Not need eyes,' Brippoki reasoned. 'Neber leave nest.'

He then marched on the spot and saluted.

'Soldiers?'

'Thojers,' he approved. 'Liket workers...'

No wings for flight, no eyes for sight, but via gesture he conveyed their big, strong jaws and enormous great heads, flat at the front, which looked very frightening to all the other insects.

'Him bite hard,' he said, 'when dey pight!'

Still other kinds he mimed were feeble creatures, with bodies – he pointed at the old map – pale yellow, and – he took up four pieces of paper – winged.

'Him made, gibbit young ones tucker special way,' he said, lip-smacking over the sugar-bowl.

More highly developed, they had eyes and wings, the only class to ever leave the nest.

'Come out nest,' Brippoki shook his head, 'neber go back.'

Those that left their homes, never returned.

Shut up in a special cell, right at the centre of the nest, was the queen.

Sarah began to suspect his purpose.

The queen grew from a winged insect, fed on a diet of special food.

'Royal jelly!' Thara exclaimed.

'*Uah*,' agreed Brippoki. 'Liket choogar.'

He took an extra spoonful for good measure, and stirred it into his tea.

Brippoki then puffed out his cheeks and, body distended, pretended to swell to enormous size. The queen, she looked like a large, fat grub with a tiny head. Trapped inside her royal chamber, far too swollen up to move, she laid thousands of eggs every day, the workers labouring hard to bring her enough food. Her only function was to lay more eggs. She was the mother of all termite brothers and sisters.

'All dipperent,' said Brippoki, 'all same.'

The ordinary white ants died every day, but the nest and its queen did not die.

'Immortal,' said Sarah.

'Eh?'

'Immortal. It means they never die.'

Brippoki shrugged.

'We not know how long queen live,' he said, 'but must die, some time.'

Sarah fiddled with the tea things, replenishing their cups.

For a time it appeared his wicked fable was done with, only for Brippoki to continue. By all of his various ways and means he explained how the winged insects, flown from the nest, were like seeds from a plant…starting new nests.

'White ants go ebery place they want,' he said, stirring. 'Eat it all up inside. Eat the wood,' he stamped his foot, ''t' make their clay, turn it stone.'

Draining his cup, he rose to take hold of the nearest chair by its legs.

'Eat their way up,' he said. 'Eat their way in.'

His hands ran up and down either side of the chair.

'Don't see 'em,' he said. 'Happen 'pore you know it! One day… *Pok*!'

Broad lips parted, he poked a finger right through the wicker of the seat. Sarah might have protested, had she cared in the least for any of the furnishings.

'Insides all gone,' he said. 'Eaten away. Eberywhere, toc, toc…' he searched for the new word '…hollow.'

Brippoki fell silent.

Well, that had given her plenty to think about.

'Me talk longa you plenty pella,' Brippoki announced.

Replacing the chair, he sat back – on the hearthrug close to her feet – and somewhat definitively folded his arms.

'Mouth belonga me, shut up,' he said. 'Mouth belonga you openpellow now.'

Sarah detected a hint of mockery in his rounder pronunciation, just as he closed up his mouth, seemingly for good.

'Thank you,' she said, quite sincerely, and opened her notebook.

It was her turn to spin the yarn.

CHAPTER XLIII
Monday the 15th of June, 1868

THE MARK OF CAIN

> 'Thy father is a chieftain!
> Why that's the very thing!
> Within my native country
> I too have been a king.
> Behold this branded letter,
> Which nothing can efface!
> It is the royal emblem,
> The token of my race.'
>
> ~ 'The Convict and his *Loubra*', traditional

'Our hero,' Sarah smiled, 'has just been granted pardon for his crimes.'

After a short prayer for my delivery I took my leave of my dear friend Gilbethorpe, and went to the Governor to return thanks for his mercy to me. The Governor received me as if I had been one of his own children. I was sent on board His Majesty's Brig *Lady Nelson*, where I remained till his excellency was pleased to order me to stop at New Zealand with one of the natives, till he call for me on his way home to Britain.

But the wind blew up so hard when the Governor came on the coast of New Zealand that the ship could not reach the land. I now being left in the isle of New Zealand, I took my travels in the country, where I was treated with every kindness by the inhabitants. No man that is really weak in his heart need be afraid of living among the New Zealanders, they being the only heathen country that I ever found as detests that abominable act which so many has being committed in all parts of the world. I mean the twenty-ninth Act.

The New Zealander says if he has no children that he is without God's blessing. This is one reason they take ten wives, so that if one misses, the other will hit. Also they say if they go to work in the morning eating or drink, that the crop will be blighted if any person commit any filth on the land that is tilled. He is momently put to death. For they say that if they eat of any thing out of that ground where the filth of their bodies lie they all will die.

Brippoki nodded sagely, appearing to approve.

No man must sleep with his wife in time of putting the grain in the ground. If a man goes nigh a woman when she is sick, it is death. Every man delivers his own wife of her children, for which he and she do not handle anything that they eat for eleven days. They are fed, or eat off the ground. They must not come under the roof of any house that has been consecrated by the priest for the said time. They both stop in the open wilderness, where every woman in that country goes to be delivered. And at the time appointed the priest goes and takes the child, and the mother and father follows him together with all their friends to a run of water, where the child is dipped three times under the water, and then is named. Then the father and mother are free.

They say that after death the soul ascends to the top of a mountain that is in that country, and moan in a most dreadful manner for leaving this earth, with their face towards the sun rising. After which moaning, they say the soul descend through this mountain under the bottom of the sea, where all of them are in a most horrid style torturing one another's souls. This mountain has been a volcano, but the fire bursting through the bowels of the earth some depth below the surface of the water, the whole body of the sea came in and put the fire out.

'At the bottom of this page,' Sarah explained, 'was drawn the crude outline of a volcano. Like a triangle, but with a hole at the top…you know what a volcano is.'

'*Uah*,' he grunted.

'I suppose it to mean a volcano, and it contains a sort of prayer or lyric within, interrupting the rest of the text on that page. No prayer or song I know of.'

'Tell me song,' urged Brippoki.

'Yes,' she said, 'I was going to. I was just…

while

I live.

I

must do as I

Can.

I must die.

But still to thee

Most merciful God

Repeat my mournful song.

She took a second look at the arrangement of words on the page. It resembled the ziggurat steeple atop St George Bloomsbury, a stone's throw distant.

'That was it,' she said. 'Shall I…?'

'*Uah*.'

There is only one way of ascending it. That is by taking one particular fish directly it is caught and stripping the flesh off the bones raw, and put it to your nose. You can then go to the top where there is a round hole, and as you walk round it you can see into the bowels of the earth, as far as your sight will go. It strikes the most greatest horror on the human mind of any sight that was ever seen on earth. It appears like a furnace come to its full heat. The New Zealanders call this hell. They all say that night and day they have seen souls on their road for this place of punishment, after departing from the body.

At these sundry details of Maori custom and belief, Brippoki had been variously nodding or shaking his head, and sometimes tugging at his beard. As Sarah read on, the shaking of his head became more violent. She badly wanted to ask after Brippoki's own beliefs in these matters, in particular about what happens to the soul after death. Wary of scaring him away again, however, she bit her tongue.

They say the soul is like our shadow. This I believe by seeing my own stand before me one dark night.

Brippoki's lips curled back and he started to gibber. His whole body quivered. The risk of him flying out of the window was already very grave. Sarah could only press on.

They say a man and woman fell from Heaven on that isle. This was the beginning of their generation on, and the man and woman had a great many children. And when the children grew up, the first part of them run away from their father and mother, each boy taking with him a girl. And when they had got a long way in the country they all counselled together what they should do if their father came after them and found them out. The eldest was for killing the old man. The youngest said:

– No, my dear brothers and sisters. Don't let us kill our poor old father. But I tell you what let us do. Let us disfigure our faces with frightful marks so if ever our father finds us out he will think we are all devils, or at least he will not know us. And as I am the youngest, if I can bear the pain I am sure all of you can.

So the eldest marked the face of all his brothers and sisters that was with him, and the youngest marked the eldest. There were fourteen of them, seven boys and seven girls. And they settled in such a remote part of the country that it was by their reckoning 30 years before the old man found them out, after they had left him. But as they say, their father knew them all by the marks they brought with them into the world.

And when he returned home he took the rest of his children and showed them the marks on their finger ends, and told them the meaning thereof. And also he told them he should soon die and go to Heaven, and at the end of the world he would bring all of them to Heaven with him, telling them at the same time they must not be frightened at their brothers' marked faces whenever they should come to war against them.

– For your war will be great with them, and this is what your war will be about. In the first place, as soon as I am gone you will all mark your faces with the marks that I have showed you all, which is the marks that God gave you all in your mother's womb. But the mark they have put on their faces is a mark that the devil told them to put on because then I should not know them. So this will be one dispute. The other will be about their ingratitude to me in running away from me when all of you were young. But they shall fall into your hands to till the land for you.

So the old man died, and to this day the New Zealanders make war one with the other about what their first fathers told them.

Sarah hunched over her notebook, the better to see it by candlelight.

Brippoki, who had calmed himself with the urgent sipping of more tea, watched her intently.

Probably she should have relented and re-lit at least one gas lamp, except that would present her too clear a view of Brippoki's near-nakedness. His bare buttocks, earlier, had been distraction enough.

Clearing her throat, she resumed the narration.

The mode of burying a chief –

'*Rangatira*,' Brippoki affirmed.

'Yes,' she said. 'You already knew that word, didn't you.'

She waited him out.

'Went from *Guniah* up Lake Wallace,' said Brippoki, 'to *Wuhrm-numbool*.'

His mouth seemed to writhe with distaste.

'Him took us cross the large water,' he said. '*Rangatira*.'

None the wiser, Sarah at least felt persuaded that he knew the word's meaning, and recognised the implicit connection to Tippahee from the *Memoirs*. She continued reading.

The heart is taken out of the body and buried in a wood, where no one must go, under the pain of death, only in those times when they go to bury the heart. The body is tied together just like a fowl put in order for roasting, then is taken to a large lagoon where it is decorated with bows, and for six or seven days and nights all sorts of romantic scenery is performed. Their dresses are made of flax and dog skin that grows in that country, the outside of which is worked most neat, with a variety of birds' feathers. Their heads are also dressed with feathers, the sight of which is a most beautiful view. But their prayers is most affectionate and dismal to relate.

The whole of them men women and children go to the side of the corpse and scar themselves in a most dreadful manner with glass, till they are so sore that they can bear no more. The blood runs from their bodies in a most desperate manner, and their cries is melancholy. At the concluding of those ceremonies the whole multitude fall in ranks like soldiers and taking their distances from the corpse about four hundred yards all stand hand in breast, and then the whole body advance in one motion with all their implements of war, and springing from the ground at the same time, so that you can feel the earth shake under your feet for some distance from them. They advance to the corpse three times and retreat without turning back. They shout all in one voice, in a most dreadful manner, pronouncing all vengeance against all souls in the next life that shall molest this soul of their departed friend till they all die and come to assist him in battle.

This is their belief, that when they die they are at war one with the other.

Humming or moaning a dismal tune to himself, his wild eyes no longer focused on anything much at all, Brippoki exhibited symptoms of increased restlessness. Sarah hurried to bring the troublesome text to a close.

The women and children are most desperately frighted in those practices, though they perform the same duty as the men, some laughing, some crying and some singing. Then the body is taken into the woods, where it is put on a stake, where it remains till it rots. And this is the end of the funeral in New Zealand.

They also say that once, when they had a very heavy battle with the savage race, that they saw a cloud descend from the heavens and a most dreadful storm arose which was the cause of their gaining the conquest over their enemies.

After I had been amongst them seven months I consented to be marked in the face, whereby I received my wife with all the power that country possessed.

There was more, but not much more, and this seemed a natural point in the story at which to break. Sarah's notation from the day was nearly exhausted, and so was she. Still, she wanted to know what Brippoki made of the Maori, in hope of hints at least towards his own people's belief system.

Whilst she yet formulated how to tackle such a delicate topic, Brippoki dashed for the window and disappeared. Sarah threw down her notebook, angry with herself for allowing him to escape without so much as a word. His nerves were obviously frayed near to breaking by her reading of the transcript.

She shut the window.

In the wake of Brippoki's abrupt and thankless departure, Sarah reflected sourly on the text just read. After all of his ramblings in the Australian Bush, Druce glossed over a perhaps more important period in his life almost too hastily. He made no mention of his flogging, subsequent desertion, nor indeed – as per either ship's log or the 1810 *Memoirs* – Te Pahi or Tippahee by name. Still unsure of Brippoki's motive even by this point, Sarah had elected to follow the author's dubious example. She held on to the hope that, if relevant, she could always bring it up later.

The speed with which Druce dealt with his time in New Zealand, it was all very abstract, reading more like a dry report…including not a single personal comment, anecdote, or day-to-day event. What a wasted opportunity. She had no real way of knowing what had passed between them; certainly nothing to indicate why the Maori king, or chief or whatever, should grant Druce his daughter's hand in marriage.

Sarah wondered to what extent events had suited Druce's purpose, or inclination. It might well have been the case that, in this instance, Druce was the gull: a European considered of use to the natives, and no more.

Her own experience was enlightening, but frustrating. Within an hour or two's investigation that same afternoon she had apprehended more of the Maori of New Zealand than it seemed she ever might with regard to the Aborigines – even at first hand.

Enjoying her final hour in the library, Sarah had consulted closely two very different books. She devoured the papers of the Church Missionary Society, principally an article by the Reverend Samuel Marsden in their Missionary Register for 1816, on Maori beliefs. Then, from the horse's mouth, *OLD NEW ZEALAND: being incidents of NATIVE CUSTOMS AND CHARACTER IN THE OLD TIMES by A PAKEHA MAORI* (Frederick Edward MANING); and a rollicking adventure it was too.

They were, admittedly, a rare breed, but as it turned out there was a word, or phrase rather, appropriate to men like Druce – *Pakeha Maori*, 'European Maori'.

In almost any public forum, the native inhabitants of New Zealand were generally equated with the Aborigines of Australia: the Admiralty clerk, for one, appeared to make of them no distinction. Sarah could scarcely admit to understanding Aboriginal behaviours, and yet had felt compelled to study the Maori as encountered by Joseph Druce, who had lived among them, as one of them.

The *Pakeha Maori* were said to live in a half-savage state, or savage-and-a-half state, being far greater savages than the natives themselves. This, according to a man who should know: 'The New Zealanders,' Maning had written, 'will not be insulted with impunity, nor treated as men without understanding; but will resent, to the utmost of their power, any injury attempted against them.'

In truth, the islanders shared more in common with their European invaders than did either race with the Australian Aborigine.

On the few occasions where she found the two native races held up in direct comparison, what seemed most immediately obvious were the differences between them. The Maori were quite unlike the native Australians. They dwelt in hilltop forts, called *hippah*, and cultivated the surrounding farmlands. A warlike race, they lived in a state of constant feud with their neighbours. They would contest, and to the victor the spoils, the defeated tribe surrendering their land and property to be enslaved – or worse. The Maori were certified cannibals. The last words of a dying chief at Hokianga, North Island, were reputed to be, 'How sweet is man's flesh!'

She had seen Brippoki eat some revolting things, but surely this could not be true of either him or his people.

The natives of New Zealand recognised the concept of leadership: they were ruled by tribal chieftains, their *'rangatira'* – men like Te Pahi.

It was said that Te Pahi, on his visits to see the white governors in Sydney, had come into a good deal of contact with the Aborigines of Australia. He held them in a contempt as great as they had respect for him and his kind, if not an outright fear of them (one of Te Pahi's sons had menaced an Aboriginal group with his spear, and every last one of them fled). Witnessing their displays of weaponry, he had approved the boomerang, but condemned their use of a parrying shield. He judged the pace of their combat 'too slow'. All in all, the Maori warrior chieftain had condescended to the Aborigine character.

Only after some half an hour's reading had it even occurred to Sarah that Te Pahi was one and the same man as Druce's father-in-law, Tippahee, the so-called 'king of New Zealand'.

It seemed telling that, for a fellow living in Australia a goodly portion of years, Druce not once made the slightest reference to its natives, nor even his least association with them.

Sarah did not have to try so very hard to imagine what it must be like, to be so thoroughly disregarded.

A New Zealander, asked by Maning what God was like, had replied, 'An Immortal Shadow.'

An intelligent spirit or shadow, according to the Reverend Marsden – what Druce understood as their concept of the soul. Frederick Maning, the *Pakeha Maori*, disagreed. The idea of a supreme being never occurred to them, he wrote, and the word the missionaries used for God, *Atua*, meant – indifferently – a dead body, a sickness, a ghost, or a malevolent spirit.

Hell was *Te po*, world of darkness or night, or perhaps *Reinga*, a realm across the seas; the Maori appeared to have more than one hell.

Sarah glanced towards the table and the trussed corpse lying there, the bound and burnt offering a Maori chief in miniature.

'If one half of the world does not know how the other half live,' wrote Maning, 'neither do they know how they die.'

The Maori seemed to her to spend the better portion of their lives killing and dying. No wonder they needed many hells. A plethora of conceits in control of their spiritual lives drove them to a great many acts utterly horrific to her sensibilities.

Muru were their complex rights of plunder – easiest to encompass if compared to the Aboriginal notion of justifiable revenge. The strongest manifestation of this principle was the mighty *Utu*, 'satisfaction' or 'payment', although the purest summation seemed the more wrathful 'retribution'. *Lex talionis*, in other words, the code of the Babylonian king Hammurabi: an eye for an eye, tooth for a tooth...life, for life.

Tapu, or as she guessed it, 'taboo', smothered their lives like a spider's web, in both this life and the next. *Tapu* involved everything held most sacred among the Maori: birthright; a certain level of class distinction bound up with rights of ownership; and the prosecution of any trespass. To avenge breach of *tapu*, or at the command of a witch, their own dreadful *Atua* entered into a man's body and slowly ate away at his vitals; an infestation very much worse than woodworm, just as Brippoki had earlier suggested.

The means of guarding oneself against the shadowy terrors of *tapu* were almost too terrible for her to contemplate. The *matua* (elder relation) of a *Pakeha* slain by a Maori had then swallowed his eyes!

Sarah shivered with disgust.

She disposed of Brippoki's gift, the dreadful pigeon carcass, and, moving room to room, shut up the house for the night.

Lambert slept soundly.

Glad, Sarah prepared for bed herself. Catching sight of herself in the bathroom mirror, she tried one more time to visualise Druce's tattooed visage – marked in the face, like a divine fingerprint; the mark of Cain.

She took up her Bible from the bedside table.

And Cain walked with Abel his brother: and it came to pass, when they were in the field, that Cain rose up against Abel his brother, and slew him.

And the LORD said unto Cain, Where is Abel thy brother? And he said, I know not: Am I my brother's keeper?

And he said, What hast thou done? the voice of thy brother's blood crieth unto me from the ground.

And now art thou cursed from the earth, which hath opened up her mouth to receive thy brother's blood from thy hand...a fugitive and a vagabond shalt thou be in the earth.

And Cain said unto the LORD, My punishment is greater than I can bear...and it shall come to pass, that every one that findeth me shall slay me.

And the LORD said unto him, Therefore whosoever slayeth Cain, vengeance shall be taken on him sevenfold. And the LORD set a mark upon Cain, lest any finding him should kill him.

AND Cain went out from the presence of the LORD, and dwelt in the land of Nod, on the east of Eden.

Sarah extinguished the candle, and lay staring into the sudden plunge of darkness. Cain was marked, not for death, but so that he would be spared: in that way, his punishments might be everlasting.

CHAPTER XLIV
Tuesday, June the 16th, 1868

DISINHERITANCE

'Wolves shall succeed for teachers, grievous wolves,
Who all the sacred mysteries of Heaven
To their own vile advantages shall turn
Of lucre and ambition; and the truth
With superstitions and traditions taint.'

~ John Milton, *Paradise Lost*

Under more cloud than sky, Brippoki lies flat on a bed of leaves within his shelter of branch. He is inert. Deadman's stories of the South Islanders have impressed him mightily – a warrior race so fierce, they take their battles beyond the grave.

Dull heat and lack of sleep drifts his mind back to warmer climes, and the days before he is simply 'the one from Brippick Station', all alone in the World – there, perhaps even more than here. Days when he is no longer a boy but not yet a man; when he is only a boy; when he is a baby; and before he is born.

The *Wudjubalug*, his people, are proud desert folk. They belong to the land, as the land belongs to them. They give thanks daily for the sunlight and the breeze.

Many stars gather about the moon, when he is only a boy. Hunting is good.

Then their land is gone. No land no more. The whitefellows come, *Ngamadjidj*. White men come, and never stop coming. They take the land and don't want the blackfellows on it. Shoot them blackfellows, long time, plenty, plenty. All round, by Christ, blackfellows coming up deadfellows.

For the water, the grass and the trees, they come. They bring strange animals to eat the grass and drink the water. The trees they chop down and chew up to make their houses, and put up their fences. They bring new grasses – yellow grass, ear grass. His people try to lead them away from the sacred sites, but they take them anyway. Fences grow up, and blackfellows are told to keep away. No more burning the grass. No digging for roots or cutting trees for firewood.

Blackfellows are shot on sight, and even in the cold and wet their *gunyas* are burned as a punishment.

No kangaroo no more, no hunting. Less stars now, in the night sky.

His people move on, deeper into the desert. *Ngamadjidj* come after. They got all the trees, got all the grass, and now they want to take the rocks! Digging holes deep in the earth, they expose all her secrets. Bring the Lowerworld closer.

Brippoki turns the bright burning coin over and over between his fingers.

The whitefellows were wicked before, with iron sticks in their hands. Wanting for gold makes them even more wicked.

The earth soon becomes tired, and her people starve.

When he is only a boy, his people, they got no use for the white man's Dreaming. Where they walk freely provides all they need. No need for things.

With the land taken away, they begin to hang about the whitefellow houses. No more hunting for them. They are sent to a 'reserve', where the land is *nungkarpa*, shit. Everything around them comes from shit, or turns to shit. They make their *gunyas*, *mia mias*, out of it. They wear shit and they eat shit. Lost, without status, clinging listlessly about the croppy settlements, his people become rag-wearers, bone-pickers, fringe-dwellers reliant on charity. *Ngamadjidj* laughs at them – worthless, drunken beggars grovelling for scraps.

The No learn to need for things, wanting billy-tea, wanting sugar, flour for damper, jerky; and rum, lots of rum. Rum helps them to forget the pain, the sickness, the bad liver, No country. Forget everything.

Wudjubalug land stretches from *Jerry Warrack* to *Woppoon*, and there, *lubras*, but no men. The men are up country. There, no *lubras*, only old *gins*. Men forget their women, and the women forget their men. Mothers forget their little ones, and the fathers forget their senses. No fuck, no childhood, no learning any more.

Good marriage must come of good skin – from bad skin comes only bad marriage. As the peoples become less, it is harder to make a good match. To have no land is to have no life. Rum is gifted instead; rum, for *gin*. No good children now no country. Newborns are killed to save them starving.

No more children come, just shit, disease and booze. They die, like flies; when he is no longer a boy, but not yet a man.

Sand turns to clay, to stone. No more No way. That just how it is. Clouds, passing.

Sarah was taking quite the chance, leaving the house soon after an early dinner. Lambert was too preoccupied with his reading or his memories to either notice or care what she did, so long as she was not too late returning.

St James's Hall, Piccadilly, on the warm evening of a warm day; impulse had brought her here, impulse and *The Illustrated London News*.

'CALENDAR. Tues. JUNE 16: Meeting of the Anthro. Soc., 8pm.'

The world couldn't be explored, or its peoples understood, solely from the reading of books. She required expertise.

Ten minutes after eight and Sarah Larkin crept into the theatre lobby. The Anthropological Society of London boasted a membership of eight thousand; there were 706 Fellows, 29 honorary Fellows, 42 corresponding members, and 104 local secretaries – and not a single woman to be counted among them. She had checked.

'By Jove, Beaven…what do we have here?'

Sarah hung back, fearful.

'Cruel massa stole him wife, and lily piccaninny.'

'Piccaninny Circus!'

She overheard remarks from of a small group of gentlemen, stragglers from the main party already gone ahead. Resplendent in evening dress, they gathered around a gaudy wall-poster, an advertisement for the Christy Minstrels: the Hall, most nights, was the venue for a 'Banjo and Bones' Black and White Minstrel Show – 'Very Popular'.

The most porcine of the Fellows struck an unlikely pose. 'So,' he said, 'we have the irrepressible Negro…black yourself up and play the banjo, Blake. I, the bones, Collingwood the tambourine!' They launched into an improvised chorus of the Minstrels' most famous song, 'Beautiful Dreamer' – very ragged, for all the polish of their appearance.

One of them broke off to hold open a door. 'Sambo,' he mock-chided. 'Come along, o' we shall miss de main event!'

'Don' drag yo' heels, lazy Bones!'

Their noise receded into the bowels of the building.

Sarah moved forward to take a look for herself at the image on the poster: white men in blackface – not unlike Brippoki, his features clogged with dried Thames clay, but reversed.

'Sure,' it read, 'to Run and Run.'

At any second a member of staff might approach, question her presence, and then all would be in vain. Sarah ducked into a stairwell at one extreme, making for the upper galleries. She ran into a Fellow on the intervening stairs, and froze. As the man passed her by she bobbed slightly, cannily keeping her eyes averted. Despite the lack of lace on her black bonnet, Sarah guessed she appeared more serving girl than lady, and for once felt glad of her dowdy dress. She entered the gods at the very top and crept down to the front.

'…served the Society well, being the site of our A.G.M. two years ago…'

The grand hall filled and the meeting convened, opening remarks were already under way.

'In the five years since the Anthropological Society came into existence, we students of man, in wishing to combine all of our partial studies under the one name, have fought for that very right,' said the main speaker. 'The cry nowadays is no longer, "Anthropology is not a science!" The question of today is rather, "What does anthropology teach?" And this is but the latest and most gratifying sign of our progress. With the very greatest pleasure, may I present to you our first Society president, Dr James Hunt, "The Best Man in England"! Come to the stand, James.'

Thunderous applause.

'Thank you,' said their president. 'Th-thank you, too kind.'

Sarah crouched low on the seating, near to the back of the deserted Upper Circle. It was hard for her to observe closely, but Dr Hunt appeared quite elderly, with a large moustache and a shaggy mane of grey hair.

The assembly eventually quietened. Dr Hunt took a deep breath.

'Anthropology,' he said, 'I make no apology, is a self-proclaimed science…'

And in that vein he carried on, his articulation, at times, almost impenetrable. Sarah knew his name from the frequent listings in the newspapers for his many books, among them *Impediments of Speech: On Stammering and Stuttering: its Nature and Treatment*. Also *The Irrationale of Speech: or, Hints to Stammerers, by a Minute Philosopher*. 'Write what you know', so the saying went.

'…Australia the puh-resent home and refuge,' said Hunt, working hard, 'of creatures crude and quaint…'

His comments met with a ripple of indulgent laughter, and Sarah's renewed interest.

'…creatures,' he persisted, 'that have elsewhere p-p-puh, p-p-p-puh…given way, to higher forms.'

Dr Hunt paused, and smiled in a fashion most unpleasant.

'This applies equally to the Aboriginal,' he said, 'as to the p-platypus and the ka-ka-kangaroo. Just as the…former reveals a mammal in the making, so does the Aboriginal show us what early man must have been like.

'There can be no doubt, that in the juxta-puh-sition of the…superior and inferior races, the latter will always become extinct if they attempt to compete with the civilised…the civilised man. Those who disdain the new nation of Australia may wish to think it denigrated, or else de-nigger-ated. But, when the Noble Savage knows his place, in subordination to the civilised, his extinction need not take place.'

Sarah looked down from her seat amongst the gods, and was displeased.

The first of the evening's guest speakers was called to the podium: Charles Staniland Wake, a noted ethnologist. He looked to be a relatively young man.

'All human societies begin in the state of nature,' he began, 'but most of them have progressed since then.' His opening gambit met with loud laughter and generous applause. 'The state of nature,' he continued, 'is one in which humans have not yet appropriated land as property. Ancient Greek and Roman historians agree it was the invention of agriculture that gave rise to property rights in land. All societies progress through distinct stages of civilisation. Adam Smith enumerates four: Hunting, Pasturage, Farming, and Commerce.'

Sarah frowned. Hadn't Sir John Lubbock nominated five?

'Each stage,' said Wake, 'corresponds to its political and economic institutions, including that of property. Hunters knew no property. Pastoralists needed, and thus developed, property in their livestock. Farmers developed property in their land. And a Commercial people such as we ourselves have invented the most complex property arrangements of all to suit our needs.

'Furthermore, every race has its stages: race and civilisation but different phases of the same great question. As some of you well know, I call this "the Psychological Unity of Mankind".

'I will typify the five races of man in reverse order,' he said, airily, 'as a bone thrown to any Degenerationists present.'

Five now.

'Last,' said Wake, 'the position of maturity, or rational state, which typifies the European. At the period of early manhood, or empirical level, stands the Oriental. The third stage, of youth, or emotional behaviour, characterises the Negro. Next, the period of boyhood, or wilful level, typified by the American Indian. And finally, at the level of the child, or selfish stage, the Australian Aborigine, one of the most legendary and backward races in our wide-ranging experience.'

Provoked, Sarah edged forward in her seat.

'The natives of Australia show approximately the condition in which man generally must have existed in the primeval ages. According to Dr Seemann, who is with us tonight...' Wake nodded into the audience at a certain point '...Australian Aborigines are the oldest as well as the lowest race of man. Australia, as with New Zealand, could be construed a unique haven for less evolved forms. Dr Hunt has already specified some best-known examples of the marsupial *genera*, their existence now confined to New South Wales and Van Diemen's Land. So it is that in the Australian seas we find the *Cestracion*, a cartilaginous fish which has a bony palate, allied to those called *Acrodus* and *Strophodus*, so common in the Oolitic and Lias, predating the Cretaceous.'

Murmurs and nodding all around; everyone seemed to approve this properly scientific dialect of hoots and screeches.

'Australia,' said Wake, 'must therefore be described as the oldest of the great continents, and the least altered...a country in its dotage, which from time immemorial has retained its character unchanged. Thus, "New" Holland may be likened to an old man, tottering towards the grave.

'Look to the desert-like interior, the great number of its salt lakes, the rivers terminating in swamps...it is almost dead already. All is hopeless stagnation.

Corals surround the whole, such calcified growths forming where the ground is gradually sinking. The leaves are dull, the flowers do not smell, and the fruits, without any exception, are tasteless and insipid. The whole of this vegetation and the animals depending on it must disappear before the country becomes a fit abode for the white man. Environmental conditions such as these,' said Wake, 'are unfavourable to mental and physical development, and have caused the inferiority of the lower races, the remote and highly pigmented inhabitants of Africa, Asia, America, and Australasia. Progress is only possible for these peoples with the aid of the more advanced European.

'In conclusion, Australia has done playing its part, and must now prepare for vast changes.'

Applause. C. S. Wake stood down. The chairman was upstanding.

'Thank you, Charles,' he said. 'The floor is now opened for your responses... The Chair recognises Dr Hunt.'

The old gentleman stood and turned, but did not take to the stage. 'I met with a cricketer at the Athenaeum Ball,' he said, his mouth forming that exact shape, 'a man I took to *be* one such advanced European. He captains the Blacks cuh-currently touring our great nation.'

Lawrence.

'I attempted to pay him a compliment, on the good behaviour of his charges. I will not burden you with d-d-duh...de-d-...' Hunt hung his head in frustration a moment, before continuing '...the nature of his reply, except to say I f-f-fear...he has been rather too much in their company.'

Dr Hunt could try reciting the liturgy, thought Sarah, a temporary cure reputed to work for the Queen's chaplain, Charles Kingsley. Or there was one of Bate's Patent Appliances: they too advertised in *The Illustrated London News*.

'The Chair recognises Lord Brockbank.'

'The Australian Cricketers insist on demonstrations of their "Aboriginal Sports", the chief of which...beating each other about the head with "*waddies*", and boomerang experiments...have been modified to suit European mildness of taste.'

'*Waddy*, you say?' another man interjected.

'It is a primitive sort of club,' said Brockbank. 'The native is so fond of his *waddy* that even in civilised life he cannot be induced to part with it. Indeed, never seems happy without one in his hands.'

'The Chair recognises Mr Wood.'

'The *waddy*,' added Wood, 'is the Australian panacea for domestic strife. Should one of his wives presume to have an opinion of her own, or otherwise offend her dusky lord, a blow on the head settles the dispute at once by leaving her senseless on the ground.'

'Hmm,' mused another gentleman. 'Where can I get one?'

'I too saw them in action at the Oval, recently…'

The Chair straightened his spine. 'Mr Bouverie-Pusey,' he announced.

'Thank you,' replied the new voice. '…At the Oval much fuss was made over their boomeranging, an elegant refinement on the art of stick-throwing. I was so impressed, I went home early.'

'Underestimate the boomerang at your own risk. In the right hands it can be a deadly-accurate weapon!'

'Mr Wood,' said the Chair.

'It is,' Wood elaborated, 'a very versatile invention. They also use it for skinning, for digging, and as a musical instrument.'

'Oh, really?' said Bouverie-Pusey. 'I now wish I had stayed.'

'I desire to make some remarks on the subject of native mortality.'

'The Chair recognises… Who are you, sir?'

'Mr Murray, of Sydney, Australia.'

A loud murmur arose. Sarah craned her neck, trying for a better view of a fellow buried somewhere deep in the audience.

'Members only knowing about the rate of mortality in European countries,' said Murray, 'will be startled on learning how frequently deaths occur amongst us. In an unhealthy season, sickness, such as influenza, assumes a much more serious and deadly character among the natives. The customary number of deaths is very greatly increased…'

Another voice filled the chamber. 'Everyone who knows even a little about aboriginal races is aware: those of a low type, mentally, are at the same time weak in their constitution.'

The Chair identified the speaker as a Dr Lawson.

'When their country comes to be occupied by a different race much more vigorous, robust, and pushing than themselves,' he said, 'they rapidly die out.'

'That,' retorted Murray, 'is my point. The rapid disappearance of aboriginal tribes before the advance of civilisation is one of the remarkable incidents of the present age – '

'They are too weak, as I say, to withstand any disease,' said Dr Lawson. He returned to his own point. 'Once sickly, there is little or no hope of recovery. Constantly exposed to the weather, the roofless Aborigines are extremely susceptible to "colds". Before a southerly wind they crouch under every cover they can find… The influx of Europeans has enabled them to procure articles of clothing or blankets the value of which, at such times, they thoroughly appreciate. But the first warm day sees all these benefits thrown aside. Not infrequently, fever and other diseases are actually produced through the careless use of damp coverlets. Their deaths arise through the improper use of clothes.'

Another Fellow stood, ready to speak.

'Compared with Europeans,' continued the doctor, 'the ordinary native is slight in frame and feeble in constitution, easily brought low by sickness, and pining away often from unaccountable causes, principally pulmonary complaints, aggravated by their own thoughtlessness and roving mode of life.'

'Thank you, Dr Lawson…you have finished?' checked the Chair. 'Thank you for your enlightening contribution. Mr Bouverie-Pusey?'

'Have not these races lived their appointed time?'

'Have a heart!' someone cried out, the voice sounding somewhat familiar: Sarah tried, but could not identify who had spoken.

'A heart, sir?' Bouverie-Pusey took up the challenge. 'Unless it be a bullock's, and well cooked, to have a heart is a mistake! We are men of science, not Romance.'

'Then perhaps it is time you heard from a man of religion.' An elderly gent lurched to his feet, steadying himself on the back of the seat in front. 'I am not so sure myself,' he croaked, 'what message Mr Murray was attempting to impart, but let me say this. Sprung from the Mother Country, modern Australia is Protestant by law. Directives from London continue to insist on religious instruction as essential, in deterrence of immorality and to the preservation of order. But around Perth, where I myself have ministered, our Sundays are far from high and holy.'

'What do you mean by this?' demanded the Chair, as if rankled by an interloper. 'Are you talking about the Blacks, or the Whites?'

'The settlers, sir,' came the reply, 'their schooling in life so harsh, they know of no kindness. Their days are given over to drinking, gambling, and hunting for sport. And I regret to report, not all of the shooting is confined to kangaroos…'

Sarah gasped.

'The Aboriginal character is not without blemishes, to be sure, nor above dishonesty when it suits them, but there can be no denying they have been set the very worst of examples. Even a blind eye might see that.'

'The Chair recognises Mr Reddie.'

'I agree with the kind gentleman. Yet how might we benefit the Australian Aborigine, given what success we have had with the morals of our own refuse population?'

'Mr Reade?'

'The specimens of Africans which have been received in America are pretty much the same as if the inhabitants of Whitechapel had been sent out to any country as specimens of Englishmen.'

Clambering to the stage, Hunt strode forward to address them all. 'However poor the stock,' he roared, 'I will not stand for this comparison. If there is one truth most clearly defined in anthropological science, it is the existence of well-marked psychological and moral, moral distinctions…in the d-different races of man.' Hunt grasped the lectern and drew himself up higher. He swept the room bodily, like a searchlight. 'Utopian ideals,' his words rang out, 'universal equality, fraternity, and b-brotherhood…' he blasted '…are chimeras! They have no place!'

If this was the Best Man in England, Sarah felt she might prefer the Worst.

A small voice from the back broke the stunned silence. 'If the Aborigines are inferior to all other races of mankind…if this truly is the case, all other races of mankind must be more highly endowed than I, for one, ever thought they were.'

Dr Hunt leant forward, his elbows jutting like pincers. 'Mr Murray is a very profound thinker.'

A howling chorus arose from Hunt's running dogs. In the face of unbeatable odds, Mr Murray sat down. The matter appeared almost settled.

Another voice, thin and wheedling, piped up. 'The native is redeemed by his contact with the White man, not corrupted,' it said. 'I wish to make that clear.'

'The Chair recognises Wood.'

'But does Wood recognise the chair?'

Laughter.

'It is a question for our times!'

'Gentlemen! Mr Wood?'

'In proposing the following example, I leave it for the individual member to decide, but mark it for the attention of the reverend gentleman in particular,' he condescended. 'A goodly number of natives are now enrolled among the police, and render invaluable service to their community, especially against the depredations of their fellow Blacks, whom they persecute with a relentless vigour that seems rather surprising to those who do not know the singular antipathy which invariably exists between wild and tamed animals…

'The Australian native policeman,' Wood concluded, 'is to the colonists what the "Totty" of Southern Africa is to the Boer and Englander, what the Ghoorka or Sikh of India is to the English army, and what the tamed elephant of Ceylon or India is to the hunter.'

Sarah could feel her heart, hardening.

'I wish to add to this point, as it returns us to another.'

'Mr Bendyshe?'

'To whit, when we get an Indian into broadcloth or an Australian into uniform, we think the great experiment of our civilisation has been successfully accomplished, and that our "travelled monkey" is a promising type of all his kind. But in truth he is only a talking parrot, a well-bred wolf, a performing tiger, whose congeners still in the forest are what they ever were. Their ability to follow the trail of a tribe or individual, their recognition of the latter by his footsteps, even in the sand, and their skill in building a native hut of branches, which it appears no European has yet been able to accomplish satisfactorily, only place them on a level with the dog and the bird.

'Had they shown an ability to depart from their traditional habitudes of thought and action, and to adopt in their place, however imperfectly, the higher modes of life introduced by the colonists, there would have been some hope for them; but of this they seem utterly incapable, and therefore their doom is sealed. Without the forest to live and breed in, they ultimately perish, like beasts in a menagerie.'

'For shame, sirs,' a lone voice was shouting. 'For shame.' Sarah was almost surprised it was not hers. A general kerfuffle arose, ruffled feathers, some boos. Sarah heard again the same protestant voice she had thought to recognise earlier. 'We are not monsters,' it cried, 'we're moral people! God knows our business.'

Hastily she crept forward.

'Sir,' replied the Chair, curtly. 'Identify yourself!'

'The Reverend G. Alston.'

Only by leaning precariously over the edge of the balcony could Sarah see him, as he broke out of the crowd and into the central aisle

'Look to yourselves, gentlemen,' he declared, firmly. 'Look to yourselves!'

'Are you leaving? Goodbye!'

The Reverend Alston was a former associate of Lambert's, one of the few whose position and opinions she had always respected; her immediate impulse was to follow him out.

The Chair moved to restore order. 'Mr Row?'

'With all respect due to Mr Bendyshe, despite the current trend in scientific thinking there is a very great gap between man and the animals.'

'Mr Reddie…'

'With regard to Mr Row's excellent observation, supposing for a moment the Darwinian theory to be true, when Mr Wallace addressed the Society, he said that since man has reached such a high condition the law of natural selection no longer applies to him.'

'But does it not apply in the case of the monkey,' asked the Chairman, 'which is developed into man?'

Laughter.

'It ceased after man was developed. And I recall a pertinent remark of Dr Hunt's on the occasion. He said what a poor natural law it must be, if mortal man can so easily revoke it.'

The man himself stood, creating an expectant hush.

'W-w… W-w-would…' Dr Hunt gave up and simply beckoned.

Dunbar Heath, as Chair, interposed. 'Would you like to come to the front, Mr Wood?' he said. 'Come to the front. Our next speaker, gentlemen, is the

Reverend J. G. Wood, who has very kindly agreed to share with us a preview of some findings from his forthcoming treatise, *The Natural History of Man.*'

To applause the Reverend Wood took to the stage, another small man in black suit in a large room too entirely filled with them.

'Whenever a higher race occupies the same grounds as a lower, the latter perishes…and the new world is always built on the ruins of the old. Such is the history of the Aboriginal tribes of Australia, whose remarkable manners and customs are fast disappearing, together with the natives themselves. The poor creatures are aware of the fact, and seem to have lost all pleasure in the games and dances that formerly enlivened their existence. Many of the tribes are altogether extinct, and others are dwindling so fast that the people have lost all heart and spirit, and succumb almost without complaint to the fate that awaits them.

'In one tribe for example, the Barrabool, the births recorded during seventeen years were only 24, being scarcely two in three years, while the deaths have been between eighteen and nineteen per annum. Mr Lloyd gives a touching account of the survivors of this once flourishing tribe. "When I first landed in Geelong, in 1837," he reports, "the Barrabool tribe numbered upwards of 300 sleek and healthy-looking blacks. A few months previous to my leaving that town, in May 1853, they showed me with outstretched fingers the total and unhappy state of the local population: nine women, seven men, and one sickly child. Enquiring after my old dark friends of the early days I received the following pathetic reply."'

Screwing up his face, Wood parleyed an idea of Aboriginal speech. '"Aha, Mitter Looyed, Ballyyang dedac, Jaga-jaga dedac!"' Wood looked up from his various papers. '*Etcetera,*' he said, 'many others named equally "dedac", meaning as one might expect that they were dead.'

The man might as well have painted his cheeks with bootblack. Sarah thought she might leave. If she could only glean something of Brippoki, but nothing good could be learned from these men. Nothing. She stood.

'This one tribe,' Wood went on, 'is typical of the others, all of whom are surely, and some not slowly, approaching the end of their existence. They are but following the order of the world, the lower race preparing a home for the higher. Do not mourn them excessively, for the Aborigines perform barely half of their duties as men. As it has been noted, this vast country was to them a common. They bestowed no labour upon the land. Their ownership, their right, was nothing more than that of the Emu or the Kangaroo.

'In due process of time white men have introduced new arts into their country, clearing away useless forest and covering the rescued earth with luxuriant wheat crops, bringing also with them herds of sheep and horned cattle to feed upon the vast plains which formerly nourished but a few kangaroo, multiplying in such

360

numbers that they not only supply the whole of their adopted land with food, but their flesh is exported to the Mother Country. The superior knowledge of the white man thus gave to the Aborigines the means of securing their supplies of food, and therefore his advent was not a curse, but a benefit to them.'

'Hear, hear!' Various members of the audience expressed their hearty approval.

'They could not,' said Wood, twinkling his eyes, 'take advantage of the opportunities thus offered to them, and instead of seizing upon these new means of procuring the three great necessaries of human life…food, clothing, and lodging…not only refused to employ them, but did their best to drive their benefactors out of the country, murdering the colonists, killing their cattle, destroying their crops, and burning their houses. The means were offered to them of infinitely bettering their social condition, means they could not appreciate, and, as a natural consequence, they have had to make way for those who could. These I term the unvariable Laws of Progression. The inferior must always make way for the superior, and such has ever been the case with the savage.'

'Hrrrah, hrrrah.'

Copious applause. Sarah's head was spinning. She had to sit down again.

Wood bowed and backed away as the secretary took the stand.

'I thank Messrs Wake and Wood for their most excellent speeches,' he said. 'Almost everywhere, save in the older and more civilised nations, we see one world of people passing off the stage, and another, more highly developed world coming on. In a few years the surface of the earth will be utterly altered. Whole races that now rule supreme over immense tracts will have passed away for ever, and civilisation will turn to better account the lands that have so long been the undisturbed home of the "black fellow". A new era will be inaugurated, and human responsibilities vastly multiplied.'

More applause.

Somebody within the audience rose to their feet.

'Such a worldwide reform has never before occurred,' he said, 'but if so, may it not, at some far distant date, occur again? Europe, now pre-eminent in all the attainments of man, may have it for her destiny to repopulate the globe, and then to tarry in her onward career. It may be the lot of nations now springing into existence at the antipodes to outstrip her in the pursuit of knowledge, and, when ages shall have passed away, to supply, in their turn, a nobler race, a more perfect humanity, to the lands which now rank foremost in civilisation.'

Sarah understood the reference made to that same newspaper article, inspired in part by Aboriginal cricket at Lord's, so annoying to Lambert. The very notion sparked off a good deal of disgruntled murmuring.

Not to be outdone, the unknown speaker raised his voice louder. 'The New Zealand offspring of the imagination of our great essayist may be no unreal creation of the imagination,' he supposed, 'and England may yet be indebted to her descendants in the south for a people who shall as far surpass her present occupants as the civilised Englishman of this day excels the half-barbarous Maori.'

Whether he was being brave or foolish, the commentator was howled down.

'The Chair recognises Dr Bertholdt Seemann.'

'It is not wort'while to waste time in discussing the dream of Gibbon or Macaulay respecting the New Zealander,' he said, 'in his looking at the ruins of London! These speculations are only interesting as showing the profound ignorance of Anthropological science in men of genius and learning.'

Boomerang-like, the comment rebounded on the Fellow who had thrown it out.

Dr Hunt checked at his pocket watch, nose twitching. He looked like Tenniel's white rabbit from Lewis Carroll's *Alice*; but, when he spoke, the part voiced was that of the Mad Hatter.

'Scientific societies,' he spat, 'are not intended to be theatres for the display of the eccentricities of their members, or f-f-for the ventilation of individual crochets or crudities, but for the real advancement of science. I do not know at this moment of *ernnhny* race who has raised themselves since we first *gnnnuu* them.'

'*Mstrrh* Wood?'

'The *owrahrr* mode of dealing with *theeze* people is the safe one to adopt with *ahhrr* savages…never trust *uhhm*, and *nahrahhr* cheat *ruhhm*.'

'*Grrr Ga?*'

'*Hahrrr rahhrrr snarrrrl ra raa. Nhgggnnr.*'

'*Vvrrr. Shhhhha aahuunnnr gurrrrnn. Pcha, pchaa. Grrrawaa.*'

They were old baboons, sucking at plums and vomiting. Sarah fled. Her feet tripped and thumped on the carpeted stair. She had to grope for the brass handrail, salt tears streaking her cheeks and running into the corners of her mouth. Pharisees! Near-sighted Pharisees!

Let them alone: they be blind leaders of the blind. And if the blind lead the blind, both shall fall into the ditch.

The distance from Brippoki's chosen camp to Number 89 Great Russell-street is about four miles, negotiated at a steady jog.

Dragging his heels, he arrives at the Guardian's house later than usual. He arrives to find the window-glass shut and the house in darkness.

Brippoki creeps around the tops of the buildings opposite. Huddled into a crouch, arms clasped over his head, he forces his heartbeat to slow.

A firebug shivers from room to room. Thara *baiame*. The Guardian sits with the father.

The light retreats, is snuffed out. Brippoki sky-walks around to the rear of the house, swinging from the branches of the tall trees there.

He observes Tharalarkin in the small room behind that of the father. She stands – dressed in a long white cloth he has seen once before – combing out her silvered hair. Unmoving, she stops and stares long and hard into the looking glass. She stands and stares until his limbs grow stiff, until long after steam from the hot tap has smoked her reflection, wiping out all trace of it.

CHAPTER XLV

Wednesday the 17th of June, 1868

MISSING LINKS

"With few associates, in remote
And silent woods I wander, far from those,
My former partners of the peopled scene;
With few associates, and not wishing more
Here much I ruminate, and much I may,
With other views of men and manners now
Than once, and others of a life to come."

~ William Cowper, *The Task*

As sure as day gives way to night, so eventually the night passes once more into day. In order that he might gather up the dew from where it spangles the longest grass, Brippoki rises early from his couch.

Hunger as much as thirst aggravates his wants. Pickings are slim – more so than back in the World, even deep in the desert country. He takes up a small spade of wood fashioned between idle hours, his *karko*. With this he can dig for grubs, edible roots, even a frog should one be sleeping under the ground. From each he may suck sometimes no more than a sip of liquid, and then roast them on the ashes of his modest fire. This bright morning, half an hour's steady work only wins him a few stems of reed from the marshy bog. These he fires and then chews at length, to extract the softer parts, and as much goodness as they might grudgingly yield.

Wading in amongst the reeds, half burying himself in the mud – all that remains of the small canalside brook as it dries up – chills Brippoki's blood. Lying supine beside his campfire, he builds it up again, until sufficient to roast a dish of water-beetles.

Brippoki reaches into his *coolamon* to retrieve the strands of bark fibre prepared a few days earlier. He has, meantime, been rinsing them in the cleanest water he can find, and laying them out in the sun to dry. Sitting with one leg tucked beneath the other, he selects two small pieces of the teased bark and, under an open palm, begins to roll them along his outstretched thigh.

With the skill of muscle memory he weaves the fibrous threads into string, *kaargerum*. Such menial tasks fell to him when only a boy, working alongside the women.

A man's True life does not begin at birth, or during infancy, spent among the womenfolk, when he has only a number for a name. Without status, without sex, without even a proper name, he is called *Kertameru*. Only slightly older, and Brippoki is stolen away by the *Curadgie*, to undergo the first of the ceremonies that would lead to his eventual manhood. The *Curadgie*, foremost among his mob's elders, is a very wizened old man, able to foresee events before they happen, and to communicate with the restless spirits of the departed.

Life's journey is no smooth path – so says the *Curadgie*, a clever-man among his people. It is a series of obstacles that must be overcome – knots, along a string – positions an individual must be qualified for, in order that they may then be occupied. Rights of way and rites of passage, each stage of life carries with it its own test, its own ritual, and its own price. These are lessons Brippoki knows all too well. He bears the scars inside and out, each badge of pain an indelible mark.

Although he can never speak of it to anyone, Brippoki remembers his first rites of passage – the ordeal of it – clear as day.

Not ceasing in his labours, Brippoki begins to rock back and forth where he squats, on his heel. His eyes lack focus. He sings.

'*Wiltongarrolo kundando.*'

His voice, pitched high, quavers. '*Kadlottikurrelo paltando.*' 'Strike with the tuft of eagle feathers, strike him with the girdle'…

He is drenched from head to toe in blood, drawn hot and fresh from the arm of a *bourka*. The anonymity of early childhood ends this day. Still just a boy, he is no longer a number, but receives the first of his names – *Parnko*. Limits are imposed on the *goorong* he is allowed to eat, the living embodiments of the sacred totems. The flesh of the red kangaroo is forbidden him, as are the females or young of any sort; likewise the white crane, *linkara*; the wallaby, *meracco*; the pheasant; three kinds of fish; and two of turtles, *rinka* and *tungkanka*. *Wilya kundarti* now by status, he is allowed to carry a *wirri* for killing birds, and his first *karko*, with which to dig for grubs.

It is in his fourteenth summer that he is ready to enter the third stage of his life. Like every other male child, he must endure the trials of man-making before he can be fully accepted as a mature adult, through rites of circumcision.

Early one morning the boys are seized from behind, a tight band fastened across the eyes of each. They wail in fear of their lives. Their captors lead them a few thousand paces distant from the camp, out of sight and earshot of any of the women or children. They are made to lie on the ground, and covered over with a possum-skin cloak – unable to see what the men are about to do. He hears a curious sound, an intermittent thump, like the limping of a cripple – first one, and then others joining. The air soon fills with dust. He can tell from the grit between his teeth, the drought on his tongue. Above them starts a terrible groaning, among them whimpering, and then dampness. One of his brothers has wet himself. A shriek and a beating of limbs as someone is seized and dragged out from beneath the cloak. Upside-down, through a chink of material, he witnesses the fate of the unlucky boy. Then another, and then rough hands grab at his ankles, and it is his turn. Pulled free of the skins, he breaks free of the elders' grasp and falls flat on his face, only to jump up and run full pelt for the tree-line. Barely ten paces and the heavy body of a Red Ochre Man brings him down, drags him back. The dust of enchantment is blown into his eyes, clouding his vision. Pulled up by the ears, loud cries are ringing in them. The Men, all the men of his clan, little more than silhouette and shadow, they circle him in single file. A *katto*, or long stick, passes from hand to hand.

More of a blur then, bodies in motion – the young bodies of his fellows, frozen. The *katto*. Stamping feet, groans, cries. His tears. The *katto*, all hands on the *katto*, the press of bodies, smell of sweat. His own body is picked up and thrown through the air. His eyes burn. The eyes of the *Curadgie*, face to his face…

Blood. He tastes blood.

> '*Mangakurrelo paltando,*
> *Worrikarrolo paltando,*
> *…Turtikarrolo paltando!*'

Brippoki pauses to wipe the sweat from his brow, and to staunch his bitten lip.

After the operation the new beings are kept in isolation, well away from the taint of females, until such time as they are fully healed. Living on a vegetable diet, their heads are constantly anointed with grease and red ochre, bandages wound around them but no blindfold. At the last, they are crowned with ornamental feathers. For some moons following circumcision a *yudna*, or pubic covering, is worn. When it is removed, according to custom, his boyhood will be over. Having survived his ritual death, the worthy individual is reborn a man.

Bripumyarrimin throws his head back and roars out his anguish. Shame runs down his cheeks – his short breaths puffing out, then in.

His *yudna* finally removed, the worst of his fears is confirmed, his non-status revealed for all to see. The sacred cutting has been denied him. Uncircumcised, he remains a child, and condemned as such. In outrage, in bitterness, many times he vows to do the necessary himself, but his trembling hands shake too much. Self-mutilation, he knows, will not make him any more acceptable in the eyes of his people.

The other children and his erstwhile peers laugh to see him. Among the adults, it is worse – they will not look at him. He is the *Murrumbidgee Biam*, a supernatural being who has taken the form of a *guli*, a black man, but one whose lower extremities are deformed. Such a one may compose ritual songs and *corroboree* dances, but is also reckoned to carry diseases, especially those leaving telltale marks on the face.

Brippoki, forever since, makes a point of never sitting cross-legged on the ground, as is that foul creature's custom.

Sarah lay in her bed, unwilling to greet the new day. She shivered with a chill rage all the more bitter for its impotence.

Coming away from St James's Hall the night before, she had lain in the bath for over an hour, beyond midnight even. As with the clay whose ghost still clung to her shoes, she feared she might never think herself clean again.

In disparaging the Australian Aborigines, the buccaneer William Dampier had set a dangerous precedent: lethal, in fact, precisely because it had persisted. Through decades of hearsay, reportage and gossip posing as official record, it had become horrifically bloated, out of all proportion with the real, human dimension. Ludwig Leichhardt, in his *Journals*, described his party being received as 'pale-faced anthropophagi' – refreshing insight and honesty, given the circumstances. In quest of exploration they had perpetrated evil. What evils, Sarah wondered, might yet arise, through the dogged pursuits of those self-appointed men of science, the Piccadilly Misanthropes.

Men might talk, but that was no guarantee they knew their subject, not even first-hand; to that extent, her experience might in fact be the greater. The twist of the Society Fellows' 'logic', their outrageous justifications, resembled nothing so much in her mind as the smooth-talking language of professional murder. Far from being in denial, perhaps they simply didn't know any better.

Worst of all, nor could she.

Science itself was not necessarily evil, but much evil might be done in its name, when allowed to be so inexact. Turning in the bed, away from the light, Sarah thought it a wicked irony: that a greater truth could be found in the world of myth.

The Golden Age, as according to Ovid, was a period when the earth itself produced all things spontaneously. Men were content with the foods that grew without cultivation, and to know only their own shores. Once Saturn was consigned to the darkness of Tartarus, however, the world passed under the rule of Jove, bringing a definitive end to such halcyon days. The Golden

Age was replaced by one of Silver, inferior to it in every way: only Gold did not tarnish.

Leichhardt, Mitchell, and men like them, were the heralds of that new age of Silver.

Then, according to that same legend, other metals would come on in swift succession, increasingly base. In an age of hard Iron, modesty, truth and loyalty would flee before deceit, violence and criminal greed, and sailors spread their canvas to the winds.

That age was already here.

Australia, once the fabled land of milk and honey, had itself passed into myth, undergoing its metamorphosis into a land of mutton and corn.

Mr Gilbert's ghost, invisibly speared through the clavicle, would haunt Sarah for evermore: with his death, any ideas she entertained of a peaceful resolution between black fellow and white had been dashed. She knew then that bloody conflict was inevitable, was occurring, had occurred – the retribution harsh. Gentle Gold could not help but give way to weapons forged in the age of Iron. Hands would be bloodstained, and the virgin earth blood-soaked.

'RRuhhHr!'

Refusing all offers of help, Lambert struggled to gain a sitting position. The best Sarah could do was to dart forward occasionally and adjust the bedding behind him, to provide more support.

'Hrrugh! Hkcough!'

Eventually she was able to present him breakfast, although it had already gone cold. He munched, slowly.

'Look,' he murmured, 'at what your old father is reduced to…an old slugabed.'

'You have not eaten your egg,' she said, flatly.

'It is very good of you…to treat me to eggs,' he said, still chewing at his last mouthful, 'but if I have another this week, I'll be bound. More…than I am already.' Lambert mopped his lips and any dribbles from his moustaches. 'I sleep very fitful,' he said, 'and wake with a lingering fever. My joints ache, my teeth are rattling loose, and to top it all, I cannot even enjoy a good motion any more. *You* eat the egg!'

He shoved his plate away.

Sarah did not react. Lambert eyed her.

'"Life itself is a disease,"' he declared, '"a working incited by suffering."'

Sarah half-smiled: self-consciousness, effacement even, from him was a rare thing. He acknowledged that his ability to complain was itself a sign of life.

'Carlyle?' she asked, removing the tray. 'Or Novalis?'

'Either,' said Lambert. He gave a little belch, hand balanced across his mouth. 'Both.'

He still wore his nightcap.

Lambert knew that she had been out for some hours the evening before, come home late, taken a bath. He knew that she lately kept secrets under his roof – kept them from him. He strongly suspected there was a man involved: there usually was, where a woman's secrets were concerned. He could not begrudge her that. His darling girl was a woman now. It was good, for the best, if someone could be there for her when he was gone.

She seemed very distant, and her mood was not bright. Lambert donned the aspect of good cheer.

> '"As Time and Hours passeth awaye,
> So doeth the Life of Man decaye.
> As Time can be Redeemed with no cost,
> Bestow It well…and let no Houre be Lost."'

Sarah stared at him blankly: sat up in the bed, propped on a bank of pillows, Lambert looked more gnomic than ever.

'Don't stand there staring, girl!' he shouted, but playfully. '"*Behold and begone about your business!*"'

Sarah took up the breakfast tray and turned out of the doorway. The second she was out of sight she scooped up the egg with her fingers and swallowed it. Ugh. He had sprinkled too much salt.

Lambert sat, patiently aware that she lingered just outside. Her head popped back around the doorjamb. 'I shall sit with you this afternoon,' she said, with seriousness of purpose.

Lambert merely nodded, and in a trice she was gone. Life…the very image of the woman who was life to him, and she was gone. Life might only be understood backwards, yet must be lived forwards. He must look forward.

Looking forward, Lambert saw the tip of his nightcap, dangling.

Taking two pieces at a time from his *coolamon*, Brippoki adds fresh fibres to his *kaargerum*, the string as it grows under the steady movement of his other palm. Hands working, his mind drifts. Unwilling thoughts, helpless to stop themselves, turn to his lost years as a youth – when he is no longer a boy, yet not a man.

Ngamadjidj, the whitefellow, comes in numbers far more than the *guli* can count. *Ngamadjidj* come, kangaroo go…blackfellows famish away.

With every passing day their anguish grows. *Walypela* keeps on coming, deeper and deeper up country, driving them further into the Bush. The land that has been theirs for countless generations is lost to them. Their birthrights are denied. Is it nothing, for them to receive nothing in return? But what can be given that is of equal value?

The forests and plains disappear, squatter settlements spreading over the whole of the country. There are more of the white man's *gunyas* than stars in the sky. Nothing else remains, as far as the eye can see.

Through soot and smoke, Brippoki looks out over London.

The days do not grow straight, as spears of grass. They are strands of spider web. He lives as his people came to live – hiding in the back country, deep in the territory of their enemies. It is country unfit to live in, offering little means of support, a place where, unless canny, a man might starve.

Deftly, he draws the two ends of the string back along his thigh, exerting a firm pressure to twist them tightly under, then rolling them with a swift motion down towards his knee.

The *walypela* problem is, they have no concept of fair exchange – only taking, never giving. Out of respect for the dead, and as a duty to those unborn, between the living there must be payback. This is the only correct way to conduct one's life – to acknowledge oneself as part of a continuum.

In the Reading-room at the British Museum, Sarah suffered hot flushes and felt her mind wandering. The day promised to be another hot one – bright, and hot. The library's ventilation was quite inadequate, too cold in the winter, too hot in the summer, and in England all four seasons often came the same day. It was not good for people. It could not be good for the books.

She turned over the brittle pages of Druce's manuscript, ready to resume her transcript. The new section began with a list headed 'The Names of the Ships'.

> 'First, *King George*, Captain Aflahen.
> 2. The *Inspector*, Captain Poole.
> 3. The *Betsy*, Captain Walker.
> 4. The brig *Venus*, Captain Steward.
> 5. The schooner *Governor Bligh*, Captain Grownns.
> 6. The *Ferret*, Captain Skelton.
> 7. The *3 Brothers*, Captain Worth.
> 8. The *George & Vulture*, Captain Brown.
> 9. The *King George*, Captain Moody, to whom I presented
> the said jewellery.'

Sarah didn't know what jewellery he meant. Nothing else was said of it.

> '10. The *General Wellesley*, Captain Dalrymple, which ship
> I completed with a valuable cargo after been done.'

The material went on to repeat that period of his life covered in his 1810 *Memoirs*, with several notable additions. No mention of the quest for gold dust, made so much of elsewhere.

The penmanship of the manuscript shifted; the curlicue of each letter 'd', significantly developed, indicated the presence of yet another new scribe – Dalrymple's identity abbreviated, with suitable flourish, to 'Capt. D.'

As the steady hours passed, the heat only increased. From somewhere across the Reading-room's vast circumference resounded a loud clatter, the fainting collapse of some other poor soul. James Hornblower, junior assistant to the Department of Printed Books, delivered to her designated seat the latest volume Miss Sarah Larkin had requested.

She looked up: he handed her the book – the compilation of *Tracts* containing the *Memoirs of Mr. George Bruce* from 1810; lost to them for a fortnight and at long last successfully re-ordered.

'Thank you, Mr Hornblower,' she mumbled thickly.

'Are you all right, miss?' enquired the fair-haired clerk.

He heard the break in her voice, and readily perceived that she was in some distress. When she looked up again, he saw the dark circles under her eyes.

'I-I'm…yes. Please,' she requested, 'leave me be.' She waved a weak hand and averted her face. 'I'll be all right.'

Events within the compared texts more than normally upset her, shortly bringing Sarah's work to an abrupt close.

Retreating back to the house, she lingered by their own bookshelves, over a section generally avoided: only a few titles, kept on one particular shelf – a chapbook, some poetry and plays for children, but mostly popular travel books, voyages of discovery, strange new lands and stranger people. Travellers' tales best expressed her mother's love of the exotic – a complement to her father's natural histories, Sarah supposed, but a curious collection for someone who, so far as she knew, had never been anywhere in her life except for Norfolk, Kent, and London.

How the spines had faded. Some titles Sarah remembered, others not at all. She couldn't find the one she had vaguely felt she wanted. Perhaps it wasn't a book after all.

The touch and feel of every object brought with it unwanted associations, emotions tender and exposed. These were among her mother's favourite things. *Modern Voyages* by the Reverend John Adams, another slim volume next to it; she picked it up.

The Shipwrecked Orphans.

Sarah felt unbearable heat, and a pressure behind the eyes. She fumbled to slide the book back into place, a thickness of mucus welling in her throat.

The *guli* belonging to the scrubs are strangers in their own country, the land no longer their own. Life having no meaning, violence, whoring, begging and theft become their new ways. The only escape from the misery of their days is in the bottle. No good blackfellows, all same like croppy, convicts and drunken sailors. Many times he is witness to the use of the flogging triangle, sees his clan brothers led away, linked in chains – brothers, father.

In his twentieth summer, the time comes for the man-child to receive the marks of adulthood. His back, shoulders, arms and chest scarred, he may yet enter into the fourth stage of his life cycle, *Wilyaru*.

> '*KARRO karro wimmari,*
> *Karra yernka makkitia…*'

As he works, Brippoki sings the cutting song. He feels the traces of the knife glow hot across his upper arms, his chest and shoulders, aware and proud of the emblems of his clan – the complex arrangement of dots, circles and long, livid lines that distinguish them from their neighbours.

> '*Karro karro kauwemukka…*'

As he endures the pain of his transformation, that same ancient skin-song fills the air. The words help to soothe his pain, guard his life against deadly dangers.

> '*Makkitia mulyeria,*
> *Karro karro makkitia…*'

His boyhood name, which is only shame to him, shall disappear in a sandstorm of new titles. During the cutting, he is called *ngulte*. The incisions made, until they begin to scab over, he is *yellambambettu*. After the sores have first healed, *tarkange*; when the skin rises, *mangkauitya*; and when the scars are at their glorious height, he will be *bartamu*.

The wounds are made very deep, and, to ensure they heal over in suitably elevated fashion, impacted with a mixture of sacred herbs and clay. His body becomes one with the land – their ritual homeland, lost to them since the incursions of *Ngamadjidj*.

As the scars criss-crossing his body prove, Brippoki has undergone the agonies of man-making.

The pain is almost too much. He sings louder.

With the change in appearance he will become a new and more powerful being, unrelated to that man-child he once was. His great pain is the pain of becoming, to be suffered in stoical silence, sufficient for him to earn full rank.

Finally accepted, cut in *Wilyaru*, his manhood, he stands to gain his new name, one that will reflect his new and adult status, come at last.

Only it never happens. A party of settlers armed with rifles interrupts the initiation at its most crucial point. Unceremoniously scattered, they flee for their worthless lives into the depths of arid scrubland. Without meaning, their lives are worth less.

Brippoki falls silent.

'All things,' Lambert insisted, 'living or no, come from the hands of the Creator, and retain the same distinctive characteristics they were blessed with.'

Sarah sat with her father because she had said she would. She made no mention of her night-time excursion to Piccadilly; it could serve no purpose. Instead, Sarah had made the very great mistake of telling him of her probable intent, to attend Sir John Lubbock on the occasion of his Thursday afternoon lecture to the Royal Institution. Lubbock was an evolutionist of the first order, a literal neighbour to Charles Darwin. This immediately set Lambert on his back foot.

'From the very beginning,' he said, 'the image of man rises before us noble and pure.'

Sarah was supremely tired of being lectured at, without resort to her own questions or opinions.

'As far back as we can trace the footsteps of man?' she asked.

Lambert was genuinely taken aback.

'Who have you been talking to,' he demanded, 'that you make the empirical demands of science?'

Sarah fell stubbornly silent. Nothing could be further from her mind, except her heart. Excluding itself, science found the whole world mad; and in that it shared much with religion.

'"And God said, Let us make man in our image, after our likeness. So God created man in his own image, in the image of God created he him. Male and female created He them."' Lambert laid a cool hand against her hot cheek. '"And God blessed them, and God said unto them, Be fruitful, and multiply, and replenish the earth…"' he paused for breath '"…and subdue it."'

Sarah's face was a picture.

Lambert relented a little. He knew of her sympathies.

'Yet, rather than convert by the holy sword,' he said, smiling, 'is it not preferable we use a bat? And may the best man win!'

If he was spoiling for a fight then she would give him one.

'You mean,' she said, 'survival of the fittest?'

'Evolution?' A flash of lightning. 'EVOLUTION?' A bolt of thunder. 'You *dare* speak to me of evolution?' Lambert railed. 'In *this* house?'

Sarah's mouth was working. She did not see the problem: Herbert Spencer had coined the phrase, although it had taken Darwin's *Origin of Species* to make it common currency – and they counted the works of both men under their roof.

'God created all things,' Lambert insisted, 'and each after its own kind. Every herb bearing seed, every tree yielding fruit, every fish, every fowl of the air…the beasts of the field and every creeping thing that creepeth upon the earth. They were not "evolved" one out of the other! The foundation of my argument is taken from the first book of Moses.'

Lambert leant a little forward in his bed, pointing a finger.

'I take the Word of God as my authority. By what right does Mr Darwin make himself a higher authority? He discovers what he finds in the world of Nature…which is itself the Work of God!'

'Father, you are – '

'Darwin's theories run contrary to revelation, and against Nature…against all that man's science knows of its workings! Has gravity a "fixed law"? The elements or their 64 chemical constituents, are *they* evolved? Fire, from air? Air, from water? Has carbon evolved from hydrogen or oxygen from nitrogen? Or vice versa, perhaps?

'No, only animals and plants…even Darwin dares no further.'

With one hand Lambert smoothed the top-sheet. 'No doubt a whale had hind legs once upon a time. One needs only go to the College of Surgeons, where they exhibit his thigh-bones, to see the proof! The poor creature languishes in the condition of a Chelsea or Greenwich Pensioner, his legs and feet quite gone…'

'Eh?' Sarah perked up.

'Protoplasm! We are to believe ourselves the descendants of…of slime! Oh, his ideas are not new, his precious theory but another revival, as old as Lucretius. The ancients would have it that everything had been fashioned out of mud. Hardly…*huk, hchaa*…original!'

Lambert carelessly gathered up a corner of bed-sheet and coughed into it. Sarah hated it when he worked himself up into a state, and not only for the risk it presented to his delicate health.

'This so-called law…of "natural selection", from which all living beings result! "The struggle of Life"? I'll show you struggle, my man!' His great meaty hands clutched thin air, throttling all competition. 'Bring on your ear-worming catchphrases, and I'll crush the Life out of every one!'

Lambert, lover of bird-life, of plants, had at one time approved the works of the eminent naturalist Mr Charles Darwin. The publication of *The Origin of Species*, however, had come as a shock, the worst in an age of shocks. So much so, he would no longer contemplate eating off the Wedgwood.

'Darwin, you ape. Transmutant! In one fell stroke you have attempted to pave over the Garden of Eden, arrest the Fall of Man, and most unforgivably of all, forgive… *You*! Forgive *us* Original Sin? Should I take your words over the Word of God?' Lambert shook his grey locks. 'I must then give up my black gown. The old sublime faith in God and heaven is gone!'

Having half-deliberately made the mischief, Sarah supposed she had to answer it. 'Darwin is a devout man,' she said. 'He does not mean to speak atheistically.'

'Oh, he professes to love his Maker! The Church, my girl, can be too Broad!'

Lambert Larkin watched her carefully, marking the shifts of colour in her cheek since he had brushed it: first blanching, when he had raised his voice, then blushing brighter than before. With a determination he found impressive she had forced her mood to cool. Only the line of her jaw betrayed her. Her lips were tight; and, he knew, set against him.

'There is evidence of a grand design to be found in Nature,' said Lambert, more calmly, 'and in this respect alone, Darwin is correct. It is the Voice with which the Deity proclaims Himself to man. But if a man believes it discovered in this debased sense, then he is doomed forever, a slave to his own wants. He *will* struggle for life! And a mortal struggle it shall be.

'The theory of evolution,' he rattled on, 'overlooks a most important point, and that is the enormous gap existing between the last stage of the animal and the first stage of man. How is it that we cannot trace the steps by which the *simiae* are advancing, until they approach the condition of men? Show me if you will where the one...' Lambert laughed at the inherent absurdity '...turns into the other.

'Darwinism supposes a human infant, from parents that were not human. How was the child educated...by a monkey? We ourselves, as men, with all of our accomplishments, are scarcely able to prevent our masses falling back into the state of brutes...savage man hasn't the ability to advance by himself!'

'If that is so,' started Sarah, 'then how do you explain – ?'

'If,' stated Lambert, oblivious, 'at the Creation, man had been cast out into the savage forest an orphan of nature, naked and helpless, he would have perished long before he learnt how to supply his most immediate wants.'

Sarah was arrested by a sudden vision of the fugitive Bruce.

'Abel, the shepherd,' offered Lambert, 'was anything but a savage.'

'You say the first man cannot have grown from an infant,' Sarah found herself saying, 'yet accept the idea of him being fully formed.'

She stated fact in order to frame a question, a conversational ploy she had learnt in dealing with Brippoki.

'Of...' Lambert was flabbergasted '...of course! There is less of the miraculous in supposing him to have been created a man, than as an infant without human parents,' he reiterated, spelling it out carefully. 'I believe it, as I believe in God...because it is impossible to believe the Universe exists without a Cause which is unseen.' Some small measure of desperation entered into his voice. 'Male,' he said, 'and female...created, thus perfect, and thus endowed... give us the proposition by which we can understand the whole human race! We would have no history, and no civilisation, without faith.'

His voice fell to a whisper. He searched her face for some trace of compassion.

'Without, all is dark, unintelligible...and irrational. To acknowledge the Lord,' said Lambert, 'is to know peace. Secure in the knowledge of His existence, all doubts cease. Why then should a man...or any person...born and brought up in the knowledge of Christ, choose to become an atheist?'

Lambert had been arguing what seemed the entire afternoon. Sarah was tired of explaining that neither she nor Darwin was in the least atheistic.

'What of these days, and the widespread abandonment of the gospel,' he went on, 'through sheer, unlettered ignorance?'

At some point soon, she thought, he must get short of breath.

'Now is the time when we must be on our guard most of all, the most critical of ignorance and falsehood...rather than running to embrace it.'

Sarah knew full well what, and who, he was being most critical of. Her mind was made up. She would go to the Royal Institute, and attend Sir John Lubbock, and see what he had to say, on this or any other matter.

'Our responsibilities to our fellow man have become an unspeakable burden. Unspeakable!' Lambert bemoaned his lot as a preacher out of work and favour. 'But that is the meaning of doasyoulike,' he said, 'free will. To accept, or decline. The choice exists for each individual, as it does for whole societies.'

He reached for her hand with his, and dumbly she took it up. Lambert motioned for her to come closer, and she accepted. His enormous dry hand went to stroke her on the cheek, and she barely flinched.

'The inferior creatures do not alter themselves,' he croaked. 'Man may change, but if he does so, it is by his choice. If he should become degenerate, as he surely does, it is his choice.'

He gave her permission, of a sort.

'What about the boomerang?' said Sarah. She felt determined to have her say.

'*What?*' Lambert's hand slid from her cheek.

She stated, calmly, 'It is a tool said to be, in all the world, unique to the Australians. Doesn't that show at least one small step in advance?'

Lambert gave every appearance of not listening. Whenever challenged, let alone contradicted, he would put in earplugs – more metaphorical than those favoured by Herbert Spencer, but no less effective.

'It cannot be a relic of primeval civilisation,' she reasoned, 'else how could it be confined to one race only? They have not learnt of it from any invader, for the same reason.'

'Old birds,' decreed Lambert, turning, 'are not caught by chaff.' He had not witnessed the boomerang in action at the Oval, not for himself. 'The miraculous art of "boomerang"-throwing,' he said, 'comes to us straight out of the old fairy-tales. There is sure to be a fairy princess who blesses her hero with wondrous gifts, usually a shield against dragon-breath, or a weapon of some sort. A sword, the blade of which may cut through anything. Armour impervious to all blows... Which would vanquish the other, do you think, if those two miracle forces should be opposed?'

Sarah began to wonder. Lambert, however, required no answer.

'In these same fairy-tales,' he said, 'we hear of arrows that always return to the archer. Next you will tell me their cricket bats have the powers of Harlequin's wonder-working wooden sword!'

In masquerade theatre, transformations occurred whenever the hero, Harlequin, manipulated his 'slapstick', two pieces of wood joined together so as to produce the appropriate noise when hitting another prop or character. This often provided the cue for a change of scene: ropes to be pulled, canvas flaps to fall. With cardboard, string, and endless afternoons, Sarah had patiently replicated such conjuring tricks in the toy theatrical productions of her childhood.

Lambert had had no time for them, even then.

Waving his 'wand', he affected a ridiculous, high-pitched voice. '"This bat receive, with fairy favours graced!"'

'You would not make so light of it,' snapped Sarah, 'if you had seen the wonders their team captain, Mr Lawrence, can perform with a cricket bat!'

She felt foolish even saying it.

'Pantomime tricks!' he shouted. 'Fiddlesticks! The present Australian savages are incapable of inventing the boomerang. It is the invention of their forefathers, *ergo*, their ancestors were superior.'

'Which would win, do you think,' said Sarah, 'if the Armour of God were pitched against the pious sword of the Israelite?'

Lambert's face went beetroot. '"This is an evil generation, they seek a sign. And there shall be no sign given it, but the sign of Jonas the prophet. For as Jonas was a sign unto the Ninevites, so shall also the Son of man be to this generation."'

His words were a fulsome curse. She dared equate the Bible with fairy-stories? Lambert lost all self-control; he began to lurch about in the bed, all coherence lost in a cacophony of coughs and splutters.

Sarah ran out of the room, only to return seconds later with a glass of water. She physically restrained him from collapse, pushing him back onto his bank of pillows, calming his fit, and then bringing the moisture to his lips. At length he was quieted.

She sat on the bed with him, herself reduced to a bag of nerves.

Lambert's eyes were tight shut. His lungs laboured for a time, rattling towards recovery, until he was able to take in sufficient breath to speak again.

Black smears under his eyes, he turned on her. His voice was a rasp.
"'The Greeks…ask for a reason… Jews look for a sign.'"
Sarah, in a daze, was unable to respond.
The weight of his body was so much lighter than she imagined.

As a child, when he has only a number for a name, *Kertameru* is punished for the things he does wrong, and knows the reason of it. As *Parnko*, a boy who grows towards becoming a man, he is taught *Bugaragara*, the Way of the Law. But when the white men come they break every law, every law including their own, without punishment. *Ngamadjidj* take their land, take their lives, take their *gins*, and gift nothing in return. No penalty is paid for their wrongdoing – instead, reward!

Truly, God is good and kind. If they pray to him, he forgives them everything. The white God must be stronger than *Bunjil*, than the Truth, the Way and the life. Blackfellows, the *guli*, must have greatly displeased the Ancestors to deserve such dreadful punishment.

Following the disruption of his initiation rites, Brippoki wanders the hills and desert of his former homelands, alone and disorientated. His spiritual rebirth aborted, he is hopelessly lost, in the most profound sense. The land itself transformed is strange to him.

Whether Black Cockatoo or White Cockatoo, *Gamadj* or *Grugidj*, the *guli* have always sung their territorial boundaries – Songlines, working like birdsong. No fixed frontiers exist, but rather points of exchange between different songs – a comparing of notes. Across each territory, swamp or desert, there are many different tongues. Although the words change, each song may be recognised by its melody.

Songlines interrupted, the tracks all but kicked away, they stumble in the footsteps of their Ancestors. Sickness in the land produces sickness of the mind. The melody is forgotten.

Brippoki's own Songline will always be imperfect, for having been cut short. Although he is a man, full-grown, and scarified as such, his transformation remains incomplete. Without No name, no man, he can never be admitted *bourka*, an elder. He will never be wise, or old. His secret shame is become his open curse.

Mindeye the destroyer comes, *Mindeye* the avenger. The props that hold up the sky are cut. The World is soon to end, the sky falling. These are the last words of the elders, as they die. Yet the Emu's egg still rises each morning, and at night rolls back into the black hole of the earth. *Gnowee* still searches for her lost son. The Law is broken, but the World carries on – without its people.

The sacred places are gone. With no country to call their own, there can be no more *corroborees*. Instead they gather around that great hole in the earth, the hole at the centre of all things, and await their turn.

Finding no words that can express or assuage his grief, Brippoki begins a tuneless keening. His afternoon's labours have produced a length of string – two-ply, woven from two separate strands, and strong. As it lengthens he winds it between two short sticks, driven into the ground and fastened cross-wise.

Time is endless oneness, like a circle, a loop unbroken. If a man is clever, he can find or forge a link to cross from one side to another. Equally, another one who is sly might reach out to redirect his present course, which he follows according to the signs he meets. They may also have the power to alter his destiny – for good, or more likely for ill.

Whether from within or from without, hope and anticipation, or anxiety and fear, characterise each stage of a man's life. To find the correct way forward, and protect him against the evils of another, requires a powerful charm. He takes up the string.

There, made his *min-tum*.

Grandfather chimes struck the hour of eight o'clock. The daughter hesitated on the landing outside her father's closed door; wanting neither to go in, nor to face him, but bound to do so.

'You haven't touched your dinner,' said Sarah.

'I do not want it,' said Lambert.

His words stung deliberately.

'And take out my po,' he said. 'You are forever allowing it too full.'

Insult to injury. In mute protest Sarah hung back.

'"CHILDREN,"' he said, '"obey your parents in the Lord."'

'"Honour thy father,"' she answered in kind. Sarah knew this lesson chapter and verse. '"And, ye fathers, provoke not your children to wrath."'

'"…but bring them up in the nurture and admonition of the Lord,"' replied Lambert.

The catechistic game sometimes played when she was a child had taken a serious turn. She could never win. Sarah would not stand to hear the next part from his lips: *SERVANTS, be obedient to them that are your masters according to the flesh.*

Storming downstairs, she cursed beneath her breath. Charles Darwin posited that the majority of our qualities were inherited. With every proximate step she prayed Darwin wrong.

CHAPTER XLVI
Wednesday the 17th of June, 1868

REGENTS IN EXILE

'I mourn the pride
And av'rice that make man a wolf to man.'

~ William Cowper, *The Task*

The air cools. Colours shifting in the western sky, the light gradually fades. Somewhere above the smudge of no horizon twinkles the first star of evening. Soon his brothers will join him, ready to run their nightly course.

Brippoki is glad to greet the end of days filled with sickness and thoughts of home. Hunger gnaws at his belly. Taking up his boomerang, he approaches a suitable tree, sizes up the odds, steps forward, and releases his weapon with an almost angry stroke. It strikes the ground in front of the tree and leaps high into the branches, but fails to strike any of the birds roosting there. They scatter noisily, and his main chance is gone.

He climbs the trunk instead, and recovers a rotten egg to roast on his fire. Whilst clinging there, he hides some of his shits in a fork between the higher branches.

Since the waterhole has dried up, pigeons no longer fly into his traps. With reluctance, he approaches the canal. To enter unknown waters is to risk the wrath of *Ngook-wonga*, spirit of such places. All same, he selects lengths of stick sufficient to protrude above the waterline, and, in that denuded region where he has plucked the bulrush root, drives them deep into the riverbed. He then retrieves the spear barb from his nostril, and takes up his dilly bag for a net.

Fish are scarce in these polluted regions; his catch is so small there seems little point in gutting them. Brippoki throws them on the fire whole, turns them once, and then scrapes away the scorched scales with a rusted spoon he has found. He devours them warm but almost raw, washed down with a single gulp from the abandoned egg.

The time to move on has already come and gone. Soon, he will have to.

Travelling between canalside and Guardian, Brippoki makes sure to vary his route. He favours stone or tile, keeping to rooftops and hard ground where his steps leave less trace. With each passing day of fine weather, it becomes easier. On occasion he walks on the sides of his feet, following well-worn grooves left by the innumerable carriages.

A hunter may lose the trail, yet, not having to cover its own tracks, still gains on its prey.

Brippoki takes up Thara's offer of tea with an avidity little short of desperation. Even boiled and stewed with select leaves, the brackish water near camp afflicts his bowels, but at least counters the lack of salt, which makes him costive.

Gulping liquid makes a man drowsy – and tiredness could kill. He takes only tiny sips. Of late, it is the best he can do to keep his mouth cool and moist, his thirst never properly slaked. One, two full cups are emptied before he finally relaxes.

'The next section of manuscript begins with a list of shipping,' said Sarah, returning to the task. Unusually businesslike and formal, she opened her notebooks almost immediately.

'At first I assumed it another record of those vessels on which Druce served,' she said, 'but given the context...' With barely a pause, Sarah glanced across at Brippoki. 'That is, thinking it over, I think it refers to ships calling in at the Bay of Islands while he was there.'

She seemed to have got away with saying the name, this time.

'He was living among the Maori, and had taken a wife, his consort...the Princess Aetockoe,' she said; her eyes averted, in shadow.

Brippoki repeatedly fingered a woven string, worn as a band around his waist – 'exhibiting' his charm. He stank ferociously, of fish-oil. Secured with a sort of gum, a variety of objects dangled from his hair: several small bones; what looked like a dog's tooth; a scrap of gauze. A short twig peeped from behind one ear, much as a clerk kept his stylus. His dark skin was coated with grease, and daubs of red and white as before, adornments of which he seemed inordinately proud.

Beneath such questionable finery, however, Sarah could not help but be aware of his decline. Complexion sallow, his eyes, formerly so bright, had become dull. His cheek, once full, had become sunken and drawn. Since his return he had refused whatever foodstuffs she provided, and, like some silly mother, she worried he would waste away entirely.

He appeared distracted, barely looking her way.

'So,' she said, finally, 'here it is... Druce quits New Zealand on board the *General Wellesley* with Captain Dalrymple...'

> Captain Dalrymple so earnestly requested that I go with him to the North
> Cape, and he promised me at the same time that he would not take me from

the Island let the weather be ever so bad. I went with him and satisfied him in his ideas.

He then put to sea in order to land me in the place I came from. That night we received a very heavy storm, which prevented him. Next morning he endeavoured to gain the Island, but, the storm still lashing, it was impossible. I was then obliged to take my passage with him to India. As soon as I found I was driven from the Island by bad weather, I endeavoured to console my consort of her grief, which was useless for some days.

The Captain used us with every kindness till we came to an island three thousand miles distant from New Zealand, where he proposed to me to remain to procure him a second cargo of sandalwood and to stay there till he returned, which proposals I refused. From this moment he took most bitter censure against me and in a few days afterwards turned me and my wife out of the cabin, telling us we must seek an abode for ourselves among the lascars of which the ship's company consisted.

Sarah paused.

'You know what a lascar is?' she asked.

'Yellowpella!' said Brippoki.

He sat on the carpet a few feet distant, winding a curl of hair around his fingers, and sipping slowly at his tea.

'Yes,' she said. 'An oriental, an oriental sailor.'

I had no bed, for the bed that I and my wife had, belonged to Captain D. My laying was on the timber with which I loaded her. In this miserable condition we existed till we came to Malacca. The voyage was prodigiously long (we was on the voyage from New Zealand to Malacca 9 months). The provisions all being exhausted necessity compelled us to eat the vermin, the Captain showing the example. The vermin being entirely dispersed, a silent motion in the ship was made to devour one another. There being a great many Englishmen on board as passengers, they secretly and firmly joined together to devour the black people.

'HOLO!' cried Brippoki, and started from his sitting position. His face assumed a look of absolute horror.

Witnessing his reaction, Sarah was mindful to move swiftly on.

The horrid act was to have been committed at 12. But the providential God prevented it by sending us a gale of wind at 8 o'clock the same night, which carried us to an island called Sulo in three days. The wind being fair cheered every soul that they felt not hunger. I have to say with truth that me and my consort, during a long famine in this ship, felt but very little of it for we was generally in good while the rest was in torture and pain.

'They not eat blackpellas?' enquired Brippoki, between hisses.

'No,' said Sarah.

He recovered his seat, appearing mollified; gently rocking the while. Sarah was glad of it, for stormier waters lay ahead.

> The ship being supplied at Sulo with every necessary she wanted, I then went to Malacca in her, Mr Cummings on board, who was a gentleman passenger. He went on shore and reported my case to the Governor, and all the ill-treatment I had received from Captain D. The Governor immediately sent for me. It being late in the evening when I landed, the Governor was then gone on a party of pleasure with the officers of Malacca so that I could not see him that night. When the Captain heard the Governor had sent for me on shore he ordered the people to weigh the anchor and get the ship under way. He then went to Penang, carrying my consort with him, for she was aboard.
>
> In the morning I waited on the Governor at his usual hour of doing business, where I was received in the most hospitable manner. The Governor took me wholly under his care and told me to console my mind regarding my wife, for it was in his power to restore my wife to me and make me amends for all the ill-treatment Captain D. had gave me. I was immediately clothed with the best and furnished with money and like necessaries I wanted. I wholly lived at the Governor's house. The Governor as soon as possible wrote to Penang respecting my consort, where he found she was bartered away by Captain D. to Captain Ross. The Governor wrote several times but receiving an impertinent answer every time he was fully determined to put the law in force against any person who should have detained her. He then wrote a letter to the Governor of Penang respecting me. I then went to Penang.
>
> When I came to the Governor of Penang, he told me to content myself that I should have my wife the next day. I left the Governor and returned to Captain Barrett, who had brought me there, and consulted him what I should do concerning my consort. He told me I had best go to Captain Ross who then had my wife in possession, and if he were a gentleman that considered his character, he would deliver up my wife without further hesitation. I immediately went to a tavern and got my dinner and then went to the house of Captain Ross. When I came there he was not at home, but his servant pointing him out to me in a distance from the house among a body of gentlemen I advanced towards them.
>
> He knew me, but I knew him not.
>
> As soon as he saw me he left the company and come and met me. In as polite a manner as I could I asked him if he would oblige me by pointing out Captain Ross among those gentlemen. In a very rough manner he asked me my business with Captain Ross. I told him. He then acknowledged his person to me. I solicited him in a most humble manner my wife.
>
> He hesitated awhile, asking me by what authority she was my wife. I told him by being ignorant enough to suffer the face God had given me to be disfigured, and losing my blood and suffering pain. According to the rules of her country she was mine.

He told me she was out with his wife and child and neither of them would be home that night, but if I would come in the morning at 8 o'clock, and if she was willing to come with me, I should have her accordingly. I came. He presented my wife to me, after an absence of three months. She was deeply affected, which occasioned her a flood of tears. He accosted me in a very rude manner, telling me not to make her cry, and asked me, as it was the last morning, would I permit her to breakfast with his wife, for she being so careful of the child his wife was very fond of her. To which, I consented. He never had the kindness to invite me, though at that time I did not want it.

During the breakfast time while I was waiting he conveyed my wife with his own into a room and locked the door. After I tired my patience with waiting I went up one pair of stairs to where I had left them at breakfast. I told Captain Ross I thought their breakfast was long. He replied with a half-laugh (as all rogues do) that they had done breakfast some time, and, pointing to the door of the room that was locked, told me that the New Zealand woman was in that room with his wife. And if I liked to call her, I might, and if she liked to come out, she might. But not to enter that room, for there was deposited all his riches. If I broke the door, he would have me hanged.

I went away dishearted.

I then went to the Master of the Court, whose name was MacAvoy. He knew me by the marks in my face, and he told me he would have nothing to do with it, that the business was settled.

I went away to the Governor and informed him of the whole business. The Governor made no delay, but immediately sent for my wife and ordered Captain Ross to quit that island. My wife being questioned at the Governor's respecting Captain Ross, she informed him that he had told her that *he* was the Governor of that island, and meant to buy a ship on purpose to take her back.

I was then returned to Malacca with my consort with me, where I remained till a passage was provided for me and my consort in the *Sir Edward Pellew*, commanded by Captain Stephens. I then took my passage for Bengal, where the case was tried before the Governor General, Right Honourable Lord Minto. I arrived in June 1809. Everything was arranged, and allowed 180 rupees per month from thence, I was put under the care of Squire Leyden, who was *aide de camp* to the Governor General and also was one of the twelve Masters of the Grand Lodge of London.

I was with this man three long months, where I became well acquainted with most of the signs of the Freemasonical arts, by having a free commerce to his own library. By his free will and permission he put into my hands one day a book which he privately kept locked up, and told me that it possessed the full power which Freemasons was in possession of, at the same time pointing out to me sundry places which was not to be read by one single person. This book thoroughly convinced me of all the Ideas that I had formed within my own breast for several years, my father being one. I was fully resolved to find out the meaning of it. No man on earth was able to instruct another with more wisdom, which he took every opportunity of his leisure time during the three months I was with him.

I then took my passage by the order of Lord Minto in a ship named the *Union*, commanded by Captain Lutterel, owner Mr Lone. We sailed with express order for New Zealand, my wife being pregnant. There was another woman put onboard who said she was a midwife, to take care of my consort whenever she was ill. We left the land of Bengal in the evening. The next day we see a fleet to windward, which we supposed to be a French frigate who had got English prizes. We kept them in sight the whole day. Dark coming on, we lost sight of them. The next morning the frigate was close to us. The Captain, taking her for a French frigate, ran away from her till she came so close that the shot brought her to, and when the boat came alongside it proved to be His Majesty's Ship *Cornelia*, commanded by Captain Edgehill. He immediately jumped in the boat and came on board the *Union*, where I introduced my consort. The honourable Captain seemed highly pleased and expressed the highest wishes to serve me and my consort with anything he had on board. It being due time, he honoured us with his company to breakfast. After breakfast he insisted that he would accompany us with his ship till my consort should be safe over her trouble, assuring us at the same time that the surgeon of his ship was well used in midwifery, for he attended several ladies in Bengal. He then gave orders to the Captain of the *Union* to keep close under his lee, and if my consort was to be taken bad in the night a gun was to be fired, and by day a signal hoisted at the Mizen peak. This was September 5th, 1809.

Well he might remember the dates.

My consort was taken bad on the 9th, early in the morning between 5 and 6. The signal was momently hoisted to Captain Edgehill's orders but by some neglect of the quartermaster on board of the frigate the signal was not seen for some time. I went to the Frenchwoman who was on board the *Union* and told her my consort wanted immediate assistance. She went into the cabin to my wife. I went on deck. In a few minutes I was called by Mr Lone, telling me that my wife was dying. I went to the cabin door where I found the terrified Frenchwoman with the door in her hand screaming out in shock, telling me that my wife was dead, in which I pushed her out of the cabin and shut the door.

This Mr Lone was as bad as the Frenchwoman. He was no better than a notorious rogue, and she proved to be a common prostitute for leaving my wife in the distressed manner she was in. By the ordinance of Providence I delivered my wife of a fine girl during of which time the…

Sarah blushed. 'The word as it is written is "*buste*",' she said. 'B-u-s-t-e. I leave it to your imagination.

…Lone stood at the cabin door crying out if my wife or child died he would have me hanged. As soon as the trouble was over, and everything safe, necessity compelled me to put the child into the hands of the terrified Frenchwoman, which she handled very tenderly and dressed it while I put my wife to bed.

By this time they perceived the signal on board the frigate. The doctor and Captain momently came on board. When Captain Edgehill asked how long the signal had been hoisted, he was greatly incensed against all who had the morning watch aboard his ship. But finding everything was safe he advised me to let the doctor see my wife, after which he very kindly entreated me to go on board H.M.S. *Cornelia*, to which I readily consented, accompanied by Mr Lone. After having partaken of a cold collation we then returned to our ships, and straight read our course for New Zealand, in the South Seas.

Druce's princess recovered and delivered of their baby girl, they regained the coastline of Australia – almost home.

Sarah knew and dreaded what was coming.

After the passage of three months we came to an anchor in the Derwent, one of His Majesty's settlements in the South Seas, where we found Commodore Bligh in great distress on board His Majesty's Ship *Porpoise*. He detained our ship to supply his wants. This was the cause of my missing the passage to New Zealand with my consort.

After the stay of three months at the River Derwent Governor Macquarie arrived at Port Jackson, when he gave a moment's order for all vessels to repair for headquarters. The letters were then broken open that Lord Minto sent with me from Bengal, concerning New Zealand. The Governor then assured me that nothing should be lost to dispatch me to New Zealand. I then took leave of the Governor and returned to my lodgings, when on my road I met Mr Riley, a gentleman who was secretary to the late Governor Patterson of Port Jackson, who informed me that Colonel Paterson wanted me. I went to the Colonel, where I was introduced to three rich merchants who invited me to dine with them. My wife was with me, and in good health at that time.

After dinner Mr Riley asked me if I had any objection to join with him and those three merchants in procuring cargoes from New Zealand. The next day I was sent for by Governor Macquarie, who informed me he had sanctioned my entering into a bond with Mr Riley, Williams, Cant, and Simeon Lord. I then went to the house of Simeon Lord, where articles were drawn up. In a few days after my wife took sick with the dysentery, and in fourteen days was a corpse.

Brippoki froze in mid-rocking motion. He would not look at Sarah, but appeared to listen closely for whatever was to happen next.

I went to Mr Riley to tell him of the death of her, but when I knocked at the door Mr Riley was bad so that I could not see him. I then went to the other three gentlemen, and told them I wanted some money to put my wife in the ground. But as soon as they found my wife was dead they told me there was no prospect of New Zealand, and they would have no more to do with it.

I then went to Mr Wells, a gentleman who know me. I told him how the concern has used me. He assisted me with every expense of the funeral, on conditions that I would send him flax from New Zealand, which he knew I could supply him with any quantity. As soon as the Princess was interred, I acquainted the Governor with the treatment I received from the gentleman that took me out of his hands, and that Mr Riley the chief merchant held my articles, so that I could not recover the money due to me from the concern, which was one thousand pounds. By breaking the said articles the Governor was highly displeased with the conduct of Mr Riley, Cant and Williams, and Simeon Lord, but he told me he was so busy with the affairs of the colony that he could not do anything for me. I then returned to my lodgings.

I cannot express the state of my mind at that time. I only say that sorrow upon sorrow crushed me to the earth, nay to the mortification of my very soul.

In a few days after came the true account of the ship *Boyd* being totally destroyed at New Zealand. This news drove all the merchants of that colony in such fear, that it was beyond hope of my obtaining a passage to New Zealand at that time.

I then entered on board His Majesty's Ship *Porpoise*, where I arrived in England, 1810. The war was hot, so that no account was took of me, nor New Zealand, at that time.

Sarah hated leaving Druce at such low ebb, since it stranded them likewise. Aetockoe was dead.

Sarah and Brippoki sat for a considerable while, together but apart.

Brippoki stood. Eyes flicking past hers, he shyly excused himself. 'Go now,' he said.

'Yes,' she said. She hadn't the energy to hold him. 'No, wait…'

Sarah spoke too quietly and too late. She sat alone in the room, the notebooks on her lap still open.

Clutching her grumbling belly, she sat back. She needed to rest, to go to bed.

Druce's blunt handling of his wife's passing had, on first reading, seemed almost unforgivable – the Princess Aetockoe, never much present in the narrative while alive, dismissed almost summarily in death. Yet in reciting these, his few, simple phrases, she experienced for herself the sting of a belated guilt and remorse; genuine depth of feeling finally communicated, not as written word, but by being spoken or heard.

More telling for its brevity, Druce's recounting thereby revealed – to the lonely daughter of a grieving father – a kernel of emotional truth.

Aetockoe's fate affected her so unreasonably because Sarah subconsciously identified the princess with her own mother. The barest recall of a sensation, something significant, fluttered beneath her drooping eyelids and then was gone.

'I, with the assistance of Divine aid, delivered my beloved consort of a fine female child,' the concluding part of his *Memoirs* had read: detail differed between the two accounts, but only slightly concerning the most crucial aspects. Joseph Druce went up a notch in her estimation for having delivered his own baby. And what might now become of the infant?

CHAPTER XLVII
Thursday the 18th of June, 1868

THE PROMISED LAND

'Anecdote of Captain Holloway.

"Why Jack," he exclaimed, "you are always reading the Bible!
are you going to write a commentary on it?"

"No, sir," replied Captain Holloway, "but the longer I read that
book, the greater my eagerness to return again to its perusal: I
find in it all the principles of my duty; and among other things,
To put my trust in God, and not in any child of man."'

~ *Calcutta Gazette*

Brippoki sits beside the smouldering ash of his campfire, only semi-conscious.
His eyes are open, but vacant and unseeing. Days and nights without sleep have
begun to take their toll…

It is days after the attendance of his first convocation, a gathering of many
clans along the *Wirrengren* plains – his first as an initiate, in youth, when he is no
longer a child but not yet a man. Returning to his homelands by a circuitous
route, he goes Walkabout. He walks to forget his troubles, the shame of his
deformity not least among them.

In his wanderings he crosses and re-crosses 'large star', the *Millewa*, the
brightest big one water. It is along the banks of this river – his parents returning
from another convocation – that he was first born. *Millewa yarra yarra*, ever
flowing.

He climbs *Yerrarbil*, and, having climbed *Yerrarbil*, *Kilmarbil*. The rocky tip is
a single block of granite that blots out the sky. Dark even in morning light, it
towers over the green of the surrounding grasslands, where flows *Ngin-da-bil*.
He crosses at the flats of *Warringal*, 'dingo jump up', where the *yarra* trees take
root at the very brink of the stream. Wind in their leaves sets them talking, and
they tell him which way to go. On the far side of *Ngin-da-bil* he passes into hill
country never walked before. The grey slopes are dappled with tiny white and
pale yellow blooms, like the down of a *yarrilla*-bird.

He comes to a chain of lagoons, so deep their waters return no light. White-barked eucalyptus cluster around, ironbark, bluegum, and stringybark.

The piercing shriek of a suburban train cuts into his reverie, the rattle and rhythm of its many passing carriages. Mellowed by distance, it seems little more than exotic birdcall.

From the summit of *Mullup-cowa*, the tall mountain with a little head, the smoke fingers of many campfires trace the course of the *Wimmera* through a broad landscape, forested land so uneven that only the tops of trees are visible, growing in the hollows.

The sound of a tumbling brook, the play of sunlight on purling waters through a grove of trees – winding stream, *Pat-la-panroo*. He is almost home. Feasting on *pirpir* the wood duck from the place of feathers, swamp and scrub, the green hill of *Kinganyu*, and on its far side…home.

A black dot moves across the distant country spread before him – a single warrior, running at great speed. It is, he realises, himself.

Brippoki's vision shimmers, trembles, and grows dark. He bows his head, pleasurable thought so intermingled with sadness, he can no longer tell which is which.

It was a perfect summer's day outside, the sun shining bright and not a single cloud in the sky. Sarah Larkin barely noticed.

She bent to examination of the papers recently forwarded from the office of the Admiralty. The indulgent clerk had copied out articles of correspondence in his own neat hand, with some additional commentary in parentheses.

The first of these excerpts appeared to be a copy of a letter written by or on behalf of George Bruce himself.

TO THE RIGHT HON. EARL BATHURST,
SEC. OF STATE FOR THE COLONIAL DEPARTMENT

My Lord,

In June last I took the liberty of presenting to your Lordship my humble Memorial, stating among many other circumstances that it had been my fate to reside for a considerable period among the Natives of New Zealand, and pointing out the probable services I might render to any of my countrymen who might touch there, in the event of my being permitted to return. To this I have received no answer; and from an apprehension that, amidst the multiplicity of business, the case of such an insignificant individual as myself may have been totally forgotten, I venture to present my Memorial a second time, humbly requesting that your Lordship, will condescend to inform me whether anything can be done to forward my earnest wishes to return to N.Z.

I have the honor to be, my Lord,

Your Lordships Most Humble and Obedient Servant,

GEORGE BRUCE

His Majesty's ship Namur *at the Nore, Nov 8th 1813*

[Despatch per ship *Three Bees*; receipt acknowledged by Governor Macquarie to Earl Bathurst, 12th May 1814]

Downing Street, 13th November, 1813

Sir,

I am directed by Lord Bathurst to transmit to you the Copy of a Memorial, which has been presented to His Lordship by a Person of the Name of Bruce, in which amongst other circumstances it is stated that you advised him to come to this Country; And I am to request you will report for the information of the Secretary of State how far the Allegations therein contained are correct, as far as they may have come under your knowledge.

I have, &c.,

HENRY GOULBURN

[Enclosure.]

THE MEMORIAL OF GEORGE BRUCE TO EARL BATHURST

Namur *at the Nore, 4th June, 1813*

The Memorial of George Bruce most humbly Sheweth, –

That your Memorialist is a native of Scotland, and that about ten years ago he entered His Majesty's Service at New South Wales on board the Francis *Schooner, and that he was afterwards drafted into the* Lady Nelson *Tender, in which he was, when Tipoo-hee, the Chief of New Zealand paid a visit to Captain King, then Governor of New South Wales: – that the* Lady Nelson *was appointed to convey the said Tippoo-hee back to New Zealand, and that during the passage he became much attached to your Memorialist, from his attention to said Chief during his sickness; and that you [sic.] Memorialist, induced by the earnest intreaties and great promises of Tipoo-hee consented to leave his ship and to remain behind at New Zealand; that your Memorialist remained behind at New Zealand upwards of three years, during which time he bacame [sic. &c.] thoroughly acquainted with the customs, manners and language of the natives; that he married the Daughter of Tipoo-hee, was made a Chief, and had uncontrouled authority over the Island.*

The naval clerk interjected a longer note at this point. '[Records state Te Pahi ("Tipoo-hee") was chief only of a small area around Whangaroa, Bay of Islands]'

Your Memorialist further humbly states, that the Honourable the East India Company's Ship General Wellesley *arrived at New Zealand, and that through his exertions and authority a Cargo was immediately supplied the said Ship, for which kindness he met with a very ungrateful return: – that the Natives were induced to consent that your Memorialist should accompany the Captain of the* General Wellesley *to the North Cape (the North End of the Island) under a solemn promise from the said Captain, that he should not be taken away from the Island; but that in violation of this solemn promise, your Memorialist, together with his Wife, were treacherously conveyed to Malacca; from whence, on his case being represented to Admiral Drury (who happened to be there at the time), he was forwarded to Bengal.*

Your Memorialist humbly adds, that here he was treated with distinguished kindness and humanity by Lord Minto, who paid two thousand rupees for his passage back to New Zealand in the ship Union, *under a conviction that your Memorialist would be of essential service to his Country by protecting and forwarding the views of any Ships that might touch there either for the purposes of commerce or Discovery. Your Memorialist, however, was never forwarded to his destination, but was left by the* Union *at New South Wales; which colony was at that time in a state of great confusion from the arrest of Governor Bligh. Your Memorialist adds, that he was obliged to remain at New South Wales three months, where his wife died, and that having made his case known to Colonel McQuarry [sic.], he was advised by that Gentleman to take a passage to England in His Majesty's Ship* Porpoise, *and to communicate his situation to his Government at home.*

Here was another note. '[Deposed as governor in Sydney, Bligh promised to return to England in HMS *Porpoise*, sailing instead to the Derwent, where he remained for some time. The *Union* arrived there when he was short of supplies, and he commandeered the necessary stores from that vessel. This prevented the *Union* from proceeding to New Zealand, and she was obliged to sail for Sydney instead.]'

On his arrival in England about eighteen months ago, your Memorialist represented his case to Lord Liverpool, and was by him referred to the Right Honourable Spencer Percival; but the lamented death of this Gentleman prevented his receiving any benefit from such application. Your Memorialist, having expended his little all, was obliged to enter into His Majesty's Navy and is at this time on board His Majesty's Ship Namur *at the Nore.*

The object of your Memorialist in this humble representation is to procure permission to be sent out, as well as a passage to New Zealand, where he has considerable property and where he is certain that his influence and authority over the Natives would enable him to confer great benefits on such of his Countrymen as might be induced to trade there. Your Memorialist is enabled to state, from information he received, that, during his detention at New South Wales, the Ship Boyd *having touched at New Zealand, the Natives, irritated at the treachery used towards him and his wife, murdered the whole of her Crew except a Woman and one or two Children, and burnt the Vessel; and he is convinced that, in the event of his being permitted to return, he would propitiate the minds of the Natives towards his Countrymen.*

Your Memorialist is impressed with a deep sense of the truth and importance of Christianity; and during his residence on the Island used his efforts (as far as his knowledge enabled him) to convince the Natives of the superiority of his religion over their own miserable superstitions, and he believes, that if furnished with proper books, he would be of great service in this respect, and might at least pave the way for the success of future Missionaries of the Gospel: or that, if such should arrive during his life time, he would protect their persons and forward their labours.

In the humble expectation that his case will be taken into consideration, and his prayer granted,

> *Your Memorialist as in duty bound will ever pray,*
> GEORGE BRUCE

Continuing on the same sheet, Dilkes Loveless had transcribed, *in toto*, the relevant portion of Governor Macquarie's reply.

REPORT ON MEMORIAL OF GEORGE BRUCE

12 May 1814

To Henry Goulborn Esq., Under Secretary of State, Downing St., LONDON

I have perused the above Memorial with much attention, and in Obedience to the Commands of the Secretary of State, beg leave to submit for His Lordship's information the following remarks thereon: Namely — 1stly the assertion made by George Bruce in his Memorial, in regard to my having advised him to go to England, is totally unfounded; having gone thither entirely of his own Accord — He was greatly involved in debt here, and to avoid paying them he entered himself as a sailor on board His Majesty's Ship Porpoise, *and returned to England in her in May 1810. 2ndly George Bruce (who went by the name of Dreuse in this Country) came originally a convict to this Colony, Deserted from the Govt. vessel* Lady Nelson *at N.Z., where he remained, and afterwards married the Daughter of the Chief Tippahee. 3rdly I believe he went to Bengal in the manner he describes, and practised gross impostures on that Government, representing himself as a Prince of New Zealand, and as being a Man of great consequence there, by which means he obtained considerable Sums of Money from the Bengal Govt., and a Passage back to this Colony, where he arrived about the time of my assuming the Govt. of it. 4thly It is not true that George Bruce, alias Dreuse, possesses any interest or authority in N.Z.; where he is, on the Contrary, much despised and disliked, on Account of his ill-usage and neglect of his wife, the Daughter of the Chief Tippahee; by whom he had an only child (a Girl) who is now supported in the Female Orphan School at Sydney; the poor unfortunate Mother having died here some little time before her Husband returned to England in the* Porpoise; *and by whom she was most shamefully and cruelly neglected in her last illness — 5thly to conclude these remarks, I must observe that George Bruce (whose character is perfectly well-known in this Country) is man of no principle whatever, of desperate fortune, much given to drunkenness, and every kind of dissipation, and of most profligate manners in all other respects —*

I therefore strongly recommend that George Bruce, alias Dreuse, may never be permitted to return to this Country, nor to N.Z.; in which last, instead of doing any good, he would do a great deal of injury and mischief, both to the natives of that Country, and to such European Traders as might chance to touch there — I have the honor to be, Sir

> *Your Most Obedient and Faithful Humble Servant,*
> *L. MACQUARIE*

The paperwork fell limp in Sarah's hand.

She fired off a quick thank-you to the Admiralty clerk, plus an enquiry after the *Porpoise*. She then took up the list of names, amended with those pulled from her latest transcript and the Admiralty correspondence, and tucked it back into her notebook. Making a fresh note at the top of a separate sheet – '*Female Orphan School, Sydney*' – she appended that too.

Lambert expressed surprise to see her still at home so late in the morning, but soon enough made sure to frown. She left him to his own devices: if he was healthy enough to bear a grudge, he was healthy enough to be left alone. She made ready for her afternoon's excursion. While there was still time, she wanted to drop into the library on her way.

Returned to Druce's manuscript, Sarah recognised the scrappy and erratic handwriting of its original scribe: no more exaggerated 'D's. She almost welcomed her old foe.

Even as she worked on the *Life*, Sarah's thoughts stayed with the 1813 *Memorial*. The contrast between solicitation and response had been truly shocking. Governor Lachlan Macquarie's round condemnation of the character of 'George Bruce', if anything, had sentenced Joseph Druce to his subsequent wanderings.

In the follow-up letter of enquiry, sent to Earl Bathurst from the Nore late in 1813, Druce had referred to himself as 'an insignificant individual…totally forgotten'. He thought himself ignored.

Sarah looked to the work in hand. Narrating his *Life* in his dying days, Druce had proceeded unaware of Macquarie's blistering response. All he knew was that his petitioning of the powers-that-be had been to no avail.

Druce ever expended the greater part of his energies on the offensive. The *Memoirs* amounted to little else than a list of grievances, and the *Life* not much more, the accused named and comprehensively shamed. Dalrymple, Ross, Lone, Grey, even the neglectful quartermaster of the *Cornelia* – the list she kept of those individuals who had crossed him, who had wronged him, grew ever longer. There could be no doubt, Druce considered himself sorely used, profoundly more sinned against than sinning.

In crafting a complex saga of intrigue and woes, ill-fortune and tragedy, all other players, even his wife – whose trials and fate engendered her more natural sympathy – were confined to bit-parts. The emphasis throughout was on hapless, blameless Druce, at the mercy of a relentless train of events.

A Mr Wells had met the costs of Aetockoe's funeral arrangements. His princess bride dead, his imposture revealed, Druce, no prince of New Zealand, was summarily cast off from the local merchants' scheme; probably leaving him no means to honour that debt. Governor Macquarie declared as much in his *Report*; Sarah merely put two and two together.

News of the *Boyd* massacre, with the loss of all hands, had only compounded Joseph Druce's misery, crushing any chance of his returning to New Zealand. Why else quit New South Wales?

Sarah abandoned the manuscript for a time. Nothing felt quite like the full story.

With a little diligent research she uncovered a few telling details about the gentlemen behind 'the concern', the colonial merchants who had reneged on their agreement following the sudden death of the princess – Alexander Riley, Francis Williams, Cant (or, in the *Memoirs*, Kent), and Simeon Lord – and, significantly, of their involvements with Governor Macquarie.

Simeon Lord, born 1770, had been sentenced to seven years' transportation for stealing tenpence-worth of cloth – almost exactly as Druce had been. Similarly, on arrival in New South Wales, some time in the 1790s, he was assigned in servitude to a military officer. Once emancipated, having the advantage of a few years and no doubt greater business sense, he became an employer himself, and, in a few years, local magistrate. His entrepreneurial venture in a cheap goods factory was encouraged by none other than Governor Macquarie, who 'favoured him greatly'. It was Simeon Lord who chartered the *Boyd*, the unfortunate ship calling in at the Bay of Islands for spars – where it met with a massacre.

By all accounts a man of unimpeachable integrity, Lachlan Macquarie's personal antipathy towards Bruce, '*alias Dreuse*', spiralled out of proportion. Convict, bushranger, deserter – the governor quite possibly resented Druce more for the roundabout ways in which details of his shady past emerged than for the crimes themselves, since obviously, as an associate of Lord, he was sometimes willing to overlook a dark past. Druce's accusing of Riley and Lord, with whom Macquarie was in public partnership, might have been enough to make the man deaf to his pleas, but there was more. From the very beginnings of colonisation the authorities' greatest fear had been that settlers might degenerate, or 'go native'. Further, Macquarie was said to distrust enthusiastic proponents of religion. With his tattooed face and *extempore* sermonising, Druce couldn't have picked a less sympathetic person to pray to.

Lachlan Macquarie was in business with 'the concern'.

And how stupid! How stupid of 'George Bruce' to petition as a Scotsman, to a truer Scot if ever there was one, and one already suspicious of his dishonesty. It was surely the end of his hopes of ever seeing the coasts of Australasia again.

Colonial life was harsh and unforgiving, said by many to shrivel the faith, just when it should have been inspired to greater heights. The same might hold true of any life if filled with enough disappointment. But that was the remarkable thing about Druce. All of the heartache, the hardship and disaster, had diminished his faith not a jot.

As was clear from his prayers and his constant petitioning, Joseph Druce put as much credence in officialdom as he did in God. He believed in the benevolence of higher authority, consistently so. And yet by their actions, unwittingly or no, two successive governors – Bligh and Macquarie – had frustrated his chances and confounded his hopes.

Sharpening up her pencil with a small blade, Sarah added both names to that growing list: the hated men against whom, according to the savage custom of his adopted nation, Druce might pronounce all vengeance – if not in this life, then the next.

CHAPTER XLVIII
Thursday the 18th of June, 1868

SUPERSTITION?

'Look, how the world's poor people are amaz'd
At apparitions, signs, and prodigies,
Whereon with fearful eyes they long have gaz'd,
Infusing them with dreadful prophecies.'

~ William Shakespeare, *Venus and Adonis*

'What is "superstition"? Dictionary Johnson, who was no dialectician and, moreover, superstitious, gives eight different definitions of the word...which is equivalent to confessing of an inability to define it at all.'

Gentle laughter shivered through the audience. Sarah was gratified to find Sir John Lubbock a good, clear, and so far sensible speaker. The Royal Institute's public lectures were delivered in a large amphitheatre generously lit by an enormous skylight, in Albemarle-street, a quarter-hour's brisk walk from her house.

This was already the fifth of Lubbock's lecture series *On Savages* (a follow-up to his 1865 bestseller, *Prehistoric Times*). The first half of the afternoon's talk had dwelt on 'Animal Husbandry', Sarah missing most of it. The latter part – copiously illustrated by use of the electric lamp, diagrams and the display of specimens – happily devoted itself to 'The Superstition of Savages'.

'Let us, then,' said Sir John, 'look a little further back. The original Greek for superstition is *deisdaimonia*, meaning fear of the deity. God-fearing, if you will.'

The Institute held as its object the advancement of knowledge in general, of the sciences in particular; and women were welcome to attend. Sitting a few rows from the back, Sarah observed that she was far from alone – nor even, for once, in the minority. Politician, financier, social reformer and also a hugely successful author, Sir John Lubbock enjoyed international fame, his name known to every household: still in his early thirties and a baronet to boot, he could be considered quite the catch.

'The Latin *superstitio* has more or less the meaning of the English word, said to come from *super*, above, combined with *sto*, stand, and to express the feeling of having some being standing over us...'

Sarah knew that feeling well, although she had never thought of it as superstition exactly; she had never been sure if that oppressive being was God, or simply her father.

'Theoprastus tells us, in his *Characters*, that superstition is simply "cowardice about the supernatural". The Reverend Kingsley, standing on this same platform but a year ago, perhaps had this in mind when he defined superstition as "Fear of the unknown". He argued it a physical affection, as thoroughly material and corporeal as eating and sleeping, remembering…or dreaming.'

Sir John gave a dramatic pause.

'Be that as it may,' he said, 'we will return to it…anon.'

A worm hooked to his rod, the audience rippled with another minor thrill. Sensing their delight, Sarah determined to resist his charms. Lubbock had a handsome enough face, his features open, if a little soft. His comparative youth was accentuated by that which was intended to disguise it: an extravagant but wispy goatee beard.

'We may see how superstition covers a wide range of mental attitudes and behaviours,' the man said. 'For our own purposes, superstition may be defined, overall, as that disposition to see an occult hand in events, and also, any attempt to appease that occult power.

'Turning to the consideration of savages, only the poorest ethnologist, or indeed anthropologist, would attempt pursuit of the noblest study of mankind and leave out consideration of their religions.'

Sarah felt suddenly certain Lubbock had attended St James's Hall on Tuesday night.

'According to almost universal testimony,' he said, 'that of merchants, philosophers, naval men and missionaries alike, many races of men are altogether destitute of a religion, or anything deserving of the name. While I do not dispute these findings in the least, on their own terms, I defer to Professor Max Muller, and his learned endeavour to explain the profound influence of natural phenomena on the mind of early man.'

The image of a rather shocking sculpture flashed onto the screen behind him, the chamber in daytime unfortunately too light for it to be very clearly seen. Sir John did his best not to find the poor show distracting, although impatience sounded clear in his voice.

'Among savage nations,' he said, 'their beliefs are characterised almost entirely by a fear of the unknown. They are exceedingly superstitious. The names of God, likewise fetishes, and statues, were their first attempts to express the inexpressible. Only when taken away from their original intent does monotheism collapse into pantheism. The *eidolon*, or likeness, becomes an *idol*, and the *nomen*, or name, a *numen*, or demon. Hence, the very great power of names.

'Religion is characterised by the strength of its appeal to the hopes and fears of mankind. In times of sorrow and sickness, it is of great consolation. If the names of the sun and moon, of thunder and lightning, light and day, night or dawn, cannot yield fit appellatives for the Deity, where are they to be found? Such is Professor Muller's opinion, as expressed in his *Comparative Mythology*.'

Giving up on the screen and the ghosts of ghosts manifest there, Sir John swung around.

'We suppose Christianity to have swept away pantheistic superstitions and the worship of multitudinous gods,' he said. 'They were in fact overtaken, and overlaid with a Christian meaning...transformed. Not so much god in everything but God as everything.

'The primary purpose of religion, the reason for its institution, was, and is, that man needs to see himself as more than the animal, the animal that his nature condemns him to realise he is.'

He only sought to join together the two halves of his afternoon's discussion, but for Sarah Sir John expressed powerful sentiments. In the midst of sorrow, doubts and sickness, her heart was in her mouth.

'And so, ladies and gentlemen, if the sensation of fear, fear of phenomena more powerful than oneself...if that sensation can be thought of as religion, then religion is indeed universal to the human race. Let us take, as our prime example, modern man in his most primitive form, the native Australian.'

Drawn to the very edge of her seat, Sarah had to adjust her skirts.

Sir John's political instincts had led him to cast the popular vote, but his choice was more selfish than that: a useful left-handed batsman and fast underhand bowler, the Liberal Party's parliamentary candidate for West Kent was also associated with its Cricket Club, and played on occasion for the House of Commons team.

'Among the scattered tribes of the Australian Aborigine,' he said, 'in Victoria, in Queensland, in New South Wales, there exists a belief in an All-Father deity. He goes by a great many names... *Bunjil, Baiame, Boyl* or *Baal*...'

They were *not* without God! Sarah *knew* it! She'd known it couldn't be true.

'But,' said Sir John, 'if questions are asked concerning him, the natives are very shy of giving information. In consequence of their rapid decrease in number, such reticence makes it altogether possible that our knowledge of this subject, slight as it is, will never be greater. I am therefore indebted to the observations of my esteemed colleague Augustus Oldfield, for his time spent among an Aboriginal clan calling themselves, of all things, the *Watch-an-dies*...

'*Boyl* or *Baal* is a supernatural being held in great dread. The notion of a beneficent spirit, it seems, never enters their heads. Their very ideal of divinity is, rather, that of malevolent force.

'Whereas we regard God as good, they look upon Him as essentially evil...a "God-Devil", or "God-evil". While we submit, they struggle to obtain the control of Him. We count our blessings. They think the blessings come of themselves, and it is evil that occurs as the result of malign interference.'

Sarah took copious notes on small scraps of paper, her stub of pencil working furiously. Their ideal of divinity might be evil; the clear implication, then, was that the Aborigines saw the world, their natural world, as essentially good, an Eden indeed. They performed that reversal Lambert insisted Darwin could not. Brippoki need not subscribe to any higher power for his salvation – quite the opposite.

Truth went naked, without the shame of Original Sin.

'Insofar as this is true, *Baal* is but one of many,' said Sir John, at once disallowing their god the same status as the Christian God. 'They fully believe in the existence of a host of evil demons. The whole face of the country swarms with them…all meaning harm and committing every mischief imaginable. Death and disease, ill success in hunting, the loss of personal property, every circumstance whose cause they cannot appreciate, in fact most every misfortune which it is possible can befall a man, is the work of spiritual agency, the power possessed of hostile tribes.

'On the Loddon River tribes live in dread of *Mindy*, a huge serpent. Duly invoked via incantation, he produces gales and hurricanes by the lashings of his enormous tail. Among the *Arunta*, or *Aranda*, a hollow tree is entrance to the Underworld. One lives in danger of sliding down the roots!'

God, the Devil, *and* Hell – just what part of 'no religion' did James Dredge and all of those others not understand?

'The *yumburbar*, a *bunyip*, *Mim-mie*…the list is endless. These malign spirits are encapsulated under one common classification…' Lubbock bared and snacked his teeth. '*In-gna*.'

Sarah practised mouthing the unusual word.

'With them, as I say, nearly all diseases and consequent deaths are the result of the enchantments of other tribes. Were it not for the ill will of their enemies, in fact, they think to live forever! If a native should wish death on his enemy, he will do it by means of enchantment. This power of enchantment is called *Bool-lia*.

'The *In-gna* is a spiritual agent, effecting the enchanter's fatal will. He solicits the *In-gna* according to his intent. Most are of human form, but have long tails and long upright ears. They are of human origin, being the spirits of men from other tribes. That, or else they are the souls of departed blackfellows who have for whatever reason not received the proper rites of burial. Constrained to wander the earth, they are conscripted into this veritable army of ghosts. Their chosen haunts are thickets, caves, all forms of rocky places, springs, *etcetera*…but most especially, they haunt graves. Such locations are avoided as much as possible.

'Significantly,' said Sir John, possessed of an imp all his own, 'none of these phantoms is of the female sex. From this, and other considerations, we may infer the New Hollanders believe women do not have souls.'

The audience bristled and set to murmuring; the soulless part in particular. Lubbock appeared to relish the reaction.

'One of the most melancholy things in savage life is the low estimation in which women are held,' he said, speaking more freely. 'Female children are betrothed from early infancy. Relatives nearer than cousins may not marry, but very little fruit is forbidden...and very early plucked. The girls generally go to live with their husbands at about the age of twelve, and sometimes even before that.

'Amongst such peoples, where a wife frequently changes, the relationship between father and son is weakened. Aboriginal Australian society is matrilineal, traced through its females. Out of various good causes exogamy, marriage outside the tribe, is endorsed. This leads to the regular practice of capturing one's wife by stealing her away from a neighbouring tribe...a practice readily acquiesced to by the women.'

He smiled, wickedly.

'Thus we may trace every step through the differing degrees of civilisation, from the treatment of woman as a mere chattel to the hallowed ideal of matrimony as it exists among ourselves.'

Sir John had deviated pretty far off course from his prepared notes. He sought to bring himself smoothly back into line.

'I spoke of dreams... The native Australians profess to foretell the future in their dreams,' he said. 'To them, their dreams are real life. This may be one reason behind its being almost impossible to waken them once they are asleep. Their sleep is so sound, so fast, that they are often injured rolling into their own campfires at night, suffering their burns without waking. These occasions, when their guard is most assuredly down, invite the hand of an assassin. Murders, whether for reasons of jealousy, revenge, or a whole network of other feasible wrongs, are most often committed in their sleep. And, you can be sure, there are always *In-gna* aplenty ready and willing to execute the task. Coming up behind the victim, most often in his sleep, the *In-gna* strikes a sharp blow to the back of the neck. Unless they can somehow be arrested, the effects of this blow will eventually result in death.

'At the first sign of sickness, the inflicted seeks to ascertain whether the *Bool-lia* of his own tribe is potent enough to repel that of his foes.

'The fountainhead of *Bool-lia*,' said Sir John, 'is the human body. Some procure it from the left arm, others the stomach...delicacy forbids me from identifying the most commonplace source. Suffice to say, the departed natives of Tasmania used to imagine that Europeans drew the fire, noise and smoke which they put into their muskets from that very same region, when they were only reaching for cartridges...' Sir John performed a helpful, roundabout sort of gesture – nothing too explicit – to illustrate his point '...by means of enchantment, of course.'

His anecdote produced the driest rustle of amusement. Sir John launched back into his speech.

'The spirit of the first man ever slain by an Aboriginal warrior in open combat enters the victor's body by the same route. It makes itself a new home, and thereafter becomes his *woorie*, or guardian angel if you like... When danger threatens the new host, his guardian spirit informs him of it by a kind of scratching or tickling sensation in those regions. In pre-colonial days, I should add, tribal conflict among the native Australians was almost continuous in expectation of this standard, many a murder doubtless incited purely to achieve this protection.

'In this fashion only might good ever be said returned for evil.'

The speaker then held up a finger-length object of some sort. Sarah sat too distant from the stage to make out what it was.

'Some attribute life to mere implements. They tend to respect weapons once they have seen them used to deadly effect. So they should. For many it is a lesson learned only the once.'

He brandished the mystery item in the air. It was long, and thin, and sharpened to a point at one end.

'Like the rifle's bullet...as invisible, and therefore magical, as it is deadly, there is also the death curse of the ancient pointing-bone. Simply in fear of this spell a native becomes ill almost instantly, and many perish from it.'

Replacing the object on the table, Sir John Lubbock leant further forward, balancing his weight on both sets of knuckles.

'We might easily dismiss their ghost stories, of invisible forces seizing them in the night...for us, nothing more than the after effects of a too-heavy meal, the nightmare visions of disturbed sleep. Yet it is,' he said, 'what *they* believe that counts.

'An individual who thinks himself cursed will seek out the protection of his own enchanter. He applies to that individual in whose *Bool-lia* he has the greatest faith. This person, in consideration of a certain reward, undertakes his cure.'

Sarah found herself overtaken by an unpleasant, creeping sensation: she pictured Brippoki and his golden guinea.

'Sorcerous powers are generally the preserve of the aged, but may come as early as the first grey hairs of middle age. Clever-men or *Cooragie*, as they are called, acquire their magic influence by eating of human flesh, but only twice in a lifetime...once that of a young child, and once that of a fellow *burka*, or elder. Among the powers they come to possess is the ability to bone-point, causing or curing sickness…and control of the weather. The very smartest of these clever-men are the *wammaroogo*, medicine-men or charm-men. Having the cloaking-power of invisibility, they are also able to transport themselves instantaneously over great distances. Time and space present no obstacle.

'Women,' said Sir John, 'are never sorcerers.'

The Guardian of the Wisdom of Dead Men heaved a huge sigh of relief.

'Prodigious appetite and indolence aside, another feature of this savage race most often remarked is their carelessness of the future. It is said they have little concept of an afterlife according to either state, neither great reward nor everlasting damnation…no life at all of a sensual character. Their religion, such as it is, operates independently of morality. Before Christianity, humility appears quite unknown.

'When questioned as to what becomes of them after their decease, some answer that they believe the spirit of the deceased leaves the body and makes its way to the spirit world. This immense repository of souls is, according to varying interpretation, on or beyond the great water, over the far horizon, or up above the clouds… *Boo-row-e*. But this will only happen so long as the correct ceremonies are performed.'

This sounded a little too conveniently like heaven, and a lot more like a mess of contradiction. If Sarah had learnt one thing from her time with Brippoki, it was that he was often too quick to agree. He went out of his way to avoid confrontation; and if this wasn't the definition of humility, then she did not know what was. Conversely, he stubbornly held to his beliefs, and kept them for his own. The Aborigines had every reason to conceal their greater truth from the invader, by telling them exactly what they wished to hear.

'…ascended,' Sir John was saying, 'in the shape of little children, first hovering in the tops and in the branches of trees, and eating, in that state, their favourite food, little fishes.

'When it comes to the rites of sepulture, and disposal of the dead,' said Sir John, louder now, 'their ideas of correct ceremony are different in almost every instance. Among the Adelaide tribes, a body is wrapped in animal skins or a cloak possessed in life, and placed on a bier made of branches. A day or two later,' he concluded, 'and the body is removed, being deposited, head pointing west, in a grave four to six feet deep.'

Sarah suddenly saw herself standing, *sto*, above an open grave. She could not quite make out the prone form within – or say to whom it belonged.

'In the vicinity of Encounter Bay,' said Sir John, 'four separate modes of disposal have been recorded. Only the elderly are buried. Middle-aged persons are lodged in the crook of a tree, hands and knees brought nearly to the chin, and the mouth, nose, ears and so on sewn shut. The corpse has three coverings: bark, netting, and an outside layer of sticks. A fire is lit at the base of the tree and there the wailing relatives gather. The body remains up the tree until the flesh has wasted away, after which the skull is taken for a drinking cup.

'Alternatively, the corpse is placed in a sitting posture, facing east, and exposed to the elements until desiccated, only after which it is placed in a tree. A fourth method is to burn the body, but this only happens in the case of infants or stillborn children.

'In Northern Australia a man's widow carries his head with her in a bag, the body being interred in a shallow grave. At the Flinders River, Gulf of Carpentaria…'

In his supply of gratuitous detail, Sir John Lubbock's mischief had taken a wicked turn. However much she might wish to leave, something in the style of his delivery compelled Sarah to stay.

'Only the lowest races of men,' he was saying, 'African Bushmen, many of the native Australians, Calmucks and so on, neglect to bury their dead, leaving them to the wild beasts. The Brazilians burn the bodies, pound the dust and drink it, with the hope of inheriting the good qualities of the deceased. Some savages perform their burials in ant-hills, and others inter the body upright.

'The native Australians prefer to keep away from the graves of their own people,' he said, 'but care little for their maintenance. Little prevents the bones of their dear departed from being scattered across the surface of the earth. They have frequently been seen to handle them, or kick them around with near total indifference.

'They have other strange quirks in this morbid regard. Often they will drive their sick away to die…either leave them to their fate, or spear them, so that they may cease to be a burden.

'It is considered most unlucky to utter any dead person's name.'

Sarah tried her best to maintain composure. The small noises she could not help but make began to attract the attention of those around her. They sat and stared or looked away, presuming her weak-spirited or squeamish – not at all privy to the reasons for the spillage of her feelings.

'All those not disposed of according to the correct rites become malign spirits, doomed to wander about the face of the earth for evermore, the only gratification allowed them being to do all possible evil to the living.'

She could block out neither his words, nor her runaway thoughts.

'Death,' chanted Sir John, 'Death to them is not the natural end to life, but the work of magic. They have no concept of an individual spiritual life, either before birth, or after death. Death is only utter annihilation.'

Terrible. Terrible. Sarah stood. She must return, she must return home straight away.

'So you see,' said Sir John, voice receding, 'progress in their religious ideas must be gradual indeed.'

CHAPTER XLIX
Thursday, the 18th of June, 1868

SUPERSTITION TOO?

'A rev'rent fear (such superstition reigns
Among the rude) ev'n then possess'd the swains.
Some god, they knew – what god, they could not tell –
Did there amidst the sacred horror dwell.'

~Virgil, *Aeneid*, trans. John Dryden

Sarah pulled herself together for Lambert's sake; not realising fully how far he did the same for her.

Late afternoon into evening, she indulged him by preparing them both a sumptuous dinner. Lambert enjoyed it so thoroughly that he neither resisted nor questioned, and afterwards actually apologised for his previous outburst. He said that he should like them to be able to speak freely, without fear of contradiction, as they 'used to' (as *he* used to would be more accurate, but still…).

After 27 years, they were finally able to sit and talk like adults.

'And what,' Lambert asked, 'have you learnt today, from Lubbock and his opinions *On Savages?*'

His interest seemed genuine enough. Sarah hardly knew where to start.

She simply said, 'He talked about superstition.'

Lambert took up the salt pot from his tray, tipped some out onto his empty plate, and then threw a pinch across his left shoulder. 'Like that?' he asked.

'Something like that,' Sarah granted, 'although it might work best when the spill is accidental.'

'Bah!' he sneered, playing along. 'How about this?' Boldly he crossed his knife with his fork.

'Well,' she considered, 'if we were seated at table, for fear of embarrassment I should say it was an ill omen…but I think it more taboo than superstition.'

Liking her answer, Lambert wanted more. 'Define for me, if you will,' he asked, 'the difference.'

Sarah worked the idea through in her head, to her own satisfaction. She then reached across to rearrange his cutlery.

'Defiance of taboo,' she said, 'incurs a social penalty.' As Lambert moved to interfere she slapped his hand away. 'The defier of superstition believes it incurs one that is supernatural.'

'One what?'

'Penalty.'

'You speak too broadly. But that is one thing I may always rely on,' he said. 'All superstition is silly, as the "King's Evil" is silly. A king may die any day of the week.'

Sarah frowned.

'Be that as it is,' continued Lambert, 'superstition properly belongs between a man, and whatever maggoty devils infest his brain.'

'You dismiss it entirely?'

'I dismiss it entirely. I acknowledge it, however, a commonplace. Supernatural belief is not so important, almost the lesser evil,' he said, 'whereas taboo is a social compact.'

'Then that is what I have learnt today,' declared Sarah, beginning to clear their dinner things away. 'Among so-called "savages", the opposite holds true.'

Sarah was nothing if not careful in her language. Her comments were specific to what she had so far discovered concerning the natives of Australia and New Zealand, but she did not want to get into antagonistic issues of race.

'Their widespread belief in supernatural forces,' she said, 'elevates both superstition and the breaking of taboo…makes of them a very real social force. Defiance of taboo incurs both social and supernatural penalties.'

Lambert looked surprised. Sarah impressed even herself.

'The Royal Institution should be congratulated,' he said, observing her at work. 'A superficial taste in arts and sciences is desirable in those to whom fortune gives leisure, for it keeps them out of harm's way.'

Sarah turned and placed a hand to her hip, the dishcloth swinging. 'If you think me a lady of leisure – ' she started. 'And you know for a fact we have no fortune.'

Lambert grinned. 'I have some.'

Her frown broke and she laughed.

'Has anyone ever told you?' he said. 'You have a very pleasant laugh.'

Her face clouded slightly, despite the compliment – since no one ever had.

Dishes washed, dried, and put away, Sarah returned to Lambert's bedside for a little while longer – finding it difficult, for the moment, to be apart from him. She saw that he held a finger between the pages of a new book (R. H. Hutton, *Professor Huxley's Hidden Chess Player*), received just that morning by mail order.

'You look tired,' he said.

Sarah gave a wan smile. 'It has been a long day,' she said.

'To be serious a moment,' said Lambert, folding his great hands together, 'these public lectures are useful only to those who know little, and aspire to little. Real learning is acquired through solitary studies.'

She nodded. 'I know that.'

Owing perhaps to his great suffering and the death of Aetockoe, the relation of Druce's signs and wonders still troubled her. Simple folk like the Gilbethorpes or even Druce himself held to a concept of Christianity not so very far removed from superstition, with its ceremony, its portents. The miracles performed by either Son or God the father helped to explain life's mysteries, soothe its tragedies. They seemed the prime attraction of a truly popular religion.

Sarah, feeling the need to be circumspect, searched for an example the likes of which Lambert would tolerate.

'Thinking of – ' She hesitated. 'Putting oneself in the position of a poor and simple citizen, for a moment, such as a member of the congregation of St George's in the East... You can understand,' she said, 'can't you, how the poor people, dying in their hundreds, might take to the anointment of oil, to deathbed confession and most especially holy communion, with its promise of trans...transubstantiation...the blood and the body of Christ.'

'Ironic, is it not?' said the Reverend Lambert Larkin. 'The disease took hold because of the cholera.' He eyed her with suspicion: better an atheist than a Catholic.

'But,' said Sarah, 'my question is: does that make their belief simple? Or profound?'

'They make Fear their god,' shrugged Lambert. 'They fear death.'

Unfolding his great hands, he opened up the pages of his book.

Sarah had skirted around the ignorance of savages, yet Lambert had succinctly hit upon their belief in malign gods of evil – lambasting it, as she'd guessed he would.

'Are they not then good God-fearing folk?' she asked.

She wanted to ask that question of him personally – her own upbringing having been designed to put the fear of God into her.

Lambert blandly turned the question aside. 'God is Love.'

He had never said a thing more dishonest.

'I prevail on you, then, to regret your dismissal of the Jews, and even to forgive the Anglo-Catholics their ritual.' Sarah wasn't exactly sure what she was asking, or why she asked it.

Lambert stared. 'You prevail upon me?' he asked.

He might as well have added, '*in my weakness?*'

'When men have lost sight of their Creator,' he said, throwing down his book, 'that is when false notions take His place...superstition, more or less, which soon descends into gross fetish, the worship of false idols...backward steps towards ignorance and savagery. Religion may be corrupted, as surely as morals…and civilisation is, above all, a moral state: without moral foundation, impossible.'

Sarah stood firm. 'Even within Christianity,' she reasoned, 'the fundaments of any one particular sect are held, unfairly, as superstition by the next.' She was being admirably forthright – ultimately, he would prefer it. 'What may be poison to one man,' she said, 'is still meat to the next.'

'Meat and poison,' he snarled. 'Superstition is an offence to God.'

The body of Christ – or was it a maggoty devil infesting her brain?

CHAPTER L
Thursday the 18th of June, 1868

BETRAYAL

'Arrived in London once again
His gold he freely spent
And into every gaiety
And dissipation went.
But pleasure, if prolonged too much,
Oft causes pain, you know,
And he missed the sound of the windlasses,
And the cry "Look out below!"'

~ Charles 'The Inimitable' Thatcher,
'Look Out Below'

Brippoki is on the move, heading eastwards, out towards Bow Marshes and the lower Lea Valley. Dampened bunches of green weed, piled and tied atop his head, serve both to keep him cool and as a natural disguise. He weaves through the long grasses, leaping the occasional ditch, body low to the ground to prevent him being seen. Here and there sit fishermen – idle spectators who do not concern him.

Beneath his laboured breath he hums, almost wordlessly, to the tune of 'Captain Jack's Song'. 'The European food...the pease...I wished to eat...I wished to eat.'

Expectation fills his mouth with saliva. Brippoki, low on energy, is tired of chewing on fern root. Roused from his torpor, only the thought of wild honey dares him sufficient to risk exposure in broad daylight.

Quarry sighted, he skids to a halt, hand clutching his chest in sudden pain. Ribcage tight, he collapses back, to lie in the long marsh grass – mouth working, like that of a fish out of water. Brippoki heaves a dry and gasping cough, and, for a while, lies supine in the grass.

Against a backdrop of deep blue, the pale ghost of *Mityan* hangs suspended in the clear noonday sky, more than three-quarters consumed by shadow.

Brippoki, recovered, crawls on his belly over to the nearest water pool. He drinks his fill, then loads his mouth, and rolls over onto his side, where he remains completely immobile – as if one dead.

Presently a bee approaches, poking about the marsh flowers. Hearing its unsteady hum, Brippoki holds his breath. The bee passes high overhead, examining the scene, and then closer, first to one side of his head, then the other. *Buzz-z-z-z.* Brippoki flickers not an eyelash. The bee hovers a moment more then turns, a change in its tune signifying that it is about to drink. The instant brother bee touches the surface of the pond Brippoki spits out a powerful jet of water. Seizing the stunned insect by the wings, he attaches a wisp of white goose feather with a spot of his own blood.

Let go, the bee makes for the hive with an angry drone – marker slowing it down, and making it easier for the eye to follow.

Brippoki's face, shape only just recovered from a previous beating, was a mass of angry lumps.

'You've been fighting again?' asked Sarah.

She saw similar swellings over much of his body.

Brippoki the hunter looked sheepish. 'Bumblies no sting in the World,' he said. 'Bee is our pren.' He raised a rueful sounding lament. 'Not bloody here. Here him bloody *lolly* pren!'

Bloody fine friend, he is, an English sort of bee: she was finally becoming attuned to his patter.

'They attacked you?' said Sarah. 'Why would they do that?'

His indignant expression transformed into one of delight.

'Bumbly choogar!' Brippoki crooned. 'Climb it tree, nice honey-stuff liket choogar!'

His flickering tongue protruding hot pink between swollen black lips, he resembled some species of lizard or black-headed snake.

Sarah laughed. 'There's tea on the table,' she said, 'milk and "choogar". You can spoon as much of it as you like, without fear of injury.'

She sat and watched Brippoki happily sort among the tea set, serving himself – just like a bee at a flower. What complexity of thought might even now be whirling within his skull? If she only knew how to frame the question in such a way that it would not drive him away.

Brippoki sat obediently at her feet.

She fumbled with her notebooks for a while.

They exchanged mute looks, both equally expectant.

Did Brippoki fear mention of Druce's name, Sarah wondered, simply because he was dead? There seemed no easy way for her to recap events, and so she leapt straight in.

'This next part,' she said, 'has been slow going.'

The manuscript had reverted to that same untutored hand from its very beginnings, rife with deletions and corrections.

'Also, there is also a portion I did not read yesterday.' Was it only yesterday? 'A departure from the main narrative…similar to when he was attacked on the Hospital ward, you remember? His account,' said Sarah, 'appears to leap forward, to somewhere after 1810, presumably, when he is stranded back in England, the country at war with the Maori of New Zealand…'

Sadly, this had been true for most of the century.

Brippoki nodded, and appeared to follow. 'Here it is, then,' Sarah said.

> The petition of George Bruce to the Right Honourable, the Lords of Treasury of the Royal Navy:
>
> My Lords, necessity compels me to address this honourable assembly with the horrid event that awaits the Petitioner's stay in this kingdom. That is, he shivers to say, my Lords, that sooner or later he shall stretch forth his hand with violence on the body of someone or other of the uncultivated people, for the constant assaults he receive from the lower class of people in the streets daily.
>
> Some calls him a 'Man-Eater'. Another says he is 'The Devil'. And others call him a traitor to his country. And this is because he don't satisfy them all with the marks in his face.
>
> My Lords, he wishes to inform this honourable house of the Treasury that he is the same unhappy wretch that has been raving in the streets of London like a madman, all through the insults he has received from the lower class of people and which he daily and hourly meets with in the streets, go where he will, about the marks in his face.

The original text had been corrected from 'my', and 'the marks in my face', into the third person.

> Therefore he trusts in God, that he will incline the hearts of the rulers of the United Kingdoms to take his miserable existence into their consideration, and states his wretched life to His Royal Highness so that a speedy removal may be ordered for him from this nation to any of His Britannic Majesty's isles in the South Seas, where he did his duty in His Majesty's Ships for seventeen years on discovery.
>
> My Lords, should it meet with the Petitioner's Sovereign's heart to grant him his request, the Petitioner wishes to exhort the grant of a small bit of land as a settler, or there to be returned to New Zealand where he should be ever ready to serve his King and country in anything requested of him on that island. O my Lords, should neither of those great favours be granted to the Petitioner, he, in the name of Christ Jesus our Holy Grand Master, humbly begs your pity for him and that my Lords will at least entreat His Royal Highness to send him out of this kingdom. With fortitude he will take his lot with the convicts by the first conveyance. For his life is a burden to him in this nation. O that the powerful God this day may strike the hearts of

every one of the British Empire with affection and pity for one poor creature amongst millions, whose soul and body is wracked by the loss of a harness, and distant from his child as his self-infamy.

The text at this point had virtually collapsed in on itself, requiring much puzzling to piece together any sense from it; unsurprising, perhaps, considering.

Please my Lords, to observe, my Lords, he is a cripple by the loss of two fingers of his left hand, which he lost in His Majesty's service, so that he cannot ship himself. Petitioner adds no more, but with eager hopes of happiness waits with patience for an answer. I will be in duty bound.

All excepting the word 'pray', the remainder had been struck out, although she had been able to make out some of the deleted words; and the closure, 'your humble petitioner, George Bruce.'

Putting down his cup and saucer, Brippoki crooked the little finger of his left hand and tweaked the air, like the lobster in his pot, an action that seemed to amuse him.

'*Mal-gun*,' he said. '*Mal-gun*.'

'Other stray words,' said Sarah, 'were scribbled in the margins…' She bent forward to consult her own notes. 'The solitary word "young"; intended perhaps to go with another, "child"?' Although she had nothing on which to base their juxtaposition, the singular isolation suggested something inexpressibly sad.

Brippoki instantly launched into a frenzy of urgent mumblings, whispered incantations repeated over and over. Sarah, in no mood for it, could only make out the phrase 'man-eater', and also, she thought, 'young child' – but that could just as easily have been her imagination.

Brippoki clapped his hands rapidly together.

'Very good!' he said, his face expressing the complete opposite.

A loose-leaf sheet fell from between the pages of her notebook to the floor: the official Navy list of ships on which Druce had served, forwarded by Dilkes. Bent forward to retrieve it, a sudden breeze stirring her hair caused Sarah to raise her head.

Brippoki crouched within the frame of the open window. Limbs folded, muscles tensed, he struck various fleeting attitudes. His wide and staring eyes gave exaggerated looks, white orbs aglow within his black face. A few more tics and bobs, and the frame stood empty.

Silent as a ghost he would arrive, and silent as a ghost he had departed.

She could have said something. Sarah sat a while longer, then rose herself to shut the window.

She returned to her notebook. Keen to attend Lubbock's lecture, she had rushed that afternoon's transcript, and events were not clear in her head. Even though she had lost the wayward Aborigine for an audience, Sarah decided to read the text back to herself.

I then entered on board His Majesty's Ship *Porpoise*, where I arrived in England, 1810. The war was hot, so that no account was took of me, nor New Zealand, at that time.

I was sent from the *Porpoise* to the *Thisbe*, where I lost my two fingers.

After my wounds was well, I was drafted to the *Kangaroo*, another of His Majesty's Ships. From this ship I was invalided in 1812.

I then went to Limehouse to lodge at a distant friend's house, where I remained till my money was all gone. I then consulted what I should do for a living. I told my friend of my intent. He highly approved of it. I then went to His Majesty's miniature-drawer and paid him four pound for drawing mine. My friend lent me money, and as soon as my portrait was down, my friend told me to take it to a man whom he knew to frame it. I asked the man how long he would be about it. He told me a week. I returned to my friend's house and told him what time the picture would be done. All this was done in order for me to exhibit myself in the country to get money.

But, O horrid to relate, better for me had the wild beast eat my flesh and drink my blood before ever I had entered that man's house. For, while I was waiting for my portrait being framed, a man came and invited me to go with him to spend the evening. My friend knew the man and through his persuadings only I went with the stranger. His name was Tucker. Well shall I remember it to my death.

I went with him to Bow, where he called for brandy hot. In a short time I was quite senseless, in which state I remained till the next morning, when Tucker's apprentice boy told me to my face that I behaved so bad with him that night in bed that he was obliged to quit the bed and sleep with the servant girl. My friend and Tucker see with what horror and shame I was struck with at this dreadful report. I was motionless for some time. I could not utter a word. But Tucker, knowing the horrid state I was in the overnight when he put me to bed with the boy, and as there was no harm done but the attempt, told me to think nothing about it, promising me at the same time before my friend's face it should not be mentioned. But my friend Wheatley told me I had better leave that neighbourhood for fear the boy should spread it. And, as I was senseless with liquor when it happened, so I could not prevent him was the report false. I took Wheatley's advice and left his house that day.

Men with men working that which is unseemly. Paul's Epistle to the Romans hinted at such mysterious perversions, sufficient to intrigue.

Sarah shook such thoughts from her head. She read on.

At my departure from Wheatley, he gave me a glass of rum and freely forgive me the trifle of money I owed him, and Tucker gave me every blessing his soul possessed. I took my departure from Limehouse and went to Dovert-street central London, where I had frequented at all opportunities with a woman of the town from the first hour I arrived in London.

At the appointed time, I went for my portrait. The man told me my friend Wheatley had obtained it, by telling him I sent for it. I then was fully convinced of the most abominable scheme that they had laid for me at Limehouse, to get rid of me and to obtain my portrait, to enrich their selves by hanging it up in the parlour to create custom. It was a public house that Wheatley kept.

In a short time after, I left Dovert-street and went to Lambeth, where I took lodgings. A few weeks after, I met a man in the street who asked me if I knew Duaterra, the New Zealander. I told him I did, and that I was the person who recommended him to Captain Moody on board the *Santaner* at New Zealand.

The man then told me that he was gone out to New Zealand, through the recommendation of Dr Gilliam to the society in London. He also told me that if I went to the said Gilliam, he would do all lay in his power to send me out, as it was my wish to go. I immediately went to Dr Gilliam, who received me with great hope and joy of making me happy, not only in this world, but in that to come. He introduced me to Mr Lancaster and Mr Lancaster introduced me to Mr Fox and all the committee, where every attention was paid to me, till Wheatley my cruel friend, to acquit himself of the ingratitude with which he had used me, came to the school in my absence and told Mr Lancaster the same cruel lie he raise of me at Limehouse. At my return to the school, Mr Lancaster told me to go out and never to come there any more. I went to Dr Gilliam, who told me if I had been in my senses when it happened, he would that day enter an action against Wheatley. I took my leave of Mr Gilliam, fully to go and take the life of Wheatley that night. But on my return to my lodgings the parlour was full of gentlemen waiting for me, so that I did not leave their company till four o'clock in the morning. I told the gentlemen all my pedigree. They gave me money. This stopped me from taking the life of Wheatley.

Soon after, I went to Chatham, where I was employed in the dockyard till Admiral Young came in the yard. I then entered with him. I was sent to His Majesty's Ship *Ceres*. From her to the *Namur* and from her to the *Tower Tender*, where I remained till the war was over.

This was not, then, a reference to war with New Zealand, as Sarah's first assumption had been: she realised it must be the Napoleonic War with France.

Ceres, written '*Searces*', she would have taken for *Circes*, '*Lemure*' the *Lemur*, not *Namur* ('*Namur* at the Nore'). Without the list of shipping Dilkes Loveless had supplied, she would have been…well, quite lost.

But what 'committee' did Druce speak of? What 'society'? Was it the same as that providential company of gentlemen who, by their timely appearance, had prevented Druce from committing murder? Who were *they*? A dizzying array of persons came and went in this part of his *Life*; and, again, not the whole of the story. Why, for instance, should Wheatley act so vengefully towards him, when the swindle involving his portrait had already been successfully accomplished?

Tucker and Wheatley, two more names to be added to the list – Tucker commonly written '*Cuker*'; and, like Luker before him, a fiend.

The exchange with Dr Gilliam smacked of something Masonic. Sarah wished that she knew more about the activities of the mysterious Masons.

The school committee, she guessed, must be that of the celebrated Borough-road School in Southwark, its founder Joseph Lancaster. Under the patronage of King George III, it had been Lancaster's express wish that every poor child in the dominions be taught to read the Bible. 'A place for everything,' was his maxim, 'and everything in its place.'

If Joseph Lancaster, then, at a push, that would make Mr Fox the Quaker, Joseph Fox…

Head swimming, Sarah felt a sense of coming to – awareness that she had fallen asleep in her chair, that she sat alone in a dark room, gone cold. She had been grinding her teeth. Bone curses and superstition; struggling to rise, she groaned out her stomach cramps and stretched. A long day, and too much attention paid to Sir John Lubbock's theatrics…

Still clutching hold of her notebook, Sarah took up the short candle in the other hand and made her way upstairs, pressing an ear to her father's door; cursory ablutions, and then preparations made for bed.

Unable to sleep for her whirring thoughts, and in spite of her desperate need, she sat propped, just like Lambert, on a bank of pillows. Firefly glow, the stars of a new constellation; at the end of the bed, reflected candlelight played across the brass inlay of the opened lid of the great sea-chest, filled with her mother's things. Inspired by night-thoughts of Aetockoe, the princess of New Zealand, she had woken to rummage through it early that same morning – or was it the day before? No, not yet midnight. For many years the trove had not seen light of day. She retrieved many of the objects from within: the hairbrush inlaid with mother-of-pearl, reinstated on the dresser; the old nightdress her mother wore. Sarah had only been a girl when these had disappeared into the depths of the coffer. Now that she was a woman, full-grown, the dress fitted her perfectly – too perfectly. Other hand-me-downs hung from the cupboard and curtain-rail, unspoilt but in need of airing.

More things, childhood memories, lay buried at the bottom of the chest, but Sarah had not yet touched them: never before could she have braved the day, too afraid of dissolving in tears at every moment. They were relics, preserved against the day…some vain hope, a day that would never come.

Events did not sit well with her: nowhere was the fate of Aetockoe's baby girl mentioned, or even pondered – if Druce even knew it. The *Petition* within the manuscript had read '*distant from his child as his self nfome*'.

Elusive Druce; she thought both more and less of him as the result; and Lambert too, distant from his child as his self-infamy.

The notebook lay open in her lap, ready to receive her thoughts. Her pen hovered, loaded with ink with which to darken a fresh, blank page. She wrote it out in note form.

distant from child as self-infamy

For an unlettered man, Druce was at times possessed of rare eloquence. What was that awkward phrase, that came just before?

wracked by the Loss of A haness

Sarah did her best to replicate the slant and loops of the hand she knew well from long hours in study of the manuscript.

A harness? There had been a correction above it, but the ink was too faded to make it out. 'Heinous'? That made no grammatical sense.

Traces of a rubric – against the spider-scrawl of red ink, the blaze of white page was fearsome: her eyes watered from puzzling overlong.

An '*heiress*' perhaps; or '*her highness*', meaning Aetockoe? No, he knew very well she was no real princess. 'Wracked by the loss of an heiress, and distant from his child as his self-infamy.'

His self-loathing was justified – an heiress, abandoned. But what, anyway, would have been her likely inheritance?

Sarah's eyes burned like twin coals in her head. All the crowding objects in the room appeared unstable, looming near then far: a thick mist, like smoke, and flying colours shot about before them. She knew it was her own fault, working each night in such low light conditions, all in short-sighted quest of economy. Too many years of close reading without spectacles had anyway begun to spoil her vision.

The circle of light about her rapidly diminished, the bedside candle guttering. The darker it became, the brighter seemed the glare of the open page.

She closed the book.

Phut-phut-phut came that panting intake of oxygen, the whippoorwill call of drowning wick. As if on cue the room was plunged into darkness.

The sound carried on. It came from downstairs.

'...Father?'

CHAPTER LI
Friday the 19th of June, 1868

BROKEN BONDS

'It was from out of the rind of one apple tasted, that
the knowledge of good and evil as two twins cleaving
together leapt forth into the World.'

~ John Milton, *Areopagitica*

It is another fine and clear day. *Warri* the wind shows his strength.

Brippoki enters into the canal waters. He wears a crown of marsh grass, broadleaf frond beneath obscuring his face and beard. In one hand he carries his dilly-bag, empty, and in the other a *tat-tat-ko* – a very long, tapered rod, the last joint of which is a twig tied with *witchi*, bulrush-string, in the form of a deadly noose.

Submerged up to his chin, he wades gently towards *mallanbool*, that stretch of water where he has previously planted the lengths of roosting-stick. *Warri* makes waves, disguising his approach. His liver shrivels. No diving-birds perch there.

He floats a while in hope, then catches sight of an even better prospect wending its way downstream. It glides closer, a stately white swan. He must be swift and sure – a single blow from its beak might break his arm. Leaving go of his *tat-tat-ko*, he takes a deep breath and submerges. He means to seize the legs and pull the bird sharply under, snapping the powerful neck, breaking both wings for good measure.

A boil of bubbles startles the swan. It takes immediate flight. Brippoki breaks surface in a thrash of limbs. Choking, spluttering, he is barely able to drag himself to the bank.

Kau-we? Kumpu! Kuna! Wuhrm-numbool kuna! Whatever this shit is, it does not deserve the name of water!

Only when the wind blows is the air not foul and choking. The smoke of a million fires finally clears, for the first time in days. A huge commercial gas works stands revealed, less than 500 paces north of Brippoki's campsite.

The sickly cloud and its smell have seeped into his bones, these last days. A fool to his senses, senses fouled, the willow, the stream, the rushes before him no longer seem quite natural. Collapsed within the ruins of his makeshift shelter, Brippoki shivers on a sickbed of leaves, weaker, and still weaker.

The trains scream as they pass overhead, making the ground tremble.

When the land is no good, a body must move on – but where? *Walypela* spreads himself over the whole of the earth, like a heavy, foul-smelling blanket.

Before he is born, the *walypela*, the *Ngamadjidj*, come up *Karawalla*, yellow-rain river, seen crossing the lands next to their own; and then their own. By the time he is a baby, they have already come to *Konongwootong*. Taken it. As payment for their land, the *Wootong* clan steals their sheep. The Whyte brothers shoot them all down, so the story goes. *Ngamadjidj* then come to *Mar-deer-um*. The *Darkogang Gundidj* live there. *Darkogangs* take many licks from the thunder stick. *Mar-deer-um* becomes Muntham Station.

And so the story goes.

Ngamadjidj take the *Jardwa* lands. The *Jardwa* come to live on the land the *Wudjubalug* belong to. His people make war with the *Jardwadjali*, when he is only a boy.

The land can only support one. That is the Way. More than one child at any one time, and two will starve.

Brippoki thinks of his *be-anna*, his blood father, and compassion bows his head. He is known only as *Rockootarap*, 'one whose wife is dead'

His mother, she wanders up from country far to the south, *mainmait*, and his father takes pity on her – so the story goes, from before he is born. Once she is gone, he is nothing, not belonging to No place. Brippoki is only *Kertameru*, a number, a small child at this time. His care falls to Old Aunty, his father's sister.

Blood must answer blood.

Ngamadjidj does not stand against the spears to take his punishment, so they spear the friends and relatives of the dead. His father is no good. He does not take his punishment well – a spear in the thigh makes him lame. He wanders their new lands in misery, or else hangs about the *walypela* houses, begging for food, more often drink – for rum, for gin. His dingo is shot for going after chickens, and he tries to spear Old Aunty for it.

A wife gives value when a man has none. Once *Rockootarap*'s wife, his mother, is gone, poor father mourns, but does not replace her. Got to give him respect for that.

Lambert, as a young man, would take long hikes into the mountains, exploring. He once told Sarah about extinguishing his lamp deep inside a cave, far underground, an accident revealing a natural wonder. Gradually, an ever so subtle light seemed to shine – illumination, he realised, coming from within the rocks themselves. Sarah had often admired Brippoki's black skin: unless greased, he returned no light. The hidden depths of his black eyes, however, had on occasion yielded something similar, suggesting frequencies of light that existed beyond sight – beyond average human perception, at least.

She had first suspected it when they walked the colonnades of the Royal Naval Hospital, Whit Monday in Greenwich, without an inkling of what he saw; his world view drawn from another source, the blazing blacklight of his imagination or else a unique brand of faith.

Brippoki was so very far from average.

A block south of the British Museum, Sarah sat within the nave of St George's, Bloomsbury, the blackened church with its aberrant north–south orientation. She had come here to pray for her father.

Diamond shapes, glowing pink and red; a sliver of blue; shards of yellow – others scattered across the cool dark flared so bright they seemed almost liquid silver. The sunlight faltered. Sarah blinked against a phosphorescent after-image, etched, as it were, into the air itself. Wherever she looked, there it also was, within her; a magical effect, achieved without magic – merely coloured light, filtered through stained glass, splashed against the deep brown wood of the pews.

She prayed for her father. She prayed for her mother. She prayed for Brippoki; even for Druce.

For her own sake she asked nothing, except forgiveness for what she was about to do.

Presenting the small pink card, the Ordinary Reading-ticket – her means of entry into the library – Sarah could not help but look at its reverse.

> This Ticket should not be allowed to go out of the Reader's
> possession; it must be produced if asked for at the
> Museum; and it should be preserved for renewal, or re-
> turned if no longer required.
> N.B. Readers are not, under any circumstances, to take a
> Book or MS. out of the Reading-room.
>
> Reader's Signature   *Sarah Larkin*

Without even looking at her card or noting her down in the Register, the young attendant on duty waved her through.

Not until the hour before dawn had her father finally ceased struggling for breath and fallen into a slumber. He had been sleeping soundly when Sarah had left the house.

It wasn't his first attack. Temporary setbacks, that was all they were; disturbed nights.

Dr Epps assured her sleep was the best tonic; and that, if Lambert was able to sleep at all, things couldn't really be that bad. If she wished – oh, yes, she wished very much – he would pay them a return visit on Saturday morning. She should get some rest herself, and not worry about it.

There was little chance of that.

On sunny days, the central dais appeared the focal point of the sun's concentrated eye. Sarah looked towards where George Bullen, the superintendent, sat in surveillance of the entire Reading-room. She purposely chose to situate herself at short table XVI, adjoining long table T – one of only two spots in the public part of the library where she could not be directly observed.

Really, thought Sarah, she shouldn't have been there; it was entirely wrong for her to be out. But then, she was there for *his* sake – to set herself free.

Only first, she needed to understand. She must understand.

One final circuit around the shelves led to her text of last resort: the second volume of Edward John Eyre's *Journals of Expeditions of Discovery into Central Australia, and Overland from Adelaide to King George's Sound, in the years 1840–1* – specifically, the catalogued supplement: *An Account of the Manners and Customs of the Aborigines, and the State of their Relations with Europeans*.

This well-thumbed book, opened on the desktop in front of her, was one she had formerly and very deliberately passed over because of its author, the notorious 'Monster of Jamaica'. She could hardly credit the evidence in front of her own eyes – the voice of reason coming from the least likely of sources. How could this comparatively enlightened and sympathetic overview be the work of the same man?

At the time of his account, Eyre had been living in South Australia for over a decade, as resident magistrate of the district of Adelaide and the Murray River system, a place more densely populated by natives than any other in that colony. Prior to his arrival in October 1841, frightful scenes of hostility, bloodshed, rapine and murder between the natives and settler squatters had been of frequent occurrence.

Aborigines were Eyre's constant companions, but as employees or servants. In quest of peace, therefore, he went to where no settler had ventured, to make himself familiar with tribesmen in their native state.

Out of all the many authors Sarah had consulted, only Eyre showed insight sufficient to entertain ideas of their religion, citing cave paintings discovered by Captain Grey as indicative of system and reflection in their minds, and avowing that other conclusions owed more to the carelessness and ignorance of enquirers.

Of all the experts she had attended, it took Eyre to solve the mystery of why, on that fateful Monday nearly a fortnight ago, Brippoki had fled shrieking from her parlour, quite possibly never to return.

Mr Eyre declared, 'I have never known a case of twins among the Aborigines, and Mr Moorhouse informs me that no case has ever come under his observation.'

Twins – this, she had no doubt, explained the obscene and revolting sin which missionaries among them could not even bring themselves to pronounce: child-killing.

If a child were born a twin, it and its sibling would be killed, smothered in sand. The slaughter of twins was an imperative. Given all of her burdens, her duties, the inconstancy of supply in an arid land, a mother could not spare more than one arm to carry an extra infant. Such a hardhearted act was made easier by dint of superstition. Twins were discounted as '*manu-tjitji*', malignant spirit children.

Joseph and Josiah Druce – the names alone perhaps contained unholy power; more dread lay in the combination of two together.

Brippoki is still *Parnko*, a young boy, when men from his mob camp near *Mokepille*, 'not many trees', to join with *Barbardin* and *Djab Wurrung* warriors for raids on sheep at 'spear point', now Ledcourt Station. The *Nundadjali* formerly belonged to these lands, until Briggs, the first *walypela*, at spear point shot them down. By and by he learns to live with them, and go hunting 'roo instead. Many tears are shed when he moves on.

The new boss, Boyd, has a headman name of 'Hamilton'. So the story goes, Boyd tells his man not to worry if blackfellows take a few sheep. Hamilton don't listen, and buys mantraps. He's always on horseback, more beast than man, patrolling his fences, a gun in each hand. When Hamilton comes across any hunting party, he breaks their spears and shields and spikes their water-skins. Two and two blackfellows are shot and killed out *Wurri-wurri*, along the *mallee* scrub. Rose – the stickybark next door – says Boyd complains. The men and not we are the masters, he says. The lost clans of six lands aim to make Hamilton listen, *Barbardin*, *Djab Wurrung*, *Jaggilbulug*, lake people from around *Ngalbagutja*, the moody people – and *Wudjubalug*.

A new *walypela* law goes against gathering, and any *boree* is soon broken up. In any dispute, accused and witnesses alike end up in a neck chain, rounded up and taken away for trial. Same time as the raids, *Rockootarap* goes along to the station like always, to beg a little. Seized and chained to a tree for two moons, he's off to jail in Adelaide. Never seen again.

Parnko is already 'orphan', the meaning of that name – the bottle took his father away long time before. If *Rockootarap* ever seen him, he bursts into tears, and can't even speak. He looks at the boy and sees his mother.

His mother.

One night long ago, in the dry, the men are off hunting. That night, *gins* and little piccaninnies are burning the bush, to get at the small game and make sweet new grass. *Ngamadjidj* comes along. The *gins* and piccaninnies are resting on the banks of the *Wimmera*, at *Worrowen*, 'place of sorrow'. Night turns day, sounds of thunder, and then night darker than ever.

Brippoki clings to his mother, to her bosom, the hole through it – that night long ago, when he is a baby.

'*The grand error of all our past or present systems – the very* fons et origo mali *– appears to me to consist in the fact, that we have not endeavoured to blend the interests of the settlers and Aborigines together; and by making it the interest of both to live on terms of kindness and good feeling with each, bring about and cement that union and harmony which ought ever to subsist between people inhabiting the same country. So far, however, from our measures producing this very desirable tendency, they have hitherto, unfortunately, had only a contrary effect.*

'*By our injustice and oppression towards the natives, we have provoked them to retaliation and revenge; whilst by not affording security and protection to the settlers, we have driven them to protect themselves. Mutual distrusts and mutual misunderstandings have been the necessary consequence, and these, as must ever be the case, have but too often terminated in collisions or atrocities at which every right-thinking mind must shudder. Thus, as in a circle, injustice will be found to flow reciprocal injury, and from injury injustice again, in another form.*'

'Mutual distrusts and mutual misunderstandings' – *utu, utu, UTU!* Eyre's text reminded Sarah of the indomitable Maori concept of 'retributive justice', the diabolical spirit of revenge; about the only trait they and the *Pakeha* shared with the native Australians. The law of the land of the lazy Doasyoulike was better understood as 'Do as you would be done by'.

The Golden Age of Greek and Roman legend was a mythical period, when perfect innocence, peace and happiness reigned. It was also considered the most flourishing period of a nation's history. No one seemed to consider that the two might be mutually exclusive.

The slaughters were mutual.

Frantically Sarah scribbled her notes. There was more, much more, but no time left to attend to it. Her eyes were on the clock face, and her own immediate future. A quarter to one already – Bullen would be on his lunch break. She had not yet found the courage to act. She would. She had to. Overdue since May, the library's temporary closure began on Monday. It was time for her to go, for good, for Lambert.

She blotted the pages of her copybook. They were carelessly smudged, but legible.

Sarah gingerly lifted up the volumes by Eyre, the manuscript concealed beneath. Checking to see that she was still unobserved, she slid it forth – carefully, carefully – and interleaved it with her notebooks. Her last hours, it might be argued, could have been better spent on the transcript; but in light of what she had learnt, she didn't think so.

Standing, she had the books gathered one on top of the other. Returning the volumes of Eyre to the *ad libitum* shelves, she started walking slowly and calmly towards the exit. It was not so very far. More clergymen than ever seemed present, and every single one of them looking her way. Not daring turn her head, she sensed Bullen still at his station. A warden patrolled the upper deck, almost overhead. Her breath caught: she had not thought to check above. Was she seen?

The doors stood open before her. The sound of books slamming shut shot a fusillade behind. Between the doors to the Salon and out, too late to turn back now, Sarah strode down the corridor into the Hall. Were she to look up, she felt sure she would see the glowering marble bust of architect Sir Anthony Panizzi, toppling down.

Her burden was heavy. She knew by heart the Penalty for the Infringement of Rules. A Reader, once excluded, was seldom re-admitted.

Across the threshold and into the lobby area without a single backward glance, Sarah Larkin passed out through the colonnade, never to return to the scene of her crime.

CHAPTER LII
Friday the 19th of June, 1868

FIAT LUX

'All visible things are emblems – what thou seest is not
there on its own account: strictly taken, it is not there at all.
Matter exists only spiritually, and to represent some Idea,
and body it forth.'

~ Thomas Carlyle, *Sartor Resartus*

The weather was fine, to look at: bright sunshine and a cloudless sky. It took the tattletale rattle of the window in its frame to inform on winds stronger by the hour. Sarah folded a napkin and used it to interrupt the noise.

From within the interior pocket of her skirts she retrieved Druce's manuscript, laying it on the table alongside notebook and papers. There could be no more trips to Shadwell, Piccadilly, or anywhere – to the library at the British Museum, most especially not.

What had she done?

Sarah removed the plunder at arm's length, and stared at it, almost in disbelief. She couldn't bear to handle the thing, not for a while at least.

Lambert appeared asleep. From the lightest touch of her hand however his eyelids fluttered open, and at the look on his face…she vowed never to leave him alone in the house again, not for anything.

He gave assurances that he was well, and, what was more, hungry. She made him a little broth, which he accepted gratefully, spoon after spoonful.

They passed much of the afternoon in gentle chatter, inconsequential but for Lambert's appearing to gain in strength. As evening drew close a slight cloud fell across Sarah's face, her expression fixed with serious intent.

'If… Father, you said that objects might still exist, even if they could not be seen?'

She spoke tentatively, not wishing to excite him.

'Objects?' said Lambert.

She wished to say 'persons', but dared not.

'If one of us were to look at the table, and see a table,' said Sarah, 'while the other could not…would you believe a table to be there?'

'If you see it, you say?' Lambert studied the bedside table, entertaining the idea. 'I can only think of that fable about Dictionary Johnson and Bishop Berkeley,' he said.

Of course, Sarah thought. During his sermon one day, the bishop had put forward a theory – that reality was a matter for individual sensation, rather than of physical material. The good doctor had emerged from the church, kicked a large stone, and declared, 'I refute it, thus.'

'Hm,' hummed Lambert, 'yes, I could accept the possible existence of the table.'

Naturally he sided with the bishop. Sarah was no longer sure what to think.

Lambert's active mind meanwhile turned the tables on science. 'It is,' he announced, 'much less rational to conceive of a stone, or any other inanimate object, that could start into being *without* a Creator. One might as well worship the stone!'

He nestled deeper into the bed. He enjoyed philosophical discourse.

'What of the soul?' he asked. 'Few people can claim to have seen one, yet all believe we have them. What of the Holy Ghost?' He reached one hand towards his daughter. 'We do not have to see something to appreciate its hold over us. I know the spirit of your dear departed mother watches over us still... Always keep her in mind, I beg of you.'

In the night, in his delirium, he had called her Frances; it had alarmed Sarah at first, until she realised that she wore her mother's nightdress.

'I...' Sarah almost choked '...I do.'

It wasn't true. Her recollection was hazy at best.

A little later on, no more than half an hour, and Lambert returned to the topic he had obviously been mulling over.

'There is the material world,' he said, 'a world of "phenomena". Except, larger forces are at work in the universe. Beyond the limits of what we know according to our senses, exist things beyond our ken... Not phenomena, but "*noumena*", sufficient unto themselves and without the need of our proof for their existence. To assert that we may never know them only sets a limit on our experience.'

No limits, indeed – Sarah looked towards the window.

'Nature...' he said, drifting slightly '...is itself but "the Veil and mysterious Garment of the Unseen".'

Lambert operated at the very edge of her understanding.

His head lay back on his bank of pillows.

'"The light of the body is the eye",' he quoted, Biblical verse. '"If therefore thine eye be single, thy whole body shall be full of light."' His voice, faltering slightly, turned husky. '"But if thine eye be evil, thy whole body shall be full of darkness. If therefore the light that is in thee be darkness...how great is that darkness."'

Emerging from his introspection, Lambert studied Sarah in hers: he wondered from where she had received her recent ideas. '"BEWARE,"' he said, so loudly that she jumped, '"lest any man spoil you through philosophy and vain deceit, after the tradition of men...and not after Christ."'

Once more teacher and guide, he fixed her with his concentrated eye. She scowled, ever so slightly.

'The idea,' he said, 'is the basis for knowledge. Man makes what he will of his own existence...cant, merely, should he forget that all of existence we owe to God. The tailor makes the man.'

Lambert relished the discovery that he could argue theology with his own daughter, yet knew nothing of equal say: he was able to look at her and not see the years of opportunity wasted.

'Men,' said Lambert, 'civilised men, live their lives governed by a system of checks and balances...mindful of the afterlife, fully expectant of going on to their great reward, or an eternity of punishment. Is this to be the only qualification of our behaviour? The only result?

'No. Obedience to the whole of the law is required. A physical obedience does not atone for moral sin, or vice...'

Lambert threatened to repeat the subtext of almost every sermon – original, or pastiche – ever delivered to an anxious congregation during his long life of service. But then the expected message turned on its head.

'...vice versa... Moral obedience...will not atone for physical sin.'

His demeanour, dark before, grew dark indeed.

Though his children might be starving, a man should not steal so much as a loaf of bread: Lambert's absolutism had always given Sarah pause. Here was some new dimension. She sat forward.

'"The gravitation of sin to sorrow is as certain as that of the earth to the sun,"' said Lambert. 'Wherefore do you seek out the rewards and punishments of the next life? Those rewards and punishments,' his gravelly voice turned barely audible, 'are here.'

Inexpressible agonies worked his face.

'When we suffer,' he said, through wrecked lips, 'God is often silent... I do not take that to mean...he is absent. Deny the power of the Unseen...and you may as well go mad.'

Lambert turned to her, eyes welling.

'I do fear...' he gasped. 'I do...'

He is *Kertameru*, 'first-born' – as a first child, and boy child, no more than numerically distinct. With the death of his mother, even before the disappearance of his father, he becomes *Parnko*. In whispers around the campfires, thinking him no longer awake, the others call him 'the son of gunfire'.

426

Somewhere in between his birth name and the name after death, another name belonged to his childhood – a name given by his parents, and taken from their natural surroundings – but Brippoki no longer remembers it.

He buries the bones and other remnants of his meals, and throws earth over the ashes of his last campfire.

To the north-northeast is a bank of cloud massive as *Gariwerd* – a mountain range, piled high, and just as solid-seeming. Brippoki thinks of his former home, *Kantillytja warara*, become the empty lands where he once walked.

The fourth stage of his life, as with the third, has been marred. The fifth, that of *bourka* – full man, or elder – can only be attained with the wisdom of grey hair. As a full man he should take the name of that particular place he belongs to, belonging to him.

Brippoki knows now that this will never come to pass.

A man's *goobong* is his family crest or totem, adopted from some aspect of Creation, be it animal, vegetable, or mineral. Without a mother, his father missing, he is ignorant of his very root – his *goobong*.

As dusk falls, the birds swoop and circle overhead, though their waterhole has for the moment dried to dust. Brippoki is reminded of the constancy in nature, and of its importance. *Pirpir*, the wood duck, *gunewarra*, the black swan, *otchout* the cod – each cycle of the seasons, and when it is time to mate, they return to their birthplace, the ancestral feeding grounds, site of every former and every future congregation. They return there year on year even should the rivers cease to flow and the waterholes dry up, even until the last straw is withered and gone. The earth might be covered over, water poisoned, wood disguised and trees taken away, and still they would return, unto generations out of mind – living, in hope.

As 'the one from Brippick Station', he belongs to no land. He has no true name. No longer numbered boy or youth, nor may he yet be admitted a man. Brippoki is considered a foolish sort. His initiations are incomplete. His Dreaming is at odds. A solitary individual obliged to keep largely to himself, he is treated in much the same way as a doctor or holy man would be – except without any of the skills, and therefore none of the status. Whenever possible, it is appropriate that he eats and even sleeps at different times, separate from the others. Excluded from ceremony, he maintains a respectful distance. In this regard alone might he observe his sacred duties.

He has spent his entire adult life profoundly lost and alone.

Only now that he is come to London does Brippoki recognise his Dreaming. Here in this place, far outside of the World, he finally knows – or at least suspects – what his *goobong* is.

~

Sarah sat downstairs, away from Lambert. Following his bewildering turn, her continued presence only seemed to upset him. He threw her looks, often confused, as if unsure of who she was or else thinking she must hate him. She might have administered another sleeping draught, if it hadn't smacked of knocking him out for the sake of her own peace of mind.

She wrung her hands, no longer sure of anything, herself least of all.

The clock in the hallway struck the hour of ten. With a stretch and a flex of her fingers Sarah laid the manuscript and her notebooks aside. Brippoki, apparently, was not coming – not this evening.

She could only throw herself into more work. She attended to various household chores in half-hearted fashion.

The *Life* wound down towards its close; there was only the matter of a few pages to go. Only an increased burning sensation behind her eyes, as well as faint deference to Brippoki, prevented her from seeing events through to their conclusion. In many ways she would prefer the story not to end, for that would probably mean, to her, the loss of both men. Druce, in the manuscript, had been staring death in the face so long that it was a wonder he was not dead already – although he was, of course.

No doom, however, should be accepted as inevitable, no evil ever 'necessary'.

Nearly every commentator on the Australian Aborigine had spoken of their likely extinction: it was even said that, once an Aboriginal woman had given birth to a half-caste baby, their own seed lodged no more. The destruction of Brippoki's people was undeniably a reality – but natural succession, the work of Providence? Pragmatical men of affairs might shrug their shoulders and turn their backs to the scene, but she was convinced: the way things were did not make them acceptable – and if that was naivety, then she clung to it fiercely. No law of nature dictated thus. No right in the least divine might excuse it. Man was dishonest if he summoned either in defence of his own actions. Should their extinction come to pass, it would be the work of his bloodied hand, no more and no less, and a stain on his conscience forever.

Sarah quietly cleaned out the grate in Lambert's bedroom, ready to build a new fire, then made her way back down to the parlour, meaning to do the same.

Life had been simpler once, without the shame that knowledge brings.

Lambert could make of it what he cared to, but there must be more to religion, she felt, whatever its origins; more than keeping to a set of rules; more to appeasing God, or gods, than strict obedience. Saul once claimed to have never broken a single rule, and no one could dispute that as Paul he was the better man.

The Old Testament was filled with stories of angels and demons, possession and exorcism, spirits of good and evil – a fiery brand of religion appealing to men most especially in their weaknesses. They lived their lives and often died by the sayings and doings of supernatural forces. Should the imps and saints of any one particular belief demand sway over all others? Providence, surely, allowed for more than one single path to happiness and fulfilment. Any faith, strong in itself, should confidently withstand the existence of others.

All of heaven and the earth had been created in seven days. Was it really so much harder to credit the world sicked up by a serpent, or hopping frog?

Genesis, *Exodus*, *Leviticus*, *Numbers*, *Deuteronomy*; the first five books of the Old Testament, the *Pentateuch*, were ascribed to the prophet Moses. Mosaic chronology of an entirely different order might also exist on the earth. The lead that separated differently coloured pieces of glass also served to bind them all together. If, instead, seeing them set against it, a religion sought to deny or crush all others, then that belief was weak and not worth subscribing to – for even as it saw that there were other possibilities, it made no allowances. Absolutism, moral or otherwise, set a limit to knowledge. Knowingly, it fostered ignorance.

And it was in ignorance that evil took its root.

Could a race of human beings appear so different as to make any possibility of connection painful, Sarah wondered, so that we simply needed to see them conquered in order to preserve our ideal of the civilised people we thought we were?

Only faith that was fragile sought challenge in every little thing. Only a questing faith might sow seeds of progress – truth sought not only in word, but also in action. Underestimating the capability of men like Brippoki arrested their development – in both concept and practice held them back, as surely as Adam did Eve.

Except God cursed knowledge withal.

Sarah stood for a while at the parlour window, unwilling, just yet, to fasten it shut.

She trembled to consider a universe filled with *noumena* that her God might not be the single answer to, after all.

CHAPTER LIII
Friday the 19th of June, 1868

THE FORCE OF SHADE

'Did I request thee, Maker, from my clay
To mould me man? Did I solicit thee
From darkness to promote me?'

~ John Milton, *Paradise Lost*

'Father,' said Sarah, 'what do you remember of the painter John Downman?'

Lambert's rheumy eyes, weary with sadness, circuited the room before settling on her. He resembled not a snail so much as a giant Galapagos turtle, or South Seas tortoise, flipped over onto its back.

'Downman?' he repeated.

Sarah suddenly wished that she had let him sleep: it was later than she thought.

'Sir John,' she said. 'Sir John Downman.'

Lambert's sad eyes rolled away again. He seemed to submerge within himself. Speaking at last, his voice gargled in his throat.

'He liked to play…with toads,' he said. 'I was eight. Or nine. There…in the garden, at Went House…Swan Street…on the corner of Frog Lane.'

They both smiled, their smiles quite unalike.

'Downman,' said Lambert, 'talked to the birds…and animals.' Searching the ceiling, he enumerated a distant menagerie. 'Tame toads, a favourite dove… two cats…and a pair of robins.' He smiled some more. 'They came to him when he called. He taught them…tricks.'

'What else?' she prompted. 'What else do you remember? Do you know what happened to him, after that?'

She should not exhaust him with her enquiries. He seemed short of breath.

'He very much enjoyed the company of the rich and famous,' said Lambert – slow, but steady. 'They were his favourite sitters. He was…a very good painter. Very popular…at one time.'

While resident in Town Malling, Downman had maintained rooms at No.188 Piccadilly. Even after the old man returned to London, he and young

Lambert had maintained a lively correspondence, prior to his quitting the capital for good, in 1817.

'Business...had greatly fallen off,' said Lambert. 'He was forced to retire.'

He gave Sarah a querulous look, no more than a glimmer, unsteady in his eye. Slowly and surely he shrank back inside his shell.

Sarah began to clear away the supper articles, piling them onto a tray.

~

I hen went To his majestys minetture drowor. & payd Him four pound for drawing mine. my frind lent me money. & as soon as my portrate Was down. my frind told me to take it to A man wome he kow to frame it.

Was the coincidence too fantastic? The possibility might not even have occurred to Sarah had Druce's amanuensis not written 'down' for 'done'. Done...by Downman? Fancy, Lambert would have said, finds the facts it wants. Of course she had no proof. Three doors down, on the corner of Charlotte-street, a man named Louis Hermann maintained premises as a picture dealer. She might enquire there, come daylight.

Sir John Downman had painted a great many royal portraits; Queen Charlotte, the Princess Royal and daughter of George III; Frederick the Great, King of Prussia; and those of other exalted persons such as Lord Nelson; Georgiana, Duchess of Devonshire; and Sarah Kemble, the 'Tragic Muse'. Among the great families, procuring a 'Downman Head' became a fashionable cult. Fashion, alas, was ever fickle. His heyday had been in the 1780s: if, in 1807, his favouritism had become so debased that he should portray the Larkin family, then by 1813 it feasibly might have encompassed the likes of Joseph Druce. That, or else Druce was the dupe of a street-sharp charlatan posing as the genuine article, 'His Majesty's miniature-drawer'.

In his dotage, poor old Sir John had ultimately failed in business – and where were his society friends then? Nor was his star alone in falling. Lambert's mother, her own grandmama, had been the daughter of a baronet; yet, looking at them now, who could imagine it? So, too, the Twyttens of Royston Hall had shown no favours following the family's tragic loss, the distaff side all but disowning them. How much further their fortunes could stand to diminish did not bear thinking about.

Woe unto them! for they have gone the way of Cain...clouds they are without water, carried about of winds...Raging waves of the sea, foaming out their own shame; wandering stars, to whom is reserved the blackness of darkness for ever.

Sarah lay in her bed, in the dark, clutching Druce's manuscript. Old age, ill fortune, recession and hard times, the themes within were all too close to home. A great net tightened about them, woven with the threads of immutable fate.

Every night now she struggled to fall asleep; in fear not of black night, but of what new reality morning light might bring.

Her father dealt in moral absolutes. When he spoke of light, he evoked a perfect morality, and darkness equally perfect immorality. Each was a manifestation of consciousness made palpably real; right and wrong; good, versus evil.

Without the one, there could be no sense of the other. Pure light was no more visible than pure darkness; only the two combined, extremes meeting. The innate power of darkness was as the absence of light: it was darkness that defined the essential features of persons and landscape.

Lambert, in his fealty to the letter of the Word, held progress only ever made by shining light into darkness. Yet if, like the painter, one allowed for only light and shade co-dependent to be at all effective, then the world might be more clearly understood. There might be virtue in embracing the darkness.

How completely Druce's miserable existence had come to align itself with his mother's curse, the mark of Cain indelibly inscribed on his face for all to see; cursed, as God cursed the serpent, to go upon his belly and eat clay. Sarah acknowledged him an unlucky individual, although often as not his troubles were duly his own. She also knew him as the vengeful type, his propensity for violence and bearing a grudge already noted, as well as the savagery of his temper. Often, when repeating his wrathful oaths, she found the incandescence of his rage – so ably communicated across time, through space – hard to resist.

The vivacity of his low character kept getting the better of him – and of her. Light, and leading; what, after all, was the worth of a stained glass reputation? Without the black in between, one might never make the distinction.

'Your goodness must have an edge to it,' wrote Emerson, 'else it is none.'

Druce's *Petition*, dictated within the *Life*, appeared to be a draft in preparation: even perhaps as late as 1819 he had persisted in his desire to return to New Zealand. The *Memoirs* from 1810; his 1813 *Memorial*; the *Petition*; his *Life* itself – he reinvented his story the entire time in that same forlorn hope.

Druce's choice of alias invoked the inspirational Scotsman Robert the Bruce. He maybe saw something of himself in the sufferance of that legendary spider – never giving up, and never giving in, no matter how many times his efforts were in vain; his life's work left, as he was, hanging in tatters. Ambition might ennoble, even if it extended no further than the capture of a fly.

'George Bruce' returned to England in the *Porpoise*. Sarah assumed that on board the same ship sailed Commodore Bligh, one of the very instruments of fate whose action had frustrated his earlier efforts to return to New Zealand. If ever Druce were predisposed to commit a murder, surely this then would have been it – that of the former Captain Bligh, of the *Bounty*.

A shadowy individual, that he was, and certainly vengeful in spirit, but so far as she knew Druce wasn't a murderer. Yet what might any man, 'poor muck-worm' or valiant spider, prove himself capable of, when fighting for his very survival?

The taste of blood was not so very different from that of dirt: both tasted of iron.

Joseph Druce. George Bruce. Jack alive. Joe-Jack. The villain had two faces. Driven to commit the deadliest of all sins, his soul would then be lost forever.

If Joseph Druce was not a murderer already, Sarah feared he might yet be.

CHAPTER LIV
Saturday the 20th of June, 1868

JACK ALIVE

'In dreams they fearful precipices tread;
Or shipwreck'd, labour to some distant shore:
Or in dark churches walk among the dead;
They wake with horror, and dare sleep no more.'

~ John Dryden, *Annus Mirabilis*

The great Spirit Ancestors dwell in the depths of the earth. One by one they emerge, pushing up the earth as they come. Caves, rocks and waterholes formed, these certain sacred places are revisited for all of eternity.

In the feast days of the dry the clans gather to exchange gifts on the *Wirrengren* plain, a past burning of roots and stumps, or at *Banyenong*, 'a possum a long time ago', for the purposes of a *corroboree*. The ceremonies they enact include marriage partnership, initiation rites, and the mourning of the dead.

In Brippoki's fifth summer, he travels there with Old Aunty. Father, inconsolable, stays behind. More than 600 heads from any number of mobs normally attend the festivities. Numbers this season are sorely depleted. Recent disputes and age-old scores are laid aside in their greater need for healing.

As they come near to *Banyenong*, the young men are sent ahead with the nets of greeting. In the evening, the nets are returned. At sunrise the next day they proceed, to find their hosts seated together in a clearing, patiently awaiting their arrival. The men form a long row, painted for battle and with their weapons arrayed, *gins* and children clustering some way behind. Warriors of the *Wudjubalug* form a second line opposite this first, their ranks soon swelled by the arrival of further clans, until everyone expected has assembled. From where the boy *Parnko* huddles, he watches as the *gins* advance into the space between the two parties, their heads bowed and coated with lime. Throwing down their possum cloaks and *rocko* bags, they extract pieces of natural glass, sharpened flint and shell. Hungrily these glitter in the sunshine. Howling, loud and melancholy, the *gins* slash at the flesh of their thighs, their backs and breasts. Blood pours from their wounds until they are red from head to foot, more blood than the dry ground can soak up. Their shuffling feet splash in the streams. Everyone else sits in silence, except, from each group, a designated *bourka*. One by one these stride forward, and in terms of violent outrage declaim the losses their people have suffered. At this point, the challenges and wounding thrusts necessary to satisfy the aggrieved parties should take place. Many spears – *leipa* – are brandished, but none is thrown. There have been too many losses of late for anyone to stomach more. The chief mourners stagger back behind the lines, their many voices raised in chorus. The entire company takes up the death-wail.

The circle of campfires burns brightly through the evening, each group ascribed a place according to the direction in which they have come. In turn, they take up positions at the centre of the circle, to sing and dance. Performances last the whole night through. Swallowed pride drives them on to greater and greater exertions, in their efforts to outdo and outlast one another.

Their bodies are painted with red and white ochre, heads strung with feathers or woolly with down, grass seeds stuck to the dried sacred blood let from their veins. Some carry bunches of feathers or leaves, tree limbs lengthening their own. Basic rhythms are tapped out using two short sticks, or by clashing together their weapons – *waddy*, *leowell*, *leipa*. A *bourka* of repute sets the time and tune.

'*Kartipaltapaltarlo padlara kundando*,' he sings.

The women sit before the dancers in a line or semi-circle. They wear possum skins, white down banding their foreheads, and horns of cockatoo feather. Removing their cloaks, they roll them tightly into a ball, and strike them with their palms in time to the beat.

'*Wodliparrele kadlondo.*'

Songs are sung in dialects so ancient that all meaning has been lost, and only the melody remains. The dancers shimmer by firelight, moving quick, quick, slow. Their dances portray the animals, the thrill of the hunt, great exploits in love and war. Each black limb painted with a broad white stripe, reanimated skeletons live out past glories, thighs wide apart and quivering madly.

Tears streak the faces of spectators.

He remembers. As part of the ritual call and response, before each repeat of the chorus, different solo performers 'ride' into the ring. Some introduce strange new words in English. He remembers the sound. These players of the stranger men are challenged and questioned, beaten down or forced back, or else their opponents collapse to the ground in a dead faint – scenes distressing to the young *Parnko*. He remembers the sound of their voices, in the night.

'*Kanyamirarlo kadlondo,
Karkopurrelo kadlondo.*'

Brippoki stands and sings the curse of vengeance – a song of power filled with all of the righteousness of *Bugaragara*, with invocations of *tjurunga*. His enemy is no better than a wild dog. He will sing him to sleep, steal on his camp, and strike to kill him where he lies.

He remembers all of it: the grief, the fury, and the fear.

The songs are wild that night. At certain intervals each dance halts, the entire company raising their hands to the stars, the campfires of their Ancestors.

'WAUGH!' their voices cry out as one.

'WAUGH! WAUGH!' he cries, until the approach of dawn, until his voice is cracked and gone.

They are off to see the King of Corsica.

Sarah walks the graveyard. Hand-in-hand with her mother she walks, although desperate to run. No birds sing. The light itself is smeary. Heavy rains have fallen all night, and through the best of the day. The air does not smell sweet and fresh, as it should after a storm. It stinks. What is that smell? On her left, and on their right, the topsoil has been washed away.

She sees for herself what the dreadful smell is. Sticking out of the ground, at their feet, are mottled green hands, stiff as claws. Her mouth and nostrils fill with the stench of rotting flesh...

Sarah Larkin woke to the sound of her own screaming. Her throat felt raw and tight, her tongue swollen like a slug.

She lay sweating, hot, then cold, and unable to move her head. The atmosphere seemed electrified, filled with bursts of strange light, although the room was in total darkness. It was early morning still – after midnight, but not yet dawn.

Nightmare soaked her pillow – no, not nightmare, childhood memory. Her mother, Frances, had taken her to visit William Hazlitt and Theodore, King of Corsica; in their graves in St Anne's churchyard, Soho. The cholera epidemics crowding London's cemeteries beyond capacity, the latest victims were stacked six- or seven-deep in shallow interments. It only took a rain shower to expose the bodies.

She had been walking with her mother, mottled green hand in her hand, through the graveyard.

Pulling herself together, Sarah rose to fetch a glass of water. Lingering at the doorway to Lambert's room, she heard the wet struggle of his lungs.

The night is thick, the brutal sort of darkness one can feel. A light moves about in the house opposite. Brippoki shifts position on the roof to gain a better point of vantage.

Thara moves about her *gunya*, carrying a candle. It lights up the white of her nightdress like the flame of a torch. From her chamber, she moves downstairs.

The firefly hovers in between floors for a time, and then disappears to the back of the house. Brippoki scrambles up. He is about to make his way around to the farther side when it reappears, hovering down another flight.

Thara enters the room he knows best. She stands, looking into the large mirror above the mantelpiece. She studies herself in the glass, at great length, as he has seen her do before. He is too far away to make out the expression on her face. She takes up scissors, and begins to attack her silver-streaked hair, throwing great chunks of it into the unlit fireplace.

Something then – a noise? – makes her freeze. She grasps the candle and runs up the stairs, and into her father's bedchamber. The curtains there are drawn.

She does not emerge again.

He creeps back to his former position, concealed within the eaves. The night is chill. His bones are weary, his head heavy. Brippoki dares not sleep.

Instead he scans the night for the glitter of predatory eyes.

The first tracks they discover are beneath the stony cliffs of *Merri-merri-winnum*. Soon, more are found, where the swamps of *Engottene-nurmwurm* fringe the plains of *Cattiong nyam nyam*. These are still fresh.

Their *corroboree* over for another season, his party returns home, to their lands further to the southwest, where Emu's egg rolls away.

A small stream waters the valley in which they camp. The turf around the banks is heavily scarred, the soft clay, at points, churned into a white and liquid mud. They are greatly disturbed by the tracks of mysterious *Ngamadjidj*. The No men have yet to see a white man. They consult with the womenfolk who survived that fateful night at *Worrowen*.

Ngamadjidj are horrific creatures, having two heads, as many legs as a beetle, and running just as fast. Their long and dragging footprints lead right up to the water's edge. There are also marks of a great many two-pointed toes – the white man's women, so their own *gins* say, are exceedingly ugly and smelly.

A finger of smoke rises from the far country spread before them. Some of the younger warriors are all for following the trail and taking their revenge. The wise men advise against it. So they set up camp in a hollow next to the stream, careful to keep the smoke of their own fire low.

A call from the surrounding brush alerts them. When they look up, they see white faces. Everyone scatters, shrieking at the tops of their voices. They leave behind bags and weapons. *Parnko*, he shits in terror. The stranger fellows stand their ground and cry 'cooey'. Everyone stays silent, in the trees or crouched behind them, until long after the evil has gone.

A few darks later and they meet the same party again, standing on the opposite banks of the broad *Wimmera*. Feeling safer, they take the time to study the curious whitefellows. Spears are brandished – threats, and furious reproach

– and, as evening falls, a war dance performed. The whites sit impassive throughout. In the morning, following a sleepless night, envoys from either side meet mid-river and exchange intimacies. They say they come from the sea, and present many useless gifts for which his people are obliged to give up their nets and a few weapons. They want to know where to find fresh water in the regions ahead. Directions are given to *Keyinga*, the lake.

Everyone is glad to have made peace. For the ghosts of their dead to return from the grave, and not know them, is a terror they wish ended.

The sky to the east grows lighter. Soon Emu's egg will roll around, and it will be time again for Brippoki to move on – aimless, alone, and in fear.

CHAPTER LV
Saturday the 20th of June, 1868

BECOME AS LITTLE CHILDREN

'And that inverted Bowl we call the Sky,
Whereunder crawling coop't we live and die,
Lift not thy hands to It for help – for It
Rolls impotently on as Thou or I.'

~ Rubáiyát of Omar Khayyám

Mother is close by. Father dumbfounds him with a string puzzle.

A round piece of bark, rolling along – pretending it an animal and they the hunters, some of the older boys try to spear it. One of their *teipas* strikes his outstretched arm. The tip, padded with grass, stings sharply, but does not pierce the skin. He cries and cries, and no amount of hugging will make him stop.

He climbs a tree. He falls, and does not cry. He hits the bark with a tiny, balled fist, and then sets to climbing again.

Ngamadjidj in these days is nothing more than smoke and ugly rumour. *Warri* the wind carries fire-talk down from the north, stories of trees sprouting up out of the sea, and huge winged birds. The dead return from *Pindi*, far to the west, on the backs of giant swans.

At the sight of them, the bravest warriors run away. The women hide their babies in the bushes. In their time away the dead have gained knowledge of another sort, and much of what they knew in life is forgotten. They speak a new tongue, no longer recognising family or friends.

He likes to hear Father tell these stories, but Mother shakes her head and covers her ears. Her people lived nearer the coast, where there has been long time plenty fighting. Talk of *Ngamadjidj* aches her liver.

Marriage is mostly with the *Jardwadjali*, a people ranging alongside *Wudjubalug* lands, partnerships approved according to *yauerin* – skin, or clan – and *goobong* – totem. *Yauerin, goobong* and *miyur* flow from the mother, and it is not good for menfolk to marry women of the same *yauerin* as their mother.

Brippoki's father marries late. His mother is found wandering the desert. Still very young, already she carries a child in her belly, a child belonging who knows where – taken one night, against her will, by a wicked *wembawemba* fellow, passing through her country with a party of white men. In revenge her people spear one of the no good one whites. It is said the spirit of the twice-dead man lodges in her. She wants to keep the child, and so is cast out.

No one wants her, until his father takes pity.

He, *Parnko*, is said to be the result.

And that is but one version of the stories told about him – later, with both his parents gone. All he knows for sure is that Mother was unlike the others. She kept herself and her boy apart, because, she said, they were better.

Brippoki remembers being carried, strapped across her back between her kangaroo cloak and two rush mats. Slung by his side is a bag of root, and, waving under his nose, tips of sandalwood. He is swaying back and forth very agreeably. The air fills with seedlings, blowing in the breeze – the smell of herb and lush grasses. The back of her head he knows very well, the honey scent and colour of her neck.

Of her face, he is unable to recall the slightest detail.

Sarah parted the heavy curtains.

The sun rose red and angry, all else concealed from view by a dense, caramel-coloured vapour. Only the very tops of the houses opposite were visible, and even then as dark outlines in the fog. London exhaled an atmospheric dust-cloud thick as pea soup; the recent fine weather having dried and powdered the dirt, the traffic kicked it up in vast quantity. Billowing from below, the street sounds seemed amplified – an effect, perhaps, of lost visibility, or simply greater cause to curse and blow one's horn.

An antipodean calenture: Sarah pictured herself adrift on a filthy brown sea. Distant island crags, only the tops of taller buildings pierced the veil. Spires, cut loose from context, slipped anchor to crest the waves – stone galleons, spectral and graceful.

'Darkness,' croaked a voice behind her. '"A day of clouds, and thick darkness."'

She turned towards Lambert, and then, back to the window, the featureless view. That was certainly the way things looked. He couldn't possibly see from where he lay in the bed. He must smell the laden air.

'Morning…spread upon the mountains,' said Lambert, 'people…great and strong. A fire!'

'A…' Sarah hesitated. 'You want a…?'

'"A fire devoureth before them,"' he spat, '"and behind them a flame burneth. The land *is* as Eden before them, and behind…desolate wilderness. Nothing shall escape.

'"The appearance… The appearance of them *is* of horses, and as horsemen, so shall they run. Before their face the people shall be much pained. All faces shall gather blackness."'

Beyond sense, he was still raving, as he had been half the night. He clutched at her and laughed, carefree as a small boy, calling her Emily and Fanny and even a few foul names, and seemed not to know her.

Night, for day – the air itself aglow is filled with smoke, as from a great fire.

Every street is a blind alley. The shifting mist forms a sheer cliff face, a wall that retreats at each step forward, even as its cousin, behind, advances. Brippoki stumbles along within the cloud, more calmed than confused by the lack of detail.

With a silent belch the foul smoke parts. A figure strides purposefully into view, only to disappear again a few paces further on – another, and then another. Each trails darkness. Occasionally they pause to fix and stare at one another, only for a moment, and are then swallowed up, a trick of light. Brippoki knows he walks in the midst of thousands. He can bear the measureless crowds for not seeing them all at once.

Gnowee, Mityan – somewhere in the sky lurks sun or moon. Brippoki has to take it by faith. Everything has the same colour, neither light, nor dark. The air is ash.

The air is a lie. His chest burns. He feels the weight of shadow, settling there.

'He is old,' shrugged Dr Epps. 'His mind wanders.'

Poised on the landing just outside the door to Lambert's room, they spoke in hushed tones. Lightly, and for the briefest instant, the fingertips of his right hand brushed against Sarah's sleeve.

'You've changed your hair,' he commented.

'What?'

The doctor looked a little discomfited.

'What can you do?' she asked, matter of fact.

'What can I do?' Epps replied. 'That is a good question.' He checked his pocket watch. 'I have to go.'

'But…'

'I have a train to catch,' he said, 'up country.'

The country; as soon as people made their money they would run to the country every chance they got, even if only for the weekend, admitting life in the city a slow poison. A touch of raw nature was the tincture to every ailment, the clear sky a balm.

Epps could not bear the scorn in her face. He excused himself. 'I must go,' he said. 'My own mother ails. She too is old.'

'Old', as if it were a disease. His mother, she knew, lived many hours away.

'What if,' said Sarah, calmly, 'what if he should take another turn for the worse?'

For an awful second Dr Epps looked genuinely doubtful.

'…I will come and see you first thing Monday morning,' he said. 'You have my word. First thing. How's that?'

How was that? He was always there first thing on Mondays, that's how it was!

'We'll see what…what progress he is making then,' he said. Epps showed his watch as much as checked it again. 'Really, must dash. Ten-thirty train.'

'No treatment?' she said. 'A sleeping draught?'

He considered a moment. 'I don't advise it. You'll be staying with him, I take it?'

'Yes.' Sarah felt suddenly guilty.

'That is for the best,' said Dr Epps. Running down a few steps, he paused, adding, 'The best medicine, I mean.'

Sarah remained on the landing. She listened to the sounds of Dr Epps moving about on the ground floor, shutting up the surgery, and then, finally, the front door. Only then did she turn.

Lambert was quiet now. The doctor had not seen the worst of it.

'Is that you?' he asked. A small bubble burst on his lips. 'My Angel.'

She had sometimes been his Darling, but never his Angel. Her mother was the Angel in the House.

He grasped her small, cold hand in his – gentle this time. 'My Angel,' he repeated.

Lambert's milky gaze wandered across her brow, her hair cut short.

'It…it is me,' she said. 'Sarah.'

'Sarah? Our little girl?' His features glowed with wonder.

The doorbell rang, insistent. Lambert was cooing and babbling. She wanted to wrest her hand from his, yet, at the same time, did not want to. It was probably one of the doctor's nearsighted patients – except it might be the doctor. He must have forgotten something, or locked himself out.

Running to the first floor landing, she saw the street-door letterbox open; a dark shape, bobbing beyond. Not Brippoki surely? In the way of *Kings*, he knew not how to go out or come in. The shadow moving aside, light through the front door letterbox held her frozen. An envelope popped through the slit, flip-flap. Why would the postman be ringing their bell? Sarah went down on tiptoe to pick up the letter lying on the mat. Addressed to her, it bore an Admiralty seal. She recognised the handwriting of the clerk, Dilkes Loveless.

There was no stamp.

Sarah made her way back up the stairs, slowly. The clerk had paid her a personal call? She sat by her father's bedside, Lambert's delirium only slight distraction.

She opened up the letter – more documents. She had asked Dilkes to check for Druce under any likely alias. Logs from the *Porpoise*, unlike those for the *Lady Nelson*, made no specific mention of him; other than catalogued close links between ships' personnel, there appeared to be little worthy of comment. The ship's muster, however – duly transcribed by the clerk, in an entry dated May 1st, 1810 – nominated one '*Jas. Druce*'.

Whence and whether –

– the next word, smudged, was illegible –

– or not: *Sydney*.
Place and country where from: *London*.
Age at time of entry on this ship: *30*.

His true age, falsified on deportation in 1792, would have been closer to 32 or 33. Druce's declaring himself 12 years old as opposed to 15 was probably what had saved him from the gallows.

Qualities: *Ordy*.

Ordinary seaman? Dilkes Loveless rather presumed upon her knowledge of naval terminology.

He had come to the house?

Slop clothes supplied by Navy: *4...0...6*.

Druce was said to be a slight man. These figures possibly represented his height – a level of detail that helped to make him seem that little bit more real.

Tobacco: *3/2*.
Comments: *deserter from HM Armed –*

'*Zinder*'? Tender?

– *Zinder* Lady Nelson.
Signed, *John Porteous* – Commander. *These are to certify the Principal Officers and Commissioners of his Majesty's Navy that the Articles of War and the Abstracts of the Act of Parliament were read for the Ships Company Agreeable to the Printed Instructions.*

Dilkes noted that same individual mustered May through October of 1810. A final entry read:

15 December 1810 (to) Thisby Paid off. 1.12.1+1.3.4. Boy List.

'*Jas.*' Short for James, or Joseph? Whether assumed or reclaimed, the change in name made sense if he was leaving the colony to escape debts incurred as 'George Bruce'.

Four foot six –

Sarah replaced the papers in their envelope. There was no accompanying letter, as if her faithful correspondent had been fully expecting to speak to her himself.

The return address should have been Mills & Wellman, the Receiving House at No.38. In her rush she must have put their home address, since that was written on his envelope. Dilkes Loveless had interpreted it an invitation to call on her.

Heaven only knew what trouble she courted.

Brippoki wishes an eye for an eye. *Waanyarra?* No, small bird is easier.

His spirit shakes itself loose. He rises up above, looking down to see the top of his own head, far below. High up, now higher than the housetops, he ascends swallow-swift, to soar above the dust storm on a level with the clouds.

Warri, the wind, whistles through wing tips. To the east sprouts a spinifex patch – sharp spike towers stabbing at the sky, as many spines as a cactus. Down south writhes the Serpent, choked on sail feathers caught in His gullet. Downcast looks see feet, scaled and clawed. Hidden sun glints off the metal moving parts of distant vehicles. Subtle rays fling faint shadows of larger birds onto the ground around. They cut in swathes and arcs, and circle-surround him – sharks about the small rowboats, taking them into the bay to board the *Rangatira*.

Below, complex strands flow out from the Piebald Giant, squat and patient at their centre – capped in dark blue, brooding. Above, a black star crosses the sun. *Waanyarra*, flying crow, looking down on the swift swallow's back. Crow-eye. Crow black.

Black death plunges.

Brippoki is returned, back beneath the shadow of St Paul, hard heart of London, ankle-deep in filth and the smell of the rookeries there. The air is thick and burning – the sky, stone, same as the city.

A mistake returning to *Pindi*, where dead men lurk in the wings. Bird brought low by crow, Brippoki sinks lower, buried in the graveyard for lifetimes of pain. The city crushed dry, bone-brittle, works its way into his eyes, ears, nose and throat. It suffocates the skin. Fine particles fill his mouth and scorch his lungs, catching breath. It is more than the dust of the ground, and to be feared.

He has gone for too long without sleep. His belly groans with hunger. Beyond exhaustion, only instinct now impels him. He neither knows nor cares where it is he walks – he walks to keep moving.

The coin only grows heavier.

CHAPTER LVI
Saturday the 20th of June, 1868

ARDENT SPIRITS

'Nor kind nor coinage buys
Aught above its rate.
Fear, Craft, and Avarice
Cannot rear a State.
Out of dust to build
What is more than dust…'

~ Ralph Waldo Emerson, 'Politics'

Sarah looked towards the window. The barest ray of light filtered through the filthy air. The city bled in from the outside – smoke, and a fly. What must it be, late morning?

Lambert's body shifted and grumbled. Sarah, unsure if he was awake or sleeping, sat close by his bedside, at the old preacher's worn writing desk; surrounded with paperwork, she made fresh notes.

Shortly after I shold have murdred my Poor father with A bras candelstick Wich I froo at him. but he puting his hand prevented it. I was put in to The workhous.

Only a small child, and already Joseph Druce raged. The workhouse system was a notorious national scandal. Sarah imagined the effect of such appalling rigours at an impressionable age: character-forming, defining perhaps the wayward direction his future life would take.

You wicked wrich for your disobedince to God you weill Wonder in the wildrness Like A Pilgrim Seeking for Reefouge and will find Non.

Felled by a desperate fortune, Druce's atonement for his crimes was to be a life of wandering. Under sentence of death, from the condemned cells at Newgate he was cast out of his country, not yet a man.

When the unclean spirit is gone out of a man, he walketh through dry places, seeking rest; and finding none, he saith, I will return to my house whence I came out.

And when he cometh, he findeth it swept and garnished.

Then goeth he, and taketh to him *seven other spirits more wicked than himself; and they enter in, and dwell there: and the last state of that man is worse than the first.*

Poor Joseph Druce, mired in self-pity and self-hatred: stigma writ large in his face, he was an object of revulsion, frustrated at every turn.

Before the world began, God, that cannot lie, had promised the hope of life eternal. His immortal anger seemed to be all that survived.

Sarah arched her spine, stiff and aching. She studied the tumbling air currents. Dust came from the manuscript, laid open on her lap; from any and all of the books piled up in every part of the room; from everything, and everyone – bleeding out from the inside, the pain of a hundred years more or less. Pain, bitterness, frustration, rage: Druce was an unquiet soul crying with a loud voice, screaming and shouting yet seeming never to be heard, not by any who cared to help or were empowered to do so. In the end his screams became incomprehensible – all of his mad cries and gesticulations, only able to stir minor particles in the air.

'In the dust, I write'…

Sarah shuddered against the awful silence. She listened harder. It was her father's breath that stirred the dust. They were alone, just she and Lambert. Nothing else moved in the room except for motes, faintly visible, stirred by whatever currents and collisions there were – calamity and catastrophe occurring at an atomic level.

The golden coin burning a hole in his dilly bag is spent. Knocking down his winnings, Brippoki swigs from an earthenware jug of 'Miller's EXOTIC NEAR Neat Imported Gin (medicinal)'. So pleased is he with his purchase that he leaves the shop without thinking to wait for change.

The shopkeeper, having assured himself it is no *jeton* or brassy Cumberland Jack, is doubly happy to accept the George III guinea in payment. No longer legal tender but money of account, its value is fixed at 21 shillings.

Liquid fire, or whatever it is, sold under the name of gin, London's own demon, serves its purpose. It takes away Brippoki's pains by giving him new ones. If nameless oblivion is to be his fate, he will drink to his departure beforehand.

The church bells are ringing, one, two, another one. The sandstorm covers over everything. Although, overhead, it does seem a little lighter than before…

He takes another swig. The Fire of God is healing, cleansing.

Whose God, he cannot say.

Brippoki clambers over the side of London Bridge, settling clumsily onto a broad stone parapet above one of the piers. Slugging gin, he drinks on an empty stomach. Small insects dither in the air above his crown. Specks of drifting ash settle on his skin. The sky shifts around and about. He is but a tiny black speck, sitting always at its centre.

Gunyas out on the marsh set down roots, grow in size, tree and meadow disappearing. Buried bones harden earth. Soil turns to shit, wood to stone. London Bridge is rising and falling, rising, falling.

He becomes dizzy with the unfolding spectacle – movement so rapid it approaches stillness, immobility so absolute it assumes blinding speed. Juddering steps and profound pulsations pound out the rhythms of the universe.

The Dreaming.

Breech-birthed in silence, from out of a boiling sea, the great bald head of the Piebald Giant rises. Stone fingers arrest the Great Serpent's curling progress. A livid blot, a rash, creeps along spreading arterial veins, striking out in every direction. Flushed with darker streams, they flow with obscure energy.

Brippoki answers the call of his Spirit Ancestors, wayfarers who planted first footsteps on the World. From the Creation comes the vision, and at the end is the vision fulfilled. Lifting up his arm, he pierces a large vein, drawing forth the salve of secondary holiness. His accelerated pulse makes the ritual blood spurt.

The campfires spin as the planets wheel, a whirl of beams and shadows – cool *Mityan* thick with flesh and thin in hunger, then burning Emu's egg. Mud-summer madness; at its height comes the storm, very grievous. A blinding flash of jagged lightning, crashing bolts of thunder, not from the skies but rock to rock, a storm such as there was none like it since man was on the earth.

The storm is a shelter to him. Having created it, gladly he enters in. Brippoki rides it out, wind-walking.

Envious Old Father, hidden among clouds. His lolling tongue spills sacred, secret laws. The Great Serpent shoots venom into his veins. Whipcrack reflexes jolt with electricity, stars shooting spears of light. The black sky stone falls to earth, cracking open the heaving clay.

Flames surge from between his toes to run along the ground. Brush fire! Hot coals spill from under stairs, setting light to the many houses. Within the walls, the stones themselves cry out, and the timber, shrieking, answers. Rafters, ablaze, come crashing down. The conflagration razes. Explosions, screams of man and beast, stampede – the clashing of swords and the trampling of hooves.

Wave after wave of fire engulfs the city in flame.

The bells of a thousand churches ring in his ears, their tunes playing in reverse. Blood, and fire, and pillars of smoke, the light of the sun smothered turns to darkness. A blackened disc, outside edge blazing, *Mityan* moon hangs huge in a black sky – runs, the colour of blood.

Brippoki collapses onto the superheated stone, a thorn-devil, skin stained red. Blue sulphuric acid, the elixir refined of souls dead and dying, bubbles from his torn vein.

An eternal firestorm burns the skies scarlet, the horizon a bow of flame. The entire landscape is a furnace, and, ever-present at its core, the cool head of St Paul.

Heads, severed, driven onto spikes, line the battlements of a great stone gate. Blood streams down the walls, soaking the ground, a foaming fountain at his feet. The seething river too flows red, totemic. It rushes onward, fierce and furious, towards the lip of a bottomless drop, a howling nothing.

'Let the past,' frothed Lambert, 'speak to the present. The day is come…when the present shall speak to the future. *Dies Irae!*

'"The great day of the LORD is near, it is near",' he warned. '"A day of wrath!"'

Sarah had to use all her weight to force him back down on the bed.

'All creation awakes,' shouted Lambert, 'ready to answer judgement! The noise…'

'Father?'

'The rattling wheels…the whip and prancing horses…chariots, jumping…'

She had closed the window against the insidious air. She couldn't do much about the noise. He grasped her roughly by the arms. His eyes, glassy though they stared directly, seemed to look right through her.

'Look not so far away!' she pleaded.

'"They shall run to and fro in the city. They shall run upon the wall, they shall climb up upon the houses. They shall enter in at the windows like a thief."'

'W-what?'

'"He that dasheth in pieces is come up before thy face!"'

Biblical quotes, she knew that – not any one passage, but from all over.

'What did you – *Owww!*' she cried.

His grip tightened. Eyes bulging as they searched her face, he held her very close.

'You're hurting… *Ungh*…' Sarah managed to wrench herself free, and took a step back.

Lambert studied the ceiling, or perhaps the skies beyond, her presence already forgotten. '"Multitudes, multitudes in the valley of decision,"' he wheedled, suddenly pathetic, '"for the day of the Lord is great, and who can abide it?"'

Sarah was thinking to try and engage him in conversation, when he again grew agitated.

'"WOE to him that buildeth a town with blood, and stablisheth a city by iniquity! Woe to her that is filthy and polluted, to the oppressing city!"'

Sarah tried for calm, but any word she uttered or move she made seemed only to incite him further.

'"The spoil of the poor is in your houses",' cried Lambert. '"Bones for bricks. Blood, the cement. WOE to the bloody city!"' he shouted. '"Woe unto the wicked! It shall be ill with *you*...for the reward of your hands...the reward of your hands shall be given *you*."'

The creases of his face became so deep, Sarah thought he would come apart.

'"Testify!"' he shouted. '"In the awful day of recompense, Repent! In sackcloth and ashes, Repent! Fasting, and with cries for mercy, Repent! Repent!"'

The prophet of despair lifted up his voice and screeched; helpless, useless, hopeless, Sarah buried her head in her hands.

'"If we repent not,"' he sighed, '"verily, we shall be inexcusable." "And the LORD alone shall be exalted in that day...when he ariseth to shake terribly the earth."'

A dull thudding sound forced her to look up. Hands above his head, Lambert rained blows on his exposed crown with frightening violence. Sarah leapt across the gap between them, landing bodily on the side of the bed. All of her papers fell on the floor. She paid them no heed. The blows from his punishing fists she took upon herself. Sarah hugged Lambert to her.

'Howl!' he cried. '"For merchant people cut down...all they that bear silver, cut off...their goods, booty, their houses...desolation"!'

Her slim body wracked with sobs, she pleaded with Lambert to stop. One might as well have commanded the tides to stop. Determined, he brooked no arguments.

'"This *is* the rejoicing city that dwelt carelessly, that said in her heart, I *am*, and *there is* none beside me. How is she become a desolation, a place for beasts to lie down in! Every one that passeth by her shall hiss, *and* wag his hand."'

Forcing herself upright, Sarah took her father's shoulders between her two hands. Her face looked directly into his – his face, gathering blackness. Furiously she willed him love, so that he might regain his reason.

'Remember,' she gasped, 'remember the story of Jonah and the gourd? "Doest thou well to be angry?"'

He returned only vacant looks. '"There is a multitude of slain,"' he mumbled, '"a great number of carcasses...no end to the corpses. They stumble upon their corpses... Their flesh shall consume away while they stand upon their feet, and their eyes shall consume away in their holes, and their tongues shall consume away in the mouth."'

'No!' she said. 'Oh, no...'

'"The Almighty Disposer will stretch out his hand"..."make of Nineveh a desolation, *and* dry...like a wilderness..."'

Lambert gasped and fell back.

'"Nineveh *is* of old...like a pool of water,"' he croaked, weakly. '"Yet, they shall flee away. Stand, stand! they *shall* cry, but none shall look back"..."nations, cut off...their towers, desolate...streets, waste, that none passeth by...there is no man...there is none inhabitant. She is empty...and void...and waste."'

Head deep into the pillow, Lambert's tongue curled back into his mouth. He was little more than shell.

The surface of the river is as flat as mirror glass. As above, so below – the reflected city lies silent, in ruin, a cracked dome at the centre. The crown of the Piebald Giant, bleached white, is no more than a shapeless, nameless rock pile, worn by winds and the sands of time.

Pale light, weak and failing, illuminates the scene. A great many broken buildings lie half-submerged in desert sands. Dense foliage wreathes the rest. Cormorant and *gau-urn*, the bittern, nest in the cracked rafters. Their voices sing from the windows, the woodwork all exposed. The numberless flocks of summers past, the spawning fish and all the wild beasts return.

A few paces distant a stranger sits, upright on a broken arch, rubble once part of the bridge now destroyed. He pauses from scratching marks onto a stone tablet to take in the awful beauty, peace, and quiet of his surroundings, sombre-seeming in his thoughts. Brippoki dares not approach for fear he may disturb him.

Is the fellow dark? Is he white? Brippoki cannot tell. The clothes he wears are like nothing ever seen. It almost seems for one moment he looks at himself – but that is how visions are. Asleep with eyes open, awake with them closed, he might even be a stone carving, an immobile statue.

The setting sun in one last burst tinges the pale ruins red.

From beneath the depths of West Monster Abyss and out of broken Shadwell, to the east, shadow creeps. Nurtured by day in the narrow alleyways, under arches, in damp corners of hidden courtyards, the terrors of black night unhitch themselves to come sliding forth. Stretching, lengthening, deepening, they roll across rooftops and slither down stairwells, joining, meeting, growing – spreading. Run together they form pools, above which solid swarms take to the air. The windows, gathering soot, black themselves out. Stone-bark grooves of petrified tree trunks run with a liquorice-sticky juice. The same greasy filth that seeps out of the pipes flows from swollen drains. In the middle of the streets, it meets. Each and every crevice is filled in. Scurrying figures flee in vain, swallowed up whole – disappeared within. Others, crow circling, turn silhouette. The streets and houses drown. Lanes are black, the immense buildings black. The bone factories pump out black smoke.

All of this occurs without a single sound.

A sudden spillage of ink into the sky, black sunrise inspires swift growth of bare black branches, a canopy of waving spider-legs, extended, stretching out across the firmament – thick trunk of solid blackness dragged pulsing behind.

A furious thunderhead gathers, shadow casting shadow across the ground. Tornado-twists spiral down, the air streaked with great black tears – Sky World pulling itself back down to earth.

A last wink of light, and then there is nothing, save blackness and the darkness forever, more dreadful than any night.

Only the river stays clear, its broad beam his guide. The blacker it gets, the brighter seems the light. A distant star suggests itself, a candle in an open window…

The coarse laughter of a ferryman, his lantern working below, brings Brippoki around. Dust, filling up his gaping mouth, lodges fast in his throat. Dark clouds are under his feet, and the shadow at his back.

Guts churning, Brippoki's chest heaves. He throws up on the spot.

His brow burns as his throat burns. He takes one last slug of blue gin, then dashes the clay jug across the vomitous rock, resolved to run. Feet stumble-sliding through the puke and jagged shards, he staggers towards the remote flare of light.

CHAPTER LVII
Saturday the 20th of June, 1868

THE HAUNT OF MEMORY

'Oh Thou, who Man of baser Earth didst make,
And ev'n with Paradise devise the Snake:
For all the Sin the Face of wretched Man
Is black with – Man's Forgiveness give – and take!'

~ *Rubáiyát of Omar Khayyám*

The Aborigine breezed in, quite soundless, through the open parlour window. He walked directly up to the fireplace and stared intently into the ashes. The fire was unlit; she had been meaning to sweep it out, but never quite got around to it.

His appearance was the most extraordinary yet; still naked, near enough. Objects increasingly arcane were tied onto strands of his hair: longer feathers, more teeth, and a dangling claw, either crab or lobster. Smeared with gum as before, as far as she could tell he had added horse manure to the mix.

Sarah shifted in her seat and cleared her throat, politely.

Brippoki leapt back, nearly going for the window again. He collided with a small occasional table, dislodging its lace doily.

'It's only me,' she said.

The wing of the armchair had perhaps hidden her face. Why she had chosen to sit alone in a darkened room, Sarah couldn't exactly say.

'I'm…sorry,' she said. 'I didn't mean to startle you.'

Granted, she didn't occupy her usual spot; still, she found it hard to believe that he, of all people, could be surprised by her – a turn-up for the books! She almost laughed: and would have, were it not for his pitiable state.

He was sweaty and breathless. She could smell the drink on him.

Brippoki keeps his eyes averted. He paces the carpet, warily, making sure to tug at his *min-tum* so that she sees he is protected. The Guardian has her days. It is not good to look on a woman when she is bleeding.

He remains on edge, unsure of propriety.

Thara moves to light the candles. 'I'll boil a fresh pot,' she says. 'This one has gone cold.'

As soon as she is gone from the room Brippoki returns to the fireplace. He crouches down, hurriedly reaches in and retrieves the object of his desire – stands, unsteadily. His dilly bag is lodged in its place of concealment. Hands cupping the precious trophy, he casts about for another pouch suitable to keep it in.

Sarah returned bearing the teapot, piping hot. Brippoki was grovelling in the grate again. He ducked back when he saw her, looking a trifle sheepish. Abruptly he let go the poker, as if it were red-hot – confounded by the clang of it striking the hearth. He looked tragi-comical in his guilt. The notion that he might wield it as a weapon barely creased her consciousness.

He was as dead and grey as a cast in the half-light, bathed in a fresh coating of ash. The skin of his feet appeared dry and scaly. The nails, long like talons, needed clipping. Brippoki, expanding his thin chest, gathered himself to his full height, and did his unsteady best to affect nonchalance – a valiant effort in vain: he was so very obviously liverish, more than a little green about the gills, almost blue, his rapid breathing far shallower than previously.

Brippoki sat – collapsed rather – as if strings holding him up had been cut, all the cartilage in an instant removed from his bones. Folded in on himself, he clutched and massaged the muscles of his upper arms and occasionally his calves, deficient by comparison. Formerly so bright, so sharp and swift, his distracted attentions easily wandered.

Sarah too, weary with cares, struggled to concentrate. She had left Lambert sleeping, finally quieted, or else would not have left his side at all. Clarity and recognition returned to his looks, he had drifted away with a wan smile tugging at the sides of his mouth.

She told herself he was past the worst of it – on the mend, like so many times before.

Brippoki's head lolled, drowsily. Speech seemed beyond him.

Earlier, Sarah had taken the latest batch of Admiralty papers from their envelope, intending to read out the details from the muster roll. She realised that would be to little advantage at this juncture.

Bleary-eyed, her guest waited doggedly on her. She knew what he wanted. Still standing, she took up her notebook; forgetting, in all her distresses, that Brippoki had run out on her previous reading.

'Last we saw,' she said, 'our man had been returned to England, all of his various attempts to return to New Zealand frustrated.'

Sarah started to read from the notes she had most recently transcribed: the sole reason for Brippoki's visits, for what other reason could there be?

I again went on board the *Namur*. From her I was in-leaved at Sheerness. I then came up to Gravesend, where I met a woman in great distress, and glad I was to find her so, for the husband of the said woman once relieved me in my distress, and I thought that one good turn deserved another. I had 22 pounds in my pocket, which I received at Sheerness for serving His Majesty.

It was late at night when I met Mrs Downey in the street. This is her name. I asked her where was Mr Downey. She told me he was at Northfleet at work. I told her to follow me to the Watermen's Arms where I lodged that night. I told the master of the house to give Mrs Downey whatever she wanted that night for her and the children. And I went to her house the next morning. I gave her four pound to lay out for her family, after which she robbed me of sixteen pound. But in a few days the money was returned me by the Mayor of Gravesend.

I then went to lodge at the King's Head, where I remained till I had spent all my money, and lost my papers which was worse nor all. I then went to work among the lightermen on the River Thames, till I was so afflicted with the rheumatism that I could work no more.

So he became a Thames waterman, like the 'water-poet' John Taylor. The repetitive cycle of Druce's behaviours appeared the chief cause of his woes, a self-frustrating prophecy.

Brippoki sat trance-like in his apathy. Features blank and unresponsive, he appeared morose more than impassive, sunken into a profound and personal gloom. He fingered and twirled the thong around his midriff – not proudly, as he once had, but from nerves. On a separate string around his neck he wore what looked to be the beak of a small bird, and this too he touched, almost by way of reflex. That same splendid body capable of monumental stillness was a mess of tics and twitches.

Their progress only brought on his decline. Sarah was almost loath to carry on. Something ate him up from the inside. She was losing him too.

I was then to Bartholomew's Hospital by Mr Voss, a gentleman who was my master at that time. After my recovery I returned to my master, Mr Voss, where I worked for him till I again took sick. I then went into the poorhouse. In a few weeks after which Mr Cooper sent for me in hope to procure me a passage to New Zealand. He sent me to Squire Hagin, Queen Square, Westminster. Mr Cooper told me that Squire Hagin was going to New Zealand and he would take me with him. But when I went to the Squire he told me that Government had cancelled his going to New Zealand. I returned with my heart full of grief.

Going through Fleet Street on my return home I met a Mr Thompson, who ask me if I had been to New Zealand. I said yes. He told me to call on him the next day, which I did. He then sent me to Mr Flicker and Mr Flicker sent me to Mr Pratt, where I was introduced to the Society. They took me out of the poorhouse and maintained me for a short time, till one day Mr Pratt sent for me and told me that the Society could no longer support me, for Government would have nothing to do with it. I again was turned into the street.

I then in my heart renounced all mankind. And I went and pawned the prayer book and Bible –

The oracle spoke. 'What is "pawned"?' he asked. Brippoki inflected his accent in precise mimicry of hers.

Sarah sat down closer to him to explain.

'It means he gave these things away, his prayer book and his Bible,' she said, 'for money.'

Such a clear suggestion that the author had lost his faith – more so, rejected it – upset Brippoki gravely.

'Him still *budgere* goodpella,' he expressed, sincerely. 'Him still love God, inne.'

The alternative seemed too terrible to contemplate.

'Yes,' said Sarah. 'Yes, I'm sure of it. Only his need for money is greater, at this time.'

'Behold,' he said, sadly, 'what manner o' love, that we be called the sons o' God.'

He quoted the First Epistle General of John. Sarah's mouth hung open. *Beloved, now, are we*, it went, *when he shall appear, we shall be like him. For we shall see him as he is.*

'We be called the sons o' God,' Brippoki repeated. 'Dem first words Lawrence teach to us boys, from the Holy Bible.'

Sarah felt she should very much like to meet this Lawrence.

The humble and despised Aborigines, unsuspected by the world at large, truly were the favourites of God. She wondered how much of the message Brippoki might have taken to heart, if only as a measure of the strength of his white brethren's beliefs, as opposed to his own.

'The prayer book,' she said, 'the Bible, they are but things. Faith…is something you carry inside of you.'

She tried her best to sound sincere, to soothe him.

'And every man that has this hope purifies himself, even as he is pure. Purifies himself, and "Whosoever abideth in him sinneth not".'

Brippoki was nodding, more sage than savage. 'We should love one another,' he said.

'Yes,' said Sarah. She worried how well he might know the remainder of that text.

'He says he has given up on his fellow man, that is all,' she said.

It was enough.

'You can understand,' she went on, 'how he might. Lose faith. In man. After all he has been through, I mean…turned out onto the street…'

Best to press on.

> I then in my heart renounced all mankind. And I went and pawned the prayer
> book and Bible, and then went to Liverpool. From there I went to Dublin, and
> from Dublin to Cork, where I see a ship laying called the *Guildford*. She was
> bound to Port Jackson with convicts. I asked the Captain to take me with him,
> but the Captain told me he had so many men on board his ship that he could
> not ship any more. At the same, he gave me a shilling, seeing I was in distress,
> and the Irish God bless them all for they used me like a Christian while I was
> among them.

'You see?' said Sarah.

Brippoki slumped, inconsolable. Apprehension, the threat of some sort of
ever-present danger, seemed the only thing to rouse him from these frequent
bouts of listlessness.

One eye on him, she read –

> I remained in Cork for some time, till, one day, I met a gentleman who knew
> me. He relieved me with money, and the next day sent his servant for me
> who conducted me to his master's quarters. This gentleman was a Captain
> in His Majesty's Horse Guards, the 79th Regiment. At my arrival in Captain
> Lacock's quarters he received me with open arms of friendship and brotherly
> love. He told me to make myself happy for he would support me till he either
> got me a situation or a ship from that country. In a short time after, at his
> return home from parade, with a smile of glory and joy on his countenance to
> serve me, he told me he had spoke to Captain Johnson the commander of the
> ship *Guildford* to give me a passage to New South Wales, and that I was to go
> on board the next day. My heart leapt within me for joy, and my friend fitted
> me out with everything for the voyage. The next morning I took leave of my
> friend and went on board. In a few days after, the ship sailed.

Sarah fell silent. She had reached the end of the fresh material recorded
that day, as well as the surplus from her previous session.

The intervention of yet another gentleman helper who 'knew' Druce
aroused her suspicions: were such instances of brotherly love the agency of
Christian charity, she wondered, or rather evidence of Freemasonry in action?
The *Guildford*. Guild Ford. They too favoured the First Epistle of John.

Brippoki's bearing brightened, as if he entertained genuine hopes of a
happy ending to the story – that their unlikely hero, after so much frustration
and disappointment, might actually achieve his goal and be returned to New
Zealand. He had forgotten the bare facts: the manuscript had been written at
the Naval Hospital in Greenwich, and its narrator buried there, long since. Or
could it be that she herself presumed too much? Only a little way ahead with
her transcript, she had not yet made the end of it. The ending was unknown.
Should she even dare, to hope against hope?

Sarah laid her notebooks aside and took up the manuscript itself. There were only a couple of pages left to go.

Finding the same passage, she transliterated the speech as she read it.

After four months at sea she put in to –

'S*incehiedoor*', it read. How on earth could she hope to decipher that?

'What that?' said Brippoki.

'I don't rightly know,' Sarah said. She had not even tried to pronounce the word aloud yet. She looked up.

The Aborigine's entire stance had altered. He cringed, all a-quiver, seeming electrified, staring wild-eyed at the book held in her lap.

'Oh. You mean this…?' Sarah blushed slightly, forced to admit. 'I have…' she started to say. 'It's the manuscript. From the library. I took it.'

Smiling awkwardly, she held it up so that he might see.

'This is the actual document.'

'*Wa… Wa-day!*'

'Only a day or so ago, I meant to…'

Brippoki leapt to his feet, hissing and spitting. '*Tjurunga!*' he shouted.

'W-what? Brippoki?'

Averting his gaze, he pointed.

The Book of the Law – in awe, Brippoki backs away.

A *tjurunga* is the holy of holies, a very sacred object. More than representing the Spirit of an Ancestor, it embodies Them, a portion of Their vital force, eternally fertile. Transformed over time, the essence of the Ancestor thereby escapes the inevitability of decay.

Deadman's Spirit is in the Book, as is that of his people – the Guardian included. And recklessly she flaunts it, in her lap! At this time!

Brippoki keeps his distance, lest there be even the slightest suspicion he might wish to steal it away.

Brippoki switched back and forth in front of the fireplace. Air disturbance guttered the candle in its holder. He jumped and started at his own shadow, jerking crazily about the four corners of the room; very swiftly reaching a pitch of excitement from which, it was clear, no amount of friendly persuasion could possibly bring him down.

They were so very nearly done.

Visibility hampered, Sarah struggled to make out the words.

After four months at sea, she put in to…Sincehiedoor, to water, where I took sick with the fever and –

Ague?

> – ague! I then went to the hospital, where I remained for seven long months in the most vilest pain and agony.

Brippoki set to moaning.

> At last it pleased the Almighty God to release me from death and Hell, where I surely must 'a' gone if I had died at that time. But I hope the Blessed Lord Jesus Christ spared me to save my poor sinful soul from perishing.

She prayed to hear the old familiar 'Amen'. Instead, Brippoki moaned louder still.

'Does he sleep now?' he suddenly asked.

'Yes!' Sarah, misunderstanding, answered sharply: with all of his noise, in his disarray, she still worried after Lambert.

> At –

Brippoki fell cowering to his knees.

Sarah paused, shocked – his behaviour was a constant mystery.

> At my recovery His Majesty's Ship *Congo* arrived at that port, commanded by Captain…Fitzmorris. I went to Captain Fitzmorris and offered my service. I was then entered onboard the Congo and came home to England in her.

She hurried the words.

> The ship came to Deptford where I found a woman whom I knew at New South Wales. She was in distress and as soon as I received my wages for *Congo*, which was only seven pound, I shared it with her till all was gone.

'Does he sleep?' persisted Brippoki. 'He sleep now, inne?'

Belatedly, she understood that he asked after Druce.

'Yes, he sleeps now,' Sarah said. 'But not alone.'

Whether he had actually known the woman in New South Wales or not was by the by: 'a woman in great distress' surely euphemised a common prostitute.

Brippoki quailed further. Her patience exhausted, she paid him no heed.

> I then went to London –

'*Owaaah!*' cried Brippoki.

> …in hope to get employment, amongst the lightermen, but alas the lightermen had nothing to do for themselves. I now found myself miserable beyond expression –

'*Nuuhh!*'

– beyond expression. Destitute of friends –

'*Ahoh!*'

– no money, nothing to eat –

'*EhHHNn!*'
'Brippoki, *please!*'

– no labour.

'*Ih, ih…*' He writhed on the hearthrug.
They were so close to the end. She read on.

Thus like a castaway wicked wretch as I am, I wandered the streets night and day.

'*Ihhhh!*'

Death –

'*IHHHHH!*'

Death to me at that time would have been very acceptable. Now I said in my heart, there was no God to let m –

Sarah never finished her sentence. As she had half expected, Brippoki rolled to his feet and made a dash for the window. Giddy and light-headed he fell over his own feet, or else a ruck in the carpet. Whichever, his delay gave Sarah chance to jump up: she surprised herself, acting without thinking. She stood firm in between Brippoki and means of escape.

Scrambling up and back, he shrieked at the proximity of the manuscript, still in her hands.

'Shush,' she said, arms spread… 'shushhh.'

Not taking her eyes off him, Sarah crouched down. She laid the book gently on the floor behind her. Backing off still further, he followed its progress with his eyes, and then looked for a way around.

They engaged in a ludicrous standoff.

'Brippoki…' said Sarah, very measured.

Breathing loudly, he mouthed cabalistic phrases.

'What?' she asked, in earnest. 'What is it? Talk to me. *Talk* to me! Joseph Druce…'

Brippoki, poor fellow, grew so frightened he fell over. He groaned pitiably.

Too tired to be clever, she needed to choose her words more carefully. This wasn't what she wanted… Sarah reached out, taking a bold step forward.

He screamed again, trembling, then coughed, his whole body retching. She dared not move any closer.

Wracked with spasms, he was violently sick. With so little content in his stomach, it was mainly sputum that sprayed out onto the carpet. His beard dripping, he looked dismayed, almost as if, through it all, a sense of good manners prevailed.

'Ohhh, Brippoki!' Until that moment she had not even seen the terrible wound on his arm. Her outstretched hand hovered.

'*Ihhh.*' He kept backing away, conflicted in fear and shame. He would not, could not, do her any harm: she kept pace, persevering.

'I am your friend,' she said. 'Let me…I can…'

Brippoki darted away. He ran full tilt into the opposite window frame – slammed bodily into it, setting it rattling – before falling back.

'*EaaaH!*' screamed Sarah. 'What are you…? Are you…?'

She huddled closer to the floor, closer to him.

'*WHO?*' she asked. 'Who *is* he?' She sounded too shrill – anger in her voice, and ugly insistence. '*Who is Joseph Druce?*'

'Deadman!'

He spat the word out, quite literally – still looking for a way out. *Deadman can come for them when he is sleeping.* The knowledge was forbidden. She could be killed for it.

'What is he to you? I am your friend,' she said again. 'I only want to help you. Please, tell me. Let me help you.'

'Deadman,' he said again, shuddering, shaking his head. 'Deadman from grave.'

They edged around each other, arms stretched forth one to another – hands, without touching, hers reaching out and his, fending off. At risk of hurting her he would not grapple.

Sarah could not bear to see him hurt, nor to see him hurt himself further. She could not stop him. Brippoki gained the open window.

'Don't…'

And out.

'WHY WON'T YOU TELL MEEE!' She screamed her frustration out of the window, before crumpling onto the sill. 'Why won't you tell me…let me…'

Sarah slid down the wall to the floor. She had lost him.

She sat, uselessly hugging herself.

No sound came from upstairs that might indicate Lambert had been disturbed.

Sarah had managed to hold herself together: she had not cried. She would not cry. Eventually, reaching for the sill, she hauled herself to her feet.

A breeze riffled through loose-leaf pages, scattered across the floor. Some paperwork had dropped from her lap when she'd leapt to intercept Brippoki; more, blown off the tabletop.

The precious book lay on the floor. Sarah took it up – the manuscript, Druce's *Life*.

They had come so close to the end. She found the page.

na I sed in my heart There was no God to let man suffor as I ded in A naton of plenty.
but O shourley there is A God. & A most inexsprissibel mircyful one.

Pasteboard defences crumbled. Her tears came in floods, and there was no stopping them.

CHAPTER LVIII
Saturday the 20th of June, 1868

SYMPATHY FOR THE DEVIL

'There is no one who loves pain itself, who seeks after it,
and wants to have it, simply because it is pain.'

~ Cicero, *De Finibus Bonorum et Malorum*

Sarah closed up the window. There was no telling how long it might be before she would see Brippoki again; the last time, he had disappeared for over a week.

She looked over Druce's recent *Life* in vain search of some clue or cause to explain the Aborigine's reaction.

According to the shipping list, Joseph Druce had served aboard the sloop *Congo* from November 1816 through March of 1817. The proceeding seven months he spent laid up with fever in '*sincehiedoor*' – Singapore? That would have been the middle part of 1816, the notorious 'year without a summer'. A gigantic volcanic eruption had affected weather-patterns across the whole of the planet for months on end, a dust cloud created thick enough to blot out the sun.

Does he sleep? Brippoki had asked. Was this another of Druce's prodigious sleeps?

Sarah herself felt she could sleep for a hundred years.

She went to put away the most recent documents received from Dilkes Loveless, and found that she had misplaced the envelope. Gathering up the last of the scattered pages, Sarah tucked them inside the closed manuscript, then opened wide the window again in case there was even the slightest chance Brippoki might return.

Checking in on Lambert one last time, she prepared to retire herself.

Sarah stewed in her bed. Exhausted though she was, still she could find no rest.

Some impulse made her pull back the covers, re-light and take up the candle, and crawl towards the bed's nether end. She returned to her mother's sea-chest, and the treasure buried there – a large and sturdy object, not at all fashionable as heirlooms went, the stiles foursquare, the corners not canted, more suited to a sailor's belongings than a lady's accoutrement. Lambert, she recalled, had considered it something of an embarrassment while Frances was still alive. Undoing the clasp she opened it wide, sliding to the floor beside.

A whistle or a painted chip, lead dragoon or gingerbread-dog – once the lid was up there could be no going forward, only back. Sarah dug deep, no longer afraid to unearth the remnants of childhood – her own, and her mother's long before her – toys, games, and all the emotional attachments that went with them, long lost, nigh forgotten. One by one she plucked them out: THE QUICK BROWN FOX JUMPS OVER THE LAZY DOG, an alphabetical caper; random pieces of a puzzle; an oxblood marble. Eyes fluttering shut, Sarah plunged both hands in. Her questing fingertips stroked the coarse edge of card-paper.

She extracted a large piece of folding card from the bottom of the chest, bringing the candle in closer so that she might study its design. She saw trees laden with foliage, groaning and generous, rich in emerald greens and deepest browns, and a mud track leading away into a hazy middle-ground. High on the horizon sat a huge mountain, stormy skies beyond. Sarah blew some of the dust off the image, almost extinguishing the candle. Refreshed, the foreground disclosed a mud hut, bird of paradise idling on the inclined roof. Visible zephyrs, drawn as curlicues of air, darted back and forth, and an ominous puff of smoke arose in the distance.

The flipside illustrated a tropical island backdrop. Twisted tree trunks formed bizarre and dream-like shapes, palm fronds curling. Fantastical caves, rocky outcrops and waterfalls surrounded a choice of trails into deep and dense jungle – a scene she knew by heart.

'Scenery unrivalled in its picturesqueness', ran the advertiser's puff.

'Jumble,' whispered Sarah.

In her other hand she held a flimsy paper doll, a figurine. What was this one? Her thumb wiped the base of the card – *Tabassa*.

The paper-theatrical play set had been old even when she was young: the by-line on the reverse side of the two-sheet read 'William West Toy Theatre, theatrical print publisher'. Sarah dug out an ornamental stage front in copperplate print, for framing the 'curtain'. To either side stood gaudy representations of the twin pillars of toy theatre repertory – Clown for pantomime, and Orson the Wild Man for the *mélo-drame*, a mixture of dialogue with action.

A minimum of stage machinery was required to mount any childish production: grooves cut into the stage floor for scenery and wings to be slotted through, and slid back and forth to change a scene; a trap door, for Ghosts; and, at the front, a shallow trough in which to place oil lights. The wooden stage was long gone, but all of this the front would have been arranged to artfully conceal.

'For there are *Combats*, great and small,
And *Portraits* out of number;
Processions, *Cars*, *Stage-Fronts*, and all!
To Fill one's mind with wonder.
The *Scenes* are shifted to and fro,
A *trap-door*'s in the rear,
Top-drops above, and *Slides* below,
Then *Characters* appear.
The *Drama*, too, call'd 'Juvenile',
Portrays each sep'rate Part,
And, while we thus our time beguile,
We get the Play by heart.'

Once shown how, Sarah had put on shows for her mother, and on rare occasion Lambert too. First, the characters were cut out and mounted onto pasteboard, 'Prime Bang Up and no abuse'. Then they were glued onto sticks, or thin wire – which was better: 'invisible' – ready to be pushed out onto the stage. Others might pop through the trap door – rise, and speak, the various parts read in different voices appropriate to the supposed manner of each.

But she was getting ahead of herself. Before commencing the Performance it was necessary to refer to the Drama, and to set the Scenes and Wings accordingly for the next Act. She did so.

Tabassa was chief – there were also Thingaringue, Thurm, and Arkoval, collectively '*Les Indiens*'. Even as Sarah marvelled at the tiny, colourful figures, they fell apart in her hands, rainbow-dusting her fingers.

She turned and searched among some papers at the very bottom of the box, retrieving a slender booklet, the Drama, *DES PETITS ROBINSON DANS LEUR ILE, comédie* ('*Of the Little Robinsons on their Isle*, a comedy'). It was a pastiche play based on *Der Schweizerische Robinson* by Johann David Wyss: the story of a Swiss family who leave their native land planning to settle in Australia, but during their sea voyage are shipwrecked and marooned on an apparently deserted island. First appearing as a supplement to the French edition, and the conceit of translator Isabelle de Montolieu, the title page of the battered and discoloured pamphlet bore the publication date 1816. '*Orné de douze figures en taille-douce et de la carte de l'île déserte*,' it read; and, 'dedicated to children everywhere'. Smudged and smeared, the flyleaf also bore a clumsy and childish inscription in pencil – her mother's maiden name, 'Frances Twytten'.

Sarah's hands shook as she turned over the pages.

The family of the novel – titled in reference to Defoe's *Crusoe* – were Monsieur and Madame Bonval and their sons Fritz, Ernest, Jack, and François.

The listed character to grab Sarah's whole attention, however, was 'George Tippahee, eight years of age, Indian prince'.

Tippahee?

Breath held, she scanned through the text, written in both French and English. The action began pretty much straight away.

SCENE I.

Savages kidnap Jack.

JACK: Help, Papa! He bites me, he grips me, he eats me!

Passing mention was made of Crusoe himself, and '*Vendredi*', and then some part missing. Sarah flicked through the pages ahead.

SCENE XIII.

Enter the Indians.

…the characters whose warpaint stained her fingertips.

SCENE XIV.

Fritz enters hand-in-hand with the young prince George Tippahee, decorated with feathers, shells, glass beads, and holding a beautiful red plume.

FRANÇOIS AND JACK (*ensemble*): A little savage! A wild friend! Ah! how happy we are!

They run to embrace him with hugs and kisses, which he returns in the same manner, with vim and vigour. They repeat all their friendly words, and the young Indian replies.

GEORGE TIPPAHEE: *Sucali (Amitié).*

FRITZ (*to his brothers*): Don't you just love him, better than a monkey? Delightful George Tippahee honours you with his friendship. He's a prince… the son of the King of New Zealand, no less!

Tabassa sits himself on a rock, serious as always, smoking the peace pipe with M. Bonval. George Tippahee presents Madame Bonval with the red feather.

GEORGE TIPPAHEE: For your head, the feather of friendship. Mother has told me: George Tippahee, take this present to Marie Bonval, and let Marie receive it with the love of Akotoe.

There could be no mistaking the personage of Aetockoe, Princess of New Zealand. Thrown into the bottom of a sea-chest, locked away in some remote region of Sarah's heart, sense-memory of her had endured.

MME BONVAL (*animated*): Akotoe! My God! Do I hear you right? The Princess Akotoe, the wife of George Bruce, is your mother?

George Bruce! The Sneak-thief Sailor, reunited with his Princess…

The playlet named 'Akotoe' as the mother of the fictional little savage George Tippahee. The lost child of 'George Bruce' and his consort, Aetockoe, had been reimagined a son instead of the daughter.

At this point in the text, the paper of the booklet was curiously wrinkled and worn, as if water-damaged. Even the ink itself was faded.

> GEORGE TIPPAHEE (*laughing*): George my father, Akotoe my mother. Marie is the friend of Akotoe, because Marie receives the feather of friendship with the love of Akotoe, of George, and of Tippahee.

Madame Bonval asks her husband how this is possible.

SCENE XV.

Monsieur Bonval reminds his wife of bulletins concerning the history of the sailor George Bruce and his Princess bride.

MADAME BONVAL: I know their history by heart.

MONSIEUR BONVAL: This island forms part of the kingdom of good Tippahee, father of Akotoe. In coming here, we visit the same, from where the sea captain Dalrymple, who anchored in this region, abducted George and his wife. Tippahee is dead, and, by his decree and the will of the whole nation, his son-in-law George Bruce and daughter Akotoe rule in his stead, and are presently occupied civilising their subjects.

One of the sailors from our ship, escaping the storm, and having swum to the island of Typpayassa, where king George and his queen Akotoe hold court, found help and protection there. The sailor told the royal couple of our marooned family, and set out to aid us – bearing a letter from George Bruce.

Madame Bonval, trembling, takes up the letter.

MADAME BONVAL (*reading*): 'George Bruce, king of the Typpayassa islands in New Zealand, and his wife Akotoe, extend greetings and friendship to the minister, Bonval, and his castaway family. If you wish to return to Europe, I will grant you the means: but I hope to convince you, after my own experience, that it is in the simple dress of the children of nature, and far from the luxuries of the great civilised nations, that happiness lies.'

It continued in much the same vein, with copious introductions, *politesse*, and niceties. Sarah had to lay the booklet aside a moment, and take a much-needed breath.

Madame de Montolieu, writing in 1816, had taken an episode of Druce's story – presumably from the same original source as his 1810 *Memoirs*, the tale concerning Aetockoe's kidnap – and given him his much-wished-for happy ending. Her whimsical playlet was a confection: perfectly suited to delight well-educated young girls from comfortable homes, but surely too sweet for the robust London stage. Yet circumstantial evidence suggested otherwise: to become a children's toy theatre production, it must have enjoyed at least some level of popularity. Action was usually prerequisite over and above spectacle and exotic scenery. *DES PETITS ROBINSON* was all talk, with no fighting, no grand procession, nor even any wild beasts. Tastes had changed since those far-off days; the delicacy of the early Romantics curdled, becoming gothic, and dark.

Around 1816, 1817, the craze for toy theatre would have been at its height, William West and his many rivals desperately keen for material. A story already in circulation as a street patterer's penny blood was as ripe for adaptation as anything else. Examining the jungle scene more closely, Sarah could see it had originally belonged to a different production entirely: tiny voided lettering in the corner read 'Forty Thieves No.2 – a Grand Oriental Spectacle'. Similar works in a genre *en vogue* meant certain articles of scenery could be endlessly recycled.

SCENE XVI.

MADAME BONVAL: *George, as-tu des sœurs?* (George, do you have any sisters?)

GEORGE TIPPAHEE: Sister Georgina, sister Zimee…Bella, and Mani…

Not content merely to change his only child's sex, the playwright blessed Bruce with many daughters, doubtless intended to wed the Bonvals' numerous sons. A little scene followed where Monsieur Bonval gave Tabassa a bottle of rum 'to cement their perfect union.' Tabassa balanced a child on each of his broad shoulders, and they raised a toast: to the future, presumably, one in which they all lived happily ever after.

Sarah searched around for the figurine of Akotoe, but could not find it.

Beggar urchins had their penny gaffs, for street entertainments such as *Punchinello*; Wilton's Music Hall and the like, the yards of galleried inns such as the Belle Sauvage, sometimes held matinee plays suitable for children. In his wanderings, 'George Bruce' himself might feasibly have stumbled across just such a production – witnessed a version of his own life's history in performance – one in which he was returned to New Zealand, the fabled isle of Typpayassa, after all.

Within his *Petition* Druce had spoken affectingly of the abuse he had suffered daily, called man-eater, devil and traitor, owing to his tattooed appearance. Sarah imagined his astonishment – at seeing aspects of his life played out as they might otherwise have been; on sale in a shop window, as a cut-out toy; or play-acted before an audience of stunted and ragged children on an anonymous corner, somewhere deep in the very lowest neighbourhoods, the likes of which he had sprung from and was now returned to, pilloried and destitute, living on the streets. Would they laugh? Would he cry? Stay and watch? Or flee?

A comedy? If so, Flaxman's statuettes had stepped down from the façade of the Covent Garden Theatre and swapped places. Druce might not have recognised the *mélo-drame* – transformed in the French style into a virtual fairy-tale – as his life at all.

The houses and their windows are nothing but plaster and paint – a series of canvas flats, receding, virtually featureless, all mass and colour reduced to grey-brown shades. Brippoki is himself the only solid element. Soundlessly he sprints through a luminous haze, not knowing where he is headed, nor rightly caring.

The air is still clogged – choked, and choking.

He carries a firebrand in his hand. Horses gathered at a fence float somewhere above, apparently mid-air. Slowing to a jog, for a moment Brippoki thinks he is returned to countryside, then, turning a corner, senses more than sees solemn buildings surround him – more of the same.

He stands at a crossroads. This street or that, it doesn't matter which.

Making a wrong choice, he faces another dead end. He can only turn around, go back the way he came, try a different angle. This time he comes to a full stop, facing himself reflected in a broad shopfront, neat and orderly. An instant's distraction, a blinding flash followed by a sharp crack, and click-clack, the shopfront is gone. Instead, he faces the clapped-out and overcrowded muddle of a dealership in marine stores.

Empty belly, burning chest, mind sloshing about in a soup; his head is a billy-pot, bubbling over. The scenery through which he moves is ever-changing, but never really changed.

It begins to rain.

Lambert woke to the growl of distant thunder. He felt hot, in a light sweat. Troubled dreams were torture enough, but waking to absolute darkness in the middle of the night was worse, for it was then that he felt most alone, at the mercy of haunting remorse. For how long had he been sleeping? Had he slept? There was no sense any more of time passing, and only one certainty – hurt. His head, his chest, his throat – so dry – everything.

Everything hurt.

Sarah lay in bed, the covers pulled up over her head. There could be no escape. An improvised belch of flame – enter, stage left, in a Mephistolean puff of brimstone, Joseph Druce. 'Pack my box with five dozen liquor jugs,' he said.

Sitting up, she made notes by candlelight, weak and wavering.

Pantomime was a peculiarly English rendition of *commedia dell'arte* tradition: in juvenile imitation of the burlesques of the London scene, all toy theatre subscribed to it. Studied fully as much as loved when she was young, the traditional entertainment split down the middle. The action opened with a story taken from classical myth, history, or even modern legend, stock characters assigned their various roles – Darling Columbine the heroine; Pantaloon her father; and their servant, Clown. At some point events would reach an impasse, whereupon, hey presto, the hero – there was always a hero – would be transformed into the colourful character of Harlequin, wearing his patchwork of rags. The comedy of the Harlequinade begun, the story would either be resolved, or dissolve into nonsense: it was for the audience to decide which.

Clown, of late, overstressed his part, whereas the drama belonged to all.

As both sneak-thief and sailor, Joseph Druce's story united what had once been the two most popular genres of theatre great and small – nautical adventure and brigandage – and within a favourite setting, the desert island drama. Meat-hungry stories such as his properly took hold of the public imagination, dominating the London stage, throughout the 1820s – long before Sarah was born, but only shortly after Druce's death.

Druce was done with the world, but not before the world was done with him.

He suffered for being a man ahead of his time – no longer ignored, but already forgotten – a poor man who very badly wanted to be rich, to have significance, at almost any price. No longer quite so extraordinary, his life was not unique. The same story went on all the time; everywhere amongst those who had no voice, and no one to speak for them – trampled by impersonal history.

And yet, in any society worthy of the term, all persons must possess some measure of significance; must have the right to protest an oppressor's wrongs. Few claims on the liberality of the nation could be so well founded as those of the British sailor. Instead he received the insolence of office and, spurned, the law's delay.

Sarah's pen, as it moved, darkened the page with ink. Line by line her words collided, crossing over. It was too late and she could no longer see straight, let alone think straight; nor do anything right.

She shouldn't try to rescue a man already dead, just because she could not save one living. Druce's own crimes were irretrievable, his consummate anger – pronouncing vengeance, of the most dangerous sort – scattershot. According to Emerson, her favourite authority on these matters, feeble souls were drawn to the south or negative pole. They looked at the profit or hurt of the action, and never beheld principle unless it was lodged in a person. They did not wish to be lovely, but to be loved.

This essential flaw in Druce's character, his weakness, drew her to him as surely as moth to flame. Any conscience on his part could of course be illusion, virtue after her design – the best in his kind were but shadows, and the worst no worse. Lines, words on paper, only gained form from whatever dimension she herself might lend.

'An insignificant individual as myself…totally forgotten.'

Not totally – the idea was too unbearable.

Sarah reflected at length. The surfeit of events in Druce's life obscured his essential character. The reverse was true of hers.

It wasn't so much the dead bodies that made her anxious to avoid graveyards, she realised. What Sarah feared most was the anonymity of the grave – an unmarked plot; no name, just a number; or only a name, undeserving. A life lived without consequence, nor any distinction remaining, of whom the most that might be said was the least remarkable: that she was a drudge who did no one harm – and no good either.

CHAPTER LIX
Sunday the 21st of June, 1868

THE LONGEST DAY

'Mad from life's history,
Glad to death's mystery,
Swift to be hurl'd—
Anywhere, anywhere
Out of the world!'

~ Thomas Hood, 'The Bridge of Sighs'

Sarah scoured the cupboards and prepared breakfast. Lambert, weak as he was, stubbornly refused all attempts to feed him.

She thought she heard him whisper. Sarah proffered a glass of water with which to wet his lips, and leant in close.

'Did you say something?' she asked.

'There is…none righteous,' he gasped. 'No, not one.'

The breakfast tray rested on his lap, but to all intent and purpose he was oblivious. Leaving it with him, she went downstairs.

Sarah parted the curtains in the front parlour. They were of lurid, if faded, design – '*Le Grand Opera*': carnations, roses, *and trompe l'œil* repetitions of their own tasselled top sash, kept in place with large coils of amber rope. She hated them, even as she loved and missed the parent whose tastes they preserved.

The carpet was filthy, discoloured with dust and ash. She remembered now: Brippoki had been drunk. He had been sick. She filled a bucket with sudsy water and scrubbed at the stains with a cloth. Other traces came to light. A virtual footprint, angry and dark, showed where he had stood the longest. Sarah roundly cursed her petty economies. By dim candlelight, she had missed the fierce wound to his arm.

An almighty crash sounded from overhead. Almost falling up the stairs, from the landing Sarah heard Lambert raving. She rushed to be by his side.

A teacup shattered before her face, into a score of shards.

'"The foolish shall not stand in thy sight,"' Lambert snarled and spat from the bed. '"Thou hatest all workers of iniquity!"'

The tray and all its contents, thrown across the room, lay in mulch and in pieces.

'"The LORD",' he shrieked, '"will abhor the bloody and deceitful man!"'

Sarah galloped to catch up – David, a *Psalm* of David. She hesitated to restrain her father, but in that moment he shrank and flamed to nothing, as a tissue torched by fire.

'"But, as for meee… I will come *into* thy house"' he wheedled, his voice high and breaking. '"I will come… Lead me, O LORD…make thy way straight before my face."'

His face, screwed tight, suddenly evened out, losing the worst of its creases. The skin was grey. '*Arrgh!*' he cried.

Sarah let go the soiled cloth, taking up his shaking fists in case he should strike himself again. Eventually, he quieted.

Wetting and wringing out a fresh flannel in a bowl of cold water, Sarah gently dabbed Lambert's forehead. His low moan interrupted her anxious ministrations.

He turned, examining her closely with a critical eye, no recognition in his face. She hovered over him, willing him well.

'"Wellfavoured harlot!"' he hissed. '"Mistress of witchcrafts! Children are their oppressors, and women rule over them! Behold, I *am* against theeee…"'

Lambert flinched and squirmed in the bed, resisting her touch.

'"I will discover thy skirts upon thy face,"' he spat, '"will shew nations thy nakedness, kingdoms thy shame. Abominable filth I cast on thee…thee…vile thee… I will set thee as a gazingstock."'

The hatred in his voice twisted up his features. Were his body not so weak and wasted, Sarah felt certain he meant to assault her. She backed off, shaking. Where was the doctor? She didn't know what to do!

'"The daughters of Zion are haughty,"' said Lambert. '"They walk with stretched forth necks and wanton eyes, walking and mincing *as* they go, and making a tinkling with their feet."'

He waved his fingers in a grotesque little mime, before curling them into large fists.

'"The Lord",' he roared, '"will smite with a scab the crown of their heads, and discover their secret parts…take away *their* tinkling ornaments… The chains, the bracelets, the mufflers…the bonnets, the ornaments of the legs… the rings, and nose jewels, the crisping pins and the hood, and the veils…all the changeable suits of apparel…"'

Lips glossy with spittle, his maddened eyes roved the room.

'"The glasses and fine linen…"'

'"And it shall come to pass, *that* instead of sweet smell there shall be stink, and instead of girdle a rent, and instead of well-set hair, baldness…instead of a stomacher a girding of sackcloth, *and* burning instead of beauty!"'

His eyes, screwed shut, worked indescribable pain.

Sarah too darted a look around the room. Any fine touches were remnants of Frances. Reckoning of some kind fuelled his madness: he spoke of her mother, in borrowed phrases of ultimate scorn.

'"And her gates shall lament and mourn, and she *being* desolate shall sit upon the ground,"' he wailed.

He opened his eyes again, wet with tears – no longer of rage but of sorrow. A heavy droplet rolled across his withered cheek.

'Mine,' he said, 'is a *jealous* God!'

The faraway sun gives out light but little heat, a baleful eye fixed on Brippoki's wayward progress. He wanders out among the ruins, the big empty. Down comes the rain – sharp, like flint. The dust cloud of recent days, settled, churns to liquid mud. It surges along the gutters in great gouts, bubbling into widening pools about clogged drains. The roadways begin to disappear, paving slick with slime – treachery, underfoot.

Brippoki's senses are on edge. With what light there is subdued, he can barely see five paces in front. The air is heavy, impregnated with sulphur and vitriol.

He straddles the span across the dock on New Gravel Lane, the 'Bloody Bridge', in the slang of the neighbourhood.

Dark arch, black flow, bleak prospect – he has returned to the Well of Shadows, very close to that dreadful spot where his wanderings brought him, that first dark time.

He will not be old, but once was young.

He remembers meadow grasslands filled with game, fresh water to drink, roots and vegetables to eat, wood for the fire, and a sky filled with stars – the country he loves.

The firelight of the Ancestors splashes across the surface of the *Millewa*. Stranger footsteps on the far shore, and the fires wink out all at once. Everything disappears into the dark.

Daylight now, and his mother, she is crossing that same wide river. She pushes him in front, balanced along a piece of bark. Floating, the waters rushing, he grips the bark strip tightly in his hands. *Warriarto*, his baby half-sister, is tied to her back in a bundle, dead for months. Mother still carries her with them, everywhere they go.

The next day his mother dies too.

Worrowen – shivering, Brippoki shakes his head.

Mother meant to carry his dead sister, her dead baby, until they should come to the proper site for her burial, her *miyur*. Each clan has its *mir* or *miyur*, its sacred waterhole, known to every adult and located in a fixed direction from their territory. It is the Spirit land of their birth – Ancestral home, and final resting place.

Mother came from another place. Brippoki has never known her clan. He has no idea of her, or his, *miyur*.

Everything seemed to *yandy* down to that.

Ignorant of his *yauerin* or *miyur*, he cannot take the name of just any place. His mother died before he might know it – father too. He was too young to know. There is no place he belongs to, nor any belonging to him. He will always be a child in a man's body – lost, forever.

Hard rainfall destroys the calm surface of every pool of water, from the shallowest puddle to the deepest dock. Brippoki stands alone, looking over a stone parapet. Staring down into poisonous blackness, he thinks the stretch of dark water the rough river. The turbulence is honest, and inviting.

He hears again the whispers of the willow. How easy it would be to surrender, to allow oneself to go under. Swallowed within the Serpent's slick embrace, he may at last know peace – oblivion, sweeter than gin.

The wharf's stone sides are steep and high, the floodwaters fast and furious. One single step, a bold plunge, and there will be no climbing out again.

Sarah succeeded in calming Lambert only at great length – smoothing his icy brow with a cool palm, talking softly; saying anything that came into her head. He had not spoken for some hours now, and things went easier that way. A few whimpers when she cleared away the fragments from his tantrum, the odd murmur, an occasional request for drink to be lifted to his lips; otherwise he drifted quietly in and out of consciousness, the flutter of his eyelids often the only difference between his waking and sleeping. Each time his eyes opened, he seemed to draw at least some measure of comfort from finding her sitting beside him.

She set all the fires and the lights to blazing, even though it was daytime – anything to dispel the day's damp gloom. None of it afforded the least comfort: the atmosphere of slow poison permeating the house came from within, not without.

Sarah stood a while in the front parlour, lost in contemplation. She would touch one or other of the furnishings and picture her mother, doing the same. In younger days, she had resented her father for refusing ever to speak of her. Latterly she came to understand, in sickness, as in health, the presence of Frances in almost everything that he said and did.

Light and shade in conflict gave our lives strength and colour, but too much grief, hate, fear – 'the family of Pain' – unbalanced the mind. Sarah avoided completing the manuscript. All of his pleas and prayers unanswered – beneath notice, as far as he knew – Druce's sense of isolation must have been total; her own was awful enough.

She would be having words with Dr Epps on his return.

~

Pindi is a great pit in the far west, whence the *Ludko* come – the soul-shadows of the unborn. The ghosts are so thickly packed on that island, there is no room for them to stand. These shiftless spirits wander the earth, miserable and alone. Hovering among the grass-trees, they wait for the hour of conception so that they can enter into a human body. Only after death and a proper burial, observing all of the attendant rites, do they return to *Pindi* – the place that everybody comes from, and must eventually return to.

The wind whips the surface of the waters. Rain hits from all sides, at crazy angles, soaking Brippoki beyond skin.

The seedling of a daring plan, a way he might yet save himself, is hatched within his brain. Slipping back from the brink, he tugs at the *min-tum* girding his loins, and sets off running – away from the dockside.

He heads steadily northwest. The rains cease. In the last hour of daylight clouds part to reveal the thin crescent of a new moon – *Mityan*, horned.

Head throbbing, Brippoki rues his drunkenness. He carries a glowing ember above his head. Naked body newly adorned with markings, stark outlines define his breast and shoulder bones. A wavy line is drawn down each arm, thigh, and lower leg, also bold slashes across both cheeks, and along each prominent rib. Around each eye he wears a large white circle, the 'strong eye'. The clay daubs are otherwise of red. Taking up arms – his *waddy* club and spear – he is disguised as *Moo-by*, a ferocious demon. By the pale shine of starlight it shows itself – a baring of teeth, a roll of the eyes, all dingo-dog glimmer and glitter.

Footsore, tired, and hungry, despite every caution he leaves behind traces that speak eloquently of his passing. His footprints, tracked through puddles of water, march out across the pavement behind him. He hears the sly pad of paws along a cautious perimeter, the click and drag of long nails, and scrape of sharpening claw.

To the point of death, he cannot sleep.

To preserve one life, another must be ended.

The uppermost part of the house glows like a beacon, the lamps lit in every room. Brippoki's attention is drawn to the only window that remains dark. The darkness suddenly divides. The Guardian stands revealed in the shaft of light. She looks sad.

Moo-by ducks back.

A few moments later, and she moves away from the closed window. Brippoki shifts position to get a better view. She stays in that same hole where her father lives. Thara sits nose deep in paper-yabber, like always. She shines, almost a ball of fire. Shadows thicken in the air behind her. His grip tightens on his *waddy*. He sees that she holds the Book.

Eyes in darkness, a lowly scavenger lurks, awaiting his perfect opportunity – not lacking the courage for open attack, but wise, and needful of certain victory.

Brippoki wishes for her to move away from the sick old man. She is afraid for him, when she should fear more for herself.

Approaching the end of the *Life*, concerning the death of a wife and last days' despairing, Sarah read the last of the manuscript alone. She did not want Druce's life to be over. Neither did she know how his real story ended – only that it must. At most there was a page or two of text left to go.

She pulled her chair close beside her father's bed, where he lay, snoring fitfully. Afraid that a chill might follow on from his fever, she kept a fire roaring in the grate, even on such a clement midsummer evening. Window closed against the rising winds, the heat in his room was oppressive.

> but O shourley there is A God. & A most inexsprissibel mircyful one. for alltho wicked infeddel as I am. surely the most Gracious & mircyful God. eard me one morning poring out my soul with grief & hungar.

An after-image of the line before, or premonition of the next; Sarah stared so long at the scrawl on the page that other words appeared, shimmering in the blank spaces between.

> it was very early. I was in gloster cort docktors Commons sant pools church yeard.

He spoke of the district she knew as Apothecary, very close to the cathedral. The excavations for the new Queen Victoria-street tore right through it.

> all was Silent in their bed. I set down at A door To rest my self. after wandring all night. The clock struck three. I drew A sight. & exclamed. O that it may be the last time I shall ever ear A clock strick. & bursting in to teears at the same time. grife soon Lold me to sleep. tell I was wakt by A poor man. who was goin out to seeck Labor. he told me to come to his house at night & sleep. I was glad to find such A frind. I thinkt him. & that night went To his house. the next day I met A gentlman In the street. who cuk me in A house. & Gave me bread & met. I told him all my Distrees. he told me not to mind it. for this He was sure. all the noblmen of A thority was cristions. both at the admiralty And sumerset house.

All the noblemen of authority were Christians: yet it had taken a poor man without work of his own to offer Druce charity, even if were only a place to lay his head. Only thereafter did the other gentleman give him bread, and meat, and hope.

> he told me three of their names. vis. mr croker. mr dyrer. mr lee. & he told me at The same time to go my self. to mr croker. & To mr lee. & they wold give me my sirvtud. for He was sure. they neve was happier then when they was reliving such poor creatures As me.

Druce threaded another daisy chain of names.

I returnd the gentlman thinks. & went To sumerset house. were I found mr lee. who in A most youmane maner told me he wold do all Lay in his powr to mak me happey. but I Must call in A few days. there was A Gentlman in the ofice. his name was mr masion. He see I was in distrees. he told me to com To his house the next day. I went he gave Me plenty to eat. & at the same time. gave orders to his servents. to give me blenty To eat & drink aney time in the day. when Ever I should call at his house. Lady mason Was deeply efficted at my distrees. but in A Few days after. I A gaine went to mr lee At the admarlty. he then interduced me To mr croker and mr dyer. & mr dyer interduced me to the high lords of the admirlty. were Mircy & compassion was shon me. & I was Sent to the royal hospital greenwich.

That was the end of the book.

Sarah sat in silence for a time, before bending forward to stir the remains of the fire in the grate.

CHAPTER LX
Sunday the 21st of June, 1868

ILL MET BY MOONLIGHT

'So word by word, and line by line,
The dead man touch'd me from the past,
And all at once it seem'd at last
The living soul was flash'd on mine.'

~ Alfred, Lord Tennyson, *In Memoriam*

'I have lived out…my Grace Days.' Lambert's breath was short. 'I must,' he said, 'pay my dues.'

'Hush,' said Sarah.

He was so small, so shrunken in the bed. His hair lay lank and stringy across the pillows, and Sarah wished she had lately thought to cut it for him, or at least to wash it.

'I am…fearful…' he said.

'Hush, now.'

'…of a leap…in the dark.'

'In the dark?' Sarah repeated.

Her father's eye shone a moment. Sarah laid a hand to the pillow, checking for dampness. His night-sweats had stained the bedding. She might at least refresh…

Lambert flinched. She reached across to clear a white strand from his face. He hissed.

Sarah protested. 'Whatever for?'

His pursed lips began to tremble and he forced his head aside, face dissolving into a mess of deeper creases. More was at work here than the vanity of a manful Christian.

'It was not mine to judge,' he whimpered.

'Your judgement was not your own,' she said.

Surprised, he turned. His face searched hers for understanding, saw it absent – infinite sympathy, yes, but no comprehension. None.

Lambert smiled, but his eyes were crying.

'Father!' she said.

'*Aoowwrrraarrhr!*'

He made such a cry!

'I draw…near to Calvary,' Lambert gasped.

Calvary was Golgotha, burial site of Adam's skull and hill of crucifixion. Looking at him now, Sarah did not doubt it. She knew that he was dying; and that he had known, all along. She wiped the back of her hand across both cheeks.

Wrestling with her skirts, she knelt down at her father's bedside. Pressing dampened fingers together just beneath her lips, she prevailed on Him – Him who seemed to turn a deaf ear when needed the most – to listen to the voice of her entreaty.

'"Spare thou them, O God, which confess their faults,"' prayed Sarah. '"Restore them that are penitent, according to thy promises declared unto mankind in Christ Jesu our Lord. Attend to the things which make for his everlasting peace, before they are for ever hidden from his eyes. Amen."'

Quickly she struggled to her feet, and collapsed back into the chair.

'"We have left undone those things which we ought to have done!"' Lambert spoke with a new urgency. '"And we have done those things which we ought not…not to have done…and there *is* no health in us."'

The health he spoke of, in this context of the general Confession, was spiritual soundness – its absence, she knew full well, the absence of all righteousness in ourselves; of self-respect. Rubric directed that certain lines be repeated after the minister: in her confusion, Sarah supplied the next.

'"O Lord,"' she said, '"have mercy upon us, miserable offenders."'

'No…' pleaded Lambert. 'No…' He waved for her to stop. 'My dear… sweet maid.'

He made as if to stroke her cheek, yet faltered, stopping short. He stared into his palm. She too stared at the back of that great palp, its flesh collapsed, veins hanging like slack cable – her father's hands.

'Child,' said Lambert, 'you are not answerable for *my* sins… "God gave them up to uncleanness…through the lusts of their own hearts, to dishonour their bodies between themselves"!'

Wracked with sobs even in the midst of anger, Lambert's mouth, wet and working, opened so wide and trembling that it was hard to make out his slurred words.

'Fff-fornication…wickedness…'

Another frightful roar, and he thrust his head into his hands. They tore at his face and beard.

'No, no, stop!' Sarah demanded. 'Father – !'

'FATHER?' He cut her short.

She froze.

Lambert gave a wry laugh. '"Judge not,"' he warned her, '"lest ye be judged."'

Lambert quoted scripture as he had done in his fever, nearly the whole of the day before. What scared Sarah almost out of her wits was that he was now in full command of his senses.

"'THEREFORE thou art inexcusable!'" he bull-roared. "'And thinkest thou this, O man, that judgest them which do such things, and doest the same, that thou shalt escape the judgement of God?'"

It was as if some great switch had been thrown, and he could only speak in Common Prayer, his priest's business – but with what rationale? What was it that he could not bring himself to say in plain English?

"'Thou...'" he said, "'that art thyself a guide of the blind...a light of them which are in darkness...

"'Thou that preachest a man should not steal, dost thou steal?

"'Thou that sayest a man should not commit adultery, dost thou commit adultery?

"'Thou that preachest against...against..."

'...

'I cannot speak of it... I cannot...'

He recited the commandments as handed down to Moses – not in the correct order, but in reverse. Thou shalt not steal; commit adultery – what came next?

'Who...'

What?

"'Who shall judge the quick and the dead... at His appearing and His Kingdom?'"

"'God,'" she answered, obediently. "'And the Lord Jesus Christ.'"

"'I charge thee therefore,'" said Lambert. He looked straight at her. 'You...'

'Yes,' she said. Anything.

'Yes...yes.' Lambert sounded decisive. 'You... God forgive me. You must help me...help me to confess...'

Confess what?

She did. And he did. And she could not believe it.

Her – Lambert – he was not – not the person she thought he was. She was not the person she thought she was. *Behold, I was shapen in iniquity; and in sin did my mother conceive me.* She was his daughter in name only – conceived outside of marriage; born of illicit love.

Thrown by the truth, Sarah reeled. This wasn't at all what she had prayed for. Tears – in his last hours, her father had given in to Catholic weakness, and she could not for the life of her process the matter he confessed. Belief? It went beyond belief: that you could live your whole life with someone and not know them.

No one. No one, as it turned out, was who they were first said to be.

The coffin lid splintered and she felt the skeletal clutch. A shameful family secret, long concealed, burst from the grave – her mother, strayed from the path of righteousness.

Narrow was the path, and broad the Way – and worse yet to come. More than one skeleton lurked in that hollow recess. Lambert kept it as he had kept her: in the dark, jealously guarded.

'...Put...' he sobbed, barely audible, 'put out the light.'

Sarah wasn't sure that she heard him right. She wasn't much sure of anything.

'...light of my life, ohhh...better extinguish the light of the world...'

Was this still confession?

'I put out the light...' he said.

His empty hands, thick fingers spread, were shaking.

'...and then put out the light.'

Oh, God.

Exposed at the turn of the tide, a sunken wreck rests in the riverine mud. Its rotten ribs jut, the butchered remains of a kill.

To increase his strength of spirit for a coming battle, a warrior consumes a portion of his sacred *goobong*. Undertaking Holy Communion, Brippoki swallows hard. At any other time such an act, akin to cannibalism, would be forbidden.

'I shall be hungry by and by!' he sings.

Taking up his *karko* on the end of a length of string – his *min-tum*, newly adapted for its purpose – Brippoki, as *Moo-by*, whirls it around his head. The makeshift device produces a lowing noise, much duller than intended, nothing like the roar of a true *mooryumkarr*.

His disappointment is keen – his opponent unlikely to be discouraged by the weak sound.

Brippoki makes his way inland, back to the dilapidated Greenwich graveyard. Even the dark time empty places fill with echoes of old suffering, solitary places the least lonely.

Sky filled with cloud, the new moon is no longer visible.

'A man am I!' *Moo-by* sings, louder now. 'I don't want to go back to the grave!'

The evening breeze moans louder still, stirring the treetops overhead. A burial place, likeliest haunt of evil spirits, is doubly worth avoiding. He has already risked much by returning there with Thara in tow. What more harm can now be done? Brippoki weighs the odds. Opposing his troubles is his only chance to end them – his one last chance remaining.

To be a man, Brippoki must *be* a man. He will face down the terror seeking his life in the place that he released it. Meeting on home ground, he might persuade the Spirit to return to its camp, a trial by combat as much as an ordeal of magic. In fighting back, he may reclaim his honour, and – possibly – make a name for himself.

Everybody was accountable, somewhere along the Revenge Trail.

Woe unto you! for ye build the sepulchres of the prophets, and your fathers killed them.

Sarah struggled not to scream.

Truly…

It couldn't be, but it was.

Truly ye bear witness, that ye allow the deeds of your fathers: for they indeed killed them…

Killer.

…and ye build their sepulchres.

In one swift motion, she set aside the candlestick. A single blow would not be enough.

Under a mountain was a volcano, at the very bottom of the sea. It was filled with souls, after death, torturing other souls. There, the dead waged endless war, one with another – killing, as surely as Cain killed his brother, over, and over, and over again.

Sarah kept her hands firmly pressed across her chest, lest her heart should burst from its cage.

Be not afraid of them that kill the body, and after that have no more that they can do.

But I will forewarn you whom ye shall fear: Fear him, which after he hath killed hath power to cast into hell; yea, I say unto you, Fear him.

Blackfellow lies motionless on a rock, as one dead or asleep in the sun. If he takes a piece of fish or flesh and holds it out in his hand, a careless hunter might think it easy prey. Then, when he swoops down on the offering, the blackfellow leaps up and seizes him – throws him on the fire and makes a meal of him.

This is the way to catch him crow.

If Brippoki's scheme is successful, Deadman will be obliged to enter into his liver and his service, as his *woorie*, a vital protector against enchantments – including evil spirits such as the *In-gna*.

Standing some way off, he first checks over the cleared ground around the grave for any signs of disturbance that could indicate the provenance of the murderer. Satisfied, Brippoki gathers fallen branches, which he arranges in a half-circle from head to foot, on the south side. On top of this he adds grass, and a length of log dragged and heaved into place with no little effort, covered over in turn with more disguising grass.

An attack would be most effective just before dawn, when the victim is drowsy. He means to lure his enemy with expectation of the same.

Finally in position, Brippoki, disguised as the demon *Moo-by*, forces the breath in and out of his mouth. He sits up in his grave, crying out for Deadman, and stamping his feet on the bare earth. Hands held together in front of his face beat out a matching rhythm.

Polpol the Hero Ancestor cries and sings for the dead.

'Alas! Alas! For me, the younger brother!
My elder brother has left me all alone!'

He hears the soft swish of bat wings, coming from everywhere.

It is time to race the devil.

Sun, moon, tide – *Moo-by* is fast travelling. A restless spirit of diabolical vengeance follows in close pursuit, and gaining. Through darkness he runs, between pools of light, through the crowding dead, through wastelands empty of life. Deadman comes on, never turning aside. Step by step and line by line the figure in shadow advances, relentless, unstoppable – no longer fart-catcher, three paces behind, but closing, almost on him.

Run, faster.

In a dash across open ground, speed counts for all.

At the bitter end of their race, cornered *Moo-by* turns to confront his aggressor, showing off his true colours. Casually he discards his *mooryumkarr*, making much display of throwing down his weapons. Apparently unarmed, he walks forward, a green bough carried in the hand as a sign of peace. He drags a foot along the ground, spear gripped between his toes. With a dextrous flick it appears in his hand, as if by magic.

He brandishes the spear and roars his challenge, fakes a throw, then retreats to where lie his *waddy* and modified *karko*. Picking these up, he beats them together – advances, retreats, advances, shouting the while, and furiously kicking up dust. Taking up the firebrand, he sets light to the grass and bushes.

The deathly peace and quiet of the grove is shattered.

A voice shouts, 'Is this the body I formerly inhabited?'

'We are not dead,' comes the reply, 'but still living.'

Moo-by hops from one foot to the other, shaking and pointing his spear. '*Wia ma pitja*,' he growls, '*nungkarpa lara pupinpa!*'

Brippoki contrives a convincing guttural menace. He spits and bites his beard in defiance. 'Come you, God damn it son of a bitch! BAASTID!'

Legs distended, he quivers his thighs and rolls his eyes – showing the whites. He cries out lustily, taunting his adversary, deriding their weaponry, their skills in the arts of war.

'*Yelo!*' he shouts. 'Coward! I will eat your kidney fat!!'

'I shall be hungry by and by,' a small voice says. 'A man am I. I don't want to go back to the grave!'

'Back you must go!' *Moo-by* insists. 'This place is forbidden!'

Bellowing out his triumph, he mimes victory – cooks the head of his vanquished enemy, scoops out the eyes and, lip-smacking, eats them, cheek-flesh too. Presenting a madcap dance, *Moo-by* pretends to trample the skull around, working himself into such a pitch that he picks it up and, hips thrusting, fucks its gaping sockets.

Exultant at the climax, he offers up his bare breast for the striking. A step forward and he bows his head, offering up a free hit. The death blow is invited, a mercy killing – invited, and refused. When no club falls, *Moo-by* snarls.

'*Ma pitja! Ma pitja! Miriwa!*'

With a flick of the wrist he turns his back, derisively slapping at his buttocks.

'Then begone!'

More than one fellow, overconfident, has turned to mock a foe he thought at safe distance, only for lightning and thunder to bring him down.

Body of destruction, a misshape rushes forward, clawed hands before its face. Not Deadman's Spirit but an *In-gna*, three white hairs on the tip of its tail. Uttering a terrible cry, it seizes *Moo-by* by the throat. Fighting bravely, he chokes it back. Baggy flesh there, like that of a *goanna* – grey. Attempting to take in its power, *Moo-by* hugs it close. He is too weak. Raking claws open him up. A deep cut, breast to loins, and his bowels are exposed. Flesh ripping, his kidney is removed, *weeka*, his liver, torn to pieces and gobbled up – sweet meats. Fiendish appetite feeds the True demon's red smile.

Fallen, Brippoki lies helpless. Looking down, he sees life's blood pool in the hollow of his ribcage, where his innards used to be. The raw head of the *In-gna* dips, and it drinks.

As one dead, he feels no pain. He cannot move – doomed to watch his destroyer adorn its self before his own eyes.

Wearing his intestines for a necklace, the *In-gna* regards him dispassionately, before resuming its gruesome operations. His body is tugged open wider, and the fiend takes the fat from about his kidneys, rubbing itself liberally all over, pleasuring in its victory. Musculature glistens moist as an eel. Flipped over onto his back, Brippoki feels his skin being stripped. A chill on his ribs, and then limbs are wrenched behind and broken. Sharp teeth nip through his tendons.

Another few seconds and he will be on the fire. In a last-ditch effort he reaches for his *waddy* with his one good arm, takes it up and, raining down blows, beats the bloody demon into a shapeless mass.

Doom.

> Doom.

>> Doom.

Through the depths of the earth itself, Brippoki feels the pulse-beat of the world. Agony – it hurts too much to move, to even try and open his eyes. Events are too far gone. He has failed. Might as well stay.

No, he must open his eyes. He must move.

Brippoki opens his eyes.

The dead wood whirls in the rising winds. Insides afire, his head has been struck off, lodged between hot stones, and set to bake in the hollow of a tree.

Some hours after nightfall, Brippoki has lain himself down with the dead man under his bark sheet, and, log for a pillow, face towards the blank sky, prepared himself to Dream the sleep of death. *Curadjie* men say that anyone who dares spend a night like this will thereafter be free from the influence of evil spirits – if they survive it. They only know this through having survived it themselves.

A night successfully spent on a grave binds and lays that spirit to rest, for good or ill.

His magic was weak, as he is weak – his desire to harm not as strong as that of his rival. *Moo-by*'s race run and lost, Brippoki's body lies unmoving on the ground. A cold rock hardens in his belly, his straggly beard clogged with dribbles of the drying clay he ritually ingested hours earlier – a lifetime ago. Head back on the log, he looks skyward. The cloud-cover only now begins to separate, scudding swift overhead.

He struck too early. There are still some hours to go before dawn.

Had he been successful, Deadman's *Ludko* would have returned to *Pindi*, never to die or be born again. He has the feeling he has not entirely failed. Time will tell.

Brippoki sits up and examines his side. Far more frightening than having seen himself eviscerated, he has received a mortal wound, guts replaced and the wound sewn up with thread invisible to the eye.

A death Dreamed is a death in Truth. Death does not scare Brippoki so much as he is terrified of having been cursed.

CHAPTER LXI
Monday the 22nd of June, 1868

WORLD WITHOUT END

'This town's a corporation full of crooked streets,
Death is the market place, where all men meets.'

~ epitaph

The iron tongue of midnight echoed down the hall.

Lambert grabbed Sarah by the wrist.

Sarah yet stayed her hand. She would not give him succour, or comfort. *The women of my people have ye cast out from their pleasant houses; from their children have ye taken away my glory for ever.*

With a frenzied look Lambert turned his eyes to heaven, and then away.

Furious at himself for his inability to embrace death, he alternately raged and then lay mewling at its prospect. His high and holy words, that had been comfort to so many, were but a goad to himself. His convictions drained him of all courage.

To have lived a lie, and to die in doubt – where was God the Father in this, his own hour of need? Where was his Faith?

Sarah wrested her arm from his. She wished him dead.

Lambert knew the choices he faced: oblivion after having been burnt to ashes; or burning forever without end. Moreover, the choice was not his.

What should he dread but enfolding darkness, terror by night, the pestilence that walketh in darkness – unless it be the light; the arrow that flieth by day, the destruction that wasteth at noonday. He had made an enemy of God himself, to all Eternity.

Sarah's back stiffened, her limbs chill even though fire crackled in the grate. She saw how fixedly Lambert stared ahead, and knew fear herself. If he died in this dreadful state – and it surely was dreadful – the blood would be on his head as it was on his hands; and his sufferings, everlasting.

Sarah crossed her chest – an ineffectual gesture.

'"If our heart condemn us,"' she said, '"God is greater than our heart, and knoweth all things."'

She couldn't be sure whether she made the effort in order to soothe, or with more pitiless intent – to slight him further, a man who held so tightly on to what he called his rights, over what he called his debts.

'What was it all for?' Lambert asked, weakly. 'What is any of it for?'

God, or Death, was implacable, indiscriminate – good or evil it came to all, and nothing. In the greater scheme of things the human concept of time, the span of any one life and its achievements, was meaningless – time was on Nature's side, a grand plan superseding all others; or else none. Given the circumstances, the idea of illimitable chaos no longer seemed so very terrible.

'Was it for nothing?' he asked.

'It is God's plan,' she said.

'...Of course.'

His soul, though it wandered, still aspired to heaven...where the wicked ceased from troubling, and the weary were at rest.

'"The Lord *is* my shepherd,"' he rasped. '"I shall not want."'

Lambert's voice threatened to falter, unheard – until Sarah's joined with his.

'"He maketh me to lie down in green pastures, he leadeth me beside the still waters."'

They spoke together, two souls in Abraham's bosom.

'"He restoreth my soul, he leadeth me in the paths of righteousness, for his name's sake..."'

The heart of the father must turn to the child, and the heart of the child to the father, lest the earth be smitten with a curse – and for the Final Restitution of All Things.

'Remember,' said Sarah, 'what Jesus said to Martha. "Jesus said unto her, I am the resurrection, and the life: he that believeth in me, though he were dead, yet shall he live: And whosoever liveth and believeth in me shall never die. Believest thou this?"'

Lambert wept silently.

'*Believest thou this?*' Sarah asked. Loyal beyond reason, she admonished him. '"Be strong in the Lord,"' she said, '"and in the power of his might."'

For here we have no continuing city, but we seek one to come.

She leant further forward so he might see her better, her elbows resting on his coverlet.

'"Open ye the gates,"' she said, steadfast and strong. '"Let favour be shown to the wicked",' she asked. '"Therefore..."' Sarah turned to address Lambert directly '"...prepare to meet thy God."'

She took his palms and pressed them together, herself not so composed.

The kingdom of God – Lambert marvelled. 'Lord, Lord,' he said.

'"Lord,"' said Sarah, '"now lettest thou thy servant depart in peace, according to thy word."'

Lambert wept and gnashed his yellowed teeth. He overflowed with remorse. 'I have used the head of an angel,' he lamented, 'for a writing desk.'

Sarah did not hear. Pious verses from childhood and *The Parent's Poetical Present* replayed in her mind.

'Who taught me first to read and pray
To kneel to God, his word obey,
And holy keep his Sabbath-Day,
MY FATHER.

'And, as thou ever wast my guide,
I'll sit and watch thy couch beside,
Should ill thy eve of life betide,
MY FATHER.

'My breast thy dying couch shall be;
I'll watch thy parting breath from me,
'T'will bear a blessing unto me:
MY FATHER.'

'"Be then the Lamb of Atonement,"' she directed. '"Seek ye the Lord while he may be found."'

Their voices in cracked chorus pronounced the Apostle's Creed. At the very middle point of their recital, the mention of hell, Lambert collapsed in abject tears. Sarah took the time to quieten and reassure, bringing him back to the point where they might continue – and finish.

Parched lips took in another gulp of air: he yet lived.

Lambert's final decline was swift. Thin and wretched, skin nigh transparent, he shook with fever and chills, a bundle of bones kept in place by the dry parchment of scripture.

'"In him was life,"' said Sarah, '"and the life was the light of men."'

She waited, hoping for some sign of response, but none came.

Her fingertip cleared his brow of matted hair. His eyes rolled back, in retreat from the light. The poor creature stood on the brink.

'"The light shineth in darkness,"' she said; '"and the darkness comprehended it not."'

...systole, diastole, systole...diastole...

His lips moved, forming one last word.

'...God.'

'May God forgive you,' said Sarah.

~

489

Fresh rain showers stop an hour or so before dawn, the sky filled with fast-running cloud.

On deserted marshland above the Salmon's-lane Lock, the last remnant of *gunya* collapses in on itself. It has not been built to last.

Four miles or so west, as the crow flies, leaves of discarded newspaper blow the length of Great Russell-street. Striking the iron gates that seal the grounds to the British Museum, they stick there, obscuring a sign that warns visitors of temporary closure.

Number 89 is in total darkness. All the windows are shut and the curtains drawn.

Frustrated, Brippoki turns away – but not before rummaging in the depths of his dilly bag to leave Thara something there. He would have liked to see her, one last time, gliding about in that mysterious way of hers.

'*Parramatta,*' he says, giving it his blessing.

He is afraid for her, when he should fear more for himself. Brippoki glances around the margins of the roof, where he squats, unwelcome. The shadows, they gather about him, too.

Today and tomorrow are finished. Taboo and Law broken, he accepts the guilty verdict. As long as little retribution is asked for, he is willing to die.

He is dead already. Time to move on.

The sun will rise again.

Alone walking the streets, Brippoki cuts a solitary figure. Hair shorn close to the scalp, his ceremonial garb starts to flake and fall off. Catching sight of his reflection, he sees that he looks diseased, like a mangy dog. Death in the desert so far from home is an ugly fate indeed.

Stabbing pains – he burns inside. Some agency of evil performs rites of magic on his footprint. Loud songs of vengeance declare their deadly desire: to do him irreparable harm.

He has been marked for death, and worse than death.

Between clouds, horned *Mityan* emerges. Even as his hopes swell at the sight, Brippoki chokes. The new moon shining before him is swallowed by an all-consuming shadow, and so close! So close to earth! The sky is falling!!

Brippoki runs.

'*Yaal wanning?*' he asks. Where am I going?

All of his short hairs stand on end. The air gathers at his back. His spine and chest crave release from this pressure.

Brippoki sprints full pelt, afraid for so much more than just his life. If an enchantment causes his death, the killer must be found, found and slain, or else Brippoki's *itpitukutya* – his immortal Spirit – will never know peace.

He falls sprawling in the muck of the street, immediately rising into a low crouch, eyes and ears alert. He will not go easy, picked off like some useless straggler.

Calling on the Ancestors for strength, Brippoki speeds on. A short dash into regions unfamiliar and he corrects his course, set on his destination. *Parramatta!*

Gradually the ground falls away, the sweep of ancient hillside traceable in the curve of innumerable cave-like dwellings. Half a league onward, Brippoki comes to high ground above a natural dip he has crossed many times, east to west and back again, on his trips to and from the Guardian – never yet to linger there, nor run it north to south.

In the distance looms the Piebald Giant. He wears a spider's face.

Standing on the rise, unable either to see it or to smell it, Brippoki hears the rush of water passing down below. Panting, he dangles each exhausted limb in turn, before heading on – into the valley.

Great earthworks piled to either side pen him in, constraining his course. He is confounded by a dizzying dimensional maze. Underfoot, overhead, rail, road, and watercourse meet. Fleet of foot he skips through thick and thin, across black pools, barely disturbing their surface. Through gaping sewer and exposed storm drain, he senses for himself the persistence of lost current. What was once a lively creek runs alongside, much reduced, a vile rivulet. Deep red in colour, it is filled with dung, and guts, and blood, dead cats and dogs and parts of larger animals. Fouled and foetid, the gas arising almost causes him to pass out.

He has stumbled blindly into the valley of shadow – *Pindi*, the ditch, a massive burial pit – through which runs the river of death.

Pure clear waters, gushing, a hillside of saffron, gardens sweet with herb; he despairs that a place something like home is come to this – leafless trees, warped rocks, a blunt depression where even weeds fail.

In perennial flow from one form into another, Brippoki's vision of the landscape fractures and endlessly re-forms – silt rearranged by rain and flood, permanent echoes of itself. He often sees more than one shape at any one time, and sometimes, in the dizziness of near-blackout, none at all.

What is desert, saltbush and stone, was once swamp, filled with grass and long rushes, lake and fresh water. One Big Ant-hill Creek – London, before London – is a fine valley. Woods lie to the east, to the west green hills, a low ridge of forest rolling, open country out in front. A gentle incline, lush with grass, is sure sign he approaches water. There, ahead – full and flowing, and broader than expected – winds the river. Clear waters sparkle through the evergreen trees on its banks. Within those flashes of dazzlement Brippoki gains greater insight, fleeting glimpses of his former freedoms and a better life back in the World – the land of his birthright, so long denied him.

This is the Dream of the Clay – what was, what is, and shall be again.

Tide-marsh and inlet, the swamp itself swamped is still there, home to Frog, Bug, and Bird. Hawk, Sparrow, Fox, Owl and Mouse; the earliest settlers remain – still alive in the dead city, as he is.

Every time it rains, a little more soil is returned. Bird flying over shits out a seed. Seed lodges in the brickwork. Green shoots crack the stone paving; roots burst pipes.

All it takes is time.

Quality of light changing, the landscape shifts again. Brippoki shrinks back from the soft margins – mud, cold and grey.

A breath on the back of his neck makes his hackles rise. Whispering in his ear and he turns, wild-eyed. The air is still. He is alone. Penned in between festering timbers and rotten brick, he looks up. All that's visible is a thin streak of purple – no sky, only a wound in blackness.

Impact.

He comes to, lying half in a puddle of filth. Dragging himself to his feet, rebounding wall to wall, a flinch at every touch, he staggers on.

Termite towers rise to the southeast, many hundred heads high. They are living in this way, piled one on top of another, shitting on each other's heads. Briefly the apparitions glow in the half-light, and then fade.

A sharp brick escarpment dagger-points in that same direction. Crossing over a borderline only visible on maps, Brippoki passes into the parish of St Sepulchre. From the vale, through the gate of death, into the jaws of death – he emerges into a vast marketplace, a smooth field within the shadow of an ancient city wall.

He is enveloped in a billowing cloud of steam. As it clears, Brippoki turns on the spot, attempting to recover his bearings. An enormous building, red brick and limestone, now fills the space where the field stretched before. A long, white body laid out on the ground, it reminds him of the sailors' Hospital in Greenwich – a palace. The walls are high, and so long their ends extend almost out of sight. Octagonal pavilion towers stand to each extreme. Warrior-women guard the entrance, and fire-breathing serpents. Beneath the triangular pediment, ornate iron grille-work shows off all the lurid hues of fresh bruising.

Curious, Brippoki moves closer, to peer through the bars of the gate.

The central aisle of a massive arcade extends forward. Flooded with light, the long hall appears hollowed out, eviscerated. Cast-iron roof supports high overhead are long ribs draped in Nottingham lace. Gate open, he walks the Grand Avenue. Long rails run left and right, festooned with meat hooks. A forest of fresh carcasses hangs there, orderly as a plantation. Bare stalls, either side, heave with more of the phantom flesh, torsos and limbs hacked into prime joints and manageable portions. Huge bins brim with hearts, livers, strips of kidney fat, carefully folded. Severed heads are neatly stacked. All of the bright white tiles and gutters have been hosed clean. In the midst of this most polite of slaughterhouses, men whose stark overalls are soaked in drying blood sit down to a hearty meat breakfast.

Stone-cold dread knocks at Brippoki's liver. Stripped flesh exposes bone, a pointing-bone that curses. The thin finger of a corpse, scraped clean, jerks knucklejoints in balled wax. The murderers mouth with their sticky lips. Chanting, pointing, they rise from their feast table. Brippoki's soul grows mad with fear.

Slip-sliding on the slick surfaces, his legs collapse in a tangle. Fallen on the floor, thick with blood and sawdust, he cannot at first will his limbs to move, not for the hurt and ache in his head or the energy drained from his body. Inclined to sleep forever, he instead rolls back over onto his feet and forces himself to rise, knowing the alternative.

Being boiled, burnt alive, dragged by the heels behind carriages – in the shadow of Old Bailey rise the gallows and the stake.

Sticky with blood, some his own, he daubs the walls as he passes. Back into the open, day for night, Brippoki staggers deeper into this butchers' quarter.

Dizzy with pain, he lashes out to either side with his *waddy*. From every cellar and basement comes the chunky sound of cleavers, hatchet blows rained onto chopping blocks – the bellowing, roaring, bleating, squealing of every condemned man and beast. Blood gushing, they gurgle and shudder, not dead – forever dying. The gutters foam red, stench terrifying.

The darkness smiles to see the fatal wounding.

Defenceless out in the open, Brippoki seeks refuge, away from the boiling vats of glue, and the air thick with feathers.

He escapes the jaws of death into a No Man's Land, the mouth of Hell.

Between Holborn Circus in the north and Ludgate to the south, road, rail and bridge construction runs the gamut.

Plagued by the sweats, he sways at the fringes of great earthworks. Layers of earth, peeled back, reveal the Lowerworld beneath: timber supports, a mess of pipes and shaft holes, seemingly bottomless – a steaming pit that casts a devilish glow. Flexed toes and digging heels struggle for purchase in the turned mud. These tracks he cannot hope to cover.

As the ground grumbles and shakes, the hellish light glares fiercer. Darts of flame sear the blackness. A multitude of carriages follows, each so hot on the heels of the other that they almost touch. Screeching to a stop, the metallic centipede vomits out damned souls, then bores a new tunnel. These shells of men do not linger but march mechanically on, disappearing into the surrounding gloom.

'I fell down a dreadful steep hill,' dreams Deadman, 'and came with great violence against an iron stanchion.'

Brippoki backs off. He rolls in the sand and mud, quite deliberately, letting it stick to the blood and feathers until quite numb.

Deadman, in His sleep, in His dreams, He comes for him.

Scrambling, springing, frantic, Brippoki maintains his course for the river, the piercing Serpent, crooked Serpent. A wild longing has seized him, an unseen power.

Flame lick around the mouth of Ludgate. The air, hot and thick, fills with the drone of angry bees.

Liquid fire flows along the gutters, jumps up all around. It lights up the night, illuminates the bellies of huge birds. As overheated windows pop, a rain of glass shards slashes his skin. He dares not any more look up. Falling beams, explosions; Brippoki hears the whoop and scream of thousands engulfed in maelstrom.

The city, the whole city is afire.

The bells ring backwards, from St Barts the Greater, St Mary's and St Bride's…a babel, confusion of voices…

Wall and ditch, fluke change of wind; Brippoki runs for cover. Stumbling, writhing, climbing – what impulse drives him?

Naming is the province of the Ancestors, the binding act bringing them closer. Only Named, may one be Known.

He must discover his True name whilst still *Wilyaru*, or else stay lost forever.

The Piebald Giant, crowned in black cloud, glowers over all. An inscrutable colossus, stirring, He heaves His head and shoulders free. The entire dead city destroyed, another is rising up through it.

The fronts of the charnelhouses grow dark. Brippoki casts aside the firebrand, a burnt-out stick, reduced to charcoal.

He sees the light. Crackling air and rolling thunder, he alone is darkness in a city turned to light. The clashing of swords, the trampling of hooves, is replaced now by a sound even louder – the rumble and roar of engines, blasts on innumerable horns, and squealing brakes. Chariots rage in the streets, flaming with torches, jostling one another in broad streams – torches, running like lightning. The earth shakes underfoot.

Weaving through this new traffic, Brippoki runs for the river, where gates open and the meat- and moon-palaces dissolve.

Huge angry moon behind him, the waterhole in front, he seeks the snakehead of the Great Serpent Thames to defend him – *Parramatta*. His shield is of red, his warpaint scarlet.

'Black friars!' shouts a warning voice. 'Blackfriars!'

Meteors run, cross their javelins. Brippoki teeters, poised in that same spot he has ever stood – on the edge of forever, the threshold of an empty page, with anger at his back.

Brippoki turns.

A gigantic black nail fixes him to the spot, and from out of that darkness leers forth a Great Head, shrouded in mist.

It is come – it is there with him, right in front of him.

Blank eyes burn, ablaze with cold fury – inhuman, insane – face, to his face, hideously marked and screaming blood vengeance. The eyes are of haliotis shell, whites gleaming malevolence – nostrils flared, chin jutting, the large wide-open mouth breathing hot fire, devouring.

Deadman reaches for him, closer, clawed hand clasping, bone finger grasping, and with His touch, darkness and death. Brippoki shrivels up like grass.

That roaring sound now deafening, the net pulls taut. Brippoki's fevered eye takes one last look. The lights of the city quiver on the water, far below.

A burning crown lights up his head.

Panatapia, red hill rising – his chest distends. Silent, from nowhere, an invisible spear released from the pointing-bone comes sliding out his front. He tastes blood, from the heart, in the mouth – he resigns himself, run out.

An instant later, an eternity, the barest perceptible outline shows in the space where he once stood.

Surging currents flush the colour of blood.

Brippoki cannot move. Conscious of what goes on around him, he is being put into a hole in the ground.

He is *Kertameru*, an infant, placed in a hole his mother has dug for him, in the dirt, where he must remain. The hole is shaped like a basin, at such an angle that he cannot easily crawl out.

'Sit along this hole,' she says to him, 'until I come back for you.'

And secure in this simple impression, he passes out of mind.

Gnowee, the sun, peeks over the horizon, still in search of Her lost son. He sees the light, and whence it flows, and in it, his joy.

Nothing grows here, nothing walks – the empty earth, pitted with hollows, wants for the water of life. And yet the Clay itself is imbued with the essence of all things, every man, every creature, every invention that will ever be. All aspects of life are seeds therein. Hidden just below the surface, they slumber.

Wichety-grub man, Honey-ant man, crying out their names, call on them. Sun, moon, stars come bursting forth, each with the immortal cry, 'I AM!'

Snake man, Cockatoo man, and in the sky, Southern Cross. As with the bloom after sudden rainfall, the frogs that have buried themselves emerge. The city comes alive in rivers of nectar, clouds of seed, the fish, the insects, the flowers and feasting birds. The landscape is not dead after all, but as the desert truly is – Dreaming.

Honeysuckle man, Bandicoot man, and he, they are lying in the cold embrace of earth. At the last he knows his True name. His golden hair glitters like a spider's web lit by sunrise. He is ageless, a young man who will never be old.

A dweller in the earth, he stands proud alongside them all, and sings the World into being.

London is covered over within the net of his sacred song.

CHAPTER LXII
Wednesday the 24th of June, 1868

WHO SAW HIM DIE?

'Our birth is but a sleep and a forgetting:
The Soul that rises with us, our life's Star,
Hath had elsewhere its setting,
and cometh from afar.'

~ William Wordsworth,
'Ode: Intimations of Immortality'

'Larkin,' the man said, 'Sarah Larkin. Hello. You were at Went House, although we were never formally introduced. Charles Lawrence.'

He jogged forward down the front steps of the lobby; extending a hand as if to shake hers, before thinking twice. Immediately Lawrence noticed the dark circles under her eyes, suggestive of late nights, perhaps more. Tall and thin, spare of figure, she was possessed of that sort of beauty not so readily apparent. Rather, it bore study – or else crept up unawares.

'It is…a pleasure to make your acquaintance,' he said.

He looked at her slightly askance.

'We could wish for better circumstances,' she said, her voice cracking.

'Where is he?' she asked. 'I'm sorry. I don't wish to be rude, it's just…'

'Of course,' said Lawrence. 'Follow me.'

He led her away from the cab-stand, up the steps, through the arched passageway of Guy's House, and into the hospital.

'They made contact with me yesterday to tell me he had been found,' he said.

'And me,' said Sarah, 'this morning.'

The doorbell had rung a number of times, the past few days, but she had never answered.

'No,' asserted Lawrence, 'that was me. I sent for you…sent word to you.'

She turned her head to search his face, searching hers. A thousand questions crowded all at once – yet the most important had been asked.

'He drifts in and out of consciousness,' said Lawrence, striding ahead. 'But a number of times now, he has mentioned you by name.'

He held open a double-door for her, assessing her frankly as she walked through. The object of his attentions swung around to face him too suddenly. They exchanged slight but honest looks.

'My name?' said Sarah.

'"Thara",' lisped Lawrence – almost suggestively.

She looked away.

'Yes,' she whispered, '...that's it.'

Mild, distracted, she appeared somewhat dismayed at the rush of bodies all around them. They walked together in silence across courtyards between buildings, along corridors that seemed interminable, and with every ward they passed she hesitated, as if half expecting to be directed into it.

'How did you – ' she said. 'I mean how did you know where to...?'

He too paused, to produce a crumpled paper from his pocket.

'He was carrying this,' said Lawrence. 'One of the few things he had on... uh, had on him.'

The envelope bore her address, in Dilkes's handwriting. Tucked inside, her fingers felt something alive. Sarah jumped. She fished out a fetish, bound with twine and tiny feathers, a glue of some sort, and made with her own hair.

Lawrence had mercifully averted his gaze to allow a moment's privacy; still, she again caught him looking at her, sideways on.

'He places great stock in you,' said Lawrence.

They gathered quietly by the bedside.

Sarah gasped to see Brippoki's cheekbones, the surrounding flesh sunken. No longer coated in ash, his skin had nevertheless taken on its pallor.

'Where did you find him?' she asked.

'Not I; some young mudlarks,' said Lawrence, 'and lucky that they did, else the river would soon have claimed him. Found his body by first light...stretched out, deep in the mud, just about as far in as he might go. The mud had almost closed over him by the time they pulled him out.'

'When?'

'Monday, towards low tide,' said Lawrence, 'beneath Blackfriars Bridge, so I'm told.'

Sarah ceased to look the prone body over, and raised her eyes to his, in wonder.

Lawrence shrugged. 'Perhaps he fell,' he offered.

Sarah no longer cared what anyone thought. She moved in closer, to examine Brippoki's face. A burning fever consumed him from the inside out.

'They cleaned him up,' said Lawrence. 'No bones broken, but sickly. Once the stink of mud was removed, they bled him. He raves a bit, every now and then…moves his legs slightly, as dogs do when dreaming.' Lawrence watched her brows crease, and her soft lips as they parted. 'His brain is inflamed, they say.'

Brippoki's eyelids flickered open. Sarah moved to a position where he might see her.

'Conscious,' cautioned Lawrence, '…but not lucid.'

'Have they fed him?' she asked.

'He refuses all food.'

'But they have made the attempt…? Pass me some water.'

She gestured behind, without looking at either Lawrence or the jug and glass on the bedside table. He obliged. Ever so gently she tipped some of the liquid to Brippoki's lips.

Lawrence warily eyed one or two of the passing staff. He said, 'Do you think you ought to…?'

'Someone ought to,' insisted Sarah.

Brippoki knew her; she saw it in his eye.

'Hello,' she said.

His jaw worked. She gave him more water, drew in closer: the noise of the ward, the moaning from the beds and the troop of shoes back and forth across the bare boards, was fearsome.

'*Pringurru*,' Brippoki gasped.

He was struggling to remove the covers, exposing his bare flesh; Sarah hesitated to help. He rolled over, arm bent back, pointing to his lower flank. She could not see anything – no wound, nor mark.

'I…I don't…'

His hand feels for his *min-tum*, the cord worn round his waist. Finding it gone, he panics. He falls back, urgently miming – a young woman plaiting a cord of kangaroo hair, passing the line around her head once, taking care to fix the knot in the centre of her forehead. The line then goes around his body, a second knot placed where the spear went in. Flapping wildly, his hands stroke his flesh towards that same point to show how to force out the bad blood.

Lawrence stepped forward.

'Miss Larkin,' he said, apologetic, 'he's delirious…'

Sarah ignored his protests. Brippoki's hand drew a line from his waist towards her mouth. He made loud sucking noises.

'Oh, really. NURSE!' Lawrence cast around for help. 'Doctor? NURSE!'

He took Sarah by the shoulders. She shook him off, even as she took a step backwards, almost into his arms.

Brippoki's face distorted horribly, hands flying about his fretted lips. His sheets, kicked about, were in disarray.

The figure of the matron overtook a junior nurse, hanging back. She took firm hold of the patient, forcing him back down on the bed. At her touch, the air instantly seemed to go out of him. All imprecation ceased, Brippoki went limp as a rag doll, limbs dangling.

'Fetch Dr Wilks,' ordered the matron.

'He's just coming,' came the nervous reply.

Sarah stared dumbly at the lace doily on top of her cap, atop her bun, at the tassellated brooch at her throat.

Dead fish eyes turned on Sarah and Lawrence; fell on Sarah's black dress.

'Miss Loag,' said the doctor, and smoothly took over.

Matron marched around to their side of the bed. 'Come away,' she said. 'You have him agitated.'

Well aware of Lawrence's discomfiture at her back, Sarah stood defiant. Brippoki had been asking something of her.

'It will do his chances of recovery no good at all,' Lawrence hissed in her ear. 'Come away.'

At that, Sarah meekly obliged.

'He hasn't his right mind,' said Lawrence.

Maybe so.

He escorted her outside. They walked around the park, an enclosure within the middle of the hospital complex. It was cloudy, but humid, and late in the day.

Wishing to alleviate Sarah's distress, Lawrence clutched at straws.

'With the help of the surgeons, he may yet recover,' he said.

'"And prove an ass",' she replied. Her features softened, not wishing to seem unkind. Lawrence marched, virile, she working to keep up. A good man, if not especially handsome; his sad and sorry face seemed a stranger to laughter.

'How is the team?' Sarah asked.

'In Hastings,' said Lawrence, a tad curtly.

In his absence Norton captained the team; the press had been told his hand was injured, 'a very nasty crack on his finger, which will incapacitate him from playing for some time.'

He discarded another in a rapid succession of lit cigarettes. A lively creature filled with character, Sarah Larkin seemed now that much calmer than he – intelligent, and without the need to show it off. Even by London standards her complexion was remarkably pale, quite unlike the frazzled damsels of Australia. These otherworldly looks attracted; an echo of home.

'It surprises me that you know Cole,' he said.

Her grey eyes were drops of seawater.

'As a friend,' she said, 'only recently, Mr Lawrence.'

'Please,' said Lawrence. 'Call me Charles.'

He wore a muffin hat over fine, straw-coloured hair. Pale-suited, his unpressed trousers looked as if they had been slept in, or rained on, or both. His jacket, equally shapeless, was all pocket, straight up and down. Sarah sensed considerable force held in reserve: baggy casual clothing did little to conceal the team captain's muscular frame.

His hands, strong and tan, looked empty without a bat to clutch.

Lawrence caught her looking.

'He is…difficult,' Sarah confessed, 'to understand.'

Some folk might think Brippoki slow, but his thoughts ran silver-quick.

Lawrence merely nodded. Among a group of men at best difficult to know, King Cole had always been one of the most remote.

'This may seem odd to ask,' she said, 'but is anyone with you from New Zealand?'

'No,' he laughed. 'That was a misprint.'

Mystified, she tried again. 'So the word "*rangatira*"…that means nothing to you?'

Lawrence's weathered cheeks turned a whiter shade of pale.

Once news of their plan to take the team to England had reached the ears of the Board – the Central Board for the Protection of Aborigines – the Melbourne newspapers had regularly published letters of protest. As a result, the authorities in Victoria had sought to put an end to their touring: the waggon ride to Warrnambool undertaken so that they might smuggle the team into neighbouring New South Wales.

On the 22nd of October last they had gone to Queenscliff, ostensibly for a day's fishing. Near to the mouth of Port Philip Bay, their little rowboats had come alongside the steamship *Rangatira*, out of Melbourne. The coastal vessel then took them on as steerage passengers up to Sydney, whereby they were spirited out of the colony and, a few months thereafter, the country.

'No,' said Lawrence, 'nothing.'

Her fierce eyes saw through him, bright and clear.

'I'm sorry,' he mumbled.

They were beckoned back into the block designated Hunt's House, to where Brippoki lingered on the ward.

'Our intent was to relieve the pressure on his brain. Although we have opened the veins of both arms as well as the temporal artery, he has not recovered. I believe it is only a matter of time.'

The doctor introduced himself as Samuel Wilks. The hospital chaplain, he informed them, had performed the last rites. Aside from nursing staff, a second man of middle age lurked nearby. Crooked and furtive in posture, he wore a white coat liberally splashed with blood – disconcerting enough, yet he also carried about what appeared to be a chunk of flesh, set in a small dish, which he would occasionally raise up and examine under one of the T-stalk gas-lamps dotted throughout the ward. Now that the natural light was fading they had all been lit, lending the scene an oddly festive glow.

Brippoki lay supine and unresponsive in the bed, as if merely awaiting the end to come.

He is standing among a crowd of children, looking down at a man laid in the mud. Then he floats a few feet above their heads, the heads of his friends, *Nei*-Thara and Lawrence. They sit together beside a *wirkatti*, a bier or burial platform, the body of a blackfellow sleeping between.

Taking a closer look at the body they attend – enveloped in cloth, rolled round and tight – he sees it is the body he occupied in life. Why, then, do they not wail and bloody themselves? They better have laid his head towards the east…

Two stranger males dressed in white step across. Facing each other, one stands at the head, the other at the foot. They are talking quietly among themselves. He decides to stay a while, and visit with them.

'Did he move?' said Sarah.

Lawrence stopped talking.

'He looked at me.'

Brippoki looked first to one, then the other of them. They huddled in closer, shoulder to shoulder. With a weak smile, he approved.

'What did you say?' said Sarah. 'He said something. What did he say?'

Lawrence sat back. He told her, 'I think he said… "Mate".'

Brippoki started, ever so quietly, to sing.

'What are those,' asked the doctor, 'more nonsense words?'

His songs all sung he is weary of breath. He feels himself drawn away, a sensation something like flying. His vision closes in, growing dark. Willingly he leaves behind all the kindness and the cruelties he has known.

Brippoki fell silent. The others looked to Dr Wilks, who leant over to check.

'He has fallen asleep,' he said.

Sarah and Lawrence exchanged an uncertain glance.

'By which,' said Wilks, 'I mean the long sleep. The stream of life has stopped.'

Lawrence threw down his cap. 'I can't wait to quit this country,' he snapped. 'In Australia, a spade is called a spade and death is death!'

It was true what they said: that you could never go home again.

'My sentiments,' said Dr Wilks, 'exactly. But straight talk is unpopular.' He indicated a quotation, framed above the bed.

'Are you willing to tend to the formalities immediately?' he asked.

'I am,' said Lawrence.

Wilks began to dictate aloud to the registrar. 'Entry for 24th June, number...?'

'Two One Seven.'

'217...' Wilks looked at Lawrence. '*Name of deceased?*'

'Charles Rose,' he replied, 'alias King Cole.'

'*Date of admission*,' continued Wilks, consulting a chart, '22nd of June, number 814. *Age?*'

Lawrence looked uncertain. 'Twenty-eight?'

'*Ward*,' Wilks looked around, 'Stephen. *Physician... Date of death*, June 24th. *Disease*, acute pneumonia. Recommend post mortem.'

The other doctor moved a little closer, his face a rictus.

Sarah had to look away. Her eye went to the quotation overhead. '*While they beheld, he was taken up; and a cloud received him out of their sight. (Acts i:9)*' Others were hung above each of the beds in the place.

She was struck full force by the unspeakable nature of tragedy.

Brippoki was dead.

'*Hour of death...* 9.30.p.m., near enough. Residence?'

Lawrence answered, 'Queen's Head public house, Borough High-street. Mrs Sarah Willsher, proprietor.'

Wilks flicked an eyebrow. 'Temporary residence?'

'Yes, it is. It is where we...'

Cole was dead.

'...where I am staying.'

'As for the mortal remains...' Wilks gestured for the registrar to shoulder his form for the moment and turned from the bed. The twisted figure in the bloodied coat stepped further forward. 'This is Mr Alfred Poland,' said Wilks, 'a surgeon doctor whose skill and science are indisputable...his dexterity and rapidity without equal...'

The fellow could not tear his avidity from the body in the bed.

'Guy's, you understand, is a teaching hospital...' continued Dr Wilks. He placed an arm around Lawrence's shoulder. 'An important centre for the study of morbid anatomy. The specimen, speaking frankly, is unique, an opportunity...'

Showing the requisition slip, he unsheathed his pen. 'Will you give your consent?'

Sarah stepped in.

'No,' she said. 'His body will not be opened to exhibition.' Turning to Lawrence, 'We absolutely refuse.'

Aboriginal ideas of future happiness relied on proper rites of burial being performed: Brippoki's paradise might well be denied him were his body no longer whole.

'An inspection at least must be made,' insisted Wilks, 'if only to confirm diagnosis. That is the way we do things here.'

'And it is when you apply theory of one sort to a problem of another that you receive nonsense in reply,' said Sarah.

Her horn was of iron, her hooves brass. She stood firm.

Nonplussed, the doctor looked to Lawrence. 'Do you claim the body?'

'Yes,' said Lawrence, newly inspired. 'We do.'

Wilks sighed and turned to Alfred Poland. 'Cover him up,' he said. 'I think we're finished.'

Sarah, declaring a need for air, returned to the hospital grounds. Lawrence accompanied her. Seeking shelter from a short rain shower, they found a stone alcove – according to its plaque, part of the old London Bridge, removed in 1832.

Above them in the night sky, a pale moon trailed by a little the bright star Rex.

Sarah fixed her eyes firmly on the ground beneath her feet.

Lawrence reached into his pockets, only to find his cigarettes all gone. 'Dammit,' he said. 'Excuse me. I keep wondering how it is that he ended up in the river?' Of course he wanted to know where Cole had been all this time, but took her very presence for his answer, making it a question imprudent to ask. 'And without his clothes,' he said. 'I fear he was the victim of a robbery.'

Many a poor soul, rolled for a shilling, was ditched in the black depths of the Thames.

'Not a robbery,' said Sarah, with some confidence.

'I don't believe he could have been merely drunk,' said Lawrence.

She said nothing.

'It's so hard to maintain order, with alcohol around,' lamented Lawrence. 'And it always is. Publicans help arrange the fixtures, provide refreshments and our accommodation! Try as I might, I cannot keep it from them. They are every day in touch with cricket-lovers who think it kind to drink their health and chat, and the poor fellows are quite helpless to refuse.'

He started to pace back and forth.

'When I remonstrate with them, they say to me they are not slaves and should have what they like in a free country. It is always the other gentlemen's fault and they are just being friendly, which is largely true, so whatever else can I do other than forgive them, and keep hoping for improvement.'

He turned to her, in search of sympathy.

'They behave very obedient,' he said. 'Will do anything to please me, and their best, all things considered. But the demon drink affects every one of them differently. Tiger likes a quarrel and wants to fight. Charley tends to sulk. Others play harmless games and tricks on each other, or endlessly profess their love for me.' Lawrence showed a wan smile. 'I became their professor before we left Australia, so long as I promised not to develop anything they would tell me, and this had a good effect.'

He perhaps meant confessor, just as much; Sarah made no comment.

'King Cole was such a regular fellow, and always good in attendance…'til of late,' he mused. 'That's what I don't understand.'

Guilty conscience kept his mouth running – and hers shut.

'Dick-a-Dick has often helped us out,' said Lawrence, frustrated. He resumed his pacing. 'He'd make any Temperance Society a good secretary. Dick's horror of drunkenness is such that he visits condign punishment on any of his brothers who indulge too much. And he lays it on strong, believe me. An awkward customer, when his blood is up.'

Lawrence sighed.

'Hah,' he said, 'listen to me. These are just a few of the troubles we managers have to contend with. The schedule we have embarked on is gruelling.'

'For you,' said Sarah, pointedly, 'more than them?'

'For us all,' said Lawrence.

Moderation might be best recommended, in all things.

He saw that she looked up at the window whereabouts the body lay.

'He was peaceful at the end,' he said. 'Going gently, without a fight.'

'Yes,' she said.

'A good sport.'

Something in Sarah rebelled. 'What umpire should he appeal to that is fair?' she said. 'It's not always the best man who wins.'

Somewhere in the distance, a clock struck the quarter hour before ten.

'It's getting late,' said Lawrence, 'you must be tired, and wanting to get home. Shall I call you a cab?'

Sarah shrugged.

'Once the king has gone from the palace,' she said, 'there is nothing to look at but walls.'

Lawrence didn't know what to make of that.

'I never thought of homesickness in quite those terms,' he said at last.

She stood. 'Does it really surprise you, so far removed from all they know, that he should perish in his pride?' Her voice communicated surprising bitterness. 'I ask you how they are, and you tell me where. And perhaps that is the same thing for them. If they are, as you say, constantly drinking, then it shows that they are poorly and depressed. He was separate from his brothers, as you call them, his only possible consolation.'

Lawrence thought of Sundown, and what little he had gleaned from him.

'I believe,' he said, 'it was his choice.'

'His choice?' she said, surpassing bitterness. 'To be here?' Sarah looked around them, her voice breaking. 'To end *here*?'

'His ties were less binding than you might think,' said Lawrence quietly. 'His consolation, less.'

She waited him out.

'He has 'istory, as the Blackies like to say,' said Lawrence. 'Except they don't, if you follow me, like to say it. I overhear things…and those tend to hold more water.'

Sarah stayed on, her interest provoked.

'*Wembawemba*, or somesuch…that's a word, I believe, to say "half-caste".'

Despite their standing so close together, and alone in the dark, Lawrence's voice fell to an urgent whisper.

'It's no secret,' he said, 'or rather, it is an open secret…the settler communities have always had their "*gin*-men" or "combos", white men who…who go with Aboriginal women.' Lawrence winced. Some blackfellows, he knew, entertained ambitions in the opposite direction – Johnny Mullagh, for one. Fruitless ambition, he trusted. 'Well,' he said, 'the practice isn't confined to just stockmen or drovers. The middle classes also indulge.'

'What is your point?' she said.

'White blood. And they whisper his grandy was no drover's boy, either.'

'It was his grandfather?'

She *was* smart. That gave Lawrence pause.

'Father's side, mother's side, I really don't know,' he said, 'but yes, I assume it a generation or two back. I mean, you couldn't tell just from looking at him.'

She met his stare even as it narrowed. Half-caste, quarter, eighth – what did it matter? Perhaps everything.

She nodded her head, slowly.

'It has turned chilly, don't you think?' he said. 'Let's walk on.'

Lonely for some days now, Lawrence felt in expansive mode. 'There'll be sad faces when I get back and tell the other lads the news…although I dare say they never acted overly fond. Not one has asked after him, even though he's been missing for some weeks…'

'Oh?' said Sarah. That came as news.

He said, 'They cut their hair and beards, you know, in mourning for the dead…'

She instinctively put up a hand, straightening her bonnet.

'…and paint themselves in white.'

'The Israelites did no less,' she murmured, 'in the time of Moses.'

'Such is the curious belief they hang on to,' said Lawrence, 'even today. That white people are dead. Their own dead, in fact, returned to life. Although we have changed colour, we feel compelled to return to those same places we frequented, back when we were alive. When we were black. Does this shock you?'

'Not…entirely.'

'In early colonial days, they almost welcomed death…hoping to come back, loaded down, as we are, with guns, arms, and provisions.' Lawrence clasped a weary hand to the back of his neck. 'Except, the names of the dead,' he confided, 'must never be repeated. They refuse even to hear of them. I got into terrible trouble once, for mentioning Jellico by name – '

Sarah caught him short. 'You mean to say there have been others, before this one? Other deaths?'

'Regrettably, yes,' he said '…before.' A rash of fatalities, in fact. 'I was not always their captain!'

Sarah turned and stalked on ahead.

'I have tried my best,' he said, 'to expose them to wholesome influences, generally.'

She had noted earlier the weakness of his chin.

'The management,' he was saying, 'cannot be held responsible – '

She rounded on him. 'He was in our charge, Mr Lawrence. We let him down.'

'No, Miss Larkin,' said Charles Lawrence, 'you are mistaken. He was his own man.'

Sarah turned aside. '"Thus conscience does make cowards of us all."'

Her liquid eyes would meet his no more.

'So,' she said, relenting, 'what will you do now?'

'Conclude matters here,' he said. 'Rejoin the team.' Their next match was in Halifax, come the weekend. 'Continue with the tour until our return to Australia. What else can I do?'

The ensuing silence was left for him to fill.

'And you?' he asked.

'I shall go home, Mr Lawrence,' said Sarah. 'Isn't that the best that any of us can hope for?'

Threshing her skirts, she bustled ahead.

'May I walk you,' he asked, 'a little further?'

'No,' she said. 'I think I shall go my own way.'

The funeral would have to be organised, and shortly.

'Shall I see you again?' he called after her.

'Goodbye, Mr Lawrence.'

Nothing was inevitable. Some things, however, were intended; and others simply never meant to be.

507

CHAPTER LXIII
Wednesday the 24th of June, 1868

THE SLEEP OF REASON

'We do not rush from darkness to light – the twilight
precedes the blaze of the day.'

~ 'Land for Aboriginies', *The Age*

Lambert, who lived by the Word, had died by the Word.

'...God.'

In closing his eyes, some time before dawn on the Monday, more so since, Sarah could not yet free herself from the links of heavy chain contained in that one word – the Father, the Son, and Holy Ghost.

Why create an Eden, and then set within it a tree whose fruit was forbidden?

Why create deadly poisons, madness, disease, death and starvation; flies, rot and excrement; all the great and petty evils in the world. Why the Serpent, Lord of Flies, of Lies; lies themselves.

Why foster ignorance, attaching to knowledge such a dreadful cost?

In every Eden there lurked a snake.

Sleep on it. Sleep.

No rest.

Sarah reached over, fingers fumbling for a box of lucifers in the dark, striking, lighting the candle at her bedside, scrabbling for a pen, dipping it in the ink; eyes half closed against the pain of the light, scribbling herself a blind note, another in a series of notes; blotting, laying the pen aside, extinguishing the light, turning away on her side.

She turned and turned again in the bed, her mind racing, only to give in and reach for the matches again.

A sleepless soul, there could be no rest, no rest in a world where the one half of mankind was continually at the mercy of the other; if not at the mercy, then at the throat.

And even then, the halves were not themselves equal.

The grandfather clock in the hall chimed the half-hour, and, what seemed moments later, chimed the hour.

She had known for herself the thrill of omnipotence, experienced as a child – tempted, as Adam and Eve were, by the God of the Garden: alternately she would tear crumbs from a picnic roll until the pigeons clustered thick around, and then stamp her foot to make them scatter.

Why should the Father of Jealousy behave any differently?

Why, and why, and why, and why…

Her hatred of all that he stood for was the greatest mark of her absolute devotion.

She had been brought up in the absolute integrity of the Word. Covenants, of course, like shackles, were made to be broken. Should terms be disputed, cases lacking remedy in common-law courts sought equity from the highest Court of Justice, in Chancery – a place where, she knew too well, even an angel might be tried and found guilty. The only certain outcome was the loss of one or both parties, and a curse on both their houses.

Sundered from Mother Church, Father from Daughter Church, Godhead collapsed.

Was she not her father's daughter?

I.
Am.
Not.
Who was my father?

Not Lambert; who had killed her mother for it.

Who was her father? Who was her mother?

> 'Love, by harsh evidence,
> Thrown from its eminence…'

…nothing but a body found floating in the Thames, homeless, and anonymous.

Had she more family, similarly unaware that she existed?

Of all the secrets brought to light these last few days, not knowing one's relations was the hardest to come to terms with. She had thought she knew her mother, insofar as she could know her; past all dishonour, she was beyond judgement now; and Lambert, too. She did not care to think of who he might have really been, all that time.

But then, who was her father?

Another life kindled in her bosom, one filled with nothing but possibilities. Had she a sister? Had she a brother?

> 'Or was there a dearer one
> Still, and a nearer one
> Yet, than all other?'

She surely knew better than to trust to dreamy hoping. This last month, for the first time in a long time – perhaps ever – she had begun to consider herself an independent object. She should not so swiftly wish away her freedom; so hard fought, and harder won.

Sarah stood at the front window, staring into the depths of the gulf. Only in hindsight could the costs be counted, of all the unwilling sacrifice made. Her frequent tears were as much of anger as sorrow. The grief she choked down only added to that growing knot of cold fury.

Sarah turned her back to the window, studied her shadow a while, and then eventually returned to the bed. In extinguishing the lamp and attempting to doze, she laid herself bare to fitful snatches of dream.

Druce on board the *Thisbe* ('vile Wall') waved a crab-like claw: his hand with two of the fingers missing – his wife and his child perhaps, whom he had abandoned, but was unable to leave behind.

She opened up the pages of the book containing the manuscript, only to find it filled with her own handwriting…

Sarah awoke with a start.

She listened to the night-time creaks and breathings of brickwork and floorboards, against the background hum of the city. She sensed the distances contained within them, between one another and from her self.

Phantom limbs could ever be felt, it was said, long after they were gone. The ache remained of what was lost.

The blood of prophets had been shed since the foundation of the world, from the blood of Abel to the blood of Zacharias. Our forefathers stoned the prophets, and we continued in the amiable custom, judgement not our own but that of other people. Her faith in God's goodness had slowly perished, like Zacharias, in that gap between the altar, tomb of martyrs and marriage, and the temple, in which God resides.

She still believed, but could not forgive. God existed and God was evil – or at the very least oblivious of his creation, mankind; which amounted to much the same thing. She was wrong before, in her thinking: God resembled nothing human in thought or deed. The Australian Aborigines, according to Lubbock, had it more correct. Their Spirit Ancestors laid down the living Law, but in their own behaviours – murder, rape, cannibalism – set no standard for man. They were, in very essence, inhuman. And, unlike the gods of Ancient Greece, they neither solicited nor expected obeisance or worship. They were oblivious.

God was no friend to the Aborigine, but an unforgiving or rather uncaring deity. Hapless man was inherently good. The Christian God, meanwhile, relied for his benevolence on Original Sin – man's inherent evil.

If Druce's faith had acted guarantor of sorts of his good behaviour, then this idea had perhaps preserved Brippoki from his own inner demons: once he thought that protection gone, all hope went with it.

Allowing her mind, for one moment, to enter into the perspective, the relationship, of a flower fairy – no, a lowly insect, hidden among the grasses; then, seen from this new angle, even human activity resembled that of uncaring gods, heedless giants striding across the earth. Except in this equation we were not gods, as we might think – we were the ants.

Beware of false prophets… Ye shall know them by their fruits.

A good tree cannot bring forth evil fruit, neither can a corrupt tree bring forth –

But why keep returning to the Bible? A lifetime's habit, ingrained, she had seen for herself how the words, the semblance of wisdom therein, could be turned to a virtual infinity of individual usage; an endless hall of twisted mirrors, reflecting only what the user best wished to see, or show.

Suffice to say, good fruit could not come from a source that had been corrupted. A thorn tree did not suddenly sprout mulberries, or juicy grapes.

Wherefore by their fruits ye shall know them.

Thorns also, and thistles; she considered herself secondary to Lambert, and subordinately under God's grace, no longer – that was just the chain, binding in fetters, by which the young and strong were held in willing subjection to the old and weak.

She had awoken, as if from a long slumber.

She had dreamt, in her sleep, an England of spring meadows and gently rolling hills, where farms and tall church spires dotted misted vales. On waking, the air turned parched and arid, and glowed hot white; then by night, in a featureless desert of cracked earth, hanging icicles formed under blasts of chilling wind. Both desolation and a curse…

Sarah had never acknowledged that her life, up until then, could be called living; but she had not gone so far as to think it a lie.

Hers was a rude awakening, from dreams that were false.

CHAPTER LXIV
Thursday the 25th of June, 1868

DARK MONARCH

'Once to every man and nation comes the moment to decide,
In the strife of Truth with Falsehood, for the good or evil side.'

~ James Russell Lowell, 'The Present Crisis'

'Bit of hard going.' The old man thrust his spade deep into the turned earth.

Lawrence could only agree.

'Not enough rain to speak of,' the digger observed, resting his arms across the handle. Stalled, clearly done for the time being, he tipped his cloth cap to the back of his head and surveyed the dappled skies.

Graveyards within central London long since filled to bursting, the earthly remains of Charles Rose – King Cole – were being interred in Victoria Park Cemetery, out towards the east beyond the slums of Bethnal Green.

Lawrence watched the wind stir the trees, crows hopping along their branches.

'I dug this ground when it was brick field,' said M'sieu Gravedigger, 'and I dug it when it was market garden. I suppose that I s'll carry on digging it now that it's f'r plain burying folks.' He adjusted the spade in the earth, saying, 'Twelve and half acres 'ere…with more 'n' a half million in 'em.'

The parson walked up, a tall and thin man all in black. He asked, 'Just you, is it, sir?'

'Yes,' said Lawrence. 'Just me.' Not meaning to exclude him from their exchange, he half-inclined his body towards the groundskeeper. 'A sorry business,' he said.

Staring awkwardly at his feet since the arrival of the priest, the digger appeared to take offence. He climbed up out of the freshly dug hole and, grumbling, took up his distance.

Lawrence's gaze fell across the nearest in a line of three common deal coffins. The Surrey Cricket Club had kindly offered to cover costs, the funeral expenses anyway negligible: Cole was to be stacked in a pauper's grave. There was little need for ceremony without the team in attendance. Lawrence planned to rejoin them that same evening, so they might hear the sad news from him directly, before any newspaper should announce it.

His players suffered in their performance: they were homesick, as Miss Larkin had surmised. With morale already low, Cole's passing could only depress matters further.

Sundown, like Cole, was *Wurdiboluc* – whether brother by blood or just some obscure relation, Lawrence had given up on puzzling their kinships: it might anyhow be prudent to send him home, sooner rather than later. Aboriginal grieving, in line with their unique beliefs, contained power sufficient to kill.

Lawrence observed the priest's lips moving. 'I'm sorry?' he asked.

'My part is done,' the parson said. 'I wondered if you wished to add anything.'

Lawrence rummaged in his pockets, pulling out notation for a short speech he had prepared: even with no audience, he owed Cole that much. Moving to the graveside, he stumbled slightly before finding surer footing.

'Cricket,' read Lawrence, 'is full of glorious chances, and the goddess who presides over it loves to bring down the most skilful players.'

The priest, standing hard by, huffed slightly. Lawrence looked up, uncertain, before reading on.

'A loyal comrade…no seeker of praise, here lies King Cole, the embodiment of Bush mateship. He stayed in for a considerable time, but the merry young soul was ultimately bowled.'

He had cribbed the closing sentiment from a recent match report, relating an occasion when Dick-a-Dick had worn Cole's cap.

They lowered the coffin down.

It was over: one of his charges dead. Lawrence's worst nightmare had been realised.

He took up a handful of earth, as directed.

'"FORASMUCH as it hath pleased Almighty God of his great mercy",' intoned the priest, '"to take unto himself the soul of our dear brother here departed, we therefore commit his body to the ground. Earth to earth, ashes to ashes, dust to dust, in sure and certain hope of the Resurrection to eternal life, through our Lord Jesus Christ, who shall change our vile body, that it may be like unto his glorious body, according to the mighty working, whereby he is able to subdue all things to himself."'

Dirt pebble-dashed the cheap coffin's lid.

'"I HEARD a voice from heaven",' the priest resumed, '"saying unto me, Write…"'

Lawrence, looking down into his calloused palm, found it empty.

~

In a public bar along Bethnal Green High-street, not far from the burial ground, the team captain swallowed another swig of beer. He drank alone.

'Lawrence is the black sheep,' the papers jibed, 'because he is white!'

Journeying alongside the Blacks had, he felt, led to the growth of his understanding of the world – or at least the limitations of mankind. In the innate decency of their natural character, his native players were so much more than savages, the naïve infants or even blanks they were so often mistaken for. The longer he spent in their company, the more he earned their respect; and they his. Familiarity bred contempt only for those who would denigrate such essential humanity, and continued so to do, almost every day.

It was no better in Australia.

Oh, surely they were rude and unmoulded – when not being mulish, over-generous to a fault. Yet a willingness to adapt and an eagerness to please were countermanded by their keeping the greater part of themselves remote. Even as events modified their more immediate environment, they cultivated an inner world, resolute and unchanging. What was perhaps a source of strength also proved their fatal weakness: they could only take so much, and then no more. Their character cast and fired in their disturbed imagination, any alteration too great threatened to shatter them completely.

As his dear colleague Hayman had said, it took time to know the Aboriginal character – longer, perhaps, to appreciate it. And time on the world's stage was a luxury they were not afforded.

King Cole was laid in his grave, Lawrence's high hopes with him.

'Another,' Lawrence said, placing a shilling on the bar. 'Keep 'em coming.'

Neither the most skilful player nor the steadiest, even as Cole's captain Lawrence couldn't very well denounce the poor fellow in his elegy. The battered copy of *Tom Brown* lay on the sticky bar before him; he had pulled quotes, as he took so much else, from that book serving as his personal Bible. Within its curled pages, a fine balance was ever maintained between joy and pain, a man's duty to himself and to others, and the will towards personal betterment – the very objects he had most lost sight of.

Taking up the book, Lawrence eyed the wise verse from *Ambarvalia*, by Clough, the Rugby poet, an epigraph heading the chapter 'Tom Brown's Last Match'. In search of guidance he began to flick back and forth through the pages, wherein so much of the text had been underlined, and margins annotated. His vaunted ambition – to make his living, while at the same time doing real good – had fallen to mere money-making. The tour turned a healthy profit for its investors. George Smith, financier, over from Sydney – cousin to George W. Graham, their accountant – intended to purchase stallion bloodstock for shipping home. William Hayman's stake matured nicely. Lawrence himself was fourth in the concern.

He paid for his silence only now. Meantime, they kept losing. Some losses were harder to bear.

"'Derry down, then fill up your glass, he's the best that drinks most.'" Lawrence, well in his cups, motioned again to the barman. The Reverend Cotton's 'Cricket Song' echoed and re-echoed. Lessons could be learnt from cricket, all right. Not all were of benefit.

> 'And when the game's o'er, and our fate shall draw nigh
> (For the heroes of cricket, like others must die),
> Our bats we'll resign, neither troubled nor vex'd,
> And give up our wickets to those that come next.'

~

Victoria had been Queen longer than Sarah had been alive. In 27 years as one of Her Imperial Majesty's loyal subjects, she had known conquest, mutiny, epidemic, abolition, and countless wars – the country even coming close, once, to revolution – without ever really experiencing any of it.

Mother had died in 1854, shortly before Sarah's thirteenth birthday; the past was never spoken of thereafter, current events at most vaguely discussed. Little to live for, save day-to-day business between these four walls. Hers had been the life of a nun – contemplation of life, not life itself.

Sarah was standing at the front window, as she had late into the night, in the parlour this time. Having gained her freedom, she little knew what it meant, or what to do with it. Unmarried, an only child, she could not assume the duties of sister-in-law or maiden aunt. She was effectively redundant; no innocent, but ignorant, an artless girl who had needed a modern-day Le Huron, the savage out of Voltaire's *L'Ingénu*, to show to her the country in which she lived – a realm of ignorance and poverty, and, worst of all, willing ignorance of poverty: old England, sick and sad at heart.

The city, even unto its hospitals and churches, had become a nightmare scene. She looked in from outside of it – belonging nowhere in it.

Intimacy with the details of Druce's tortured *Life* were not, on their own, necessary for her to have approached greater understanding: poverty respected neither class nor capability; not intellect, prudence, labour or health. There was nothing deserving at all in poverty – vice no singular promoter, nor, heaven knew, virtue any great defence.

Everyday trials and tribulations, the struggle for existence, brought down the tyranny of the Word. Religion was an irrelevance in the face of such suffering, just as she was – moral superiority, morals themselves, impossible to maintain, while the broad mass of people existed beyond reach of the gospel.

Who more truly lived in denial? Who more truly lived? Living hand to mouth, by the hour, freed poor folk from the curse of intellect holding her in thrall. She might be better off unable to afford such torturing luxury, the time on her hands all her own. Or was this but the first, halting step in her uncertain decline – poverty, fear of poverty, her selfish regard, all rooted in the same spiritual sickness.

She must keep faith. The sheer effort it took to change one's self might take many years, oceans even, but it was always possible to move forward.

Almost unconsciously, Sarah touched her hand against the cold window glass.

Not until that day Brippoki arrived on her doorstep had her own self awoken, from within as much as without. She would not allow her new life to be so soon over, now that he was gone.

Sarah dressed and took a turn around Russell-square, wandering, directionless. A wise heart rarely found in the house of mourning, she strove to restore her equilibrium.

She paused beneath the shade of a London plane tree, *Platanus X hispanica*, the most common of trees, planted widely throughout the city as it was the only kind to thrive in a polluted atmosphere. Plain as its name, it was not without aspects of beauty. By virtue of its mere existence the evil world was done some good.

She removed one of her gloves, to stroke the mottled bark's rough surface.

Only a month since she had been to see him play in his first match at the Oval, and now he was dead and buried. She had known the appointed time, and she had known the appointed place; Captain Lawrence had been kind enough to make certain of that. Sarah preferred to honour Brippoki her own way – his way, most likely: in silent communion with nature. If she was wrong, he must forgive her. They had put Lambert Larkin in the ground on Tuesday, in Malling. She could not face a second funeral inside a single week.

Her goodbyes said privately, Sarah tried to picture Brippoki as she wished to remember him – seated atop One Tree Hill, beneath the elm.

She found herself picking at the bark. Friable, it came off in sizeable chunks. An area about the size of her fist was now exposed – the layer beneath, disclosed to the air, noticeably lighter in colour.

Sarah took a step back and, guilty for the injury, replaced her glove. Turning, she looked up, searching somewhere above the drifting clouds.

When we died, as in our dreams, we returned to the place that we came from.

'Weep, weep.'

Heels grinding the gravel path, she spun about.

A childish giggle issued from among the highest branches of the tree; Sarah moved side to side, trying to see where. Taking a step or two further from the trunk, she almost collided with a perambulator. Deep within the shifting leaf-shadows, and sufficiently high up, she could not make out the face, not even to determine the colour of his skin – but it appeared to be a boy of about eight years old. He could have been black but was more likely white, and filthy – a sweep's boy, a small white child, sitting tall in a tree and laughing at her.

Much later, Sarah again occupied the front parlour, her chair pulled up close to the windows; no longer staring down into the street; content merely to look out occasionally, at the night skies.

She wondered if she could have helped Brippoki any better, now that he lay beyond all help – but if so, how? Lambert had always led her to despise the phrase 'if only': in a universe directed by God's purposes, regrets were immoral.

Bitterness was futile, and twisted a life. Sarah thought, if anything, she should be grateful to Druce, and, yes, to Lambert, for the example they had set. Only in taking back the responsibility for her own life could she look down into the grave without bitterness.

Sarah's fingers worked, turning over and over the small object in her hand.

Things her elders would call – had called – supernatural, primitive tribal societies accepted as part of the natural order, the intangible accredited with power to affect the tangible, and indelibly so. Ghosts, Holy or otherwise, achieved dynamism through the strength of their belief – beliefs making for reality.

Some sort of connection existed between Brippoki on the one hand and Druce on the other; she was not meant to know what it was, only to bear witness to the blood sacrifice, part of a ritual; living proof. Brippoki, gentle soul, had believed a vengeful spirit unleashed. His sensitivities had caused him no little distress and a very great fear: fear of a figment something like his personal Nemesis.

According to what she had learned of his complex mythology, that vengeful spirit would often employ another agent to do its dirty work. Druce himself was dust, a ghost; less substantial than Wall, more a Moonshine sort of man, made up of lantern, dog, and thorn-bush. If he were the killer then she was his mouthpiece, the one to deliver his curse.

Had she herself embodied the '*In-gna*'?

And last of all he was seen of me also, as of one born out of due time. Therefore whether it were I or they, so we preach, and so ye believed.

Harbinger of doom, or doom herself; for all she knew the tail of a fiend lurked concealed beneath her skirts. It could not have been any worse if she had killed him herself, and either buried or burned all evidence.

Sarah clutched her free hand, which had been resting on Druce's manuscript, to her racing heart. She knew something, a little, of Aborigine custom. Should she disclose to anyone her suspicion of his death by haunting, Brippoki's erstwhile fellows might feel it their obligation to seek out the killer – be he or she alive or dead. And if the guilty party could not be discovered, then another of his people would do as well: as and when the opportunity presented itself, sooner or later they would enact their dreadful revenge.

When it came to knowledge of secrets, she began to understand the responsibilities of holding one's tongue.

The murder unsolved, late revelation of Brippoki's heritage, his white blood, drove Sarah once more to consider that long list of names, names of those who had wronged Druce during his lifetime, trawling for possible suspects. Captain Lawrence had intimated rumours of a figure in authority, a governor perhaps, or ship's captain at least. Grose, King, Bligh, Macquarie…for whatever reasons, there had been a quick turnover among the governors of that colony. Each of them had some recorded association with Joseph Druce; and they were also, presumably, in daily contact with the native population, if only as their servant underclass. Dalrymple, Simeon Lord – who knew? It could be one of any number of early traders, chancers and swindlers who had chanced to cross paths and swords with the unfortunate man. Seventy-six years had elapsed since the date of Druce's transportation in 1792 and the present moment – the span of up to at least four possible generations, maybe more.

Hic Occultus Occulto Occisus Est: thus read the epitaph of Kaspar Hauser. 'Here an unknown was killed by an unknown.'

Really, there was no way for her to know. Here she was, still trying to make sense of the evidence when more often than not there was none, or else none that could be qualified, the larger part of the story already over, long before she was even born.

Pale face reflected in the window glass, Sarah looked to herself, not recognising that creature staring back, strange and new. She surprised herself at the immediacy with which was willing even to think along these lines, able by now to enter into the mindset of men as different as either Brippoki or Druce.

'In consideration of a certain reward…'

Sarah opened up her closed palm. In it lay the whittled carving of a small boat. She had found it on the windowsill about an hour earlier. A crimson impression creased her palm from where she had clutched on to it so tightly, for so long; gladly she endured the vague ache of her tendons.

Brippoki had perhaps intended to represent the *Rangatira*.

His superstitious belief proved inspirational in another way. Any ghost story necessarily entailed belief in a return from the dead: if not the resurrection exactly, then at least notions of an afterlife. By the same token, his ultimate conviction in what threatened and probably killed him revealed – to her mind at least – an aspect of hope. Both Lubbock and Lawrence had intimated Aboriginal concepts of an afterlife, one entailing a return across the oceans, supposedly home; even so far as wearing the skin of a different colour. They entertained ideas concerning the persistence of the soul...its migration, after death, into the living body of another, be it animal, vegetable, or white man; and, perhaps, of a better world.

Mutability of matter, immutability of soul – the flower may bloom and die; buried, the bulb lives on. Lambert would have liked that.

Christ preached that he rose from the dead, and yet some still argued against the feasibility of resurrections, the Feast of Trumpets, the Feast of Tabernacles. If there was no resurrection, then Christ had not risen: preaching was in vain, and her faith also. Her faith, which was above all a quest for truth – even if it might never be grasped. What was real, except for what the mind told you?

Man feared death in uncertainty of his status in the afterlife. Neither Lambert nor Druce had departed in peace, whereas Brippoki...his eyes had smiled, finally, in recognition – as if to say 'you've been a good friend to me'. He himself absolved her.

She alone might unite Druce with Brippoki in her thoughts, so that they were reconciled, although dying at the opposite ends of the earth from where they most wanted to be. Gladly, or so it seemed, Brippoki returned to that place he came from, wherever it might be – the same timeless realm perhaps where Joseph Druce took stock. They walked in conversation along the shores of Eternity; awaiting, as one, the messenger to bid them embark.

The grandfather clock began to strike the late hour, soon joined by the sound of church bells. Standing at the opened window, Sarah heard none of it – her mind half the world and months on the ocean distant.

More than one path existed to glory and to God; a longer path, and more treacherous, than any she could have imagined...

There was more than one truth.

No one should judge another for the meat they chose to eat, for the drink they chose to drink, in respect of their high and holy days, of new moon or their Sabbath days.

For we wrestle not against flesh and blood, but against principalities, against powers, against the rulers of the darkness of the world, against spiritual wickedness in high places.

DEATH OF KING COLE, THE ABORIGINAL CRICKETER

Cricketers will regret to hear that King Cole, one of the celebrated Black Eleven now on a professional visit to this country, died last Wednesday eve in Guy's Hospital. His death was caused by inflammation of the lungs, and his loss is severely mourned by his mates and all who knew him.

Daily Telegraph
27 June, 1868

THE ILLUSTRATED LONDON NEWS

REGISTERED AT THE GENERAL POST-OFFICE FOR TRANSMISSION ABROAD.

No. 1490. - VOL. LIII.   SATURDAY, JULY 4, 1868.   WITH A SUPPLEMENT,
FIVEPENCE.

BIRTHS AND DEATHS.

The following is the return by the Registrar-General of births and deaths in London, during the week ending Saturday, June 27: –

The deaths registered in London during the week were 1454. It was the twenty-sixth week of the year; and the average number of deaths for that week is, with a correction for the increase of population, 1304. The deaths in the present return exceed by 150 the estimated amount, and exceed by 226 the number recorded in the preceding week.

METROPOLITAN NEWS.

A complimentary dinner was given last Saturday to Sir John Young, who has been succeeded in the governorship of New South Wales by the Earl of Belmore. The colonial department was represented by the Duke of Buckingham and Mr Adderley, and of the guests a large number were connected to the Australian colonies. In response to the toast of his health, Sir John Young sketched out a great future for Australia; for although fortunes might not be made as rapidly as they once were, the general progress of the people was satisfactory, and wealth was increasing. He attributed the prosperity of the colonies to the marked absence of intemperance, and to the indomitable energy of the people.

THE AUSTRALASIAN COLONIES.

The arrival at Portsmouth of his Royal Highness the Duke of Edinburgh on Friday se'nnight, and the complimentary dinner given to Sir John Young on the following Saturday – very apposite incidents – naturally bring the Australasian colonies under the public notice at home. The Prince, we rejoice to know, has completely recovered from the dangerous wound inflicted on him in New South Wales by the pistol-ball of an assassin.

We hardly dare contemplate what might have been the state of feeling, from the palace to the rudest hovel, had the dastardly attempt upon the Duke's life proved effectual. Happily, there is no need that we should do so. The empire has been mercifully spared a great calamity.

It chances that the colony in which the murderous attempt was made had been presided over during the preceeding six years by Sir John Young, whom, on Saturday last, within a few hours of the arrival of the Duke of Edinburgh, several colonists of New South Wales, Victoria, Queensland, and Tasmania, just now residing in London, entertained at dinner. The presence of the Duke of Buckingham and Chandos, the Secretary of State for the Colonies, and of Mr. Adderley, M.P., the Under Secretary, on the occasion, will be regarded by the public on both sides of the world as a sufficient assurance that the crime which had nearly cost us one of our Royal Princes has in no way been taken to cast a shade upon the loyalty of the colonists amongst whom it was perpetrated.

The two incidents thus brought into juxtaposition may serve to fix our thoughts for a moment or two upon our antipodean colonies. We know not that they can be justly said to be looked upon by Englishmen in general with frigid indifference. There are but few families in this country some member of which has not cast in his lot with the people of one or other of Her Majesty's Australasian possessions, and whose feelings, consequently, are not interested in the well-being of those infant empires. If for the most part, as Sir John Young intimates, Abyssinia is better known to the British mind than Australia, if no great excitement can be got up here over the political crises that happen there, it is yet a mistake to set down these phenomena to any lack of sympathy between the mother country and her daughter. Parents are not necessarily devoid of affection for their children because they do not estimate the joys and sorrows, the red-letter days, and the "black Fridays" of all their juvenile tribe at the same importance as the young ones themselves. We know that nations, like individuals, must bear the yoke in their youth – we hope, not without reason, that early discipline will develop manly qualities – and if we do not make so much fuss over colonial trials as the colonists themselves regard as indispensable to any proof of strong attachment, it is far more owing to pre-occupation by matters to which we are bound to attend than to any conscious neglect of interests which we might and ought but do not attend.

No statement made by the late Governor of New South Wales will be received with more general satisfaction than that in which he concisely submitted to his audience several indications of the substantial prosperity of this group of British colonies. That they should be more distinguished for energy in business than for political propriety and statesmanlike wisdom is one of the inevitable results of their position. Individual affairs

necessarily take precedence of the affairs of the community in new and thinly-peopled territories. There the first law of life is to subdue and replenish the earth, and man's business is not so much with his fellows as with Nature. But whilst the Australians are making rapid advances in material comfort and even affluence, and by their people's industry are causing the wilderness to smile, we are not to imagine that they are indifferent to the demands of on the one hand, or the benefits on the other, of well-planned social organisations. At great expense, with unfaltering determination, and not without many personal risks and some loss of life, they have put down that form of brigandage which took the name of bushranging, and have thereby achieved the most indispensible condition of civilisation – the security of life and property. Sir John Young testifies of the colonists that they are a most orderly and law-abiding race. In some respects, indeed, they have the advantage of the mother country. Unrestrained by many of the antique conventionalisms which impede our progress, they have happily solved some problems which continue to puzzle us at home. They have not now to fight the battle of religious equality; they have settled on a broad and permanent basis the question of the education of the people; they have made some considerable advances in regard to the means of a higher intellectual culture; and they are encouraging, and to a gratifying extent have succeeded in establishing, habits of sobriety.

Where solid advantages like these are possessed by young nations, political struggles, even when intense, can involve no very serious issues; and great latitude may, with comparative harmlessness, be given to party spirit. We who remain at home may catch the echoes of these colonial strifes without any serious alarm as to which way they may chance to be decided. They do not touch the bases of colonial prosperity. A quick succession of Ministerial crises and frequent general elections, which, after all, do not remove existing dead-locks, might be perilous here; but there they do not reach down to the depths of the social system. No doubt, they have their passing inconveniences; but their tendency, in the long run, is to give breadth and power to political experience. And this is precisely the qualification which new self-governing communities stand most in need of.

Even in regard to political economy, in which our colonists are under the greatest temptation to get astray, we entertain no feeling of concern as to the future. The laws which determine the wealth of nations are sure to vindicate themselves, sooner or later, in countries where thought and speech and action are free; and those laws are better learned by practice than by theory. Of course, there will always be, in Australia as elsewhere, a balance of good and evil. Utopias exist only in the imagination, and will not bear the touch of facts. But, at least, our kinsfolk on the opposite side of the world are to be congratulated, if not envied, as regards their position. The countries of their adoption are in the freshness of manhood. They will bequeath to prosperity a rich inheritance.

They add strength and grandeur to the empire to which they cling with so enduring an affection. They are spelling out lessons which may be of unanticipated service even to the whole world. *The return of the Duke of Edinburgh furnishes us with a fitting opportunity for recognising them as members of the British family. We greet them heartily, and bid them "God speed!"*

EPILOGUE

THE LAST OF ENGLAND

'The World was all before them, where to choose
Their place of rest, and Providence their guide.'

~ John Milton, *Paradise Lost*

The dove had disappeared, not to return again.

On the 27th of June England declared fresh war with the New Zealand islands.

Barely two months later and Sarah Larkin set her eyes to the horizon: bright and sunny skies to the east held the promise of a Greater Britain.

Their tiny craft leapt the waves; they slapped at the underside, increasing large. The nervous passengers sat well in order. Everyone returned their looks to the shores they left behind; all except for the crew – and Sarah.

There would be no more death – neither sorrow, nor crying – no more pain: the former things had passed away. She looked forward to new heavens and a new earth.

DeVitt and Moore's Australian Line of Packet-ship the *Parramatta* was due to sail from the outflow of the Thames, calling first at Plymouth, and then direct for Sydney. The emigrants had gathered at Blackwall Pier, the masts of sailing vessels loading in the East India Docks towering high above their heads; they awaited there the departure of their ferry for boarding; the main ship, out in the Channel, made ready to receive them.

Sarah discreetly cast her eye over the huddled bodies, now that all were gathered close in the boat. Aside from a gentleman in incongruous carpet slippers, everybody wore their Sunday best: men in earthen suits of fustian or corduroy, the women pretty in their bright dresses. Even Sarah wore the finest of her mother's outdoor garments, the cut adjusted to suit – neither thing dared while Lambert remained alive. Her outfit had been only slightly dirtied by a trip on the railway.

None of them was rich; anybody wealthy would presumably be joining them on board by other means. Principally intended for the families of stricken shipbuilders and ironworkers, the East-End Emigration and Relief Fund in most instances provided. The colonies of Victoria, New South Wales and South Australia likewise assisted, to promote immigration. Sarah did not consider herself above charity, so long as it had no direct connection to the Church. According to Aboriginal notions of a Supreme Being, man and God lived independently of each other; and it seemed a fine arrangement.

Her roving eye fell on the bo'sun, a strapping figure with a ruddy, tanned face. Turned a certain way, and beheld in a certain light, he could be mistaken for Sergeant Padraig Tubridy out of Leman-street Police Station; the fellow compared favourably with that kind-hearted rogue, as few men could. She had never enquired, on that June afternoon, as to whether or not the sergeant was married – a question flitting across her mind on many an occasion since. He was, no doubt, and had a dozen children at least to show for it: he had looked the sort. Many an Irishman made this same trip that she now undertook. Maybe somewhere on that wide continent such a one, a real man, as good, waited for her.

The bo'sun caught her looking and tipped a wink.

The steward, taking register, called out to the pale creature seated close to the prow, staring fixedly out to sea. 'And you, ma'am,' he shouted above the sounding furrows, 'what is your name?'

Realising that she was addressed, the young woman pinked and turned. 'My name...?' Buffeted by the stiff sea-breezes, her hand reached up to clear her face of loose threads of hair. 'Larkin,' she said, 'Miss Sarah Larkin.'

Sarah looked beyond the steward at the cliffs of her homeland fading from view. The hot sun created a heat haze, but also lit the long coastline as a streak of silver, cut through it like a slash. Above soared the sky, a coalescent dome of deep blue, colour never so pure when seen from inland.

Nineveh was laid waste, and none bemoaned her. The dark history Sarah had dealt with went beyond black. She had seen men that were as phantoms, and phantoms that were as men: it was a waking dream, a living nightmare written in dust, dissolving now.

Emancipist and free object, her purpose held:

'To sail beyond the sunset, and the baths
Of all the western stars, until I die.'

Sarah dearly wished to witness the happy Aboriginal freedom she had read about, that tonic simplicity, even as it disappeared from view.

Governor Eyre's recommendation of sympathy and benevolence, to 'succour, teach and improve', felt worthy of the attempt. Not a mission, as such – she knew better than that now, thanks to Brippoki. Rather, on behalf of people so little known and very greatly misunderstood, she would convey their message to the colonists, so that the lives of the forgotten might not be so easily forgot. In some regard she might help mitigate those evils which the occupation and possession of their country so unnecessarily inflicted. She would devote herself to redress of those compound wrongs, even if it took her lifetime.

She prayed to blue heaven, so spacious: 'Keep ye judgement, and do justice.'

Coming to, their craft had more than passed the halfway point; the other passengers now sat facing in her direction. Most looked more than a little daunted, others confident. The older ones just looked sad. Sarah also turned. The ocean crossing could not frighten her with its dangers. She had prospects.

The bo'sun, shouting, pointed out their ship now in sight, a white sail fixed among the scattering seagulls. He swivelled his body around, to squint in raw appreciation of their passions, insolently favouring those females among the party he figured unmarried, and calling them every one his 'pretty butterflies'.

Blithe to their heaving progress, Sarah laid a palm to the cool brass of her mother's formidable sea-chest. She only took what could fit within it, and no more. Her former life, disassembled, could never again recover its shape, and deliberately so.

She brought with her Druce's manuscript. Even after everything he had gone through, Druce still clung to hope, to his faith: by hook and by crook she would see him get his wish, and be returned to New Zealand.

Deep in the pocket of her dress, she firmly grasped hold of the carving – like a charm – that Brippoki had gifted her in his final days. Everything ahead would look new and strange, but already her journey felt a homecoming.

'The *Parramatta*, ladies and gentlemen. A splendid new frigate-built ship, she is,' the steward advertised. 'A1 tip-top, only thirteen years old, John Williams her commander. This fine vessel has a full poop, unusually large cabins for first class accommodation, with desirable opportunities for a few second cabin passengers,' meaning themselves, 'and will carry on board an experienced surgeon.'

A few people gulped at that.

'Once on board,' the steward advised, 'I will be coming around to collect the bedding-money. Please have ready your fees of one pound, or ten shillings for each child…' he smiled '…further to the terms of your freight or passage.'

Coming close, they could now quite clearly see the white letters painted across the stern of the much larger vessel.

A large woman at the back raised her voice high above the roar of the billows. '*Parramatta*,' she asked, 'is that a word?'

'Yes,' shouted back the steward, 'the name is taken from the earliest pioneer settlement, in the days of the First Fleet…now the second town in that colony, about fourteen miles distant from Sydney. Other towns include Windsor, Liverpool, Campbell Town, and Newcastle.' He found that listing familiar sounds lent his passengers comfort.

''Afore that,' rumbled the bo'sun; slyly, and speaking less formally, 'it were a local Aboriginal word.'

'Does it have any meaning?' someone close to him asked.

'Yes, it do,' he affirmed. 'It means "head of the water".'

The steward carried on in singing Australia's praises, but Sarah paid him no heed. Their small boat was turning, and in another few minutes would be coming up alongside.

'Don't look so gloomy, my lovely!' the bo'sun said. He spoke to her directly. 'We s'll be there before you know it.'

That word, gloom…

Sarah turned her face aside, looking further out to sea. She followed in the footsteps of a traveller from a timeless land. *He lives there, still.*

Turning back, she returned the bo'sun's gaze; smiling, quite openly.

Later, if he was fortunate, he might even hear her laugh.

'Like the Egyptians and Ancient Hebrews
We were oppressed under Logan's yoke
Till a native black lying there in ambush
Did give our tyrant his mortal stroke.
My fellow prisoners be exhilarated
That all such monsters such a death may find
And when from bondage we are liberated
Our former sufferings shall fade from mind'

~ 'Moreton Bay', traditional

Nyuntu Anangu Tjukurpa Wiltja Nga Palya Nga.
'Your Aboriginal dreamtime home. Wish you peace.'

Acknowledgements

In no particular order (you're all first): David Kendall, Corinne Pearlman, Andreja Brulc, James Hollands, Simon and Susan D'Souza, Kim Neville-Harman, Ravi Mirchandani, Frank Wynne, Woodrow Phoenix, Jason Pratt, Lilian Hillyer, Eddie and Annie and, bah, even Hayley Campbell, Sean Morris, Cathal Coughlan, Faithless, Shriekback, Robin June, Aaron Cometbus, Peter Ackroyd, Ed Wood and Simon Campbell of Waterstone's Quarterly and all at Pleasant Studio, Margaret Curd, the Hawthornden International Retreat for Writers, Hawthornden posse (Kate Rhodes, Leslie Brody, Carolin Window, Shelley Leedahl, Janne Moller), Arvon folk (Jan Woolf, Kay Stopforth, Jo Hurst, Xanthe Wells, Gill Farrer-Halls, Stephanie Hunter, John Thynne, Hardish Virk, Ioana Sandi, Lindsay Clarke, Adam Thorpe), Ivor Watkins and John Rennie at *East End Life*, Peter O'Shaughnessy, Graeme Inson and Russel Ward for *The Restless Years*, Peter Sculthorpe, John Greenway, John Nicholson (London Revisited Walks and Talks), Tim Mars ('Approaches to Doom'), Donald Payne (*aka* James Vance Marshall), Professor Stephen Hopper (Kew), Joanna Latham (*KANYINI*), Ray Newton (Wapping Trust), Madge Darby, Brian Nicholson, Thames Lighterman Eric Small, David Kemp and Molly Potts (Malling Society), Mr Madgerly (West Kent Hunt), Margaret Friday (Dreadnought Librarian, site tour of former Infirmary of the Royal Naval Hospital), Lorraine Finch (very helpful guide within the Chapel and Painted Hall at the Royal Naval Hospital, Greenwich), National Maritime Museum Curator of Paintings Roger Quarm, Neil Rhind MBE ('Thomas Noble's Blackheath'), Clare Nelson, head of Research and Development at Trinity College of Music ('The Greenwich Pensioner' by Dibdin), the British Library, the Newspaper Library, Colindale, Tower Hamlets Local History Library (Christopher Lloyd and Malcolm Barr-Hamilton), Public Record Office, National Maritime Museum Library, Wellcome Institute, Docklands Museum, Greenwich Local History Library, National Library of New South Wales (Martin Beckett, Microfilms Librarian, Original Materials Branch; Jennifer Broomhead, Intellectual Property and Copyright Librarian; and latterly, Julie Wood and Kevin Leamon), all residents at No.89 Great Russell Street; and, last but certainly not least, all at Myriad – Candida Lacey, for keeping faith; Vicky Blunden, for endurance and pollarding; Linda McQueen, for her interest, insight, and scary mind. My sincere apologies to anyone that I might have forgotten.

No thanks at all to: wood pigeons, Clancy focken Docwra, and house flies.

Sources

The use of an apposite or commentary quotation at the start of a chapter is a recognised form common in nineteenth-century literature (see, for instance, *Tom Brown's Schooldays*). These are called epigraphs. Some are taken from newspaper articles; others, snatches of traditional song; there's Biblical verse included; but mostly, they are taken from works of literature, including poetry. All sources are deliberately contemporary or else works in print prior to 1868.

I have limited the attribution of quotes *in situ* to author and title, so as not to distract. For those who wish to know more, here they are again (where incomplete) in more detail:

LITERATURE

Opening Quote: Thomas Carlyle, *Works*, 'On Cholera'

I *Rubáiyát of Omar Khayyám*, 2nd edition (1868), trans. Edward FitzGerald, verse 79. See also: X (verses 89, 90), XXIX (46), XXXV (32), LV (52), LVII (88), XXXII (100)

XI Ralph Waldo Emerson, *Essays*, Essay III (1844), 'Character' (also XVII, XXIII, XXV)

XIV Ralph Waldo Emerson, *Essays*, Essay VI (1844), 'Nature'

XXIV Wordsworth, Ode: Intimations of Immortality from Recollections of Early Childhood, V (ditto XXVII, LXII)

XXVI Alfred Lord Tennyson, In Memoriam CXXIX (ditto LX)

XXX Ralph Waldo Emerson, *Essays*, Essay VI (1841), 'Friendship'

XLI Ralph Waldo Emerson, *Nature; Addresses and Lectures* (1849)

XLIV John Milton, *Paradise Lost*, Book XII

XLIX Virgil's *Aeneid*, trans. John Dryden (1697)

LIII John Milton, *Paradise Lost*, Book X

LVI Emerson, *Essays*, Essay VII (1844), 'Politics'

JOURNALISM

II *Rugby Magazine* (preface, *Tom Brown's Schooldays* by Thomas Hughes)

III *Bell's Life* in London, 23 May 1868

V *Bathurst Times*, 1867 ('THE ABORIGINALS AT BATHURST', reprinted in *The Australasian*, 11 Jan 1868)

VII 'The Aboriginal Eleven v. the M.C.C. (Melbourne Cricket Club)', *The Australasian*, 29 December 1866 (also VIII (i))

VIII (ii) *The Illustrated London News*, 9 May 1868

IX *Ballarat Star*, editorial, 4 Feb 1867

XXXIII George Godwin, *London Shadows* (in *Building* magazine)
XXXVIII *Bell's Life* in London, 23 May 1868
XXXIX W. B. Tegetmeier, *The Field*, 23 May 1868
XLVII *Calcutta Gazette*, 30 March 1809
LXIII 'LAND FOR ABORIGINIES', *The Age*, 28 Oct 1858

TRADITIONAL SONG

IV, XVIII, XXVIII, XXXIV, XLIII, L, and the first closing quote.

BIBLE

Attributed in situ – *all according to the King James version of the Holy Bible*
VI, XVI, XL, XLII

OTHER

XV Dr John Dee, *General and Rare Memorials pertayning to the Perfect Arte of Navigation* (1577)
XXI Dr John Dee, 'This Petty Navy Royal, The marveilous Priviledge of the Brytifh Impire', in *General and Rare Memorials pertayning to the Perfect Arte of Navigation* (1577)
XXXVII *The Christian Topography of Cosmas, an Egyptian Monk*, *circa* 547 AD

Picture Credits

PART I

'The Aboriginal cricket match on the M.C.C. ground (Melbourne, 1867)'
Engraving by Samuel Calvert, appearing within the *Illustrated Melbourne Post*, 24 January 1867/printed and published by Ebenezer and David Syme, proprietors of *The Age* newspaper, Elizabeth-street, Melbourne, Victoria. The original copy is owned by the National Library of Australia, Identifier: nla.pic-an23148191.

PART II

'Ludgate Hill – A Block in the Street'
Etching by Gustave Doré, from *London: A Pilgrimage* by Gustave Doré and Blanchard Jerrold, first published by Grant & Co. of London in 1872.

PART III

'The New Zealander'
Etching by Gustave Doré, from *London: A Pilgrimage* by Gustave Doré and Blanchard Jerrold, first published by Grant & Co. of London in 1872.

A F T E R W O R D :

About *The Clay Dreaming*   534

About Ed Hillyer   542

ABOUT THE CLAY DREAMING :

'The life of an individual is a miniature of the life of a nation.'

~ J. W. Draper

The spark of inspiration for *The Clay Dreaming* came from an article in my local paper: 'Not over for Cole', by Ivor Watkins (*East End Life*, 7–13 October 1996). That spark was then fanned into flame by a second article in the same 'Eastend History' series, appearing almost a year to the day later, called 'From Limehouse Lad to Maori chief', by John Rennie (*East End Life*, 6–12 October 1997). The first article concerned the Aboriginal cricketer King Cole; the second was about a Greenwich Pensioner – the Royal Naval equivalent to a Chelsea Pensioner – named Joseph Druce, a man who had led a most extraordinary life and lived just long enough to tell the tale.

Here on the one hand was a native of Australia, remembered only for playing the very English sport of cricket, and on the other, an English boy deported for his crimes to the crown colony of Australia: a rogue adventurer who subsequently came to live among the Maori of New Zealand, as one of them, the rank of Chief conferred on him in 1806 – the very first of the *Pakeha Maori*, literally 'European Maoris'. It seemed to me as if their lives and lifestyles had – in the most simplistic of senses – somehow crossed over, or been exchanged: black for white; between northern and southern hemispheres; Old World for New. My imagination went into overdrive, wondering how there might be a connection or connections made between the two of them.

What brought the disparate and obscure life stories of these two men home for me, as a housing co-op tenant living in Mile End, in London's East End, was the discovery that King Cole (aka Brippoki, aka *Bripumyarrimin*), an Australian Aborigine, was buried only a short distance away from my house. Joseph Druce, buried just across the river Thames in Greenwich, had been born a roughly equal distance away from where I lived, in fact just to the south of me in the neighbouring Tower Hamlet of Stepney.

It took the every-now-and-then labour of some years for me to locate the grave of King Cole. I searched for it around the wide green spaces and most obscure corners of vast and leafy Victoria Park, having read that he had been interred within the grounds there. All the while the truth was hidden in plain sight. He was buried in nearby Meath Gardens, Bethnal Green – once a portion of that same great park, but separated since by a few major roads. There's no telling the exact spot; the graveyard itself disappeared long ago. The small park is now open space. In commemoration of him a single, simple stone block rests in the ground, arbitrarily placed beside a pathway and beneath a twisting Eucalypt. The burial plaque reads:

In memory of
King Cole, Aboriginal cricketer,
who died on the 24th June 1868

Your Aboriginal dreamtime home. Wish you peace.
Nyuntu Anangu Tjukapa Wiltja Nga Palya Nga

Eucalyptus pauciflora donated to the Aboriginal Cricket Association
by Hillier Nurseries Ltd.
Planted on Sunday 26th June 1988

Of only 46 words comprising this brief dedication, my own family name is among them. I cannot overstate the shock of this discovery. That sealed it. I just had to write this novel. Thereafter, Brippoki's grave marker (I prefer to think of him by that name, even though, and ironically, it is as much of a given name as 'King Cole' ever was) became something of a literal touchstone for me in the creation of this book. I felt (and feel) a certain responsibility to tell his untold story – to flesh out the bare (and now misplaced) bones of the man who travelled such a long way only to die here. I like to pay him a visit every now and again, pull up the *boree* log, sit down, and have a chat. I feel that he has on many occasions encouraged me to persevere in the learning of my craft and, ultimately, to see the writing of this book safely through to its completion. That, and to dare envision an Aboriginal experience of Victorian London, something which I felt couldn't help but be compelling…

Winkling out record of Joseph Druce, his lifetime and achievements, proved no less protracted and troublesome. Although the original 1997 newspaper article had tipped me off to the existence of his *Life of a Greenwich Pensioner*, I couldn't find trace of it anywhere. Once again, the solution to the riddle was right under my nose. The very excellent Local History Library in Bancroft Road, Mile End, furnished me with photocopies of a piece from the East London Record No.4 (1981). The excerpted article – by a Mr Ralph Bodle, from Kaukapakapa, New Zealand – was entitled 'The Road to Transportation'. He had been engaged in researching Madame Isabelle de Montolieu, author of a French translation of *The Swiss Family Robinson*; a lady who had also, by curious happenstance, written a play, which she added to the second edition, published in 1816, wherein 'she created a character based on a newspaper report she had read about George Bruce, whose real name was Joseph Druce'. I read (and for some time thereafter still somehow managed to overlook) this vital clue: he'd changed his name!

For Ralph Bodle, the discovery of Druce's *Life* had been a happy by-product of his own researches. As revealed in a footnote to his brief article, the Mitchell Library, State Library of New South Wales, had acquired the original manuscript, and there it nowadays resides. The Greenwich Pensioner had eventually found his way back to Australia!

'Soon after being admitted to Greenwich Hospital in 1817,' the article said, 'he produced a 19,000 word manuscript known as *The Life of a Greenwich Pensioner* […] presented to John Dyer, secretary of the Hospital, possibly before Druce's death in February 1819.' And so, in 2002, with the help of my old mucker Mr Eddie Campbell (formerly of Glasgow, Scotland; currently of

Brisbane, Australia), I was able to establish contact with the trustees of the Mitchell Library, and arranged to be sent a photocopy, taken from a microfiche recording of the object itself.

That was a Holy Grail moment. Finally, I held a facsimile of Druce's manuscript in my hands – accurately reproduced down to the marbled cover, and with every scratch and slip of the pen. Entirely handwritten, the work appeared to be the work of diverse hands, and was therefore most likely dictated by an illiterate Druce to various of his fellow inmates, most of them barely any more literate than he. While painstakingly decoding passages of intense detail concerning the man's earliest experiences and humble origins, early thrills soon gave way to doubt and dismay, as the storyline gradually dissolved into fitful raving and endless imprecations to God, 'the Almighty Disposer of Events'. Diamonds, certainly, glittered in the rough, but you could hear the man dying, there on the page, via his feverish ramblings.

Once I realised the full significance of Druce's change of name, of course, it proved the key to unlocking an entire cabinet of curiosities. As soon as I started looking instead for 'George Bruce', the evidence piled up. The British Library furnished me with the 1810 *Memoirs* (of Mr George Bruce). He was mentioned by that name in the Australian Dictionary of Biography; J. A. Turnbull's *A Voyage Round the World*; Barrington's *History of New South Wales*; MacNab's *From Tasman to Marsden*. The Historical Records of Australia included some of his Memorial correspondence. Each entry threw up more pieces for the puzzle, and led on to further discoveries.

Moving on into the twentieth century, *The HOME*, a swish periodical somewhat resembling *Vogue*, included Bruce among its article series of *Picturesque Rascals* by C. H. Bertie (issue for 1 March 1935). Trips to the Public Record Office in Richmond produced ships' logs and musters, Pensioners' admission papers, Burial Registers, and more…

Perhaps none of this revelation would ever have been possible without reference to that 1981 article by Mr Bodle. I have not been able to trace his present whereabouts; but wherever you are, sir, I salute you – '*sucali*'.

Finally able to locate and read the Druce manuscript for myself, I subsequently gained permission for its co-option and usage within my own storyline, very kindly granted by its current owners, the Mitchell Library. It appears to have come into their possession via the good graces of Thomas Whitley of Blackheath (South Australia, not South London), in November 1898. How it might have made its way there from Greenwich, well…I provide one possibility. I have sprinkled the actual text of Druce's *Life* liberally throughout my own storyline, intervening at some length in order to edit down some of its excesses of religiosity, and where necessary improve slightly the narrative sense of it. Still, it is Druce's life experience expressed in the man's own words – and what, after all, could be better?

FACTS INTO FICTION...

'...no man can write anything who does not think that what he writes is for the time the history of the world; or do anything well who does not esteem his work to be of importance. My work may be of none, but I must not think it of none, or I shall not do it with impunity.'

~ Emerson, Chapter I from 'Nature', part of *Nature; Addresses and Lectures* (1849)

Without either Brippoki or Druce, there could be no story. This book then, most of all, is for them, and to both gentlemen, my sincere and eternal gratitude; I hope to have done you some little justice in our sharing of stories, conveying an idea of your struggles and at least a little of your pain.

As far as possible, the roles assigned to each of them in this otherwise fictional story accord with what few facts are known about their actual lives and essential character, although very little exists in the case of King Cole – not much more than the dates of his death and burial. However, identity and motives have been embroidered or invented for the purposes of turning their lives into a work of historical fiction (the weighty tome you are at this minute most likely struggling to hold within your hands). With regard to Joseph Druce, the novel, as I say, incorporates portions of the unpublished manuscript that he dictated during the last years of his life, and which is, wherever possible – within bounds of relevance and comprehension – quoted verbatim. Druce is also, however, reinvented here (a miracle he himself performed more than once within his lifetime...). As some readers may have gathered, there is more going on here between the lines, and in the blurring of fact and fiction; but that is perhaps for another book, and for another time.

Thus, this historical fiction is based on real lives. Evidence of those lives persists all around. If you'd like to read details of the boy Druce's actual criminal trial, the Proceedings of the Old Bailey for 1674–1834 can be found at www.oldbaileyonline.org. Not for the last time the crafty weasel lied about his name, so you'll be wanting William Druce, theft: burglary, 13 Apr 1791 (ref: t17910413-7). And to see the record of Druce's sentence of death commuted to transportation for life – lest we forget, for the theft of two (actually nine) silk handkerchiefs – see 14 Sept 1791, ref: o17910914-1, under the name now of Joseph Druce. Fascinating stuff. (One Saturday in March 2004, I was in the Tower Hamlets Local History Library on Bancroft Road, busy with my researches, when a juvenile gang was spotted stripping down my pedal bike, outside. Trailing them unnoticed, I managed to trap them inside their own garage. When the police eventually turned up, the door was opened for them to be arrested and cautioned. I got my wheel back. Nor did the irony escape me – time changes little. But they should consider themselves lucky to have got off so lightly.)

Druce's many letters to the press, and articles written about him, can be found in the newspapers of the time. His own 1810 *Memoirs*, 1813 Memorial and other documents are often unofficial compilations of material that first appeared in the Calcutta journals and Sydney press. I've discovered more of his correspondence since finishing the novel, and I'm sure there's more out there yet to be unearthed. His associations with prominent early colonial figures such as Matthew Flinders, Captain Bligh and Dr Caley are likely to throw up further documentary evidence of his activities – although under what name is anyone's guess.

Certain other related objects might also still survive somewhere, their significance long since forgotten. In Rotherham, in August 1868, the remainder of the Aboriginal team signed a cricket ball – a prize lurking in someone's loft perhaps, the names scrawled upon it a mystery to the current owner, awaiting rediscovery. If you live up that way, please do have a look, eh? The portrait of Druce's tattooed face by the 'King's miniaturist' may also be out there. That the painter was John Downman is my own conceit, but I chose him not only to reinforce the Malling connection, but also because, given their relative and depleted circumstances at the time, it is entirely possible that it was indeed Downman that painted Druce's portrait. The painting was made, that much is certain, probably destined to become a curio in some drinking establishment. A *moko* tattoo on the face of a white man would make it hard to miss. I'm keeping a lookout.

'George Bruce' also left behind a living relation in his daughter with Aetockoe, a trail I intend to explore further. So far any attempt to trace living descendants has met with failure. Even so, I'm confident that they exist. If that's you, get in touch.

Another key resource in my research was *Cricket Walkabout*, by John Mulvaney and Rex Harcourt, an excellent handbook detailing the various Aboriginal Australian Eleven tours, culminating in their trip to England in 1868. My portrayal of Charles Lawrence and co. was largely based on the wealth of archive material referenced within this work, which often led me back to the original newspaper articles. In various ways many of my researches were also extrapolated from there. The plot of *The Clay Dreaming* itself works like a filter, through which I have sifted a wealth of found material, most of it contemporary and much of it out of copyright, wonder-stuff that might not otherwise be seen but which is the best expression of the times, then and now. Incorporated are articles of news, commentary, reportage and crucially, whenever possible, *vox populi* (eyewitness accounts): the sights and sounds of the living streets recorded word for word, for the accents, the vocabulary and the intonation.

Into the mix I have added considerable flights of fancy, the boomeranging arcs of the imagination. Sarah Larkin, for instance, is a wholly invented character. Much of the Town Malling connection in particular was arrived at via walking around the graveyard there, checking for suitable names and dates on the stones. Lambert Larkin is loosely based on the Reverend Lambert Blackwell Larking, Vicar of Ryarsh; and his wife Frances Twysden of Royden Hall (all but reinvented) also plays her part. In real life this couple produced no children. As regards relatively minor characters such as William South Norton,

Dilkes Loveless, the rest of the Aboriginal team and so on, they represent names co-opted from contemporary records, but their personalities herein are largely fabricated for story purposes. If anyone – cricketing pundits, but in particular living relatives – feels that I have been unfair to their memory in any event, *mea culpa*, but this is expressly literary fiction with a historical setting, and changing the names of those involved would have reduced the whole enterprise.

Other characters have perhaps unexpected connections in other forms of literature. To any fans of Sergeant Padraig Tubridy (as well as those seeking raucous tales of the Afghan frontier) I hereby refer your kind attention to issue 15 of *Frontline Combat*, and *Two Fisted Tales* numbers 16 and 21 (both titles EC Comics, in print since the 1950s). The handsome sort appearing there I believe to be a close relative of our Tubridy, if not the fella hisself. See also, from DC Comics in the 1970s, *Our Fighting Forces* 124, and *Star Spangled War Stories* 162 – never reprinted, so a bit harder to find. All stories are by John Severin and Jerry De Fuccio, two very excellent gentlemen resident in the former crown colonies of North America.

TALES OF THE CITY

Robert Vaughan (not the one from *The Man From Uncle*) wrote in 1843, 'Our age is pre-eminently the age of great cities.' This novel is very much a portrait of London as I know it, and its people as I know them, past, present and future. I readily confess it to be, much like Lambert Larkin's sermons, a Frankenstein's monster: numerous passages stitched together, impressions taken from hugely disparate sources, thanks largely to the splendid collections housed within the British Library (where I spent so much time they could demand rent), all engendered by the spark of truth, and my source of electrical current an original galvanic battery. (Even as Joseph Druce raged and died in a Greenwich hospital, so ran the vitalist debate of 1814–19 on the origins of life itself. This is in part what inspired Mary Wollstonecraft Shelley to create her own *Modern Prometheus*, an early classic of Gothic Romance literature.) Further jump-starts of voltage were supplied by the likes of Peter Ackroyd (in his superb *London: The Biography*) tipping me off to a deluge of quoted sources, from which I was then able to glean choice nuggets. My hat is tipped, too, for their resurrected art and language having brought extra life to my book, to the works of Louis Simond, Blanchard Jerrold, Gustave Doré, Johannes Vorsterman, Henry Mayhew, Henry James, Friedrich Engels, J. E. Ritchie and the Reverend Harry Jones, amongst far too many others to list here.

CURIOUS AND CURIOUSER

Funny things aplenty happened on the way to this forum. Here are just a few: my decision to make Dr Hunt of the Anthropological Society a stammerer, based on a whim, later turned out to be the truth. According to adverts in *The*

Illustrated London News he had written books on the subject. 'Plum-sucking baboons' attack Druce within his manuscript on the exact same calendar date that the meeting of the Anthropological Society (a real event) occurred some 51 years later – I couldn't have arranged it better myself. The name of Larkin that I had fictitiously adapted has, it transpires, a genuine connection with Druce – anyone who knows of the sordid local history establishing the mansions of Blackheath (South London, not South Australia) will perhaps know what I mean. A few days after I wrote an imagined version of the sights taken in on a London to Greenwich boat-trip in 1868 (detail, alas, cut from the final draft), I found them perfectly visualised in a Greenwich Local History Library wall display, 'PANORAMA (from memory), made by Ernest George Cattermole (15 years old), 1858' – he would apparently play it out in scroll form for family and friends. Go and see it if you can, it's lovely. Referring to the layout of Hardwick's Naval Hospital plan of 1843 (held at the Wellcome Institute, ref: V13339) I discovered the mid-east section of lawn designated 'Drying Ground for Lieutenant Loveless', the place where he exclusively was allowed to air his laundry. This turned out to be the exact same spot, down to the yard, in which I situated him on the occasion when we first meet him, enjoying his sandwich lunch – in a passage I had written only a day or two beforehand.

Perhaps it all seems like small-potatoes from a distance, but at the time it really felt as if I was on to something – and it just kept happening. On more than one occasion entirely relevant facts and names would leap out at me, even when whirring fast-forward or back through a blur of microfiche, far too fast for the eye to follow. It took some years for the various threads of my narrative to come together, and several more before the weave began to make some kind of sense. I strove the entire time to understand the compulsion felt to find or else forge connections between characters and events in order to tell these two stories in one. If ever in doubt – and there was plenty of that – I often took reassurance from the confluence of what had seemed at first disparate fact and figures. My efforts, my thoughts, my researches were at times very definitely being directed. Serendipity is one word for it. I followed in footsteps.

LAST WRITES

'Perhaps from the other side of life any death, no matter how seemingly pointless, may become the centre of a glittering web of meaning.'

~ Brian Boyd, *Vladimir Nabokov: The American Years*

No question about it, the days of Industrial Revolution were a 'bleak age' to pass through. Most of its workers subsisted in conditions of extreme poverty. 'Till the Bishop of London called the attention of the public to the state of Bethnal Green,' wrote the Reverend G Alston, 'I believe that about as little was known at the West-end of the town of this most destitute parish as the wilds of Australia or the islands of the South Seas.' This quote, from radical paper *The Weekly Dispatch*, was reprinted in the Chartist newspaper *The Northern Star* No.338, 4 May 1844.

By this time a half-century or so of European incursions had all but eradicated the Australian Aborigines in the very regions Alston evoked, where they had lived undisturbed for at least 50,000 years. The statistics, where they are recorded, are truly terrifying. Jardwa people (also 'No') formed the nucleus of the Aboriginal cricket team. They had suffered an 80 per cent reduction in population in less than ten years (between 1836 and 1843), effectively decimated year on year. The Australian Gold Rush, starting in 1851, only served to escalate matters – the processes of attrition having already been well established. By 1857, 139 Jardwa remained out of an estimated 3,000 at the time of first contact (all figures are taken from *Aboriginal Languages and Clans, 1800-1900*, Monash Publications in Geography). As the novel indicates, many players were already the last remaining members of their clan groupings (moieties, or 'mobs'). We are dealing, by the 1860s, with the remnants of a nomadic culture wherein entire language groups have already been extinguished. In the words of Alexis de Tocqueville (1805–1859): 'Here civilization works its miracles, and civilized man is turned back almost into a savage.'

Brippoki was Wudjubalug, or Wotjobaluk, of the Wergaia (when it comes to adapting phrases from a strictly oral culture into Roman alphabet, the results are at best gestural – something I have attempted to suggest by rendering the word differently each time it is mentioned in the text, according to the differing speakers; the Jardwa Dick-a-Dick, Captain Lawrence, and Brippoki himself). He is said to have come from lands around the Wimmera River, then a fertile region of Southeastern Australia, around Adelaide. I have endeavoured to suggest a regional dialect and manner of speaking analogue to surviving Wudjubalug phrasing, wherever I could find it, but I make no pretence towards accuracy. In all honesty, he exists – within the framework of this story – chiefly as a work of imagination. I heard another author say in interview, when challenged because she hadn't included the point of view of indigenous characters in her story, 'That's not my story to tell.' Brippoki's isn't my story to tell either – but I can't let that stop me from trying. He came to London and died here. He's lying there in the ground, somewhere beneath my feet. Since he's no longer around to tell his story, and was probably never given the opportunity, I've attempted to tell one for him. I very much hope that he likes it. *Budgere pella?*

To sum up, then: Andy Croft, radical poet and publisher, in *Now Or Never* 14, confidently declared: 'the most important theme for writing to explore is […] the possibilities – and the limits – of being human in your time and place'. He also expressed his theory of 'moral vocabulary – the need to bear witness, to testify on behalf of the speechless against the Pharisees; the powerful, the hypocrites and the liars'. I came to these words having already completed my book, but they neatly encapsulate for me the fuel that powered my narrative engine, and what it was that through it all drove me on to the finish line.

ABOUT ED HILLYER :

Where were you born and where did you grow up?
North London born and raised (Southgate, Barnet, Finchley); East London settled (Stepney, Mile End and now Wapping). I love being close to the river, cycling canalside, and the sense of being firmly embedded in (an ongoing) history – Captain Bligh lived on the next street over for a time, Flinders House is the next block over; the painter William Turner had an affair in my local pub. I hope to.

Did you read widely as a child?
Any books would have been hand-me-downs from older siblings. *Ferdinand the Bull* was an early favourite. My first word was 'diplodocus'. And I caused a stir at school for paraphrasing Wordsworth at about 6 years of age ('I wandered lonely as a grain of sand...'); precocious little lordling – I must have been insufferable. I was also very big on comic books: *Tintin*, *Asterix*, moving on to *Conan the Barbarian*, *Spider-man* and such (President Obama and me, we've so much in common). Still read them today – as well as produce them, of course.

What was your favourite subject at school?
Art, probably, because my ability at drawing made me popular. English, and History. That's all pretty much stayed with me. I hated Thursdays – Physics and double Maths.

What was your career before you began the novel?
...it says here – as if that's all over! I'm a comic-book creator by trade: writer and artist, editor, and sometime tutor. And it's not so much a career, more a catalogue of misfortune relieved by the occasional happy accident. After 23 years at it, I do at last seem to be reaping some sort of reward for dogged persistence – or else sheer longevity.

Which authors do you most admire?
Vladimir Nabokov for his cruel, fond heart, wordplay and tendency towards wilful obscurity; Richard Condon and Walter Mosley for their pulp majesty; Stan Lee and Jack Kirby for their vocabulary and imagination. Film-makers are as big an influence: Terrence Malick, Powell and Pressburger, Ridley Scott, Anthony Minghella and Gillies Mackinnon.

What is your idea of perfect happiness?
Bed.

MORE FROM MYRIAD EDITIONS

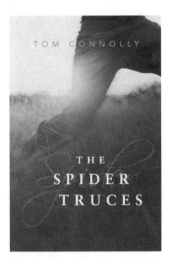

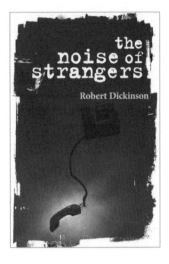

"Lyrical, warm and moving, this impressive debut is reminiscent of Laurie Lee."
Meera Syal

"A funny, moving and quirky coming-of-age story. Hugely enjoyable."
Deborah Moggach

Against the vividly described background of 1980s rural Kent, this moving portrait of a father-son relationship shifts effortlessly between evoking utterly convincingly the terrors and joys of adolescence and the pleasure and pain of being an adult.

Ellis is obsessed by the spiders that inhabit the family's crumbling house – and also by a need to find out more about his mother, whose death overshadows the family's otherwise happy existence.

ISBN: 978-0-9562515-2-7

An Orwellian dystopia in the guise of a fast-paced thriller, this is a coolly satirical novel laced with humour, suspense and intrigue.

After years of civil conflict, gated communities separate government workers from the Scoomers cruising the streets in their battered Fiats.

But when Jack and Denise witness a fatal car crash one night, this precarious security is ruptured.

Through conversations between characters, leaked tapes of official meetings, transcribed phone calls, fly posters for prayer meetings, and provocative articles in an illegal newspaper, this haunting vision of corruption and surveillance is at once deeply unsettling and frighteningly familiar.

ISBN: 978-0-9562515-1-0

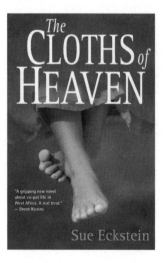

"One of those brilliant books that offers an easy, entertaining read in the first instance, only to worm its way deeper into your mind. A modern Graham Greene – fabulous...fictional gold."
Argus

"Graham Greenish with a bit of Alexander McCall Smith thrown in, very readable, a charming first novel...very humorous."
Radio 5 Live Up All Night

"Entertaining and rewarding... an excellent début. If you like Armistead Maupin, Graham Greene or Barbara Trapido, you will love this."
bookgroup.info

"Populated by a cast of miscreants and misfits this is a darkly comic delight."
Choice

ISBN: 978-0-9549309-8-1

"Skilfully evokes the era and the slow-moving quality of childhood summers, suggesting the menace lurking just beyond the vision of her young protagonists. A study of memory and guilt with several twists."
Guardian

"This emotionally charged thriller grips from the first paragraph, and a nail-biting level of suspense is maintained throughout. A great second novel."
She

"Such is the vividness of the descriptions of the location in this well structured and well written novel that I want to get the next train down. On the edge of my seat? No way – I was cowering under it."
shotsmag.co.uk

ISBN: 978-0-9549309-4-3

MORE FROM MYRIAD EDITIONS

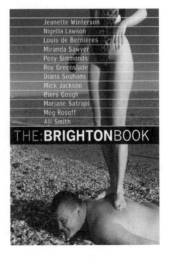

"An exquisitely crafted début novel set in a post-apocalyptic landscape. I'm rationing myself to five pages per day in order to make it last."
. *Guardian Unlimited*

"An all-too-convincing picture of life...in the middle of this century – cold and stormy, with most modern conveniences long-since gone, and with small, mainly self-sufficient, communities struggling to maintain a degree of social order. It is very atmospheric...leaves an indelible imprint on the psyche."
BBC Radio 4 Open Book

"A decidedly original tale. Psychologically sophisticated, it demands our attention. Ignore it, O Philistines, at your peril."
bookgroup.info

ISBN: 978-0-9549309-2-9

"*The Brighton Book* is a fantastic idea and I loved writing a piece with crazy wonderful Brighton as the theme. Everybody should buy the book because it's such a great mix of energy and ideas."
Jeanette Winterson

"Packed with unique perspectives on the city...*The Brighton Book* has hedonism at its heart. Give a man a fish and you'll feed him for a day. Give him *The Brighton Book* and you will feed him for a lifetime."
Argus

A celebration of Brighton and Brightonians – resident, itinerant and visiting – in words and pictures, with original contributions from Piers Gough, Lenny Kaye, Nigella Lawson, Woodrow Phoenix, Meg Rosoff, Jeanette Winterson and others.

ISBN: 978-0-9549309-0-5

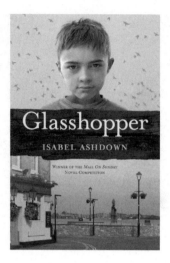

"Tender and subtle, it explores difficult issues in deceptively easy prose...Across the decades, Ashdown tiptoes carefully through explosive family secrets. This is a wonderful debut – intelligent, understated and sensitive."
Observer

"An intelligent, beautifully observed coming-of-age story, packed with vivid characters and inch-perfect dialogue. Isabel Ashdown's storytelling skills are formidable; her human insights highly perceptive."
Mail on Sunday

"Isabel Ashdown's first novel is a disturbing, thought-provoking tale of family dysfunction, spanning the second half of the 20th century, that guarantees laughter at the uncomfortable familiarity of it all."
'Best Books of the Year'
London Evening Standard

"An immaculately written novel with plenty of dark family secrets and gentle wit within. Recommended for book groups."
Waterstone's Books Quarterly

ISBN: 978-0-9549309-7-4